The
BRIDE'S
Prerogative

Susan Page Davis

BARBOUR
PUBLISHING

For more information about Susan Page Davis, please access the author's
website at the following Internet address: www.susanpagedavis.com

Cover design: Faceout Studio, www.faceoutstudio.com

Published by Barbour Publishing, Inc., P.O. Box 719, Uhrichsville, OH 44683,
www.barbourbooks.com

*Our mission is to publish and distribute inspirational products offering exceptional
value and biblical encouragement to the masses.*

 Member of the
Evangelical Christian
Publishers Association

Printed in the United States of America.

★ THE SHERIFF'S SURRENDER ★

Dedication:

To my first son-in-law, Tyler.
Thank you for taking such good care of
our daughter and grandchildren,
and for building great memories with us in Idaho.

★ CHAPTER 1 ★

Fergus, Idaho
May 1885

Gert Dooley aimed at the scrap of red calico and squeezed the trigger. The Spencer rifle she held cracked, and the red cloth fifty yards away shivered.

"I'd say your shooting piece is in fine order." She lowered the rifle and passed it to the owner, Cyrus Fennel. She didn't particularly like Fennel, but he always paid her brother, the only gunsmith in Fergus, with hard money.

He nodded. "Thank you, Miss Dooley." He shoved his hand into his pocket.

Gert knew he was fishing out a coin. This was the part her brother hated most—taking payment for his work. She turned away. Hiram would be embarrassed enough without her watching. She picked up the shawl she had let fall to the grass a few minutes earlier.

"That's mighty fine shooting, Gert," said Hiram's friend, rancher Ethan Chapman. He'd come by earlier to see if Hiram would help him string a fence the next day. When Cyrus Fennel had arrived to pick up his repaired rifle, Ethan had sat down on the chopping block to watch Gert demonstrate the gun.

"Thank you kindly." Gert accepted praise for shooting as a matter of course. Now, if Ethan had remarked that she looked fine today or some such pretty thing, she'd have been flustered. But he would never say anything like that. And shooting was just work.

Fennel levered the rifle's action open and peered at the firing pin. "Looks good as new. I should be able to pick off those rats

5

that are getting in my grain bins."

"That's quite a cannon for shooting rats," Gert said.

Ethan stood and rested one foot on the chopping block, leaning forward with one arm on his knee. "You ought to hire Gert to shoot them for you."

Gert scowled. "Why'd I want to do that? He can shoot his own rats."

Hiram, who had pocketed his pay as quickly as possible, moved the straw he chewed from one side of his mouth to the other. He never talked much. Men brought him their firearms to fix. Hiram listened to them tell him what the trouble was while eyeing the piece keenly. Then he'd look at Gert. She would tell them, "Come back next week." Hiram would nod, and that was the extent of the conversation. Since his wife, Violet, had died eight years ago, the only person Hiram seemed to talk to much was Ethan.

Fennel turned toward her with a condescending smile. "Folks say you're the best shot in Fergus, Miss Dooley."

Gert shrugged. It wasn't worth debating. She had sharp eyes, and she'd fired so many guns for Hiram to make sure they were in working order that she'd gotten good at it, that was all.

Ethan's features, however, sprang to life. "Ain't it the truth? Why, Gert can shoot the tail feathers off a jay at a hundred yards with a gun like that. Mighty fine rifle." He nodded at Fennel's Spencer, wincing as though he regretted not having a gun as fine.

"Well, now, I'm a fair shot myself," Fennel said. "I could maybe hit that rag, too."

"Let's see you do it," Ethan said.

Fennel jacked a cartridge into the Spencer, smiling as he did. The rag still hung limp from a notched stick and was silhouetted against the distant dirt bank across the field. He put his left foot forward and swung the butt of the stock up to his shoulder, paused motionless for a second, and pulled the trigger.

Gert watched the cloth, not the shooter. The stick shattered just at the bottom of the rag. She frowned. She'd have to find another stick next time. At least when she tested a gun, she clipped the edge of the cloth so her stand could be used again.

Hiram took the straw out of his mouth and threw it on the

ground. Without a word, he strode to where the tattered red cloth lay a couple of yards from the splintered stick and brought the scrap back. He stooped for a piece of firewood from the pile he'd made before Fennel showed up. The stick he chose had split raggedly, and Hiram slid the bit of cloth into a crack.

Ethan stood beside Gert as they watched Hiram walk across the field, all the way to the dirt bank, and set the piece of firewood on end.

"Hmm." Fennel cleared his throat and loaded several cartridges into the magazine. When Hiram was back beside them, he raised the gun again, held for a second, and fired. The stick with the bit of red stood unwavering.

"Let Gert try," Ethan said.

"No need," she said, looking down at her worn shoe tips peeping out beneath the hem of her skirt.

"Oh, come on." Ethan's coaxing smile tempted her.

Fennel held the rifle out. "Be my guest."

Gert looked to her brother. Hiram gave the slightest nod then looked up at the sky, tracking the late afternoon sun as it slipped behind a cloud. She could do it, of course. She'd been firing guns for Hiram for years—since she came to Fergus and found him grieving the loss of his wife and baby. Folks had brought him more work than he could handle. They felt sorry for him, she supposed, and wanted to give him a distraction. Gert had begun test firing the guns as fast as he could fix them. She found it satisfying, and she'd kept doing it ever since. Thousands upon thousands of rounds she'd fired, from every type of small firearm, unintentionally building herself a reputation of sorts.

She didn't usually make a show of her shooting prowess, but Fennel rubbed her the wrong way. She knew he wasn't Hiram's favorite patron either. He ran the Wells Fargo office now, but back when he ran the assay office, he'd bought up a lot of failed mines and grassland cheap. He owned a great deal of land around Fergus, including the spread Hiram had hoped to buy when he first came to Idaho. Distracted by his wife's illness, Hiram hadn't moved quickly enough to file claim on the land and had missed out. Instead of the ranch he'd wanted, he lived on his small lot in town and got by on his sporadic pay as a gunsmith.

Gert let her shawl slip from her fingers to the grass once more and took the rifle. As she focused on the distant stick of firewood, she thought, *That hunk of wood is you, Mr. Rich Land Stealer. And that little piece of cloth is one of your rats.*

She squeezed gently. The rifle recoiled against her shoulder, and the far stick of firewood jumped into the air then fell to earth, minus the red cloth.

"Well, I'll be." Fennel stared at her. "Are you always this accurate?"

"You ain't seen nothing," Ethan assured him.

Hiram actually cracked a smile, and Gert felt the blood rush to her cheeks even though Ethan hadn't directly complimented her. She loved to see Hiram smile, something he seldom did.

"Mind sharing your secret, Miss Dooley?" Fennel asked.

Ethan chuckled. "I'll tell you what it is. Every time she shoots, she pretends she's aiming at something she really hates."

"Aha." Fennel smiled, too. "Might I ask what you were thinking of that time, ma'am?"

Gert's mouth went dry. Never had she been so sorely tempted to tell a lie.

"Likely it was that coyote that kilt her rooster last month," Hiram said.

Gert stared at him. He'd actually spoken. She knew when their eyes met that her brother had known exactly what she'd been thinking.

Ethan and Fennel both chuckled.

Of course I wouldn't really think of killing him, Gert thought, *even though he stole the land right out from under my grieving brother. The Good Book says don't kill and don't hate.* Determined to heap coals of fire on her adversary's head, she handed the Spencer back to him. "You're not too bad a shot yourself, Mr. Fennel."

His posture relaxed, and he opened his mouth all smiley, like he might say something pleasant back, but suddenly he stiffened. His eyes focused beyond Gert, toward the dirt street. "Who is that?"

Gert swung around to look as Ethan answered. "That's Millicent Peart."

"Don't think I've seen her since last fall." Fennel shook his head. "She sure is showing her age."

"I don't think Milzie came into town much over the winter," Gert said.

For a moment, they watched the stooped figure hobble along the dirt street toward the emporium. Engulfed in a shapeless old coat, Milzie Peart leaned on a stick with each step. Her mouth worked as though she were talking to someone, but no one accompanied her.

"How long since her man passed on?" Ethan asked.

"Long time," Gert said. "Ten years, maybe. She still lives at their cabin out Mountain Road."

Fennel grimaced as the next house hid the retreating figure from view. "Pitiful."

Ethan shrugged. "She's kinda crazy, but I reckon she likes living on their homestead."

Gert wondered how Milzie got by. It must be lonesome to have no one, not even a nearly silent brother, to talk to out there in the foothills.

"Supper in half an hour." She turned away from the men and headed for the back porch of the little house she shared with Hiram. She hoped Fennel would take the hint and leave. And she hoped Ethan would stay for supper, but of course she would never say so.

★ THE SHERIFF'S SURRENDER ★

★ CHAPTER 2 ★

From across the street, Milzie Peart watched two women enter the Paragon Emporium. She would make that her last stop before heading home. Libby Adams always let her warm up by the stove, and sometimes she let Milzie have a broken packing crate. Once the store owner had even given her a cracked egg.

She turned away, wishing she had enough money to buy something to eat. Her scant supplies at the cabin always ran low this time of year, but this spring had turned out worse than other years. Bitsy Shepard, who owned the Spur & Saddle Saloon, had given her a biscuit earlier and shooed her off, but it wasn't enough to fill her belly.

As Milzie pulled her woolen coat closer around her thin frame, a button popped off—the last of the metal, army-issue buttons. In the dusk, she saw it roll across the packed earth and under the weathered boardwalk that led to the Fergus jail. She went to her knees, heedless of the dirt grinding into her already filthy skirt, and stuck her hand beneath the edge of the walk. "Now where are you hidin'?"

A door opened, and she jerked her head up to see who was leaving the sheriff's office. A man hurried down the steps ten yards away, leaving the door wide open. Not Sheriff Thalen. Milzie couldn't make out his face in the dusk, but this man moved quicker than Bert Thalen. Not so broad through the shoulders either.

She expected him to come down the walkway, but instead he

glanced her way, then slipped around the side of the building. She couldn't say she recognized him. He wore a dark coat and felt hat, like all the men hereabouts.

She shivered. Her joints creaked as she hauled herself to her feet. She would have to improvise a way to keep her late husband's old army coat closed—unless she could get the sheriff to lift the planks and retrieve that button for her.

She looked toward his office. The door still stood open to the chilly May evening. Bert ought to shut it. For the last fifteen years, Thalen had presided over the town's only jail cell. His office also held a desk and a woodstove. Smoke poured out the chimney. Milzie wasn't sure she wanted to ask his help, but she wouldn't mind warming her hands at his stove. Though the snow had been gone several weeks, the nights still dipped to near-freezing temperatures.

She shuffled to the jailhouse and winced as she slowly mounted the two steps. A whiff of cooking food tickled her nose. Baked beans. She peered inside. No one stood on ceremony with the sheriff of Fergus. You wanted something, you just walked in. Still, she hesitated, squinting into the dim interior. The outer room appeared to be empty, but she heard the fire sputtering in the box stove. Its heat felt good, and she eased inside, leaving the door open so she could see by the fading light that entered with her.

No one was in the cell—the barred door stood open. The sheriff must be in the back room. Or maybe he'd gone out and his visitor had missed him.

The tiny back room was smaller than the cell, with a bunk in it. The sheriff slept there if he had a prisoner, Milzie knew. He'd stayed there when he had her husband, Franklin, locked up for disorderly conduct years ago.

She edged closer to the stove. The warmth of the fire lured her, step by step.

"There now." She held out her chilled hands. Her knuckles ached as the delicious heat spread through her.

At the back of the stove, a pan of beans simmered. The smell nigh made her ribs rub together. Before she could stop herself, she grabbed the wooden spoon that rested against the edge of the pan and raised it to her lips. The sweet, hearty flavor filled her mouth and nostrils. Beans cooked with onions and salt pork, mustard and molasses.

She looked over her shoulder. Bert Thalen could walk in at any moment. Reluctantly, she set the spoon back in the pan and limped toward the doorway to the back room. If he was here, maybe he'd find her button and give her a plate of those savory beans.

A stick of split firewood lay on the floor near the doorway. She grabbed the doorjamb to brace against and stooped to pick it up. Her hip ached, and she straightened, panting. She caught her breath, trudged slowly to the wood box, and dropped the stick in. Sheriff ought to take better care of things.

Again, she limped to the doorway. If he was in there, he was sure being quiet.

Golden light from a small window in the west wall of the building illuminated the room. The sun had just hit the horizon, and its last fiery rays streamed in, showing the empty bunk and a small stand with a bowl and pitcher.

Bert Thalen lay sprawled on the floor beside the bunk, staring up at the ceiling. His face was a horrible purple red. Or maybe it was just the reflection of the sunset.

Milzie took two steps into the room and stared down at the sheriff for a long minute. He didn't blink. A dark ooze stained the floorboards under his head. A large, shiny safety pin held his suspenders together on the near side. Milzie stooped and unclasped it. Her aching fingers resisted, but she managed to pin the front of her coat together where the last button had been.

She walked slowly out to the stove again and scooped the wooden spoon into the beans. The sheriff wouldn't be needing those.

★ CHAPTER 3 ★

Libby Adams flipped the bolt of black bombazine over several times, spreading yards of the sturdy fabric on her counter. She could tell from long practice when she had laid out the four yards Mrs. Walker wanted. She could have cut it to within two inches without ever consulting her yardstick, but she measured it anyway, under the eagle eye of the mayor's wife. Mrs. Walker always bought dark colors and practical fabrics.

While Libby folded the cloth, Mrs. Walker browsed the notions counter, selecting buttons for her new dress. Her husband, meanwhile, hovered in the emporium's hardware section. The few groceries they had chosen were already tallied and waiting in a crate, but the mayor usually wound up cooling his heels while his wife shopped for her personal wants. He found rancher Micah Landry eyeing a posthole digger and greeted him with relief. Libby's part-time clerk, Florence Nash, was diligently restocking the cracker and candy jars. A housewife selecting soap and lamp oil was the only other customer at the moment. Well, Milzie Peart huddled near the box stove, but she seldom bought anything. Libby was tempted to ask her to leave. Her body odor, worsened by the heat, kept other customers away from the stove.

Mrs. Walker brought her sundries to the counter and placed a card of a dozen black buttons and a paper of straight pins on the folded length of fabric.

Libby smiled at her. "All set, ma'am?" She'd known Mrs. Walker for years. Their husbands had been friends in the old days.

But the mayor's wife kept herself slightly aloof, and Libby never felt herself on an equal footing with Orissa Walker.

"You don't have any new silk floss?"

Libby tried to keep her smile from drooping. "Not yet. I've ordered a better selection, but these things take time."

She hoped her investment in expensive embroidery threads didn't prove a poor one. Only a few women in Fergus had time to fritter away on decorative arts, and she knew she might never sell all the skeins of fine floss she had ordered. Still, some of the girls who worked at the Spur & Saddle or the Nugget were handy with a needle, and they all liked to add fripperies to their costumes. Libby shuddered when some of them entered the emporium wearing scanty dresses, but they were good customers. For them, she maintained one of Fergus's best-kept secrets: a supply of garish satins and sheer muslins stored in the back room. She had even special-ordered ostrich feathers, satin garters, and beribboned, glove-fitting corsets for Bitsy Shepard and her employees. Mrs. Walker would probably die of apoplexy on the spot if she saw the items that Libby procured for Bitsy. In the year and a half since Isaac's death, Libby had been forced to support herself, and that meant ordering merchandise that would sell.

The sleigh bells on the door jingled, and the door swung open. Cyrus Fennel charged in, bringing a blast of cold air. His gaze settled on the mayor's wife.

"Mrs. Walker! Is your husband here? I went by your house, but—"

"I'm here, Cyrus." The mayor stepped away from the wall of hardware. "You wanted to see me?"

Libby shivered. "Shut the door if you please, Mr. Fennel."

Cyrus glanced at her and hastily closed it. "I beg your pardon, ma'am. Charles, we have a crisis."

"What is it?" The mayor stepped closer, as did Micah Landry and the shopping housewife. Florence paused with a handful of jawbreakers suspended over an open candy jar. Mrs. Walker eyed Fennel critically through her small spectacles.

Cyrus held the mayor's gaze. "Bert Thalen is dead."

Libby drew a sharp breath, and the others gasped.

"What happened?" Mayor Walker asked.

"I don't know. I was coming from Hiram Dooley's place, and I stepped in to have a word with Bert. He's lying on the floor in the back room of his office, dead as a plucked chicken."

"Oh dear." Walker fumbled in his pocket and produced a handkerchief, with which he dabbed at perspiration on his brow. "I suppose we'd better get someone to lay him out."

"You'd best come and take a look," Fennel said. "Thalen's the law around here, and there's no one else we can fetch to tend to him."

The mayor cleared his throat and glanced at his wife as he shoved the handkerchief back in his pocket. "Hmm. Well. . .I suppose Hiram Dooley will make a coffin for him."

"But someone needs to take some kind of official notice that he's dead," Fennel persisted.

"We don't have a doctor," Mrs. Walker pointed out unnecessarily. Everyone in Fergus was painfully aware of the fact.

"It would take days to get someone up here from Boise," Landry said. "You'd best look at him, Mayor."

"Hmm. . .well, I suppose."

Fennel and Landry headed for the door. The mayor followed with slower steps. He glanced back at his wife. "You'd best stay here, m'dear. I shan't be long."

"Nonsense. I'm coming." Mrs. Walker wrapped her woolen cape snugly about her and walked away from the counter, leaving her purchases behind. "We haven't had a funeral in more than a year."

The Walkers and the housewife went out. Libby glanced over at Florence and said, "Or a wedding in twice that long." She tore a length of brown paper off the roll beneath the counter and wrapped Mrs. Walker's material and sewing notions. On the boardwalk outside, several people hurried past.

"Sounds like word's gettin' around." Florence screwed the lid onto the jar.

Libby felt a sudden urge to go over to Thalen's office. The mayor's wife was right about Fergus; the town had spent a dull winter. The sheriff's death was big news. Bert Thalen had been a friend of her husband's when Isaac was alive, God rest his soul.

Susan Page Davis

Besides, as owner of the emporium, she ought to get the details so she could tell her customers all about it. The store was empty. Milzie Peart must have slipped out while the others were talking.

"You mind the till," Libby told Florence. Quickly she took off her apron and grabbed her coat and bonnet.

A farm wagon approached from the north end of town, but Libby tore across the street before it came within hailing distance. A knot of curiosity seekers had gathered outside the sheriff's office. She sidled up to Gert Dooley.

"What happened to the sheriff?"

Gert glanced at her then turned her attention back to the office door. "Dunno. I was just dishing up supper for Ethan Chapman and Hiram when Griff Bane came pounding on the door and told Hiram he needed to get over to the jail 'cause Bert was dead. Hiram and Ethan are in there now with Griffin, the mayor, and Cy Fennel."

Libby nodded. Griffin Bane owned the smithy and livery stable. Most likely the sheriff, a widower who lived alone just outside town, would be laid out over at the stable. Fergus lacked a lot of things besides a doctor, an undertaker being one of them.

The mayor came out of the sheriff's office and latched onto the handrail by the steps. His face held a greenish cast, and his knees seemed a mite wobbly.

"Folks," he called out, and the crowd went silent. "Folks, our beloved sheriff, Bert Thalen, has breathed his last. I've asked Hiram Dooley and Griffin Bane to take care of. . .what needs to be done. Funeral tomorrow at the graveyard, one o'clock sharp."

The people began to murmur. A few walked away, but more arrived, having just received the news or seen the gathering.

The mayor joined his wife on the walkway. "Well, m'dear, we need to retrieve our bundles from the emporium."

"Mayor, wait!" Cyrus Fennel hurried down the steps. "There's something else you need to take care of, Mr. Mayor."

Everyone halted, eager for more news.

Walker frowned at Fennel. "What is it, Cy?"

"Why, we'll need a new sheriff. I think you should appoint someone."

16

"Sheriff's an elected position," Gert called out.

Fennel's eyebrows lowered. "We can't leave the position open while we wait for an election. Can't go long without a lawman."

"You could appoint someone temporary-like," Micah Landry suggested.

Mayor Walker hooked his thumbs in his coat pockets and stood for a moment, staring toward the doorway. At last he said, "I'll take that under advisement."

The people let out their pent-up breath and shuffled away. Hiram Dooley and Ethan Chapman emerged from the office, and Gert advanced to meet them at the bottom of the steps. Libby followed on her heels.

"What happened in there?" Gert asked her brother.

Hiram shrugged.

Ethan said, "Not sure. Looks like he might have fallen and hit his head on the edge of his bunk. He's lying on the floor beside it."

"Tripped and fell?" Gert probed, frowning up at the tall rancher.

"Maybe." Ethan didn't sound convinced. "Coulda been heart failure, I guess."

"Bert was a strong man," Libby ventured.

Ethan glanced her way and nodded a greeting. "Miz Adams. He was gettin' along in years. Must have been well past fifty."

Closer to sixty, Libby thought, but she kept silent. Her husband, Isaac, had been fifteen years her senior, and he would have been fifty this spring. His friend, Bert Thalen, was several years older.

Gert persisted. "So somehow or other, he hit his head."

"All I know is, the mayor wants Hiram to build him a casket." Ethan clapped the gunsmith on the shoulder. "I'll help Griffin move the body over to the livery, and then I'll come help you."

Hiram nodded.

"That's it?" Gert asked.

"Well. . .I'd say someone needs to examine the body closer. Someone who knows what they're doing." Ethan gritted his teeth. "There's some blood on the floor, and it looked like he whomped his head pretty hard. Stove his skull in some."

Hiram nodded, and Gert eyed her brother critically, as though

17

his silent opinion counted more than Ethan's.

"I did notice one other thing when they rolled him over," Ethan said.

"What was that?" Gert asked eagerly.

Ethan stuck his hand in the pocket of his Levis and pulled it out, then turned it over and opened his fist. A coin lay in his broad palm.

"A penny?" Libby stared up into Ethan's face, but he was looking at Gert.

"It was underneath him," Ethan said. "Probably doesn't mean anything."

"He might have had it in his hand when he died." Gert's forehead wrinkled.

Ethan nodded. "Might. And dropped it as he fell."

Griffin Bane appeared in the doorway. "Hey, Ethan, you ready? I can use some muscle here."

"Coming." Ethan shoved the penny back into his pocket and hurried up the steps.

Gert eyed her brother. "I suppose you need to see if you've got the right lumber for a coffin."

Hiram nodded, his lips clamped together.

"Well, come on then." Gert turned toward their nearby house. "Finish your supper first though. I'll put Ethan's plate in the pie safe until he comes back. If he doesn't forget and go home without his supper."

Brother and sister moved off, and Libby felt suddenly chilled. Full darkness had fallen, and she quickened her steps toward the emporium. Closing time had arrived, but if she stayed open, folks might come in to talk. The emporium made a good meeting place—not as good as the saloons, but a respectable place where decent women could gather. And when they did, they were apt to purchase an item or two.

Her speculation proved correct, and small groups of people wandered into the emporium over the next two hours, drawn by the lights. They leaned on the counter or clustered about the stove, debating the recent state of the sheriff's health and possible candidates to take over the office.

Libby sent Florence home at eight o'clock, and soon afterward, she locked the door behind the last lingerers. She locked her cash box in the safe in the back room. Heading up the stairs to her living quarters, she shivered. The apartment was cold, so she left the stairway door open to let some of the warmth up from the store. She set her lamp on the table and washed her hands. While she prepared her solitary meal, she thought about what Bert Thalen's passing would mean to the town. Her husband had respected him. Libby felt less secure just knowing Bert was dead. Cyrus Fennel had a point: Though Fergus was not a lawless town, it might become one if it had no sheriff.

When at last she lay down to sleep, she slid her hand under the pillow beside her—Isaac's pillow. The sheets were cool, but the polished wood of the Colt Peacemaker's handle felt the same as always. Solid. Dependable. Libby wished she knew how to handle the gun better. When Isaac was alive, she never worried about guns. Now she felt safer just having it handy. If someone broke in, she could point it at them. Chances were they'd listen to her. But maybe it was time she learned to load and shoot the big pistol.

★ CHAPTER 4 ★

The mayor took center stage at the funeral the next afternoon. He spoke at length—too much length, Ethan thought—about Bert Thalen's contributions to the town. Ethan had pulled his hat off for the service, as had all the other men, and the wind cooled his ears to the point of discomfort.

"Bert was liked by everyone." The chilly wind caught Walker's thin voice, making it hard to hear at times. "When we came looking for gold back in '63, Bert Thalen, Isaac Adams, Cyrus Fennel, and I met up in the assay office. We immediately became friends. Bert was square. He always kept his word, and if another miner needed help, he'd lend a hand."

The mayor went on, but Ethan let his mind wander. True, most folks respected Bert, at least enough to keep electing him sheriff every fall for the last fifteen years. But he did have a temper. Thalen's ranch bordered Ethan's, and they'd ridden fence together several times. Ethan had heard Bert cuss and carry on when things didn't go his way. He liked his tobacco chaw, and he'd gotten set in his ways. But he was all right—better than most men would be if they wore the star.

Cy Fennel took the mayor's place at the head end of the grave, facing the crowd. Word had traveled fast, and most of the town's one hundred or so residents had turned out, along with a few outlying ranchers.

"I well recollect the first winter we prospected in these hills." was putting on a bit of a folksy tone today. "My wife, Mary, and I homesteaded, but I spent a lot of time the first two years out on the claim I'd filed with Bert, Charles, and Isaac. The first winter, we got caught in a blizzard. We like to have froze to death. Cold! Wasn't it cold?" Cyrus shook his head. "Yup, those days it took a lot of grit to survive out here."

"It ain't no picnic nowadays," called Micah Landry, who ran a few cattle on his ranch out Mountain Road.

Everyone laughed uneasily.

"Yes, sir, Bert was a tough one." Cyrus nodded soberly, not focusing on anyone in the crowd.

He opened his mouth as though to speak again, but Mayor Walker called out, "Anyone else want to say something about Bert?"

"He was always a gentleman, and I never saw him drunk."

The crowd swiveled around to look at the speaker, Bitsy Shepard, who owned the Spur & Saddle Saloon.

"He encouraged me to keep the business after Isaac died," Libby Adams said.

Her voice was so quiet that Orissa Walker piped up with, "What'd she say, Charles?" No one had any trouble hearing the mayor's wife.

The murmuring increased, and Walker raised both hands. "Now, folks, quiet down. Let's have a psalm and a prayer, out of respect for the dead."

Griffin Bane stepped forward holding a worn, leather-covered book. His thick eyebrows nearly met as he opened it. If Ethan hadn't known him so well, he'd have thought Griff was angry. But he always scowled like that on somber occasions.

"Psalm 23," the blacksmith said. " 'The Lord is my shepherd; I shall not want.' "

A lot of the townsfolk recited the chapter along with Griffin, without the aid of a Bible—mostly older folks. The town had yet to acquire a church or a man to fill the pulpit and bury their dead. Some of them heard scripture only in snippets at funerals and such. For years, the only times Ethan had heard preaching came when he rode to Silver City or Boise.

Still, he didn't need every-week services to remember the

verses he'd learned as a child. His mama had coached him for weeks until he could recite the Shepherd's Psalm and the Old Hundredth word perfect for his Sunday school teacher. But that was before they came to the ranch near Fergus.

" 'Yea, though I walk through the valley of the shadow of death, I will fear no evil,' " Ethan recited softly, along with Griffin and the others. " 'For thou art with me; thy rod and thy staff they comfort me.' "

He glanced over at his friend Hiram. While the gunsmith mouthed the words silently, his sister, Gertrude, spoke evenly, in unison with Griff. Only three Bibles were in evidence besides Griffin's. Libby Adams held hers open at the middle, while Orissa Walker clutched one close against her chest. To Ethan's surprise, Augie Moore, the bartender at Bitsy's place, also held one and followed along as Griffin read.

" '…And I shall dwell in the house of the Lord forever.' " Ethan hoped Bert had crossed into the house of the Lord. "Amen." Griff clapped his hat on with one hand while flipping the Bible closed with the other.

Ethan started to put his misshapen felt hat back on, but Mayor Walker said, "Cyrus, would you lead us in prayer?"

Cy Fennel cleared his throat, and all the men dropped their hands back to their sides, holding their hats ready. Hopefully, Cyrus would have the sense to make it quick.

"Dear Lord, we ask You to take Bert into Your house and let him live in bliss forever among the angels. Amen."

"Amen," Ethan said firmly, though he wasn't sure they'd be rubbing elbows with the angels when they passed over.

As he at last pulled his hat low over his ears, the mayor spoke again.

"The ladies have laid out refreshments in the schoolhouse, but before we partake, there's a bit of town business we need to tend to. We'll try to keep it brief, but we need you all there. And I'm told we've got beans, corn cake, and dried apple pie, with sundry other delectables for when we're done. So get on over to the schoolhouse."

The crowd broke ranks, turning their backs swiftly on the

open grave. Hiram and Griffin circled the mound of dirt at the foot end of the hole, where they'd stashed a couple of spades that morning. Gert Dooley stayed nearby, watching the people leave in an arrow-straight line for the schoolhouse.

"I can help." Ethan stepped up beside Hiram. "You two did all the digging this morning."

Hiram shrugged and dug the blade of his spade into the pile of loose earth.

"Thanks, Ethan. We'll be fine." Griffin hefted his spade.

"I don't mind," Ethan said. "Hiram, why don't you take your sister over to the schoolhouse? It's chilly out here. Gert would probably appreciate getting inside."

Hiram paused and looked uncertainly from Gert to Ethan and back. "You go on," he said at last.

Ethan shook his head and reached for the spade handle. Gert was a nice young woman, but he'd rather stay out in the cold a little longer than let the whole town think he was walking out with her. He'd decided long ago not to go down the courtship road.

Hiram eyed him for a long moment then handed him the spade and brushed off his hands. He turned and crooked his elbow for his sister, and they followed the others. Gert held her back as straight as a poker. A belated thought crossed Ethan's mind that he may have insulted her without meaning to.

He plied the spade vigorously, hoping the work would warm him up. May 5 ought to be warmer than this, but the distant mountains still held their snowcaps. Griffin labored silently with him. They had nearly leveled the pile when Gert came puffing back to the graveside.

"Ethan!" She pulled up, panting. "You're needed at the schoolhouse."

"What for?" He straightened and stared at her.

"Just come. Quick. Folks are getting impatient to eat." She turned away and walked back the way she'd come.

Now why had she asked for him and not Griffin? Ethan looked over at him, but the blacksmith merely shrugged.

"I never knew people in Fergus to keep the food back waiting for anyone," Ethan said.

"Mm. Like one pig waits for another." Griffin stuck his spade in the dirt. "Come on, we might as well see what the fuss is about."

They trudged together toward the rough log building on the edge of town. Fergus had a scanty school roll these days—seemed most of the children had grown up or families with young'uns had moved away. Isabel Fennel, Cyrus's daughter, kept school for fewer than a dozen pupils.

As they stepped into the schoolhouse and removed their hats, the warmth and smell of many people close together hit Ethan, but subtle food scents softened it. Griffin followed him through the small cloakroom into the back of the classroom.

"Here he is," boomed Augie Moore.

"Yeah, Ethan."

He looked toward the voice but couldn't pick out the speaker. From the front of the room by Isabel's desk, Mayor Walker spoke.

"Ethan, come on up here, please."

Ethan arched his eyebrows and put one hand to his chest as if to say, "Who, me?"

The mayor nodded. "That's right, son, come right up here."

Slowly, Ethan walked the aisle, feeling at least fifty pairs of eyes boring into him. People packed all the benches, and at least a dozen men stood along the walls. He stopped a yard from the mayor and stood still with his hat in his dirty hands. "Yes, sir?"

"Ethan, I'm appointing you as interim sheriff of Fergus until we have a chance to organize a proper election."

Ethan's jaw dropped, and immediately he snapped it shut. No use looking like a fool, even though he felt like one.

Mayor Walker continued. "The people agree with me that you're the best choice for the job, so I'll just pin Bert Thalen's star on your coat, there, and—"

"Hold it." Ethan stepped back and threw one hand up as the mayor leaned toward him with the business end of the star's pin pointed at his chest. "I'm not sure I want that job, thank you."

"Nonsense. You've lived next to Bert for a long time, and you've helped him plenty. He even deputized you when he had to throw those ruffians off Cold Creek a couple of years back."

"That's right, Ethan," Cyrus said jovially from where he

leaned against the log wall with his arms folded. "You're just the man for this job. Young, healthy, strong, and always on the right side of the law."

Someone started clapping, and the crowd took it up.

"Hey, Ethan! Speech!" voices called out.

He turned to face the crowd and held up both hands, in one of which he still held his hat.

"Folks, please."

"Let him speak!" The mayor couldn't seem to talk loudly without going shrill. The shouts subsided.

Suddenly all was as quiet as the moment after an owl screeches. Ethan swallowed hard.

"Folks, I dunno where this notion came from, but the truth is, I don't think I'm qualified. Besides, my ranch doesn't leave me time to perform official duties. The sheriff has to spend a lot of nights in town. I just can't do that."

"Hogwash!"

Ethan felt the blood rush to his face. That would be one of the stagecoach drivers. He was only in Fergus two nights a week. Did he even qualify as a citizen?

Cyrus Fennel again spoke up, and everyone looked toward him. "Now Ethan, it's only until we have time to sort things out and find someone permanent. But you meet all the requirements for the job."

"I do?"

"Well, sure." Cyrus unfolded his arms. "Besides the things I mentioned before, you don't have a family."

Ethan gulped. He surely didn't want a job where they wanted you to have no wife or kiddies to notify when you got killed.

"I—"

"And you served in the army."

Ethan's heart sank. The last thing he wanted aired in public was his part in the so-called Indian wars six and eight years ago.

"You know how to shoot and how to act under pressure," Cyrus went on. "And you've got good horses and guns. The town wouldn't have to provide those."

Mayor Walker said quickly, "Of course, we'll pay you with that in mind. Same as we paid Bert. All the business owners in town will kick in."

Ethan frowned. "I don't want the people to have to scrape up money to pay me."

"You mean you'll do it for free?" Augie yelled.

"No, I didn't say that."

The room erupted in shouting and whistling.

The mayor picked up the stick his daughter used as a pointer during classes and tapped it on the desk. "Here, now. Settle down. Of course we'll pay the sheriff. It's a dangerous job."

"That's right," Cyrus said as the people calmed down. "Can't ask Ethan to leave off working his ranch anytime we need him without pay."

The mayor stepped closer and bent his neck back to look up at Ethan. "Truth is, I can't think of anyone else who's as well qualified as you are. Can't you help us out for a few weeks?"

Ethan looked out over all the faces—the rawboned ranchers and weathered old-timers, the resolute women and the young men determined to make a go of it in Idaho Territory. Hiram stared at him with gray blue eyes, his mouth in a straight line, offering no persuasion, merely waiting to see what his friend would decide. Beside him, Gert gazed at him with the same solemn eyes and thatch of straw-colored hair, but her plain face held an eager sympathy that somehow made Ethan wish he wanted the job. Gert worked hard, and someone ought to do something nice for her now and then.

He shifted his gaze. If he didn't watch it, he'd find himself a lawman out of sympathy. Sure, the women of Fergus were unsettled by Bert's death. He'd heard several asking this morning how the sheriff had died and if the town was safe. Did duty demand that he saddle himself with Bert's job just to allay their anxiety?

The faces of the women finally turned the corner for him. He wouldn't sleep tonight if he walked away from here knowing Gert and Bitsy and Libby Adams and Mrs. Walker and all the ranch wives were afraid. Most of them had followed men here with at least an implied promise that civilization would prevail in Fergus. Ethan couldn't let the whole town down.

He cleared his throat and looked at Mayor Walker.

The older man's eyes widened. "Well? What do you say?"

Ethan reached his hand out slowly, and the whole town exhaled as he took the metal star.

★ CHAPTER 5 ★

All semblance of order disappeared after the mayor declared it was time to eat. Gert squeezed between people to get to the front of the room where the tables of food were set up. She found her apron and joined several other women to help dish up beans and stews.

People in Fergus had practical funeral customs. Women took food and aprons. Men took tin plates and cups and their appetites. After the deceased was laid to rest, an hour of good food and conversation followed, as sure as the corpse stayed in the grave.

Libby smiled wanly at Gert as she tied her apron strings behind her back. "Afternoon, Gert. What did you bring?"

"Four pies."

"Good for you. I hope there's some left for us."

They didn't converse much as they served the long line of townsfolk, at least three-quarters of whom were men. Some of the ranchers made cheeky comments to the women serving the food. Gert noticed that they teased Florence, the young clerk from Libby's store, the most. A few made comments to Gert. A couple of men stared outright at Libby. Though most folks knew she wasn't looking to remarry, a few diehards continued trying to impress her.

"Well, Miz Adams," one cowpoke from Micah Landry's ranch said with a grin as Libby plopped a large square of corn bread on his plate. "You look purty as a peach orchard today."

"Thank you, Parnell. I've never seen a peach orchard, but I'll take that as a compliment."

"It's a mighty purty sight, ma'am."

Libby chuckled. "Thank you. Next."

"Oh, wait," Parnell cried. "I was gonna ask if I could call on you, ma'am."

"No, thank you," Libby said. "Next."

Gert marveled that Libby could brush off a suitor so serenely. Parnell huffed out a breath. "But—"

"Just move along, Parnell," said the next man in line.

Gert straightened her spine and dipped her spoon into the bean pot without meeting the man's gaze. Jamin Morell ran the Nugget, the new saloon in town. Gert held him personally responsible for the noise on the Nugget's end of the street on Saturday nights.

"Thank you, ma'am," he said.

"You're welcome." After he'd stepped over in front of Libby for corn bread, Gert sneaked a disapproving glance at him. His suit must have come from back East. The material was finer than what Libby stocked at the Paragon Emporium, and anyway, Gert doubted any woman in Fergus could tailor that well. His swirly-patterned silk waistcoat would be something to stare at if she didn't have to worry about him staring back.

Jamin beamed a toothy smile at Libby. "Good day, ma'am. That looks delicious."

Gert turned to serve the next man in line.

"Howdy, Gert."

Ethan's strained smile melted her heart. She could tell he'd hated to take the sheriff's position, but when he saw the need, he'd stepped up and accepted the duty. Ethan Chapman had to be the finest man in Fergus. After Hiram, of course, though her brother had slacked off on taking part in civic activities since Violet died. Before that, Hiram used to talk and even laugh with his customers. He'd squired Violet around town when she needed to shop, and he'd offered to help ranchers who were laid up. All that politeness and neighborliness had ended when Violet drew her last breath.

Well, no sense thinking about that. Right now the town's new sheriff was smiling at her.

"Congratulations, Ethan," she said softly. "I think the mayor chose the right man for the job." Of course, Cy Fennel did the actual choosing, and Mayor Walker had carried out his wishes, as always, but she would never say that to Ethan. It was fitting that he'd been chosen, no matter who orchestrated it.

He gritted his teeth. "I don't know about that, but it seemed someone needed to do it, and we wouldn't get any food until they did."

Ethan could always make her laugh. She loved it when he spent time with Hiram and coaxed a smile or two out of him as well.

"You'll do a good job." She ladled a generous serving of beans onto his plate.

"This your mess?" He nodded toward the bean pot.

"No, Annie Harper brought 'em. I brought pies."

He glanced down the tables toward where the desserts waited. "I'll be sure and get some. I know they'll be good."

Gert was still smiling when she turned to the next in line— sour-faced Orissa Walker.

An hour later, she and the other women scraped out the pans and retrieved the biscuits and pie they'd hidden away to be sure they got something.

"I should get back and open the emporium," Libby said as she sank onto a bench.

"I could open for you, Miz Adams," Florence said. She sat down, balancing her plate and a tin cup of cider.

"We'll both go," Libby replied. "As soon as we finish eating and cleaning up."

"You've done enough," Gert said. "We've got plenty of women to clean up. If folks will remember to take their dishes, there won't be much to do anyway. Hiram will put all the benches back."

The crowd continued to thin. Bitsy Shepard and Goldie, one of her saloon girls, collected the four large pans in which Bitsy's contribution for the meal had arrived—sliced roast beef, a mess of succotash, a mountain of mashed potatoes, and a deep-dish dried pumpkin pie big enough to feed two dozen people.

"Thanks for sending all that food, Bitsy," Gert called.

Bitsy's gaze lit on her, and she smiled. " 'Tweren't nothing."

"Sure it was," Libby said. "Most folks hereabouts don't eat that well unless they go to the Spur & Saddle for Sunday dinner."

Bitsy flushed, which Gert thought a remarkable feat for a saloon owner of twenty years' standing. "I do thank you." She and Goldie hustled toward the door, their satin skirts rustling. Gert wondered if they'd chosen their least flamboyant dresses for the funeral. Bitsy's was a deep wine red, and Goldie's too-short green overskirt showed a ruffle of gold beneath and a scandalous hint of dark stockings.

Gert turned back to Libby and Florence. "Bitsy always thought a lot of Bert."

"Yes," Libby agreed, "but she'd have done the same for anyone in this town."

Libby took the prize for genuine sweetness, Gert decided. Some of the town's women wouldn't give Bitsy the time of day. But Libby always had a kind word for anyone—a ranch hand, a saloon girl, or the mayor's prim wife. She was more than passably pretty, too, with her golden hair and vivid blue eyes—the way Gert had always wished her own had turned out, instead of this scraggly hair the color of dishwater and eyes like the smoke coming out of the chimney when Hiram burned greasewood. No wonder all the men in town hankered after the lovely widow. But Libby gently discouraged all who came courting.

Gert lifted her last forkful of roast to her mouth. Bitsy surely could cook, no denying that. Or maybe the rumors were true and Augie Moore did a lot of the cooking for her during the day, putting on his bartender's apron when the men began to gather after supper.

Libby stood. "If you're sure you don't need me. . ."

Gert shook her head and waved a hand at the nearly empty food tables. "Git. There's barely a thing left."

Her friend hesitated and looked around the hall. She leaned close to Gert's ear. "Have you heard anyone say for sure how Bert died?"

"Just what Ethan said yesterday. He hit his head."

"I can't help thinking about it and wondering."

Gert studied Libby's face. "You mean. . .maybe someone hit it

31

for him? Nobody's said as much."

"Good. I probably worry too much." Libby turned toward the door. "Come on, Florence. If we don't hurry, we'll miss some business."

As the two left the schoolroom, Gert's gaze drifted again to Ethan. He stood near the stove with the mayor and Cyrus. She wondered what Mayor Walker was saying so earnestly. To one side, Jamin Morrell sat sipping from a tin cup. He almost seemed to be listening to the men's conversation. Gert had no use for Morrell. He'd come to Fergus a year past and opened the Nugget Saloon on the opposite end of Main Street from Bitsy's establishment. Not that Gert approved of Bitsy's business, but compared to the Nugget, the Spur & Saddle was practically genteel. Morrell took a long pull from his cup, and suddenly Gert wondered if he'd sneaked a bottle of spirits into the schoolhouse.

After a moment, the two older men clapped Ethan on the back and left him. Cyrus went out the door, and Mayor Walker joined his wife and a couple who owned a ranch east of town.

Gert busied herself setting the few remaining pans closer together so she and Mrs. Landry could clear off one table. No sense letting folks see her making calf eyes at her brother's friend—the new sheriff, that is. She smiled to herself. Ethan might not be overly comfortable with his new position, but she couldn't think of a better candidate for the job. Not another man in Fergus could be as impartial and honest as Ethan Chapman.

"Hey, Gert."

She jumped and looked up to find the object of her thoughts looking at her with brown eyes fit to make a schoolgirl swoon.

"Ethan."

"Seen Hiram?"

"I think he went back to the graveyard with Griffin. They wanted to make sure the dirt got tamped down good."

Ethan nodded and turned his hat around in his hands, holding it by the brim. "Thought I'd ask Hi to go over to the sheriff's office with me. The mayor and Mr. Fennel think I oughta go over it to see if there's anything that will tell us more about Bert's. . . demise."

She nodded. "Hiram will go with you if you ask him. Just don't expect him to hold forth with his opinion."

Ethan actually smiled. "Right. He's restful, your brother." Still, he stood there, turning the hat round and round. "I guess I'll have to sleep in there some now."

Gert searched his face. Fatigue etched little lines like pine needles at the corners of his eyes, and his eyebrows drew together.

"I don't expect you need to stay there tonight. Bert only slept there when he had prisoners, didn't he?"

"I guess. But I'll have to make arrangements for someone to tend my ranch when I'm in town."

"Don't you have any ranch hands?" Gert asked.

"I had two last year, but I let them go in the fall. You know, Spin and Johnny McDade. Couldn't afford to pay them all winter."

She nodded. The two had ridden over from Boonville last summer, if she remembered right. Good, steady boys. "I expect they'll come back, now that it's warming up again."

"Maybe. If so, they'll watch things for me while I'm sheriffing, I guess." Ethan sighed. "Can't say I like this turn of events."

Gert laid her hand on his sleeve for an instant. "You'll do fine, Ethan. Just fine." She pulled her hand back lest he think she was being forward.

"Well, thank you kindly. Guess I'll go see if Hiram's done." He walked toward the door and clapped his wilted hat on when he reached it. As he half turned to close the schoolroom door behind him, his gaze again met Gert's, and he gave her a curt nod.

She stood looking at the closed door for a long moment until Mrs. Landry called, "Gert, is that Laura Storrey's dish?"

Ethan walked out of the school yard and looked toward the grave site. Sure enough, Hiram and Griffin were out there, filling in the last few shovelfuls of dirt. He took a few steps toward the graveyard, then stopped.

Since when did he need a friend to go with him into a scary, dark place? Not since he was a boy. Maybe it was time he faced reality. When his enlistment expired after the Indian wars, he had come back here looking for some peace and quiet. He minded his own business and worked his own land. Now the townsfolk wanted him to mind everyone else's business and make sure no one tried to mess with their property. Not Ethan's choice, not by a long shot.

But that seemed to be the hand God had dealt him. He frowned and pulled his hat off so he could scratch his head. Somehow it didn't seem quite right to think of God dealing him a poker hand.

"You understand, Lord," he mumbled. "It's what You gave me, I reckon. So I guess that means I have to play it out."

He sighed and turned back to the school yard. He'd left his paint gelding tied to the hitching rail there before the funeral. Little did he expect when he'd left his ranch this morning to come home a lawman. He might never get that fence strung.

Scout stood with his head drooping, sound asleep.

"Hey, fella."

The paint whickered as Ethan untied the lead rope and stowed it in his saddlebag. He took out the bridle and held the bit up. The gelding smiled then opened his teeth enough for the curb to slip into his mouth. Ethan slid the headstall over Scout's ears and buckled the throat latch. He stood stroking the horse's long, sleek neck for a moment, knowing he was stalling.

At last, he tightened the cinch and swung into the saddle. Scout minced around toward the ranch. "Not yet, boy. We got one more stop to make." Ethan reined him the other way, toward the center of town.

The main street seemed strangely subdued in the waning afternoon. Half the buildings stood empty since the bust that had followed the gold rush, but usually folks were about this time of day. Ethan guessed they'd either had enough socializing at the funeral or had gathered in small groups indoors to keep discussing the recent events.

Scout's hoofbeats echoed off the facade of the three-story building that used to be a boardinghouse. Those were the days, when the miners poured into town to have their gold dust weighed and find a hot meal and a stiff drink. But the boardinghouse had stood vacant for nigh on ten years. Ethan had been only eleven when his family moved here, but the town's population had been at least triple what it was now. He remembered the time when three general stores served the needs of the hundreds of miners with claims in the area.

A few of the old buildings had been cannibalized for lumber, but most were still owned by someone who objected to such activity. In fact, a large proportion of the vacant buildings were owned by Cyrus Fennel. He'd bought up a lot of property, in town and outside it, when the boom collapsed. Cyrus kept saying the town would prosper again and then he'd make a fortune selling the storefronts and empty houses. And if anyone tried to steal lumber off one of his buildings, Cyrus put the law on them. Ethan wondered if he'd have to lock people up for pilfering boards. Lumber was in high demand here.

He came to the jail and pulled gently on the reins. Scout obliged by stopping. Ethan gazed toward the weathered building. No smoke puffed from the chimney, and from outside, the jail looked like one more abandoned house.

Scout shook his head and nickered.

"Take it easy, fella." The saddle leather creaked as Ethan lowered himself to the ground. He felt old today. He was only twenty-nine—at least, he thought it was twenty-nine. That or thirty. But he felt like an old man.

Was it because Bert Thalen was fixing to be an old man, and now Ethan had to take the old man's place? The town had always had an old sheriff. Ethan remembered Sheriff Rogers from back when he was a kid. Rogers had supposedly been the first sheriff, elected when the young town erupted with gold seekers. Then Rogers retired, back in '70, and the town elected Bert in his place. Bert had quit placer mining by then and taken up ranching. He must have already been over forty then.

Ethan tied his horse to the hitching rail and looked up at the gray sky. "All right, Lord, I guess I've got to be sheriff. But I don't have to be old, do I?"

He strode purposefully toward the jail, refusing to enter like a doddering oldster. He flung the door open. The dim interior smelled of ashes and scorched beans. A pan with crusted-on food sat on the cold stove. The door of the single cell was open, just as it had been yesterday. Inside, a wooden bunk was attached to the far wall, which had a small barred window. A straw tick and a chamber pot were the only other amenities.

Ethan glanced around the outer room. Across from the stove stood Bert's desk and a chair. In one corner, a stool sat beneath several posters tacked to the wall. Hanging from a nail was a large key Ethan assumed went to the cell door. A kerosene lantern hung from the ceiling. Another window—also barred—shed a little light on the surface of the desk. A few sheets of paper and a tin can holding a pencil lay on the scarred desktop.

He walked four paces to the door of the small back room. Bert's bunk—where Ethan would probably spend more nights than he wanted to—took half the floor space. On the bare board floor beside it, a dark, irregular stain marked the spot where Bert's smashed head had rested. A shelf held two cups, two tin plates, assorted silverware, a bullet mold, a can of kerosene, and a tobacco tin. In one corner, a mismatched china bowl and pitcher sat on a low stand, and near it on the wall, a grayish towel and one of Bert's flannel shirts hung from pegs.

Ethan felt the small room closing in on him. His ranch house, with two snug bedchambers, a loft above, and a huge, open kitchen and sitting room, would make three of this jailhouse. He inhaled deeply and recalled Gert's words to him at the school. He wouldn't have to stay here unless he had prisoners.

"Thank You for that, Lord."

Yesterday the old sheriff had lain on his back, here by the bunk, with his feet sprawled right about where Ethan stood. He stepped aside quickly, then gave himself a mental kick in the backside. He couldn't avoid the spot where Bert died forever. He'd have to sleep in the dead man's bunk.

"At least I can wash the bedding and clean up that bloodstain." He stepped forward, deliberately planting his boots where Bert's body had lain on the planks, and yanked the crazy quilt off the bunk. Beneath was only another straw tick. A small pillow covered with a linen case lay at one end, and he shook the pillow out and wrapped the case up in the quilt. Dust filled the air and set him coughing. If it ever warmed up outside, he'd empty out the tick and the pillow and fill them with new straw.

Bert probably never dusted or swept this place. Ethan had yet to see a broom, though there must be one somewhere. He walked back into the outer room, seeking the tools he needed. A bucket half full of water sat between the stove and the wood box. He hadn't noticed it before. He could get more water and scrub the floor in there. And if he couldn't find a broom, he could walk over to Hiram's and ask to borrow Gert's.

He opened the stove and stooped over the wood box. Plenty of kindling, but tinder seemed in short supply. He grabbed a split log and began peeling off slivers and placing them in a strategic heap in the belly of the stove. Over them he built a tepee of kindling sticks. Bert had left a matchbox conveniently on the back of the wood box. Ethan lit the tinder and blew to coax the tiny flames.

He eased the stick he'd taken the splinters from into the stove, then stretched to reach another log. As he started to put it in the stove, he looked at the stick and jumped back, dropping it. The firewood clattered to the floor, thunking his knee on the way down.

Ethan stared down at the stick of wood. Slowly he stooped and retrieved it. He held it up by one end, like he would a gopher snake by its tail. The dark blotch wasn't much—just a reddish smear on the edge of the light, rough wood. As he brought it closer and peered at it, he nearly gagged. A clump of graying hair was lodged in the dark spot where a sliver had split from the rest of the log.

"Ethan?"

He jumped and turned toward the doorway. Hiram ambled toward him, frowning. His gaze traveled to the firewood and back to Ethan's face.

"I found this in the wood box." It sounded stupid. Ethan stepped toward his friend and held out the split log. "See that?" He pointed to the dark patch and the hairs.

Hiram raised his eyebrows. He reached out and took the two-foot piece of wood by the other end.

"It must have been there last night when we took Bert out of here," Ethan said.

Hiram nodded. "Musta been."

"Yeah. Must have." Ethan swallowed hard. "Good thing we didn't build the fire up and toss it in the stove without noticing."

Hiram's eyes were plain gray in the dim light. "How come. . . ?"

"What?" Ethan tried to follow Hiram's thoughts as he studied the wood again. "That's got to be Bert's hair and blood."

Hiram nodded again.

"I wonder if there were wood slivers in his scalp." The thought bothered Ethan. They should have paid more attention. "Someone hit Bert with that stick of fir."

Hiram eyed Ethan thoughtfully. "Not his heart."

"I'd say not."

Hiram pursed his lips and said nothing.

"If it'd been a woman, we'd have had the ladies lay her out," Ethan said. "They'd have changed her clothes and washed the body. They'd have cleaned the wound in the back of his head— her head. Oh, you know what I mean, Hi. They'd have noticed things."

The gunsmith nodded and scrunched his face up in distaste. "Gert said as much. Said we ought have changed Bert's shirt. But he was wearing his best one when he died."

"If we had, maybe we'd have looked closer. Did you notice anything odd about that gash on the back of his head?"

"Only that there wasn't any blood on the edge of the bunk where everyone said he must've hit his head."

"Yeah." Ethan walked over to Bert's desk and sat down in the oak chair behind it. "I guess I wanted it to be that way. There wasn't anything in the room that could have been a weapon. I didn't want to think someone did him in."

"Nobody wanted to," Hiram said.

"We could ask Griff. Maybe he noticed something."

"He'da said so."

Ethan nodded. Hiram was talking more than he had in years, but the things he said were small comfort.

"All right, what do we do? There's nobody to tell."

Hiram laid the stick of wood carefully on top of the desk so that the stained end stuck out off the edge.

Ethan rubbed the back of his neck. He hated being the sheriff. Less than two hours, and the job already scared him silly. Was a murder investigation his first duty? "All right, let's think about this. Maybe there's a U.S. marshal somewhere in the territory."

Hiram shrugged. "Boise, maybe?"

"Yeah. I'll send a telegraph message to Boise. That's good thinking, Hi. I'll ask who the territorial lawman is."

That settled, Ethan felt much better. He stood up. "Right. Let me finish building that fire. While the water for scrubbing the floor heats, I'll go to the telegraph office. Yeah. That's what I'll do." He looked at the stove. The door still stood wide open, and his little kindling pile was consumed. The flames had vanished, leaving the one split log forlornly smoldering.

He stepped toward the wood box, but Hiram put out a hand to stop him. "Go." Hiram reached down for another supply of kindling.

"Right." Ethan strode to the door and looked back. "Thanks."

★ CHAPTER 6 ★

That evening, Ethan walked to the mayor's house. He'd sent his terse telegram. After that, Hiram had helped him clean up the jail, though they couldn't completely get rid of the blood stain on the floor in the back room. Gert had offered him a small rag rug the Dooleys had used by their back door for some time. It neatly covered the spot.

He'd ended up eating at Hiram and Gert's again. Ethan had to admit, Gert Dooley did two things very well: cook and shoot. He'd have to be careful not to wear out his welcome in her kitchen now that he'd be spending more time in town. The three of them had agreed over coffee and bread pudding that he needed to advise the mayor that he'd found evidence of foul play and initiated contact with the U.S. marshal.

The Walkers had a comfortable frame house on Main Street. It boasted a wide front porch and yellow paint, which made it stand out from all the weathered board buildings. Lantern light glowed through the checked curtains. Ethan knocked on the door, and a few seconds later, Orissa opened it. Her hair, as usual, was fixed in a high bun that seemed to pull her face up into a tight grimace.

"The mayor's not home." Mrs. Walker never referred to her husband as Charles. He was always *my husband, the mayor*, or *Mr. Walker.*

"Where might I find him, ma'am?"

She huffed her displeasure. "I'm sure I don't know."

Ethan took that to mean Walker was at one of the saloons. Where else would Fergus men go in the evening?

"Thank you kindly." He descended the steps and headed south on Main. The mayor being the mayor—and having to maintain his civic dignity—Ethan figured he would choose the Spur & Saddle over the Nugget.

As he passed a few businesses now closed for the night, some homes with lanterns glowing inside, and as many empty storefronts, the burden of his new office settled on his shoulders.

People complained about the noise and carryings-on at the Nugget. A lot. Would he have to wade through the drunks every Saturday night and attempt to keep order? Maybe he'd have a talk with Jamin Morrell before his first Saturday night as sheriff rolled around. It was only two days distant, which didn't give him much time to strategize. What did Bert do about the Nugget? Ethan always spent weekends quietly on his ranch, beyond the reach of the music and shouting, but he'd heard people talk about it. Miners and cowboys rode miles on Saturday to sample the offerings of the tiny town of Fergus.

He gained the boardwalk in front of Bitsy Shepard's establishment. The murmur of conversation reached him as he opened the door. Cigar smoke wafted through the air. The scent of a good dinner lingered, and the quiet atmosphere almost comforted him. A man could come here without embarrassment. He could even bring his wife, if he had one, on Sunday when Bitsy closed the bar and served a fried chicken dinner to all and sundry. Once when they rode fence together on opposite sides of their property line, Bert Thalen had told him that he was seldom called to the Spur & Saddle. Bitsy ran a tight ship, with Augie Moore as a competent bosun. Ethan understood that to mean that Augie didn't take any nonsense from the patrons.

Bitsy herself worked the room tonight. As Ethan entered, she stood next to a table where three men were seated. All were focused on Bitsy, who had changed her deep red funeral wear for a shimmering blue and silver dress with a plunging neckline. Other than that, the dress was quite modest, and Ethan tried to keep his attention on those other features. Even so, he nearly stepped on

41

young Goldie, who carried a tray of drinks toward a table of card players in the corner.

"Oh, excuse me, miss." He jumped back out of Goldie's path.

"Don't mind if I do, Sheriff." Goldie gave him a saucy smile, and Ethan blushed to his hairline.

Walker sat at the table Bitsy graced with her presence, so Ethan turned in that direction, being more careful where he stepped. The room held a dozen ranch hands and miners, in addition to a handful of the town pillars. One of the pillars beckoned to him.

"Say, Sheriff, how are things in town this evening?" Cyrus Fennel called as he approached.

"Quiet so far, Mr. Fennel."

"Glad to hear it." Cyrus took a puff on his cigar and blew a stream of smoke toward the ceiling.

"Mr. Walker, I'd like to talk to you, if you've got a minute," Ethan said to the mayor, who sat on Fennel's left.

Bitsy smiled at the men. "Well, enjoy your drinks, gents. Bring you anything, Sheriff?"

"No thanks, ma'am."

She nodded and moved away, greeting the cowhands at the next table as though they were long-lost relatives.

"What is it, Chapman?" The mayor's shrill voice almost made Ethan smile. How many times had he imitated that tone to make Hiram laugh? The realization that he now answered to the mayor, when this morning he'd answered to no man, made his stomach churn. That and the cigar smoke.

"It's about Bert Thalen."

"God rest his soul," said Oscar Runnels, who ran a freight business consisting largely of several dozen pack mules.

"What about him?" The mayor cradled his glass between his hands and smiled up at Ethan as though he hadn't a care in this world, which he probably didn't, this far from Mrs. Walker.

"Well, I. . ." Ethan glanced at Cy Fennel and Oscar Runnels, suddenly wondering if he'd ought to spill all he knew in public. "Could I have a private word with you, sir?"

"Official town business at this time of night?" The mayor's voice escalated into a whine. "Just spit it out, Chapman. Is it about Bert's personal property?"

"No, sir. It's about. . .about how he died."

"Hit his head," said Fennel.

"That's right." Walker nodded vigorously, almost slopping his drink. "And we gave him a right good sendoff this afternoon."

"Well, sir. . ." Ethan saw that the miners and poker players had begun to take an interest in their conversation. He pulled up a chair and sat down so he could lean close to Walker and drop his voice. "It's true his head hit on something, all right, or rather, something hit his head. And I think I've found out what that something was."

The three men at the table stared at him. The others in the room had resumed their conversations, and Augie poured another round for two men leaning on the bar.

"Not his bunk bed?" Cyrus asked.

Ethan shifted his gaze to Fennel. The man's steely eyes made his neck prickle. Best to bring in the fact that Hiram could corroborate what he'd found. "No, sir. Hiram Dooley and I set out to redd up the jailhouse after the funeral, and we found a stick of firewood with blood and hair on the end of it, like someone had been smacked hard with it."

Fennel took a quick drink from his glass. The mayor continued to stare, but Runnels asked, "Where'd you find this here stick of wood?"

"Er, yes," Walker added.

"In the wood box beside the jailhouse stove."

The three sat in silence for a moment. Ethan waited for them to say something. He hadn't ever thought about it much, but Cyrus often seemed to speak when the mayor was addressed. Sure enough, he spoke next.

"If that was used as a weapon against someone, why didn't the person who used it throw it in the stove and burn it up?" Cyrus asked.

"That I don't know, sir."

"So, what are you going to do about it?"

Ethan gulped. He remembered Gert saying, 'I think the mayor chose the right man for the job.' But what did Gert know anyway?

Guns and bread dough, yes. But law enforcement? She knew as much as he knew about tatting lace, which was nothing.

"I've sent a telegram to Boise," he managed. Fennel and Walker looked at each other.

"That's probably best," the mayor said grudgingly.

"Are they going to send a deputy marshal up here?" Cyrus again had the probing questions.

"I haven't heard back yet."

"I suppose we should inventory Bert's things," Oscar said.

"Yes, we should." Cyrus picked up his glass. "I told the mayor earlier that I went by Bert's place this afternoon to make sure his livestock was all right and there weren't any animals in the barn. His horse is over at the livery. The cattle will be all right in the pasture for a day or two, but we need to make sure no one steals them or the things in his house."

The mayor nodded decisively. "That's a good job for you to do tomorrow, Chapman. Take a couple of fellows with you and list everything of value." He turned to Cyrus. "Where's Bert's son living now?"

"Oregon City, I think."

Ethan cleared his throat. "I guess I can get an inventory made and send it to him. Peter Nash would have his address at the post office."

"Well, there's not much else we can do, is there?" Walker took a deep swallow that emptied his glass. He set it on the table with a thump. "I need to get home, gentlemen." He rose and donned his hat. "Sheriff, keep me informed."

Cyrus and Oscar pushed their chairs back. Ethan surmised the interview was over. As Fennel pushed past him, he said, "Yes, Chapman. If there's going to be federal lawmen coming here, we need to be prepared."

Ethan stared after them, holding his hat. Didn't they care that Bert was murdered? Weren't they anxious to have the killer apprehended? They didn't seem worried about anything except government men coming to Fergus and upsetting their routine.

"So Bert's death wasn't an accident."

He turned his head. Bitsy stood at his elbow, looking at the door where the men had just exited.

Ethan wished Walker had let him tell him in private. Too late now. Everyone at Bitsy's place knew, and the news would be all over town within an hour.

Libby hurried down the stairs Friday morning to let Florence in at the back door of the Paragon Emporium. Punctual as usual, Florence untied and removed her bonnet, revealing the rusty red locks that clashed with her rosy cheeks.

"Miz Adams, you'll never guess what Myra Harper told me this morning."

Libby smiled as she headed for the counter. Her daily preparations for business would take most of the half hour that remained before opening time.

"You're probably right, Florence, so just tell me."

"The sheriff was murdered."

Libby stopped in her new high-topped, eleven-button calfskin boots and eyed her clerk cautiously. "Bert Thalen was murdered?"

"Well, sure. Not the *new* sheriff."

"I should hope not."

Florence giggled. "Me, too. Sheriff Chapman's a sight cuter'n Sheriff Thalen ever was."

Libby tried to scowl at her but failed. Ethan *was* a well-favored young man, and she supposed it was only natural for eighteen-year-old Florence to sigh over him, though Ethan probably had ten or twelve years on her.

"Now, Florence, don't speak ill of the dead. After all, you've no idea how Bert Thalen looked thirty years ago. Could be he was the handsomest man in the territory."

The girl giggled again as she hung up her bonnet. "I doubt that, ma'am. He was a nice man, but handsome he was not."

Libby sobered. "So, someone killed him? It wasn't an accident?"

Florence sidled up to the counter, puffed up with importance. "Myra stopped at the post office for her daddy's mail, and she asked Papa if he'd heard." Florence's father, Peter Nash, kept the post office on the family's front porch, and Florence was privy to a lot of gossip. "She said she had it from her father, and that he'd heard it from the mayor, who got it straight from Ethan Chapman last evening. Someone clobbered the old sheriff over the head with a stick of his own firewood."

Libby stared at her for a moment then swallowed. "I see." She leaned over so she could read the case clock near the front door. "Florence, I'm going to get the cash box out and run over to Gert Dooley's for a minute. You go ahead and get the ledgers out, and if Mrs. Harper brings eggs and milk around, pay her the usual rate."

She went to the storage room, opened the safe, and took the cash box out. She carefully put back most of the money, leaving only five dollars in change to start off the day. After closing the safe door on the rest, she carried the cash box out into the store and set it on the shelf beneath the counter. Florence had laid out the ledgers containing the regular customers' accounts and was now dusting the selection of housewares with a feather duster.

"I shan't be long." Libby tied on her bonnet and grabbed her gray shawl. She dashed out the back door and around to the alley between the emporium and the stagecoach office. A wagon rattled down the street, and a couple of people ambled along the boardwalk. She ran across and down to the Dooleys' house, set back from the street. Gert would be up and about her morning work. Libby hurried to the back door.

Gert answered her knock almost at once. She'd tied her pale hair back in a careless knot, and several strands had escaped and fluttered about her face. If Gert would just tend to herself a little more, she could be quite pretty, but she never seemed to care about the impression made by a crooked apron or untidy hair.

"Why, Libby Adams, what are you doing here so early?"

"I'm sorry, Gert. I hope I'm not disturbing you."

"Not at all. Can you take a cup of tea? Hiram's gone with Ethan Chapman and Zachary Harper to inventory Bert Thalen's belongings."

"No, really I can't. I'm glad to hear they're looking after Bert's things. I just came to see if you'd heard the. . .well, I guess it's a rumor."

Gert folded her arms across the front of her apron. "A rumor?"

"Well, yes. That Bert was murdered."

Gert shook her head regretfully. "It's no rumor. That there is the honest truth."

Libby raised her hand to her lips. "Oh dear. I was afraid of that."

"My brother was at the jail yesterday when Ethan found what they're calling evidence. Someone cracked Bert across the skull with a stick of fir from his wood box."

Libby's stomach went a little twitchy, as though she'd drunk a glass of sour milk. "Are they sure?"

"Oh yes, they're certain."

"Well, I. . .I don't know what to say. Are we safe in this town?"

"Now, that's the question, isn't it? Ethan's got no idea who did it, which means it could be anyone."

"Anyone?" Libby licked her dry lips.

"Anyone at all." Gert nodded firmly, and another strand of hair slipped from her coif.

Libby raised her chin. "If I bring Isaac's pistol over here after closing time someday, can you show me how to shoot it?"

Gert arched her eyebrows. "Sure, I could. What have you got?"

"It's his old Colt."

Gert nodded slowly. "Oh yes. A Peacemaker, isn't it? Hiram made a new walnut grip for that gun four or five years back."

"Did he? I don't remember. I never paid much mind to it when Isaac was alive."

"I'm surprised you haven't sold it by now." Gert eyed her with speculation in her gray blue eyes. "You might feel safer with something like that behind the counter."

"I sleep with it under my pillow." Libby flushed as soon as the words were out. Would Gert think her a ninny?

"Not loaded, I hope? If you don't know how to handle it, I mean."

"I had Cyrus Fennel check it for me after Isaac passed, to be sure it was empty. He offered to buy it, but I told him I thought I'd hang onto it for sentimental reasons."

Gert nodded. "Come by tonight if you want. We can shoot out back. Or we can ride out of town a ways if you want more privacy."

"Thank you, Gert. I appreciate that."

Libby bustled back across the street. Cyrus was opening the door of the stagecoach office and tipped his hat to her. Libby ducked down the alley and around the back of the emporium. Folks saw her as self-sufficient. Now she was one small step closer to being safe.

★ CHAPTER 7 ★

There now, hold it steady with both hands, and this time, don't jerk. Just squeeze gently." Gert gave Libby an encouraging smile and a nod.

"What?" Libby cocked her head toward her shoulder. "You had me put wool in my ears, and now I can't hear you."

Gert leaned closer and spoke with exaggerated enunciation. "Gently. Take it slow and easy."

Libby nodded and turned to focus on the target. Gert had hung a hank of knotted dried grass from a fir tree branch fifty feet away. She liked a bright piece of cloth or a slip of white paper for a target, but last year's crop of grass stood up free for the taking. The dry stalks were pale enough to stand out against a dark background of woods or a black rock.

Gert placed her hands on her hips and waited. Libby took aim, wavered, straightened her shoulders, and looked down the big pistol's barrel again.

"You're taking too long," Gert said.

"What?"

Gert sighed, leaned in close, and yelled, "The longer you wait, the shakier you'll get."

Libby raised her eyebrows and nodded, her lips parted as she considered the instructions.

"Put it down to your side," Gert yelled, pantomiming the action.

Libby lowered the pistol. It nearly vanished among the folds of her dark blue skirt.

"Now, when you bring it up, do it all at once, and shoot when you first focus on the target."

Libby nodded, but her eyebrows drew together and she looked far from confident.

"Like this," Gert shouted. She turned to face the target, drew up her pretend gun, raising her left hand at the same time to meet and steady her right. "Pow!"

She looked over at Libby.

"Did you hit it?" Libby asked.

Gert laughed and gestured for her to proceed. Her pupil was far too pretty and proper to be toting a Colt Peacemaker.

Libby inhaled deeply, held her breath, swung the pistol up, and pulled the trigger.

Mildly surprised that she'd carried through, Gert looked barely in time to see a fir twig flutter down. Libby hadn't hit the target, but she'd clipped the branch just below it.

"Good job." They both laughed.

Libby dug the wool out of one ear. "I've only got three more bullets."

"You shoulda brought more."

"That's all I had."

Gert frowned. "Don't you have more in the store?"

"No. I guess I should order more."

"Yes, you should. Don't you stock ammunition regularly in the emporium?"

"I wasn't sure what to order for this gun. Isaac used to do all that. Lately I just reorder what people are buying."

Gert grinned at her. "You're just too dainty to be true, Libby. The bullets for a Remington rifle same as Ethan uses will fit that pistol, right as rain."

A muffled shout drew Gert's attention toward the dirt track she and Libby had followed out from Fergus after supper. Cyrus Fennel, on his big roan, had pulled up at the edge of the road and hailed them.

Gert and Libby both stuck their fingers in their ears to ream out the wool.

"Did you say something?" Gert called to Fennel.

"I most certainly did. I asked what you ladies were up to."

"Just shootin'," Gert said.

"I see that. You usually shoot behind your brother's house, Miss Dooley."

"It's my fault, Mr. Fennel." Libby advanced toward him, holding the Peacemaker at her side between the folds of her skirt. "I asked Gert to give me a shooting lesson off where the whole town couldn't see. I guess we were close enough for you to hear us though."

"I was on my way home for supper and heard a few shots. Thought I'd check to make sure everything was all right."

"We're fine," Gert said.

Cyrus kept the rein short, and the gelding pawed the ground. The big man shook his head. "I'm not sure it's safe for you ladies to be out here shooting. What if I'd ridden up on that side of you?"

"You'da been foolish if you had," Gert said.

Cyrus glared at her. "Someone could get hurt. Miss Dooley, I know you're quite the marksman—or should I say markswoman? But still, you don't know who might be on the other side of those trees."

Gert puffed out a breath. Where to start? Anyone could see they fired only in the direction of a steep dirt bank that would catch all their lead. Yet he insinuated that he wasn't safe riding down the road behind them. Of all the nerve.

Before she could speak, Libby took two more steps, bringing her to within a few yards of the horse. "It's my fault. I heard Bert Thalen was murdered, and I wanted to be able to defend myself if need be, so I got out Isaac's pistol and determined to learn to use it."

He shook his head. "It doesn't do for nervous females to keep loaded guns. You could injure an innocent person. Why don't you let the sheriff worry about the killer, Mrs. Adams?"

Gert scowled. "What if the killer strikes again before the sheriff can stop him?"

Libby glanced at her and nodded.

"Oh, ladies." Cyrus sighed. "Let the men of Fergus worry

about public safety. I'm sure Sheriff Chapman will find out what really happened to Bert. If he *was* murdered, it was likely by some miscreant he tried to arrest. That person won't hang around town waiting to be caught."

"Thank you for the advice," Libby said. "I do feel better knowing men like you are looking out for our well-being."

Cyrus tipped his hat. "Good day, ladies." He turned his roan and cantered toward home.

Gert looked at Libby. After a long moment, Libby's mouth skewed into a grimace. "Nervous females, my foot."

Gert smiled. "You've still got three bullets. And you've got more .44 cartridges back at the store, right?"

"I sure do."

"Then let's see if you can shoot that bunch of straw down, and then we'll go home."

That evening, Ethan slowly approached the Nugget. His palms sweated and his throat was a little dry, though it was chilly. He walked steadfastly, giving his sidearm a quick pat. His first visit to the Nugget had better not be on a rowdy Saturday night. Tonight would be bad enough. Best to show his face and let Jamin Morrell know he'd keep an eye on things regularly.

He hesitated before pushing the saloon door open. A sour rendition of "Camptown Races" plinked from the piano inside, and the fumes of tobacco smoke and liquor made him brace himself. Could his mama see him from up in heaven? He hoped not. Although his purpose in entering the den of iniquity was innocent, Mama most certainly wouldn't approve.

He shoved the door open a little harder than was necessary, sending it flying back to bump the wall with a thud. Everyone in the Nugget swiveled and stared at him. The girl at the piano in the corner stopped playing and sat with her hands still poised over the keyboard.

Morrell had been leaning on the bar, conversing with a customer, but he straightened when he saw Ethan and smiled at him.

"Well, Sheriff. Welcome to the humble establishment."

Ethan cleared his throat. "Evening, Mr. Morrell."

"It's a quiet night tonight." Jamin looked over at the bartender, Ted Hire, who was wiping up a spill on the polished surface of the bar. "Ted, set up a glass for the sheriff." He turned back to Ethan. "What'll it be, Sheriff?"

Ethan stepped forward. "No, thanks."

"Oh, that's right." Jamin slapped his temple as if he were the most forgetful old codger in Idaho Territory. "You're on official business."

Ethan didn't contradict him, but they both knew he'd never darkened the door of the Nugget since it opened last summer. Jamin probably knew he never drank liquor. Morrell was sharp. Ethan figured he knew which men in town imbibed and which didn't, and which ladies liked a nip now and then as well.

"Just stopping in to tell you to call on me if you need any help keeping the peace," Ethan said. His right eye tried to twitch. He stared hard at Morrell, determined not to blink.

"That's kind of you, Sheriff." Morrell pulled a gold watch from his vest pocket, consulted it, and put it away. "You're welcome here anytime. Mr. Tibbetts and I were just discussing how badly this town needs a doctor. Isn't that right, sir?" He looked to the dust-covered rancher leaning on the bar for confirmation.

"We sure do." Tibbetts upended his glass and drained it. When he set it down, the bartender refilled it without asking.

Ethan nodded. "Can't argue with you there." If they'd had a doctor when Bert was killed, the doctor could have looked at the dead man's wound and maybe known right away poor Bert had been murdered.

"A physician would be a fine addition to the community." Morrell settled again with one elbow resting on the bar.

"Need a bank, too," called a man who sat at a small, square table holding a half dozen playing cards in one hand. Ethan recognized him as one of Cy Fennel's stage drivers.

"Yes, indeed," Morrell said. "That's another thing that would help this town grow."

"How about a preacher while you're at it?" Tibbetts blinked

at Jamin. "That's what my missus is always sayin'. We need us a preacher."

Jamin started to laugh then sobered. He flexed his shoulders. "Your missus may be right, Jim." His eyes narrowed.

Ethan wondered what the saloon keeper was thinking. When a town got a church and a minister, it usually forced restraint on its houses of entertainment. Surely Morrell didn't favor that.

Ethan glanced around. Besides Tibbetts and the poker players, only two other customers and the girl at the piano kept Morrell and the bartender company. The night was young, of course, but it gave him satisfaction to think Bitsy Shepard had kept the greater part of the saloon traffic despite the new competition.

Thoughts like that always muddled Ethan, since he knew deep down that any saloon was bad. As a nondrinking citizen, he'd avoided both and ignored their existence. But as sheriff, he'd need to make his presence felt and even cooperate with the owners to keep things from getting out of hand. Saloons being legal, he had to live with the facts.

But that didn't mean he had to linger.

"Have a nice evening." He nodded to Morrell.

"Come again, Sheriff."

Oh, I will, Ethan thought as he strode toward the door. *I surely will.*

As the door swung shut behind him, he heard someone say, "I dunno if the new sheriff's man enough for the job."

He stood still for a moment on the steps, fighting the urge to charge back in there. But he wouldn't know who the speaker was, and besides, that wasn't the way to prove him wrong. Only time and diligence would do that. He walked on toward the jail.

On Monday afternoon Libby took off her apron and hung it behind the counter. Finally the air held the warmth of May and the promise of summer. She wouldn't need a wrap today. She'd chosen a large needlepoint handbag in which to carry her pistol and a supply of ammunition. She reached for a crisp green calico poke bonnet that would be perfect headgear for a spring day.

"Florence, I'll be back by three o'clock." Traffic in the emporium was always light after noontime, and her clerk could handle it without her.

"Yes, ma'am." Florence's hazel eyes held a hint of solemnity as she looked about the store.

Libby went out the back. She didn't like people to see her leave by the front door. The mayor's wife might try to go over and talk Florence down on prices, thinking she could get a bargain from the inexperienced girl. Libby smiled at the thought. For the first month of Florence's employment, Libby had made her repeat over and over before opening each morning, "Only Mrs. Adams makes deals with customers."

She lurked in the alley between the emporium and the stagecoach office until she was sure no one paid any mind to the foot traffic on her part of the street. As she dashed across the way, she noted smoke puffing from the jail's chimney. Ethan must be in his new office. He'd been sheriff less than a week, but he seemed to take the position and its responsibilities to heart. Already she'd heard complaints. When Ted Hire came in wanting some lamp oil, he'd mentioned how the sheriff had come into the Nugget three times on Saturday night and told the boys to keep the noise down. It put a damper on the usual hilarity, to hear Ted tell it.

At the Dooleys' house, she cut straight around to the back. Gert had already saddled the two horses she and her brother maintained. Hiram Dooley's Sharps rifle protruded from a leather scabbard on the saddle of Gert's dun mare, Crinkles. The other horse, Hiram's docile bay gelding he called Hoss, stood with his head drooping, eyes closed, and tail swishing now and then. His reins hung down from the bit, the only restraint Gert had used on him. That was about all the excitement Libby liked in a horse.

"Howdy," Gert called with a smile.

"Good afternoon. Am I late?"

Gert glanced up at the sky. "Not on my account."

"Are you sure Hiram won't mind if I take his horse?"

"No, he's got the mayor's rifle in. He'll be working on it all afternoon, I dare say."

Gert unhitched Crinkles and swung the mare's head around. "Need a boost?"

"Well. . ." Libby gathered Hoss's reins and moved him to an uneven spot in the ground, where she could stand a few inches uphill from him. She was able to lift her left foot to the stirrup from there. "I'll be fine," she called, but Gert led Crinkles over anyway.

"Forgot to put the stirrups up. Go ahead and mount. I'll run 'em up the leathers once you're on."

Libby swung up and threw her leg over, struggling to arrange her skirt and keep her bag from bumping Hoss's side.

"You ought to alter one of your skirts," Gert said. "It'd be easier to ride in."

"Oh, I know." Libby had ridden sidesaddle before she'd come west to marry Isaac Adams, but out here, the practice was out of fashion. She doubted the town of Fergus boasted a single sidesaddle.

Hiram's legs were a good deal longer than hers, and her toes slid out of the stirrups. In seconds, Gert had adjusted the straps. "All set?"

"Feels just right." Libby bounced on her toes, and Hoss swung his head around, fixing her with a reproachful gaze. "Sorry, Hoss."

Gert hopped easily onto Crinkles's back. Her divided skirt settled with modesty about her. Libby decided she would look at the pattern book when she got back to the emporium. Maybe it was time she had the practical Western version of a riding habit. Gert gathered her reins and clucked. Crinkles set out at a swift walk. Libby squeezed Hoss. When he didn't move, she kicked him lightly, and he shuffled off in the mare's wake.

They ambled behind the row of houses and businesses that faced Main Street and soon were beyond the edge of town. Gert urged her mare into a quick trot, and Libby, with some effort, persuaded Hoss to keep up. They rode to a stream that gushed down out of the mountains on its way to the river. This time of year, the streams around Fergus looked as though they meant business, but by the end of July, most would be bone dry.

Gert led her up the ravine to a secluded spot between the hills, where she halted and jumped to the ground.

"Are we on Ethan Chapman's land?" Libby asked as she dismounted. She looked about for a place to tether her horse.

"Bert Thalen's ranch, actually, but he won't mind." Gert didn't seem to notice what she'd said about the dead man, or if she did, she hadn't considered it disrespectful. Libby liked Gert, but sometimes she seemed a little indelicate.

Gert looked at her. "Did you know that Ethan heard back from Bert's son?"

"No, what did he say?" Libby asked.

"He wants Ethan to sell off his livestock and keep an eye on the place until he decides what to do with it."

"Oh my."

"Griff Bane said he'll buy Bert's horse. Ethan thinks Micah Landry might buy the beef cattle." Gert added, "Don't worry about Hoss. He'll ground tie."

"Even when we start shooting?"

"Yes, he's too dumb to run away."

Libby let the reins fall and looked about. "It's beautiful out here. I should get away from town more."

"You can ride Hoss or Crinkles anytime," Gert offered.

"Thank you. Isaac used to keep a team and wagon, but I sold them after he died. Too expensive. I just hire freighters to haul stuff for me."

"It's an extravagance for us," Gert admitted. "Hiram and I like to be able to ramble around when the fancy strikes us, so we put up with these nags."

Libby pulled some small pieces of bright flannel from her reticule. "You asked for some scraps of cloth."

Gert's eyes lit. "Thanks. Those are perfect." She nodded toward a knoll a short distance away. "I'll set up the targets over there, and we can shoot from beside the stream."

Libby watched her easy gait as she went to prepare the mark. Gert walked like a boy, though she must be twenty-four or more. Libby could remember when she'd come all the way from Maine to help Hiram's wife, Violet, with her new baby. Or such was

Gert's intention when she set out on the long journey. As soon as Violet Dooley had learned a baby was on the way, she'd sent a gushing letter, begging Hiram's little sister to come stay with them and help her keep house when the child arrived. Gert had gladly answered the summons.

She was sixteen when she arrived, of that much Libby was certain. Tall, raw-boned, and gangly as a colt. No one considered her a beauty. Gert had plain, honest features and a temperament to match. She probably could have married in those first few years here in Fergus. But she'd arrived to find her brother in mourning, with Violet and their sweet baby buried out near the schoolhouse. Gert had made it plain to all that she'd come to help her brother. Any young men who'd fluttered about the gunsmith's house soon learned she didn't intend to cook and clean house for anyone but Hiram. And so, eight years later, she still lived in her brother's home.

As she piled up a few stones and anchored a bright slip of cloth on top for them to aim at, Gert frowned in concentration. She wasn't homely, Libby told herself again. Some might say so if they saw her gritting her teeth like that, with worry lines creasing her brow. But Gert had potential. Libby wished she could coax her into the emporium when a new shipment of fancy goods came in from St. Louis. But it was the bar girls who hurried over in search of ways to pretty themselves up, not plain, honest Gertrude.

Gert finished constructing three targets at varied distances and walked back toward her. Libby realized she didn't have her gun out of the bag yet. She took her handbag down from the saddle and walked toward the stream. Gert went to Crinkles and drew Hiram's rifle from the scabbard.

"Ready?" She walked over to Libby's side with the Sharps resting on her shoulder.

"I haven't loaded yet," Libby confessed. "Go ahead and shoot a few rounds."

Gert shrugged as though it was nothing to her.

"That's a nice rifle." Libby nodded at Gert's weapon.

"Hi got it off a miner. He'd gone broke on his claim and needed enough cash to get out of the territory. Someone told him the gunsmith might buy it." Gert shook her head. "Of course Hi gave him more than he should have."

"Your brother's got a soft heart."

"No, he didn't like the look of the fellow. I think he wanted to make sure he got far away from Fergus."

Libby laughed. "I hope he didn't give more than the gun was worth."

"Did I say that? He could have got it for less though." Gert swung the Sharps up to her shoulder.

Libby jumped at the sharp crack. To her, it seemed Gert fired as soon as the rifle reached a horizontal position.

"Sorry," Gert said. "We didn't plug our ears yet."

Libby reached into the depths of her reticule once more for a wad of wool. Within a few minutes, they were taking turns firing their weapons. Gert aimed at the farther marks while Libby shot at the nearest.

After firing six rounds in succession, Libby lowered the Peacemaker and exhaled in disappointment. She looked over at Gert and said loudly, "I'm just no good at this."

"I was watching. You're getting closer. Remember what I told you last time—aim, steady, squeeze."

"I thought I was doing that."

Gert lowered the stock of the rifle to the ground. "Load up again, and I'll pay closer attention, but I think you're improving."

Libby noticed a woman walking toward them from the direction of the road. "There's Mrs. Landry."

Gert swung around. "Sure enough."

"Hello," Emmaline Landry called.

"She lives out here, doesn't she?" Libby asked.

Gert nodded toward the nearest hill. "Yonder. Her man's ranch backs up against Bert and Ethan's spreads."

Emmaline trudged along holding her skirt up a few inches. She still wore her apron and had a smudge of flour on her cheek.

"I misdoubt my eyes. What are you ladies doing out here? I heard shooting like a battle and thought I'd better investigate."

Gert laughed. "No fighting, Mrs. Landry. We're just having a little target practice."

"Shooting? Whatever for?" The rancher's wife looked at Libby.

"Now, Gert I can understand. But you, Miz Adams?"

Libby smiled. "Yes, ma'am. I've decided I no longer want to be helpless. Part of my husband's legacy to me was this pistol. After what happened to Sheriff Thalen, I thought it was time I learned to use it."

Emmaline's eyes darkened. "The other day, one of our neighbors had a bucket of milk stolen—bucket and all. Can you believe it? But what's that you're saying about the sheriff? We was at the funeral, and all I heard was he'd fallen and hit his head."

Libby looked at Gert, and Gert inhaled and pulled her shoulders back.

"Sheriff Thalen didn't bump his head," Gert said. "He was murdered, and that's the honest truth."

Emmaline's jaw dropped. "No."

Libby nodded. "I'm afraid so, Mrs. Landry. We've no idea who did it, and so I asked Gert to teach me to shoot. If anyone comes creeping around the emporium at night, I want to be ready."

"That's not a bad idea. Are you planning to do this again?"

Gert looked inquiringly at Libby. "Maybe. If Libby wants to practice again."

"Could—" Emmaline looked over her shoulder toward the road and back again. "Could I join you? Micah's got a shotgun I think I could handle."

"Sure," Gert said.

Libby smiled. "You'd be welcome. How about Thursday afternoon?"

"Suits me." Gert hoisted the Sharps onto her shoulder.

"I'll be here." Emmaline caught her breath and lifted her skirts. "I 'most forgot. I left bread in the oven. Thursday!" She ran for the road with her shawl and bonnet strings fluttering behind her.

★ CHAPTER 8 ★

Cyrus Fennel was nearly sober when he entered the Nugget on Saturday evening. He'd already visited the Spur & Saddle, where he'd shared a drink with Oscar Runnels. The Nugget wasn't his usual haunt, but he wanted to speak to a couple of the men who worked for him on the stage line, and he had reason to believe he'd find them at Jamin Morrell's establishment.

He pushed open the door and squinted in the thick smoke. At a corner table, he spotted Ned Harmon and Bill Stout, one of his shotgun messengers and the driver he'd ridden in with that afternoon. The two were deep in conversation with Griffin Bane, the owner of the livery stable. Cyrus strode over to the table.

"You boys going to be in shape to take the coach on to Silver City in the morning?"

"What? We don't get our Sunday off?" Ned scowled up at him.

"Not this time. The Mountain Home coach broke down. Don't know when they'll get here. You'd best call it an early night and show up ready to roll at sunup."

"Sure, Mr. Fennel." Bill Stout looked up at him and hiccupped.

Cyrus turned and walked over to the bar.

Ted Hire smiled a welcome and shouted over the loud voices and off-key music from the piano. "Mr. Fennel. What can I get you, sir?"

"Whiskey. And don't serve those two men any more tonight, you hear me? They've got to work tomorrow."

"Yes, sir, I hear you loud and clear." Ted set a glass on the bar and filled it.

A lull in the tinny music set off snatches of conversation.

"—twin calves, both bulls."

"—told the mayor that was hogwash."

"—ladies shootin' up a storm, out the Mountain Road."

Cyrus turned and homed in on the last speaker—a miner he'd seen before but couldn't put a name to.

Ralph Storrey, who had a small spread at the south edge of town, said, "Oh, that's likely Hiram Dooley's sister. She can shoot the whiskers off a gnat at a hundred yards."

"There was three of 'em," the miner said, but the rest of his sentence was drowned out by a shaky rendition from the piano of "My Grandfather's Clock."

Someone jostled Cyrus's elbow, and he spilled part of his drink. He whipped around. A young cowhand stepped back and yanked his hat off.

"Sorry, sir. Don't pay me no nevermind."

Cyrus gritted his teeth. No point in making a scene over it. When he turned around again, Ted had already wiped up the spill.

"Let me refill your drink, Mr. Fennel."

When the girl finished the song, the card players were still discussing the female shooters.

"I say the women of this town don't seem to know their place," said a hardware salesman who had come in on the afternoon stage with Ned and Bill.

"That's right," Storrey grunted.

By now Cyrus had downed two and a half drinks, counting the one at the Spur & Saddle, and he thought the salesman showed a rare sense of propriety.

"I've got to agree with you, mister," he called out. "I saw a couple of ladies out shooting last week. Said they wanted to be able to defend themselves."

"Ha!" Ned yelled. "Ain't that what you got a new sheriff for?"

"That's right," said one of Micah Landry's cowpokes, who lounged at another table with the saloon girl now hanging over him. "Old sheriff died one day, and we got us a new sheriff the next."

"Well, them ladies don't seem to think much of the new lawman," said the miner. "Iffen they did, they wouldn't be out shootin' when they'd oughta be tendin' their young'uns."

The salesman nodded. "They should be home keeping house."

"My daughter Isabel would never go gallivanting around doing such things," Cyrus said.

"Well, you never know," drawled another cowhand. "She ain't got no man to keep house for but her father."

The saloon went as silent as a church.

Cyrus slammed his glass down on the bar. "What do mean by that, you jolt-headed lunk?"

The cowboy and three of his friends stood. Ted quickly scooped all bottles and glasses off the bar.

"What'd you call me?" the cowboy asked.

Cyrus squinted at him. This was no time to back down. "I said you're a—"

"Easy, now," Griffin Bane said, rising. All eyes swung his way. "You gents got no call to get riled up. If a few ladies feel safer knowin' how to fire a rifle, where's the harm?"

"I'll tell you where's the harm," Cyrus said. "They're like to blow somebody's head off while they're out blazing away at sticks and old bottles."

"The sheriff oughta put a stop to it," said Bill Stout. Cyrus wondered if he said it just to stay on his good side, but he nodded in Bill's direction.

"*If* the sheriff can do that," Ralph Storrey said. "I'm not so sure the new sheriff could handle a pack of gun-totin' ladies."

The young cowboy who had slopped Cyrus's drink laughed. "Yeah, he ain't got a woman. Maybe he's scared of petticoats."

"The new sheriff happens to be a friend of mine." Griffin's heavy words again cut through the bluster.

"Yeah? Well, he's s'posed to be a big Injun fighter, but I ain't seen him do nothin' since he come back to Fergus." Landry's cowhand glared at Griffin through the smoke.

Cyrus wondered, not for the first time, if pushing the mayor to appoint Chapman as sheriff was such a good idea. They wanted a man they could control, but Ethan was showing initiative, telegraphing the U.S. marshal on his own and patrolling the town regularly. If there was going to be real trouble. . . He reached for his whiskey glass, but Ted had moved it.

"Give me another drink," he snarled. Ted produced the glass from beneath the bar and poured while darting glances toward the men and the door.

Bane still stood glaring at the young cowboy. "Take back what you said about the sheriff, you buffoon."

"Make me."

"As for keeping the law in town," Cyrus began, reaching for his glass, "time will—"

"And speaking of the new sheriff," Ted shouted in his ear.

Cyrus jerked his head toward the door. Great. The one time he nearly lost control of himself, and that annoying young man they'd pinned a badge on had to walk in. The fact that he'd seen him half an hour ago at the Spur & Saddle, when he'd only imbibed one drink, wouldn't help now. He pulled in a deep breath. "Sheriff Chapman."

Ethan nodded gravely. "Mr. Fennel. I see you're making the rounds tonight."

Cyrus clenched his fists. "Just came to remind a couple of my men that tomorrow's a workday on the stagecoach line."

Ned Harmon jumped to his feet, swayed a little, and sat down again.

Bill Stout shoved his chair back and stood more slowly. "That's right, Mr. Fennel. We're calling it a night; ain't we, Ned?"

"Whatever you say."

Bill latched on to Ned's collar and pulled upward. "Come on. Let's get over to the livery and get some shut-eye."

"Hold it, boys," Griffin said. He walked over and stood deliberately in front of Cyrus. "If your men are going to bed down in my stable all the time, I think it's time we came to a financial understanding."

Cyrus felt his jaw twitch. If he couldn't see Ethan watching him with keen, dark eyes over Bane's shoulder, he'd have hit him. His drivers had sacked out in Bane's hayloft for years without any question of pay.

"It doesn't cost you a cent to let them sleep there," he said through his teeth.

"It's still my barn." Griffin's solid form didn't budge, and neither did his stare.

"I'm sure we can work this out, Griff." Cyrus managed a smile. "You know we've got no boardinghouse in this town anymore. The boys have to sleep somewhere."

"That's right." Ned raised one hand, as if what he said carried vast importance.

Griffin Bane still scowled at Cyrus. "Correct me if I'm wrong, but don't you own the building that used to be the boardinghouse?"

"Yes, I do." Cyrus didn't like the quiet that bespoke the men's attention. This run-in would be all over town by morning. He'd better come out looking good. "If someone wanted to rent the place and open up the business again, I'd be happy to discuss it."

"Maybe you should put that daughter of yours to keeping a boardinghouse," the salesman said, and all the men but Cyrus and Ethan laughed.

Cyrus's eyes flashed. "My daughter is the town's schoolmistress."

"That right?" The salesman shrugged. "Beg pardon."

One of the bar girls swaggered toward Cyrus. "I'd like to keep a boardin'house, Mr. Fennel. You could set me up to run it for you."

Ted scowled at her. "Good thing Mr. Morrell ain't around to hear you say that. You just be glad you've got a job here."

"Where *is* Mr. Morrell tonight?" Ethan asked, looking around.

"He went to Mountain Home a coupla days ago. He ain't back yet." Ted shot a nervous glance at Cyrus. "I heard the stage broke down in Grand View. Likely he's staying there tonight."

"Yeah," Ned Harmon said dolefully. "They got a boardinghouse in Grand View."

"You insolent—" Cyrus drew back his hand but suddenly recalled that the person who had raised the topic was the sheriff. He lowered his hand and cleared his throat. "Well, I'll be heading home. You boys get over to the livery and hit the hay." He frowned at Griffin Bane. "Come by the stage office tomorrow and settle up with me. We'll discuss how much it's worth to let a squiffed messenger and a reckless driver sleep it off in your barn."

Cyrus clapped his hat onto his head and strode out the door. As he passed the sheriff, Ethan said, "Have a good evening, Mr. Fennel."

"Yeah," called the hardware salesman, "and you might want to think about that boardinghouse. It's mighty hard to get a room in this town."

On Sunday afternoon Gert forced herself to attack her overflowing mending basket. She and Hiram always spent Sundays in quiet occupations—no shooting or splitting wood. Occasionally Gert experienced vague twinges of self-reproach, not so strong as guilt, telling her that sewing didn't constitute a proper pastime for the Sabbath. But since they had no preacher to tell them so, the full weight of conviction eluded her, and she told herself that tranquil industry, performed away from the prying eyes of their neighbors, could not possibly cause one of weaker conscience to stumble.

Her brother sat near the window, patiently carving and smoothing a gunstock for one of the stagecoach line's "shotgun messengers," the men who kept watch on the Wells Fargo stagecoaches.

Gert groped the bottom of her basket for a darning egg, gasped when she found a needle instead, and jerked her hand out.

Hiram paused in wielding his sandpaper and cocked an eyebrow.

"Stuck myself." She sucked the injured finger. She'd always categorized sewing as a necessary evil. A few minutes later when she was sure she wouldn't bleed all over her project, she snatched one of Hiram's shirts from the basket. Buttons first. The darning could wait until she'd worked her way down the layers in the basket and prospecting for the egg was no longer so hazardous.

A knock at the kitchen door annoyed her slightly, as she'd just gotten her needle threaded. People dropped in at all hours to seek Hiram's services, but since he didn't like to talk to anyone, Gert was the designated door opener and greeter. She laid her mending aside with a sigh and rose. Her brother watched with mournful eyes as she walked across the room, but he never paused in rhythmically sanding the piece of walnut.

Gert swung the door open to the mild May sunshine and stared in surprise at her visitor.

"I want to join your club," Bitsy Shepard said.

"Club?" Gert tried not to be rude, but Bitsy's idea of Sabbath wear was one garter short of shocking, which made staring almost mandatory. Her deep blue satin dress, shot through with threads of silver, had been caught up over one knee with a rosette of ribbons to reveal a frothy underskirt of vermilion net. Though Bitsy wore a dainty hat with two bright feathers curled down over her left eyebrow, it didn't detract from the effect of her low-cut bodice. Gert cast a quick glance over her shoulder to be sure Bitsy was out of Hiram's line of vision. "Did you say 'club'?"

"Yes. I heard you have a shooting club for ladies."

The question of whether Bitsy would qualify to join any association for ladies barely grazed Gert's mind. It was the word *club* that seized her attention.

"Oh, it's only me and one or two others. Mrs. Adams wanted to learn to handle her husband's pistol after Sheriff Thalen was killed, and then a couple of ranchers' wives joined us to practice loading and shooting, what with all the petty thievery that's been going on lately. It's not a club."

"I don't care what you call it. I want in." Bitsy's deep red lips quivered, and Gert realized two things. Bitsy was upset, and her lips matched her underskirt.

She glanced once more toward her brother's chair. Hiram, bless his heart, must have overheard enough to realize who had come calling. He'd taken his gunstock and sandpaper and retreated to his bedchamber. Gert inhaled deeply and stepped back.

"Would you like to step in for a minute, Bitsy?"

For the first time, Gert admitted a saloon girl to her home. Of course Bitsy was more than a saloon girl, some might argue. As owner of the Spur & Saddle, she was a businesswoman, the same as Libby Adams. Even as she thought as much, Gert knew comparing Bitsy and Libby was inherently wrong.

"Do you have a weapon?" she asked.

Bitsy hiked her skirts up even farther and leaned over to disengage something from a loose pocket hanging between her petticoat and net underskirt. She straightened, tossing the dark hair back from her powdered brow, jeopardizing the stability of her hat. The feathers quivered next to her temple.

"I've had this since I was fourteen." She held out a pistol not much larger than the palm of her hand.

Gert stared at it for a moment. "May I?"

"Sure."

Bitsy surrendered it, and Gert walked over to the window to hold it up in the light. The beautiful little gun had a black walnut stock, smoothly curved into a bird's-head shape. The round barrel, only about three inches long, was flattened along the top. Silver fittings on the stock bore engraved swirls and the gun maker's name.

"I don't know's I've ever seen a genuine Deringer before." Gert held it tenderly and gazed at the big hammer spur and the low sight on the end of the engraved barrel.

"Oh? I thought they were pretty common." Bitsy stepped closer.

Gert looked up at her quickly. "Would you mind if I showed this to Hiram?"

"Well. . .no, I guess not. There's nothing wrong with it though. I just don't have any ammunition for it. Haven't shot it in years. I figure it's time I brushed up my shooting skills."

"You're not the only one who feels that way."

"Well, with Bert being killed in broad daylight. . ." Bitsy choked a little, and Gert wondered just how close Bitsy and Bert had been.

"I think my brother would like to see this." Gert crossed to Hiram's bedroom door and tapped on the pine panel. "Hi? Can you come out and look at a pistol?"

A moment later, he opened the door a crack and peered out at her, eyebrows arched in skepticism.

"Miss Shepard's got a gun for you to look at."

Hiram opened the door a little farther and shuffled into the room, looking everywhere but at Bitsy. Gert stuck the pistol into his hand. He gave a curt nod in the general direction of their visitor without ever making eye contact and gave his attention to the gun.

Gert watched his face. She could tell by the way he inhaled slowly, his lips slightly parted, that he'd fallen in love. He cradled the weapon tenderly and examined it from both sides. He rubbed the cross-hatched lines carved into the butt and stroked the iron barrel—round at the front, octagonal where it fit precisely into the stock. He opened the lock and peered into the breach.

At last he looked up at Gert and smiled.

Gert touched his arm gently and turned to Bitsy.

"My brother says it's the real thing, made by. . ." She glanced back at her brother. "What was his first name?"

"Henry," said Hiram.

"That's it. Henry Deringer Jr. of Philadelphia. Most of the ones you see nowadays weren't really made by him, and they're not nearly so nice."

"Can I get bullets for it?" Bitsy asked.

Hiram nodded.

"It's a percussion pistol," Gert said, frowning. "Most of the newer ones they *call* derringers take cartridges. But I'm sure we can fix you up. If Libby Adams doesn't have what you need at the emporium, you can ask her to order it. I know she has powder, caps, and patches. Or you can make your patches. But it looks like a large caliber to me." She looked to Hiram.

He nodded. "Fifty-one."

"Ouch," Gert said with a smile. "You don't have a mold that size, do you, Hi?"

Her brother shook his head.

"What does that mean?" Bitsy took a step toward them, and Hiram stood his ground but pulled his shoulders back a little.

"It takes an odd-sized bullet," Gert said. "Libby might have some lead balls that size, but I doubt it. Where'd you get fixin's for it before?"

"A friend brought me some. But that was in St. Joe, years and years ago. Like I said, I haven't used this since I came to the territory. I've. . .let Augie handle any roughnecks lately."

Gert shrugged. "Well, one way or another, we should be able to fix you up."

Bitsy eyed Hiram up and down, and this time he did step back. "Do you know anyone else in town with that size firearm?" she asked.

He shook his head.

"If anyone had one, he'd know it," Gert said.

"Maybe I should buy another gun." Bitsy raised a hand and brushed her hair off her brow, setting the feathers dancing.

Gert felt a soft touch on her sleeve. "What is it, Hi?"

He held the little pistol up and gazed meaningfully into her eyes.

Gert smiled and said to Bitsy, "My brother says, will you sell the Deringer? He'd like to buy it."

Bitsy blinked her artificially long lashes and turned her gaze on Hiram. "He said all that?"

Hiram's face flushed, and Gert suppressed her annoyance. Bitsy had lived in Fergus long enough to know Hiram rarely spoke the way other people did.

"Yes. If you're interested, he'll make you an offer. Maybe enough so you could buy a new revolver."

Bitsy smiled. "Sorry. I'd keep it even if I couldn't get the bullets for it. It was given to me by—" She stopped and shrugged. "Sentimental value, you might say."

Hiram nodded and handed the Deringer to Gert, though Bitsy was only two feet away. He turned and oozed back into his room, closing the door quietly.

Bitsy stared after him. She opened her mouth as though to speak and then shook her head. "Well, then, I need some bullets."

"Libby's closed today for the Sabbath," Gert said. "You can ask her tomorrow. If she doesn't have them, she can order them from Boise."

"All right, thanks. And may I shoot with you and your friends?"

Gert looked over Bitsy's colorful costume and knew she had to make the decision at once and not back down. What would Libby say? That was easy. Gert wasn't so sure about Emmaline Landry.

"Of course. We're meeting here tomorrow afternoon at two. We've been riding out of town so's people don't complain about the noise."

"Do I need a horse?"

Gert couldn't imagine Bitsy riding astride in one of her flimsy outfits. "Maybe we can get a wagon from Griff Bane this time. If you want to come regular, we'll work something out." She passed the small pistol to Bitsy.

"Thanks." Bitsy hiked up her skirt and stuck the Deringer in her pocket. "I should probably tell you, I'm not just doing this because I'm scared. I do have employees who can take care of me and my place if I need 'em to. But I heard Cy Fennel and some of the other men have been grousing about you and your friends taking up shooting."

Gert stared at her. "Mr. Fennel? What does he care?"

"He thinks it's not ladylike. And he's not just been saying it. He's been saying it over at the Nugget."

"Ah." Gert began to see the light. The saloon that comprised Bitsy's competition had begun harboring men who complained about independent women. She'd never considered Bitsy a friend, but in that moment, she felt a streak of sisterhood toward her. Anyone who disliked Cy Fennel must have other good points as well. "You're welcome to come shoot with us anytime. Anytime at all."

★ CHAPTER 9 ★

Ethan took a quick ride around his pastures Monday morning. His herd of Hereford-cross cattle seemed to be doing all right, though he'd paid them little attention for the past week. He'd have to plant his garden soon and brand his spring calves. Then it would be time to cut hay, and his barn roof needed some work. His whole place would go to ruin if he didn't give it some care.

He looked around and with a sigh turned Scout toward the road to Fergus. He hated to head in to town again, but his conscience wouldn't let him stay at the ranch and feel comfortable. Someone in the town always seemed to want the sheriff's attention. Saturday nights had taken the starch right out of him, having to haunt the two saloons. And what about finding out who had killed Bert Thalen? He'd thought about it many times but seemed no closer to learning the truth.

At least they'd completed the inventory of everything of value in the house, woodshed, and barn, and gotten that in the mail to Bert's son. Ethan and Hiram had cleaned the food out of Bert's house, boarded up the windows, and put a lock on the front door to keep vandals out. So many details to consider. And the marshal in Boise was no help as far as the murder went. He'd sent word to carry on. What did that mean?

Ethan wondered what Mayor Walker would say if he told him he didn't want to be sheriff any longer. Maybe he should up and quit.

At midmorning he tied the paint gelding to the hitching rail in front of the jail. His gaze swept the main street. He was surprised to see Gert and Bitsy enter the emporium together. He'd never known Gert to socialize with the saloonkeeper. Not that Bitsy was a bad sort; she just wasn't. . .

The blood rushed to his cheeks. Bitsy was the type of woman his mother had taught him to stay away from. Gert, on the other hand, while neither wealthy nor elegant, was nevertheless a lady. What would bring those two together?

His curiosity got the better of him, and he crossed the street and edged through the door to the Paragon Emporium. Libby Adams stood behind the counter, showing something to Gert and Bitsy. Both seemed riveted by whatever it was she displayed.

Mrs. Adams's shop girl, Florence, kept busy at the far end of the store, arranging items on the shelves. Three or four other customers browsed, and Ethan decided he could imitate them and hear the ladies' conversation. He spotted a harness hanging on the front wall and hastened to stand near it, with his back to the counter.

"Yes, I can get a supply of lead balls for you," Libby said. "Are you sure you don't want to get one of the new cartridge pistols?"

Bitsy said, "Hiram Dooley seemed to think this was a well-made gun and would work fine."

"That's right," Gert put in. "And when you get the ammunition, we can test fire it for you if you like, just to make sure."

"All right. Let's order some lead then."

Bitsy's cocky laugh carried throughout the store, and a man who'd been reading labels on packets of garden seeds looked toward the counter. Ethan forced himself to study the tooled leather headstall on a bridle. That would look fine on old Scout.

"You know," Gert said, "you might want to lay in a few small pistols, Libby."

Ethan could hardly believe she'd said that. Since when did Gert tell a merchant what to order? He strained to hear her quiet tones.

"A gun like that isn't as accurate as something bigger would be," Gert went on, "but it sure would slip nicely into a lady's reticule. And if a ruffian gets too close, it'll blow a big hole in him."

Ethan caught his breath and forced himself to keep still,

though he'd never in his life heard women calmly discuss blowing holes in ruffians.

"And it's the ones who get too close that you have to worry about," Bitsy said. "Ladies in this town are having to think about their safety."

"Might be a good idea to order some," Libby conceded. "I hate to order anything I can't sell, but I've had two women in here in the last few days asking me about firearms. I don't usually order new guns, but now and again someone will bring in an old rifle to trade for supplies."

"If you do decide to stock handguns," Gert said, "make sure you get ones with common-sized bullets. You don't want to have to order special ammunition for everyone in town."

"Sorry to put you out," Bitsy muttered.

"It's no problem," Libby said. "But I'd have some cash tied up in the stock if I started ordering new pistols. I'll think about it."

The man pondering the seeds had edged over next to Ethan, who recognized him. Zachary Harper farmed and ran a few beef on the south edge of town.

"Howdy," Ethan said.

Harper jerked his head toward the counter. "You hear that, Sheriff? Women talking about buying guns and bullets. You gonna let them do that?"

"Can't see why not," Ethan said.

Harper pulled back and scowled. "Why, if my missus wanted a gun, I'd take the back of my hand to her." He turned his stony gaze toward the cluster of females at the counter. "Those ladies don't have enough to do, that's what. And not a husband among 'em."

Ethan felt the blood rushing to his face, though he wasn't quite sure why. "Settle down, Mr. Harper. They've got a right to own firearms if they want, same as we do."

Florence finished her task and approached the counter, carrying an empty crate. The door opened, and Mrs. Walker entered.

"Gettin' a little crowded in here," Harper mumbled.

"Hello, Mrs. Walker," Libby called, and then, "Well, hello, Sheriff Chapman. Didn't see you come in. May I help you with something?"

"No, thank you, ma'am." Ethan touched his hat brim and hastily followed Harper outside.

Harper shuffled off toward his farm wagon. He'd climbed onto the seat before Ethan thought of what he *should* have said inside the emporium. Yes, he ought to have said that if those three ladies had husbands, they might not be so worried about their safety. Too late to say it now though. Harper had already turned his team toward home. Guess he'd decided to come back another time for his seed.

Ethan ambled across the street, still thinking about Gert and Bitsy egging Mrs. Adams on to buy weapons suitable for ladies. He paused to stroke Scout's flank and looked back across the street.

"Morning, Sheriff," Oscar Runnels called as he strolled toward the stagecoach line's office.

Ethan waved, still lost in thought. Instead of going to the jail, he took the path around the Dooleys' house, into the backyard.

Hiram sat on the rear stoop, meticulously spreading varnish on a gunstock. He looked up at Ethan with those innocent gray blue eyes.

"Hello, Hiram." Ethan stuck his thumbs into his belt. "Did you know your sister's over to the emporium with Bitsy Shepard?"

Hiram quirked an eyebrow and shrugged.

"Know what they're doing?" Ethan asked.

"Nope."

"They're telling Miz Adams what to order for guns and ammunition."

Hiram pulled an actual smile, as though he was proud of his sister.

Ethan eyed him cautiously. "I didn't know Gert was friends with the likes of Bitsy."

Hiram carefully set the gunstock on end, leaning it against one of the railing's slats where it wouldn't get knocked over, and stood. "She come over here yestiddy." He sighed and shook his head, a dreamy look on his face. "Purtiest little thing I ever seen."

Ethan stared at him in disbelief. "Bitsy Shepard? No, Hiram!"

His friend blinked at him and frowned. "No, not her." Hiram

75

stooped and picked up the can of varnish and his paintbrush. "Miz Shepard's got a genuine Deringer."

"Whew." Ethan wagged a finger at him. "For a minute there, you had me worried. So what's this business about ordering guns for women?"

Hiram shrugged.

"Yeah, that's about the size of it," Ethan agreed. "Harper didn't like it though. He was in the store, and he heard 'em talking. He'll tell Cy Fennel, too."

Hiram leaned over the railing and spit in the grass.

"Yeah," said Ethan. "But Harper will do anything Fennel tells him to. I expect that's why he's on the town council."

Hiram said nothing, but his eyes had a way of speaking.

"What?" Ethan asked sharply. "You think I'm under Cy Fennel's thumb, too? Now you're making me mad."

Soft footfalls and the swish of a skirt caught his ear, and Ethan turned toward the path. Gert was rounding the corner of the house. She pulled up short and looked at Ethan, then Hiram, then back at Ethan again.

"What are you mad about?"

"I'll tell you. I'm thinking of turning in this badge, that's what."

"Why would you do that?" Gert breezed past him. Hiram stepped aside so she could enter the kitchen. When her brother started to follow, she glanced at the can of varnish. "Uh-uh. That goes in the barn."

Hiram ducked his head and went down the steps. As he headed for the stable, Ethan wasn't sure whether to follow him or not.

"You eating lunch here?" Gert asked from the doorway. She was already tying on her apron.

Ethan cleared his throat. "Well, I dunno. I ain't been asked. And your brother thinks I'm letting Cy Fennel tell me what to do."

Gert's pale eyebrows drew together. "Did he say that?"

"He said plenty."

She smiled. "I'll just bet. You'd best go do your sheriffing business and come back in an hour. We'll talk over lunch."

Ethan looked down at his scuffed boots and nodded slowly. "Thanks, Gert."

"Anytime."

He turned to the path and plodded next door to the jail. It stood as empty as it had all week. What was the sheriff supposed to do all day, anyhow? Maybe he should have stayed out at the ranch, after all. Not for the first time, he wished someone would give him a job description. Yesterday Mrs. Storrey had sent her boy to fetch him because her neighbor's boar got loose and had rooted up her yard. The day before, Clem Higgins allowed Ethan should make his brother, Nealy, patch up all the windows he'd shot out of their cabin when he was drunk. Ethan wasn't sure he could force a man to fix up his own property, but he encouraged Nealy Higgins to do the right thing. Nealy, being a reasonable man when he was sober, had agreed to do it if Clem bought the panes. But really, was this how Bert had spent his days?

Ethan headed out into the street. The Mountain Home stagecoach rolled up before the Wells Fargo office. Jamin Morrell got out. The messenger hopped down and carried a wooden chest into Fennel's office. The payroll for the stagecoach line, no doubt. The town needed a bank. Fennel, Morrell, Bitsy Shepard, and Libby Adams all had safes in their places of business. Other people probably did what Ethan did and stashed their money in a cracker tin or under the mattress.

He strolled along the street, greeting people he met. Most replied cordially, and the crotchety mood Hiram had inspired began to dissipate. By the time he reached the Spur & Saddle at the south end of Main Street, Ethan felt much better. Augie Moore was heading into the saloon carrying an armload of firewood.

"Mornin', Sheriff."

"Mornin', Augie."

The street petered out into a trail across the prairie. Ethan crossed it and ambled down the other side. Maybe tomorrow he'd stay out at the ranch. If anything serious came up, everyone knew where he lived.

He passed the mayor's house, the feed store owned by Mayor

Walker, and two vacant buildings. The post office was next.

"Oh, Sheriff!"

He stopped and turned his head. Peter Nash, the postmaster, hurried out of his tiny office, the closed-in porch of his weathered house.

"This mail came for Sheriff Thalen, so I guess you should have it."

Nash shoved a rolled-up sheaf of papers into his hand.

"Thank you, Mr. Nash." Ethan broke the string that held the bundle together and unrolled it. Wanted posters. He stared at the first one, his mind racing. Maybe a known desperado had come to Fergus and murdered Bert Thalen. If nothing else, he should study these posters so that he'd recognize any of the criminals depicted on them if they rode into town.

He hurried back to the jail, where he spread the posters out on Bert's desk. Three train robbers and a horse thief. It seemed unlikely any train robbers would come to a town without a railroad. Unless they wanted a place to hide out. Ethan scowled and shuffled the papers. The horse thief looked awfully like the picture he'd seen of President Cleveland in the Boise paper.

He sat back and sighed. He was kidding himself if he thought one of these hooligans had sneaked into town, killed the sheriff, and left again without being seen. The wood box across the room sat innocently beside the stove. Ethan had placed the stick he believed to be the killer's weapon on the shelf in the back room, to be sure no one tossed it into the stove by mistake on a chilly evening. But really, what good would it do him to keep it? And what good would he do the town as a lawman? His chances of finding the killer looked pretty slim.

An hour must have passed, or near enough. He got up and trudged to the Dooleys' back door. Enticing smells hovered on the gentle breeze. Corn bread. Bacon? No, ham.

And something spicy. Oh, if Gert had baked a pie. . .

He shuffled up the steps and raised his fist to knock. Gert opened the door.

"Right on time."

She stepped back and let him in. Ethan slid his hat off and

78

hung it on a peg next to Hiram's near the back door. Hiram already sat at the table, and Ethan took the place he customarily occupied when he ate here. Which was often. Come butchering time, he'd bring them a side of beef to make up for all the vittles he'd eaten with them.

"Ethan, would you ask the blessing, please?"

Alone at the ranch, he'd gotten out of the habit, but Gert always reminded him of more civilized days and places. He bowed his head, wondering if Hiram spoke the blessing when the two ate alone.

"Lord, bless this food and the hands which prepared it."

"Amen," said Gert.

Hiram's amen was spoken by his eyes only, but he plainly appreciated his sister's efforts.

"Now, what's this about you throwing down your badge?" Gert scooped a boiled potato out of the ironstone dish and plopped it on her plate, then handed him the bowl.

Ethan set the dish down between him and Hiram.

"I'm not doing much good as sheriff. The customers at the Nugget quiet down for a few minutes when I walk in, but overall, I'm not lowering the rate of alcohol consumption in this town."

"Can't expect to do that." Gert frowned as she skinned her potato. "But if there weren't any sheriff, those rowdies might tear the whole town apart. You're a calming influence, that's what you are."

"Well, what about the murder?"

Brother and sister stared at him in silence. At last Gert said, "What about it, Ethan?"

"I'm not going to catch the killer. How can I? We've got no clues except for a bloody stick of firewood. Bert's dead and buried, and we've no idea who did it. What good is a sheriff who can't keep the town peaceful on a Saturday night, let alone solve murders?"

"Don't sell yourself short. You've only started the job. And I don't think anyone expects you to bring in the killer single-handed." Gert reached to the middle of the table and speared a slice of ham.

They ate in silence for a few minutes. At last Gert rose to fetch the coffeepot.

Ethan gave her a sheepish smile as she filled his cup. "Mighty good corn bread, Gert."

Her face lit up for a moment. "Thank you. I expect you'll feel better about your new job now that you've got a full belly. Of course, a piece of apple-berry pie might tip the scales."

"What kind of berry is an appleberry?" Ethan asked.

Hiram laughed aloud.

"Not an appleberry," Gert said. "It's a pie made out of dried apples and blueberries from last summer."

She bustled about for a moment and brought him and Hiram each a generous slice.

Ethan took a bite. The apples and blueberries went surprisingly well together.

Gert poured her brother's cup full of milk. "How about you, Ethan?"

"No thanks, just the coffee. Oh, and these are mighty good appleberries."

She snorted and resumed her seat at the table.

When they had finished dessert, she refilled his coffee and sat down again, watching him. Ethan took a sip from his cup and set it down. Gert had something on her mind. Like her brother, she would speak when she was ready. Unlike Hiram, she was often ready.

"Listen to me, Ethan Chapman. This town needs a lawman. Not just any man, but an honest and diligent man. I'm not just talking about the carryings-on at the Nugget. We've got a killer in Fergus."

The blunt statement jarred him. "Are you scared, Gert?"

"Maybe." She frowned and tossed her head. "Think about what would happen if you went over to the mayor's house today and gave him your badge."

"I expect he and the town council would appoint someone else to do the job."

"Maybe so, but who? What man in this town could do as well as you?"

"Seems to me anyone could. Besides..." Ethan shook his head. "Hiram here seems to think I'm Walker's puppet, or rather, Cy Fennel's."

"Why would he think that?" She didn't look at her brother but fixed her stare on Ethan.

"Just for agreeing to be sheriff, as near as I can tell. Because that's doing what they want. You know Hiram looks down on anyone who does what Fennel wants."

"Hogwash." Now Gert turned her ire in Hiram's direction. "You quit making Ethan feel useless, you hear me? We need him in this town. If you get him to feeling bad, he'll up and leave."

"That wouldn't be a big loss," Ethan said.

"Oh yes it would. It'd be one less decent man in Fergus. Don't you get all proud of your humility on me, sir. What would happen if we got someone like Augie Moore for our sheriff?"

"Augie?" Ethan stared at her, startled.

"Yes, Augie. I've heard it whispered that he'd be a good sheriff. He could knock heads together with the best of them—maybe better than some. But the man's got no morals; you understand me, Ethan?"

"Well, I..."

"Of course you do!"

He winced. "I reckon."

Gert nodded. "That's right. Now, I dunno if you can catch Bert Thalen's killer or not, but if I get my purse stolen and I need to go tell the law, I don't want to go to someone like Augie Moore about it. Or Jamin Morell or Zachary Harper."

"Well, if you put it that way..."

"I do."

"All right. I hear you." Ethan looked over at Hiram, who nodded. "Yeah, I hear you, too."

Gert crossed her arms and sat back in her chair. "Hiram apologizes for making you mad earlier."

"Oh?" Ethan glanced at her brother again.

Hiram gave a grudging nod.

"So. No more of this 'I don't want to be sheriff anymore' business." Gert picked up her cup and sipped her coffee.

Ethan hadn't felt so much a part of a family since he'd left home ten years ago to join the army and come home from the Indian wars to find his parents dead and buried.

"I still don't know why they picked me." Ethan shot a quick glance at Hiram. "And don't you say it's 'cause they can push me around."

"Partly it's because you've got no family," Gert said.

Ethan didn't like that thought, but it wasn't the first time he'd had it. Bert hadn't had a family either, other than his grown-and-gone son. Did Fennel and Walker want a lawman whose family wouldn't be destitute if he got killed?

"You're not needed at home all the time," Gert said.

"I have work to do at my place. I may not have a wife and young'uns, but I've got stock and a homestead."

Gert pursed her lips. "I reckon you do. Whyn't you post a bill on the jailhouse door saying the sheriff will be out to his ranch if needed."

"I dunno. Think folks would cotton to that?"

"Womenfolk do like having the sheriff within hailing distance," she acknowledged.

Ethan reached absently for his cup, but it was empty. Gert rose and brought the coffeepot over. She refilled his cup, and Hiram held up his for the dregs. Ethan took a swallow. The brew was strong and bitter now, and he got a few grounds in his swig. He grimaced and swallowed them down.

"I don't want to give up my ranch." He hadn't really meant to say it aloud, but it seemed it was either/or. Sheriffing or ranching.

"Don't," said Hiram.

When his best friend spoke, Ethan always listened.

Gert set the empty coffeepot on the sideboard. "Hi's right. This is a temporary job. Just do the best you can, at least until they hold an election and you know if you're going to keep on being the law."

"I could decline to run for the office."

Hiram shook his head.

Gert eyed her brother and said, "You're right again, Hiram. You may not be the best shot in town, Ethan, or the scrappiest fighter, but you're honest, and you're not afraid to call a spade a spade."

Hiram nodded.

Gert's eyes blazed as she gathered steam. "If I had to pick a man in this town who would stand up against evil when it came his way, I'd pick you, Ethan Chapman. So, no matter why the mayor picked you, I'd say he picked right." She scowled across at her brother. "You got anything to say, mister?"

Hiram shook his head.

★ CHAPTER 10 ★

Milzie Peart rubbed her belly. Her root vegetables and flour had long since given out. She had a few lead balls for her husband's old rifle, but no gunpowder. She'd tried to snare a rabbit, without success. With only a quart of dry beans and a few herbs left, she knew it was time to make another foray into town.

The people in Fergus shunned her, mostly. Bitsy would maybe give her a bite. Or she could go through the trash heaps in hopes of finding something. And if Libby Adams would give her a few seeds, she could plant some sort of a garden and maybe harvest a few crops later on. She'd have died last winter if she hadn't put by so many turnips and carrots. When her cabin burned in early March, she'd been able to salvage only a few things and set up housekeeping in the cave that Franklin had shored up as part of his mining claim. Nothing good had ever come out of the cave, so since he died, Milzie had used it to store things.

After the cabin's ashes had cooled, she'd hauled the charred box stove step by step over to the cave's entrance. If it had been any bigger, she never could have done it. That was two months ago. She'd hung on to life by her broken, sooty fingernails since then, huddled up in the cave when she wasn't out foraging for firewood or something to eat. She'd sifted the ruins of the cabin and come up with a few things she could use—one blackened pot, a few nails and hinges, a fork and a tin cup. She'd even found a crock of sauerkraut that hadn't shattered and burned. That had kept her going for near a week.

What she wouldn't give for a mouthful of fresh beef now. Some nights she lay awake on the rock floor thinking about stew. Broth teeming with potatoes and onions and chunks of beef as big as hen's eggs.

Eggs. Sometimes an egg found its way into Milzie's pocket when she ventured about town. She kept away from the ranches with dogs. Lots of women in town kept a few hens, and on occasion she'd borrow an egg with no one's permission but the biddy's.

It had turned warm, and she didn't need Franklin's wool coat today, though she'd miss its deep pockets. A sugar sack would do for any bits she collected. She wound a raveling shawl that had once been blue about her shoulders and left the cave.

An hour later, she hobbled around behind the Spur & Saddle. Franklin had spent many an evening here. She wished she had a penny for every dollar he'd spent on drink. That would get her through a winter, it would.

Voices came from inside the kitchen. Likely that brawny Augie Moore was cooking. He was a good cook, but he didn't like folks to know it. Milzie smiled. Did he expect people to think Bitsy stood around all day in her fancy clothes hacking up chickens? And those little saucepots of girls who worked for her couldn't cook; you could bet on that. Nope, the barkeep did most of it.

She shuffled over to a small window and squinted against the glare of the sun. Sure enough, there was Augie, back to her, pounding away at a huge lump of brown dough. Rye bread, maybe. Just thinking about it set her to hankering for it. Over in the corner, another man hunched over a bucket into which he dropped potato peelings as fast as he could get them off the potatoes. He raised his chin to speak to Augie, and she recognized him. Old Ezra Dyer. He used to have a claim on Cold Creek. Had he given up sluicing at last and moved into town? Maybe he'd bring the bucket of peels outside and she could carry some off. Men always peeled potatoes too thick. Likely she could make a good soup out of his leavings.

"Hey!"

She jumped. Augie glared at her, raising a floury fist toward

85

the window. Milzie scooted back out of his sight. She'd best move along and come back later, when he was tending bar. That was the best time to forage for scraps at the saloon.

She walked down the street, keeping to the back side of the businesses, until she was certain she'd passed the mayor's house on the other side. Then she eased through an alley. Not many people were about, and she picked up her skirt and trudged across the street, winding up in front of the feed store. A couple of men lounged on the steps talking, so she didn't stop, but in passing she noticed where a bag of oats had spilled a little of its contents. Probably a mouse had chewed a hole in the sack. She could come back later and scoop up that handful of oats. It might grow out back of her cabin, where Franklin used to grow oats when they'd had a mule.

The emporium was the first building she dared enter. Like a shadow, she scooted away from the door and behind the racks of merchandise. Libby Adams and her redheaded clerk girl were at the far end of the store, where the yard goods and ready-made clothing were displayed. Milzie padded past a pile of flour sacks to a table heaped with canned goods. It would be easy to slip a tin of fruit under her shawl.

"May I help you with something today?" Miz Adams smiled. Her eyes sparkled a bright blue, even inside the store, where the light wasn't good.

Milzie straightened her bowed shoulders as far as she could. "Why, I was in town today, Miz Adams, and I wondered, would you have any extra seeds?"

"Seeds?"

"Yes'm. You know, to plant. A few beans, maybe, or squash."

"Oh. Well. . ." Libby glanced toward a shelf where neat little sacks and paper packets sat in an orderly array.

"I don't need much," Milzie said quickly. "I thought p'raps you'd spilled a mite when you was a-measurin' things out for someone."

"Well, I might have something in the back room." Libby nodded. "Yes, I think I might. Would you like to wait just a minute?"

"Yes'm, be happy to." Milzie hobbled toward the stove in the middle of the emporium. They hadn't built up the fire today, but habit drew her to the gleaming firebox. A couple of minutes later, Miz Adams came from the back room with something in her hand. Milzie eyed the twists of paper Libby held out to her.

"Here's a bit of carrot seed, and a few squash, and enough peas for a row."

"Thankee, ma'am." Milzie bobbed her head and put the paper twists into the sugar sack she'd hung at her waist. She shuffled slowly to the door.

Where next? She'd had no food yet. True, she'd got some seed. That was good, but it didn't help now. Milzie looked back up the street toward the mayor's house. No, she wouldn't try to forage in the mayor's slops, at least not in daylight. His wife would likely get the sheriff if she caught her. A vague notion entered Milzie's mind that there might not be a sheriff anymore. She'd seen Bert Thalen laid out dead and cold.

She walked slowly past the stagecoach office and saw Cyrus Fennel inside, sitting at a big desk. That was one man she didn't care to meet up with. She glimpsed the blacksmith shop on the next corner, and the livery stable beyond it. If she could slip in there, she might be able to sit down in the hay for an hour or two. She might even pick up some corn or oats from the barrels of horse feed.

A shortcut took her behind an abandoned store building, past the smithy, to the back of the livery. Used to be another man who ran the livery, back during the boom. But he'd gone away. Now the smith owned the livery, too. Like as not, he barely made a living from the two businesses nowadays, with the town's population so small.

Five horses stood in a corral munching hay. She hobbled past them to a path between two fences. In a second enclosure, four big horses stood in the shade. Probably a team for the stagecoach. The others looked like saddle horses, none of them too spirited. Must be the ones the liveryman rented out. Slowly she sidled up to the back door, beside the manure pile. It was partway open, and a wheelbarrow full of dung sat just inside.

Milzie peeked into the barn. Across the dim, hay-strewn floor, two men stood talking near the big front door, which was rolled wide open to the late morning sun. She recognized one as the owner. Bane, that was his name. His bushy hair stuck out beneath his hat brim, and his voice boomed and echoed off the barn rafters high above.

"Well, if you think you know who did it, you ought to tell the sheriff."

The other man, middle-aged and as wrinkly as the Idaho prairie, shook his head. "I don't know any better than you do. I'm just saying if Thalen was really murdered, the law ought to have found out who done it by now. And if Chapman wants to be the sheriff, he ought to do what a sheriff does."

"Which is?" Bane towered over the older man.

"He ought to find out who killed Thalen. People don't like to think we've got a murderer runnin' loose in this town. My wife hates to walk down the street to the emporium by herself anymore. She's right upset about it. Says the kiddies ought not to be walkin' clear out to the schoolhouse without a grown-up to watch out for 'em, in case the killer shows up."

Milzie slithered through the opening and along the shadowy wall. Harness and tools hung on pegs, and she tiptoed past them and around the end of a tall wagon tongue that stood leaning against the wall. To one side, a tie-up stall held several large barrels, and she figured they were full of grain. She slid into the small area and noticed an enameled cup and a biscuit tin on a shelf formed by the framing members of the stall. Curious, she moved closer and stood looking down at the tin. She used to buy Huntley & Palmer biscuits once in a while, back when Franklin was alive and they had a little cash to spend at the emporium.

She reached out and caressed the smooth green metal. The gold lettering and swirls formed a pleasing design. She was vaguely aware of the men's conversation as she opened the tin. The wad of paper money inside made her catch her breath. If Bane had that much cash money, would he miss the few coins in the bottom? Quicker than she could blink, the coins were in her little sack.

Sunlight filtered through a knothole and glittered off something else inside the tin. She smiled as she picked up a huge safety pin. Milzie stroked the smooth metal. The pin was open, and she stuck it through her shawl, then eased the cover of the tin shut. Her gnarled fingers were barely strong enough to squeeze the pin closed.

The men's voices seemed louder. Were they walking toward her? She ducked behind the barrels and hunkered down.

"I heard some ladies are starting to carry pistols," Bane said.

"Tomfoolery." The other man sounded annoyed.

Milzie blinked, wondering if that was true. Maybe the schoolmarm could tote a gun to the schoolhouse to protect the scholars. She couldn't feature Miz Walker with one though. Maybe Bitsy Shepard. She was tough as two-penny nails. Milzie peered over the tops of the barrels. Assured that the men were still occupied, she thought she might sneak out the back without being seen.

"Well, I'd best get back and see if my wife's done with her shopping," the older man said. "Like as not, she's run up a bill I won't be able to pay till harvest."

Bane laughed and said good-bye, then turned toward the back of the barn. Too late, Milzie realized he'd probably come back here and finish the job he'd started of cleaning out the stalls.

The closer he got, the smaller she tried to make herself. She squeezed down and back into the corner, soundlessly contracting into a heap of rags. Bane grasped the wheelbarrow's handles and pushed it out the back door. She heard the *creak-thump-whup* as he tipped it up and emptied the contents at the edge of the manure pile.

When he rolled the barrow back inside, he took it to one of the stalls along the side of the barn and shoveled manure into it. Milzie relaxed. He had no inkling she was there. Maybe she could sneak out while he worked in the stall.

Furtively she crept out of the tie-up he used as a grain bin. Only a half dozen more steps to the door, and dark shadows masked the back wall. She took one step. Bane turned with a shovelful of manure, and she stiffened against the wall. A horse collar she'd bumped slid off its peg and thunked to the floor. Bane jerked his head up to stare, and Milzie dove behind the nearest barrel.

She heard his steps, cautious and stealthy. Her poor old heart raced. He was coming over here. If he caught her, he'd find the coins in her pocket and call her a thief. She held her breath. Maybe she could duck past him and out the door.

The barrel was shoved aside, and she jumped up, pushing past the huge shadow, toward the streak of light shining in the door. She forgot about the wagon tongue. Her foot caught it, and her shin connected, too. She sprawled in the straw and covered her head as the heavy thing fell.

Bane gave a gasp almost simultaneous with the thud of wood on bone. The barn shook as the big man and the wagon tongue hit the floor together. Milzie scrambled over them. Her hand landed on the spongy expanse of Bane's stomach, and she yanked it back. The man wasn't moving.

She hesitated until he pulled in a long, shuddering breath. Relief swept over her. She hadn't killed him. Clambering over his massive body, she saw a knife lying on the floor just beyond his limp hand. He would have stabbed her if that wagon tongue hadn't hit him. She scooped up the knife and darted out the back door. The horses lifted their heads and stared at her. Milzie hobbled around the corner of the corral and flattened herself against the wall of the smithy, between it and the livery. She stood panting and listening for pursuit.

★ CHAPTER 11 ★

Cyrus hustled outside as the stagecoach rolled down Main Street. The driver, Bill Stout, halted the team outside the office door in a flurry of dust. The shotgun messenger, Ned Harmon, jumped down and saluted Cyrus with a touch to his hat brim before opening the door of the coach.

Four passengers stirred inside. Good. Maybe the line would work its way out of the slump they'd had the last couple of years. More people were coming through Fergus this spring than usual.

"Mrs. Brice. Nice to see you back again." Cyrus offered a hand to the woman exiting the coach. "Watch your step. I trust you had a good trip to Portland?"

"Good to be home, Mr. Fennel."

"How is your daughter?"

"She's well, thank you." Mrs. Brice turned away to see to her luggage. By this time, two miners had climbed down.

"Good day, gentlemen," Cyrus said.

"Fennel," one replied with a nod. They went toward the boot of the coach for their kits.

"Thank you for taking the stage."

The last man out was a stranger. He eyed Cyrus as he straightened his jacket. "Is there an establishment in this town where I can get lunch?"

"We don't have a restaurant as such, but there are a couple of places where you could get a sandwich," Cyrus said. Again he thought of the abandoned boardinghouse. He wasn't about to set up one of Morrell's draggle-tails to run it, but maybe it was time to consider finding a couple or a respectable widow who could keep a few guest rooms open and serve lunch to the stagecoach passengers. To the customer at hand, he pointed down the street. "At the Spur & Saddle, they're apt to have a pot of stew on the stove. Or at the other end of the street is the Nugget, where it's strictly cold fare, and then only if you're lucky."

The man looked toward Bitsy's, then toward Jamin's.

"How long before the stage leaves?"

"Twenty minutes," Cyrus said. Ned had unloaded all the disembarking passengers' luggage. He signaled the driver, and Bill clucked to the team. He'd get the horses to the livery so Bane could swap them out. Then he and Ned would wolf down a biscuit or two with a beer at the Nugget and be ready to drive out again.

The passenger checked his pocket watch and marched toward the Spur & Saddle. Cyrus wasn't sure he liked advertising the saloons. The men of the town had begun to polarize over Bert Thalen's death. Those who drank at the Nugget on Saturday nights seemed to think Ethan Chapman wasn't doing his job and should be replaced. Over at the Spur & Saddle, the men seemed more inclined to support Ethan and cooperate with him if he came up with a plan to catch the killer. Personally, Cyrus doubted the new sheriff had any desire to track down the murderer. But he seemed to be doing a fair job of keeping down the shooting and yelling at the Nugget.

Oscar Runnels approached along the boardwalk, carrying a leather satchel. "Am I too late for the stage?"

"Nope. They just went round to change the teams. You've got at least fifteen minutes. You buying a ticket?"

"That's right. I've got to go to Silver City today."

Cyrus went into his office and opened the drawer where he kept the ticket books. Oscar pulled out his wallet, and they made the exchange.

"Good day for traveling," Cyrus noted.

Running footsteps thudded on the boardwalk outside. Ned Harmon caught the doorjamb and stood panting, blinking in at them.

"What is it, Ned?" Cyrus asked.

"Griffin Bane. He's layin' on the floor at the livery, out cold. We thought he was dead, but then he cussed, so he's not. But someone chucked him on the head a good'un and maybe robbed him."

"What's that?" Runnels asked. "Someone's hurt Bane?"

Ned nodded. "Bill's with him. I misdoubt he'll come to 'fore Sunday."

"What about the team?" Cyrus asked.

"Team ain't ready. They's still in the corral."

"That's not good." Cyrus pushed his chair back and grabbed his hat. "We've got to keep the schedule."

Oscar brought his fist down on Cyrus's desk. "What are you frettin' about the schedule for? Send that slacker to fetch the sheriff!"

Cyrus saw the good sense of that and barked at Ned as he strode for the door. "Go round to the jail and see if Sheriff Chapman's there. If he's not, check Hiram Dooley's kitchen. Chapman's over there at lunchtime some days."

Ned bolted across the street. As Cyrus hurried toward the corner, he could hear Oscar panting along behind him. The stagecoach stood outside the livery, the tired team hanging their heads. Cyrus entered the big pole barn. Bill Stout was carrying a pail of water in through the back door.

"Where's Bane?" Cyrus called.

"Yonder." Bill didn't stop walking, and Cyrus met him beside the prone figure of the blacksmith. Without another word, Bill tipped the bucket and poured a quart or so of cold water in Griffin's face.

Griffin sat up spluttering and waving his arms. "Wha. . . wha—Hey!"

"You all right, Bane?" Cyrus asked.

The big man blinked up at him and rubbed his sleeve across his eyes. "My head." He clutched it and moaned.

Bill tipped the bucket again. When the first splash hit Griffin's head, he dodged to the side and swiped at Bill's kneecap.

"Quit that! I'm awake."

Cyrus extended a hand. Griffin grasped it and rose with a groan.

"What's going on?"

Cyrus turned toward the door, where Oscar had paused. Ethan Chapman and Hiram Dooley pushed past Runnels and skidded to a stop beside the three at the back of the barn.

"What happened, Griff?" Ethan put his hand on Bane's arm. "Are you hurt?"

"My head is killing me." Griffin put his hand up to the top of his head and pulled it away, holding his fingers up in the light that streamed through the back door.

"You're bleeding." Bill set the bucket down.

"I was attacked. Someone was hiding back there near the grain barrels. He jumped out at me and whacked me on the head with something." Griffin swayed on his feet.

"You'd best sit down," Ethan said.

"He needs to get the team ready." Cyrus cringed at the anger in Ethan's eyes. "I suppose Bill and Ned can do that." Ned had arrived behind the sheriff and Hiram and now stood panting between Cyrus and the timid Oscar Runnels, who edged closer to the group.

Hiram touched Ethan's sleeve then jerked his head toward the corral behind the livery. He marched outside.

"Go with Hiram, boys. He'll help you get the teams switched." Ethan looked toward Cyrus. "Is Bill driving the next leg?"

"Yes. He and Ned are taking the coach as far as Silver City."

Ethan nodded. "All right, Griffin, what say you sit down and tell me what happened? See if you can remember anything else." He pulled a keg over, and Griffin plopped down on it.

"Too bad we ain't got a doctor," Oscar muttered.

"I couldn't see him very good." Griffin puckered up his face. "He musta been a big fella though. He hit me powerful hard."

"Bane must have been out cold for half an hour or more," Cyrus said to Ethan. "He hadn't even started to get the replacement team ready for the coach."

"I woulda." A belligerent gleam flashed in Griffin's eyes as he scowled at Cyrus. "If that robber hadn't jumped me, I'da had 'em ready and waitin' when your boys got here."

"Robber?" Ethan asked.

"Well, why else would he have attacked me?"

Ethan lifted his hat and scratched his head. "Maybe you'd best look around and see if anything's been stolen."

"That's a good idea." Griffin started to rise and sank back down on the keg. "Hoo, boy, I'm a little woozy."

"How many horses did you have in the corral?" Ethan asked.

"Horses?" Griffin swiveled to look out the back door and groaned again, putting both hands to his head. "Uh. . .the team of four in the corral on the west side and five saddle horses on the east. And old Sal in the front stall yonder, in case someone came in wanting a mount right away."

The men looked toward the stall nearest the front door of the livery, where they could see the back end of a chestnut horse. The mare stood placidly, swinging her tail now and then to brush off the flies.

Ethan walked to the rear door and perused the corrals. "Looks like all the horses are accounted for."

He stepped aside as Hiram came in, leading a big sorrel gelding.

"Hitch him right there, Hi." Griffin pointed to an eyebolt in the wall with a rope dangling from it.

"I'd best get back to the office and tell the passengers the stagecoach will be delayed a few minutes," Cyrus said.

He and Oscar walked across the barn floor and out into the sunshine.

"Crazy thing," Oscar said.

"Yes."

"Makes me a little skittish, what with old Bert being killed in broad daylight a couple weeks ago."

Cyrus stopped and eyed Oscar for a moment. Bert Thalen and Griffin Bane had both been whacked on the head. What if the women were right, and the killer was still in Fergus? "You go back and see if they find out anything's missing. I'll tell the other passengers the coach will be right along. But don't you say anything on the ride. You hear me, Oscar? Folks will get unstrung if you spread rumors about killers attacking people all over Fergus."

"I wouldn't say anything like that."

Cyrus nodded. "I think we'd best keep this quiet if we can. Go back and see if the sheriff's found out anything."

After Bill and Ned rumbled off with the stagecoach, complaining loudly that they'd had no lunch and taking Oscar along inside the coach, Ethan turned to his friends.

"Now, Griffin, think carefully. How tall was the man who hit you?"

Griffin winced and scratched his chin through his beard. "He was hiding till I got right up close. Then he jumped out. I don't rightly know."

"You think he was as tall as you?"

"Could be. I was facing the light from the doorway, and he was over there in the dark." Griffin looked up at him suddenly. "He smelled."

"Smelled how?" Ethan asked.

"Like a bear. Foul."

Ethan considered that. Maybe a trapper had come down out of the hills and thought to find some easy money in town. "You said your knife was taken. Anything else?"

"I keep a little cash in a box over near the feed barrels."

"What's it look like?" Ethan asked.

"It's a biscuit box. Green and gold."

Hiram had stood by in silence, but now he scurried to the corner stall and returned a moment later with the biscuit tin. Griffin took it and raised the lid. He grunted, staring at the contents.

"Looks like your money's there." Ethan nodded at the wad of greenbacks in the tin.

"No, there were some coins in the bottom." Griffin took out the small bundle of bills and frowned. "I had some change."

"How much?"

The big man shrugged. "Four bits at least. Not more'n a dollar all told."

"That's not much." Ethan scanned his face, wondering how seriously Griffin took the loss of a few coins.

"Why'd he take the change and not the dollar bills?" Hiram asked.

"Good question," Ethan said. He hated to imply that Griffin's memory was spotty, but it did seem odd. "You sure you didn't take them out?"

Griffin nodded. "I just put them in there yesterday. And a horse-blanket pin." He looked down into the box again.

"Horse-blanket pin?" Ethan leaned over the tin once more. "Where is it?" He looked at Hiram, but he only shrugged. It seemed a strange item for anyone to steal. Ethan almost said as much but clamped his mouth shut. Griff might think he doubted his word. But it was odd. Deep down, Ethan figured he was mistaken. The pin would turn up, jumbled in the straw or tucked onto a shelf, forgotten.

Griffin stood slowly. "I sure don't feel like doing much this afternoon."

Without speaking, Hiram walked over to the half-cleaned stall where Griffin had left his wheelbarrow. He picked up the shovel and began to work.

"He's a good friend. You take it easy and let Hi help you out." Ethan looked up at Griffin. "You want me to do anything about this?"

"Not much you can do, I guess. I want you to find the robber, but I don't guess that will be easy."

Ethan looked down at the metal box again. "You don't have a safe, do you?"

"Naw. I don't have that much money lying around. I never have more than five or ten bucks. But still, if someone's sneaking around town stealing and killing people. . ."

"Some folks are scared," Ethan acknowledged.

"Those women who are shooting all the time," Griffin said. "You oughta put a stop to that, Eth."

"Why? If it makes them feel safer. . ."

"Someone's going to get hurt. Next thing you know, one of those ladies will get shot during one of their practice meets."

Ethan ran a hand through his thick hair. "I been meaning to ask Gert about that. I've heard folks talking, and I wondered how many women are involved. So far as I know, it's only a few."

"A few is too many."

Ethan noted that Hiram paused in his shoveling and looked toward them. He must have heard his sister's name mentioned. First there was the conversation Ethan had overheard at the emporium. Then Ted Hire at the Nugget had said Gert was rallying some women to learn how to shoot, and Ethan had wondered if it was so.

Gert was an odd girl. She wasn't all soft and stylish like Libby Adams, but she had a kind soul. She'd left her folks back in Maine to come help her brother and his family when they needed her. She fed a crusty cowpoke-turned-sheriff every time he showed up on her back stoop. And he'd seen her feed stray cats and give a man who couldn't afford to pay for Hiram's work a chance to split wood in exchange for a gunsmithing job. If she really had started teaching women to shoot, her motives were honorable. But he should talk to her about safety, if nothing else. The livery owner wasn't the only man in town grousing about it.

Hiram pushed a wheelbarrow full of manure out of the stall and trundled it past them. He stopped just inside the back door and stepped to the side near the grain barrels. In the shadows, he stooped and lifted a long wagon tongue and stood it up against the wall. He picked up a horse collar, which he hung on a peg.

Ethan brought his attention back to the injured man. "I'll look into it, Griff."

★ CHAPTER 12 ★

Libby was aware when Milzie Peart entered the emporium. She didn't like to have Milzie come in and loiter. Customers didn't like it. At least it was warm enough now that they didn't have to keep the stove hot. The heat always magnified Milzie's stench.

But Libby couldn't run her off the way some did. She felt sorry for the old woman. As she measured out coffee for one of the rancher's wives, she tried to keep an eye on the stooped figure. Milzie had asked for seeds last time she was here. Libby wasn't sure she hadn't walked out with anything else. Usually she gave the old woman a little something to nibble on, figuring it might keep her from pilfering. If the other customers cleared out, she'd give Milzie the last few crackers from the nearly empty case beside the counter.

When the rancher's wife left, another woman stepped up to the counter. Libby smiled but again wished she could choose her clientele. One of the girls who worked for Bitsy at the Spur & Saddle smiled shyly back at her.

"Vashti." If that was really her name, which Libby doubted.

"Yes'm. Miss Bitsy said it's a good idea if we girls get ourselves a sidearm. She said you could help us."

"Oh. Uh. . ." Libby glanced around the store. Milzie was only a few steps away. "I have some small handguns." She took three from beneath the counter and laid them out for the girl to see, wondering if she shouldn't ask Vashti to come back Monday before she opened the store—or even tomorrow while the emporium was closed. But she hated to do business on the Sabbath. The shipment of pistols had arrived only yesterday with one of Oscar's mule teams, and she still could barely believe she was selling them like this. But what did it matter if the whole town knew she had stocked some handguns and would sell them to women? Word of mouth would probably bring her more business.

Vashti picked up the smallest one. Its pearl grips seemed to ripple as the light struck it. "I like this one."

"All right." Libby reached for the roll of brown paper. "Let me wrap it for you."

"Thanks, but I'll put it in my bag."

Libby cleared her throat and glanced toward the door. Jamin Morrell was just entering. He nodded at her, smiling as he removed his hat.

"Good day," Libby said. "Can I get you anything, Mr. Morrell?"

"Carpet tacks," he said.

"Oh yes. Right over there near the nails." Libby pointed toward the hardware. She glanced around and saw that Florence was busy measuring ribbon for Mrs. Ingram "If you can't find them, I'll be over in just a minute."

Jamin nodded and headed for the hardware.

Vashti seemed to have shrunk into her silk shawl. She studiously avoided looking around toward the rival saloon's owner.

"Now you'll want some ammunition," Libby said in what she hoped was a smooth, professional tone.

"Is that the same size as Miss Bitsy's?" the girl asked.

"No, it's a smaller caliber, but it's a good piece."

Vashti leaned close and whispered, "I'm hoping Miss Dooley will teach me to use it."

"Oh." Libby tried not to let the smile slip. What had she started? When she'd gone to shoot with Gert on Thursday afternoon, they'd been joined by Emmaline Landry, Bitsy, and two other women. Word was getting around Fergus, and women were responding eagerly. She stooped and pulled out a box of cartridges. "It's fifty cents extra for the ammunition."

While Libby wrapped the box, Vashti dug into the ridiculously small satin pouch that dangled from her wrist. "My friend Goldie wants a gun, too. I'll tell her you've got some left."

A rancher carrying an ax handle and a tin of tobacco came and stood behind Vashti, ogling the young woman's back as he waited. Libby took her money and handed her the change and her package.

"I'll see you at the shooting practice on Monday." Vashti watched her, expecting a response.

"Uh, yes, I expect so," Libby said.

By the time she'd totaled up the rancher's purchases, Mr. and Mrs. Robinson had entered. Mr. went straight for the tools, while Mrs. made a beeline for the ready-made clothing. Morrell was still in the hardware, and Milzie had wandered to the far end of the store. Mrs. Ingram approached the counter with her notions and a bolt of muslin. Libby forced out another smile and told herself a busy store was a good thing.

"How many yards would you like?" she asked Mrs. Ingram.

"Six, please. Did you hear that the livery was robbed yesterday?"

Libby gulped. She didn't like to think about other business owners having trouble. "Yes, I did."

"They say Griffin Bane was attacked in broad daylight." Mrs. Ingram shook her head. "I'd think it would take a brazen criminal to attack a man as large as Mr. Bane."

"I. . .suppose so." Libby measured out the material. "Lovely and warm this morning, isn't it?"

More customers came through the door. A few minutes later, she looked up into Jamin Morrell's face.

"Oh, Mr. Morrell, I've neglected you."

"That's all right. You've been busy, and I found what I needed."

Libby glanced toward the yard goods. Several people browsed the merchandise, but Milzie was nowhere to be seen.

"Looking for the old woman, by any chance?"

"Well, yes." Libby fingered the lace at her collar. "I was going to give her some crackers."

"She left a moment ago." Jamin leaned toward her over the counter and lowered his voice. "You might want to check over your stock of safety pins."

Libby stared at him then looked toward the open door.

That evening, Gert walked slowly up the street toward the Walkers' house. She didn't really want to spend the evening quilting with a half dozen older women, but Orissa Walker had made a point of inviting her. The flying geese quilt would go to the Walkers' married daughter in Silver City. Libby had promised to meet her at the quilting bee, so Gert had agreed. She trudged along the board-walk with her sewing basket—minus her overdue mending—on her arm.

Orissa welcomed her with a dour face and ushered her into the parlor. Isabel Fennel was the only other woman within twenty years of Gert's age. Where was Libby? She didn't ask. She figured she had to put in at least an hour without the risk of being thought horribly rude and becoming the subject of the quilters' gossip as soon as she left.

She settled in between Annie Harper and Isabel on one side of the quilting frame.

"How's school?" she asked Isabel.

"Not bad. We've another month. Then we'll break for the summer."

"I expect you'll enjoy a bit of a rest when the term ends."

Isabel's lip curled as she eyed her, and Gert felt her face flush. Was her face dirty? Why did Isabel look at her that way?

"I don't suppose I'll rest much this summer." Isabel bent over her needle.

Gert blinked. Had she just been snubbed? If this were Boston, she might just care.

"Do you know if the sheriff's found out who robbed the livery?" Mrs. Runnels asked as their hostess sat down in the chair nearest the door.

"No, I haven't heard anything new," Orissa said.

"Seems to me he ought to have arrested someone by now," murmured Annie.

Isabel humphed. "Ethan Chapman is incompetent. Father

says he has no clues at all on Bert Thalen's murder, and now this. Why they picked him for sheriff, I have no idea."

"A poor choice to protect us." Mrs. Runnels jabbed her long needle down through the layers of the quilt.

A knock at the door summoned Orissa, and a moment later she ushered Libby into the parlor.

"Hello, ladies. I'm sorry I'm late." Libby smiled at the circle in general, but she gave a pert nod when her gaze rested on Gert.

"Sit right down, Elizabeth," Orissa said. "You can work on this part and stitch your way over to meet Bertha."

Libby slid into the seat between Orissa and rotund Bertha Runnels. She soon had her needle and thimble out, and the work progressed, along with the chatter. No one mentioned that the husbands of the married women present were probably out at one of the town's two saloons, knocking back whiskey. Instead, they focused on domestic topics. Gert let it flow around her as she made the boring up-and-down stitches.

She glanced across at Libby, who stitched industriously with a slight smile on her lips. She always looked as though she'd welcome an adventure. Funny, Gert thought of Libby as her own age, though the widow was probably eight or ten years her senior. Isaac Adams had been a friend of Cy Fennel and Charles Walker, but he'd married a younger woman. Libby never spoke to her of truly personal topics, but Gert had the distinct impression she'd loved her husband. She liked to think Libby had enjoyed some happy years with Isaac. Few of the married couples in Fergus seemed content. Rather, they survived.

"Gert, I can't say as I approve of this latest enterprise of yours," Mrs. Walker said.

Gert jerked her chin up and stared at her, unsure of how to respond.

Libby jumped into the silence. "If you mean the shooting club, I do."

"Club?" asked Annie. "What's this?"

Gert felt her cheeks flame, but Libby's musical laugh rang out.

"That's what some of the women call it. We practice shooting together two afternoons a week, and Gert instructs us. We're all learning to protect ourselves."

Orissa shook her head. "The mayor thinks it's nonsense."

"The mayor is on hand to protect his wife," Libby pointed out. "Some of us ladies have no husband or son or brother to defend us in time of need."

"Well, my father says it's dangerous, and someone's going to be killed by accident," Isabel said.

Gert scowled. Leave it to Cyrus to say that.

"We're extremely cautious whenever we shoot, aren't we, Gert?" Libby asked.

Gert looked up at her. Libby's rosy cheeks and gleaming blue eyes would qualify her for the girl on a soap advertising card. Libby smiled gently and nodded ever so slightly.

"Oh yes," Gert responded. Better to follow her friend's lead than to get upset and cause more talk. "We always follow safety measures."

"More than you can say for some of the men," Annie Harper muttered.

Bertha nodded, frowning. "I heard Emmaline Landry has joined."

"That's right," Gert said. "Her husband's out on the range a lot, and she wanted to know how to use a gun in case a drifter showed up at the ranch."

"She joins us on Thursdays," Libby put in.

"It's a wonder Mr. Landry lets her," Isabel said.

"She probably doesn't tell him." Bertha shook her head in disapproval.

Libby surveyed their project. "My, isn't this quilt coming along nicely?"

"Yes, we've made good progress." Mrs. Walker stood. "I think it's time for tea."

"Let me help you." Libby jumped up and headed toward the kitchen with Orissa. Gert wished she could make a graceful exit through the front door, but Libby had rescued her so kindly that she didn't want to leave her friend alone.

Right now all she wanted to do was get home and fix a bite for Hiram. She pictured him sitting alone in the front room, reloading cartridges for his rifle. Poor man. Loneliness had settled over him. She tried to be good company. She'd rather be sitting with her near-silent brother than with this bunch of cats. And without her, Hiram was practically helpless, though she would never utter such a thought aloud.

"Good coffee." Ethan raised his mug in Hiram's direction before he took another swig. "You make it?"

Hiram just nodded, but he smiled as he picked up his horse's bridle and a rag.

"I don't know what to do next," Ethan said. "Oh, not tonight. I know what I have to do tonight. Go over to the Nugget again and tell them to pipe down." He cocked his head to one side and listened. Was it his imagination, or could he hear loud music and laughter from the saloon? "It's what I should do about the crimes that's got me puzzled. What does a lawman do when he can't figure out who's committing crimes in his town?"

Hiram frowned and polished away at the leather cheek straps. "You've asked everyone if they saw anything."

"Yes, I think I've talked to every adult in Fergus, and a few of the children and horses."

Hiram laughed.

Ethan stretched out his long legs and sipped his coffee again. "Did I tell you Spin and Johnny showed up at my ranch on Monday?"

Hiram nodded and picked up a can of neat's-foot oil. He tipped it up, sloshing a little on his rag.

"They're taking care of the place while I loaf around town doing nothing." Ethan shook his head. "Useless, that's what I am." He looked around the Dooleys' comfortable kitchen. Did the plant on the windowsill and the bright tablecloth make the difference that marked this as a home?

"Do you think the same person jumped Griff as killed Bert?" Hiram asked.

"I've thought about it, and I can't begin to tell you. It would seem likely."

After a few minutes of silence, Hiram put the bridle aside and walked over to the cupboard near Gert's worktable. He returned with the coffeepot in one hand and a plate of ginger cookies in the other.

"Thanks. Gert make these?"

Hiram nodded and set two cookies on the table in front of his own chair and topped off his cup of coffee.

"Gert's a good woman," Ethan said around a bite of cookie. He'd almost said *girl*, but she wasn't a kid anymore. He chewed appreciatively. She knew how to bake. And shoot. And sew. And do a thousand other things. Hiram was a lucky man to have a sister so steady and diligent. And willing to keep house for him.

"She's all right."

That was high praise from her brother, as Ethan was well aware. He'd heard tell how Gert had come on the stagecoach to Boise, before it ran all the way to Fergus, and Hiram had driven over there to fetch her. She'd come three thousand miles of hard road, expecting to find Violet and a new baby to care for. Instead, Hiram had met her with the news that he was all alone now. That was back while Ethan was off in the army. And Gert had stayed. She'd grown from a lanky girl to a competent housewife—only she wasn't a wife.

"Has she got a name, other than Gert?" he asked. Somehow, he felt she ought to have a softer name, the same way he sometimes thought she ought to have a softer hairdo or a fancier dress.

"Trudy." Hiram sat down again and shoved half a cookie in his mouth.

"Trudy? Oh, of course. Gertrude."

Hiram nodded as he chewed. When he'd swallowed, he said, "Our pa used to call her Trudy."

They lapsed into silence again. Ethan pictured a little girl with flaxen braids tagging along after her big brother. That would have been in Maine, though, not out here. What did Maine look like? Lots of forest that came down to the ocean shore? Maybe he'd ask Gert someday. Hiram wouldn't string enough words together to give him a proper picture.

When his cookies were gone and his mug was empty, Ethan stood and stretched. "Well, Hi, thanks for the grub. Time to mosey."

"Watch yourself."

Ethan nodded and went out the back door, grabbing his hat from a peg on the coatrack. The noise from the Nugget hit him as he rounded the corner of the house. With a sigh, he headed north on the boardwalk, past the jail and the vacant boardinghouse.

"Trudy," he said to no one.

★ CHAPTER 13 ★

Ten women showed up for shooting practice on Monday, counting Gert and Libby. Gert could barely trust her eyes.

"Where'd they all come from?" she asked Libby as they dismounted.

"Word gets around." Libby ground tied Hoss and took the Peacemaker from her saddlebag.

Gert hefted her Sharps rifle and walked slowly toward the waiting women. Bitsy and the two girls who served drinks and who knew what else at the Spur & Saddle had come in their short skirts and low-cut blouses. Emmaline Landry had brought her neighbor, Starr Tinen. Both wore faded housedresses with aprons tied over their skirts. Florence was there. Libby had given her the afternoon off, leaving Oscar Runnels's oldest boy, Josiah, who helped her unload shipments of new merchandise, to watch the store for an hour. And to Gert's surprise, Annie Harper and her oldest girl, Myra, had come.

Annie walked toward her with a sheepish smile on her face and an old shotgun resting on her shoulder.

"Hello, Gert. Will you take two more pupils? I told Myra about this club, and we both decided we wanted to learn to shoot."

Gert eyed her for a long moment. "You could have asked Mr. Harper to show you."

"I'd much rather learn from you."

"Pa's got no patience," Myra noted.

Gert nodded. She wouldn't want to learn shooting—or anything else—from an impatient man, and she'd seen Mr. Harper lose his temper over little things. What would he say when he heard his womenfolk attended the gun practice?

"Well, let's see your weapon. You got shells?"

"Only eleven. Figured I'd stop by the emporium for more on the way home."

Libby glanced at Gert. "I keep having to order more ammunition. It's a hot commodity in Fergus right now." She turned her lovely smile on Annie and Myra. "We're glad you ladies could be here."

"I had no idea how popular this shooting circle was." Myra turned wide eyes on Gert. "Miz Dooley, I've never fired a gun before. You'll show me how to do it right, won't you?"

Gert looked over the cluster of eager women and pulled in a long, slow breath. She straightened her shoulders and smiled at Myra. "I surely will. But this is a lot of people. We'll take turns in an orderly manner. Everyone gather in close. First, let's talk about how we make sure none of us gets hurt while we practice." She looked at Libby and gave her a firm nod.

"Ladies," Libby called in her cheerful voice. "I didn't know how many of us there'd be today, but I've brought a small prize for the lady who shoots her personal best today." She held up an embroidered velvet needle book.

"Aw, now ain't that fine," said Emmaline.

"And if more than one of you qualifies, I'll bring extra prizes when we meet next on Thursday."

They murmured approval at Libby's promise. She was an excellent merchant, Gert noted, and would no doubt have all these ladies inside the Paragon Emporium ere nightfall.

An odd, unpleasant smell struck Gert's nostrils. She turned slowly. Another woman had come quietly down the path to join them.

"Mrs. Peart!"

Milzie grinned at her, revealing a gap where one of her front teeth had once resided. "Miz Dooley. Miz Adams. Ladies." She looked around the circle of faces a bit defiantly. "Mind if I shoot with you'uns?"

Gert eyed the Hawken rifle resting on Milzie's shoulder. With its heavy barrel and chunky stock, the gun would take down a grizzly with one shot if need be.

"This here was my husband, Franklin's, buffalo gun." Milzie lowered the stock to the ground and stood waiting. "I got some bullets for it, but no powder. Thought p'raps I could borry a mite."

Gert's stomach churned as she surveyed the old woman. Her heart did a little squirming, too. She tried to ignore the stench that hovered around Milzie. The other nine women were as silent as the school yard on Saturday, waiting for her to either cast Milzie out or. . .

She forced herself not to look to Libby for aid. This was a matter for the Almighty. *I think I hear You whispering in my ear, Lord.* She looked straight into the watery gray eyes.

"You're welcome here, Milzie. Show me what you've got for ammunition. We can help you with powder for today. But let me check your rifle over first, to make sure it's safe for you to fire."

Hiram jumped from his chair when Libby followed Gert into the kitchen. Libby hoped she hadn't embarrassed him by coming home with his sister after the shooting practice.

"Hello, Hiram. Gert said I'd best consult you before I place my next order for ammunition."

His soft, gray blue eyes widened, and his pale eyebrows rose. "Ma'am?"

Hiram didn't come into the emporium much. Libby seldom thought about him, but when she did, she pegged him as a quiet young man, probably about her age, who liked peace and solitude. In another time and place, she could imagine Hi Dooley as an artist or an inventor. Here in Fergus, he was the sad-eyed gunsmith.

Gert pulled off her bonnet and hung it on a peg near the door. "We've got all sorts of ladies coming out of prairie dog holes with odd-sized guns. Libby needs to know for certain what ones will take the same size cartridges. Then there's the odd ones, like Bitsy's Deringer. Annie Harper's got a shotgun—"

Hiram blinked, and Gert went on as if he'd spoken aloud.

"Yes, Annie was there, and Myra, too. You know, her big girl. They both want to learn to shoot in case the killer comes around when Mr. Harper's away."

"Killer?"

Hiram's single word set Gert off again.

"You know what I'm talking about. The man who murdered Bert Thalen and tried to kill Griffin Bane. All the ladies in town are scared, and the men don't seem to be doing anything about it. Except for Ethan. I know he's trying to run down the killer, but so far, he hasn't had any luck. And the ladies are nervous, I'll tell you."

Hiram drew in a breath as though he would speak, but then he closed his mouth and shook his head.

Libby stepped forward and smiled. "So, Hiram, if you wouldn't mind, I'd appreciate your advice. Milzie Peart brought the oddest rifle today."

"That gun's the size of a cannon." Gert snatched her apron from a hook and tied it on. "You ever seen it? She said it was her dead husband's gun."

"Once. Big old Hawken." Hiram nodded as if he could see the thick barrel and heavy stock.

"That's right. And Milzie has no idea what load it takes."

Hiram scratched his head. "That one can handle most any powder load. But you don't want to turn her loose with it, do ya?"

Gert had neared the cupboard, but her step faltered. She turned to face Hiram and brushed back a wisp of hair that had come loose and fluttered about her cheek. "I couldn't send her away."

Libby nodded. "I know how you feel. She comes into the store, and other people don't like it because she. . ." She stopped, feeling an unwelcome flush creep up her cheeks. Even though Milzie wasn't present, Libby couldn't bear to speak ill of her. "Well, she looks. . .unkempt."

"And she smells," Gert added.

"Well, yes."

Gert opened the cupboard and took out an empty pottery bowl. Her jaw dropped, and she stared at her brother. "Don't tell me you ate all those cookies."

Hiram ducked his head. "Me 'n' Ethan."

"Oh. Well, that makes it all right then." Gert slammed the bowl back onto the shelf and shook her head. "I'll tell you, Libby, since Ethan Chapman took the sheriffing job, I don't think he ever eats at home anymore."

Libby smiled as she watched Gert's jerky movements about the kitchen. "Well, you're so handy to the jailhouse."

Hiram's eyes lit, and he nodded at her with a slight twitch to his lips. Libby nearly laughed aloud, but Gert kept up the injured air.

"That man eats twice as much as my brother, and that's the truth."

Libby started to speak but caught herself. *Perhaps he needs a wife.* That's what she'd wanted to say. But something about Gert's agitation told her this wasn't the time to tease. If Gert had feelings for the sheriff, teasing might cut deep, especially if Ethan didn't look at her in the same light.

Ethan hadn't showed an interest in ladies since he came home from the Indian wars. He'd seemed a normal, fun-loving young man before he went away, but now his face stayed frozen in serious lines. He kept to his ranch. Unlike a lot of former cavalrymen, he didn't frequent the saloons. The single women had hoped he'd enter the limited social circle of Fergus, but he'd disappointed them. Even Florence had sighed over him for a while, but she'd given up, declaring Ethan immune to feminine charms. Libby wasn't so sure. The fact that he and Hiram Dooley had drawn together made her think they understood their mutual sorrow. They could be friends without talking about Hiram's dead wife and baby or the Bannock War, or whatever it was that kept Ethan bottled up.

And Gert was in the middle of it. She probably saw Ethan more than any other woman in Fergus, and she saw him more often than she did any other man except her brother. Why shouldn't she have feelings for him? But if Ethan didn't wish to marry, Gert could expect nothing more than a broken heart. No, this wasn't the time to tease her.

Libby cleared her throat. "I've made a list of the women's firearms, Hiram. When I get back to the store, I'll inventory what I have for ammunition, but we go through a lot when we practice.

The shipment I got last week is nearly gone already. I plan to order in a large supply. If you can give me a few guidelines, I'll make sure no one has trouble getting the proper cartridges again." She handed him a slip of paper.

Gert lifted the lid on the teakettle sitting on the cookstove. "Say." Her smooth brow wrinkled. "Where's my kerchief?" She touched her hand to her neckline, feeling inside her collar.

"You took it off out in the valley," Libby said.

"Yes. It was warm in the sun. I stuck it in the saddlebag. But when we put the horses up, I took everything out again, and I didn't see it."

Hiram shrugged and bent over Libby's list. His light hair spilled over his brow, and he pushed it back absently with almost the same gesture Gert used.

"Get this for Milzie." He pointed with his pencil to where he'd written the ball size and powder grains for the load. "The rest looks fine. But if you think some others might bring muzzle loaders, you may want to lay in some extra lead balls in a smaller size." He scrawled another note. "You usually have plenty of powder."

Libby nodded and took the paper. "Thank you. I've decided to go to Boise on the stagecoach and see about the order. When I send it by mail, they don't always ship exactly what I want."

"When are you going?" Gert asked.

"Maybe Wednesday, if Florence thinks she can handle the store all day. And now I'd better get back over there. Florence went ahead to the store alone, but she may need me."

As she turned to leave, she noted that Gert had set out a large mixing bowl, a crock of rolled oats, and another of brown sugar. She grabbed a small jar of cinnamon off the shelf. Unless Libby was mistaken, Hiram and Ethan would soon have a new supply of cookies.

★ CHAPTER 14 ★

Would you mind stepping over to the stagecoach office with me?" Libby asked the next morning.

Gert had come to the emporium for more brown sugar, but if Libby needed a favor, she allowed she had time. "If you like."

"I do."

Libby turned to Florence. "I'll be back in a few minutes." She reached for a smart blue bonnet that matched her store-bought woolen dress. Gert walked with her to the door as Libby tied the wide ribbons under her chin.

Once outside, Libby leaned close to Gert. "I don't like going over to Mr. Fennel's office alone."

Gert raised her eyebrows and pulled Libby to a stop near the wall of the store. "Does he. . .bother you?"

Libby smiled sheepishly. "Not really. Sometimes he comes out of his office and looks at me when I'm outside washing the front window or helping someone carry out their bundles. He stands on the boardwalk down there and. . .just watches. That's all."

"Think he's sweet on you?" Gert looked down the sidewalk toward Fennel's place of business. "He's been widowed nigh on three years now."

Libby grimaced. "To be honest, he came around once and asked me to take Sunday dinner with him at the Spur & Saddle. It was only a month after Isaac died, and I didn't want to. It seemed in poor taste for him to ask me so soon."

"Some folks remarry mighty quick out here."

"Yes, but. . .I don't *need* a husband. Isaac left me with a good business and a tidy sum of savings. Not that I'd say that to just anyone, you understand."

Gert nodded soberly. "That's one reason I stayed on with Hiram. So's he wouldn't think he needed to go looking for a wife to replace Violet."

"Poor man," Libby murmured. "He cared deeply for Violet."

"Yes, he did. And if he'd gone to baching it after she died, the women in this town would have inundated him with kindnesses he didn't want."

"Perhaps so. But. . .supposing someday he decides he *wants* to marry?"

"Then I'll move out. I could find employment, I expect. Or I could go back to Maine."

"Are your folks still living?" Libby asked.

"Yes. Our pa builds boats. That's where Hiram learned to use tools, in Papa's shop."

"That's interesting. But now he's out here where there's no call for boats."

"He likes guns. He likes anything mechanical, really. And if I ever thought he'd formed an attachment for a lady, I wouldn't stand in his way. I'd like to see Hi happy again."

Libby nodded. "I expect he feels the same way about you. If you decided to take a husband, I mean."

Gert huffed out a breath. "No chance of that."

"I don't know why you say that."

"Look at me. I'm just. . .just Gertrude Dooley, spinster. The gunsmith's sister, homely and drab."

"You're not homely, and you don't need to be drab." Libby could tell her words made no impression. She took Gert's arm. "If you ever need a job, come and see me. Come on, now. Let's get this done."

They walked the short distance to Cyrus's office. The sign WELLS FARGO CO. swung over the boardwalk. Fennel sat at the desk inside but jumped up when they entered.

"Ladies, welcome! How delightful to have you here. How may I be of service today?"

Libby stepped forward. "I'd like a ticket to Boise on tomorrow's stage, please."

"Happy to oblige." Cyrus turned to a set of shelves beside his desk and took out a ticket book. "Business or pleasure, if I may ask?"

"Business," Libby said.

"Ah. Scouting new merchandise for the Paragon Emporium?"

"You might say that."

Cyrus looked at Gert. "And are you riding along as well, Miss Dooley?"

"Nope."

He nodded and made out Libby's ticket. "That will be three dollars and thirty cents, please."

Gert winced at the amount, but Libby opened a small purse and counted out the money.

"I'll have a crate or two on the way back," Libby said. "Will that be all right?"

"So long as we don't have a coach full of passengers who have a lot of luggage." Cyrus stood and handed her the pasteboard ticket. "Will it be heavy freight?"

Gert laughed. "Not unless you call lead heavy."

"Lead?" Cyrus frowned at her.

"Well, I was thinking of picking up some braid and yarn, too," Libby said. "They're not heavy."

"Oh no, not at all. But. . .lead? Are we talking about bullets?"

Libby nodded. "I need to get some special sizes of ammunition. Some of my customers have found it hard to obtain bullets to fit their firearms."

Cyrus's face went stony. "For the shooting ladies?"

"Well. . .some of it," Libby admitted.

"I'm not sure I can let you do that."

"What?" Libby's face froze with her mouth open and her eyebrows lost up under the brim of her fetching bonnet.

"It might not be safe for other passengers for you to carry a quantity of ammunition over these mountain roads."

"That's ridiculous," Libby said. "People carry guns and bullets on the stagecoach all the time. It's expected of your shotgun messengers."

"Ah, but not cases of live cartridges. We don't carry kegs of gunpowder either. Too volatile. The stagecoach line has the right to refuse dangerous cargo."

Libby turned to stare at Gert, her mouth open and her lovely eyes wide. Gert had the distinct feeling she needed to help her friend out of this mess, especially since she was the one who'd mentioned lead.

"You've already sold her the ticket."

Cyrus glared at her. "That was before I knew what she was planning to carry on our coach."

Gert threw her shoulders back. "So you'll refuse to let her board the stagecoach?"

"She can ride to Boise anytime. She just can't bring back a large quantity of ammunition."

Libby held out one hand toward Cyrus. "Maybe I'll hire the freighter to haul it in. Though some of my customers won't be happy with the delay."

"Hogwash!" Gert stepped between Libby and Cyrus. "You're only doing this because you don't like us women out there learning to protect ourselves. You're one of those pigheaded men who thinks women should be home knitting and baking biscuits all day."

"I beg your pardon."

"Gert, dear, please don't overset yourself." Libby tugged gently on Gert's sleeve. "Please, we'll find another way to deal with this. Now, Mr. Fennel, if you'd kindly refund the price of my ticket—"

"We don't generally do refunds," Cyrus said.

"Of all the nerve!" Gert shoved Libby aside. "I've never seen anything so rude and stingy in my life. You're the one who won't let her bring her merchandise on the coach, and it hasn't been three minutes since you took her money. That is the meanest, nastiest thing I've ever—!"

"Morning, folks. Is there a problem?" A shadow darkened the door as the deep voice cut her off. Gert whirled and looked into Ethan's face. His brown eyes kept the gentle, coon-dog cast they always held, but his jaw tightened as he took in the scene.

"Sheriff, you're just the person we need." Gert grasped his arm and pulled him into the office. "Mr. Fennel says Libby can't carry a stock of ammunition on the stagecoach, and now he refuses to give her back the price of her ticket."

"Gert, really. It's nothing." Libby's face went scarlet. "It's only three dollars and thirty cents."

"But you bought that ticket in good faith not five minutes ago."

Ethan stepped forward with both hands raised. "Ladies, please." He stopped only a pace distant from Cyrus and looked him in the eye. "Mr. Fennel, what's the problem here?"

Cyrus's mouth drooped, and he reached for his pen. "I suppose I can make an exception this once and refund your money, Mrs. Adams. But I'll not have you transporting dangerous cargo on the stage."

Gert opened her mouth again, but Ethan caught her eye, and she divined from his expression that this would be a good time to keep silence. "I'll be outside," she muttered to Libby.

The bright sunshine nearly blinded her, and she wished she'd remembered to wear a bonnet. She'd thought she could get by without it on a quick run across the street to the emporium. Now, if she had a bonnet that matched her eyes, like Libby had. . .no, that wouldn't work. Gert's would be a lackluster gray blue, not at all attractive.

The fact that Cyrus had backed down when the sheriff appeared didn't appease her anger. Fennel wasn't the only man in this town who seemed to think women couldn't handle their own affairs and needed a man to tend to business for them. Men who thought that way found her and the ladies' shooting group offensive. Gert wondered if it didn't threaten their pride. The men of Fergus somehow felt less heroic and manly if their women carried weapons. Well, in her book, the men of Fergus needed to show some evidence that they were capable of protecting their women and children. When they proved up, the ladies would be happy to back off and let them do all the defending and strutting they wanted.

Libby and Ethan came out of the office.

"You got your feathers smoothed down now?" Ethan eyed her doubtfully.

"Not hardly."

He shook his head. "You said some fighting words in there."

"He was being downright churlish to Libby."

"Well, now, that may be, but it's your opinion. The man's got company policies to deal with, but he made an exception."

"Exception!" Gert kicked at the bench outside the office and wished she hadn't. Her big toe smarted. "He's still mad at her because she wouldn't—" At that moment, Gert glanced Libby's way and took note of her stricken face. The widow had revealed Cyrus's advances to her in confidence. Gert's chest hurt as she realized how close she'd come to blabbing her friend's secret on the main street of town, in a place where Cyrus could probably hear every word she said through his flimsy office walls. She ducked her head. "Forget it."

"Yes, that would be best." Ethan's eyelids stayed halfway closed as he looked at her. Probably he meant for her to see he wasn't happy with her performance, but all Gert could think was how the sunlight threw elongated shadows of his lashes onto his cheek. Odd that she'd never noticed his eyelashes before.

She turned away swiftly and nearly bumped into Libby.

"Come on, Libby; let's go over to my house. I'll bet Hiram would make a run to Boise for you to fetch that ammunition. Let's give him the list."

"It can wait."

"No, it can't. We have practice again Thursday afternoon, and you've got three women with no bullets. How can they learn to shoot if they haven't got bullets?"

"Here comes the stage," Ethan said, and Gert raised her chin, looking down the street. Cyrus came to the door of the office, holding his gold pocket watch, and the three of them stepped aside in unison to allow him plenty of room on the boardwalk.

"Right on time."

As the stagecoach drew up in a whirlwind of dust, Ethan drew Gert back a step. Cyrus was now between them and the direct path to the emporium. If they wanted to go there immediately, they'd have to go out into the street, around the coach and team, or else elbow through the people now descending from the vehicle.

"Look," Libby hissed, and Gert stared toward the open door of the stagecoach.

Cyrus was helping a woman of about thirty-five climb down, and her gaze swept the street. Her crisp black traveling dress held the inevitable wrinkles and dust of the road through the valley, but her pleasant expression gave Gert a jolt of anticipation. The woman's hem nearly touched the boards underfoot, which bespoke an Easterner, but her dress was well cut from a serviceable fabric meant to withstand the rigors of the journey.

Behind her, a man disembarked. His bowler hat and worsted suit also pegged him as an outlander. He met the woman's gaze with a tired smile.

"Well, Apphia, we've made it at last."

"Welcome to Fergus." Cyrus extended his hand to the man. "I hope you had a pleasant journey."

Instead of the usual complaints about the rough roads and jolting coach, the man grinned. "Indeed we did, sir. I'm Phineas Benton—the Reverend Phineas Benton. This is Mrs. Benton. We hope to make Fergus our new home."

Gert gasped. Mrs. Benton looked her way and smiled again. "Hello."

Libby leaped toward the woman, and Mrs. Benton held out her gloved hand. "I'm glad to see some civilized ladies live in town."

"My dear madam, you have no idea how happy we are to see you. I'm Elizabeth Adams, and I own the Paragon Emporium, behind you."

Mrs. Benton looked over her shoulder. "An impressive establishment, Mrs. Adams."

Libby turned and yanked Gert forward. "This is my friend, Gertrude Dooley. Her brother is a gunsmith, and Miss Dooley makes her home with him."

"Pleased to meet you, Miss Dooley." Mrs. Benton took her hand and bowed her head.

"H–hello." Gert tried not to stare at the woman. Even with a layer of travel dust, the dark hair that framed her face looked thick and glossy, and her warm brown eyes radiated sincere satisfaction.

Cyrus nodded toward Ethan. "This is Sheriff Chapman.

Sheriff, may I introduce Mr. and Mrs. Benton?"

Ethan bobbed his head and briefly shook hands with them. "Sir. Ma'am. Welcome."

"Are you a preacher?" Gert gulped as they all stared at her. Stupid thing to say. He'd told them he was a reverend.

Mr. Benton's laugh rang out and echoed off the facades of the empty buildings across the street, but his expression was not unkind. "Indeed I am, ma'am. That's why we've come here from St. Louis. Could one of you please direct me to a Mr. Jamin Morrell?"

"Morrell?" Cyrus's jaw sagged. "You want to see Morrell, Reverend?"

"Why, yes. I assume he's chairman of the pulpit committee. He's the one who invited us to come and minister here in Fergus."

★ CHAPTER 15 ★

Cyrus was never one to let flies settle on him. He turned to Ethan and smiled. "Sheriff, I believe the mayor ought to be notified of this happy event. Would you mind stepping over to his house and telling Mr. and Mrs. Walker that a man of the cloth has arrived in town?"

In his attempt to carry out Cyrus's idea swiftly, Ethan practically fell over the Bentons' luggage. Within a couple of minutes, the mayor was pumping the reverend's hand and beaming as though he'd personally issued the call to shepherd the wayward flock of Fergus. Orissa Walker, her color high and her hat slightly askew, also welcomed the couple and insisted they retire to her parlor for refreshment.

"How kind of you," Mrs. Benton said.

"We should be delighted." Her husband held his bowler hat to his chest and bowed as though Mrs. Walker had lifted a burden from his shoulders, which she probably had. No doubt the minister and his wife had wondered where they would have their next meal.

Libby excused herself so she could get back to her store. As the Bentons bid the gracious widow good-bye, Cyrus heard Orissa whisper to Gert, "Can you run to Annie Harper's for me? See if she and Myra can help prepare a company luncheon in my kitchen?"

Gert nodded.

"We'll have the Bentons, the town council members, and of

course the mayor and myself. If you're able to help, I'd be most grateful."

Gert made no commitments but scooted away on the other side of the stagecoach. Cyrus told the shotgun rider to carry the Bentons' luggage to the mayor's house until further arrangements were made. Nick Telford, the driver, gathered the reins and started the team toward the livery.

"Cyrus, you'll accompany us home, won't you?" the mayor asked.

"Certainly. But I need to take care of one small item first."

As the Walkers herded the new clergyman and his wife toward their home, Cyrus strode quickly down the boardwalk to the telegraph office. A quarter of an hour later he had his reply—Phineas Benton's credentials stood up. Such was modern-day America—pace for fifteen minutes, and someone in St. Louis considered your question and sent you an answer. He still wasn't sure how saloon keeper Jamin Morrell had managed it, but the Reverend Phineas Benton was the genuine article.

When Cyrus reached the Walkers' home, Oscar Runnels had already heard the news and answered the summons. He sat in the parlor drinking tea and inquiring about the Bentons' trip and whether they were related to the Bentons of Lewiston. The two other council members showed up soon after—Griffin Bane and Zachary Harper, whose wife presumably raced around the kitchen while her hostess sat languidly conversing with the Bentons. Someone was out there anyway. Pleasing smells emanated from the Walkers' kitchen.

After answering questions about their trip, Mr. Benton looked around at the assembly. "So, the church council is complete? I expected to see Mr. Morrell here."

The mayor shot Cyrus a panicky glance, and Cyrus cleared his throat. "Well, now, sir, that's a funny thing. You see, we didn't have a formal pulpit committee, or even a church committee or board of deacons. The men you see here make up the town council. We've hoped for several years to bring a minister to Fergus but were never able to do that. There is no congregation as such. That is, there will be, I'm sure, but you'll have to start from scratch, so to speak. And Jamin Morrell is. . . Well, I doubt he'll be one of the charter members."

"Oh?" The minister held his gaze with an innocent expression, and his wife also stared at him with raised brows. Cyrus wished he didn't have to break the news, but someone had to explain.

Mrs. Walker saved him the trouble.

"Jamin Morrell is the owner of the vilest saloon in town. He's a man of few morals, if any. Begging your pardon, Mr. Benton, but I cannot conceive of a reason why he invited you here." Orissa's wrinkled brow smoothed out again as she paused and dredged up a smile for the parson and his wife. "But we are all glad that you came."

The men chimed in with quick assents.

"I. . .see." Benton eyed his wife askance, and it was obvious that he didn't really see. "But. . .why did Mr. Morrell undertake to contact us?"

Cyrus set his teacup aside and leaned forward. "Mr. Morrell is a shrewd man, sir. He knew the ladies—that is, the people—of the town wanted a church and a minister. It's my guess that he saw providing one as a way to gain respect in the town."

"You may be right," Walker said. "He's been trying ever since he moved here last year to get other folks to take him seriously as a businessman and a contributor to the community. He doesn't like being looked down on because of his profession."

Mrs. Benton frowned and turned to Orissa. "Do you mean to say that he would use us as a means of persuading people to look on him and his. . .business more favorably?"

"Why, I. . ." Orissa swiveled toward her husband. "I'm sure I don't know."

"Could be," Griffin Bane said. "Morrell runs a rowdy place over at the Nugget. Some folks wish he'd never come to town. Of course, others frequent his establishment." The blacksmith went red under his beard and glanced at Cyrus.

Cyrus returned his gaze steadily. The men of this town would stick together—and if no one started naming patrons of the Nugget, they'd be fine. He did wonder how the preacher's arrival would affect business in the saloons. Might keep the family men away for a few weeks. Bitsy would suffer more in that case than Jamin. But in the long run, people who were going to drink would drink.

"I see," Mr. Benton said again.

"You won't leave on account of Morrell being the one to ask you here, will you?" Zachary Harper asked. "You'll break my wife's heart if you pack up and go. She was all excited when she heard we had us a preacher at last."

Benton reached over and patted his wife's hand. She smiled tremulously at him.

"No, we won't leave," he said. "God works in mysterious ways, and we're here to stay."

Luncheon pleased all the diners and proved remarkably palatable, considering the amount of time the cooks had had to prepare it. Cyrus wondered if Gert Dooley and others in the neighborhood had brought over dishes they'd prepared for their own families.

"I'd still like to meet Mr. Morrell and thank him," Mr. Benton said.

"Why don't we ask the sheriff to show you around the town after lunch?" Cyrus asked. Inwardly, he congratulated himself on coming up with this brilliant notion. Chapman was polite and discreet, if a bit of a dolt. He could keep the Bentons busy for an hour while the mayor and council hashed over the unexpected developments. He smiled at Mr. Benton. "While you're gone, the council can discuss living arrangements for you and where you can begin holding services."

"You said there's no church building."

"No, there's not," the mayor said. "We do have a schoolhouse."

"We've got a dozen vacant buildings in town," Griffin said. "This used to be a mining boom town, but most of the people left after the ore played out. Why not use one of those empty buildings for a church? At least temporarily."

The suggestion bothered Cyrus, since he owned those buildings. No one would want to pay him for the use of one for worship services. On the other hand, Isabel hated having to rearrange the classroom after a community event. No doubt she'd be out of sorts if the council gave the minister permission to use her schoolroom for services. His daughter obeyed his decrees, but that didn't mean she wouldn't find subtle ways to make her displeasure known.

"Er, we can discuss the matter," he said quickly.

Six hours later, Cyrus wandered into the Nugget for a much-needed drink. Lately, if he went to the Spur & Saddle to drink, word got around. Why should the town care if he put a little whiskey back? He had a suspicion it was Bitsy's doing because he'd spoken out against the shooting club. For the last couple of weeks, she'd made snide comments every time he went in there. All right, if she didn't want his business, he'd take it elsewhere. The Nugget wasn't as quiet and comfortable, but at least he could have a drink there without worrying someone would count his refills and tell his daughter how many.

Jamin Morrell sat at a corner table with a couple of ranchers. When Cyrus entered, Morrell rose and headed over to the bar.

"Set up a whiskey for Mr. Fennel, Ted. He deserves a lot more than that for offering the new preacher free rent on a house."

Cyrus smiled, though it had irked him to no end when the mayor and the rest of the council had pressured him to do it this afternoon. Word of the decision had run through the town like a prairie fire, and now folks thought he was generous.

He'd argued with Charles, Griffin, and Zachary that if a preacher should be paid, so should a landlord. But he was the only one with vacant real estate in town. At last he'd agreed to give six months' free rent on one of his empty houses to the Bentons. If they didn't find other living quarters during that time, they could discuss a rental or purchase agreement with him.

"Not a problem, Morrell." His tone was more jovial than he felt. So long as the rest of the town never found out how bitterly he'd fought the free-rent proposal, he could play the hero as well as Jamin. "You deserve some credit yourself, persuading Mr. and Mrs. Benton to come to our fair town."

Jamin shrugged. "It was a long shot. That's why I didn't tell anyone. Didn't want to get the people's hopes up. But I knew someone in St. Louis who might know someone, so I sent off a letter."

"Well, we owe you a big debt. Been wishing we had a preacher for a long time." Not that he personally had wished it. He'd have to spend Sundays sitting through dull sermons now, but at least they'd have someone to perform weddings and funerals, and most of the ladies would be happy.

Cyrus sipped his first whiskey. He still thought there must be more to the story. Isabel and half the matrons of the town had nagged their menfolk for years to get a preacher for Fergus. The town council had written several letters to towns back East and even splurged on a newspaper ad in Boston, hoping to entice a man to come, with no results. But when Morrell got the idea, he asked a friend a favor, and presto—a bona fide, ordained minister showed up!

The argument over whether to use the schoolhouse for church services, build a sanctuary, or designate some other building a temporary church had lasted even longer than the one over housing the couple. Not everyone in town would attend church, and some didn't want to see the town subsidizing it. The council had discussed asking the members of the community for donations. At last they'd agreed that it really wasn't a town problem. The church members should bear the expense of a building to meet in. But since all the town pillars wanted a church and a minister, they would encourage the townspeople to contribute to the cause.

After much wrestling, Cyrus had agreed to open the old Jonnason Haberdashery building, between the jail and the telegraph office, for services. The people interested in having a church would clean it and provide seating. And a small rental would be paid to Cyrus from the church's offerings.

Mr. Benton had found this arrangement satisfactory, and Cyrus had left him after giving him and Mrs. Benton a tour of their new "church" and housing. Orissa Walker offered to let them stay at the mayor's house until the ladies got their new lodgings ready. She also promised to line up a bevy of local women to help clean both buildings. Griffin had offered to canvass the residents for basic furnishings for the new parsonage. All was accomplished so quickly that Cyrus's head spun—or perhaps that was partly due to the second and third glasses of whiskey Ted had poured for him. He still had the feeling he'd gotten the short end of the stick, but at least Charles and the others had agreed he should be paid for use of the haberdashery.

"The way I see it," Morrell now said, "having a preacher will help this town grow. The population dropped off after the mines played out, but it's still a nice little town. It will be even better with a few more businesses, a few more families. . . ."

A few more customers. That's what he was thinking, wasn't it? Cyrus nodded. "I like the way you think, Morrell. Well, mostly. You're a real businessman."

Now, if only the ladies of Fergus would get distracted by the cleaning frenzy and forget about their little shooting club. The very existence of the group peeved him. It wasn't right.

Maybe if he kept on the preacher's good side, he could bend his ear and get him to say something from the pulpit that would make the women see how wrong it was for them to be out shooting up the hillsides when they ought to be doing what they were doing this minute—cleaning and cooking.

A vision flitted through his mind of the town's ladies, led by the timid Mrs. Benton, lovely Libby Adams, and belligerent Gert Dooley, all marching toward the Nugget carrying axes and signs that read: DEMON RUM.

No. Not in this life.

"Ted, better pour me another."

"It's so nice of Hiram to do this for me." Libby totaled the columns of figures listing the amount of each cartridge size she wanted and her estimated cost.

"Well, with the new preacher coming and all, we need you ladies to stay here to help them get settled." Ethan smiled at her. "I think it's great that you've made a donation to start the church fund."

Libby circled her total and reached for the cash box. "I hope it will inspire others to do the same. The congregation needs to buy that building from Cy Fennel as soon as possible." She counted out several large bills. "I've wired ahead for a case of Bibles, too."

"That's a good idea. Folks will be wanting them, now that we're going to have church regular. I might even buy one myself."

"You don't have a Bible, Ethan? I'm surprised at you." Libby lowered her voice. "I hope Hiram doesn't mind carrying all this money."

"Griffin's going with him."

"Wonderful. But who will tend the livery?"

"He's got Josiah Runnels and Ezra Dyer ready to swap the stagecoach teams out. If anyone needs to have blacksmithing done, they'll have to wait."

Libby arched her delicate eyebrows. "I'm surprised Griffin would go to so much trouble. Loaning us a wagon and team was generous enough."

"Well, Griff isn't sure he approves of the shooting club, but he's starting to disapprove of Fennel. He may be doing it partly to make him mad."

"Ah." Libby nodded. "I'm afraid Gert's and my doings have caused people to take sides. I'm sorry about that."

"Don't be. You ladies are right to want more security."

Libby looked around as Florence entered the back door. "I don't like to trust this delicate an order to Oscar Runnels and his mule teams. They're slow, and besides, after what happened yesterday, Cyrus might forbid Mr. Runnels to do it for me. It's just as well Hiram and Griffin are willing." She handed him the money and her list. "Thank you, Ethan."

He nodded and stepped out onto the boardwalk. The sturdy freight wagon came down the street, with Griffin holding the reins and Hiram sitting beside him. They pulled up in front of the emporium, and Ethan stepped into the street. Two rifles lay at the men's feet.

"You two take care."

"We will," Griffin said. "If you don't mind looking in at the livery once or twice, I'd appreciate it."

"Maybe you can look in on Trudy, too," Hiram said.

"Trudy? Who's Trudy?" Griffin's bushy brows lowered, and he leaned away from Hiram, the better to stare at him.

Ethan grinned and ignored the question, hoping his face wouldn't go too red in front of the blacksmith. "I'll do that. Here's Miz Adams's list." He handed the cash over with it, and Hiram quickly stuffed both in his vest pocket and buttoned it closed.

"See ya tomorrow night." Ethan stepped back up on the boardwalk and waved.

Griffin clucked to the horses and set off down Main Street, then turned his head again to stare at Hiram. "Who's Trudy?"

Ethan laughed and headed across the street.

"Sheriff!"

He stopped on the walk in front of the jail and turned toward the call. Micah Landry trotted up on his bay mare and dismounted.

"What is it, Mr. Landry?"

"My wife, that's what."

"Is she hurt?" Ethan's neck prickled at the anger in the rancher's voice.

"Not yet, but she might be soon. I've had enough of this shooting society."

"Oh." Ethan gritted his teeth and prepared to hear a passionate rant.

Micah wrapped the mare's reins around the hitching rail and stepped up on the boardwalk with him. "Emmaline is wasting two afternoons a week now, going out to yak with a bunch of misguided women and shoot off a passel of lead. Do you know how much ammunition she's used in the last three weeks?"

"I have no idea."

"Two boxes of shotgun shells, that's how much. I told her we can't afford a dollar a month for shooting practice. And what'll we do when one of those women gets shot?"

"Easy, now. I'm sure they're being careful."

Micah balled his hands into fists "Don't tell me to take it easy. I want my wife back in the kitchen where she belongs. That's my gun she's using, and it's my money she's spending on shells."

Ethan swallowed hard and put one hand out toward Landry.

"This is really between you and Mrs. Landry. She's not doing anything illegal that I can see."

"Well, there oughta be a law against it. Women shouldn't be able to take a man's gun without asking and shoot off his supply of ammunition. What if I want to go hunting and there's no shells left?"

Cyrus Fennel came down the sidewalk and ambled over to where they stood. "What's going on, Micah?"

"My wife. She's out shooting all the time with those other women. I'd like to take Gert Dooley and—"

"Watch it, now," Ethan growled. "Miss Dooley told me your wife asked to join them, not the other way around. It sounds to me as though you and Mrs. Landry need to sit down over a pot of coffee and discuss this in a civilized manner."

"We tried that this morning, and it weren't civilized. Sheriff, you've got to disband that club."

Cyrus clapped Landry on the shoulder. "Now, Micah, have you told the missus you don't want her going to these club meetings?"

"I tried, but she just kept saying how much she enjoys getting out and talking to the other ladies. I says, 'How can you talk if you're all blazing away?' But she says she likes it and that she feels safer now that she knows she can hit a man if she needs to."

Cyrus's graying eyebrows rose. "Did you take that as a threat?"

Landry's jaw dropped. "Threat? No! What are you talking about? I never thought. . . Why, you don't suppose this is about women's rights, do you?"

"You just don't know with today's females. Bloomer costumes and the Women's Christian Temperance Union. . ." Cyrus shook his head, frowning. "I have to say I'm glad my daughter hasn't neglected her duties to join the shootists."

Ethan cleared his throat. "Gentlemen, I don't think you should take this too seriously. The ladies want to feel safe because they're left alone for long periods of time. They want to know they can defend themselves, that's all. Now, I have work to do. Good day." Ethan tipped his hat and turned his back. He walked to the jail fighting the urge to look back.

★ CHAPTER 16 ★

After the first Sunday service, Cyrus and Isabel left the new sanctuary just behind the Walkers. Pastor and Mrs. Benton stood at the door, shaking hands with the parishioners.

"Now you be sure and come over for dinner as soon as you're done here," Orissa Walker said loudly enough for all those still in the building to hear.

"Thank you," Apphia Benton said.

Her husband smiled and took Mrs. Walker's hand. "We'll be there shortly, my good woman."

Cyrus nodded at Mrs. Benton and shook the minister's hand heartily. "Good sermon, Reverend."

"Thank you." Phineas Benton's face barely contained his ear-to-ear smile. "And thank you again for your generosity, Mr. Fennel."

Cy left the building and put his hat on. Isabel came out behind him.

"Are you coming straight home, Pa?"

"I may drop in to see someone for a minute. Go ahead and get dinner on though. I'll be right there." A month ago, he might have gone to the Spur & Saddle for his Sunday dinner, but Bitsy's venom was too much to face lately. He'd as soon eat at home. But first he wanted to stop by the Nugget. He went to the back door and knocked.

Jamin Morrell came to open it in his shirtsleeves.

"Well, Mr. Fennel, what brings you out?"

Cyrus nodded with a half smile. "Just thought I'd tell you, the church service was packed. But I think the reverend was disappointed that you didn't show up."

Jamin laughed. "It'll be a hot day in January when I start going to church."

He walked inside to a table in the corner, where he had writing materials spread out, and picked up a stoneware mug of coffee. "Just catching up on some correspondence and bookkeeping." After a quick swig, he set the mug down and slid a sheet of paper over the one he'd been working on.

Cyrus had glimpsed the salutation of a letter: *Dear Dr. Kincaid.*

"Why do you keep the Nugget closed Sundays if you don't believe in religion?" he asked.

Jamin gave him a tight smile. "Everyone needs a day of rest, Mr. Fennel. If Bitsy Shepard wants to serve chicken dinners instead of taking a day of rest, let her. I doubt she makes much profit from it. I give my employees the day off. You can tell the reverend that if you want. He can do his business on Sunday, but don't expect me there."

Cyrus left him, noting peevishly that Morrell could at least have offered him a cup of coffee. Oh well, Isabel would have dinner ready at home.

As he walked, he pondered how he could bring the Reverend Mr. Benton over to his way of thinking about the shooting club. Dooley and Bane had driven all the way to Boise to fetch the ammunition Libby Adams had wanted to bring in on the stagecoach. On his visit to the emporium yesterday, he'd seen several new guns displayed. Those hadn't been there before. Oh, she'd ordered in Bibles, too, the hypocrite. Did she think that could offset the way she encouraged all those women to defy their husbands? Much as he admired her golden locks and sweet visage, he was glad he hadn't pursued an entanglement with Libby. She would buck him all the way on both domestic and business matters, unlike his pliable and obedient daughter.

Maybe he and Isabel could entertain the Bentons for dinner next Sunday. If he could get the minister away from distractions, they could have a serious talk about a woman's place in society and how the shooting club was detrimental to the town and the congregation. Reverend Benton needed to understand the danger of an organization that prompted women to abandon their duties in the home.

Milzie set Franklin's Hawken rifle against the stone wall of the cave and carefully unwrapped her bundle. She had so few possessions she took great care to make sure they stayed in a safe place. The bundle consisted of her ragged shawl, for which she was thankful. That, with a wool skirt, one bodice she'd made from one of Franklin's old shirts, and a tattered nightdress, made up her entire wardrobe. She'd saved Franklin's wool, army-issue coat the night of the fire, and her shoes, but they were nearly in pieces now. Her stockings had long since worn through at the toes and heels.

The cave served her better as a home than it had as part of Franklin's mining claim. He'd dug about inside for weeks, twenty years or more ago, hoping to find some ore, but without success. It only went back thirty feet or so into the rock. Frank had shored up the ceiling while he was at it and built a little shelf on one side of the opening, between two timbers. An old lantern hung above it. Her only furniture was a wooden crate she'd salvaged and used as a stool.

She peered at the jumble of items she'd brought back from her latest trip into town. The light streaming through the cave entrance revealed her new treasures, mostly bestowed on her by the ladies of the shooting club.

The bright red kerchief was a prize she'd almost passed up. She felt guilty as she stroked it. Miz Dooley likely would miss it, but it was so cheery, she couldn't walk off without it. And she could tie it about her throat when the weather turned cold again. She'd also picked up a few brass shell casings after the shooting practice. She wasn't sure what she would do with them, but they must be good for something. A bread roll and a clump of raisins— Bitsy Shepard had slipped her those, bless her heart. And Miz Adams had brought her a few crackers wrapped in brown paper. The final item was one she'd found when she cut behind one of the ranch houses on her way home: a button that looked all shiny in the sunlight, like silver. She held it up to the light. The design resembled a knot, cast in metal. She stroked it lovingly and placed it on the shelf.

The shell casings looked fine, next to her neat row of shining safety pins, including the big one from the livery. She raised her hand to her mouth and licked the spot on the back where she'd been burned in March, the night the cabin went up in flames. It didn't hurt much now, but the skin was still rough. She folded the red kerchief and set it next to the blacksmith's knife and the matchbox that held the few coins she'd found at the livery last week.

The shooting club was the greatest adventure she'd had in years. Franklin's Hawken bought her entrance into the company of the finest ladies in Fergus. True, she was reduced to "borrowing" ammunition to practice with. Libby or Gert brought her powder and lead for two or three shots each meeting. She was getting good at shooting, too. Under Gert Dooley's tutelage, her aim had improved dramatically. Milzie had visions of bringing down a pronghorn for meat someday. Wouldn't that be fine?

Her pitiful inventory mocked her. How would she survive with only these few things? But she'd made it through since March, and the warm weather was on her side. She'd planted the seeds Libby Adams gave her a couple of weeks ago. Already, feathery little carrots sprouted in the garden spot behind the charred remains of the cabin.

She would rest today and forage again tomorrow. Today she'd saved one lead ball for the Hawken. Somehow, she'd figure out a way to salvage a bit of powder next time and bring it home to the cave. And sometime soon, she would go hunting.

Gert drove the wagon to Bert Thalen's ranch on Monday afternoon with Libby and Mrs. Benton on the seat with her. In the back rode Florence, Annie, Myra, Vashti, and Bitsy. Libby had hired the wagon from the livery so that Mrs. Benton could attend the shooting practice in comfort.

When Gert reined in the team, six more women, wives of

ranchers and miners, awaited their arrival. They swarmed around the wagon to greet the ladies from town.

"Ladies," Gert called, standing up on the wagon, "it gives me great pleasure to introduce Mrs. Apphia Benton."

Mrs. Benton smiled warmly and nodded at the women assembled on the meager grass.

"Some of you met her yesterday at the church service," Gert said. "For those of you who may not have heard, she is our new minister's wife."

The women crowded in closer, and Emmaline reached up to help Mrs. Benton descend from the wagon seat.

After allowing a few minutes for greetings and chatter, Gert nodded at Libby, who raised her melodic voice.

"Ladies, if I may have your attention, please. Since our numbers have grown so, Miss Dooley and I have formed a plan for dividing the shooters into teams. Each team leader will be responsible for seeing that safety procedures are followed and that all targets and debris are cleaned up before we leave."

The women nodded and murmured their approval. With Ethan's permission, they continued to meet in a draw on Bert Thalen's ranch, but he had warned them that the site of their meetings would probably have to be moved if Bert's son sold the ranch or decided to come live on it.

"Before we name the team leaders," Libby said, "Miss Dooley has one other announcement."

Gert tried to smile, but her stomach lurched a little. She wasn't used to speaking to a crowd. "It has come to my attention that certain people in the town have given our group a name." The women waited in utter silence. Gert swallowed and went on. "They're calling us the Ladies' Shooting Club."

"Could be worse," Vashti said, and they all laughed.

Gert was able to smile then. "Yes, it could." She'd thought of several possibilities herself, none of them good. "I wondered if you would like to formally enact a resolution to take the name 'Ladies' Shooting Club.' That would make us an acknowledged organization."

"Acknowledged by whom?" Bitsy called.

Gert looked at Libby, a panicky dismay squeezing her innards.

"Why, by us, of course," Libby said, still smiling, and a ripple of amusement ran through the group. "And by all the kind gentlemen who have shown their support in various ways—the sheriff, Hiram Dooley, Griffin Bane, and others."

Annie called out, "The way I see it, if a man isn't carping about our shooting habits, he's on our side."

"What good will naming the club do?" Emmaline asked.

Gert looked to Libby with a silent plea for her to continue. Libby rose to the occasion.

"As an entity, we can have a voice in the town. Miss Dooley and I thought the club might even approach the town council concerning safety. We could urge them to allow the sheriff to deputize men to help him patrol the town at night, for instance."

"Why couldn't we help with that?" Myra asked.

"Hmm, I'm not sure the town fathers are ready for that." Libby reached to squeeze the girl's arm and looked over at Gert.

Gert cleared her throat. "May I hear from those in favor of this resolution—to be hereafter known as the Ladies' Shooting Club of Fergus?"

"Aye," chorused the women.

"Any opposed?"

Blessed silence greeted her. "Thank you. The resolution is enacted. And now, I would like to institute a new tradition for the club. I'd like to ask Mrs. Benton to lead us in prayer."

"I'm delighted to be here with you as a part of this group." Mrs. Benton pushed a wisp of dark hair back beneath her bonnet. "Thank you all for your welcome. Shall we pray?"

The ladies bowed their heads—even Vashti, after Bitsy elbowed her sharply.

Half an hour later, as the teams worked smoothly through their shooting routines, Gert moved from group to group to give pointers on aiming.

In Emmaline's group, she heard Apphia say to Goldie, "Why of course you would be welcome at the church services. No one would turn you away from the Lord's work." The saloon girl eyed her dubiously.

When Gert reached Libby's team, her friend gestured for her to join them.

"I was thinking that perhaps on Thursday you could give us all a lesson in gun cleaning." Libby's blue eyes glinted with eagerness.

"Sure. That's a good idea." Gert looked over the orderly ranks of women and frowned. Milzie was hobbling away, past the row of tied horses and toward the road. "I gave Milzie her last bullet and powder load, but she's leaving, and I don't think she's fired it yet."

★ CHAPTER 17 ★

Ethan stretched the wire tight while Johnny McDade pounded in staples to hold it to the fence posts. The bottom of the box of staples showed, and Ethan looked anxiously toward town.

"Sure wish that brother of yours would get back here."

"No doubt he's flirting with that redheaded gal at the emporium," Johnny said.

Ethan shook his head. Spin McDade, the older of the two brothers at nineteen, considered himself quite a ladies' man. Sending him into town on an errand was a risk, but he'd figured the two boys wouldn't get much done on the fence if he went, and he hadn't wanted to send the younger brother with cash. Of course, Libby would probably have opened an account for him if he'd sent a note, but Ethan liked to keep his debts cleared up. Credit could ruin a man, or so his pa had always said.

A few minutes later, Ethan saw a telltale plume of dust where the road ran behind some scrub pines. "Maybe that's Spin coming."

"We can hope." Johnny picked up the jug of spring water they'd brought along and tipped it back for a long swallow.

Spin and his horse appeared at the edge of the new pasture they were fencing—not that it produced much grass, but it would hold a few cattle while Ethan gave his north range a chance to recover from spring grazing. The leggy bay gelding cantered toward them.

"Hey!" Johnny waved his hat and grinned at his brother.

139

Spin pulled the horse to a halt and jumped down. "I got the staples. Miz Adams asked me to tell ya the shooting club will meet this afternoon."

"What's that?" Johnny asked. "Do we want to join this here club?"

Ethan laughed. "I don't think so. It's for women."

The two young men stared at him. They hadn't been into town much since they'd joined Ethan for the summer, and apparently they hadn't heard about the controversial new society.

"Some of the women in Fergus are learning to shoot. Since Sheriff Thalen was killed, they've wanted to learn to defend themselves. Mrs. Adams is just keeping me informed. They usually meet on Thalen's old property, not far from here, so don't you boys go riding over that way. They might blow your heads off." Ethan nodded toward Bert's land.

"I heard some shooting over thataway on Monday," Johnny said.

"Does Florence Nash go?" Spin asked. "I might want to join if she does."

"I told you, it's for women only." Ethan reached for the box of staples Spin pulled from his saddlebag.

"How much time did you spend following Florence around the store?" Johnny asked.

His brother smiled. "She's a peach. I might just need to ride into town with you Sunday, Ethan. She told me they're having church services now."

Ethan nodded. "You can both go if you've a mind to. Your ma and pa would be pleased, I'm sure." No doubt Spin would find his way onto the Nash family's bench that served as a pew, but that was all right. As big as he talked, Spin generally behaved himself, and Florence was a nice girl.

"You aiming to settle down?" Johnny stared at his brother in disgust.

"Maybe."

Johnny scowled and shook his head. "I never."

Ethan and Spin laughed.

"How about you, Ethan?" Spin asked in a man-to-man tone.

"You ever think about settling down?"

Ethan grunted and pulled his work gloves on. "I consider myself settled."

"Aw, come on." Spin bent to help him lift and string the wire. "Don't you ever think about courtin' a girl?"

"No. I try not to."

"Why ever not?" Johnny asked, retrieving his hammer.

"I just don't want to think about getting married, that's all."

"Well, that Miz Adams is mighty pretty," Spin said.

"Hush," Ethan said, not unkindly. "Let's get this fence up."

"And there was another girl came into the store while I was there. Gert, they call her. Not so pretty as Miz Adams, but she seemed pert and likable."

"I told you to hush. Mrs. Adams and Miss Dooley are too old for the likes of you, and I told you, I'm not ready to settle. Now are you gonna work, or am I gonna have to pay you off and hire someone else?"

Ethan bent his back into the grueling work. When they'd strung the wire as far as he'd planted fence posts, he wielded the post-hole digger, and Spin followed, driving more posts in with a sledgehammer. Johnny chinked them with small stones when needed. By noontime, all three were drenched in sweat and ready for a meal.

As he wearily mounted Scout, Ethan considered the rest of his day.

"After we wash up and eat, you two can work on the barn roof." They wouldn't work so hard they suffered from it, but they'd make a little progress.

"You going into town?" Johnny asked.

"Reckon I should. Folks like to see the sheriff's face now and then."

He wondered if he could count on supper at Hiram and Trudy's. He smiled to himself. He'd taken to thinking of her as Trudy, and the more he cogitated on it, the better he thought the name fit her. He might even take her a little something as a token of his gratitude. But what? He wouldn't want her to start thinking like the McDade boys, that he ought to settle down. So nothing personal.

He thought back to when he'd left Fergus to join the army. He'd been only a couple of years older than Spin was now. Young, carefree, idealistic. That was before he helped chase the Bannocks all across the Idaho Territory and followed the Sheepeaters high into the mountains. Back then, he might have sparked a girl and dreamed of setting up to have a family. But now. . .now when he thought of families, he remembered the faces of the starving Indians they'd chased down. Memories of their skirmishes sickened him. And what woman would want to spend her life with a man haunted by wailing Sheepeater children?

No, a woman like Libby was better off on her own. She seemed content with her business and her friends. And Trudy? She had her brother to fret over. She didn't need another man whose past rose up to haunt him.

So that was that. He'd take them some beef when it came butchering time. But no flowers or candy for. . .

The image of Trudy as a little girl with flaxen braids flitted across his mind.

Libby sat up in bed, her heart pounding. She strained to hear. Something creaked, but the two-story building made its own noises when all else was quiet. Something different had yanked her from sleep.

She heard it again—stealthy footsteps in the rooms below. She could barely breathe. Someone was in the back room of the store, where her desk sat and the safe huddled in the corner behind a stack of crates.

She slid her hand under Isaac's cool, undented pillow. The Peacemaker fit her hand like an old friend.

Her dressing gown lay draped over a chair, and she slid it on, tying it firmly about her waist, then picked up the pistol. Shoes would only betray her.

As she listened, the footsteps sounded again. The intruder had left the back room and gone to the main floor of the emporium. What was he after? Had he tried to open the safe? She took a trembling step and stopped to listen again. She heard quiet thumping and shuffling, then snapping. Three quick steps took her to the door. She turned the knob with excruciating slowness and pulled the door two inches inward.

With an eye to the crack, she squinted toward the staircase and saw a glow. He must have lit a lantern...or a candle. The glow flickered on the ceiling and walls over the stairs.

Smoke hit her suddenly, a roiling wave of it, and she gasped, which only sucked more into her lungs. She shut the door, not worrying about the sound it made. For a moment she stood groping for a reason. She'd had no fire in the stove downstairs for weeks, and she hadn't even lit her cookstove in the upstairs apartment tonight. How could there be—

The acrid smell reached beneath the door and choked her.

★ CHAPTER 18 ★

Libby threw the door open and dashed to the top of the stairs, clutching the pistol before her. Smoke rolled up the stairwell. Pulling in a deep breath, she hurried down. The air seemed clearer at the bottom of the flight, though she could now see flames rising from a heap on the floor between the counter and the racks that held housewares and baking supplies.

She looked all around. No one moved through the thickening smoke in the big room. On tiptoe, she approached the site of the fire. Merchandise had been piled up in a mound—clothing, stationery, and seed packets. Combustibles. No hardware or pots. Things that would burn quickly. A sudden flare-up in the blaze drove her back several feet. Something had caught and sizzled. Lard, maybe, or bacon?

She laid the Peacemaker on a shelf and grabbed a wool blanket. The fire bucket always sat near the pot-bellied stove, even in summer. She shoved the blanket into it, trying not to slop the precious water. The heavy cloth soaked her nightclothes. She stood and carried it to the blaze. Choosing the part that burned most fiercely, she flipped the wet cloth over it, slapping at the fire and jerking her blanket back. The hot floorboards made the bare soles of her feet smart, but she couldn't stop. Several times she swatted at the flames and glowing embers. A flaring brand rolled toward her, and she lifted her robe and nightgown, jumping back.

She soaked the blanket again and returned to her task until the blanket began to smoke. The fire bucket was nearly empty, so she upended it on the fire and edged around the burning pile. She managed to squeeze past the end of the counter. The bucket of drinking water was nearly full. She picked it up and hurried back to the fire, coughing so hard she spilled some of the water. Aiming for the spot that persisted in burning the worst, she swung the bucket and threw the water on it. She jumped back, lest the swash throw hot embers on her.

The smoke thickened, and flames kept licking at the heap. More water. Libby ran through the storage room. The back door was unlocked, but she wouldn't think about that now. She ran to the rain barrel and scooped her pail full.

As she hurried back inside, sloshing water against her legs and again soaking the lower part of her nightclothes, she wondered if she should run for the nearest neighbors. But as she threw the full bucket onto the fire and a great deal of water ran off it and flowed across the floor, she decided she could put it out if she persisted. If she ran for Peter Nash or the mayor, the fire might grow beyond their ability to stop it.

She made three more trips before she was satisfied that the flames wouldn't leap up again. Exhausted, she leaned against the counter, panting. Her wet clothing was covered in soot, and she assumed her face looked as bad. She went to the front door and threw it wide open. What difference would it make now to leave the doors open? Already her domain had been breached.

Slowly she climbed the stairs and opened all the windows in her living quarters to clear out the smoke. Her feet were sore, but nothing worse than a sunburn, so far as she could tell. In her bedchamber, she lit the lantern and pulled the curtains. Dawn was upon her, and there was no point in going back to bed. She wasted no time but dressed carefully. Her hair would smell of smoke until she washed it, but at least she could scrub the soot from her face and hands. At last she felt presentable. Time to go for help.

She stopped partway down the stairs. The fire was out. Should she even bother her neighbors? The sheriff was the man she needed. A moment's thought, and she went out the front door, closed it firmly behind her, and dashed across the street and down the walk. The jail loomed still and dark, but already lantern light shone through the side kitchen window of the Dooleys' house. Libby hurried to the back and knocked softly.

Gert opened the door cautiously.

"Good morning! Forgive me for coming so early," Libby said.

"What is it? Is something wrong?" Gert's nose wrinkled as she threw the door wide and stepped back so Libby could enter.

"Yes. Someone broke into the emporium and started a fire downstairs. I was able to put it out, but I'd like to talk to the sheriff before I open the store."

"Oh, Libby! Are you all right?" Gert grasped her wrist and looked her over. "You're not hurt, are you?"

"No, I'm fine. I want to go back and start cleaning up right away. It's a mess, but I hope to open the store on time. Do you think—"

"Hiram's getting up. He'll go right away for Ethan. Maybe you should wait until the sheriff gets there to start your cleaning."

Libby shook her head. "No, I wouldn't be able to open on time if I waited. I want to get all the burnt stuff out and air the building well. I'm not sure how badly the floor is damaged, but if I can help it, I won't give the ruffian who did this the satisfaction of closing my business." Her voice choked, and Gert put her arms around her.

"There now. If some outlaw broke in and vandalized your store, you really oughtn't to be over there alone."

"He's gone now." Libby swiped at her tears, wishing she had strength enough to keep from crying. "Oh, Gert, why would anyone do this?" A little sob leaped out of her throat, and she put her hands to her face.

"Sit down." Gert led her gently to the table and pulled out a chair for her. "I'm fixing you a cup of tea as soon as I tell Hiram and get him on his way. Then I'll go over with you, and we'll do whatever's needed."

"You don't have to. You've got your own work to do."

Gert gave a little snort. "I've got nothing more important than fixing breakfast for a man who's capable of doing it himself."

Libby arched her eyebrows. Gert had never before implied that Hiram might not need her quite so much as she wished. "All right." She blinked back her tears and searched her pocket for a handkerchief.

Gert left the room and returned a moment later with Hiram on her heels. The gunsmith stopped in the doorway and eyed her mournfully. At last he spoke.

"You're all right, ma'am?"

"Yes, I am, Hiram. Thank you for asking."

"I'll go to the ranch for Ethan." He strode to the back door, grabbed his hat, and left.

Gert went to the stove and lifted the teakettle. "He offered to check through the store and your rooms, but I told him you'd rather he fetched Ethan. But I'm going with you, and no arguments. You might have been killed." As she spoke, she measured tea into a pot and poured hot water on it. Then she brought their cups to the table and pushed the sugar bowl toward Libby. "I don't expect you've eaten anything, have you?"

Libby shook her head. "But I don't want to lose any time—"

"Just a bite." Gert brought a tin box from the cupboard and opened it to reveal several cold biscuits. "Leftovers, but with a little cheese, they'll go down. You'll be glad later that you had something."

Libby supposed her friend was right, though she barely tasted the biscuit and wedge of sharp cheese Gert placed before her. The tea comforted her.

"Thank you."

Gert put the last bite of her own biscuit into her mouth and stood. She reached to gather the dishes and carried them to the dishpan. "Come on, now. I'll take care of these later. Shall I bring my mop?"

"I've got everything we'll need in the store," Libby said.

Together they walked across the street and up the boardwalk. The early sunlight streamed down Main Street. Libby opened the door of the emporium and led Gert inside to the site of the fire.

Water had run over the floor, pooling in spots and draining through cracks between the floorboards in others. The pile of charred merchandise stank, and the air still held the strong, acrid stench of smoke.

"I'll prop both doors open," Libby said. "I've got the windows open upstairs." The storeroom had no windows to open. Isaac had designed the building that way on purpose, partly for security, and partly to give him more wall space for shelves and stacks of goods.

She took her broom, mop, and bucket from the back room.

"Maybe we should start with a shovel." Gert eyed the wet, ashy pile distastefully.

"Good idea. And I've got a wash boiler over there in the hardware section. We can fill it and carry it out back. I'll get Josiah to haul the trash off later."

"Right," Gert said. "Let's just get it outside for now."

Libby walked quickly to the apparel section and grabbed two pair of men's heavy work gloves. She took one to Gert. "Here. I don't think we want to touch that stuff without gloves."

They set to work, removing all of the ruined items. For twenty minutes they said little. Libby gasped when she recognized some of the wrecked merchandise—the remaining unsold Bibles.

"Wicked."

Gert peered over at the charred leather and paper. "Oh, Libby. I'm so sorry."

Libby sighed. "I've felt a little guilty, anyhow, making a profit from selling the scriptures."

"I don't think you need feel badly about that. Folks in town were glad to get them."

Libby sat back on her heels and wiped her brow with the back of her wrist. "It could have been much worse. So much worse."

The sleigh bells hanging from the door jingled softly as Ethan brushed past them with Hiram close behind.

The sheriff strode toward them and halted, staring down at the stinking mess on the floor.

"This is where it happened?"

Libby nodded. "A pile of merchandise from all over the store—things that would burn easily. Cloth, paper. I'm guessing some lard to help it burn faster."

Ethan frowned.

Before he could speak, Libby said, "I guess you wish we hadn't started cleaning, but I want to open on time today. That is. . ." She faltered, looking to Gert for reassurance. "You don't think it's too smelly, do you? A lot of the other merchandise might be ruined from smoke. I wonder if the flour will taste like it. And the bolts of cloth—I suppose I could wash them if the smell won't air out."

"Let me look around for a few minutes, please, before you do any more," Ethan said. "Where did you put the burnt stuff?"

"Out back." Gert nodded toward the door behind the counter as she pulled off her work gloves. "We made a heap behind the store and figured Josiah could take it away later."

"All right, but I'll want to look at it before he does. Mrs. Adams—"

"I think he burned nearly all the seed packets," Libby said absently, looking at her depleted shelves. "But it's late in the season. Most folks had got what they wanted for seed."

"Did you see the person who did this?" Ethan asked.

She jerked her head around to look at him. "No. I. . ." She was shaking. That was odd. She held her hand out before her, curious at the way it trembled.

Gert stepped forward and put her arm around Libby's waist. "We've been working hard. Why don't you come sit down in the back room while you talk to Ethan?"

"I'm all right." Libby pushed back a lock of hair and wondered if her face was all sooty again. "I didn't see anyone, but I heard someone walking around down here. I think that's what woke me up. Probably he was gathering the things to burn. I heard footsteps and thuds. It frightened me, so I got up and went to my bedroom door. Then I smelled the smoke."

"You put the fire out all by yourself?" Ethan asked.

"Yes. It. . .wasn't that big, but it put off a lot of black smoke."

"There was an empty lard pail in the junk we hauled out," Gert said.

Ethan nodded. "I'll have you show it to me later. Now, Mrs. Adams, think hard. You're sure you didn't see anyone?"

"No one."

"How do you think he got in?"

"The back door wasn't locked." She shook her head. "I know I locked it last night. I always do. But I suppose. . ."

"I'll look at it." Ethan knelt and examined the floorboards. "The fire doesn't seem to have burned through the floor, but it's charred here." He looked up at Hiram. "We could replace these three boards, couldn't we?"

Hiram nodded. "I can go get what we need right now."

"Oh, you don't—" Libby stopped. Hiram was already out the door.

"He'll fix it good as new," Gert said.

Libby looked toward the case clock. It was nearly six in the morning, and she had only two hours to get ready for opening. Florence would help when she arrived at seven thirty. Libby sent up a quick prayer of thanks that she'd put all the ledgers in the safe last night.

"If you could make me a list, I'd appreciate it," Ethan said. "You can do it later today when you have time. Put down anything that's missing from your inventory. And if you know it was in the fire heap, check it off. If you're not sure, and something was maybe stolen, let me know." He stood and walked around, peering under the tables and racks. He paused by a set of shelves that held blankets and linens. "Does this weapon belong to you?" He turned, holding Isaac's Colt pistol.

"Yes. It was my husband's. I brought it downstairs with me and left it there when I began fighting the fire."

Ethan brought it to the counter. "You'll want to put it back in a safe place before you open for business." He stood for a moment, looking down at the countertop. Then he looked up slowly. "Could you come here for a moment, please, ma'am?"

Libby walked over to stand beside him.

"Do you know how this got here?"

Libby looked down to where he pointed. Near the pistol on the otherwise bare countertop lay a penny.

★ CHAPTER 19 ★

Ethan watched Libby's face as she looked down at the counter and spotted the coin.

"I suppose I could have dropped it there when I was putting the cash box away last night. You don't think the arsonist left it?" She reached for the penny.

Ethan touched her sleeve, and she stayed her hand.

"If you don't mind, I'd like to take it," he said. "I can give you another to replace it if your cash doesn't come out right."

Gert stood at Libby's elbow, staring at the coin. Her wide, gray blue eyes met his gaze. "You found a penny under Bert Thalen's body after he was killed."

"Yes." Ethan slid the coin off the countertop and tucked it into the watch pocket of his vest. He'd never owned a watch, but the penny would be safe there.

Hiram entered through the front door carrying a long board. Ethan looked it over. It was about the same width as the floorboards of the emporium. "You got more if this isn't enough?"

Hiram shrugged. "Thought I'd cut three short lengths off this. It ought to do."

"All right, I'll be with you as soon as I poke through the trash pile out back."

Gert stepped forward. "I'll show you where it is, Ethan. I'm sure Libby wants to straighten up the merchandise and start that list you asked her for. And maybe change her outfit before she opens for business."

Libby looked down at her rumpled and stained clothing. "If you don't mind, I'll do that next. Now that most of the filth is outside...although I suppose I'll be weeks getting rid of all the ash and dust." She looked around with a hopeless air.

"We'll help you," Hiram said softly.

"Thank you." Tears glistened in Libby's eyes. "I'd like to freshen up before Florence arrives." She turned and glided toward the staircase, hidden behind a partition that held tinware and kitchen utensils.

Ethan looked to Gert, and she pulled in a breath. "Come on. I'll show you the trash heap. You got gloves?"

He shook his head, and she picked up the pair Libby had discarded. "If these don't fit you, I'm sure she wouldn't mind if you took another pair from the store."

Ethan pulled them on and flexed his hands. "They're a little tight, but they'll do."

Gert stepped over the board. Hiram stood by the hardware table, sizing up Libby's selection of crowbars. Ethan followed her into the back room and paused.

"This is where she does her paperwork?"

Gert turned toward him. "Yes. And stores all the merchandise she hasn't put out yet."

"She's got a safe." He looked around for it.

"I think it's over there in the corner." Gert pointed beyond the desk and chair at the end of the room.

Ethan walked over and looked past the desk. A pile of wooden crates hid the corner from view. In the shadows of the windowless room, he could barely see. On the desk he spotted a fancy oil lamp.

"Mind lighting that lamp for me?"

Gert stepped to the desk, and he sidled around the stack of crates and ran his hand over the wall. As the glow from the lamp flared up, his hand touched cool metal. Gert came around the crates and held up the lamp.

"The safe looks fine," she said.

Ethan nodded. There was no evidence that anyone had tampered with it. So why had the arsonist broken into the store? Would they be able to tell if he'd stolen anything? Or had he just come to wreak havoc?

"Libby could have been killed this morning," Gert said softly.

His stomach lurched. "I thought of that. You don't think this lunatic's intention was to burn her alive, do you?"

"I don't know. He could have been more efficient, if that's what he wanted."

Ethan swung around to face her in the cramped space. "How?"

"He could have set the fire right at the bottom of the stairs so she couldn't come down. But no, he put it out in the open space in front of the counter, away from the walls. And he could have thrown more lard on it or dumped a couple tins of lamp oil. Down at the far end of the store, she's got at least a dozen cans of oil. He didn't even touch 'em. I only saw one lard pail in the pile that burned. It's like he wanted to make a lot of smoke and bother, but he wasn't intent on murder."

Ethan thought about that for a few seconds. "I think you're right. But that penny. . ."

"Yes. That's important, isn't it?"

He nodded slowly. "It must be. It's just like the other one."

Her eyes flared. "Exactly?"

"Yes. An 1866 Indian head cent. I saved the other one in a tin over at the jailhouse. I'll compare them, but I'm sure they're the same."

"He left you a message."

"Why do you say that? Whoever killed Bert couldn't have known at the time that I'd be the next sheriff."

Her brow furrowed as she puzzled over it. "Are we sure about that?"

Ethan caught his breath. "That's. . .reaching a little."

"I know, but—" She glanced over her shoulder. Ethan heard the sound of nails screeching as Hiram tore up the floorboards in the main room. "Just think for a minute. What if the mayor already had you in mind to replace Bert?"

"You're saying the mayor killed Bert?"

"No, I'm not saying that. But what if Cyrus did?"

"Cy Fennel? Trudy, are you loco?"

Her lower jaw dropped, and she stared at him. "What did you call me?"

Ethan gulped. "I'm sorry. I didn't mean you're loco." Why was she looking at him like that? He pulled off his hat and ran a hand through his hair. "Look, I'm sorry."

"You said that."

"Well, just forget about that, all right? We're talking about this criminal. There's no way he could have known. Even if the murderer was Cy Fennel—and I'm not saying it was, 'cause that's crazy—but even *if*, I still say there's no way he could know I'd take the job. Because I almost didn't."

"Why did you?"

He looked into her eyes and couldn't speak for a moment. The lump in his throat nearly choked off his breathing. He couldn't tell her he'd taken the badge because of her hopeful eyes. When had Gert-Trudy Dooley become the reason for the way he lived?

He broke the stare and let out a breath. "Look, right now we're talking about this fire, all right?"

"I thought we were talking about Bert's murder."

"No, *you* were talking about Bert's murder."

"Because of the penny."

Ethan shook his head. "Look, it's close in here with the smoke and the lamp and all. Let's go out back and look at that trash heap."

She set the lamp on Libby's desk and blew out the flame. "You know the same person did this as killed Bert."

"We don't have proof."

"The pennies are proof."

"No, they're not."

She stamped her foot and then scowled at him. "There's a connection."

"I'll give you that." He couldn't recall seeing her so worked up about anything, ever. The color in her cheeks and the spark in her eyes made his stomach gyrate, which rattled him more than finding the penny. He took her elbow and steered her toward the open back door. "Let's get outside where there's some fresh air."

The crisp morning breeze refreshed him better than a cool drink of water. Folks were stirring, and he could see Zach Harper, across three back lots and a field, walking toward his barn. Fergus was waking up to another day.

Ethan paused just outside the door and stooped to look at the latch and the jamb.

"Someone definitely tampered with this." He stuck his head back inside and squinted at the woodwork. Apparently Libby didn't use a bar on this door but trusted the brass lock. Her husband had probably installed it not too many years ago. "Let's look at the burnt stuff."

Gert walked ahead of him to a heap of smelly, charred refuse. She stooped and picked up a broom. The straws were coated in soot. "This is everything Libby and I hauled out. She didn't want to leave it in there, and I can't say as I blame her."

"No, me either." Ethan took the broom from her and used the handle to poke among the debris. He wished he could have seen it the way it was when Libby found it.

"They burned the new Bibles. That upset her." Gert's voice quavered, the first sign of vulnerability she'd shown. "We need to find out who did this, Ethan."

She looked up at him, and a tear shivered from the corner of her eye and streaked down her dirty cheek. He wanted to comfort her. Wanted to pull her into his arms so bad he could almost feel her head on his shoulder.

"Aw, Trudy."

She jerked her shoulders back. "Why did you call me that?" She stepped toward him with her hands clenched as though she would pummel him.

Ethan jumped back. "Hey, I'm sorry." He held up both hands, dropping the broomstick. How on earth had he let that slip out? "Your brother told me that your pa used to call you that." She stopped and considered his words, so he kept talking. "I guess I've been thinking on it some, about how it must have been when you were a girl. But I won't say it again, I promise."

Her lip twitched and she sniffed. "I don't. . .mind it."

"You don't?"

She shrugged. "Not so's you'd notice it."

"Oh. Well. . ." He studied her cautiously. Was she mad at him or not? Just because a woman said she wasn't upset didn't always mean it was true. He cleared his throat. "I'll do everything I can to find out who set the fire."

She nodded, staring down at the pile of refuse. "You can't deny that whoever did this was leaving a message. If not for you, then for someone."

"I'm not saying you're right, but who? What's the message, and who is it for?"

She bit her lower lip and shrugged. "I don't know what, but... for the town, maybe?"

★ CHAPTER 20 ★

Tidying up the emporium and inventorying the merchandise proved time consuming, especially with constant interruptions from horrified patrons. News of Libby's misfortune had spread throughout the town, and it seemed everyone had to come in person to inquire about Mrs. Adams and see the damage. Most seemed disappointed that the industrious friends had helped Libby clean it all up and even replaced the burnt floorboards before the news got about.

"My oh my," Mrs. Walker wailed, surveying the clean new rectangle on the floor. "Why, Mrs. Adams might have burned to death if she hadn't woken up."

"That's right." Laura Storrey looked over the rearranged shelves. "Did she lose much merchandise? I hope that darling lavender silk I had my eye on didn't get burned."

"Let me help you look for it." Gert steered the woman toward the yard goods. Mrs. Storrey bought six yards of the expensive material, which seemed none the worse for the smoke.

At the end of the day, Libby swayed on her feet as she closed up shop, and Gert determined that her friend must get some rest. That evening and the next morning, she gathered names of women from the shooting club who volunteered to give Libby a couple hours of help. Gert labored over her list the next morning, arranging it into a schedule. Myra helped her get the timetable to all the women.

Hiram presented the mayor's repaired rifle when she returned to fix lunch.

"Can you test this for me?" he asked. "I need to get it back to the mayor and then get over to the Bentons'."

Gert was more curious than annoyed at the interruption in her busy morning. Hiram rarely visited other homes. "What are you going over there for?"

"I told the parson I'd build him a stand to use until we get a proper pulpit made."

Gert put cotton in her ears, took the Winchester rifle out behind the house, and fired a half dozen rounds. When she finished, she saw Apphia coming up the path. "Here," she told her brother as she handed him the rifle. "Tell the mayor it shoots a little right of center. I expect he knows. Otherwise, it's fine. Now, I'm going over to help Libby. Mrs. Benton's going with me."

Hiram blinked at her. "No dinner?"

"On the back of the stove." She picked up the basket she'd packed to take with her and met Apphia at the back door. Together they stormed the emporium. Gert marched straight to Libby.

"You come upstairs with me for something to eat. Mrs. Benton will help Florence man the store for the next half hour. After that, we'll send Florence home for her dinner, and you shall have an hour's rest."

"Rest during the day?" Libby stared at her. "I can't do that."

"You can, and you will. We've got other ladies from the club coming in later, and we'll all take turnabout to help you mind the store and do any more cleaning and counting you need to do for the next couple of days. Annie Harper is bringing your supper over this evening at closing time."

Libby burst into tears. "Gert, I don't know what to say. You've been so good."

Startled, Gert patted her back awkwardly. "There now. Come on upstairs. You're worn to a stub."

Libby submitted after that, and Gert set out the stew and sourdough bread she'd brought over. For the first time, she sat down at Libby's kitchen table and ate lunch with her. She made sure Libby ate a full portion then tucked her into bed under the loveliest wedding ring quilt she'd ever seen. Libby's rooms above the emporium might have stood in a mansion. Had she brought the beautiful furnishings with her when she married Isaac, or had they ordered them one piece at a time over the years? Sometime when Libby wasn't exhausted, she'd ask.

Downstairs, Florence had shown Mrs. Benton the rudiments of adding a purchase to a customer's account, and Gert sent the girl home for her noon hour. She and Apphia did a brisk business.

After waiting on several townspeople and a couple of ranchers in succession, Gert caught her breath and looked around. They'd done all right, she and Apphia, though they were slow at locating some items people asked for. She'd gone to the right woman in time of crisis. The minister's slender, dark-haired wife carried on with stamina and dignity. At the moment, Apphia was talking to Milzie Peart over in the staples section. They appeared to be having a pleasant conversation.

Mr. Dyer came in just then.

"Well, Miss Dooley. I don't usually see you here. Is Mrs. Adams all right? I heard she had some excitement yesterday."

"That she did, sir. She's fine, but she's taking a short rest. May I help you with something?"

"Maybe so. Miss Shepard needs sugar and potatoes. She says I'm not to bring home any punky ones."

Gert shrugged. "We'll do our best. You know how hard it is to get firm potatoes this time of year."

"I allow you're right. Just two or three months till we have a new crop though. I can hardly wait."

Gert smiled and took his basket from his hands. "This way, sir, and you can choose your own spuds if you wish."

While she and Ezra picked over the sprouting potatoes and chose the best for Bitsy's Sunday dinner crowd, Gert overheard a bit of Apphia's talk with Milzie.

"I do wish you'd come Monday after the shooting practice," she said. "We'll have tea, and you can tell me about your ranch."

"'T'ain't much of a ranch," Milzie mumbled. "Since Frank died, 't'ain't much of anything. I put in a few vegetables though."

"Ah, you enjoy gardening. So do I."

Gert figured it was more a matter of survival than a hobby

for Milzie, but she said nothing. She silently applauded Apphia's courage in inviting the filthy old woman into her home. Maybe if all the women of the shooting club followed her example, they could influence Milzie to take better care of herself.

A few minutes later she took a broken candy stick from a jar on the counter and slipped it to Milzie. She was sure Libby wouldn't mind. Milzie shuffled out of the store with a gap-toothed smile.

★

On Monday the ladies gathered at Bert Thalen's ranch as usual. Milzie looked different when she arrived, and at first Gert couldn't figure out why. Then she realized the old woman had washed her tattered clothes. Her arms and face looked less dirt-encrusted, too, and Gert almost thought her hair was a shade lighter than she'd seen it before.

Of course. Today Milzie was invited to Apphia's for tea. Mrs. Benton had confided to Gert and Libby that she hoped she could convince Milzie to accept a gift of some new clothing. Gert wasn't sure the old woman would take new things outright and had suggested used items. After a moment's thought, Apphia had decided to offer her a blouse she'd had for two years. Still serviceable, it showed a little fraying about the cuffs. Libby had gleefully added a shawl that had snagged on the wooden shelves, so that it now had an imperfection. She'd entrusted it to Apphia earlier.

"Tell Milzie I don't want to try to sell it, since it's got that snag."

They'd decided that was enough for one day. If things went well, the club members could see that Milzie had a new skirt, shoes, stockings, and underthings before fall. And here she was, ready to go meekly home with the impeccably groomed Mrs. Benton for tea.

"I don't know how she lives all alone in that cabin," Gert said, shaking her head. She rummaged in Crinkles's saddlebag for the three bullets she'd brought for Milzie. She'd long since stopped expecting to be repaid for them.

When their hour of practice ended, she called the women all around her and praised their orderliness and the improvement she'd noted in their aims.

"I'd like to thank you all for your help over the last few days," Libby said. "Things are back to normal now, though we'll be short of a few items in the store until Mr. Runnels brings my next shipment from Boise."

Gert looked around at the sober faces. "Ladies, I've one more bit of business. As you know, there's been a rash of crimes in Fergus. Serious crimes. Murder, assault, arson. We've shown how we can support one another. I propose that we endeavor, as an entity, to help the sheriff foil the criminal who has been making mischief and striking in violence."

"What could we do?" asked Vashti. She looked almost wholesome today, without any cosmetics. The skirt she wore came down nearly to the tops of her smart tan boots.

"I'm thinking the biggest thing we can do is stay alert," Gert said. "Watch out for anything suspicious. And we could help prevent more crimes just by being watchful. We can look out for each other. Those in town can check in on one another during the day and the evening. Those outside town can call on each other more often to be sure no one's been attacked."

"And if something does happen, we can fetch the sheriff, like you did for Mrs. Adams the other day," Florence said.

"That's exactly what I mean. Let us help one another, especially the women who live alone or whose men are away a lot. Let's help each other stay safe."

Annie Harper began clapping, and the other women picked up the applause. Gert felt her face flush with the thrill of having an idea accepted and approved.

"Let's make a list then. Anyone willing to help out in ensuring safety for others, tell me and I will put down your name." The women crowded around, and Gert listed all their names but Milzie's. The old woman hung back, looking anxiously toward the westering sun now and then.

"We need to take this list to the sheriff and see if he can make use of our abilities," Gert said when she'd finished it.

"Would the sheriff be over to his house today, do you think?" Emmaline Landry asked.

"I passed him on the road on my way out here," said Bitsy, who had arrived a few minutes late.

"Then he's likely in town," Gert said. "Shall we go to him as a group? Those who live in town, I mean. I'm sure some of you ranch ladies need to get back home."

Milzie's frown grew more pronounced as they talked. Gert caught Mrs. Benton's eye.

"You'll excuse Mrs. Peart and me, won't you?" Apphia said. "We had made other plans for this afternoon, though we're more than willing to serve."

"Of course," Gert said, and Milzie perked up immediately. "And if you wish to ride back into town in the wagon with Mrs. Harper, she can drop you off right in front of your house."

Six of the fifteen women left for their scattered homes, and the rest rode their horses or the wagon back to town. Milzie smiled nearly all the way, swinging her legs off the back of the Harpers' wagon. At the new parsonage, Annie halted the horse, and Apphia hopped down.

"Here we are, Mrs. Peart." She reached up to help Milzie clamber down.

Gert waved to them. "Have a nice afternoon, ladies. We'll let you know what the sheriff says."

Annie flipped the reins, and the horse plodded on to the hitching rail in front of the jail. Gert jumped down and waited until Annie, Myra, Libby, Bitsy, Vashti, and Florence joined her. They were missing Goldie, who reportedly had taken to her bed with a catarrh, but otherwise, all the women who regularly attended had come to shoot today.

Gert smiled. "Ready?"

"Ready," they chorused.

She turned and led them up the boardwalk. If Ethan wasn't at the jail, she would feel pretty silly. They'd have to track him down. What if he was at the Nugget? Maybe Vashti or Bitsy would peek through the door to see. But he was more likely chewing the fat with Hiram.

Before they even reached the stoop in front of the jail, the door swung open. Ethan stood, tall, rugged, and flustered, in the doorway.

"Ladies! To what do I owe the honor?"

Gert cleared her throat. "Sheriff, we represent the Ladies' Shooting Club of Fergus, and we're here to offer our services in helping you catch the miscreant who is terrorizing our town and prevent further violence."

His eyebrows shot up. "Well, now." He looked them all over for a long moment then shifted his gaze back to Gert's face. "And what services does that entail?"

Gert gulped and took a step toward him. "We have some ideas. We also have a list of fourteen able-bodied women who can help in any capacity you see fit." She fished her list from her pocket and held it out to him.

Ethan leaned forward and took the paper from her. He perused it for a moment then looked up. "Would you like to come in, ladies? I don't have many chairs, but this seems like an idea worth discussing."

Gert couldn't hold back her grin as she glanced at the other women. Florence and Myra were grinning, too. Even Libby wore a restrained smile.

"I can see the sense of this," Ethan said a few minutes later. He'd let Annie Harper, as the eldest, have his chair and brought a stool and a short bench from somewhere in the shadows of the jail so four more women had seats. Vashti and Gert stood near the desk, and Gert had outlined her vague ideas of how the ladies could help.

"Thank you, Sheriff," she said. "We appreciate that you're taking us seriously."

"I can see that I'd be foolish not to." Ethan smiled. "Now, ladies, I know some of you have jobs, but if you're serious about this, your enthusiasm and energy can be assets to the town. I've noticed that several of the women on the list live a few miles outside town."

Gert nodded. "They couldn't do a lot, but they're willing to give a few hours a week."

"Good. Let's say Starr Tinen and her mother-in-law could

check a couple of times a week on Mrs. Peart and the Robinsons—
they're the last two places out the Mountain Road. That would
be extremely helpful. I've pondered on how we'd know if one of
the outlying ranches was attacked. I'd hate to think someone had
trouble and no one knew about it."

"I've got an idea, Sheriff," Annie Harper said. "What if the
Robinsons and Miz Peart had something like a flagpole where
they could run up a signal? If the nearest neighbors could see their
signal in the morning, they'd know the other folks were all right.
But if there wasn't any flag flying, why then they'd know they
needed to go and check on their neighbors."

"I like that idea," Libby said. "In fact, since the Paragon
Emporium was attacked last week, I've wondered how I could get
word out if I needed help again. I could hang a white towel out
my bedchamber window each morning when I rose. Florence or
Annie ought to be able to see it from their backyards."

"That's true," Florence said. "And if one morning I didn't see
it, I'd run over to the store early to make sure you were all right."

Ethan nodded. "Good thinking, ladies. Let's set up pairs of
women who can check on businesses in town. Look to see if
windows or doors have been broken, for instance."

"Like my back door was broken in," Libby said ruefully.

"Exactly. They could check in on the elderly folks in town,
too, to be sure they were all right," Ethan said. "And since the
fire at the emporium, I've worried that someone is lurking about,
waiting for a moment to do more harm where least expected.
He might bother the school children on their way to and from
the schoolhouse, for instance. If he wants to make mischief, there
are plenty of opportunities."

Annie nodded. "It's a long walk to school for some. We could
send two ladies in the morning to walk the children to school
and have two more meet them when school's out. I'm sure their
mothers would appreciate that."

"That's right. Of course, school will soon be out for the summer,
but we could put this plan in motion until the term ends." Ethan
looked at Gert and held up her list. "Would you help me work
out the details, Miss Dooley? We can match up the pairs for their

assignments, according to where the ladies live and the best times for them to carry out their duties."

"I'd be happy to." Gert felt her face flame, but none of the others seemed to notice. All were murmuring their approval and telling each other when their own most convenient hours to be on watch would fall. Gert met Ethan's gaze. His dark eyes glittered, and his left eye twitched—almost a wink. His smile widened, and she found herself looking forward to working on the list with him. Perhaps over a piece of mince pie.

★ CHAPTER 21 ★

Libby and Vashti waited outside the schoolhouse for Miss Fennel to dismiss her class. They could hear the children reciting their lessons. Isabel's voice broke in as she spoke sharply to one of the Ingram boys. Vashti rolled her eyes skyward, and Libby smiled.

"I recall my school days with fondness, but something tells me this isn't Willie Ingram's favorite way to spend his time."

Vashti chuckled. "I never did more than three grades all told. We moved around so much, I never stayed in one place long enough to finish a reader."

Libby wondered how the girl had separated from her family and come to work at a saloon in an Idaho mining town gone bust. Vashti's enthusiasm for the shooting club had surprised her, and Bitsy had allowed her extra time off this afternoon to fulfill the duty Gert had assigned. Without her cosmetics and lurid costumes, Vashti might almost have passed for a schoolgirl herself. Libby doubted she was older than Florence Nash. The thought that wholesome girls like Florence and Myra Harper wound up working in saloons all over the country grieved her, but she had no idea what she could do to change that. Getting to know Bitsy and her girls through the shooting club had altered her attitude toward them.

The schoolhouse door burst open, and a handful of boys pounded down the steps. They paused and stared at the two women.

166

"Good afternoon, boys," Libby said. "We're here to see that you get home safely."

"Ha! That's a good one." Willie Ingram, his little brother, and Tollie Harper breezed by them and ran toward town. The girls and a couple of smaller boys emerged from the building at a more moderate pace.

Behind them, Isabel Fennel stopped in the doorway and eyed Libby and Vashti. "May I help you, ladies?"

"We've come to see the children home safely," Libby said.

Vashti nodded with vigor. "Sheriff Chapman assigned us this duty."

"What's that?" Isabel frowned and came down the steps.

Libby looked after the children, who had gained the road and would soon be out of sight. "The Ladies' Shooting Club is taking on some civic duties, one of which is to ensure safety for the school children and women who live alone. Would you like us to walk you as far as your home?"

"No, thank you. That's not necessary." Isabel looked them over as though not quite sure what to do with them, especially Vashti. Libby wondered if she even recognized the saloon girl. Perhaps she was trying to place her.

"Well, your father's ranch is close by," Libby said. "If you're sure you don't want an escort, we'll go after the children."

"Thank you, I'll be fine." Isabel's upper lip rose into a little peak on the left side as she spoke, and she swept Vashti with a disapproving gaze.

So, she had catalogued the bar girl. Libby nodded and turned away.

"'Bye," Vashti called and scurried after her, muttering.

"Did you say something?" Libby asked.

"I said, 'Fussy old bat.'"

"Oh!" Libby shot her a sideways glance. "We'd better hurry. The children are so far ahead of us, I'm afraid we won't do any good."

"We'd best tell their mothers what we're doing, so they can tell the kiddies to wait for us tomorrow, no matter what that priggish old stick does," Vashti said.

"Yes," Libby said. "Er, I can inform the mothers."

"Can you? That's good, because I'll need to get ready for work soon."

Libby held up her skirts and kept pace with the saloon girl.

Milzie tried to hold the Hawken steady as she aimed, but her arms shook. Was it because the gun weighed so much, or because of the hunger that gnawed at her belly? The jackrabbit hopped a few steps farther. He blended in so well with the low brush that she could barely see him.

She braced herself and held her breath, lining the sights up with the ornery critter. But he hopped again. Now or never. He'd soon be out of sight. Milzie pulled the trigger and fell back from the recoil.

"Oof." She sat up, rubbing her shoulder. Must have forgotten to hug the stock up close like Gert had shown her. The rifle lay a couple of feet away. She hauled herself shakily to her feet and walked over to where the rabbit had been. Clean missed it. No surprise.

Oh well. According to Gert, if she'd hit it with this load, she'd likely have blown it to bits anyway. She'd have been lucky to find any bits to put in her stew pot. She shook her head and trudged back toward where she'd stood when she fired. Now, where'd the Hawken got to? It was right here, wasn't it?

She peered all around at the grass and shrubbery. Nothing. She turned and looked toward where she'd seen the rabbit. Maybe she was a few steps this way. . . . Or had she stood farther away?

After twenty minutes, nearly ready to give up the search, she stepped on the gun's stock. The barrel lay all but invisible in the grass. Exhausted, she crumpled in a heap beside it. Better rest awhile before she tried to tote it home. Must be near a mile. And better stick to foraging. At the end of a day's picking through trash piles, she'd have more to show than she had today.

Gert had just hung up her dishpan after doing Tuesday's supper dishes when a frantic pounding came at the front door. Her pulse thudded. She glanced at Hiram, who sat at the table. He looked up from the new Bible she'd bought before the fire at the emporium.

"Who can that be?" she asked.

Hiram only raised his eyebrows. Gert wiped her hands on her apron and hurried across the sitting room to the seldom-used front door. She opened it, and Isabel Fennel all but fell in. Gert seized her arm to steady her. The schoolteacher stared at her, gulping in quick, shallow breaths.

"Isabel. Come in. Is something wrong?"

"I'm frightened."

Isabel's pale blue eyes looked bigger than usual in her pinched face. Her hairdo showed the wind had been at work during her short walk to town, and her shawl lay askew over her shoulders.

"Come sit down," Gert said. "What's happened?"

Isabel took the offered chair and put one hand to her brow. "Nothing, really. I shouldn't have come." She stirred as though to rise. "Forgive me for intruding."

"You're fine." Gert laid her hand lightly on Isabel's shoulder. Isabel had recovered herself somewhat and had thought better of blurting out her troubles. "I was about to make myself a cup of tea. Would you join me? My mother always made tea when things seemed a bit out of kilter."

"Well. . ." Isabel looked around the dim room toward the kitchen, where the glowing lamp illuminated Hiram at the table. "I don't want to disturb you and your brother. I saw your light. . . ."

"You're most welcome, and you won't disturb us." Gert lit the small lamp on the side table and hurried to the kitchen before Isabel could change her mind. Her heart still pounded from the jolt of Isabel's interruption as she took down two teacups. The kettle steamed on the stove, and she quickly measured loose tea into the pierced tin ball and lowered it into her plain brown teapot.

Hiram watched her in silence for a moment then bent his head over the Bible. How could he be so calm when a woman who had never entered their home before came pounding on their door? That seemed to happen a lot lately—maybe he'd acclimated to it better than she had. Gert took a deep breath and fixed a tray with two cups, the teapot, and the sugar bowl. If Isabel asked for milk, she'd have to go out to the root cellar.

She carried the tray carefully to the sitting room and nudged aside a few of Hiram's tools so she could set her burden down on the bench beneath the window facing the street. "Do you take sugar?"

"No, thank you."

Gert hesitated but knew it would be impolite not to ask. "Milk? I have some—"

"Just black, please," Isabel said.

Gert exhaled and sat down opposite her with a smile. "Here you go. Careful, it's very hot."

Isabel raised her cup, blew on the surface of the liquid, and took the tiniest of sips. "Thank you."

"Now, tell me." Gert waited, wondering what had brought Isabel here. Cyrus Fennel's daughter had never sought out either of the Dooleys for company, though she was about Hiram's age. So far as Gert knew, she hadn't befriended Violet either, but preferred solitude or the company of the older women in town. She must have had a terrible fright to come here for refuge.

"I. . .I walked into town this evening looking for my father."

"Oh." Gert sipped her tea to cover her confusion. Apparently Cyrus hadn't shown up for supper at the ranch, which lay outside town, barely half a mile beyond the Nugget Saloon. "Did you look in the stagecoach office?"

"Yes, I went there first." Isabel swallowed and looked away. "He wasn't there. His office door wasn't locked, but. . ."

Gert nodded. She could guess where Cyrus was, but she didn't like to say it.

"I. . ." Isabel cleared her throat. "I thought I'd stop at the emporium, but apparently I was a few minutes too late, and Mrs. Adams had just closed. As I came back along the boardwalk past the alley. . ."

"Yes?"

"There was a man in there. In the alley, I mean."

Gert put her cup down. "Just. . .loitering, or walking through the alley?"

"As I walked by, I noticed him leaning against the wall of Papa's office. He was in the dark, and I couldn't see his face, but he frightened me." Isabel shuddered.

"Perhaps he was waiting for your father to come back." Yet if the office was unlocked, why not wait for Mr. Fennel inside? It did seem odd. And Libby used that alley often to get from her back door to the street. What if the man was watching the emporium? Waiting for the emporium's lights to flicker out and Libby's apartment lights above to come on? There was a small window on that side in Libby's kitchen, Gert was sure. She'd seen it the day after the fire, when she'd eaten lunch with Libby. It overlooked the low roof and false front of the Wells Fargo building. The idea caused her pulse to take off again, though Hiram had repaired the back door of the emporium and installed a new lock and a sturdy bar as well.

Isabel leaned back in the chair, curling her fingers around her teacup. "I didn't like to walk all the way home alone. I thought of going to the Walkers', but I'd have had to pass the alley again, and. . .well, I looked across the street and saw your light."

"I'm glad you did," Gert said. "Isabel, you're welcome here anytime. And if you ever feel uneasy to be alone, I hope you will call on me or another of the shooting club women. We want to make sure all the women in this town feel safe."

Isabel took a sip of her tea and swallowed before she met Gert's gaze again. "Yes, Libby Adams and. . .and a girl came to the schoolhouse yesterday and again this afternoon to see the children home. Will they come every day?"

"Someone from the club will come all week, morning and afternoon."

"Thank you. Perhaps I shall accept the offer of walking with them tomorrow. Of course, school recesses on Friday for a month's vacation."

Gert nodded. "We'll come anytime you need us. The sheriff has approved our schedule of checking on people in pairs. If we can help you in any way. . ."

In the kitchen, Hiram's chair scraped the floor softly, and a moment later he stood in the doorway.

"Would you like me to fetch your pa, Miss Fennel?"

Isabel turned her head and stared at him. Gert suppressed a smile. She could almost hear her thoughts—*He talks!*

"I. . ."

"It's no trouble," Hiram said.

"I'm not sure where you'll find him." She looked down at the rug Gert had braided during her first long winter in Idaho Territory.

"This town's not very big. I'll find him."

Gert considered jumping up and telling him how Bitsy had revealed Cyrus's defection to the Nugget during the past few weeks but thought better of it. Hiram probably knew that, seeing as how Ethan stopped in nearly every day and told her brother all his official business.

Hiram went silently out the back door. Stillness settled over the house. Gert sipped her tea and cast about for a new topic.

"This shooting society," Isabel said at last. "Can just. . . anyone. . .join?"

Gert pulled in a sharp breath. Did that question have a right answer? After all, the club's members included several saloon girls and the new minister's wife; elegant Libby and slatternly Milzie. "We're open to just about any female."

"And do the women supply their own firearms?"

"Yes." They sat in silence for a long moment, and Gert scarcely dared breathe. Was Isabel interested in joining their ranks, or was she simply probing into something she found incomprehensible?

"I believe I should like to come next week after school is out."

Gert exhaled and reached deep for a smile. "You would be most welcome."

"I doubt Papa will approve." Isabel frowned and set her cup on the side table. "I could buy a small gun, I daresay. They can't be too expensive. And I've saved the biggest portion of my salary for more than ten years."

"I'm sure Mrs. Adams can help you find something suitable," Gert murmured. Indeed, Libby had educated herself over the past few weeks, devouring catalogs from gun manufacturers. She'd told Gert ruefully that she had to limit herself to make sure she didn't spend more time reading up on guns than she did studying the scriptures before bedtime.

Isabel met her gaze. "And do you instruct those who've never. . ."

"Yes, ma'am. We're bringing all the ladies along to where they feel confident in handling their weapons."

"If you're sure no one will object, then I'll look forward to next Monday."

"Oh, absolutely certain. We meet at—"

The back door burst open and Cyrus Fennel strode through the kitchen.

"Isabel! What's the meaning of this?"

★ CHAPTER 22 ★

Cyrus could scarcely believe that his daughter sat in Gert Dooley's parlor.

"I was worried about you, Papa." Isabel stood to face him.

Guilt and annoyance struggled inside him, and annoyance won. After all, Isabel had gone crying for help to the woman who had set out to make a fool of him. Gert had even gotten the minister to speak out in favor of the shooting club from the pulpit. Cyrus gritted his teeth and managed to keep his voice down. "It wasn't my intention to make you fret. We had some trouble with the harness on the stagecoach team this afternoon, and after I'd done with that, I stepped out to talk to someone."

"Is your business finished now?" Isabel asked. "I'm ready to go home, but it's dark now, and I don't wish to walk alone."

Was she trembling? Cyrus scowled at her. "I need to lock up the office."

Gert stepped forward. "Isabel saw a man hanging around the alley beside your office."

"So your brother told me. I'll check to make sure no one's lingering about."

Gert looked past him, and Cyrus realized Hiram had come in behind him and stood silently in the corner. The man was altogether too sneaky.

"Hiram, we should go check on Mrs. Adams," Gert said. "After what happened last week, I don't like the thought of a man loitering about beneath her windows when she's alone."

Hiram nodded.

"Well, Isabel, gather your things, and we'll head out." Cyrus looked at Gert and forced himself to do the right thing. "Thank you for helping her, Miss Dooley. And if you'd like, Isabel and I can check on Mrs. Adams."

"Yes," Isabel said, "and I'll tell her that I'll come around Saturday and look at those handguns she has for sale."

"What did you say?" Cyrus reared back and stared at his daughter.

"I'm joining Miss Dooley's shooting club, Papa. If you're going to be out evenings all the time, I need to know how to handle a gun."

Cyrus swung his arm back. "How dare—"

Gert pushed between them. "It's not *my* club. All the ladies together have made it a success, and now we're working with the sheriff to keep the town a little safer. To protect women and children from *violence*." She spit out the last word and glared at him.

Cyrus's head spun. He hadn't had *that* much to drink tonight, but the room seemed to sway nonetheless. "Isabel!" He looked around and focused on her with difficulty. "I forbid you to join that society."

Isabel straightened her shoulders. "Papa, you always used to come home in the evening. Since Mama died, you've stayed in town a couple of evenings a week. Fine. But if you're going to make the Nugget your regular stopping place all week long and leave me alone at the ranch, then I need a way to protect myself. I will go to the shooting club."

She wrapped her shawl closer and stepped toward the front door. Cyrus's head felt as though it would explode. Never had his daughter defied him. Never! She'd grown from a sweet little girl into an awkward, plain young woman, and now suddenly she was more than thirty years old and a virago bent on humiliating him. No wonder she'd never had any serious suitors.

Isabel stepped toward the door, and Hiram scooted around to open it.

"Come, Papa," she said over her shoulder. "We'd best get over to the office and lock it up." She looked back at Gert. "And we'll go around and knock on Mrs. Adams's back door. Thank you for the tea."

"You're welcome," Gert replied. "I expect I'll see you both in church."

Cyrus stumbled down the front steps and followed Isabel toward the street, fuming. A dozen retorts fluttered into his foggy brain, but when he turned to look back, Hiram had closed the door.

"I didn't mean to call her Trudy, but it slipped out, and she got all ruffled and feisty." Ethan leaned his crossed arms on the fence of Hiram's corral. The moon shone down on Crinkles, Hoss, and Scout as they lazily picked mouthfuls of hay from the pile Hiram had thrown out for them.

"She doesn't seem mad at you now," Hiram noted, sticking a straw in the corner of his mouth.

"No, she got over it quick. I think it surprised her, and I promised I'd never say it again, but I need to be careful."

"How's that?" Hiram's gray blue eyes showed just beneath his hat brim.

"So's she won't get mad again."

"Huh."

Ethan loved Friday nights in June. The warm breeze flowed over them. The town lay peaceful, though he'd stroll around to the Nugget and the Spur & Saddle in an hour or so, just to make sure things stayed calm. Behind them, Gert clattered about in the kitchen, washing up the supper dishes.

"I sort of started thinking about her as Trudy." Ethan put one foot up on the bottom rail of the fence and waited for Hiram to comment. When his friend remained silent, chewing his straw and watching the horses, he added, "Shouldn't have done that. Now it's getting hard to think of her as Gert, and when I talk to her, I want to say Trudy."

"My fault."

"No, it's not."

"Shouldn't have told you."

Ethan sighed. "I've known you both a long time."

Hiram grunted.

"And sometimes I thought how hard she has it and how she ought to have things a little easier. Face it: life's hard on a woman out here. They work all the time, and for what? A lot of sorrow for most of 'em."

Hiram pushed his hat back and looked over at him. "That why you never got married? 'Cause you didn't want to offer a woman a life of hard work and little to show for it?"

Ethan eyed him in surprise. Hiram seldom asked personal questions. "Well. . ."

His friend shrugged and looked away. "We're talking about my little sister."

"Are we?" Ethan asked.

"I thought we were."

Ethan considered that. Was this entire conversation about Trudy? He'd thought they were talking about frontier women in general, with Trudy as an example.

Gert. He meant Gert.

"I s'pose it is, partly. And partly because I never. . ."

Hiram swung around and looked at him with his eyebrows arched.

"I never felt worthy," Ethan said.

Hiram settled back down against the fence again, chewing and looking. Finally he threw the straw aside. "How's that?"

"Well. . .when a man offers a woman marriage, he's offering her his name and his property and his reputation."

"At least."

Ethan nodded. They agreed on that. Hiram had given the whole package to Violet.

"So he'd want to be sure he could offer something worthwhile. And. . .well, I don't feel I've got it."

Hiram sighed. "Are we talking about Gert now, or are you just philosophizing about what a crackbrained cowpoke you are?"

Ethan stood up straight. "Aw, Hi, I never thought seriously

about. . . No. No, I'm not talking about Tru—about Gert. Just, you know, life in the territory."

"All right then. Just checking. Because if you were getting all addlepated over Trudy—"

"Gert. Her name is Gert."

"Right. But if you *were* getting addlepated over her, she'd be Trudy to you, wouldn't she?"

Ethan hesitated only an instant. "Fair enough."

Hiram nodded. "So. You're saying you're no better than a dirt clod, so far as your prospects for being a husband."

"That about sums it up."

"I couldn't agree more, but I'm afraid our reasons would be different."

"What's that supposed to mean?"

Hiram shook his head. "Tell me why you're disqualified from settling down and being a family man, and don't give me this 'hard life for women' malarkey. Their lives will be hard enough out here, whether you marry one of 'em or not."

"That's true, I guess." Ethan glanced toward the kitchen door. He could sure use a cup of coffee right about now, but this wasn't a conversation to have where Trudy could hear. Or Gert. Either one of them. He shook his head to clear it. "When I went away with the militia, I was young and idealistic. I was set to protect the settlers and save the territory. And to put those Indians on the reservation and make 'em stay there."

Hiram gazed off over the corral, but Ethan could tell he was listening.

"You know, my pappy tried to tell me there'd be days I wished I didn't go. Hi, there was things that happened. . . . I get all worked up just thinking about it, all this time later."

"Some things never get better."

"You got that right. But I'm telling you, if I'da known! The first skirmish I was in, over by Silver City—that went all right. I don't know as I even shot any Indians. I kept loading and firing, and. . .well, after a while, we'd won. But later on, after the excitement died down and we got out into the hills, chasing after them and half freezing to death and the other half starving, it wasn't nearly so palatable. The Sheepeaters were the worst. It was war, and I knew that meant there'd be some bloodshed, but it's a whole lot different when you get pinned down on a mountainside and the Indians set fire to the mountain below you."

"You never told me that."

Ethan shook his head. "We clawed our way out, but it's something you never forget. And it didn't make us feel like showing mercy when we finally caught up to 'em." Ethan pulled his hat off and threw it on the ground. He was shaking all over, even though it was warm. "Some things just ain't right, no matter which side you're on."

"I'm sorry, Eth. I saw a big change in you when you came back, and I knew you took it hard, but. . ."

Ethan let out a long, slow breath and stooped to retrieve his hat. "Is something wrong with me to feel so strong about it seven years later?"

"No. There's nothing wrong with you." Hiram's hand came down on his shoulder. "I expect you've gone before the Lord about all that."

"Many, many times."

"Well. . ." Hiram sighed. "If you did anything wrong, He's forgiven you. You do know that?"

"Yeah. I guess."

"God doesn't lie. He says He'll forgive us. He does."

Ethan nodded. "I've just felt so. . .I don't know. . . . Not just dirty. Corrupted. It wouldn't be fitting to tell a woman about the things I saw and did, but how can you live with another person and not tell them about things you think about so often?"

Hiram leaned on the fence again and spoke slowly. "I'm not saying it's a small thing, but if that's what's kept you from thinking of having a family. . .well, the right woman would understand and overlook the past, particularly knowing you'd confessed to the Lord."

"I s'pose."

"Oh, she would," Hiram said.

Ethan got the feeling he wasn't talking about a hypothetical right woman.

"Well," he said. They stood in silence for a moment.

The back door of the house opened, and Trudy called, "Hey, you two, your coffee's like to go bitter it's been simmering so long."

Hiram nudged him, and they walked toward the house together.

★ CHAPTER 23 ★

Thank you for going with me." Apphia Benton handled the reins capably as Gert settled onto the wagon seat beside her.

"I missed Milzie, too, at the club on Thursday. I hope someone's checked in on her, but I'm afraid we have to communicate in person until we all get telephones out here." Gert puffed out a breath.

"You told me she's been faithful at the meetings," Apphia said.

"Perfectly. I believe it's been good for her—and the rest of us, too. A lot of the members never see another woman for weeks at a time."

At the end of Main Street, Apphia clucked to the horse. The bay gelding loaned to them by Griffin Bane stepped out in a smart trot. Gert looked up at the sun. They'd be back in town before noon, and she could do her usual Saturday cleaning.

"I haven't been all the way out this road since last fall. It's looking dry already, and we've barely passed the summer solstice."

"Yes, it *has* been dry," Apphia said. "I wondered if you usually have more rain this time of year."

"Some years." Gert pointed to a low house nestled between the brown hills. "That's the Landrys' place. You know Emmaline."

"Yes. Her whole family came to services last Sunday. I was so pleased."

"It surprised me, too. I didn't expect Micah to bring them."

"Well, I hope to get Milzie into church as well," Apphia said.

Susan Page Davis

"We had such a good visit on Monday. But then she didn't come Thursday. . . ."

Gert eyed her carefully. Could she have truly enjoyed serving tea to Milzie? Just the thought of inviting Milzie inside the Dooley house made her shudder. The smell would take as long to get rid of as the smoke stench in the emporium. Gert's limited acquaintance with the Bentons had raised her opinion of the clergy. Both Apphia and her husband seemed to have tender hearts toward the poor and the needy.

"I worry about her, too." Though her own concern might not be so pure-hearted as Apphia's, Gert spoke sincerely. She'd actually missed Milzie's snaggletoothed smile, and the three charges she'd prepared for the Hawken Thursday morning still rested in her saddlebag. "That's the Robinsons' house," she said a few minutes later. "I see Lyman out working his garden. Do you want to stop?"

"Perhaps on the way home. I confess I'm anxious about Milzie."

"That's fine." Gert waved to Mr. Robinson. He lifted his head as the wagon passed and waved his hat.

"How old are they?" Apphia asked.

"Both in their sixties, I'd say. They have a wagon and a mule, but the trip into town is a major undertaking for them. I don't know as they'd do it on a day they couldn't shop, too."

"That's a major drawback in the congregation. The parishioners are so scattered. My husband and I have tried to get around to all those who've come to services so far, but we've several ranches to visit yet."

"Milzie's is the last one out here," Gert said. "It's around that bluff, probably a good half mile from the Robinsons'. Maybe a mile. And they can't see each other's houses, so I don't know as the flagpole idea would work too well for Milzie. We couldn't expect her to climb up the hill every morning. Although her husband's mine is above the cabin."

"She told me about Frank's passing." Apphia shook her head. "I'm not sure how that woman has survived the years alone out here."

182

They rounded the hill that stuck out, blocking their view, and Gert looked forward, seeking the roofline of the cabin. Something didn't look quite right. She caught her breath and seized Apphia's wrist.

"What is it?" Apphia asked.

"Hurry. Her cabin's flat."

The horse trotted into what should have been the dooryard, but the only welcome they received was the view of a charred heap of ruins where the Pearts' modest home had stood for more than twenty years.

Apphia held the reins while Gert climbed down from the wagon and walked over to the burned-out cabin. Tears filled her eyes and choked her. How could she not have realized something was horribly wrong?

She stumbled back to the wagon and looked up at Apphia through stinging tears. "This isn't new. It's been awhile."

"But. . .where has she been living?"

"I don't know. Let's tie the horse and look around."

They walked slowly about the site of the cabin.

"She's started a little garden," Apphia said, stooping to pull a clump of grass from a crooked row of peas.

Gert spotted the root cellar, but it was empty. She turned slowly, looking over the valley. Apphia walked back to the ruins, shouting, "Milzie!"

"The mine," Gert called. Apphia turned toward her with her lovely dark eyebrows arched. "Up there." Gert pointed to the cave opening a short way along the hillside. Apphia walked quickly to join her.

"Do you think she could be in there?"

"Maybe. We should check. Franklin tried to mine it, but there wasn't much in these hills. I think he took a little gold out of the creek—that's what they lived on—but not the hillside."

They toiled up the path to the dark cave entrance.

"This would be a difficult walk for Milzie." Apphia turned to look back. "When she comes into town, does she walk all that way?"

"I expect so, unless she catches a ride with the Robinsons."

"It would take her a couple of hours to walk that far."

Gert nodded. "She shouldn't be out here alone. Especially with no house. I wonder when that happened."

When they'd approached to within two yards of the cave entrance, she stopped.

"Milzie? Are you in there?"

The wind ruffled her hair, but no one answered.

Gert stepped forward, her heart racing. "I hope there aren't any critters in there." She and Apphia stood in the opening, squinting into the darkness. "Look." Gert stepped into the cave and pointed to a heap of cloth on the floor.

"Is that a blanket?" Apphia asked.

"I think it's Franklin's old wool coat she wears in the winter." Gert looked around, spotting a few other items. "There's a lantern." She took it down and checked the reservoir. "No oil."

"Here's a candle stub." Apphia picked it up from a rude shelf between two framing members against the rock wall.

"I don't see any matches." Gert looked closely at the shelf. "If we come calling again, we'd best bring some, and some lamp oil or a few more candles."

"Do you really think she's living in this cave, poor soul?" Apphia's face softened as she took in the meagerness of Milzie's existence.

"She must be." Gert fingered the small items on the shelf. "I wonder if she'd let us move her into town. She's so independent."

"But she's been accepting small gestures from the club members." Apphia opened her crocheted handbag. "I don't suppose we should be in here without her permission. I'll leave the gingerbread I brought for her." She took out a small parcel wrapped in a napkin and laid it on top of the coat.

"I hope animals don't get it before Milzie does." Gert spotted a covered crock on the floor and dragged it to the opening, where she could see its contents. She lifted the lid and sniffed the mass inside.

"What is that?" Apphia leaned closer.

"She's fixed a batch of camas root. Not much of that grows around here. She must have found a patch down by the river." Gert put the lid back and replaced the crock. "It's good nourishment, I guess. The Indians set a lot of store by it. That may be helping Milzie keep from starving."

"Poor thing. The town ought to do something. Do you suppose she *would* let us move her?"

Gert stared at her. "Well, ma'am, I don't know. And I can't think where you'd put her. You don't really have room in your little house, and. . ." She let her words trail off but couldn't repress a shudder. "I do feel sorry for her."

"Maybe the Robinsons could tell us when the cabin burned." Apphia pulled her shawl around her.

Gert took a last look around. "At least we know she's not in here now. But where is she?"

Milzie took her time Saturday morning, leaning on her stick as she walked across country toward town before the sun got hot. She stopped by the Higginses' cabin. Nealy and Clem weren't around, so she took a drink from their well and poked around the yard a little. They wouldn't miss the egg she took when they had at least three more that she left untouched in the chicken pen.

At the Landrys', she gathered the courage to knock at the back door. Emmaline opened it and promptly greeted her.

"Well, good morning, Milzie. Would you like a slice of corn cake? We've some left from breakfast."

Would she! After thanking the donor and devouring the food, Milzie ambled on until she was less than a mile from town. By then, her old legs didn't want to go any farther. She found a thicket to curl up in where she wouldn't be readily seen if anyone passed by. A good nap used up several hours. She awoke when a horse fly landed on her nose. The sun was high overhead, and she felt lazy. But she needed to get her stiff bones moving if she wanted to complete a foray into town and get home before dark.

Milzie knew every dump in Fergus. The trash heaps on the outskirts of town rewarded her.

At the pile belonging to the Spur & Saddle, she picked a large tin can to aid in her cooking and put it in her sack. A china cup with the handle broken clean off. Next, she found a good-sized shard of a broken looking glass. One of Bitsy's girls must be in for some bad luck. She frowned as she looked at her partial reflection. With a shrug, she wrapped the glass in a sheet of newspaper and stuck it into her bag.

She made her way down the back side of Main Street and paused behind the Dooleys' house. The gunsmith puttered about the place, but she saw no sign of Gert. Too bad. Milzie liked Gert, and she had a light touch with biscuits.

At the emporium, she had better fortune. Miz Adams greeted her with a smile.

"Well, Milzie, how are you? We missed you on Thursday."

"Had the grippe."

"Oh? I'm sorry to hear that. I hope you're over it now."

"Middlin'." The truth was, clouds had rolled in on Thursday, and Milzie hadn't wanted to risk being caught several miles from home in a downpour. But that wouldn't sound like a very good reason to miss the shooting club.

Another customer entered the store. "Excuse me, won't you?" Libby asked. "Make sure you see me before you leave. I've got a little something for you."

Milzie wandered about the store for a good twenty minutes. Miz Adams had gotten in enough new bolts of cloth to cover a tabletop. Milzie surreptitiously ran her hand over them. The soft nap of the corduroy pleased her. Franklin liked corduroy pants in cold weather. They didn't itch like wool. It was too hot for summer, but wouldn't she love a skirt from that brown bolt for fall? Likely women didn't make skirts from corduroy though.

The flannels were even softer. She wanted to put her face right down and brush her cheek against the fabric.

"May I help you, Mrs. Peart?" Florence Nash, the red-haired girl, stood right next to her.

"You jumped me," Milzie said.

"I'm sorry."

Milzie looked toward the counter. Libby was handing a wrapped parcel to Oscar Runnels. No one else waited for her to tot up an order. Milzie ignored Florence and shuffled toward her.

"Oh, Milzie, I haven't forgotten you." Libby smiled again. She sure had a pretty smile. Her teeth were just as white as the bleached muslin bolts. She ducked down behind the counter for a minute then stood again. "I've been saving these for you." She placed a pair of knit stockings on the counter. "They came in mismatched. Can you imagine? See how one's a little larger than the other? I can't sell them like that. Could you use them by any chance?"

"Surely." Milzie reached out a shaky hand. Soft, whole stockings. "Thankee, ma'am."

Libby hesitated and looked about the store. "You know, it's time when I like to sit down for a minute. There aren't many customers, and Florence can look after things for a bit. Would you like to have a little refreshment with me in the back room?"

Milzie could scarcely believe it. Since joining the shooting club, she'd received invitations from the cleanest, nicest women in town—not to say the richest, necessarily, though Libby Adams probably qualified there—but some of the best. Tea with the minister's wife on Monday had nearly been enough to lure her into church. Hot tea with sugar and cream, little quarter sandwiches, boiled eggs, and cookies so small it took four to make a mouthful. Her mouth watered just thinking about it.

In the storage room, Libby let Milzie sit in the big chair by her desk. She took a cut glass bottle and two tumblers from a cupboard and poured each glass half full of red liquid. Milzie stared at the lovely swirling beverage.

"This is raspberry shrub." Libby smiled again. "It's my grandmother's recipe. I try to get enough berries every summer to make a good batch."

"It won't be long before the berries come on," Milzie said with what she hoped passed for a sage nod.

"That's right. This is my last bottle from last year." Libby sat down on a stool nearby and raised her glass to her lips.

Milzie lifted hers and smelled the liquid. It surely did smell of fresh raspberries. Her stomach clutched. Emmaline's corn cake was long gone. She took a sip. The sharp juice, sweetened, but not too much, slid down slicker than a greased eel. No fermentation. Miz Adams wouldn't offer anything like that, of course. Milzie gulped the rest and lowered her glass with a sigh. Libby's glass was still nearly as full as when she'd started.

"That's mighty pleasin'. Thankee."

Libby kept smiling but didn't offer more. "So you're feeling well now?"

"I am. You can expect to see me on Monday."

"Good." Libby stood in a swirl of challis skirts and rustling cotton petticoats. "Now, Milzie, I've put aside a few more things. Don't take them if you don't want to, but if you can use them. . ." She opened the cupboard again, put the ornate bottle away, and brought out a couple of tins. "A can of oysters and one of pears. Can you use those?"

"Oh yes, ma'am." Milzie opened her capacious sack, and the cans disappeared inside. "I do thank you."

Libby nodded. "You're welcome. I need to get back to the store now, but we've had a good visit today."

"Yes, yes." Clearly the hostess expected her to precede her back into the emporium, so Milzie went.

"Good day, Milzie," Libby said when they reached the store.

"Good day to you." Mrs. Walker was looking over the housewares, and she watched critically. Milzie made a deep bow to Libby. "I shall see you on Monday." She turned, chuckling, and walked as steadily as her tired old bones would allow toward the front door. Mrs. Walker's horrified expression was worth the aching feet she'd have tonight.

She made her way down the boardwalk, uncertain where to go next. Should she head for home? Her sack would grow heavy, and she might need to rest along the way. Maybe she would take a rest right now. She slid between weathered buildings and found a spot behind the smithy where she could lean against the back wall. Inside, the blacksmith was working at his forge. She liked to hear the *whoosh* of the bellows and the *cling-cling* of the hammer. She leaned back and closed her eyes. So far, she'd had a good day.

Sometime later, she awoke. The blacksmith had stopped working. A horse nickered, and she looked toward the back of the livery. The big, bearded man came out of the barn, leading a solid chestnut horse. He opened a gate and released the horse into a paddock with three others. The stagecoach must have come in.

She looked up at the sky. The sun would set soon. She'd best get going. Already she doubted she'd be home before dark, but that didn't worry her much. The moon would be near full tonight, and the air would be cooler once the sun was down. She picked up her sack and headed back to Main Street.

As she passed one building, an open door drew her. It was an office. She looked up at the sign. Of course. Wells Fargo. This must be where Cyrus Fennel conducted his business. The coach was nowhere in sight. She peeked inside. A desk, shelves and cupboards, and a man crouched behind the desk, as though taking something from a low drawer.

She didn't care for Fennel, but he was rich. Maybe he would give her something out of respect for Frank, God rest his soul. Everyone else had been kind today. Why not see if the richest man in town felt generous?

She stepped forward. "Evening, Mr.—"

He looked up suddenly. Cold, angry eyes glittered in the dimness. The face beneath the hat brim wasn't right. Who was he? He stood, and she thought she knew, though why he should be in here... Maybe he worked for Fennel now.

"You!" He stepped around the desk toward her.

His harsh voice frightened her, and she backed toward the door. She fetched up against a wall instead, beside a small box stove.

Suddenly the silhouette of his hat and something about his nose sparked a memory. "You came out of the jailhouse the night Bert Thalen was killed."

His eyes narrowed, and he advanced toward her, his lips curled in a snarl. "You meddling old woman!" He reached for her.

Milzie tried to duck past him, but she was too slow, and he had her cornered between the stove and the wall. She dropped her sack of plunder and held her stout walking stick with both hands. Why was he angry with her?

He snatched the stick and tossed it aside as thought it were a twig. As his hands closed about her throat, she groped for something else—anything.

She grasped a poker and swung it up. He grabbed it and wrestled her for it. She stared into his eyes as they both stood clutching the sooty poker. He gritted his teeth.

"You should have stayed home, old woman."

He yanked the poker from her. Milzie shrank back against the wall and raised her hands before her face.

★ CHAPTER 24 ★

Cyrus polished off his second whiskey and shook his head as Ted Hire raised the bottle to refill his glass.

"Not tonight, Ted. I'd better get on home, or Isabel will be beating the bushes for me." The Nugget was filling up anyway, and he didn't like to stay there on a Saturday evening. The noise at the saloon always mounted steadily after the sun went down. He'd rather go home and settle down in his comfortable chair before the fireplace. "I'll take a bottle of that good whiskey with me though."

As Ted bent to retrieve a fresh bottle, Cyrus pulled out his wallet. He settled his account and picked up the bottle—not as good as the stuff Bitsy kept. He'd have to speak to Jamin about that. He turned toward the door just as Ethan Chapman stepped through it. The noise level immediately fell.

"Evening, sheriff," said Nick Telford, the stagecoach driver. He had settled in early at a corner table and was playing poker for pennies with a few friends. An inveterate gambler, Nick had been known to lose his entire month's pay a penny at a time. Cyrus figured that was his business. Nick would win one week, and Bill Stout the next, and then Parnell Oxley. At least the currency circulated in the local economy.

"Howdy, boys." Ethan's gaze swept over the poker players, skipped quickly past the saloon girl carrying drinks to two cow hands, and landed on Cyrus. "Mr. Fennel."

Cyrus gave him a curt nod. He wished he'd have gotten away

before Ethan walked in to see him carrying his bottle.

Jamin Morrell entered from the back room and called out cheerfully, "Well, Sheriff! How's life in the fair town of Fergus tonight?"

"Quiet so far. Doesn't look like you're having any trouble in here."

"Not a bit," Morrell assured him, though he hadn't been in the saloon at all for the last half hour. Of course, Ted probably would have fetched him in a hurry from out back or wherever he'd been if someone had started tearing up the place.

"Well, excuse me, gentlemen." Cyrus held the bottle down at his side, away from the sheriff, and walked toward the door. "Have a pleasant evening."

He went out into the cooler evening air. The sun was low, and his long shadow stretched before him as he crossed the street diagonally. He continued up the boardwalk to the stagecoach office. Time to lock up and head for the ranch. He left his horse at the livery during the day, but lately his relationship with Griffin had seen some strain. He'd either have to confront the blacksmith or find someone else to house the stagecoach teams and his personal mount. That didn't seem practical. He reached the office and pushed the door open with a sigh. Griffin worked hard, but he had a stubborn streak. Too bad. It would be so much easier if he'd just go along with—

Cyrus stood still, staring at the dark heap on the floor beside the stove. What on earth?

Ethan left the Nugget and walked slowly up the boardwalk toward the jail. What now? He could relax for an hour or so then check the two saloons again. Drop in on Hi and Trudy? Didn't want to wear out his welcome. His discussion with Hiram last night had crossed his mind many times throughout the day. Had the time come to face up to the past and let go of it? That would mean thinking about the future, and he usually shied away from that.

Across the street and up half a block, Cy Fennel lurched out of his office, still holding the bottle of whiskey he'd carried at the Nugget. He must be drunker than Ethan had realized. He staggered to the edge of the boardwalk and retched.

Ethan paused, wondering what to do. Should he go get Cyrus and walk him over to the jail, where he could sleep it off? He'd leave the cell door unlocked, of course. But if he did that, Cy would be furious later. Maybe he should go to the livery, get Cy's horse, put him on it, and head him toward home. No, he might fall off halfway there and break his neck.

Cyrus straightened and looked about. He focused on Ethan and lifted his free arm.

"Chapman! Quick! Come over here."

Ethan blinked. He didn't sound drunk. He raised his chin and stepped into the street. *Lord, let me not have to mix it up with Cy tonight, please.*

He was only halfway across when Cyrus lunged down from the walkway and met him in the street.

"It's old Mrs. Peart!"

"What?" Ethan stared at him. Was the man right out of his befuddled mind?

"Millicent Peart. In my office. Go look."

Ethan struggled to make sense of that. Only one thing to do. He walked over and stepped onto the sidewalk. His boots thudded with each step to the office door. It was nearly dark inside. Before his eyes fully adjusted, he spotted a huddled figure on the floor near the cold box stove. It couldn't be. He stepped closer and stared down at her. Cyrus's words began to make sense. The poker lay beside her. He bent down and then stood up quickly. No wonder Cyrus had emptied his stomach. There'd be no question of how Milzie Peart died.

A shadow darkened the room even more. He swung around. Cyrus stood in the doorway, staring at the crumpled form on the floor.

"What happened?" Ethan asked.

"She was in here when I came over to lock up. Almost didn't see her."

"Can you light a lantern?"

Cyrus hesitated, and Ethan didn't blame him. The sight was bad enough in the gloom. When Cy reached for the kerosene lantern that hung over his desk, Ethan held out his hand. "I'll do it. You go 'round to Dooleys' and fetch Hiram for me, would you?"

Cyrus's brow cleared. "Sure. I guess he'll need to build another box. Oh, matches are in my drawer." He nodded toward the desk.

When he'd left, Ethan stood still for a moment. *Lord, show me what to do. This is getting scary, and I've got no notion how to stop it. Please, Lord.*

Slowly, he moved around the desk and opened the top drawer. Sure enough, a box of safety matches rested inside. He lit the lantern and adjusted the wick. He had no reason not to look at Milzie again. Might as well get it over with.

He set the lantern on the edge of the desk, pulled in a deep breath, and turned toward the body. From the distance of three yards, the brutal destruction of her skull wasn't evident. He took a step toward her, bracing himself. Footsteps hurried along the boardwalk outside, and he paused. A moment later, Hiram appeared at the door. His gaze bounced from Ethan's face to the still body on the floor. He grimaced.

"Looks like someone took Cy's poker to her," Ethan said.

Hiram nodded and inched closer.

"I suppose we need to look her over a little better than we did Bert." Ethan forced himself to approach the body. Blood ran over the floorboards around her head. He knelt down, careful to stay out of it.

"Poor thing," Hiram said softly, crouching beside him.

"Where'll we take her?" Ethan asked. "Livery stable?"

"I sent Cyrus to ask Griff. Old Cy was white as my granny's Irish table linen, and he didn't seem eager to come back here."

"Understandable." They sat staring down at her. "I hear a good undertaker can fix a person up so's they look natural again," Ethan said.

"It would take a lot of fixin'."

"Yeah." Ethan swallowed back bile. "Maybe we should get an old blanket or something to put her on before we move her."

Hiram nodded. "Gert might help clean her up a bit."

"Don't want to ask her."

"Me neither."

After a long pause, Ethan said, "Maybe one of the older ladies?"

"We could ask."

Between Milzie and the door lay a grimy flour sack. Ethan leaned over and pulled it to him. Lumpy metal items clanked together. He opened it and peered inside.

"Cans and a wad of newspaper." He pulled out a pair of dark stockings.

Quick footsteps heralded a new arrival, and they both looked toward the door. Phineas Benton entered, panting and adjusting his waistcoat. "Gentlemen, can I be of assistance?"

Ethan stuffed the stockings back into the sack and stood slowly. "I don't think so, Pastor. This woman's good and dead."

"So Mr. Fennel informed me. He stopped at my house on his way to fetch the smith." Benton doffed his bowler hat and looked at the body with mournful eyes. "Is there anything I can do to help you, Sheriff?"

"Well, Hiram and I were just saying we should get a blanket or something to put her on and tote her over to the livery. We usually lay folks out over there because we don't have a. . .what you'd call a mortuary."

"Indeed," Benton said. "Perhaps I can find something, though most of our bedclothes were newly donated by the parishioners."

"Ask my sister, Gert," Hiram said.

Benton glanced at him and nodded. "Thank you. Shall I go now?"

"Please," said Ethan.

The preacher turned to go then looked back. "My wife will, of course, volunteer to assist the ladies who prepare the body for burial. I believe she was acquainted with Mrs. Peart, though I myself had never met her."

Hiram and Ethan exchanged looks.

"That'd be fine," Ethan said.

"Perhaps Mrs. Walker would help, too."

Ethan doubted that, but he said nothing.

"Gert will probably want to be there." Hiram looked down at the floor.

He was right; Gert *would* want to do a last service for one of the shooting club members and a senior resident of the town. Ethan still didn't like the thought of her seeing this grisly sight and handling the bloody corpse. "There's time to worry about that later. Just see if Miss Dooley can give us something to wrap her in, and we'll get her over to the livery."

"It shall be done." Benton tipped his hat and flitted out into the night.

Ethan looked at Hiram, whose lips twitched. "Yeah, he strikes me that way, too. A mite formal for Fergus, but his heart's good."

A moment later, Griffin arrived with Bill Stout and Ned Harmon, who had planned to sleep in his hayloft. The parson returned with a ragged old bedspread, and they began the grim task of transferring the body.

"Easy now," Griffin said as he carefully slid his arms under Milzie's torso. "Get that cloth under her head when I lift it."

Ethan was glad he'd wound up with Milzie's feet. He might have joined Ned outside vomiting if he'd taken the spot Griffin had. This wanton destruction of an old woman took him back to the atrocities he'd seen during the Indian wars.

Once Milzie's head was covered, things moved along quickly. The old woman wasn't very heavy. Bill and Griffin started carrying her out, but Griffin paused and shook his head.

"Just let me carry her, Bill," the big man said. "You come along and make sure the blanket ain't draggin' or nothin'."

Ethan called after him, "I'll be over in a few minutes, Griff." He turned back into the room. Phineas stood near the desk, his hat in his hand, with the air of a footman awaiting his command.

Hiram, however, knelt near the pool of dark blood.

"Ethan."

"What is it, Hi?"

His friend reached into his pocket and pulled out a jackknife. He opened one blade and bent low over the stain. Using the blade, he prodded at something resting in the blood.

"For your collection," Hiram said softly. He stood and wiped the small object on his shirttail then held it out to Ethan.

"What is it?" Benton asked.

Without looking, Ethan replied, "An 1866 Indian head penny."

★ CHAPTER 25 ★

Much later that evening, Gert poured coffee for Ethan and Hiram at the kitchen table.

Ethan rubbed a hand across his eyes. "Thanks. Mrs. Benton will come after breakfast with Annie Harper, and you can all go over to the livery together to work on the body." When he glanced up at her, the dark shadows beneath his eyes stood out. A few weeks of sheriffing had aged him. "Are you sure you want to do this?"

"Of course. I wish I'd done more for her while she was alive. She never begged outright, but I could see she was hungry."

Ethan blew on his coffee and took a sip.

"Libby said she pilfered a few things from the store," Gert said. "She felt sorry for her and started giving her leftovers—broken crackers, dented tins, the last pickle in the barrel."

Hiram's eyes spoke to her with his direct gaze and quirked eyebrows.

"You're right," she said. "I'd best tell Ethan."

"Tell me what?"

"Mrs. Benton and I drove out to Milzie's place this morning to visit her."

Ethan's brows shot up, but he waited in silence.

Gert cleared her throat. "We, uh, got a surprise. Milzie's cabin had burned flat."

"What? When did that happen?"

"No one seems to know. Milzie wasn't home, but we saw signs

197

that she's been living in the cave up the hill where Frank tried to mine."

Ethan nodded. "I know the place."

"Well, she wasn't anywhere around, so we stopped at the Robinsons' on the way home. Lyman and Ruth said they didn't know. Can you imagine? They live that close to her, and they haven't been up to her place since last winter. Ruth's been poorly this spring, I guess. She said Milzie stops in now and again, and they usually give her something to eat. But when we told them the cabin was burnt, they seemed shocked. Lyman took on a case of guilt, saying he ought to have checked on her. But they'd seen her several times this spring, so they figured she was the same as usual."

"Too bad. I think your shooting club did more for her than anything." Ethan raised his cup again.

Gert went to the pie safe and took out the leftover flapjacks she'd saved. "I figure it had to happen in the night, and no one saw the smoke. The last Lyman could tell me for sure that he'd seen it standing was early February. You two want a pancake with jam?"

Ethan looked at Hiram before answering. When Hiram nodded, he said, "Don't mind if I do."

Gert put the plate on the table between them and took the jam pot from the cupboard. She gave them each a knife, and they set to work spreading the flapjacks with jam, rolling them up, and wolfing them down. She'd meant to save them over for Hi's breakfast with a couple of eggs, but no matter. These two had done a man's work this evening, and they deserved a snack.

Ethan ate three and then licked his fingers. "Sugar's good for folks who've had a shock."

"How shocking was it?" she asked.

"Worse than Bert. A lot worse. I hate to have you ladies see her like that."

Gert shrugged. "Someone's got to clean her up. I mean, you can't just bury a person all. . ."

"Her clothes are right filthy, too."

She sat down at the end of the table, with Hiram and Ethan on either side of her. "We should have done more."

Hiram scrunched up his face as though he'd eaten a mustard pickle. "Do more for someone else."

"That's a good thought," Gert said. "I felt like a hypocrite after Apphia and I saw how she was living."

"It's not your job to make sure everyone in Fergus is eating three square meals a day." Ethan's face flushed a bit, and he added quickly, "Though I'm grateful for the meals you've served this stray."

"Well, I think Hi's right that we can do more for other people. There's a lot of folks living hand to mouth around here. How long since anyone's seen old Jeremiah Colburn, for instance? He's got a flock of sheep on his place east of here, but I don't recall seeing him for a long time."

"I heard Zach Harper mention him the other day," Ethan said. "He'd come and wanted to trade three roosters to Zach for a hen. He gave him two."

"Well, good." Gert rested her elbows on the table and her chin in her hands. "I just hate to think of these poor old people dying alone."

Hiram drained his coffee cup and set it down. "Milzie wasn't alone."

Sadness swept over Gert, and a painful lump rose in her throat. "I've been thinking about it." She pressed her lips together and nodded. "I don't know what Milzie was doing in Cyrus's office tonight, but it could have been anyone who was attacked—anyone who went there at the wrong time. It could just as easily have been Isabel who was murdered."

Ethan frowned, and the lines at the corners of his eyes deepened. "Hiram told me about the other night when Isabel saw the man in the alley."

Gert wasn't surprised that her brother had told Ethan the tale. They talked a fair amount when she wasn't around, and Hiram took Ethan's new responsibilities as seriously as Ethan did. "What if she'd gone looking for her father tonight instead of that night?"

"Yes." Ethan turned his cup around slowly, as though studying its design. "I've kept an eye out since, for men loitering about in the evening."

Hiram inhaled deeply. "You think that fella might have killed Milzie?"

"I don't know. What do you think?"

Hiram set his jaw for a minute then shrugged.

"Well, I have ideas about who killed Milzie," Gert said.

Ethan eyed her cautiously. "Plan on telling me?"

She hesitated. She wouldn't want him laughing at her. On the other hand, she'd had nothing to do but think while he and Hiram did their duty over at the Wells Fargo office tonight. Maybe she'd had more time to cogitate on it than either one of them had.

"Who found Milzie's body?" she asked.

"Cyrus Fennel. He'd been over to the Nugget. I saw him leave the saloon carrying a bottle. I left shortly after he did, and I saw him come out of his office all in a dither." Ethan gave a grim little smile. "I thought he was drunk. He got sick."

"So did Ned Harmon." Hiram stood and took his mug to the stove, where he refilled it with coffee.

Gert started to tell him he'd be awake all night if he kept drinking coffee, but she thought better of it. Hiram was thirty-three years old, and he could drink coffee if he wanted to. "So Cyrus was the first to see the body."

Ethan nodded. "So far as we know."

"And who found Bert Thalen's body?"

"Uh...I guess it was Cy—hey, you don't think—" His forehead furrowed like a plowed field. "You're not saying one of our leading citizens is going around killing folks, are you?"

"I'm not saying anything. I just think it's very interesting that we've had two murders in this town in the last six weeks, and the same person found both bodies." She looked at Hiram. "Don't you find that interesting, Hi?"

He pursed his lips and nodded.

Ethan slapped the table. "You two beat all. Cyrus was here the day Bert died, to pick up his rifle. I saw you shoot it, remember?"

"Yes. But he left here, and we started eating supper."

"He said he found Bert dead and then ran over to the Walkers', looking for the mayor."

"And at some point, he told Griffin Bane," Gert added.

"That's right. I think Cy saw him on the street. And I recollect he found the mayor in the emporium, so pretty near everyone in town heard about it."

Gert nodded. "And tonight he goes into his office alone and comes out yelling murder."

"Not exactly. But you're right that he found both bodies." Ethan pushed back his chair. "Gert, you're almost making me believe it, and that's not good. I saw Cyrus just a few minutes before he sounded the alarm both times."

"Think on it," she said.

"I will. But right now I'm heading home to get some sleep. I'm frazzled, and there's a lot to do tomorrow." He reached for his hat and set it firmly on his head. "Wish I'd brought Scout over here instead of leaving him at the livery."

"Milzie's all covered up," Hiram said. "You won't have to see her again."

Ethan nodded without meeting his gaze. "Well, good night. Thanks for helping out, Hi. And Gert, thanks for the eats and the advice."

She watched him go out and close the back door gently behind him.

"What's the matter?"

At Hiram's question, she realized she was scowling. Just the fact that she was disappointed exasperated her. She clawed at her apron strings. "That man."

"He's a good man."

"I know it."

Hiram cocked his head to one side and waited.

"He called me Trudy last week, and I said. . ." Still her brother waited. She wished she hadn't started. Her face was heating up, and she hated that. "Why did you tell him about that anyway?"

"Sorry."

"No, you're not."

"If you're mad, I am."

"I'm not mad. Not at you."

"At Ethan?"

She tugged the knot loose and pulled off her apron. "I told

him I didn't mind, but he went back to calling me Gert."

"That bother you?"

"Yes."

"You want me to call you Trudy?"

"No."

Hiram nodded and carried his and Ethan's dishes to the worktable and set them down. He walked over to her and stooped to place a light kiss on her cheek. "Didn't mean to cause a stir. Though some folks beg to be stirred."

He took a candlestick from a shelf and lit the taper, then shuffled off through the sitting room.

"Humph." Gert lit a candle and blew out the lamp.

☆ CHAPTER 26 ☆

Milzie's funeral drew far fewer mourners than had Bert Thalen's, though the Ladies' Shooting Club was well represented. Libby stood between Gert and Apphia in the graveyard near the schoolhouse, while Phineas Benton gave a proper sermon. The only other men present, besides Ethan and Hiram, were Griffin Bane, Micah Landry, and a half dozen old-timers who had known Frank Peart. Through gossip at the emporium, Libby had learned that the curious paid their respects at the livery stable before Hiram sealed the coffin.

Cyrus Fennel and the Walkers did not attend. Isabel maintained her father was laid out by the shock of finding Milzie's body. That seemed a bit lily-livered for a strapping big man who'd seen a great deal of life, but Libby didn't question her. Isabel stood on the other side of Gert, stiff and stony-faced.

"I'm surprised Mrs. Walker didn't come," Apphia murmured to Libby when her husband finished his homily.

"Cloudy," Libby whispered back. She didn't like stretching the truth, but she considered saying unkind things about people to be a worse trespass than covering their pride with a white lie. The truth was, Orissa Walker never admitted the existence of people like Milzie. If the old widow ever entered the emporium while she was shopping, Orissa ignored her and checked out as soon as possible with a twitching nose. Libby knew for a fact that the preacher had asked her to help lay out Milzie's body, and Orissa had made an excuse, so he'd gotten Annie Harper instead. It made Libby sad, but people don't change their ways easily. When Apphia got better acquainted with Mrs. Walker, she would probably understand why the mayor's wife didn't attend this funeral.

As the Reverend Mr. Benton began his benediction, large raindrops splatted down on the women's bonnets. Apphia ran up her black umbrella and stepped closer to Phineas to shelter him as he prayed. Libby opened her pearl gray sunshade—an extravagance she couldn't resist when it came in a shipment of new ladies' wear from St. Louis. It was a perfect match for her best gray dress. She edged closer to Gert to share its meager cover. In her gray silk, with black gloves and a hat she'd snatched off the millinery shelf this morning, she considered that she'd perhaps overdressed for Milzie's funeral. How she'd starved for places to wear pretty clothes these last few years! At least they had church now. She could wear the outfit again on Sunday and even change her gloves and hat for something less somber.

The people around her said a hearty "Amen," and she jerked her eyes open. Shame on her for letting her thoughts meander to fashions during prayer. The congregation broke ranks and swarmed toward the schoolhouse. Those who had umbrellas walked slower. The men clapped their hats on and ran, leaving the open grave for their attention after the downpour.

The mourners' state ranged from damp to drenched by the time all crowded inside, and Hiram immediately went to the stove and laid a fire. The assembly being about a third of the one at Bert's funeral, Libby judged that they would have plenty of food. All of the women had brought at least one dish, and they far outnumbered the men. The Ladies' Shooting Club had turned out to the last woman. Gert and Apphia had made sure all the ranchers' wives were notified. As a result, the luncheon dishes were nearly as varied as at the last funeral. With fewer males eager to eat it, the ladies could enjoy a leisurely feast and visit.

While the rain drummed on the roof, they dished up the food and settled in to do it justice. The men gravitated to one side of the schoolroom, and the women claimed the other side without protest.

Libby noted that Bitsy, Vashti, and Goldie wore cloaks

she'd ordered in recently—black satin lined in jewel tones. They had an air of parrots in crows' feathers, as their bright skirts peeked out from beneath the somber folds of the cloaks. As the room warmed, they soon laid their wraps aside, and the saloon girls again displayed their bright plumage.

Gert wore the dark blue wool dress she wore to church on all but the hottest days. Again Libby wished she could dress the young woman in something more attractive. Apphia's two-piece lilac dress might be slightly outmoded by Boston standards but was far more stylish than the baggy cotton or woolen housedresses most of the women wore.

Libby joined in the conversation that burgeoned around her. At first the women talked about Milzie and what a shame it was she'd died.

"Did you see the dress Mrs. Adams gave us to lay her out in?" Annie asked Starr Tinen.

"No. I'll bet it was pretty."

Libby felt her color rise. She hadn't intended for anyone else to know about that. Gert had come to her early that morning, explaining that Milzie's clothing was so caked in blood and soil that she couldn't get it clean. With hardly a second thought, Libby had drawn her to the racks of ready-made clothing and helped her choose a dark cotton dress. She wished now she'd done more for Milzie in life. Why had they all held back? Of course they'd suspected the old woman would take advantage of their kindness, and perhaps she would have. But did that matter? What did God expect of them when a neighbor lacked for decent clothes?

"Does anyone know whether the sheriff has caught the killer yet?" Starr asked.

"I don't think so," Annie said. "Gert, do you know anything new?"

Across the room, the men had talked cattle and water rights, but during the lull before Gert answered, Libby heard one of them say, "—cold-blooded killer."

Several voices rose at once.

"Sheriff, when are you going to make an arrest?" That sounded like Micah Landry.

"Folks in town are scared out of their socks," said Oscar Runnels.

Ezra Dyer jumped up off his bench, knocking Oscar's plate out of his hand.

"Sheriff, you've got to do something, and I'm not whistlin' Dixie. You got to find out who's doin' the killin' around here."

Ethan stared at the old man and held out one hand toward him. "Now, Mr. Dyer, settle down. I'm doing everything I can to find out who's responsible for this."

"Well, what about the other crimes?" Micah Landry asked. "We still don't know who killed Thalen or who attacked Griff Bane in broad daylight."

"Yeah," Oscar chimed in. "And don't forget the fire at the Paragon. Mrs. Adams could have been toasted, and you ain't found out who did that yet either."

"Hold on now," Ethan said, but half a dozen voices drowned him out.

Only Griffin was able to bring silence, when he rose from his seat and towered over them.

"All o' ya's, shut up!"

Ethan was grateful for the quiet that followed but wished he had a voice as authoritative as the blacksmith's.

"The fella who robbed me was a big man." Griffin peered around at the others from beneath his bushy brows, as though daring them to contradict. "I don't think it was anyone from in town. I'd have recognized him. If he hadn't sneaked in and got the jump on me, I'd have had him. And then Milzie would be alive." He clenched his meaty hands. "I take that kinda personal."

Ethan stood and set his tin plate down. "Gentlemen, I'm with Griffin. I take it personally, too. I think every man in Fergus needs to take this personally. Because the next person who's clobbered or robbed or burned out of his house could be any one of us." He pulled in a deep breath. Everyone in the room, including the twenty or so women, hung on his words. He made a quick decision and hooked his thumbs in his belt. "I'd like to make an announcement. I wish the mayor was here, but two members of the town council are with us, so I guess that's good enough."

"What is it?" Ezra asked.

"I'm going to deputize two or three men to help me find the killer. I'll spend my time working on it until we run him down."

"I'd be honored to help you, Sheriff," Griffin said.

"Thank you."

The others clamored to be deputized. Ethan held up both hands. "Easy, now. I need men who can help me patrol the town at various times of day and night. So far, all the crimes have taken place in town."

"Not my oatmeal cake that got stolen off the windowsill," Laura Storrey called.

Ethan winced. "There have been some smaller crimes both in town and out in the countryside." He had his ideas about that—especially since Libby had admitted she was certain Milzie had stolen from her. But the thought of Milzie bludgeoning Bert Thalen was ridiculous, and she certainly hadn't beaten herself to death. "I'm not sure those incidents are related to the more serious crimes. Folks, I'm asking you to be patient. Give me three good men to help me. The town might want to consider some small compensation for their time."

"You can't guarantee it'll do any good," Oscar said.

"That's true, I can't. But I hope we'll catch this man. And I think we have a better chance if everyone is careful. Don't go out alone at night. Lock your doors. Don't leave your womenfolk alone."

The men looked at each other. Some nodded, and others just frowned.

"I'll accept Mr. Bane's offer of help," Ethan said. He shot a quick glance toward Hiram, but his best friend shook his head almost imperceptibly. That was all right. Hiram would help him whether he wore a badge or not. "I also thought I'd ask Zachary Harper. He's not here today, but—"

Annie Harper shoved her stool back and stood. "Sheriff, maybe you'd ought to consider who's here supporting Milzie Peart today. And who came to your office not long ago offering their help."

Ethan felt an annoying tickle at the back of his neck. He took a deep breath. "That's also true, ma'am. You ladies have done a superb job of escorting the schoolchildren for the last week or so, and also of checking up on some of the widows and elderly folks. I appreciate that."

"Well, we ladies are behind you," Annie said. "But we want to see some results."

Gert stood up.

No, Ethan pleaded silently. *Not you, Gert.*

"Sheriff, we'd like to extend our offer again. The women of the Ladies' Shooting Club of Fergus will help you in any way we can. Just tell us where you can best use our assistance, and we'll be there."

"Thank you."

"Aw, now that's just foolishness," Micah Landry protested.

"Sheriff, why do you let them waste all that lead, anyway?" Ezra Dyer asked.

Across the room, Emmaline stood.

"You sit down," Micah shouted.

Emmaline glared back at him. "Sheriff, we women are not only willing; we're prepared. We all have weapons, and we've trained ourselves to use them. Which is more than we can say about some of the men in this here town."

"Ha! Most of those weapons are *our* weapons," her husband yelled.

Vashti jumped up and stood on her bench, momentarily showing a shapely leg as far up as her garters. "Sheriff, you've got more than two dozen pretty good shots right here in this room, and I'm talking about this side of the room."

The men erupted in angry shouts. Ethan wasn't sure what to do. He could pull his pistol and fire a round into the ceiling, but then they'd have to fix the leak in the schoolhouse roof. Micah lunged toward him, and Ethan tried to retreat a step but tripped over his bench and sprawled backward, taking Oscar with him. Griff took a swing at Micah. The town threatened to go to pieces without the aid of the skulking killer, until a shrill whistle pierced the air.

Everyone froze for an instant. People cringed and swiveled

toward the sound. Hiram sheepishly lowered his fingers from his mouth and shrugged. Griff bent toward Ethan and offered him a hand up.

"Folks, listen to the sheriff," the blacksmith shouted.

Ethan flexed his arm and rubbed the elbow he'd hit going down. "Thanks, Griff. Hiram. Let's all settle down and talk about this reasonably."

Hiram and Griffin immediately took their seats, and the other men slowly complied, grumbling a bit as they did. Behind Ethan, the swishing of skirts told him the ladies had resumed their positions as well.

"All right. Here's the way I see it. We have the best chance of catching the killer if we're all alert and careful. Griffin, I'll deputize you, Oscar, and Zach. You all live in town and can give a few hours a day."

Oscar nodded, and Griffin said, "Sure can."

"Good. And Griff, maybe you can make some stars for the three of you. I haven't found any extras over to the jailhouse."

"I can do that."

"Now, we men can take turns patrolling in town during the night, but as you all know, most of these crimes have taken place before nightfall. So be careful." He swung around to look at the women. "Ladies, we'll continue your daytime patrols in pairs." Everyone remained quiet, and he felt the pressure lift from his chest. "Thank you all. I appreciate your willingness. Mrs. Harper, will you please tell your husband I'd like his aid?"

"I surely will," Annie said. "But aren't you going to deputize any of us women?"

Ethan's adrenaline surged again. Was there any good way to answer that? His gaze met Gert's, and her gray blue eyes bored into him—eager, passionate, and expecting him to do the right thing.

"I. . .guess I could do that. Miss Dooley, we appreciate *all* you ladies' willingness, but I'll only officially deputize two of you for now. I think you and one other—whoever is your next best shooter."

Gert's eyes narrowed and she gave a slight nod. "That would

be Libby Adams or Bitsy Shepard."

Libby said hastily, "Thank you, Miss Dooley, and you, too, Sheriff, but my business has kept me so busy lately that I'll have to decline."

Ethan looked at Bitsy. She wore a frothy green dress and a black hat with unnaturally brilliant red and green feathers drooping down over one eye. She threw her shoulders back, which also thrust her bosom out—not that Ethan took special notice.

"I'd be pleased to assist in this matter, but I'll have to do my patrolling before the supper hour, due to my business commitments."

"Thank you, Miss Shepard. That should work out just fine." Ethan exhaled and looked around. "It sounds as though the rain has let up. Thank you all for your attention. Those I've named, please come over to the jail for the swearing in."

The people stirred and stood, talking over the turn of events. Women began packing up their dishes.

Ethan edged over beside Hiram. "You need me in the graveyard?"

Hiram shook his head.

"Thanks. Because I think I've got my hands full."

On the way out, Ethan caught up with Griffin and tapped him on the shoulder. "Wait up. I want to ask you something."

Griffin turned to face him in the muddy school yard.

"You never found any coins on the floor after that fella robbed you, did you?" Ethan asked.

"No, he got away with my little stash."

Ethan put his hand up to the back of his neck and rubbed his damp hair. "I still can't figure out why he didn't take all your money."

"Me neither." Griffin's dark eyes flickered.

"But what I was getting at was—did you find any other coins? Ones that might not have been in your cracker tin? A penny on the floor, maybe?"

"Nope. I don't think so."

Ethan nodded and clapped him on the shoulder. "That's all right. I just wondered. Say, how do you feel about taking one of the deputized ladies with you while you patrol?"

Griffin frowned. "You were in a bit of a squeeze there, weren't you? I suppose we can't get out of it, and if they went around on their own and got hurt, you'd never hear the end of it, would you?"

"No, I wouldn't." Ethan gulped. "I was thinking of sending Bitsy Shepard out with you for a couple of hours."

"Suits me," Griffin said. "Bitsy's all right. It's a good thing you didn't pick any of those young girls though."

"Yeah, I figured Gert's position as head of the shooting club made her a logical choice, and I let her pick the second woman. Gert's pretty levelheaded."

"She is," Griffin said.

Gert came out of the schoolhouse with Mr. and Mrs. Benton. Both ladies carried their empty dishes, and the pastor toted his big Bible and a black umbrella. Griffin's gaze lingered on them, and a protest reared up in Ethan's breast. Was Griffin looking at Gert and seeing Trudy? Naw. Griff was thirty-five—more than ten years older than Gert. Yet no one would look down on a woman in her mid-twenties who married an older man. Look at Libby Adams. Her husband must have been at least a decade older than her. Ethan did some quick mental ciphering. Near as he could tell, Gert was about five years younger than he was, and that seemed ideal to him.

He rubbed his scruffy jaw. Where had those thoughts come from, anyway? Gert had lived in Fergus for eight years, and no one had courted her. Why should he think every man got the idea at once? Maybe because his own feelings toward her had changed?

Griffin moved away. "All right, I've got to stop by the livery and make sure the team for the afternoon coach is ready, but I'll be over to the jail in a little while."

Gert walked to where Ethan stood with the mud oozing over the toes of his boots.

"Care if I walk with you, Ethan? Hiram's going to fill in the burial plot now. I told him to wait till things dry up a little, but he doesn't want to go off and leave the grave open."

"Sure, that's fine." He'd almost ridden out here this morning but left Scout in Hiram's corral after he learned his friends were walking. It wasn't all that far back to the center of town. Phineas

Benton invited several of the ladies to ride back with him and his wife. The preacher had made some sort of agreement with Griffin about the regular use of a wagon and horse.

Gert waved and spoke to everyone who passed them.

"Nice sermon, Reverend," Ethan said as Pastor Benton and his wagonload of ladies lumbered by. Soon he and Gert were more or less alone, walking steadily and dodging puddles.

"Thank you for treating us womenfolk as equals," Gert said.

"Oh well. . ." No point in saying they wouldn't *quite* be equals, and he didn't want the ladies out patrolling in the middle of the night. He'd deal with that later if he had to. "You're welcome."

"I've been thinking a lot about the murders," she said.

"Still think Cy did it?" Ethan smiled at her.

"You think it's funny."

"No, I just don't think it's feasible."

"Big word for a cowboy."

"Cowboy turned lawman."

"Oh, you like it now?" Her eyes were more blue than gray as the sun struggled to put in an appearance.

Ethan shrugged. "I'm not saying I want to keep this job forever, but I don't see the city council hurrying to hold an election either."

"That's true." Gert trudged along in silence for a minute. "Well, I expect they'll wait and reelect you when they reelect Charles Walker in the fall."

A month ago, Ethan would have protested violently. Now, somehow, that didn't seem so bad. Of course, if he truly wanted to keep the office, he'd better start finding some clues to solve the murders.

He glanced at Gert from the corner of his eye. She'd worn her hair down today. Beneath her bonnet, the locks settled about her shoulders. He liked it. Of course he'd never say so.

"I have given your suggestion about Cy Fennel some thought. But we know for a fact was at the stagecoach office at the exact time Griff was robbed at the livery. I figure that rules him out."

Gert made a soft little sound—not a snort or a sniff, but he could tell she wasn't happy with this conclusion.

"What one thing bothers you the most about these crimes?" he asked.

"You mean besides the fact that two people are dead?" She eyed him with calculation in those eyes.

Ethan nodded. "I'd like your take on the whole situation."

She held his gaze for a moment but stumbled when she stepped in a dip in the road. He reached out to steady her.

"You all right?"

"Yes, thanks."

Maybe he should offer her his arm. Something in him squirmed at the thought. Not that he'd mind touching her, but someone might see, and then the whole town would think he was courting Gert. And would that be so bad? He wasn't sure yet. His resolution never to take a wife, nearly seven years old, still bound him, though lately its grasp on his will had grown weaker. Best to keep his distance until he either hardened his resolve or decided to fling it aside.

"You know about the pennies we found." He eased away from her a bit as they walked. "Tell me what you think they mean."

"Nothing, except. . ."

"Except what?"

"You won't laugh? Because you laughed when I said maybe Cyrus did it."

"I won't laugh." He was pretty sure he hadn't actually laughed about that other idea either, but there was no point arguing over it.

"I think they mean the same person did all the crimes. At least. . .at least the two killings."

"So do I. What about the fire at the emporium?"

She nodded slowly. "Had to be."

"But with the murders, the pennies were under the bodies. After the fire, it was on the counter."

"He wanted to make sure you found it," she said. "If he'd left it with the burning stuff, he had no guarantee that the fire wouldn't grow and it would get lost in the ashes."

"Hmm. You may be right."

Her chin wrinkled as she frowned. "Or not. I mean, a store is a place where anyone could drop a penny or leave one on the counter after counting up the cash in the evening."

"Not one from the same identical year," Ethan said.

She lowered her lashes. "You said the one from Milzie's murder was the same year, too."

"That's right. All three of them."

"Well, then, the year must be significant." A cloud covered the sun, and her eyes were gray again as she looked up into his face.

"So 1866." They walked on in silence for a while, and Ethan was very conscious of Gert-Trudy beside him. Her head came just about to his shoulder. Her natural stride was nearly as long as his own, and he easily adjusted to hers.

"What happened in 1866?" she asked.

"That's what I'd like to know. My family moved here that year. I was ten years old." He sighed, thinking back. "Fergus was a boom town, full of hard-drinking miners. A lot of people lived in tents. I think there were four saloons."

"Hiram and I were just kids then, back in Maine. He was fourteen, and I was five years old."

Trudy at five. Again he pictured a little girl with blond pigtails tagging along after her big brother. He glanced over at her. "I haven't told anyone else about the pennies. Just you and Hi. Of course Libby knows about the one at her store."

"She was there when you showed the first one, too," Gert said.

"And the preacher was with Hiram and me when Hi found the one in Cy's office. I figure I won't let it be known in general though. If it really is a clue. . ."

He fell silent, wondering what one did with clues. He'd pondered this one until his head hurt.

They reached the jail and went inside. Ethan waved Gert to the chair behind the desk and brought the stool over for himself. They studied each other for a long moment in the gloom.

At last, she leaned forward, resting her hands on the desk. "Ethan, I'm sure you have the mental resources to outwit this killer. I've been thinking hard on it and even praying about it. Praying for you, that God will help you find out who did it."

A painful longing made his throat constrict. How long since

someone had cared enough to pray for him? And would God really answer those prayers and make him smarter? That would be a miracle. Trudy seemed to think he had some brain power already, but he felt as stupid as a fir stump. Still, she had faith in him.

"Thank you," he said. "I appreciate that."

She untied the strings of her bonnet and pulled it off. Her hair fluttered and settled again in gentle waves. He didn't think she'd ever looked so pretty.

He cleared his throat. "One thing that really puzzles me."

"What's that?"

"Why wasn't there a penny when Griff Bane was attacked?"

"The robber left in a hurry."

"Maybe."

She inhaled and stared up at the wanted posters on the wall. "What if it fell in the straw on the floor, and you just didn't notice it?"

"I thought of that. But remember how the man we're after put the one on the counter at Libby's, to be sure we'd find it?"

She nodded. "So you're thinking he'd probably do the same at the stable—make sure it didn't get lost."

"That's right." He leaned back on the stool with his head against the wall. Again the silence stretched between them. A sliver of an idea pricked the extreme edge of his mind. He sat up. "What if the person who killed Bert and Milzie was the same person who set the fire at Libby's, but he wasn't the same person who attacked Griff?"

She sat perfectly still, holding his gaze. After about ten seconds, she nodded. "All right. You may have something there."

"Tru—" He caught himself, but her eyes had grown round. She watched him, her lips slightly parted, waiting. Ethan swallowed hard. "Your hair looks nice that way."

Now, where had that come from? He'd told himself *not* to say that. And yet he wasn't sorry. Unless she got mad again. Then he'd be plenty sorry.

In the utter silence, a voice called from the front step, "Sheriff, you in there? I'm here to take my oath."

The door opened, and Bitsy sashayed in. She wore a red dress with an abbreviated skirt. Beneath the hem, matching baggy trousers pouffed above her shoes. Ethan looked helplessly at Gert.

She smiled. "Bitsy believes the ladies should wear bloomer costumes when we go on patrol. I haven't decided what I think of the fashion. I've divided one of my skirts for when I go riding, but I have to admit this trend is practical."

Ethan opened his mouth and closed it again. Bitsy's costume was awful. More awful than her revealing saloon wear. More awful than Milzie's rags. How could any woman think such an outlandish getup was attractive? But he couldn't say any of that. Maybe sometime when he and Trudy-Gert were alone, but certainly not with Bitsy standing right there in front of them wearing it.

Behind Bitsy the door opened again. Oscar Runnels and Zach Harper entered.

"We're here," Zachary said jovially. "Thanks for picking me and not my wife, Sheriff."

Bitsy glared at Zach, and Gert hid a smile. Oh yes, dealing with deputies was going to be quite an experience.

★ CHAPTER 27 ★

On Sunday morning the old haberdashery was filled for the morning service. Before Phineas Benton stood to lead the first hymn, Gert looked back toward the door. Two black-cloaked women slipped in and found a seat in the next-to-last row of benches. Gert nearly whooped for joy. She had formed a pact with Apphia and Libby to pray until Bitsy and her girls accepted their invitations to church.

A sharp intake of breath caused her to turn around. Isabel Fennel sat right in front of her and Hiram, beside her father. Isabel, too, had seen the newcomers.

"Isn't that those two girls from the saloon?" Isabel hissed.

"Yes, Goldie and Vashti. Isn't it wonderful?"

Isabel's eyes narrowed. "I. . .suppose so."

"They need the Lord," Gert whispered.

"Well, yes." Isabel faced forward.

Gert glanced at Hiram. He shook his head slightly. So, he'd heard. He knew how burdened Gert had felt lately for the ladies of the shooting club, including the saloon girls. She'd told him the overwhelming guilt she'd felt when she realized she'd been remiss all these years in not sharing God's Word with others. The Dooleys had kept up their faith, though they'd gone without church. They hadn't even owned a Bible until recently. That had bothered Gert now and then, but she'd reminded herself that, when she came west, she couldn't carry much. Besides, the children of the Dooley family had never owned their own Bibles. Their parents had one, but more would have been an extravagance. So she and her brother had gone without.

They hadn't lived as heathens. They still asked the blessing at each meal, and Gert prayed often, and she'd vaguely missed spiritual training and fellowship, but she hadn't given much thought to her neighbors' spiritual needs. Since the Bentons' arrival and Libby's procuring Bibles, Gert and Hiram had devoured the scriptures. Principles she'd learned as a child struck her with new clarity. She wanted all of the ladies of the club to learn as she was learning and to believe as she believed.

Most of them claimed at least a superficial faith. The saloon girls seemed the farthest from the fold, with Milzie a close second. Apphia had made Milzie her own project, hoping to win the old woman through kindness. Too late for Milzie now.

In her own heart, Gert had taken on the saloon women. They may not see their need for God, but in her new vision, their need hung out where all could see, like their brightly colored dresses flapping on a clothesline. Gert now believed she was no better than Goldie or Vashti. She lived virtuously in her brother's house instead of upstairs at the Spur & Saddle. But only her faith in Christ gave her an eternal advantage over the girls, and she longed to share it with them.

Cyrus sat in front of Hiram with his spine rigid and his shoulders unmoving during the service, except when they stood to sing a few hymns. Apparently, he had recovered from his prostration. As soon as the final song and benediction ended, he turned around and buttonholed Hiram.

"Say, Dooley, I've mentioned to the reverend that we ought to have some new pews for the church, or at least put backs on some of these benches."

Hiram nodded. "Might be able to."

"Well, an hour and a half on a rough bench with no back support is too long. I expect I'll be stiff all day."

Gert smiled at his inspiration to initiate some improvements in the sanctuary. She stole a quick look toward the doorway. Goldie was shaking hands with the Bentons, but Vashti had already disappeared through the portal.

"Now, since it's for the church, do you think you can donate your time?" Cyrus asked.

Gert's anger boiled inside her. Cyrus didn't want to do anything that would cost him a penny, but he expected other people to donate money, materials, and labor.

Hiram said, "I'll ask the pastor what he thinks."

Isabel had turned and was looking at her with her habitual sour face. Gert met her gaze and tried to smile.

"I don't expect I'll be able to come to shooting practice tomorrow," Isabel said.

"Oh? That's too bad."

Cyrus picked up his hat and said to her, "I've got to see Bane for a minute, Isabel. I'll be back."

"That's fine, Papa." After he walked away, Isabel turned her attention back to Gert. "My father wants me to start work on the old boardinghouse tomorrow."

"What for?"

"He wants to open it for business, the sooner the better."

Gert glanced over at Hiram. Her brother watched Isabel with his big gray blue eyes but said nothing.

Isabel took her gloves from her handbag and pulled them on. "He said he's gotten requests from stagecoach passengers for meals and rooms in town." She flicked a glance toward where her father stood in conversation with Griffin and leaned closer. "He's also had some sort of falling out with Mr. Bane, and he wants a place where the drivers and shotgun messengers can sleep."

Gert winced at the thought of Isabel keeping house for the likes of Ned Harmon and Bill Stout. "And he wants you to run that big place all alone?"

Isabel shrugged with a little sigh. "I told him he'll have to hire someone else before the summer term of school opens. A married couple would be best." She lowered her voice to a fierce whisper. "I will *not* give up my schoolroom to run a boardinghouse."

"I'm sorry," Gert said. "I hope it goes well for you."

"Well, I hate to give up the shooting club, too. The ladies have been. . .nice to me. Of course, Papa's still furious at me for joining. He's upset with the parson, too, for letting Mrs. Benton join. Papa thinks the parson should tell all of us ladies to repent and lay our weapons on the altar."

Gert chuckled. "Pardon my saying so, but your father doesn't know much about women."

Isabel's brow creased. "I'm beginning to wonder why Mama ever married him." She clamped her lips shut as though embarrassed that the thought had escaped through them and looked over her shoulder. Cyrus was now deep in conversation with Charles Walker and Zachary Harper. "Anyway, I wanted you to know that I probably won't be able to shoot anymore."

"You could come over to my house after supper if you wanted to keep practicing."

"I wouldn't want to trouble you."

"No trouble. I shoot out behind our house for Hiram when he's fixed a gun. It won't take but ten minutes to shoot off a few rounds and keep your aim up."

A gleam of hope lit Isabel's eyes. "You'd really let me do that?"

"Sure. You've improved a lot in the few sessions you've had. I'd hate to see you give it up now. These long evenings, we may as well make use of the daylight."

A genuine smile spread over Isabel's face. "Thank you! I'll do it if I'm not too tired tomorrow."

"What will you do at the boardinghouse tomorrow?" Gert asked.

"I'm to scrub down the kitchen and dining room first, and two bedrooms. Papa wants me to start serving lunch by Thursday if I can, but I told him I won't do it unless he gets a decent cookstove in there, and tables and chairs for the diners. I can clean, but I can't make furniture, and I won't serve food on packing crates."

"Good for you. Does he have extra furniture?"

"He's got some. I think there are bedsteads and a few other pieces upstairs in the boardinghouse from when it used to be open."

"That will be a lot of work, getting the place ready."

"Yes, it will."

"Maybe I can come give you a hand in the morning."

Isabel cleared her throat and looked away for a moment. "I'm not sure Papa would pay for extra help."

"I'd come as a friend, just to help out." Gert picked up the new Dooley Bible and handed it to Hiram.

Isabel's mouth hung open for a second. "I. . .don't know what to say. Your offer is very generous."

"I don't mind helping." Gert smiled. "Could be some of the other ladies from the club will help you, too, if they have time."

Isabel stared at her as though she couldn't believe a word Gert had said. Her father strode past them toward the door and called to her without pausing. "Come along, Isabel. I'm finished."

Gert felt like blasting him, but after all, they were still in church, sort of. Isabel scurried into the aisle and followed him.

When Gert turned around to see if Hiram was ready to leave, Ethan stood next to him.

"Howdy." He nodded at Gert. "Hiram, I need to do an inventory of Millicent Peart's belongings. I wondered if you'd be free to ride out to her place with me tomorrow. From what the ladies told us, there's not much to see, but I need to make a record of it."

Hiram nodded. "If I'm not too busy putting a back on Cy Fennel's bench."

Ethan pulled back and scowled at him. "What's that about?"

Hiram waved one hand in dismissal. "I'll go with you. Come to the house when you're ready."

They walked outside together, pausing to shake Pastor Benton's hand at the door. Ethan walked with them as far as the path to the Dooley house, where he halted for a moment.

"Well, I'll head over to the livery and get Scout."

"Would you like to eat dinner with us?" Gert had debated all the way down the street whether to ask him or not. He was eating half his meals at their house now, but he'd rarely come into town on Sunday until the church services commenced. Hiram was fixing a shotgun for Augie Moore and would probably want to continue the project after dinner, but he wouldn't care if Ethan sat around while he did it.

"Thanks, but I let the boys go home over the weekend, and

I'd better get out to the ranch." Ethan tipped his hat. "See you tomorrow, Hiram. . .Trudy."

Gert watched him walk across the street. Slowly she turned to her brother.

"Did you say something to him?"

Hiram touched a hand to his chest. His eyes widened, as though asking, "Me?"

"Oh, never mind." Gert slipped her hand through his arm, and they strolled around to the back door of their house.

★ CHAPTER 28 ★

Ethan knocked softly on the kitchen door at Hiram's the next morning. He usually came to town later, but he had a lot to do today. Trudy opened the door and surveyed him with calm, grayish eyes.

"Morning."

"Morning yourself." He held up the dirty sack he'd brought. "Thought Hiram and I could go through this sack of things we found near Mrs. Peart's body before we go out to her place."

She nodded. "He's out in the barn."

"I'll just go on out there then." He held her gaze for a long moment, trying to think of something else to say. He didn't want the conversation to end so suddenly. She might be off who-knows-where by the time he and Hiram came back from the Pearts' homestead. "Uh. . .will you be around later, when we come back from Milzie's?"

Trudy leaned against the doorjamb. "I'm planning to help Isabel this morning. Her father's set her to cleaning up the old boardinghouse so they can serve meals and house the stagecoach workers and passengers. But I'll come back to fix lunch, if that's what you're worried about."

"Wasn't worried."

"Oh." They stood there in silence, she at the kitchen door and he on the worn path below the bottom step. "You boys will be ready for something to eat when you get back, I expect."

"That's kind of you. I expect we will."

She nodded, and for an instant, a smile lit her features. Ethan found himself returning the smile.

"Go on," she said with a wave of her hand. She stepped inside and shut the door.

He found Hiram spreading fresh straw in the horses' stalls. Ethan sat down on the feed bin and waited for him to finish. A minute later, Hiram stood his pitchfork against the wall and walked over.

"Milzie's bag?" Hiram nodded toward the sack.

"Yup. Figured we could go through this first. I looked at it some, and I showed it to Bitsy and Oscar. I figure it's stuff Milzie picked up the day she was killed." Ethan stood and emptied the sack on top of the feed bin. He pushed the black socks and two tins of food to one side. "Libby told me Milzie came to the emporium that day, and she gave her these things. The rest of it's junk."

"You didn't put the stuff from her pockets in there, did you?" Hiram asked.

"You mean that busted egg?" Ethan wrinkled his nose. "That got thrown away with her clothes."

Hiram nodded toward the things on the feed bin.

"Well, this here"—Ethan picked up a china cup with no handle—"matches the good china Bitsy uses for the Sunday dinner. She said Milzie probably found it in her trash heap. The rest is just a tin can, a couple of nails, and an old ox shoe. Oh, and there's a piece of a mirror in that newspaper."

Hiram picked up the wad of paper.

"Careful," Ethan said. "It's sharp."

Hiram unwrapped the shard, turned it over in his hand, and laid it down with the other things.

"That's it." Ethan looked down at the meager assortment and shook his head.

"Stuff she found in the rubbish?"

"I reckon, except for what Libby gave her."

Hiram took Hoss's bridle from a peg on the wall. "I'll get my nag."

Gert carried her broom and a bucket half full of water down

the street toward the old boardinghouse. She wore her oldest housedress and had tied a linen dish towel over her hair. She still couldn't find her red kerchief, but she needed some protection from spiders and such. At her waist, a cloth bag of rags hung against her apron.

Maitland Dostie, no doubt on his way to the telegraph office, where he presided, passed her on the boardwalk. He eyed her speculatively but murmured only, "Miss Dooley."

"Good morning." Gert fought down the urge to explain why she went about so early in a patched dress carrying a pail of water. He'd hear soon enough that the boardinghouse had reopened.

Her destination lay between the jail and the Nugget, but the saloon was quiet despite the early morning bustle of the town. Out front of the boardinghouse, a horse and wagon stood tied up at the hitching rail, and a rock propped open the door of the rambling building. In the wagon bed lay a mop, a broom, a small crock, a basket, and two tubs.

Gert mounted the rickety steps. Maybe Hiram could fix those— if Cyrus would pay him. He wouldn't want to do anything that would help line Cyrus's pockets unless he received compensation. Gert understood, but as she'd told him last night, she wanted to help Isabel even though she wouldn't be paid.

Isabel had never befriended other young women in the town. It was about time she learned what benefits friendship could bring. Hiram had taken that information in with his usual calm. He rarely interfered with Gert's actions and never criticized her decisions. Sometimes she wished he would say more, but usually she counted it a blessing that she lived with a quiet man.

Thumping echoed through the empty building. Stepping into the shadowy interior, she called, "Isabel?"

"Out here," came the faint reply.

Gert crossed a large, open room to a door that led into what she guessed was the kitchen. Boards covered the two windows on the outside, but the back door stood open, admitting a thin stream of light. One window's lowest board had been removed, and she saw a flash of blue through the dusty glass. She set down her broom and bucket then walked over to the back door.

Isabel stood outside, wielding a claw hammer. "I'm trying to get these boards off so we can see what we're doing." With a grunt, she ripped one end of a board free from the window frame.

"Let me help you." Gert stepped down into a tangle of prickly poppies and grass. Neither of them stood tall enough to reach higher than the two bottom boards on each window.

"I don't suppose you have a ladder," Gert said.

"No. There may be a stool or a bench inside."

Gert went to search for one. By the time she came back with a wooden crate, Isabel had done all she could and stood panting against the clapboards.

Gert placed her crate beneath the first window and held out her hand for the hammer.

"You really came," Isabel said.

"Sure." Gert could only manage to take down two more boards from each window.

Isabel laid them neatly by the back stoop. "It's enough for now."

"Yoo-hoo!"

Isabel jumped and stared toward the doorway. "Who can that be?"

Gert laughed.

Isabel climbed one step and called through the vacant rooms, "We're out here, in back."

A moment later, Annie Harper came through the door and stood on the stoop eyeing Gert's handiwork.

"Hope you don't mind," Gert said to Isabel. "I mentioned to Annie yesterday what you were doing, and she said she might be able to come for an hour or two."

"Myra's with me, too," Annie said. "She's lugging a pail of warm water."

Isabel blinked several times and pulled in a deep breath. "Thank you. I. . .don't know what to say."

Annie reached out and squeezed her shoulder. "This will be fun."

"Fun?" Isabel looked doubtfully up at her.

"Of course. I don't get to work with other women very often.

We can sweep and scrub and talk. Let's get at it."

Isabel threw a tremulous smile in Gert's direction and followed her inside.

Myra had set down her pail of water just inside the kitchen. "What first, Mama?"

Annie looked at Isabel. "The kitchen?"

"Yes, please. Then the dining room. If we get to it, I'll want to do the hallway and stairs next, and two bedchambers for guests."

"I think it's fine that you're going to serve meals. This town needs another decent eatery." Annie picked up Gert's broom and vigorously attacked the floor.

Gert didn't try to determine what Annie was counting as the first decent place to eat. If they got too specific, Isabel might take offense, since the Spur & Saddle was the only place Gert could think of where folks could get a good meal, and that was only at noon on Sunday, though she'd heard that lately Augie kept a stew simmering for desperate travelers.

"This is a good, big kitchen," Gert said. "Once we wash the windows and scrub down the shelves, you'll have a wonderful place to work."

"Maybe we could paint the walls a cheerful color," Annie said. "Do you like yellow?"

Isabel looked around at the drab, dark board walls. "That would be lovely, but for now, I thought I'd work on getting the place clean. Then I need to lay in supplies. Papa wants me to serve luncheon to the coach passengers on Thursday."

"Will you do all the cooking and cleaning yourself?" Myra asked, wide-eyed.

"Well, I. . ." Isabel faltered and wrung out a rag in the warm water. "I'm not sure."

"I'll bring over a couple of loaves of fresh bread Thursday morning," Annie said. "If you want, that is, so's to be sure you've got plenty for your first day or two."

Gert nodded. "And I'll bring you some dried apple pies."

Isabel stood motionless with the rag in her hand. "I. . .thank you both. It would certainly ease my mind a bit for the opening day."

Gert's mind whirled as she calculated how many of the local

men might decide to drop in to taste the cooking on Thursday. When word got around, Isabel might build a regular lunchtime clientele. "I could make pies for you regular, if you'd like."

Isabel's face softened. "Would you really? I'm not so good with pastry. I suggested to Papa that we might find someone to do part of the baking."

"I'd be happy to," Gert said.

"Think about what your time is worth. I'll have Papa order all the supplies."

Gert smiled. "Sure. But for the first day, it will be my gift to help you succeed."

"Yes, my bread, too," said Annie.

"That sounds delightful. I do appreciate it." Isabel stood and headed for the nearest tier of shelves. "Oh. . .how many pies do you think we'll need, Gert?"

"Hard to say. Maybe you could start with half a dozen on Thursday and see how much you sell. If you get a lot of business, I could do six on Mondays and again on Thursday."

"Those are shooting club days," Myra called from where she wiped the first layer of grime from the windows with a dry cloth.

"That's right. But I should be able to make pies in the morning." Gert rolled up her sleeves. "We'll see how it goes, shall we?"

Annie's voice lilted out in a sudden burst of "Rock of Ages." Isabel stared at her. Myra joined in with her sweet alto, covering her mother's wobbles.

Gert smiled at Isabel. How long since she'd heard singing outside of the last few weeks' church services? She picked up a rag and hummed along as she soaked it and wrung it out.

A few minutes later, as the quartet came to the end of the third verse, a red-tinted shadow loomed in the open front doorway. Gert looked up from sweeping the hearth where the old cookstove had once stood.

"Well, Bitsy, I'm glad you could make it." She straightened and walked over to greet the newcomer. Not so long ago, she'd thought of Bitsy only as "that saloon woman." She smiled at the wonder of the changes seen in Fergus over the past six weeks. They had a church, women had been recognized as volunteer law enforcement officers, and she now claimed Bitsy Shepard as her friend.

Bitsy grinned and held up a basket. "Augie's cinnamon rolls for when you ladies need sustenance."

"Wonderful," Gert said.

Annie called, "Well, Bitsy, I must say your outfit looks very practical. And such a cheerful color."

"Why, thank you." Bitsy preened just a bit, the better to display her bloomer costume. "It's good for working without showing your garters. A bit more discreet than my usual wear, but—can you imagine—some of the gentlemen find it shocking."

Myra nodded, grinning at her. "I can imagine it. Papa said that very thing when he came home from the jailhouse on Saturday."

"Now, Myra," her mother said gently.

"But it's true, Mama." Myra stepped eagerly toward Bitsy. "He came home fussing like an old woman. 'That Bitsy Shepard was wearing pants, I tell you. Shocking. Just shocking.' Didn't he say that, Mama?"

Gert smothered a giggle at the young woman's impression of her staid father. Annie apparently found Zachary's reaction to the fashion less amusing than Myra did. "Now, Myra, stop it. You'll embarrass Miss Shepard."

Bitsy let out a loud laugh. "Don't fret about that, Miz Harper. I haven't been embarrassed since I was twelve years old. Now, who's got an extra scrub rag? Let me at the dirt. I've only got an hour to help you, but I'll send Goldie over for a spell when I go back to the Spur & Saddle."

A small sound came from Isabel's throat. She'd stood still since Bitsy's appearance, her hands poised above the basin of water she used to scrub down the work surfaces. She hadn't moved or said a word, but her face had turned a mottled pink.

Gert sidled over to her. "Are you all right, Isabel?"

Isabel swallowed with effort. "I'm just. . .surprised. I didn't expect. . ." She darted a glance toward the vision in red.

Bitsy's painted eyebrows wriggled. "Oh, I see." Her face turned thoughtful and she set down her basket. "Well, Gert, I'll be going." She turned toward the door.

★ CHAPTER 29 ★

Ethan and Hiram rode into the narrow flat spot before the site of Frank Peart's old cabin. Even though Trudy had told him the house had burned, Ethan cringed at the sight. The fieldstone chimney loomed over the charred beams and boards. He couldn't identify any large items in the ruins. No bedsprings—but then, Frank and Milzie had probably done without. There had been a stove. Trudy had mentioned seeing it in the mine above.

Hiram dismounted and let his reins trail. Hoss immediately lowered his head and began to crop the meager grass. Ethan followed him, ground tying Scout. Together they approached the burned-out square.

"You reckon the person who set the fire at the Paragon did this?" Hiram asked.

Ethan pushed his black hat back. "I dunno."

Hiram kicked at a length of charcoal that might once have been part of the door frame. "If he did, how would we find his penny?"

"Good question." Ethan looked up the hillside. "Come on. We're not likely to find much here. We'd best check the cave."

"Milzie will have salvaged anything useful." Hiram pulled his rifle from the scabbard on his saddle. Ethan eyed him in surprise. "In case we run across a rattler."

The path to the old mine entrance held ruts and gouges. Old Milzie must have struggled to haul things up the incline. When they reached the dark opening, Ethan pulled his pistol and hesitated. Hiram fished in his shirt pocket and produced a small tobacco tin. Since he didn't smoke, Ethan's curiosity was piqued.

"Gert said to bring matches."Inside, they found a short candle, and Hiram lit it with a lucifer from his tin.

A quick sweep of the cave assured Ethan that no critters had moved in. Split and crushed rocks showed them where Frank had prospected for gold or silver, but the cave ended in a hewn niche extending not more than six feet beyond what appeared to be the back of the original cavern.

Ethan and Hiram gathered up Milzie's pitiful store of household goods and carried them out into the sunlight.

"Pins." On a flat rock, Ethan laid out fourteen safety pins, from one a half inch long to a large horse-blanket pin.

"This looks familiar." Hiram handed him a knife with a four-inch blade. The haft, about as long, was made of polished deer antler.

"Griff Bane's knife." Ethan stared at Hiram. His friend nodded. Ethan exhaled and shook his head. "How could she get this?"

Hiram cocked his head to one side. "What if she went in the livery after Griff was attacked, saw the knife, and picked it up?"

Ethan thought about that. "Don't you think she'd have tried to help him? Or told somebody he was hurt?"

Hiram drew in a deep breath and raised his shoulders. "What, then?"

"What if. . ." Ethan took his hat off and scratched his head. "What if she hit Griff?"

"Laid him out?"

Ethan nodded. "I know it sounds crazy, but. . ."

"Naw."

They stood in silence. It seemed unbelievable to Ethan that anyone would see the blacksmith injured and not try to help him. But Milzie hadn't been exactly stable. "Griffin was sure about the knife. Said he'd pulled it out when he heard a noise. He had it in his hand when that fella jumped him. And when he came to, it was gone."

"I thought maybe Ned or Bill had swiped it when they found

him out cold." Hiram turned his guileless gray blue eyes toward the cave entrance. "Doesn't seem likely Milzie would have gotten it from one of them."

"No, but she's known to have walked off with things she fancied. These pins, for instance. Libby said something about pins, and didn't Griff mention a blanket pin?" Ethan picked up the largest of the pin collection. "I'm betting this belongs to Griffin, though there's probably no way to prove it. But that knife, I'm 99 percent sure about, and Griffin can confirm it."

Hiram's Adam's apple bobbed as he looked down at the other items they'd found. "What else ya got?"

"Some shell casings. And some money. Not much." Ethan laid out a few coins. "Griffin also said some change was missing. And there's this." He laid a wrinkled but folded red kerchief on the rock beside the pins.

Hiram reached out one finger and touched it. "That bears a fair resemblance to one Gert had. She missed it one day after their shooting club met."

"When?"

"Back along when they first started meeting. Libby came home with her one day to talk about buying ammunition. While she was there, Gert missed it."

The fact that Milzie stole from people all over town troubled Ethan, but that didn't prove anything so far as the murders and other crimes were concerned. He looked down on the burnt cabin again. "I sure wish we'd known what dire straits she was in."

Hiram nodded.

"Trudy and I—" Ethan stopped and felt the blood rush to his face. "That is, Gert and I agree that whoever hit Griffin isn't the one who did the murders. He didn't leave a penny at the livery."

"Unless Milzie picked that up, too." Hiram held the knife up and looked closely at where the tang fit into the hilt.

"Never thought of that," Ethan admitted. "She could have stolen the penny."

"Any 1866 pennies in that collection?"

Ethan examined the coins carefully. "Nope. But she could have spent it."

"Maybe so." Hiram's brow furrowed, and he picked up one of the safety pins. "Bert."

"What about him?"

"His suspenders were loose."

Ethan felt a fearsome dread in his chest. He wasn't sure he wanted to go where Hiram was leading him. "Just exactly what are you getting at?"

Hiram squeezed his lips together and very slowly writhed in a shrug.

"No, Hiram, come on. You know she can't have killed Bert."

Hiram's eyebrows shot up, and his eyes widened.

Ethan shook his head. "Because he was a lot taller than her, for one thing."

"Could have been bending over near the bunk."

"Oh, and she left the penny under his body? You think Milzie would do that? Next you'll tell me she clobbered Griff, too. Hi, think about it. She stole coins. She didn't leave them for other people to find. And she wouldn't set the Paragon Emporium on fire. Libby gave her more stuff than just about anybody."

"Not until after the fire."

Ethan frowned. "You're making my head hurt again. But there's one thing that proves Milzie wasn't the killer."

Hiram nodded slowly. "She's dead."

"That's right. And she died in a way that shows someone else killed her. And that person left the penny in her blood. The same person left the pennies when he killed Bert and when he set the fire at the emporium."

Hiram laid the knife and the safety pin on the rock. "All right. I'm with you so far. But has there got to be another killing before we learn who did it?"

"No, Bitsy, wait." Gert grabbed Isabel's forearm and squeezed, none too gently. She stared into the teacher's face, wanting to scream at her, but no suitable words found their way to her tongue.

Annie filled the silence. "Bitsy, you don't need to go. It's very kind of you to want to help. Why, any woman in our shooting club who needs a hand will get it."

"That was my understanding." Bitsy hesitated. "But if I'm not wanted. . ." She lowered her head. "I thought things were different in town now. In the club, at least."

"They are." Gert let go of Isabel's arm and walked over to Bitsy. "The club has taught us all a lot of lessons, and you, Bitsy, are one of this town's most valuable business owners. Your selflessness in patrolling and serving as a deputy sheriff to help others is exemplary."

Bitsy licked her violently red lips. "Thank you, Gert. I was hoping I could be a neighbor, too. I've never had much chance to do that." She flashed a bitter smile. "I'll see you later at the club meeting." Again she turned away.

As she reached the door, Isabel stirred.

"Miss Shepard!"

Bitsy stopped, hovering like the red sun at dawn. Slowly she turned, eyeing Isabel through narrow slits of eyes edged by thick black lashes. "Yes?"

Isabel's lips trembled. She took two steps forward and extended her right hand. "You. . .are welcome here. Thank you for coming."

Bitsy met her in the middle of the floor and took her hand for an instant then released it. "I'm glad to be here."

"Then if you'd care to assist me, I was about to begin on the dining room floor."

Gert let out her breath in a slow stream. *Thank You, Lord.*

They all fell to work and soon had both kitchen and dining room transformed. Myra took a broom to the top of the staircase and swept her way down. As she reached the bottom step, Goldie arrived carrying a coffeepot wrapped in towels.

"Hurry, Miss Bitsy! My arm's about to fall off."

Bitsy dropped her mop and dashed to take the pot from her, then faced them all with a big smile. "Wipe your hands, ladies. Time for a morsel. Then I must get back to my own work. Goldie can stay awhile and help you get those bedrooms gussied up."

They sat on the stairs, a crate, and two stools Isabel had unearthed. Bitsy poured the coffee with the dignity of a duchess, and Goldie removed the linen napkin from the roll basket and passed it to the damp, dirty women. Gert's hair had come loose and hung about her shoulders. She pushed it back and took one of Augie's cinnamon rolls. The smell of them alone set her mouth watering.

With the first bite, she closed her eyes. "Mmm. If I could make anything half this good. . ."

"What?" asked Myra.

"I'd patent it."

Gert opened her eyes in time to see Isabel take her first bite and chew slowly. A look of adoration crossed her face. Her eyes brightened. She swallowed, and her lips pursed.

"Miss Shepard. . ."

"Yes, Miss Fennel?"

"Do you. . .sell these rolls at your place of business?"

Bitsy chuckled and waved her hand. "Naw, Augie just makes them for the girls and me now and again."

"Usually for Monday breakfast," Goldie piped up.

"I was wondering." Isabel hesitated. "Do you suppose Mr. Moore would have the time or the inclination to do some baking for the boardinghouse?"

"What a novel idea," Bitsy said. "He's quite busy at the Spur & Saddle, but if you'd like, I shall ask him."

Gert pictured the brawny, bald bouncer creating fancy breads and pastries for prim and proper Isabel's clients. She took another bite of the confection. *I always knew anything was possible with You, Lord, but after this morning, I truly believe it.*

Ethan walked to the mayor's house after lunch at Hiram and Trudy's. He'd rather be anywhere else right now than on his way to Charles Walker's house. He'd as soon be with the dozen women out shooting in the ravine on Bert's ranch. But a summons from the town council could not be ignored by an employee. Since Ethan had accepted his pay at the end of May and hoped he would soon receive a full envelope for the month of June, he supposed that obligated him to go when the council summoned him.

Mrs. Walker met him at the door, and he handed over his hat to her. In the parlor, Charles and the four town councilors were enjoying coffee and cigars. Ethan's eyes watered in the blue smoke.

"Coffee, Sheriff?" the mayor asked.

"No thanks. I just had some." Ethan took the only vacant seat in the room—a horsehair-covered armchair.

"Is there any progress on this crime spree, Sheriff?" Walker got right to the point, and Ethan had a feeling the council had talked about it before he arrived.

"Well, sir, I've been working hard on making sure it doesn't happen again. Setting up patrols, checking on the—"

"Yes, yes," Walker said in his squeaky voice. "We know all about the deputies and the ladies patrolling in scandalous costumes."

Ethan eyed him for a moment. So far as he knew, only one of the women had adopted the bloomer getup, and he'd bet the council wouldn't designate her a lady. He decided to take a different approach.

"I've been able to narrow the field of suspects."

That got their attention.

Cy Fennel leaned forward and tapped the ash from the end of his cigar into an ashtray on the side table between him and Oscar Runnels. "Care to enlighten us?"

"I have evidence that leads me to believe Bert Thalen and Milzie Peart were killed by the same person."

"What sort of evidence?" Zach Harper asked. The lopsided stars of sheet metal Griffin had made for him and Oscar were pinned to Zach's vest and Oscar's waistcoat. Griffin's was somewhat better crafted and had been burnished so that it shone a bit. He must have taken more pains on his own.

"I'm not sure I want it to get about yet," Ethan said. "If the killer knows everything I know, he might not play into my hand."

"Oh, that's good, Sheriff." Oscar held his cigar up in front of him and savored the words. "Play into your hand." He nodded.

"It's nonsense," Cyrus barked. "This isn't a poker game. Tell the council what you've found so far."

Griffin stroked his beard. "Yeah, Ethan, you might tell your deputies, too."

Ethan shoved the hair back off his forehead. Another thing this town needed, besides a bank and a doctor, was a barber. "Well, Mr. Fennel, you know your daughter was frightened by a man in the alley near your office a few nights before Millicent Peart was killed."

Cyrus harrumphed and crossed his legs. "What's that got to do with anything?"

"Mrs. Peart was killed in that same office, only four nights later. It's my thinking that an unknown assailant waited for you on that first occasion, planning to assault you when you returned to your office that evening. Your daughter's appearance and the subsequent commotion scared him away. But on the evening Mrs. Peart was in town, he again waited for you to come and lock up for the night."

"I'd only stepped down the street for a minute." Cyrus looked around at the others as though seeking their assurance of his innocence.

"Oh, I know that," Ethan said. "I saw you myself at the Nugget."

Cyrus cleared his throat and tapped his cigar on the ashtray again, though it had hardly burned down.

"You make a habit of it?" Griffin asked. "Going out and leaving the stage office unlocked?"

Cyrus shrugged. "Occasionally I step out and leave the door unlocked, if that's what you mean. So what? Do you lock up the livery stable every time you stroll over to the post office?"

"S'pose not." Griffin sank back against the sofa cushions.

"What are you getting at, Sheriff?" Zach asked.

Ethan looked around at them. None of them was stupid, but most of them he considered a bit shortsighted. "I think that person had it in for Mr. Fennel. It's my theory that the same killer who did in Bert Thalen planned to give Mr. Fennel the same treatment. But on the second time he tried, his plan was again interrupted, this time by Milzie Peart. She wandered into the Wells Fargo office and found him lurking there, waiting to attack Mr. Fennel."

"And he attacked Milzie instead." Oscar's eyes widened in his round face. "By George, Sheriff, you may have something there."

"That's ridiculous." Cyrus straightened and glared at Ethan. "Folks thought he was hanging about Mrs. Adams's place. He did set a fire there earlier, you know."

"But this time he did his mischief in your office."

Cyrus's face reddened. "That's a lot of flapdoodle. Who would want to kill me?"

Ethan shrugged. "I haven't figured that out yet."

"Well, someone wanted to kill Bert," the mayor noted, his voice rising. "No one knew of any enemies he had either. Unless it was someone Bert put in jail back along. But that doesn't make much sense to me."

Oscar swept his cigar through the air, trailing smoke. "I figure the person who killed Bert was a lunatic who hated lawmen."

Ethan frowned and shook his head. "Then why didn't he attack me last week instead of Mrs. Peart? And why did he wait in Mr. Fennel's office, not mine?"

"Interesting questions, Sheriff, but this isn't getting us any-where." The mayor pulled out a handkerchief and blew his nose.

The thick smoke brought tears to Ethan's eyes. He swiped at them with the back of his hand, but that made his eyes sting more. He coughed. What would they say if he opened a window to clear the smoke out?

"So you don't think the fire at the emporium is significant?" Cyrus demanded.

"On the contrary, I think it's tied in with these killings, but I'm not sure how just yet. And I don't know why he set a fire there instead of attacking Mrs. Adams, as he did Bert and Mrs. Peart. That fire was deliberately built to make a lot of smoke but not to burn the whole building. And the arsonist made enough noise to wake Mrs. Adams. He didn't intend to kill her."

"Well, our womenfolk are frightened, I know that. We need a man who can see this job through." The mayor lifted his cup and took a sip.

Things weren't going well. Ethan clenched his teeth and wished he could get back to work. Let them call him incompetent if they wanted to. He was doing the best he knew how. But the looks on Walker's and Fennel's faces told him that his best didn't equal enough.

Zach sat forward. "Do you suppose this lunatic has set out to ruin the town? If you're right and he didn't intend to attack Mrs. Peart but was waiting for Cyrus, that would be two prominent business owners he's gone after. Bert wasn't a business owner, but he had a lot to do with town business."

"Don't forget the livery," Oscar said. "He attacked Griffin, too."

"Maybe." Poker game or not, Ethan still wanted to play it close to his vest. He didn't want to say anything about the pennies. Not yet. If he had to reveal that later, fine. For now he'd keep it to himself and the Dooleys. A few people knew some of it, but no one but Ethan, Hiram, and Trudy had all the facts. And would it hurt to let the town council think the killer also pulled off the incident at the livery? "Anyway, with my new deputies helping me patrol at night and the shooting ladies keeping their eyes peeled by day, I hope we can avoid another crime."

Zach stubbed out the end of his cigar in the ashtray. "So you think he might be planning to strike again?"

"Are you thinking he'll go after Cy?" Oscar asked.

"Yes. He failed last time—and got the wrong person. So next time he'll try to make sure he gets it right." Ethan met Cyrus's gaze. "If I were you, sir, I'd take extra precautions. Don't sit up alone late in your office. Lock the door when you go out. Take someone with you on your way home to the ranch."

Cyrus's face had taken on a grayish hue.

Zach leaned back in his chair and frowned at Ethan. "What if he attacks someone else in town?"

"It's possible he'll go after one of the other business owners. He might attack one of the saloons, or the telegraph office, or the feed store. We just don't know what's going through his head. But I don't think these attacks were random. He planned them."

"Why do you say that?" Walker asked.

"He made preparations."

"What kind of preparations?" Cyrus shifted in his chair. "It's my understanding he used a piece of Bert's firewood to clobber him with and my poker to bludgeon Mrs. Peart. He used Mrs.

Adams's merchandise to fuel his fire. Seems to me he used what came to hand."

All of their eyes drilled into him. Ethan wished he hadn't said so much. The men waited. Nobody smiled.

"All of that is true," he conceded. "But if this man who was seen loitering in the alley is our killer, then I'd say he waited for the right moment. He knew what he intended to do. It happened that the wrong person came along."

"Hmm," said Oscar. "That doesn't sound like much preparation to me."

"Or much evidence." Cyrus looked at Mayor Walker. "Charles, perhaps you want to tell Chapman what we decided earlier."

Walker cleared his throat. "Certainly. Cyrus here—that is, we all decided we'd like to see this killer apprehended, and soon."

"Of course," Ethan said. "We all would."

"Yes, well. . ." Walker glanced at Cyrus, who nodded. "If you can't show us some results soon—say within a couple of weeks, why we'll just have to appoint a new sheriff, that's all."

Ethan's heart clunked against the bottom of his belly. They were going to take the position away from him so soon? Who would replace him? He couldn't imagine any of the men in this room doing more than he was doing to protect the town or figuring out who had killed two citizens.

He hadn't wanted to be sheriff, but he'd done his best. It struck him all of a sudden that he liked being sheriff of Fergus. He'd wrestled with the crime issue. He'd tried to make the town safer. And he didn't want to give up now. He had to be close to solving the riddle of the pennies. If they took his badge away, would the next sheriff they picked be able to do more than he could?

He wanted to keep this job. But he couldn't let them know how much. Cyrus was mean enough to push him out sooner if he knew.

Ethan shrugged with one shoulder and put a boring drawl into his voice, which was hard since it was scratchy from the smoke. "If that's what you want to do, Mayor, it's up to you. I think I can solve these murders. I'm getting close, but I need a little more time."

"Well. . ."The mayor's high-pitched quaver grated on Ethan's nerves and made him shiver.

Cyrus struck a match and lit a fresh cigar. "Two weeks, Chapman. That's it."

⭐ CHAPTER 30 ⭐

On Wednesday evening Libby waited inside the door of the emporium until she saw the Nash family walking down the street toward the church. She opened the door and called to them. Florence and her stepmother, Ellie, paused and waited for her to lock the door and hurry over to join them. When Peter realized the women lagged behind, he called to his two boys to wait. Libby was glad she didn't have to walk the short distance alone.

Together they headed for the old haberdashery and the mid-week prayer service. They'd only begun the custom three weeks ago, but already prayer meeting had become one of the highlights of Libby's week.

Florence wore the new dress she and her mother had sewn. The plaid cotton had come in Libby's last shipment of yard goods.

"Your dress came out very well, Florence," she said.

Florence smiled. "Thank you, ma'am. Mama likes the pattern so much, she's going to make a dress for herself after it."

Libby nodded to Ellie. "It should suit you well."

"Thank you. I've got a piece of gray flannel I thought I'd make up for fall. Oh my!" Ellie had spotted Libby's new, basket-shaped, French bag of soft leather. Idaho Territory might be a few months behind the New York fashions, but Libby refused to bypass them completely and stick to the basics.

"I saw them in the latest catalog and couldn't resist." She held it up so that Ellie could see it clearly. No need to mention the pearl-handled Smith & Wesson revolver inside. She'd decided to add it to her arsenal, leaving the heavier Peacemaker at home under her pillow except for shooting practice. The little gem of a pistol in her bag allowed her to go armed wherever she pleased and still appear dainty.

Mr. Nash held the door open for them, and the ladies entered the old store now used as a sanctuary.

Just inside, hugging the back wall and peering at the crowd with wide, frightened eyes, stood a young woman dressed in claret-colored silk. She clutched the edges of a fringed gray shawl before her bosom, but even so, the white expanse of her neck hinted at a low neckline. Rosettes caught up the skirt in front, exposing the girl's clocked stockings and shoes with scandalously high heels. Opal, the new girl from the Nugget.

Fearing she would tear out the door, Libby stepped toward the anxious young woman. Before she reached Opal's side, Apphia Benton scooted down the aisle and reached for the girl's hand.

"My dear Opal. Welcome."

Libby watched with interest. Opal had come into the emporium last week and purchased a fan and some perfume. But how did Apphia know her? The minister's wife must have expanded her outreach to Bitsy's rivals. Libby stood entranced as Peter Nash herded his family toward a bench halfway down the aisle. Ethan's ranch hands, the McDade boys, appeared, and the older one managed to end up seated beside Florence.

"Won't you come and sit with me?" Apphia asked the saloon girl.

"Oh, I..." Panic filled Opal's eyes as she flicked a glance toward the front of the room. Perhaps she had guessed correctly that the pastor's wife usually sat in the front row.

Libby stepped toward them and smiled. "Good evening. I'm Libby Adams, from the emporium."

Opal met her gaze and nodded slowly. "I remember you."

"Would you like to sit with me? I'm all alone tonight." Libby gestured toward a bench in the next-to-last row.

"Thank you," Opal whispered. She caught her breath and turned to look at Apphia.

"It's all right, my dear. I'll find you afterward, and we can visit for a few minutes." Apphia smiled gently at both of them, nodded, and turned toward the front of the room.

Libby entered the row and sat on the bench. Perhaps she should have suggested Opal enter first. The girl might feel the urge to bolt if Pastor Benton launched into a fiery exposition.

Two rows ahead, Libby saw Gert and Hiram sitting with the Harpers. Across the aisle, Goldie and Vashti claimed seats. Goldie glanced over at them, and her eyes widened. She elbowed Vashti, who leaned forward and stared past her. She glared at Opal and turned to face the front with a flounce of her black cloak.

Libby would have laughed if they were anywhere but church. Apparently, the competing saloons' employees harbored deep resentment toward one another.

Opal drew in a shaky breath. "I oughtn't to have come."

"I'm glad you did," Libby said.

"I have only an hour," Opal said. "Mr. Morrell says if I'm late coming back, he'll never let me go again."

"I'm surprised—" Libby stopped short and felt her face flush.

"That he let me come at all?"

"In the evening, I was going to say," Libby admitted in hushed tones.

"Well, I wanted to come Sunday morning, but I was ailing."

"Perhaps he'll let you come next Sunday."

Opal nodded judiciously. "Mostly we can do what we want Sundays. He said I've got to be back tonight by eight o'clock. It's never busy on Wednesday, but most of the traffic we get is after eight." She shot a surreptitious glance across the aisle. Goldie was staring at her malevolently. Opal caught her breath.

"Don't mind them," Libby said. "They're good girls, really. They're always well behaved when they come to the shooting club."

Opal's eyes sparked. "I heard tell about the club. I. . .I want to learn. Would they let me?"

"I expect *all* the members would welcome you."

Pastor Benton stood at the pulpit and raised both hands. "Let us pray."

As she bowed her head, Libby prayed silently, *Lord, thank You for bringing this wayward one in. You know her heart. Let her see Your love here.*

Ethan walked past the haberdashery as the opening hymn rang out. He wished he could be inside, singing along to "What a Friend We Have in Jesus." Maybe sitting next to Trudy.

He ambled along the boardwalk, past the closed telegraph office and an empty building. He hummed the hymn as the strains grew fainter and kept on until he reached the Spur & Saddle. Only two horses dozed out front at the hitching rail.

Inside, Augie was behind the bar, and a cowboy leaned on it, one foot on the brass rail below, with a mug of beer before him. Bitsy rose from the round table where she'd sat with two of Oscar's mule drivers.

"Evening, Sheriff." She wore one of her frothy dresses, but she went behind the bar and fetched a glittery silver shawl before joining him near the door.

Ethan waited, nodding to the two customers. Bitsy slung a twine bag over her shoulder as they stepped out onto the street.

"Got my piece in here," she said confidentially, patting the bag. "Not that we'll have to use 'em tonight, but I like to be prepared."

Ethan smiled. "Good of you to volunteer for this hour. I know evening's your prime business time."

She shrugged, causing the shawl to slip down over her shoulder and show a bit of white skin. "Wednesday's always slow anyhow. I let the girls go to the prayer meeting. Augie can handle what little business we'll get before that's over. But as you can see, I'm dressed for business tonight. Not a deputy sheriff's usual getup, hey?"

Ethan smiled. "Not quite. Griffin says he'll take over the patrol when church is done."

They crossed to the east side of the street. The reddish light from the setting sun reached between the buildings and glittered bright off the windows of the storefronts opposite. They walked in silence for a while, past the lane to the Harpers' farm, then the Nashes' house and post office. Ethan wished she'd worn the bloomers tonight. Would anyone see them walking together? Probably at least half the town's residents were at the prayer meeting; the novelty of church services still drew most of them in.

"Oh, I almost forgot." Bitsy stopped in front of the Walkers' house and fumbled in her bag. She pulled out a piece of brass. "Griffin finally made badges for me and Gert. Not bad, eh?" She held it out so he could see it. The word *Deputy* was engraved in block letters on the five-pointed star.

Ethan nodded. "He's getting better at it."

Bitsy drew her chin in and craned her neck as she fastened the badge near the neckline of her dress. Ethan looked away. *Please don't ask me to help you with that!* He gulped.

"There!" Bitsy moved forward, and he exhaled. They moseyed toward the emporium. "That Gert Dooley is a nice gal."

"Uh, yes she is." Ethan observed Bitsy cautiously from the corner of his eye.

"I never thought she'd mix with the likes of me, but she's been nothing but sweetness to me and my girls."

Ethan could well believe that. Ahead of them, Cyrus came out of the stagecoach office and turned to put the key into the lock.

"Evening, Mr. Fennel." Bitsy's husky voice cut through the stillness.

Cyrus's head jerked around, and he straightened. "Well, well. The evening patrol, I assume?" He looked Bitsy up and down from her shoes, better suited to a dance floor, to the little ruffled cap that graced her curls.

Ethan winced, again wishing "Deputy Shepard" had put on more suitable clothes. "Bane will take over at nine o'clock," he said. "We're just making sure no one's doing mischief while most of the business owners are elsewhere."

Cyrus nodded. "I thought of that—everybody over to church. It's a good time to break into one of the stores."

"Well, sir, we'll take special care of your place." Bitsy laid her hand on his sleeve and gave him what some might consider an alluring smile. It made Ethan shudder.

Cyrus pulled away. "Thank you. I'm late for prayer meeting, and I told my daughter I'd meet her there."

Bitsy chuckled as he hurried across the street. "Can't stand that man, the old hypocrite."

Ethan frowned and cocked his head to one side. "Then why'd you. . ."

"Play up to him?" Bitsy smiled as they resumed their walk. "Cyrus used to spend plenty of time at my place, and I was glad for his business. His respectable friends came, too. But I'm doing well enough now that I can get along without him."

"Even with the new competition down the street?"

"I think so. I cater to a different clientele than Jamin Morrell. My place is a respectable house and nicely furnished. You've seen it."

Ethan nodded reluctantly. Bitsy's establishment had the atmosphere of a hotel lobby, with rugs, lamps, and padded chairs. Jamin's had rough furniture and a tinny piano. You could get wine in the Spur & Saddle, someone had told him. Jamin served strictly beer and whiskey.

"He's got sawdust on the floor." Bitsy shook her head. "I did that back in the day. You know, when these hills were full of miners. But as soon as I got a little money, I put it into decor. Paintings, wallpaper, a fancy chandelier. And I don't let people spit on the floor anymore."

"You've got a real homelike place. Prettier than most homes in Fergus."

"Sure I do. And gentlemen like to come there and relax. They'll spend a little more for a drink at my place because it's peaceful. They can sit and play cards for a couple hours and not worry about someone starting a brawl and upsetting their poker game." She looked up at him. "Did you know we make as much on the Sunday dinner as we do on Friday night drinks?"

"No."

"Yup. We served twenty-six chicken dinners last Sunday. Of course, Saturday night's our big night. Always has been, probably always will be."

Ethan hesitated, but his curiosity reared up. "What about the boardinghouse? I heard Miss Fennel is going to start serving meals."

"That won't hurt my Sunday traffic. I talked to her some Monday, and again this morning, when I went to help her redd up the place. She says she told Papa she wouldn't do any cooking on Sunday except breakfast, and if they have boarders, they can go over to my place or eat some crackers or something in their rooms."

Ethan arched his eyebrows. "She told him that?"

"You're darn tootin'. That gal has sprouted some backbone lately. You knew she'd joined the shooting club last week? Against Papa's will."

"Yeah. But she's taking private lessons with Tr—Gert, now that she's got to work all day."

"I told you Gert's a gem. Who else would do that for a pucker-faced schoolmarm who looks as though she was weaned on vinegar?" Bitsy shook her head. "I'm glad she's standing up to her father at last. He's got a mean streak, always has. I meant it when I said I don't like him." Bitsy looked up at Ethan and winked. "I only did that tonight to make him squirm. I don't like him, and he don't like me. We both know it." She nodded firmly.

They had passed the Wells Fargo office and an empty building and now approached the Walker Feed Company. Across the street, the singing had stopped, and all was quiet. The folks must be praying.

"So. . .if you don't mind my asking," Ethan said, "how come you don't go to church now? Seems all the other ladies from the shooting club are going, even your. . .employees."

Bitsy barked out a laugh. "They're my girls, Sheriff. No one in this town has illusions about their occupation." She shook her head. "But no, I don't see myself warming a pew. The decent folks in this town never said boo to me until lately. Now all the ladies in the shooting club treat me nice. I like it. It's kind of different, feeling as though I've got some friends. But I don't think God's ready for me yet."

Ethan looked away, trying not to register shock. "Miss Shepard," he managed, "I believe God is always ready."

Bitsy jabbed him with a sharp elbow. "Look!" She pointed down the alley between the feed store and the old building that used to be the wainwright's shop.

Ethan squinted against the dusk. Smoke poured from the big pole barn that stood a hundred feet or so behind the feed store.

Charles Walker stockpiled all his grain for the store in that building. The stench of the black, roiling smoke hit Ethan's nostrils.

"Fire! Run over to the church, Bitsy! Tell the men to come quick! Bring water and blankets."

Bitsy hitched her skirt even higher and jumped off the boardwalk, wobbling on her high heels. Ethan ran for the barn.

★ CHAPTER 31 ★

Gert sat with her head bowed as Bertha Runnels prayed.

"Lord, we ask that You would heal Mr. Bryce from his sciatica. Help the—"

The door crashed open, and Gert's eyes popped open. Heads swiveled toward the back as Bitsy Shepard yelled, "Fire! The mayor's barn's on fire. The sheriff says all men get to the Walker warehouse. Bring water and blankets."

Gert jumped up as the men streamed toward the door, calling to each other.

Libby struggled against the flow and came toward her. "If the buildings on Main Street catch, the whole town could go."

"Should we go over?"

"We'd just get in the way, I expect."

"We could haul buckets of water over and soak blankets for them," Gert said.

"Good idea. And I could put on a pot of coffee."

Gert looked around. "There's a back door. Come on."

She and Libby fought the tide of parishioners struggling toward the exit and gained the door near the pine pulpit Hiram had built for Pastor Benton.

Annie Harper cut them off. "You thinking what I'm thinking?"

"Bucket brigade from my place," Libby said. "And I'll donate the fixings for coffee."

Annie nodded. "I can get my big pot."

"I've got two extras in the store." Libby took her arm and

steered her past the pulpit.

Behind them, Apphia Benton yelled, "Ladies, don't panic. Let us remain here and pray while the men fight the fire."

Libby hesitated, and Gert shoved her gently toward the back door. With Annie they made their escape. As soon as they got outside, she smelled it. They rounded the corner of the haberdashery, and she halted, staring at the massive column of black smoke. From their angle, it seemed to rise from the feed store itself and the vacant storefront beside it. Not until they'd crossed the street and come even with an alley could they see the barn behind that served as Charles Walker's warehouse. Dozens of men surged toward it. Bitsy, in one of her bright silk dresses, stood on the corner yelling and pointing the way.

Gert ran to her, leaving Annie and Libby to worry about coffee and other nonessentials.

"What can I do, Bitsy?"

"Water! The men can't bring it fast enough. If you can, pump water and bring it. They've got two tubs over there where they can soak their wool blankets, but we need to keep them full. And buckets of water to throw on the fire."

"Libby's pump and the Nashes' are probably closest."

Bitsy nodded. "The men are using them, and Zach Harper's gone for his wagon. He plans to haul barrels of water, but it may be too late."

Not many women had stayed at the church. Vashti and Goldie ran across the street, holding their skirts well above their knees.

"Miss Bitsy, what can we do to help?"

"Bless you, girls. Round up more buckets. Augie's already over here, but you can get pails and big pans from the kitchen. Oh, and get the wash boiler."

The two girls hiked up their dresses and charged for the Spur & Saddle.

Gert left Bitsy on the corner to direct the people who came to help. She ran to Libby's back door and up the stairs that led directly to the apartment above the emporium. Annie answered her peremptory knock.

"Give me any buckets you won't need," Gert panted. Annie thrust a galvanized pail and a dishpan into her hands.

"Wait, Gert," Libby called. She hurried over with her keys in her hand. "I'll go downstairs and open the back door of the store. You can take anything that will help."

"I'll meet you there."

Gert pounded down the outer stairway and tossed the pail and dishpan toward the pump over Libby's well. Peter Nash already worked the handle up and down, and Griffin and Oscar, along with Jamin Morrell and two men Gert didn't know, waited to fill their own containers. Bitsy's alarm must have emptied both saloons.

At the door, Libby shoved a stack of new buckets into her hands. "Pass these out to whoever's there."

Gert hurried to the pump. "Anyone need a pail?" Augie was working the pump now, while Bill Stout and Hiram filled their buckets. She handed empty ones to Ted Hire and Cyrus. When they'd gone, Gert filled her own and hurried to the tubs where the men repeatedly brought their blankets to dunk them. Ethan met her there as she dumped two full pails into the tubs, his face and clothing black with soot. Even his badge was caked with it.

"Trudy! Keep back. You need to stay safe."

"I will." She squinted toward the barn. Her eyes stung from the smoke, and tears bathed her cheeks. Thick smoke poured from the open barn door and the spaces beneath the eaves. Inside, flames leaped among the bulging stacked feed sacks. Men soaked the siding boards on the south side of the barn. Others hurried in the big doorway with water.

"Is the whole thing going to go?"

"Maybe. A big stack of oat sacks was burning when I got here, and it's caught on the inside wall now. We're hoping we can lick it, but it will be close." As Ethan spoke, he plunged a filthy, ragged blanket into the tub. He lifted it and squeezed out enough water to keep from wasting much on his way back to the blaze. Hefting the heavy wool, he grinned at her, his teeth brilliant white in his blackened face. "Shoulda known you'd be out here helping."

"We're making coffee for all you men," she called as he turned to go.

He yelled over his shoulder, "Save me some."

"Get back!" Hiram's shout rang louder than Gert had ever heard his voice before. Men tore away from the south wall as flames ignited the siding and ripped up the height of the barn on the outside of the wall. The heat intensified, and the fire fighters couldn't approach the inferno. Suddenly the roof burst into flames.

"Mercy!" Gert turned to find Orissa beside her. Her huge eyes reflected the bright flames in her pinched face.

Gert sidled closer to her. "I'm sorry, Mrs. Walker."

Orissa turned her face into Gert's shoulder and sobbed.

"Soak the roofs of these houses," Ethan shouted. "If the empty buildings catch, the whole town will go."

A ring of men stayed as close around the barn as they could bear, smothering embers that reached the ground. The light wind favored them by sending its occasional gentle breath southward, not directly toward Main Street. The men carried bucket after bucket to the back of the feed store, the Wells Fargo office, and the vacant storefront between them. While others climbed onto the roofs to slosh the water over the vulnerable shingles, Hiram and Griffin began to carry buckets to the back of the emporium. They flooded the back porch of the store and the stairs that led to Libby's apartment.

"Think we need to do the roof?" Griffin shouted.

Hiram turned and looked toward the barn. Much of the siding had fallen away. The beams stood, outlined in flame, surrounding the high stacks of bagged corn, oats, and wheat. Without question, the whole pile had caught now.

"That fire's gonna smolder for days," Hiram said. "We can't bring enough water to drench the whole thing."

Griffin nodded. "We need to contain it."

Orissa sobbed.

Gert tightened her arm around her. "Come on, Mrs. Walker, let's go inside the emporium. You need to sit down."

At dawn all agreed the fire was mostly out. Now and then a new plume of smoke found its way out of the charred pile of grain. Ethan posted Deputies Oscar Runnels and Zach Harper to a two-hour shift to make sure the fire didn't break out again. Griffin and Hiram would relieve them for the next watch.

Ethan knelt by one of the tubs and immersed his head. Raising it, he stood and shook off the extra water. Someone handed him a towel. After he'd wiped his face, he realized it was Trudy.

"Thanks. Shoulda put apples in there so we could bob for them." He handed her the grimy towel. The skin on his face hurt as though he had a sunburn.

Mayor Walker plodded toward him and thrust out his hand. "Thanks for all you did, Sheriff."

"I'm sorry we couldn't stop it sooner." Ethan looked toward the pile of charred boards and the heaps of ruined grain.

"You did all anyone could."

Ethan nodded grudgingly. "Thank Miss Shepard, too. She spotted the smoke first. Our patrols paid off tonight. We were able to muster the men quick enough to keep the fire from ripping through town."

Walker sighed. "I had no idea anything was wrong until Pete Nash's boy ran over and hammered on my door. I stayed home last night—had a little headache." He put his hand to his temple, as though that were evidence that he'd been ill enough to dodge prayer meeting.

Ethan glanced at Trudy, who stood silently beside him holding the towel. "I hoped we could save the building and maybe some of the grain."

"I surely wish this had happened before Oscar brought in that big new shipment yesterday." Walker sighed and looked back at the ruins of the barn. "You're sure this was deliberate?"

"Pretty sure," Ethan said. "When I first got there, I could tell it started right in the front corner, not far from the door. I think he dumped oil or something like that over the full sacks on that side of the barn. I had hopes. . . ." He rubbed the back of his sore neck. "Well, no sense wishing now. But when it's cooled off, I want to poke through the ashes on that corner and see if we find any oil cans or anything like that."

Mrs. Walker came out the back door of the emporium and shrieked, "Charles! Charles, are you all right?"

The mayor gritted his teeth and staggered toward her. "I'll live, Orissa. Don't discompose yourself now."

"Oh, Charles, you've lost all your inventory."

"There, now. We've still got the store and our home. This is a great loss, but we'll get by."

Orissa's sobs rose, and he patted her shoulder.

"I'd best walk them home," Ethan said to Gert. "The mayor may have overdone it a little tonight."

"Sure." Gert turned troubled gray eyes on him. "Libby's set up coffee and whatever the other ladies brought for breakfast inside the store: sandwiches, gingerbread, doughnuts, biscuits. All the men can go in the back door, get their eats, and head out the front. But I was hoping you'd come to our place later so we could talk about this."

Ethan smiled down at her. "I'll be there. Soon as I get the Walkers home safe."

She hesitated then said, "Look around their house, won't you, Ethan? If the killer set that fire, it's possible he did it to draw people away while he busied himself at something else."

"We think alike." He had a sudden desire to touch her, to hold her in his arms, but that was preposterous. He was covered with soot. Besides, half the town milled about, and the sun had risen and illuminated the people in all their filthy exhaustion. The light breeze whistling down the hills brought anything but romance.

"Come on." He nodded toward Libby's back door.

Fifteen minutes later, after the mayor had consumed a sandwich and listened to the commiseration of a score of people, Ethan set out with him and Orissa. As they walked up the street, Orissa said, "It's a wonder the store and the old grocery didn't catch."

"Sure is. A real nine days' wonder." Her husband's voice was threadier than usual.

"Your throat sore?" Orissa asked.

"Yes. All that smoke."

"You'd both best wash up and go to bed for a few hours,"

Ethan said. They came to the dooryard, and he stopped. "Did you lock up when you left the house?"

The mayor scowled at him. "Lock up? Never do."

"Well, then, just let me take a look around before you go in."

"You think—"

"I don't think anything." Ethan shot a glance at Mrs. Walker's sharp features. "I just want to be sure it's safe."

He walked slowly to the front steps. Nothing seemed amiss, and the door was shut. He mounted the steps to the porch and reached out for the knob but stopped. Something caught his eye on the mat at his feet. He bent and picked it up, running his finger along the smooth edge. He didn't take time to examine it closely. No use getting the Walkers all upset. He opened the door and went inside.

Ethan walked through the entire house, room by room. So far as he could see, nothing was out of place. Mrs. Walker was a persnickety housekeeper. It would have been easy to see if someone had rifled the place.

At last he went out and called to them, "Seems all right. You can come in."

"Sheriff, what's the meaning of this?" Charles Walker said as he puffed up the steps. The fire had singed off half his eyebrows, and his bald spot held a sprinkling of sweat drops.

"Just checking," Ethan said.

"Do you think the same person set the fire tonight as set the one at the Paragon?" Orissa stared at him through narrowed eyes.

"I don't know, but it's possible. I wanted to be sure the arsonist wasn't up to other mischief while we were all over at the fire."

"Good thinking, son."

Ethan smiled grimly. The mayor had never called him that before. He wondered if they'd still replace him if he didn't unmask the killer in the next twelve days.

"Well, good night, folks. We'll keep watch at the warehouse, and I'll be sleeping at the jail tonight. If you need me, you'll know where to find me."

"Sure enough." The mayor wheezed in through the doorway.

"Thank you, Sheriff." Orissa followed him.

Ethan strolled slowly down the street. The stench of smoke still hovered. People exited the emporium in clusters. Through the front window, he could see Florence, Ellie Nash, and Bitsy helping Libby straighten up. Peter Nash and Augie Moore stood to one side talking with cups in their hands.

Ethan stood for a moment watching until he was reasonably sure the Dooleys weren't in there. He ambled on down the street toward their house. The Nugget was quiet, and the whole north end of the street lay subdued. No piano music, no laughter this morning. The sun eased up above the houses and the livery stable. He followed the path around to the back door of Hiram's house and knocked.

"There you are." Trudy stood in the doorway with her hair all loose about her shoulders and a spotless white apron over her blue dress. Ethan's throat ached, not from the night of breathing in fumes, but from the sight of her, so calm and content, waiting for him.

"Sorry I'm so filthy."

"Come in. I put Hiram in the bathtub, and when he's done, you can have a turn. I've got more water on the stove."

Ethan started to say there was no need but abandoned that notion. If he'd ever needed a bath in his life, it was now.

He followed her inside. She turned and leaned against her worktable with her arms folded across her chest, saying nothing but watching him. The light streamed in the window behind her, sending little glimmers off her hair. It looked almost golden, not the flat straw color he usually registered when he looked at her.

Her eyes crinkled. "What?"

"Nothing. Just. . .I appreciate it. Seems to me you hauled a lot of water in the last few hours."

"We all did."

"Well, you needn't have done more for me."

"Hiram carried most of the bathwater." She turned to the stove and picked up the steaming coffeepot. "Did you get coffee at Libby's?"

"I did, but I wouldn't be against having more. My throat still tickles."

She poured him a cup, and he took it from her. He didn't want to sit down with his trousers crusted in soot and grime, so he leaned against the edge of the sturdy pine table.

"Thank you, Trudy."

She smiled. "I'm glad I can do it."

He took a sip and savored it. "Did I ever tell you, you make good coffee?"

"Seems you might have." She waited a moment then raised her chin. "So tell me, who set the fire?"

Ethan dug his hand into his pocket and brought it out again. "Whoever left this on the Walkers' doormat."

She caught her breath and reached for the penny. "Eighteen-sixty-six?"

"You tell me. I didn't want them to see it, so I didn't look yet."

She took it over to the window and bent close. Her hair took on more golden highlights, and her face glowed. How could he ever have thought she was plain?

"That's the year, all right." She straightened and held it out to him.

Ethan took the penny, flipped it in the air, caught it, and returned it to his pocket. "Anyone could have gone over and left that on the doorstep while we were all at the fire."

She nodded slowly. "Or before he went to the fire."

Ethan raised his eyebrows. "I hadn't considered the mayor a suspect before. But you're right. He could have done it. He skipped church last night." He smiled ruefully. "I was about to embrace your theory, you know."

"Cyrus?" Her brows arched like the wings of a soaring hawk.

He nodded. "He went late to the prayer meeting."

"Yes, I saw him come in after the first couple of hymns."

"Bitsy and I met him on the street. He'd just come out of his office, and we hadn't spotted the fire yet. That fire must have been started at least several minutes before we saw it. By that time, it was putting out a lot of smoke." Ethan drained his coffee cup.

"So Cyrus could have set it and then gone back to his office." Trudy drew in a deep breath. "What now, Ethan?"

"I don't know. Most of the men in town have nearly as shaky

alibis. Someone could have set that fire twenty minutes before church time. Just got it going and walked away. Or even ten minutes before time for the prayer meeting."

"And then showed up to help put it out when you and Bitsy sounded the alarm."

"Sure." He wagged his index finger at her. "So you be careful, won't you, now? I don't want anything happening to you." He touched the tip of her nose.

Her eyelids lowered as she looked at his finger. He drew it back and winced.

"Sorry. My hands are still dirty."

She smiled. "I'll be careful."

Hiram appeared in the doorway between the kitchen and the sitting room in his stocking feet, wearing a clean plaid shirt and shabbily comfortable trousers. "Well, Eth, how's everything?" He scrubbed at his damp hair with a clean towel.

Ethan laughed. "Fine, just fine."

Hiram spread his arms, indicating his outfit. "Gert made me put on all clean clothes, even though I haven't been to bed." He shook his head. "Women."

"Oh, hush," Trudy said. "You can't sleep all day. There's too much to do. To start with, you can carry that pan of hot water into your bedroom and heat up the tub for Ethan. I didn't think it was possible, but he's even filthier than you were half an hour ago."

Hiram grinned. "Good thing I had the first bath."

Ethan picked up the potholders Trudy had left on the work counter and turned to the stove. "I'll get it. But I don't have any clean clothes to put on."

"I put out a shirt for you," Hiram said. "Don't think my britches would fit you though."

"Thanks." Ethan winced. "I've got a few things at the jail. Should have brought them."

"I can run over there for you," Hiram said.

"I appreciate that. What all do you two need to do today?"

"It's Isabel's opening day," Trudy said. "I promised her six pies by noon, and Hiram's going to take another turn on watch over at the fire."

"That's right. So you think Isabel will go ahead and open, what with all the excitement over the fire?"

Trudy shrugged. "The stagecoach will still come in at quarter to noon, fire or no fire."

"True. Well, I'll get in the tub. Meanwhile, Trudy, you tell your brother what I found over at the Walkers'." When he turned around with the steaming pan of water in his hands, Hiram was stifling his laughter, but Trudy nodded at him with a complacent, wistful smile.

"I'll do that while I make my pie crust."

Hiram winked at him. "Don't forget to wash behind your ears."

★ CHAPTER 32 ★

Gert packed two pies in the bottom of her large carrying basket. She took a light wooden platform Hiram had built for the purpose and carefully fitted it over them, lowering the legs between the pie plates. On top of this she put two more pies.

"There. If you can carry the other two..."

"Oh yes." Apphia Benton put one of the remaining pies in a smaller basket and picked up the other. "Ready?"

Together they went out Gert's back door and around the path to the boardwalk.

"Thanks for helping." Gert felt a twinge of guilt at asking her morning caller to lend her a hand. "It would have taken me at least two trips alone, and I'm dead tired."

"You poor thing," Apphia said. "At least my husband and I got a few hours' sleep after the fire was out."

"Well, I'd promised Isabel, and she's just starting to act friendly to me and some of the other ladies. I didn't want to give her an excuse to back off, even if I had to hurry things up and used canned fruit for two of the pies."

"They'll be delicious, I'm sure." Apphia smiled at her. "I'm glad Isabel's venture has gone so well, but not pleased that it means even more work for her, poor woman."

Gert had to agree. Word that the boardinghouse was reopening had already led to the rental of both bedrooms the women had helped renovate. Now her father demanded that she open up four more rooms. All passengers, as well as the stagecoach drivers and shotgun riders, must know that clean, comfortable rooms at a respectable lodging house were now available in Fergus.

"In the old days, folks didn't care much where they slept," she said. "Hiram told me the miners coming through town would sleep five or six to a room at the boardinghouse. But nowadays people think they should have a nice room to themselves, like they would at a hotel in the city."

"And Mr. Fennel is taking advantage of that."

"No surprise to me." Gert looked over at the minister's wife. "I don't mean to speak ill of Mr. Fennel. I suppose most would say he's done a lot for this town. He's stuck around here since the boom days and through the bust. He mined for gold and ran the assay office; then he bought a ranch and got the stage line's business through these parts. He's had a hand in most of the enterprises in Fergus. Now he's just turning his hand to a new vocation. He'll make it succeed."

"He will, or his daughter?" Apphia shook her head. "Seems to me that Isabel's doing all the work."

"True. Her pa bankrolls it, but she's seen to the labor."

"And her friends have helped her." Apphia's brow furrowed. "I'm not sure we're doing Isabel a good turn. The more we help her for free, the more her father will let us."

"I know." Gert sighed. "Hiram won't do any more without being paid. Not for Isabel. She's going to pay me for my pies after today, and I know she's paying Augie for his cooking, too. I keep telling myself not to go over and help her scrub anymore, but then I think of her trying to do it all herself, and I feel sorry for her."

"She's hired Myra Harper to help serve meals and wash dishes and laundry, so don't trouble yourself anymore." Apphia paused as they came to the small street that cut between the jail and the boardinghouse. The Bentons' new home lay a block to the east on this narrow street.

"Almost there," said Gert. "Let's take them around to the kitchen door." She led Apphia to the back of the boardinghouse. "I do think Isabel's father's coming around a little. He sent two of his coach riders to set up the bedsteads and move furniture for her. Told them they could work off the price of their rooms doing it."

And yesterday he thanked Hiram for fixing the steps and offered to pay him to make a sign."

"I'm glad to hear she's getting some help," Apphia said. "I fear the women in this territory often fall into the category of forced labor."

Gert opened the door, noting that all the windows on the back of the building were now free of extra lumber and sparkling clean.

Isabel, wearing a voluminous apron over her dress, looked up from where she peeled potatoes. "Oh, Gert, bless you! I wasn't certain you'd have time."

"Sure did. And Mrs. Benton came along and offered to help me truck the pies over here."

"Set them right here on this table. I can't begin to thank you enough." Isabel indicated a small table near the door to the dining room, and Gert and Apphia set their baskets down.

Myra Harper came into the kitchen carrying a stack of ironstone plates. "These are the ones we're using for lunch, right, Miss Fennel?"

"Yes, and call me Isabel. We'll be working too closely for formality."

"All right. Shall I set the tables, or do you want the plates out here?" Myra asked.

"Go ahead and set up for six at the big table. We'll take the serving dishes out, and folks can serve themselves." When Myra had left the room, Isabel brushed back a strand of loose hair and turned to Gert and Apphia. "I don't know what I'm doing, and I have to make so many decisions. If we get a lot of customers, I suppose we should take orders and fill their plates in the kitchen as they do in restaurants. But I want people to feel that Fennel House is like a home. If they want seconds, the dish will be on the table."

"That sounds right," Apphia said. "You want your guests to feel contented and cared for, not like someone you're only out to earn money off."

Isabel nodded slowly. "Yes. That's it. Father doesn't understand. He wanted me to buy the cheapest blankets the emporium could get, but I told him that if he spends a little more and puts pretty quilts on the bed or nice, commercially milled bedspreads, the patrons will see us as more than a second-rate boardinghouse. I've been praying this venture will succeed and"—she flushed and looked down at the paring knife in her hand—"and that people will say we've made a good addition to the town."

Gert smiled. "Other folks have been praying for you, too, Isabel."

Apphia walked over to her and patted Isabel's arm. "My dear, you've put a great deal of thought and effort into this. Perhaps you have a special gift of hospitality."

"Do you think so?" Isabel sighed. "I do want to go back to teaching though. I told Father he has three weeks to find someone else to do this. When the summer term opens, I want my class back."

"Are you sure?" Apphia asked.

"Yes. I don't mind the hard work, though cooking was never my strongest talent. And Myra's been a tremendous help. But I don't like the thought of men milling around. I'll have to please the paying customers, even if they're difficult. But I told Father that if any of his stage line employees try to take liberties with me or Myra, I'm done."

"I'm sure he's instructed them to behave as gentlemen when they come here for refreshment or for their rooms in the evening."

"Well, I'm not staying here nights." Isabel raised her chin. "There is absolutely no way I'll room here when there might be all men for guests some nights. At least Father saw the sense to that. He says he'll take me home to the ranch each evening."

"I'm glad to hear it," Apphia said. "My dear, you know I'm just around the corner. If you ever feel unsafe here, I urge you to dash out the back and come to me and Mr. Benton."

"Thank you." Isabel sniffed. "That's very kind. I don't expect to be working here long though."

Gert walked over closer. "The Ladies' Shooting Club can make this a regular stop. I'll ask the sheriff to look in evenings, too."

"Thank you. Father felt at first that someone responsible should be on the premises at night. When I suggested he might start sleeping here. . . Well, he didn't take kindly to the notion.

Besides, that would leave me alone at the ranch, and I don't like the isolation of it when he's not around."

"Absolutely right," said Apphia. "If the venture pays, I hope he'll hire a trustworthy couple to live here. Meanwhile, we shall continue praying for you and sending our club members to check on you. And now. . ." She looked at Gert. "We know you and Myra have a lot to do, so we'll leave you."

Relieved they had not been pressed into doing chores, Gert followed Apphia to the back door. "Good-bye, Isabel. And do call on either of us if you need anything."

Ethan breathed deeply as he left the Nugget on Saturday evening. It was good to get out into the fresh air. He didn't know how those men could stand it in the close atmosphere of the saloon. The smoke, the smell of liquor, the bar girls' cheap perfume. Give him a clear whiff of prairie air anytime. A light breeze brought him a hint of scorched corn through the twilight, but the smells from the warehouse fire had pretty much abated over the last three days.

He ambled past the boardinghouse. Instead of a blank, echoing hulk, it now showed signs of life. The windows were no longer boarded. Soft light glowed from the dining room and parlor, and candlelight shone dimly in an upstairs front window. Cyrus had paid Hiram to make an attractive sign: FENNEL HOUSE, ROOM & BOARD. The town was mending and regaining vigor.

The little jail where Ethan presided loomed dark and silent. He walked past it toward the cozy house beyond. He smiled with anticipation. Trudy had promised to patrol with him for two hours at sunset to fulfill her commitment as a deputy. He'd looked forward to it all day. Of course, they would keep it businesslike, but he'd still get to walk with her, and no doubt they would converse. These days, talking to Trudy always left him feeling warm and hopeful that something good would happen.

He strolled around to the backyard as usual. Hiram came from the barn with a bridle slung over his shoulder.

"Evening, Hi," Ethan said.

Hiram nodded with a half smile.

"Trudy ready to go patrolling with me?"

"I expect so."

Ethan let him go up the steps first and open the door to the kitchen. The oil lamp burned low on the table, but Trudy wasn't present. Hiram looked at him and shrugged then shuffled off into the parlor. Ethan leaned against the doorjamb and waited, enjoying the snug hominess of the kitchen.

A moment later, Trudy entered. He straightened and smiled. "Hi."

"Howdy." She wore a dark skirt and light-colored blouse with a short jacket over it. She'd tied her hair back, and while he waited, she reached for a bonnet. Frowning, she stayed her hand. "I like to be able to see, especially when I'm on watch. Those bonnets are good for keeping the sun off, but they block a good part of your vision, too."

Ethan chuckled. "Like blinders on a horse?"

"Something like." She looked over her shoulder toward the other room then snatched Hiram's sagging felt hat and popped it onto her head. "Come on. He won't miss it."

She reached for the Sharps rifle that stood in the corner between the cupboard and the door.

"You're taking his rifle, too?" Ethan asked.

"We *are* on duty."

"Well, yes, but it'll get heavy, don't you think?"

She hesitated. "I suppose I ought to get a pistol, but we haven't had much cash come in lately. I don't like to ask Hiram to lay out money for something extra."

"I thought he had a six-shooter."

"He used to, but he traded it a year or so ago."

"Well, I'm armed." Ethan patted his holster.

"What good is a deputy without a gun?"

He considered that. "Another pair of eyes."

"All right. Let's go then."

It was almost fully dark outside when they walked out to the street.

"Which way?" she asked.

"I just came from the Nugget, and things looked peaceful at the boardinghouse. Let's head down the street as far as Bitsy's place."

She fell into step beside him on the walkway. "Did you see Isabel at the boardinghouse?"

"No, I didn't go in. But I saw her father at the Nugget."

"So he hadn't picked up Isabel to take her home yet." Trudy scowled at that, and Ethan didn't blame her. Cyrus had been seeing Isabel home to the ranch every evening, and the sprinkling of boarders, which now included the coach drivers and shotgun riders, were left to have pleasant dreams on their own.

"Wonder if she had many guests tonight?"

Trudy said, "I took her two pies this morning after the Boise stage came in, and she was bustling around getting lunch. Myra Harper was helping her. She said she'd have two people staying tonight for sure, and maybe more off the Silver City coach this afternoon."

"Cyrus made a good decision to reopen the place."

"Yes, but Isabel's afraid he won't let her go back to teaching." She stepped down at the break in the boardwalk between a vacant house and the haberdashery. "This fella we're watching out for."

"What about him?" Ethan should have known her thoughts would go back to the criminal who eluded them.

"He seems to like fire."

He offered her a hand up onto the sidewalk at the other side of the alley. "I reckon that's true. That seems to be his weapon."

"That and bashing people's heads in."

"Yes." They walked on in silence to the front entrance of the building where the church services were held. Ethan paused and shook the locked door to make sure it was secure. He'd long since found cracks in most of the shutters or planks nailed over windows in town. These allowed him to peer into the interiors of the unused stores and houses to make sure no flames sputtered within. Two fires so far—at the emporium and the warehouse. And who knew but the Pearts' cabin fell to arson as well? But he tended to think that was carelessness with the stove on Milzie's part.

"Maybe we should walk around the back of these places," Trudy said.

"Sometimes I do. Let's make a circuit of Main Street. Then

maybe we'll go the long way around, one street over."

"All right. We can go check the livery and go up the back of that side as far as the burned warehouse, at least." A horse nickered nearby, and Trudy turned toward the street. "Look at that. Horses lined up from the Spur & Saddle all the way down here."

"That's right. It's Saturday night. Bitsy's place will be full. It was early when I stopped in at the Nugget, but quite a few men were in there getting primed. Probably by the time we get back down to that end of the street, it'll be starting to get rough." He eyed her ruefully. "Maybe Saturday night's not the best time for a female deputy to patrol."

Trudy stepped over to the edge of the boardwalk and patted one of the horses at the haberdashery's hitching rail. "It's early, like you said. If it gets too wild, you can take me home and make Hiram go with you. I just hope Cyrus goes for Isabel before it gets noisy." She made her way down the row of horses, patting each one on the nose.

Ethan smiled as he watched her. Sometimes he forgot she was a girl. She was so competent and levelheaded. She never threw a fit of hysterics.

"Isn't this Ralph Storrey's paint?" She stroked the nose of the horse on the end of the row.

"Sure enough." The rest could have been anyone's, with all the dark colors blending into the night. The bays and chestnuts all looked black, but the flashy pinto's white patches stood out.

"I always notice him when Ralph rides down Main Street. He looks so. . .I don't know. . .happy. And eager."

"He's a good horse, all right." Ethan felt a little disloyal, comparing this animal mentally to Scout. While Scout had gotten a little long in the tooth and wasn't as fast as he used to be, he was a good horse, too, and they'd have several good years together yet.

Trudy stepped down off the boardwalk beside the paint. "Hey, fella. You tired of waiting for your master?" She rubbed his snout and slid her fingers up his broad face to scratch beneath his forelock. The gelding nickered and tried to rub his head against her arm.

"No, you don't. I don't want you slobbering all over my clean clothes."

Ethan laughed. Had she changed her clothes for him tonight? She looked good.

She rejoined him, brushing her hands together. They continued on until they reached the front of the Spur & Saddle. The place was bright with lamplight. A half dozen horses dozed at each of the two hitching rails out front. Gentle music and laughter floated out to them.

"That sounds like a piano," Trudy noted.

"Bitsy's got a nice one in there."

Trudy cocked her head toward the sound. "It sounds real pretty."

"Yes."

"Who plays it?"

"One of those bits of girls." Ethan felt his face flush. He hated to admit he even knew girls lived and worked here.

"Goldie or Vashti?"

"I dunno. The one with the blond hair."

"That's Goldie."

"Mm." He shrugged.

"She's not bad at it, is she? I wonder if she practices every day."

"I don't know. The cowboys come in on Saturday night to hear her play."

Trudy gave a little bark of a chuckle as though she doubted the music was the main attraction.

Ethan shifted his weight to his other foot. "I usually go in and ask Augie if things are peaceful."

"Let's do it."

He gulped and stood rock still. "You can't. . .you can't go in there. Not now."

"What do you mean, *Sheriff?*"

"I mean that ladies don't go in there on Saturday night." It came out louder than he'd intended.

Trudy's eyes, dark, stormy gray in this light, sparked up at him. "What's the difference? Saturday night, Sunday noon, it's the same place."

"Yeah, but. . ."

"Same people running it."

"Well, yes."

"And I'm a deputy sheriff."

"I can't deny it."

"Then let's go."

It dawned on him suddenly that she wanted to see the place. "Uh, Trudy, have you ever been inside?"

After a moment's silence, she shook her head.

"Never ate Sunday dinner here?"

"Nope. Hiram and I usually stick to home on Sunday. I don't think my brother's ever been inside either saloon."

"Uh. . .I don't think you should go in. For all the reasons you never have before."

She held his gaze for a long time. At last she exhaled and reached up to settle Hiram's hat lower on her brow, shadowing her eyes. "Lots of women go there on Sunday."

"I know. And if Hiram wants to take you, he can."

She nodded, her lips tightly compressed. "All right. I'll wait here. Get going."

He patted her shoulder awkwardly. "Thanks. I won't be long."

Ethan bounded up the steps and entered the saloon, determined not to leave Trudy standing in the street more than a minute.

Two men came out of the Spur & Saddle. Gert eased back into the shadows under the overhang of the eaves. They lurched down the steps and headed for the hitching rail. After untying his horse, one couldn't seem to get the momentum he needed to bounce into the saddle. He led the horse over to the steps and mounted from the second stair. They never saw her but turned their horses toward the road that led out past Harpers' farm.

Gert left her place of concealment and walked to the hitching rail. She didn't recognize any of the horses for sure, though one compact dun looked a lot like the one Starr Tinen rode to the shooting club. Maybe her husband had ridden into town to hear the piano music. She curled her lip and patted the dun's sleek neck. "It's not your fault if your owner has bad habits."

Across the street, a solitary figure left the boardwalk and

came toward her. Gert backed up until she stood once more in the shadows beneath the saloon's eaves. With her brother's hat pulled low, she watched from beneath the brim.

The man paused and looked northward, the length of Fergus's principal street. Perhaps he considered visiting the Nugget instead of the Spur & Saddle. He faced toward her, his thin shoulders slouched. Mayor Walker. His friend Cy Fennel was down at the Nugget, by Ethan's account. Still boycotting Bitsy's establishment. As Walker approached, Gert shrank down and hoped he didn't notice her.

He reached the boardwalk before the saloon and lifted his foot to the first step. Gert noticed movement beyond him. Down the street, between the closed telegraph office and the old haberdashery, a dark figure stepped out from between the buildings. He stood still. She wondered if he was as indecisive as the mayor on where to buy his whiskey.

She saw a flash of light. The bang of a gunshot cut through the air and echoed off the fronts of the buildings on the far side of the street. Mayor Walker spun around and fell on the steps. Gert's heart squeezed, and she couldn't breathe. She wanted to duck down behind the stoop, but she couldn't take her eyes off the dark shadow that flitted toward the prone man. Would he shoot again to make sure the mayor was dead?

Without thinking of her danger, she jumped up and dashed to the front of the steps. She was a deputy sheriff. If he wanted to make sure he'd done the job right this time, he'd have to go through her.

"Leave him alone!" She threw herself to her knees beside the mayor.

The other man stopped several yards away. Light from the windows glinted off the barrel of his pistol. For a moment, Gert feared he would shoot at her. Why, oh why had she listened to Ethan and left the rifle home?

He gaped at her. His dark hat shadowed his face, and she couldn't see his features, but it looked like he'd tied a dark cloth over his mouth and chin. He raised his other hand over his head and thrust it toward her as though throwing something.

Everything happened so fast, Gert barely noticed the men pouring out the door of the Spur & Saddle. All she could take in was the mayor lying on the steps gasping, the small *click* as a tiny object hit the stair tread beside his body, and the shadowy man fleeing down the boardwalk. He ran to the horses tied before the telegraph office. In a flash, he had unhitched Storrey's paint horse and leaped into the saddle. Gert turned her attention to the mayor. He sucked in a big breath and shut his eyes. The other man disappeared with only staccato hoofbeats testifying to his flight.

"Trudy! I heard a shot. What happened?" Ethan crouched beside her. "Is that the mayor?"

She looked up and nodded. Her eyes filled with tears, multiplying the images of a dozen men who stood above her, staring.

Augie thundered down the steps with a linen towel in his hand and knelt by Walker's other side. He pulled back the mayor's jacket.

"He's bleeding bad." Augie stuffed the towel over the wound. "I think he's breathing."

Ethan looked up at the other men and singled out Ezra Dyer. "Go get Bitsy. Ask her where we can put him."

"Sure thing, Sheriff." Ezra turned and clumped through the throng.

Ethan slid his arm around Gert's waist. "Are you all right? What happened?"

"The penny man," she gasped.

He stared at her. "Wh—you sure?"

She nodded. His strong arm felt so warm and reassuring, she didn't want to move. But she had to, before they lost track of the evidence. She leaned across the mayor's body and picked up the small object by Augie's boot. It had bounced off the step above, spun, and lodged against the stair riser. She held it up to Ethan.

He turned his palm upward, giving her a place to drop the penny.

★ CHAPTER 33 ★

Cyrus ran up the middle of the street. Long before he reached the Spur & Saddle, he was gasping. When had he gotten so out of shape? He didn't work as hard as he used to on the ranch or in his mining days. Now he mostly sat around his office all day. Suddenly the run from the Nugget to Bitsy Shepard's place was too much for him. He slowed down near the telegraph office and pressed one hand to his chest. No sense bringing on heart failure.

Parnell Oxley dashed past him. The young ranch hand had burst into the Nugget with news that the mayor had been gunned down outside the Spur & Saddle. Ted Hire, the Nugget's bartender, followed Oxley. Twenty or more men crowded around the front entrance of Bitsy Shepard's saloon. Cyrus shoved aside two at the fringe.

"Let me through." He halted, staring at the tableau on the steps. It was true. Charles Walker lay sprawled as though he'd fallen on the steps in midstride. Augie Moore hovered over him, and on the other side, Gert Dooley sat on the bottom step with the sheriff beside her. Cyrus glared at Ethan. "What happened here?"

Ethan stood and pushed his hat back. "Mr. Fennel. We're about to move the mayor inside where we can tend him."

Cyrus pushed past another man and went to his knees by his friend's head. "Charles, can you hear me?" Walker moaned, and relief coursed through him. Cyrus wasn't prepared to lose the one man he called a true friend.

The mayor's eyes flickered open. "Wh. . .what happened?"

The sheriff leaned in close and laid a hand on his shoulder. "Someone shot you in the belly, Mr. Walker. We're going to take you into the Spur & Saddle. Miss Shepard's getting a room ready. Then we'll see if Annie Harper will come look at you." Annie not only served as a midwife, but in the absence of a doctor, she was known as the person best at sewing up knife cuts and setting bones.

Mayor Walker lifted one hand and grasped the front of Ethan's vest. "No! Don't take me in there. Orissa will have cats. Take me to my own house. It's not far."

"He's right," Cyrus said. He wasn't sure Orissa would stoop to entering the saloon on a Saturday night, even to see her gravely injured husband.

Ethan looked questioningly at Augie.

"I can lug him that far," Augie said. "He don't weigh more'n a magpie."

Bitsy appeared in the doorway, and the men parted for her. "We got the room all ready, Sheriff. Did someone go for Annie? And what about Mrs. Walker?"

Ethan said, "Change of plans, Miss Shepard. The mayor's talking, and he wants to go home. Sorry we put you out."

Bitsy waved her hand. "That makes no nevermind. Did you send one of the fellas to tell his wife?"

"Yes, ma'am. And then on to the Harpers'."

Augie slid his meaty arms beneath the mayor's slight form. The lamplight gleamed off his bald head. "Hold on, Mr. Mayor. I'm going to pick you up now."

"Let me help you," Cyrus said.

Augie shook his head. "The best way to help me is to run ahead and make sure his missus knows we're bringing him over there."

As the brawny man rose with the mayor in his arms, a wail reached them from the east side of the street.

"Not my Charles! Oh why? Why?" Orissa Walker, a black crow crying doom, swooped toward them.

Cyrus saw his duty and reached her in the middle of the street before any of the others moved.

"Orissa, calm yourself." He reached for her arm.

"Is he dead? Tell me."

"No, my dear. Far from it. Now, be quick and get his bed ready. They're bringing him home, and Annie will be here soon to help you care for him."

"Oh me!" She put both hands to her face and sobbed. "What shall we do? Is it bad?"

"I don't know." Cyrus swallowed hard, but the ache in his chest had worsened. "I think perhaps a prayer would not be amiss." He took her hand and drew it through the crook of his arm. Augie walked toward them with his burden. Ethan and Gert came behind him. "Miss Dooley," Cyrus called, "would you kindly inform my daughter of the reason for my delay?"

Gert stopped walking. "I can do that."

Cyrus nodded and turned back to Orissa. "Come," he said gently. "Let's get things ready."

"You need to tell me everything you saw," Ethan said to Gert. "I'll send someone else to tell Isabel."

"Send Bitsy so she won't be frightened." Gert shivered. She reached to fasten the top button of her jacket. "You need to go after the man who did it."

"Did you see where he went?"

She lifted her hand toward the north end of the street. "He jumped on a horse and galloped off toward Mountain Road."

Ethan dashed up the steps to the Spur & Saddle and spoke to Bitsy. She ducked back inside, and he turned at the top of the steps, in the light. "Gentlemen, prepare to ride out with me. We need a posse to go after the man who did this. If you're sober and you have a horse and a weapon, prepare to leave from the livery stable in ten minutes."

As he came down the steps toward her, the men dispersed, and Bitsy and Vashti hurried out of the saloon, spreading shawls about their shoulders. They headed together down the boardwalk toward the Fennel House.

Ethan reached Gert's side. "Walk with me as far as your house, Trudy. Tell me on the way what you saw."

"He was all dressed in black. I was standing there, behind the steps." She swiveled and pointed to the spot beyond the hitching rail where a half dozen men were preparing to mount. "The mayor reached the steps, and this man came out of the alley yonder. I couldn't see him well—just that someone else was coming. Then he fired a gun, and the mayor fell." She stopped walking in front of the telegraph office. Her throat burned as she recalled the moment. "He was right about here when he did it. I don't think he saw me. He started walking toward the mayor, and I jumped up. I was afraid he'd shoot Mr. Walker again."

"Oh, Trudy." Ethan slid his arm around her and pulled her close for a moment. "You shouldn't have done that."

She leaned away from him. "I'm the law, Ethan, same as you. I wasn't going to let him do worse than he'd done. I suppose if I'd stayed put I might have seen him more clearly, but then the mayor would be dead for sure."

"I expect so."

"That's when he threw the penny. I think now he was maybe just coming closer to leave it by Mr. Walker's body, but at the time. . ."

"Hey! Where's my horse?"

They both whirled toward the hitching rail. Ralph Storrey stormed down the boardwalk toward them. "Sheriff, someone's up and stolen my horse."

"When I yelled at him, he threw the penny then grabbed the nearest horse and galloped off," Gert said to Ethan. "It was Mr. Storrey's paint. He rode that way, at least as far as the smithy. After that, I don't know."

They all turned and stared northward. Several horsemen already trotted toward the livery stable.

"I'll ask Griffin if he saw anyone ride by," Ethan said.

"I'll ask Bane to loan me another mount," Storrey said. "If I lose that horse—" He stomped off down the street.

Gert took a deep breath, certain her next request was doomed. "Ethan, I want to go with you."

"No." He kept his arm around her, pushing toward home.

"I'm a deputy. And I saw him do it."

"No."

Bitsy, Vashti, and Isabel ran up the boardwalk toward them.

"Sheriff, is the mayor going to live?" Isabel grabbed Ethan's arm and clung to it.

He cleared his throat. "Well, Miss Fennel, I don't know. He's over at his own house, and your father's with him. You might want to go see if there's anything you can do. I'm raising a posse to go after the man who did it."

"We'll see her safely to the Walkers' house," Bitsy said. "Is the shooting club riding with the posse?" She looked eagerly to Gert.

Gert gazed at Ethan. "Please?"

"I can't let you ladies come. But you can do a lot of good here. Help Mrs. Harper with the mayor. The men riding with me can leave their women and children there so they won't be alone while we're gone. Gather the ladies in, won't you, Trudy?"

Gert felt her face flush. The whole town would know before morning that the sheriff had a nickname for her.

"Yes, we'll do it."

Bitsy, Vashti, and Isabel left them to hurry across the street and south to the Walkers' house.

"Now tell me quick," he said to Gert. "What did he look like besides dark clothes?"

She squinted her eyes almost shut, picturing the penny man in the shadows. "He wasn't as tall as you, nor as fat as Oscar Runnels." She looked up into Ethan's eyes and nodded. "He was young. At least he moved fast. I'm sorry I can't tell you who he was."

Ethan squeezed her hand as they reached the path to her house. "You've done fine."

Hiram came from the back of the house.

"Gert, is that you? What's going on? I heard a lot of commotion."

"The mayor's been shot."

"You want to join the posse?" Ethan asked. "I'll fill you in when you get to the livery with your horse and gun."

Hiram turned on his heel and bolted for his corral behind the house.

Parnell Oxley ran toward them diagonally across the street.

"You coming, Sheriff? Griff Bane says someone rode past the livery hell-for-leather on a paint horse."

"I'm right behind you." Ethan touched Gert's sleeve for a moment. "Don't stay here alone. Get over to Walkers'. If you go out to bring other women in, go by twos and threes." He hesitated a moment then pulled her to him.

His lips met hers, and fire shot through her. This was all wrong. He couldn't kiss her and then rush off to hunt down the killer. He might not return, and—

"Be safe, Trudy." He turned and ran after Parnell for the livery.

★ CHAPTER 34 ★

Libby held her pearl-handled revolver in her hand when she went to open her door. Gert stood on the landing outside.

"Did you hear? The mayor's been shot."

Libby sighed and lowered the pistol. "I wondered what it was all about."

"Come over to the Walkers' with me," Gert said. "Ethan's taken a posse after the shooter, and I don't want you here alone."

"A posse? They know who did it?"

"I saw him." Gert's mouth was set in a grim line.

"Who?"

"I don't know. I was waiting outside Bitsy's for Ethan. The killer came out of the shadows over by the telegraph office and shot Mr. Walker. Then he stole Ralph Storrey's horse. Ralph's madder than a wounded grizzly. I wanted to ride with the posse, but..." Her face contorted in a grimace. "We may be deputies, but we're still women. Come on. And bring your gun. I don't have one."

"Would you like to carry my Peacemaker? I've got the little Smith & Wesson now."

"I'd feel easier," Gert admitted, and Libby ran for the weapon and her cloak.

A half dozen women had gathered in the Walkers' kitchen. Apphia Benton met Gert and Libby at the door and told them in hushed tones that Mrs. Walker, Mrs. Harper, and the minister were with the mayor.

They milled about, talking quietly. Myra Harper and Ellie

279

Nash took over the cookstove and made coffee and gingerbread for any who wanted some. Libby kept several pans of water boiling in case Annie called for it. After half an hour, Annie emerged from the bedchamber, asking for clean rags. Libby and Gert searched about but couldn't find anything that looked the least bit frayed.

"Typical of Orissa," muttered Ellie. "Here, take this." She handed Annie a clean linen towel.

"How is he?" Libby asked.

"Not good. I'm afraid the bullet's done more damage than I can undo. If we had a surgeon. . ." Annie shook her head and went back into the bedroom.

A knock sounded on the door, and Libby hurried to open it. Emmaline Landry with Starr Tinen, her little girl, and her mother-in-law entered.

"Micah rode off with the sheriff's posse," Emmaline said as she removed her bonnet. "He told me to get the Tinen ladies and come here, as Arthur Tinen and his father were with the posse, too."

"They'd gone into town right after supper," Starr explained. She stooped to help four-year-old Hester untie her bonnet strings. "I was looking for Arthur to come home, and here came Emmaline with word to fort up at the mayor's house."

Emmaline shrugged. "I wasn't entirely sure what was going on. Micah wouldn't stop and tell me everything. Just that the killer had shot Mayor Walker, and the posse was going to ride him down. Told me to get to town and stay here until they come back."

"Did a single horseman ride past your place before that?"

"Not that I saw," Emmaline said.

"Me either." Starr gave Libby a pouty face as she stood. "We'd have been as safe at the ranch, now that Ma Tinen and I know how to shoot."

"Oh well," said Jessie Tinen, Starr's mother-in-law. "It's a chance to see the other ladies." She took her granddaughter's hand and walked with Hester toward the kitchen door. "So, tell me, is the mayor killed?"

"No." Libby nodded toward the closed door of the bedchamber. "But his condition is grave. Annie Harper and Mr. Benton are seeing to him, but it doesn't look promising."

"Dear, dear." Jessie shook her head.

As they entered the kitchen, the other women greeted Emmaline and the Tinens. Florence drew Starr into a corner for a gossip, and Ellie offered refreshments to the newcomers.

Gert paced back and forth between the wood box and the pitcher pump that loomed over one end of the cast-iron sink. The Walkers were one of the few families to have a pump in the house, and Libby tried to squelch her envy each time she looked at it.

She cornered Gert near the wood box. "Should we make a foray to the emporium? If they need more bandages..."

"I could go with you if you like." Gert's eagerness told Libby she chafed at the confines of Orissa's kitchen, no matter how modern the furnishings.

"Let me ask Annie if they need anything else."

Libby went to the bedroom door and tapped softly. Mr. Benton opened it. Beyond him, Orissa Walker sat stiffly at her husband's bedside, her white face more pinched than usual. Libby's heart wrenched for her. Annie's broad back bent over the swathed figure on the bed. At her feet rested a wash basin full of bloody water and drenched cloths.

Libby murmured to the pastor, "Miss Dooley and I thought we'd go together to my store and fetch anything that's needed here. I've some soft cotton Annie could use for bandages, and perhaps she could use some peroxide or salve." She shrugged, trying to think what other medicinal supplies she had in stock. She had yet to replenish some of her inventory since the fire.

Mr. Benton consulted Mrs. Harper and returned with a short list of items the nurse thought would be useful. When Libby reached the front hall, Gert waited for her. Light spilled from the door of the front room, and the gentle murmur of Apphia's voice reached them.

"They're praying," Gert whispered. "Mrs. Benton suggested it, and they've all gone into the parlor."

Libby snatched her cloak and handbag from the coat tree near the door.

"It frets me that Emmaline didn't hear anyone ride past her house before the posse came," Gert said as they went out into the cool evening. "I saw the shooter ride off, and Griff saw him go past the livery. That's the last anyone knows for sure about where he went."

"There's not much out there but a few ranches." Libby took out the key to the store.

"What if he cut off across country or circled back? He could be anywhere now."

"You mustn't worry." They reached the store, and Libby unlocked the door. They spent the next ten minutes gathering a basket full of supplies for Annie. Libby added a pound of tea and a small sack of sugar. When they left, Gert looked carefully about before they stepped out onto the boardwalk. The street was silent and dark except for lights from the two subdued saloons and the few houses on Main Street. Gert kept the Peacemaker in her hand as they walked.

"I think we should tell the others about the pennies."

Libby eyed her in surprise. "You mean the one on my counter after the fire and the one Ethan found near Bert Thalen's body?"

Gert nodded. "There was one near Milzie's body, too. My brother found that one. And. . .well, there've been others you probably don't know about."

Libby's pulse beat faster, and her throat squeezed. "When?"

"After the warehouse fire, and again tonight."

"No."

"I'm afraid so. This killer has been using the mayor for his latest target."

Libby slowed her steps. "And Ethan knew this?"

"Not specifically. Until tonight, I mean." Gert's mournful expression and ragged voice tugged at Libby's heart. "We've talked about how this outlaw seemed to be going after important people in the town. You, Bert, Cyrus. And now Mr. Walker."

Libby nodded slowly, thinking back over the last two months. "Cyrus because of Milzie being killed in his office."

"Yes. And Isabel saw a man loitering in the alley there, too."

"I remember. She and Cyrus came to tell me about it." Libby

shivered. "So you think he was lying in wait for Cyrus, not for me or Isabel."

"The more I think about it, the more I believe that."

"It's almost a relief to hear you say that—it means he probably wasn't planning to do me bodily harm. Although the fires. . ." She studied Gert's profile as they approached the Walkers' dooryard. "What would he have against Cyrus? And me and Bert and Mayor Walker, for that matter?"

"That's what we need to find out. I think it's time we brought the rest of the ladies in on this."

"How can they help?"

Gert reached to touch her arm, and they stopped walking before the front steps. "We need to figure out who's doing this. If the men don't catch up with him, he'll kill again."

Libby stared into her friend's troubled eyes. The lamplight from the window of the Walkers' front room illuminated Gert's face.

"My dear, you saw the mayor attacked tonight. You've had a shock."

"No, Libby, listen to me." Gert's voice cracked, but she went on earnestly. "I should have been able to put a name to the killer. I saw him. True, his face was hidden. I tried to help Ethan by describing the man's size and clothing and demeanor. It didn't help. Now, Ethan is a fine man, and a fairly clever one, don't you think?"

"Yes, dear, he's a very fine man."

Gert nodded and chewed her lower lip for a moment. "But if he and Hiram and I can't figure this out, we need more people. Different folks come at things from different directions."

Libby could see that nothing short of a powwow would calm her young friend. "All right, let's go in and talk to the ladies then. If the posse can't solve this case, perhaps the Ladies' Shooting Club can."

Ethan sent two men to check on the Robinsons and rode onward. Only one more homestead on this road before it petered out in the hills. Milzie Peart's. A few minutes later, he and Hiram pulled up next to the burned-out cabin. A dozen men thundered in behind them and reined in their mounts.

"When did this place burn?" Griffin asked.

"Sometime this spring." Ethan looked toward the hillside. "We'd best check the old mine, but I don't see any horse."

Hiram dismounted and dropped Hoss's reins. Ethan and Griff climbed down to join him. Ethan turned to address the other men.

"Wait here. There's a cave yonder, and we'll check it."

A minute later they stood to one side of the entrance. Hiram sniffed the air. Ethan quirked his eyebrows at him, but Hi shook his head.

"I've got matches," Griffin said. An instant later, a small light flared up in his hands.

"There's candles inside." Before Ethan could stop him, Hiram scurried into the cave. The light flickered out, but Hiram reappeared in the entrance as Griffin lit another match. The gunsmith held out a short stub of candle, and Griffin put the match to the wick.

"If he were in there, he'd have shot us by now," Ethan noted.

"Sorry." Hiram ducked his head.

"Not the most brilliant thing you ever did."

They walked into the cave together, with Hiram holding the candle high. A quick survey told them the cave was empty, and nothing appeared disturbed.

"Let's go." Ethan led them outside again. As they descended the path to the waiting posse, the two men he'd detailed at the Robinsons' rode up.

"No one's been by there until we came," Parnell Oxley called.

Ethan bent and caught Scout's reins. He looked up at the starry sky, thinking. *Lord, show me what to do.*

"We're wasting time," Griffin said. "He could be anywhere by now."

Cyrus urged his mare over closer to Ethan. "Suppose he cut off by my ranch and rode west."

"Could have, I guess," Ethan said. "Or he could be up in these hills."

"No sense going up there in the dark," Micah Landry growled.

"What now?" asked Zach Harper. "Head back to town?"

"Hate to do that." Ethan rubbed his scratchy chin. He looked around at the men. "How about if we split up? Half keep going this direction, and half go out the Owyhee Road?"

"He coulda lit out for Reynolds," Augie Moore put in.

"Yes, he could have." Ethan sighed. Probably the smartest thing would be to head back to Fergus. Most of the ranchers along the way had been alerted. The posse could go out in the morning and try to pick up the trail. He doubted they would. If they hadn't trampled the outlaw's tracks, they'd be mingled indistinguishably with the other hoofprints on the dusty roads.

"Gentlemen, I don't know as we have much chance of finding this fellow tonight," Ethan said.

"He's got my horse," Ralph Storrey called.

"I haven't forgotten that." Storrey's ranch was on the south side of town, in the opposite direction to the one the outlaw had taken. Ethan puzzled over what little he knew.

"Let's at least go out by my place," Cyrus said. "We can ask if anyone out that way heard a rider go past."

When no one presented a better plan, Ethan lifted his boot to the stirrup and swung onto Scout's back. "All right, let's go."

"So the sheriff's been collecting all these pennies from the crimes and trying to figure out who left them?" Starr's eyes shone with the challenge.

"That's right." Gert faced all the women in the Walkers' parlor and wondered if she'd made a wise decision. "I hoped the Ladies' Shooting Club, and you other ladies, too," she said, nodding deferentially to Bertha Runnels and Jessie Tinen, "could help us out. Seems to me, if we all put our heads together, we should be able to tell who the killer is."

"Well, he's not one of the posse," Goldie said. She'd come over from the Spur & Saddle with a bottle of whiskey. Miss Shepard thought they might need it for the mayor, she'd explained. Apphia had gingerly accepted the bottle and carried it to the bedchamber as though she held a wriggling snake between her fingers.

"Now, that's a good thought." Gert pointed her index finger at

Goldie. "See? I knew this would be helpful."

"So, who was in the posse?" Ellie Nash asked.

"And who did you see at the Spur & Saddle after the outlaw rode away?" Myra added.

Libby jumped up. "Excellent! Let me get a pencil and a sheet of paper, ladies. We can make a list of men we know are innocent."

Gert exhaled, feeling as though a huge rock had rolled off her chest. It wasn't the same as naming the killer, but eliminating the better part of the town's residents might bring them closer to the truth.

She looked around at the rapt faces. "All of you be thinking while she gets it."

A minute later, Libby returned with a piece of brown wrapping paper and a pencil. She settled down on the settee next to Apphia, who handed her a book to use as a lap desk.

"All right," Libby said. "Gert, you were there. Tell us which men you're certain this infidel is *not*."

"Well, Ethan Chapman, for sure. And Ralph Storrey. His horse was stolen." Gert lowered her eyebrows, mentally counting the men who had poured out of the saloon. "Augie Moore. Ezra Dyer. Mr. Tinen—junior and senior. Uh. . .Parnell Oxley. One of the Storreys' ranch hands. Mr. Runnels. . ." Gert's gaze caught Goldie's. The girl seemed barely able to contain herself. "Of course, Goldie was there, too. She might be able to tell us who was *inside* the Spur & Saddle when the shooting took place."

Names spilled out of Goldie's mouth faster than Libby could write them down. "Mr. Colburn, Maitland Dostie, Josh Runnels, Nealy and Clem Higgins. A drummer that came in on the Boise stagecoach. That feller who's got a mine down the river. Micah Landry and the ranch hand Miss Dooley mentioned. Buck, they call him."

"Well!" Gert felt a new admiration for the girl. "Anyone else?"

"Hmm. . ." Goldie's brow furrowed. "Of course, Miss Bitsy was there, and Vashti and me."

"Do you think it could have been a woman?" Florence asked. Everyone stared at her.

"I. . .I don't think so." Gert wished she could state emphatically that the killer was a man.

"All right," Libby said, scribbling the last of the names. "If anyone else can positively give someone an alibi, tell me now."

Most of the women quickly vouched for themselves and their husbands.

Isabel cleared her throat. "What about my father?"

Gert winced. "He came soon after the shooting. I believe he was. . .at the other end of town when it occurred."

"Yes, I expect you're right." Isabel's face was stricken. "I had two customers take rooms at the boardinghouse today. One was the salesman that Goldie mentioned. The other was an older gentleman who went to his room as soon as he'd had supper. Bill Stout was going to sleep there tonight, too, but he'd gone out."

"Probably to the Nugget," Gert hazarded. She wondered if the saloon girls on that end of town could give her a list of patrons.

Hester Tinen had fallen asleep on her mother's lap. Starr curled a lock of the little girl's hair around her finger as she spoke. "You know, we can't rule out anyone who was at the Nugget tonight. Unless they vouch for each other, that is."

Isabel shrank down in the corner of the sofa.

Gert pressed her lips together. She wished she could shout out, "Your father is innocent, Isabel." But she couldn't do that. She doubted Cyrus's guilt now, but could she say that for certain? And could the shooter have ridden out of town then sneaked back to join the posse? She rejected that idea. Storrey's horse was still missing, after all.

Silence hung over them for an agonizing moment. Gert inhaled deeply. "I don't think the man I saw was Mr. Fennel. Of course, I can't be certain, but Mr. Fennel is a tall man. As is Griffin Bane. When the killer mounted Mr. Storrey's horse, I didn't have the impression of an overly large man. And I'm sure I'd have recognized Mr. Bane's build, so I've ruled him out as well."

"He's quite distinctive, isn't he?" Bertha asked. A chuckle rippled through the room.

Gert nodded. "He is."

"What was this thing you mentioned about pennies?" Myra asked. "The sheriff has found a penny after each killing?"

"Yes," Gert said. "After the fires at the emporium and the mayor's warehouse, too. There are five now. One from Sheriff Thalen's murder, one from Milzie Peart's, and the one the man threw tonight. It landed on the steps of the Spur & Saddle next to Mayor Walker." Would Ethan be upset if she revealed the rest? Gert gulped and said as calmly as she could, "All five were minted in the same year—1866."

"That's a long time ago," Starr said.

Florence nodded. "The year I was born."

Libby cleared her throat. "They're common though. Gert and I have discussed this some. I didn't come to Fergus until a few years after that, but my husband was here then. I can't think of anything Isaac ever told me that could be connected to these crimes. We wondered if any of you older ladies can recall what went on in town that year. Did something happen that would make this person angry?"

At that moment, Annie and Orissa entered the parlor, and all the ladies fell silent.

Apphia stood and walked toward them. "How is the mayor?"

"He's resting," Annie said. "The pastor is sitting with him. I thought it would do Orissa good to have a cup of tea and something to eat."

"I'll get it." Ellie rose and hurried toward the kitchen.

Orissa's skin was stretched tight over her face. Even her hands were pale. Apphia took her arm and guided her to the spot she had vacated on the settee.

"We've been praying for your husband, and for you, my dear." Apphia squeezed her hand.

"Thank you. Annie is optimistic."

All eyes turned to Annie for confirmation.

"Yes," she said. "It's a serious wound, but none of the vital organs seems to be hit. We've got the bleeding stopped, and he's resting easier. We'll see what a good night's sleep will do for him."

Orissa looked around at all of them. "What was it you were discussing when we came in? Something about the town's history?"

Everyone looked to Gert. She nodded. "We were saying how the people who've been attacked by this outlaw all seem to be among the town's founders. The sheriff has some clues that point to something in the past—something that perhaps happened in 1866."

"Charles and I were here then," Orissa said. "Do you think it's someone who's carried a grudge for near twenty years?"

"It could be."

Ellie came in with a tray and took tea and a few cookies to Mrs. Walker.

"That was the peak of the gold frenzy," Bertha said. "My husband and I came the next year. The mines were already starting to play out."

"Yes. Fergus was a lawless place back then." Orissa reached for the teacup. "A thousand men would come to town every weekend."

Libby said, "We've asked all the ladies to think about what the town was like then. There were several businesses that have closed since, and the boardinghouse was in its heyday."

"The stamp mill over to Booneville had begun operating," Bertha said. "A lot of ore passed through there."

"My family was here," Isabel said quietly.

Something clicked in Gert's mind. She glanced over at Libby. "Ladies, think about this. Isaac Adams was here in 1866. A few weeks ago, his widow's business was set afire. Cyrus Fennel was here that year. Milzie Peart was killed in his office. Mayor Walker was here. Both his business and his person have been attacked."

Bertha clapped her hand over her mouth. "Cyrus, Charles, Isaac. . .they were all here when we moved to town. Of course, Charles wasn't the mayor then. He started out mining, didn't he, Orissa?"

"Oh yes. They all did. Cyrus took over the assay office in '65, I think. My husband gave up mining soon after. It didn't go as well as he'd hoped. But we'd saved enough to build a decent house and start a business." She nodded and took another sip of tea.

Gert frowned, reaching for something. "What about Bert Thalen? Was he here in '66?"

"And Milzie Peart," said Ellie.

"Well. . .I'm not sure it's so important when Milzie arrived."

"But she was killed," Starr said, her brow furrowing.

"Yes, but. . ." Gert swallowed hard. "Right now my theory is that the outlaw didn't set out to kill Milzie. He only did it because she got in his way."

"In Father's office," Isabel said.

"Yes. The sheriff and I both think the killer was waiting in there to ambush Mr. Fennel. Poor Milzie went in, and he attacked her instead."

"If that's what happened," Goldie said soberly, "then the same person killed her as shot the mayor and killed the old sheriff, but not for the same reason."

Gert nodded. "That's my thinking, all right. So why did he do these things? What made him go after Bert? And the mayor and Mr. Fennel?"

"And what about Griffin Bane?" Starr asked.

"He came to town later," Libby said with certainty. "After Isaac and I had married. He bought the smithy, and later on he took over the livery, too."

"Libby doesn't fit in," said Apphia. "From what you've told me, the killer has attacked men who were here during the town's boom years. Libby told me she came about twelve years ago and married Mr. Adams then."

"That's right," Libby said. "We were married in 1873. But Isaac had already stopped mining and established the emporium."

"That's why he didn't kill you," Emmaline said. Several jaws dropped, and she hurried to explain her thoughts. "Suppose this killer was angry at your husband. Isaac was already dead when he came, and it was too late for revenge. Maybe he thought he'd do something bad to you, his widow, but not. . ."

"Not as bad as he's done to the others," said Myra.

"If what you're saying is true, my father is in grave danger." Isabel's gray eyes pinned Gert. "That man tried to kill him and failed, perhaps more than once. He succeeded with Sheriff Thalen, and the mayor lies in grave danger under this roof. Isaac Adams is already dead. My father could be next."

Gert's mouth went dry. "That's so. And Cyrus went with the posse."

"Yes. He insisted on helping find the man who shot his old friend." Isabel's lips trembled, and she clamped them firmly shut.

Gert nodded. "I fear you're right. If anyone is in danger tonight, it's Mr. Fennel. So...what did those four men all do to cause such hatred?"

"There were a lot of gold strikes in the early years," Orissa said, her eyes unfocused as she looked back over the years. "The first miners came here in 1862 or '63, I think. Charles heard about it, and we got here in the fall of '63. I'm not sure if Bert Thalen was already here, or if he came the next spring—there were a lot of rough men about, and I stayed close in our lodgings that winter. But Bert and Charles met by spring and became partners."

Gert sat up straighter. "Business partners?"

"They had a claim together with..."

"Why, yes," Libby said. "Now that you mention that, I recall my husband telling me about it once. Isaac was in on a mining claim with the mayor and Mr. Thalen. And Cyrus, too. Isn't that right?"

Orissa nodded. "Yes. All four of them invested in a tract down the river. They thought they'd strike it rich. They sluiced out a fair amount of gold, but nowhere near as much as the few really rich claims you'd hear tell of. They each put away a stash and bought some land."

"Who owns the claim now?" Gert asked.

"I don't know." Orissa looked blankly to Libby.

"They sold it, didn't they?" Libby asked.

"Yes, I'm sure they did."

"When Isaac died, the only property I found a deed for was the emporium building and the lot it's standing on." Libby met Gert's gaze. "But if the four men owned a claim together and sold it, there must be a record of it."

"My father might have something," Isabel said, and all eyes swung her way. "He kept the assay office until business dropped so much they closed the one here. Now they go through Silver City, but he has old records in the safe at his office."

"Now, hold on just a second," Jessie Tinen said. "Arthur and I came here the year our son turned seven. Sixty-five. Right after

Arthur got home from the army."

Again the ladies fell silent. The Civil War had barely touched Idaho Territory, but those who came from points east remembered it well.

"Now, there was a big to-do, I recall, about a mining claim." Jessie sucked in her ample cheeks and frowned. "Some fella made a big fuss over it. He'd bought a claim that was supposed to be a good one, but it turned out to be worthless. Arthur decided then and there not to try mining. We bought our ranch and started working it."

A stir of excitement flickered in Gert's stomach. She turned to the mayor's wife. "Mrs. Walker, can't you remember the name—"

Orissa's face had turned ashen. She stared at the far parlor window and spoke a single word. "Morrell."

★ CHAPTER 35 ★

Morrell?" Libby and Gert locked gazes across the crowded parlor. Libby voiced what everyone was thinking. "There's Jamin Morrell, but he only moved here last year."

"The family. . ." Orissa spoke quietly in the stillness. "The man had a scrawny wife and a little boy thin as six o'clock."

Gert's eyes took on a resolve that made Libby shiver. "Did anyone see Jamin Morrell when the posse rode out?"

Goldie shook her head. "He could have stayed at the Nugget."

Gert leaped to her feet. "I'm going over there."

Libby gasped. "To the Nugget?"

"That's right. We need to get to the bottom of this."

"But my dear. . ." Apphia faltered.

"What will you do?" Myra asked.

"First, I'll see if he rode out with the posse."

"And if he's still there?" Libby asked. "We haven't any proof that he's mixed up in this business. The name could be a coincidence."

"I'll ask him if he has anything to do with it." Gert's eyes flashed a stormy gray.

"I'll go with you." Goldie stood and eased past the knees of the other women.

"Me, too," said Emmaline.

Myra began to rise, but her mother laid a restraining hand on her sleeve. "You'll stay here," Annie said, and Myra sank back into her chair, scowling.

Isabel stood and eyed Gert with a challenging air. "I shall come with you."

Gert nodded. Without speaking, Libby got to her feet.

"We five," Gert said. "That's enough. The rest of you stay here with Mrs. Walker."

"We shall be praying," Apphia said.

They stepped out into the yard. A chilly breeze off the mountains fluttered Gert's hair, and she regretted not grabbing her despised bonnet after she gave Hiram back his hat when he left to join the posse. She buttoned her jacket over the butt of Libby's pistol, now tucked firmly in the waistband of her skirt. Libby, Emmaline, Isabel, and Goldie followed her out of the house.

The five of them spread out and strode side by side down the quiet street. Libby walked closest to Gert, between her and Emmaline. Uneasily, Gert wondered if they ought to have a better-defined plan.

The sound of distant hoofbeats brought her to a halt. The other women stopped and listened. As far away as she could see in the black tunnel of the street where it passed between the Nugget and the smithy, a white patch materialized.

Isabel let out a muffled squeak. They all stood still, staring and shivering.

The horse's outline became apparent as it trotted nearer. Gert relaxed and walked forward, her hand extended toward it.

"Whoa, boy." The paint horse stopped a few yards from her and snuffled. Gert walked up to him and caught one trailing rein. "There, now. Take it easy." She stroked his neck, and the horse rubbed against her shoulder.

"Where did it come from?" Libby asked.

"This is Ralph Storrey's horse," Gert said. "The one the killer stole. I don't know where he's been, but he's just moseying toward home. Good fella."

"Should we hitch him up?" Emmaline asked.

Gert considered the options. "Ralph was here when the mayor was shot. Laura's likely still at their house south of town, not knowing what happened. If the horse comes home with an empty saddle, it'll scare her."

"Let's hitch him here," Libby said. "When the posse comes back, maybe the sheriff will want to look him over for evidence."

Gert nodded. A month ago, she'd have laughed at that idea. Now it seemed very reasonable.

After she'd secured the horse at the nearest hitching rail, the five women moved on down the street, past the telegraph office, the emporium, the feed store, the jail, and the boardinghouse.

Only two horses were tied up in front of the Nugget. At the steps, Gert hesitated a moment. Someone inside plinked out a spare rendition of "I'll Take You Home Again, Kathleen." Voices murmured, and glass clinked on glass, but for a Saturday night, the Nugget seemed pretty tame.

Gert lifted her foot and marched up the stairs to the double door, with Libby close behind her. The others followed in their wake.

When Gert shoved the door open, the four people inside stared at the women. All sounds ceased.

Gert tried to see everything at once. In the lantern light, rough tables and chairs filled the sawdust-covered floor. Spittoons sat in strategic corners. A cowboy leaned on the piano, and a raven-haired girl in frothy red and silver taffeta lace sat before it, gaping at the women in the doorway. A bearded old man sitting at a table to one side froze with a glass halfway to his lips and stared.

Straight ahead was the bar. Behind it stood a girl with golden hair, resplendent in flounces of shimmery blue satin, pouring whiskey into a glass. When she saw the women enter, her flaming red lips parted.

"M–Mrs. Adams. Ladies. May I help you?"

"Hello, Opal." Libby walked toward the bar as though she habitually visited the saloon girls at the Nugget. "We wondered if Mr. Morrell is in tonight."

"No, he. . .he went out some time ago. There was a ruckus at the Spur & Saddle, I understand." Opal's eyes flicked from Libby to Gert and beyond. When her gaze rested on Goldie, her lips flattened.

Gert edged up beside Libby. The cowboy came over and leaned on the bar, watching them.

"So Mr. Morrell rode out with the posse?" Gert asked.

"Well. . ." Opal didn't meet her gaze.

Gert looked over at the girl near the piano. "Was your boss here when you heard about the shooting?"

"Uh. . .I'm not sure." The dark-haired girl glared at Opal as though blaming her for letting these disruptive women in.

"Ted was pouring," Opal said quickly. "A cowboy came in shouting that the mayor was killed and the sheriff was raising a posse. Every man in here ran out. Including Ted."

"And Mr. Morrell?" Gert asked again, pronouncing each word distinctly.

"I. . ." Opal glanced sideways to the other girl, but she was no help. She'd come over nearer the bar and stood caressing the cowboy's mustache and smiling at him. "I'm pretty sure he went, too. I haven't seen any of them since." Opal nodded toward old Pan Rideout, the miner sitting alone in the corner, and threw another glance at the cowboy down the bar. "These two came in later. I figured we were done having customers tonight, but I guess these fellas live south of town and hadn't heard about the killing."

"The mayor's not dead," Gert said.

Opal's eyes widened. "Oh? Well, that's fine then. Guess we won't need to hold an election for a while."

Libby smiled graciously. "Rumors do get around, don't they? Mr. Walker is very much alive."

Gert squeezed close to the bar and leaned over toward Opal. "What was Mr. Morrell wearing tonight?"

Opal blinked at her. "Wearing? You want to know what the boss was wearing?"

"That's right."

"Uh. . ."

A curtain shielding a doorway behind the bar fluttered, and Jamin Morrell stepped through it.

"Ladies. I'm speechless."

Gert straightened. Behind her, the other women caught a collective breath.

Morrell walked forward to Opal's side. "Pour me a drink, sweetheart."

Opal finished filling the glass she'd set down earlier and handed it to him. Gert wondered if she'd been fixing it for him all along. Had he been hiding in the back room, listening to every word? If so, why had Opal lied?

Morrell tossed back a big swallow of whiskey and set the glass on the bar.

"Now then, ladies. To what do I owe the dubious honor?" His dark suede waistcoat hung open, and his black shirt, unbuttoned at the neck, held wrinkles and smudges of dust. His stubbly jaw clenched as he watched them. His hard gaze slid past Gert and assessed her four companions.

Goldie stepped forward before Gert could speak. "This here's a contingent of the Ladies' Shooting Club of Fergus, mister. And Deputy Gert Dooley has a few questions for you."

Morrell's eyes narrowed, and he raised his chin a tad. "Don't you belong at the other end of the street? If you're looking for different employment, I'm not hiring."

"I ain't looking. I wouldn't work here if you paid me double."

"Hush, Goldie," said Emmaline.

Morrell's gaze shifted back to Gert. She tried not to squirm as he studied her with a bit of speculation in his dark eyes. The other club members moved in around her. She felt stronger with them at her back.

"Would you care for a drink, Miss Dooley?" he asked.

"No. I want to know why you're not with the posse."

His eyebrows shot up. "Nothing like getting to the point, is there?"

"No, sir, there's not."

"My bartender and every customer who was in the place an hour ago charged out of here to ride with the sheriff. Someone had to stay and guard my business and my...other employees."

Gert's anger nearly choked her. She didn't take her eyes off him. "Opal said you went with the sheriff and the rest, but it seems she was wrong."

"She must have forgotten that I was out back going over the

accounts. Or maybe she just didn't tell you." He shot a glance Opal's way. "My employees guard me from frivolous interruptions."

Libby gasped at his rudeness, but Gert let out a short chuckle. "However you want to paint the picture, my friends and I want to know where you were when Mayor Walker was shot."

"Thank you for being so concerned about my activities." Morrell tipped the bottle up and poured himself another hefty drink. "Sure you won't join me?"

"Answer the question, Mr. Morrell," Gert said stonily.

"I've already told you. I've been here since suppertime. Ask Flora." He nodded vaguely toward the dark-haired girl who still stood next to the young cowpoke.

Gert glared at him across the bar. A hot mass churned in her chest, making it hard to inhale. "You're a liar."

"Am I?" Morrell took a swallow of the whiskey.

"Your family came here twenty years ago," Gert said with certainty. "Your pa bought a claim that was worthless. You and your folks suffered. And now you've come back, aiming to hurt the people who took your pa's money and make them hurt worse than you did."

His face hardened as she spoke. Gert's pulse accelerated, and the air in the saloon thickened.

"You don't know anything about me. I came here a year ago to start a business. I've tried to be an upstanding citizen of the community. I've made contributions to the town coffers. I influenced a preacher to come here, even though I knew it might hurt my enterprise. I even offered to serve on the school board, but the town councilors didn't think I was good enough."

His voice dripped bitterness and Gert shivered, watching him toss back the rest of the whiskey.

"That upset you, didn't it? That people didn't think a saloon keeper should be on the school board. This town owes you a lot, doesn't it? You've been paying back the men who sold your father that mining claim, making them suffer."

"You have no idea how much I suffered," Morrell said in a deadly quiet voice. "My father worked himself to the bone and died of pneumonia. If my mother's heart hadn't given out, she'd have starved to death. You have no idea what we went through because of the fine leaders of this town. Now get out of here."

Gert held his stare. "No, sir. Mr. Morrell, I'm afraid we're going to have to arrest you for the murders of Bert Thalen and Millicent Peart, and the attempted murder of Charles Walker."

"And the fires," Emmaline said in her ear. "Don't forget the fires."

Gert nodded. "The fires at the Paragon Emporium and the Walker Feed Company, too."

Morrell let out a short laugh. "Oh, ladies. How exactly do you intend to take me into custody?"

Gert put her hand to her jacket's top button. She ought to have prepared for this before they set foot inside the Nugget. Seeing only the saloon girls and two customers inside had thrown her off her guard. She pulled in a deep breath as she quickly undid her jacket's buttons and reached inside for the Peacemaker. Before she had the pistol out, Morrell had stooped behind the bar and straightened again with a double-barreled shotgun in his hands.

"All right, ladies. Don't move. Miss Dooley, I suggest you put that thing on the bar and back up a few paces. This shotgun can kill you and three or four other women quicker than you can spit." His gaze roved over the women. "Uh-uh." He moved the shotgun a hair, so that his sights covered Goldie. "Just leave that peashooter alone. I must admit, that's a shapely leg it's strapped to. Maybe I *could* find a place for you here."

Gert caught a glimpse of Goldie's chagrined face as she let the flounce of skirt fall back over her garter with its little holster. She wouldn't be able to use her weapon either. Libby's gun was no doubt still in the bottom of her handbag. Gert doubted Emmaline or Isabel was armed tonight. It was up to her.

"I'm sure we can end this peaceably, Mr. Morrell," she said. "Put the shotgun away."

"You're the sharpshooter, aren't you? Put your gun on the bar, Miss Dooley. Let's see your hands up high."

Gert shot a sidelong glance at Libby. She stood still, her shoulders squared, but her lips trembled.

"Come on," Morrell coaxed. "If I let loose with this load of

299

buckshot, every one of you will be killed or maimed. You know what it can do. Now all of you get your hands up where I can see them."

Gert couldn't swallow the painful lump at the back of her throat. Libby raised her hands slowly. Others stirred behind her. *Oh, Lord, what have I gotten us into? We could have done this so much better.* "Couldn't we sit down and talk about this?" Her voice quivered, and he smiled.

"I think we're beyond chitchat. Hands up."

Gert lifted her hands.

Without looking away, Morrell called, "Flora, take Miss Dooley's weapon."

The girl walked over hesitantly and squinted at Gert. She touched Gert's dark jacket, found the pistol, and yanked it out. Stepping back, she laid it on the bar before Morrell.

"Thank you. And now the one this little dove has under her skirt." He nodded toward Goldie. Flora lifted Goldie's hem and retrieved the small pistol.

Morrell walked around the end of the bar and skirted the group, still holding the shotgun pointed at them. "Get out, Pan. The Nugget's closed for the evening."

Pan Rideout stared at him. "But I ain't finished."

"Get out!"

Pan's face crumpled into his bushy beard. He slid out of the chair and staggered toward the door, muttering, "Man can't have a few drinks. . ."

"You, too, Jake."

The cowboy turned and stalked toward the door without another word.

"All right, now." Morrell had worked his way around the group so that he stood between them and the door. He waved the gun's barrel, indicating that the women should separate. "Mrs. Adams, please step over there, near that table."

Libby hesitated and then took a few steps.

"Miss Fennel, you, too."

Isabel stood rock still for a moment. Gert was afraid she would swoon, but she took three wooden steps and stopped next to Libby, who slipped her arm around Isabel's shoulder.

"And I think I'll keep Miss Shepard's little spitfire, too. That woman's done everything she could to keep my business from succeeding." He winked at Goldie. "Over yonder, darlin'."

Goldie swept past him, her head high, and turned to stand, arms akimbo, next to Libby and Isabel.

Morrell smiled. "Oh yes. That's quite a tableau." He glared at Gert and Emmaline. "You can go. I expect the sheriff will be gone all night out in those hills, but if you see him, tell him I'm square with Fergus now. I intended to bring Cyrus Fennel down, too, but I'll take his daughter with me instead. If he comes after her, I'll deliver what I've wanted to give him for years."

Isabel's cheeks flamed, and she wobbled. Libby tightened her hold on the young woman and leaned close to whisper in her ear.

"What are you going to do?" Gert determined not to leave the other women in his power.

He only smiled, but his expression quickly turned to a snarl. "I'm going to finish what started almost twenty years ago. The men who ruined my family won't be laughing up their sleeves anymore. Now get out!"

Gert could see that standing toe to toe with him would do no good. She grabbed Emmaline's arm and pulled her toward the door.

"We can't—" Emmaline began.

"We have to," Gert hissed as she practically tossed the woman through the double door.

Emmaline caught her balance and narrowly avoided pitching down the steps into the street. Gert seized her hand and drew her down and away from the light. Pan Rideout sat on the edge of the bottom step muttering, "I didn't finish my drink yet."

"What are we going to do?" Emmaline wailed.

Gert swallowed hard. "I'm thinking. If the men come back..." She glanced futilely toward the smithy and Mountain Road.

"What if they don't? We can't wait."

"You're right. It sounded like he's going somewhere. He might force them to leave town with him."

"Yes, or he might abuse them."

Gert winced. She didn't like to think that, but Emmaline was right. Every minute counted. "Come on, let's get some help."

Emmaline ran with her down the street toward the Walkers' house.

Across the way, the front door of the Spur & Saddle opened. Bitsy came out carrying a lantern. Vashti followed bearing a basket over her arm. Bitsy closed the door behind them, leaving her saloon dark and silent on a Saturday night for the first time in more than twenty years.

Gert pulled up in the middle of Main Street, panting.

"Well, Gert," Bitsy said pleasantly, walking toward her. "What are you doing out? When Goldie didn't come back, Vashti and I decided to go over to the Walkers' house and see if there's anything we can do."

"We need your help," Gert said.

Bitsy's brow wrinkled so deeply that she looked her age despite her cosmetics. "What is it?"

"Jamin Morrell is the killer, and he's holding Goldie and Isabel and Libby inside the Nugget."

"He threw Gert and me out," Emmaline said. "He says to tell the sheriff he's square with the town now."

"What did he mean by that?" Bitsy asked.

Emmaline sniffed. "He said his parents died after they left here. He blames the town of Fergus."

"I'll explain it all later," Gert said. "Right now we need to help those women."

Bitsy looked down the street, where light spilled out of the Nugget. "Yes. You can count on me."

"I don't know what he aims to do," Gert admitted. "I suspect he'll pack up and skip town before the posse gets back."

"But. . .will he take the women with him?"

"I don't know. He said to tell Cyrus they were even now. Cyrus was one of the men who cheated his father, and I'm afraid he might do something horrible to Isabel. I'm not sure about Libby and Goldie."

"We've got to act quickly; that's certain." Bitsy turned to Vashti. "Here, take the lantern and the food to the mayor's house.

I'm going with Gert."

"Can't I come?" Vashti asked. "Goldie's in there."

Gert touched the girl's arm. "Go to the Walkers' and tell Mrs. Benton and the others what happened. Tell as many as have weapons to meet us down near the Nugget. But everyone has to be careful and keep quiet."

"Yes, ma'am." Vashti hurried across the street toward the mayor's house.

Bitsy turned around, hiked her skirt up, and removed her Deringer from her garter. She tucked it beneath the folds of her shawl. "Ready, Deputy Dooley."

Gert smiled grimly and nodded at her, wishing she hadn't lost Libby's pistol. "Let's go then." Her voice cracked a little, and she cleared her throat.

★ CHAPTER 36 ★

Jamin Morrell watched Gert push Emmaline out the door, then swung the shotgun barrel back toward the other women. Isabel sobbed, and Libby pulled her closer.

"God is in control," she whispered to Isabel.

"Flora," Jamin said.

"Yes, Mr. Morrell?"

"You and Opal go on upstairs and pack my things for me. There's a bag in my wardrobe. I've got the wagon ready out back."

"We're leaving?" Flora asked. "Where are we going?"

"Just go do it."

The two girls hurried past him and up the stairs. Halfway up, Opal caught Libby's eye. Her face held such distress that Libby began praying silently for her. She wondered if they could somehow distract Morrell long enough for her to get her pistol out of her handbag.

Morrell laughed. "Oh yes, indeed. You ladies don't need to worry about your baggage. I'll outfit you when we reach our destination."

"Where are you taking us?" Goldie asked.

"To a new town. I've had enough of Fergus. I've purchased a business in another place, and I expect to have a much nicer saloon than this one. Better than that place down the street. And I'll have you three ladies to help me run it."

Goldie scowled at him. "You can't make us go and work for you."

"I can't?" Jamin shrugged. "In your case, I'd think you'd be glad.

304

It will be an improvement in your station."

"I doubt it." Goldie looked about the Nugget. "This place is a pigpen."

"Oh, but I'll have a lot more to invest in the new one," Morrell said. "Mrs. Adams and Mr. Fennel are both going to kick in a significant investment in my new enterprise."

Libby found her voice at last. "You'll let us go if we do?"

"Did I say that?" He looked her over and smiled in a way that made Libby feel like a mouse that stumbled into a fox den. "Fennel will give me every cent he's got in hopes of getting his daughter back." He glanced at Isabel, and his smile faded. "Maybe I will give her back. She hasn't got the looks or the carriage you have. But you, Mrs. Adams. . ." He eyed her figure again, and Libby shuddered. "Yes, I think you'll be a nice addition to the place."

"Then why should I pay you?" she gasped.

"You don't have a choice. We'll visit the bank you patronize in Boise before we head for the new location."

Goldie tossed her head. "I ain't going with you."

He threw his head back in a laugh. "Tell me that in six months."

"The people of this town won't let you carry us away," Libby said.

"Oh, you mean the good sheriff and his friends?" Morrell scratched his head and drew his eyebrows together as though thinking hard. "Let me see, didn't every man in town ride out a couple of hours ago, looking for a phantom killer? I doubt we'll see them before morning. But just in case, we'll get moving."

Flora came down the stairs dragging a large portmanteau.

"Where's Opal?" Morrell asked.

"She's packing away a few things for her and me." When she reached the bottom of the stairs, Flora straightened. "What now, Mr. Morrell?"

"Leave that there. You get out of here, Flora."

"What. . .what do you mean?"

The double doors swung open. "Hey, what's a man gotta do to—"

Morrell swung around and fired the shotgun without hesitation. Pan Rideout flew backward out the doors.

Gert, Bitsy, and Emmaline stopped when the report of a gun echoed down the street. Pan Rideout's body catapulted off the steps of the Nugget and several yards beyond, into the dirt.

Without a word, Gert picked up her skirt and ran to the old man. Tears streamed down her face as she knelt beside him.

"Mr. Rideout! Pan!"

His eyelids lifted slowly, and he frowned up at her. "I ain't even finished my drink yet."

Emmaline slid to the ground on the other side of the miner. Bitsy stood at Gert's shoulder, aiming her Deringer at the doors of the Nugget.

"How bad is it?" Bitsy asked.

"Hit him in the leg," Gert said. "Maybe the stomach, too. There's some blood on his shirt. But I'd say two or three pellets got his leg."

Pan's mouth opened wide. He stared up at her for a moment in silence then howled. His eerie shriek reverberated off the storefronts. "Owww! He done shot me! Owww!"

Emmaline put her hands to her ears. Gert leaned over the old man and grasped his shoulders firmly. "Hush, Mr. Rideout. We'll help you, but you've got to keep quiet."

"Am I killed?"

"Not yet. Now let us get you over to my house. It isn't far." Gert looked up at Bitsy. "Think we can carry him over there?"

Bitsy nodded up the street. "Help's coming. I'll send Vashti for some blankets, and we'll get a bunch of women to lug him."

The yellow gleam of a lantern approached from the far end of Main Street. Gert peered into the dimness and made out a dozen women hurrying toward them, their skirts swirling.

Florence and Vashti reached them first, with Vashti bearing the lantern.

"What happened?" Florence asked.

"That snake Morrell shot Pan Rideout for no reason at all,"

Bitsy said. "He's got Mrs. Adams, Miss Fennel, and Goldie in the Nugget. Says he's keeping them."

"Not Mrs. Adams!" Florence's face paled, and the flock of women behind her erupted in shocked exclamations.

Gert stood. "We've got to help Mr. Rideout first. He's bleeding a lot. Morrell was loaded with buckshot." She spotted Apphia in the group. "Mrs. Benton, will you take charge of him, please?"

"Of course." Apphia stepped forward.

Gert's spirits lifted. The Ladies' Shooting Club would work together as a team. "Get five or six women to help you carry him to my house and care for him there." Apphia nodded. "And Myra—"

"Yes'm?" Myra said eagerly.

"Run ahead to my house. Go in the back door. It's not locked. There's a lantern on the kitchen table with a box of lucifers beside it."

"Here, take this lantern," Vashti said.

"Good. Bring back the quilt off my bed." As Myra dashed off toward the Dooley house, Gert scanned the group. "Who can run back to the Walkers' and fetch bandages?"

"I can," said Vashti.

"All right. Ask Mrs. Harper if she can leave the mayor in the reverend's care long enough to examine Mr. Rideout. Go."

Vashti dashed off the way she had come.

"The rest of you, listen up," Gert said. "How many of you ladies of the shooting club have your weapons?"

Several said, "I do."

"Good. I'll need you. We're not letting Morrell take Libby or Isabel or Goldie out of the Nugget. That means we need to cover the front and back doors."

"What's the plan, Gert?" Starr asked.

Gert frowned. "Mostly to keep him from leaving. If he steps foot outside, we arrest him. If he resists. . ." She hesitated, wondering how it would end and what evil Morrell might do before then. Reason told her he wouldn't stay long for fear the posse would return and trap him. Blocking his flight seemed the only good option.

Bitsy cleared her throat. "We all know that Gertrude Dooley is the best shot in the Idaho Territory."

The others murmured their assent.

Bitsy looked down at the Deringer in her hand. "My little gun isn't very good in this situation, but it's better then nothing. Gert, I suppose your brother took his Sharps rifle with him?"

"Yes, he did," Gert said.

"Who here has a rifle?"

A dark-clad figure eased through the crowd, and Gert recognized Orissa Walker.

"Mrs. Walker! I didn't realize you were here."

Orissa held out a rifle to her. "When the girl from the...when Miss Vashti told us there was trouble, I figured you might be needing this. My husband can't wield it tonight, but there's no one else who can use it as well as you, Miss Dooley. I'd be honored if you'd take it to defend our town."

Gert reached out and took the rifle and a box of ammunition from her. The mayor's Winchester wasn't as fine as Cyrus's Spencer rifle, but she knew she could use it to advantage. Her brother mounted a new sight on it for Walker just weeks ago. If she remembered right, it fired a little right of center.

"Thank you, ma'am." The tears rose in her eyes once more. "I appreciate it."

Orissa nodded. "Unless you feel I can be of assistance, I believe I'll go back to my husband now."

"You do that," Gert said. "Ask Mr. Benton to pray for a peaceful resolution to this."

She and Bitsy divided the armed women into two companies. Bitsy took her group around to the back of the Nugget. Gert and her troop stayed out front, aiming their weapons at the doors while Apphia and her contingent carried Pan Rideout away.

Stillness descended on Fergus. In the starlight, Gert stared at the saloon's windows. Now and then she saw movement within. What was Morrell doing? A dim light in an upstairs window went out. She moved to where she could see the stairway inside. Opal came down carrying a carpet bag, with several smaller bags slung over her shoulders.

Morrell handed the Colt Peacemaker to Flora and lowered his shotgun. He laid it on the bar and walked deliberately over to the three captives. Libby shuddered and tried not to think about what he had just done. She had no doubt he would kill her and her two companions if they made him angry. She tried to pray, but her pleas felt more like inward screams.

He stopped in front of her and studied her face for a long moment then smiled. "Oh yes, we'll have some good times together. I think you'll like California."

Libby returned his gaze with a stony glare. Isaac had told her once that her eyes could freeze the Snake River when she was angry, which wasn't often.

Morrell turned to Isabel. His expression turned thoughtful as he reached out to push back a strand of her brown hair. "Not too attractive, but I daresay with the right clothes and some lip rouge, you'll do." He laughed. "Your father is so arrogant, I think this may be the best revenge after all. I had planned to pay him one more visit before I left town, but this is much better. I can't thank you enough for coming to me tonight. He'll be so humiliated when he learns you decided to go with me."

He ran his finger down Isabel's cheek, and she cringed against Libby.

"Leave her alone," Libby said. A rush of anger crashed through her.

"Oh no. It's time for us to leave. We want to put a lot of miles between us and the men of Fergus before morning. This way, ladies." He gestured toward the curtained doorway.

Again Libby sent up a silent prayer. Her hope lay in Gert. Where was she now? Goldie caught her eye. What was she thinking? The two of them could survive rough treatment, but what about Isabel?

"Move," Morrell shouted. He grabbed Isabel's wrist and yanked her toward the doorway.

Isabel stiffened and raised her chin. "I won't go one step with you."

309

"I think you will."

"I'd rather die."

Morrell paused an instant then let out a soft chuckle. "Would you?" He turned and took the Peacemaker from Flora's shaky hands.

Libby no longer cared whether she emerged from the Nugget unscathed. She hauled her handbag around by the strap. As she fumbled with the clasp, Morrell deliberately raised the pistol and aimed it at Isabel. "Your father won't like this solution either. Are you sure you don't want to go?"

★ CHAPTER 37 ★

Gert stood flattened against the outside wall of the saloon beside the front window. She heard Morrell's icy words. She moved cautiously so she could see through the dusty glass.

Morrell stood holding Libby's revolver aimed at Isabel. To Gert's amazement, Libby was pawing in her French handbag, no doubt going for her pistol. The dark-haired saloon girl, Flora, saw her and reached for the shotgun on the bar. Libby would be too late. And would she even pull the trigger?

Gert put the muzzle of the mayor's rifle up, almost touching the glass, and sighted.

Morrell slowly and deliberately pulled back the Peacemaker's hammer. "Last chance to come along nicely, Miss Fennel."

As Libby tugged out her Smith & Wesson, Flora hefted the shotgun and yelled, "Drop it, lady! Drop it now, or I'll shoot!"

As Morrell whirled toward Libby, Opal slung one of the bags she'd brought downstairs at Flora.

A gunshot exploded inside the saloon. Flora staggered and crashed into Goldie. Libby raised her pistol as Morrell caught his balance and focused his aim on her.

Gert aimed just a little left of his buttons and squeezed the trigger.

★

The column of men rode back into town just before dawn. Weary to the bone, Ethan drooped in the saddle. Several of the ranchers had dropped out and headed for home. Hoss plodded lethargically along beside Scout. Hiram sat on his back, swaying a little with Hoss's gait.

The street was quiet, and all the buildings on the north end were dark. Even the Nugget was silent.

"I wonder if the mayor's still alive," Ethan said.

Hiram nodded, his lips pressed tightly together.

Ethan pulled gently on the reins and turned Scout. The other men moved their horses up close to him. "Thank you all for trying. I'm going to catch a few hours' sleep, and I suggest you do the same. I'll head out again around noon and see if I can find anything we missed in the dark. Anyone who wants to join me, come to the jail then."

As the men said good night to each other, Hiram stiffened in his saddle. "Ethan, look."

"Hmm?"

Hiram pointed toward the Nugget.

"What is it?"

Hiram didn't answer, so Ethan studied the building's facade. The first rays of sunlight hit the front window to the right of the door, but the window on the left was a dull, dark hole.

"Someone took out the window." Ethan stared at it. "Must have gotten wild last night after we left."

"Sheriff, there's a light on at the jailhouse," Augie Moore called.

Ethan swung around to look toward the jail. Sure enough, a soft glow outlined the small window. Down the street, a horse neighed, and he stared at it for a good five seconds before he was sure his exhausted brain told him the truth. He turned and scanned the posse for Ralph Storrey.

"Ralph, looks like your horse is tied up about where you left it last night."

Ralph rode forward on his borrowed horse and stared toward the telegraph office. He put his heels to his mount's sides and trotted down the street toward the pinto.

Hiram cocked an eyebrow at Ethan. "What do you think's going on?"

"I dunno. But I intend to find out who's in my office."

Ethan swung down and tossed Scout's reins to Hiram. His back and legs were stiff with fatigue. He hadn't spent all night in the saddle since the last war. He limped to the walk before the jail, limbering up a little with each step. By the time he reached the door, he walked normally. He pulled his pistol from its holster and pushed the door open.

Trudy.

She sat slumped in his chair with her head cradled on her arms atop the desk. A rifle lay before her on the desktop, with the jail cell key beside it. The kerosene lamp burned low on its hook above her, casting a shimmer on her hair. As he crossed the threshold, she flinched, then sat up, blinking.

"Well! Sheriff Chapman." She stood with a crooked smile.

He walked over to her and stood looking down into her soft blue gray eyes. "Hey, Trudy." He wished more than anything that he had good news. He wanted to tell her they'd caught the killer, and that she and all the people in Fergus could feel safe now. He swallowed hard. "I'm sorry. We rode all night, but we lost him. Lost him early. He's just...gone."

A slow, shaky smile curved her lips. She put her hand up to his stubbly cheek. "You may have lost him, Ethan, but we found him."

"What?" He eyed her cautiously. "What happened? I saw Ralph's horse tied up, and the broken window at the Nugget."

"Your killer is lying on the floor over there beside the bar. It's Jamin."

Ethan drew in a slow breath. "Jamin Morrell."

Trudy nodded. "I'll tell you all about it."

A riot of questions sprang to his mind. He caught her to him and held her in his arms. "Trudy, Trudy. Are you all right?"

"Yes." She sneaked her arms around his waist, and he lowered his cheek to rest on top of her head.

In the shadows, a throat was cleared. Ethan straightened and stepped away from her, peering toward the jail cell.

"Oh, and the Ladies' Shooting Club brought you a couple of prisoners," Trudy said.

He walked over to the cell door and gazed in at the two girls from the Nugget. The dark-haired one sat on the edge of the bunk, glaring daggers at him. The light-haired one—Opal, wasn't it?—stood with her arms folded and a put-upon air.

"You going to let us out of here, Sheriff? I helped them get their friends away from the boss."

Trudy came softly over and stood beside him. "We disarmed them and locked them up for you to deal with. I don't know how big their part was in the crimes, but they were helping Morrell get ready to leave. He was going to take Isabel, Libby, and Goldie with him."

"Take them where?"

"California, apparently. He planned to make Libby empty her bank account for him in Boise first. He was going to make them work in his new saloon. But Isabel refused to go, and he was going to shoot her." Trudy's voice cracked. "Ethan, I'm so glad you're home."

He turned and folded her in his arms again, ignoring the two women observing. She sobbed and hung on to him. "Sweet Trudy," he said. "I'm going to have to hear the whole story, but right now, we'd best go tell your brother you're all right."

"Oh, if he's gone home, he'll know." Trudy lifted her head and swiped at her eyes. "Pan Rideout's in his bed."

"What?"

"Jamin shot him, too."

"Eth?" Hiram stood in the doorway. "Well, hi, Gert. Everything all right?"

"Why don't you step outside with me and Hiram?" Ethan said to her. He kept one arm firmly about her waist as they walked to the door and out to where Scout and Hoss were hitched. The rest of the men had scattered to their homes or gone to the mayor's house for their wives. The street was quiet once again.

"The ladies caught the killer," Ethan told his friend.

"I peeked through the Nugget window," Hiram admitted. "That your shooting, Gert?"

Her eyes clouded. "Afraid so. With the mayor's rifle. It wasn't my first choice, but Morrell would have killed Libby." She gritted her teeth and looked forlornly at her brother. "It wasn't such a good idea to confront him like I did."

Hiram nodded soberly. "The mayor going to make it?"

"We think so, and Pan Rideout is, too, but they'll both be laid up awhile. He's over to our house, Hiram."

"What happened to him?"

"He got in Morrell's way."

Hiram stepped closer and touched her shoulder. "You gonna be all right?"

She nodded and sniffed. "Yes, but I wouldn't want to go through last night again. Annie did wonders with the patients, but I'd be more hopeful if we had a doctor."

"Morrell told me last week he'd written some letters and hoped we'd get a physician to move here soon," Ethan said.

"Oh, and here we are patching up the people he shot while we wait."

Hiram said, "Well, he got us a good preacher."

"True. And do you know why he did it?" She looked from him to Ethan.

They both shook their heads.

"He wanted to be a big shot in town, like Cyrus and the mayor. But it wasn't enough. People still didn't respect him, even though he'd tried to act like a pillar of the community." Her shoulders drooped for a moment.

Ethan studied her tear-streaked face. She must feel as appalled as he had after his first battle against the Bannock. Maybe they could talk about his war experience after all. They might even be able to comfort each other. He tightened his hold on her just a little, and she looked up.

"You fellows must be hungry," she said. "Come on. I'll make some flapjacks."

"What about the prisoners?" Ethan asked.

"Prisoners?" Hiram's eyes widened as he looked at his sister once more.

She chuckled. "I'll send Deputy Shepard over to keep an eye on them while you have breakfast."

★ CHAPTER 38 ★

Church services began on time Sunday morning, though several benches were empty and many members of the congregation had eyes red from lack of sleep. Mrs. Walker stayed home with her husband, and Annie Harper sat with them. Several of the posse members were also absent.

Hiram and Ethan sat down on each side of Trudy, trying to hide their yawns behind their hands. Neither had shaved that morning, but she didn't mind.

Libby paused at the end of their row on her way in. Ethan stood stiffly.

"Good morning, Sheriff." She smiled at the Dooleys. "How's Pan doing?"

"Holding his own," Trudy said. "Bertha and Oscar Runnels volunteered to sit with him this morning. If his wound doesn't get infected, they plan to move him to their house tomorrow."

Libby nodded. "That's good. And Trudy, you look lovely today."

As her cheeks warmed, Trudy realized she was no longer Gert. She had begun to think of herself as Trudy, too. Ethan's eyes swept over her, she could tell without looking up. She smoothed the skirt of the light blue muslin dress Libby had persuaded her to buy.

"Yes, you do," Ethan said. "Very nice."

Trudy's cheeks blazed, and she was glad when Libby turned her focus back to Ethan.

"Are you going to let the girls from the Nugget go, Sheriff?"

316

Ethan gritted his teeth and shrugged. "I'm not sure yet. I'd like to talk to you later about what happened last night. Trudy says Flora helped Morrell when he kidnapped you ladies, but Opal helped you escape."

"I believe she did. It happened awfully fast at the end."

"Uh, would you like to sit here?" Ethan asked, stepping into the aisle.

"Thank you, but. . ." Libby's gaze shifted toward the doorway, and she smiled. "I believe I'll sit with Bitsy and her girls. I'll speak with you later, Sheriff."

"Bitsy came?" Trudy turned her head and watched in satisfaction as Bitsy, Vashti, and Goldie settled with Libby two rows behind them. Isabel Fennel crossed the threshold with her father and clung to his arm as they walked toward their bench.

Pastor Benton stood up and walked to the pulpit. Dark shadows rimmed his eyes, and he smiled wearily.

"Greetings, brothers and sisters. Our town has endured great trials, but God has sustained us. I'm happy to report that Mayor Walker is resting this morning, with no fever. We're in hopes he'll recover from his wound in time. Mr. Rideout was also wounded, as most of you know. His injury is less severe, and we expect him to make a good recovery. One other announcement—I've placed an order for hymnbooks, and Mrs. Adams tells me they should arrive in a couple of weeks."

As the congregation sang "Amazing Grace" from memory, Trudy sent up another prayer of thanks. The pastor's sermon on love for one another touched her deeply. She'd seen the people of Fergus move from separate, self-centered households to caring individuals and families watching out for one another. As she listened, she felt blessed beyond anything she deserved, having gained a new love for the women of the town and being seated on the rustic pew between the two finest men in Fergus.

After the benediction, they filed out into the blistering sun.

Trudy caught up with Bitsy before she could hurry away.

"I'm glad you came."

Bitsy smiled with a shrug that set the pheasant's feather in her hat bobbing. "It wasn't so bad. I may make a habit of it. Of course,

I've got to hurry now and prepare for the dinner crowd. Augie's been on his own the last hour, and I expect he'll need us."

Hiram and Ethan came to stand beside Trudy as she watched Bitsy and the two brightly clad girls scurry toward the Spur & Saddle.

Hiram's gaze shifted to the south end of the street. "Looks like a rider coming in."

As others filed out of the haberdashery building behind them, they stood watching until the bay horse had brought its rider close to them. The man stopped the dusty mare in the street and gazed at the crowd of people emerging from the old store in their Sunday best. Several bags were strapped to the cantle and sides of his saddle. The man looked tired. He homed in on Ethan and smiled through a couple of days' growth of beard.

"Good morning, Sheriff. Is this the town of Fergus?"

"Yes, sir," said Ethan. "Can I help you?"

"Why, yes. I've ridden all night. Is there a hotel?"

Ethan nodded down the street toward the Fennel House. "The boardinghouse is right yonder."

He looked where Ethan pointed and smiled. "Ah. That sounds adequate. I suppose I could have waited for tomorrow's stagecoach run, but I was eager to get here. And. . .I'm looking for Mr. Morrell. He invited me to come."

"Oh?" Ethan looked at the Dooleys. Hiram shrugged, and Trudy frowned. Ethan said to the stranger, "What is your name, sir?"

He leaned down and extended his hand to Ethan. "It's Kincaid. Dr. James Kincaid."

"Praise God," Trudy murmured.

Ethan released the man's hand and shoved his hat back. "Well, Doc, you've come to the right place. I hope you're not too tired, because we can put you right to work."

Trudy laughed. "One of the patients is at my house, just a few doors down, Doctor. Would you care to take a look at him and join us for dinner?"

Hiram said, "Go on ahead with him. I'll take care of his horse."

"That sounds wonderful," the physician said.

Trudy nodded in satisfaction. "Good. And after dinner, Sheriff

Chapman can take you around to meet the mayor. He's the other patient."

As Kincaid dismounted, Ethan reached for Trudy's hand. She let him hold on to it as they led the doctor toward the Dooley house.

Discussion Questions

1. Ethan Chapman doesn't want to be sheriff. He's shocked when the town fathers choose him for the job. But within weeks he is reluctant to give up the position. Why has he changed his mind?

2. Orissa Walker is known to be a proud woman, but others are not immune to this flaw. How does Gert's pride manifest itself in the story? Do you see a change in her attitude toward Cyrus? Isabel? Milzie? Bitsy? Others?

3. How does the Ladies' Shooting Club help Gert, Libby, and the other women think differently about their neighbors?

4. What reasons do Hiram, Libby, and others have to resent Cyrus? How much of this was brought on by his own actions? Do you feel Isabel was justified in rebelling against her father? Was she right to work in the boardinghouse? To insist she keep her school?

5. How does Ethan tread the line between smoothing the mayor and town councilors' feathers and doing what he feels is right? How could he have done better?

6. Ethan sees Gertrude as two separate people: plain, practical Gert and sweet, lovable Trudy. When he grieves over his army experience, close-lipped Hiram advises him to take God at his word and move on. How does this help him in his relationship with Gert/Trudy and let them merge into one? And should Hiram perhaps take his own advice?

7. Why are the town fathers embarrassed when the new minister assumes Jamin Morrell is chairman of the pulpit committee? Do their relationships with the saloon owners change after the minister arrives?

9. How do Gert and Libby decide who gets to join the shooting club? Why is the act of joining so divisive? Was Pastor Benton right to allow Apphia to join?

10. Too late, the ladies begin to help Milzie. How does Gert's approach differ from Libby's? From Apphia's?

11. Bitsy tells Ethan, "I don't think God is ready for me yet." How would you have responded?

12. Some of the residents of Fergus seem to live contradictory lives. Augie Moore, who is Bitsy's bartender and cook, owns one of the few Bibles in town. Many of the faithful churchgoers spend Saturday night at the Nugget or the Spur & Saddle. Gert and Hiram, both believers brought up in a Christian home, spend Sundays alone and silent for years, and it seems they have rarely mentioned their faith to others. How critical is it that the outward life match the inward? How did the town's history contribute to this discrepancy? What changes did you see in any of the townspeople?

★THE GUNSMITH'S GALLANTRY★

★ CHAPTER 1 ★

Fergus, Idaho
May 1886

Wait, Hiram!"

The gunsmith paused on the board sidewalk and turned around.

Maitland Dostie left the doorway of his tiny office and shouted at him, waving a piece of paper. "Got a message for ya."

Hiram arched his eyebrows and touched a hand to his chest in question.

The gray-haired telegraph operator smiled and clomped along the walk toward him, shaking his head. "Yes, you, Mr. Dooley. Just because you haven't had a telegram in the last five years and more doesn't mean you'll never get one."

Hiram swallowed down a lump of apprehension and reached a cautious hand for the paper. "What do I owe you?"

"Nothing. It was paid for on the other end."

It still seemed he ought to give him something, but maybe that was only if a messenger boy brought the telegram around to the house. Hiram nodded. "Thanks. Where's it from?"

"Whyn't you look and see?"

Hiram wanted to say, "Because if it's from Maine, it's probably bad news." His parents were getting along in years, and he couldn't think of a reason anyone would part with enough hard cash to send him a telegram unless somebody'd up and died.

But Hiram rarely spent more words than he had to, and Dostie had already gotten more out of him than usual. Besides, if someone in the family had died, the telegraph operator would know it. Wouldn't he look a little sadder if that were so? Hiram nodded and tucked the paper inside his vest so it wouldn't fly away in the cool May wind that whistled up between the Idaho mountains. He walked home, stepping a little faster than previously, certain that Dostie watched him.

At the path to his snug little house between the jail and a vacant store building, he turned in and hurried to the back. Maybe he ought to look. If it was bad news, he'd have to tell his sister, Trudy. Undecided, he mounted the steps and opened the kitchen door. A spicy smell of baking welcomed him, along with Trudy's smile.

"Just in time. I'm taking out the molasses cookies and putting in the dried apple pies." She bent before the open oven.

The woodstove had warmed the kitchen to an almost uncomfortable level. Hiram hung his hat on its peg and headed for the water bucket and washbasin. No use trying to get cookies from Trudy unless he'd washed his hands.

"Did Zachary Harper pay you?"

"No. He says he'll come by next week."

"Humph."

Hiram shrugged. Trudy got a little mama-bearish on his behalf when folks didn't come forth with cash for his work on their firearms, but he knew Zach would pay him eventually. It wasn't worth fussing over. As she peeled hot cookies off the baking sheet with a long, flat spatula, the soap shot out of his hand and skated across the clean floor. Thankful it hadn't slid under the hot stove, he walked to the corner and bent to retrieve it. The paper in his vest crackled.

"Oh, I 'most forgot." He corralled the soap and returned it to its dish. After a good rinsing, he dried his hands, fished out the folded yellow sheet of paper, and laid it on the table.

"What's that?" She stopped with the narrow spatula in midair, a hot, floppy cookie drooping over its edges.

"Telegram."

"What's it say?"

He rescued the crumbling cookie and juggled it from one hand to the other. "Don't know." He blew on it until it was cool enough that it wouldn't burn him and popped half into his mouth. The warm sweetness hit the spot, and he felt less anxious.

Trudy set the cookie sheet down and balled her hands into fists. She put them to her hips, though she still held the spatula in one. "What's the matter with you? Why didn't you read it?"

He shrugged. How to tell his younger sister that he hadn't wanted to be smacked with bad news while the telegraph operator watched him?

"It's windy out."

She scowled at him.

"I didn't want it to blow away. Read it if you want." He reached for another cookie. "Is Ethan coming over tonight?"

"What do you think?"

Hiram smiled. The sheriff spent a disproportionate amount of time at the Dooley house these days, but he didn't mind. Ethan Chapman was a good man.

Trudy still eyed the telegram as though she expected it to rear back and sprout fangs and a tail rattle.

"Go ahead and read it," Hiram said, feeling a little guilty at putting the task off on her.

"If it's addressed to you, then you do it."

He sighed and laid his cookie aside. It would be better with milk, anyway. He wiped his hands on his dungarees and picked up the paper. As he opened it, he quickly scanned the message for the "from" part and frowned. Why on earth would Rose Caplinger send him a message all the way from Maine?

"What?" Trudy asked.

He held it out to her. "It's Rose."

"Violet's sister?"

Hiram nodded. "She wants to visit, I guess." He should have read it more closely, but the idea of his opinionated sister-in-law descending on them was enough to make a bachelor quake. He and his bride, Violet, had traveled west twelve years ago, in part for the opportunities that beckoned them, but also to escape her pushy family. If Rose hadn't bothered to come after Violet died, why on earth would she take it into her head to visit a decade later? "We'll have to tell her not to come."

Trudy's eyebrows drew together as she studied the paper. "Too late, Hi. She's already in Boise."

Libby Adams lowered the bar into place inside the door of the Paragon Emporium. After a long day tending the store, it was a relief to close up shop. She threw the bolt and turned the OPEN sign to CLOSED, but before she turned away, a man appeared outside and tried the door handle.

Surprised, Libby gestured for him to wait, removed the bar, and unbolted the door.

"I'm just closing, Cyrus. Do you need something tonight?" She stood with the door open a few inches, peering out at the stagecoach-line manager, whose office lay a few yards down the boardwalk.

"I came on a social call." The tall man's smile stopped short of his gray eyes. "It's been a while since we've talked. Thought I'd invite you to dinner—say, Friday evening?"

Libby caught her breath. Cyrus and her husband, Isaac, had been friends. After Isaac's death, Cyrus had made overtures to Libby, but too soon in her widowhood, she'd felt. Cyrus's wife, Mary, was also deceased, so she supposed there was nothing improper about it. Back then, she'd told herself that his timing alone had prompted her to turn him down.

Now it was more than that. Her sharp grief was past, but she knew without any rumination that she didn't wish to form a social alliance with Cyrus. She found his authoritative manner overbearing and repulsive. Actions she'd observed over the past few years confirmed her suspicions that she would not find happiness in the Fennel household. No, if she ever married again, it would be to a far gentler man than Cyrus.

She opened the door a bit wider so as not to appear rude, but she determined not to budge on her answer. "I don't think so, Cyrus, but thank you for asking."

His face hardened. "Why not?"

"I'm content with my situation the way it is."

"Oh, come on, Libby." He leaned closer, and she drew back, shocked that his breath smelled of liquor. "Aren't you tired of being alone? We've both had enough of that. Do you enjoy living by yourself and working all day to earn a living? I'm offering you a chance to put this behind you." His nod encompassed the emporium and Libby's entire life.

His implication that she lived a bleak and pointless existence annoyed her. "I'm not ready to—"

"Of course you're ready. Neither of us is getting any younger. Now's the time, while we can enjoy life together."

She shook her head. "I'm not interested in changing my situation just now, Cyrus."

His eyes narrowed, and he studied her thoughtfully. "Not interested in me?"

"If you insist that I say it, then I suppose not." Her pulse quickened at the angry twitch of his mouth. "We've known each other a long time, Cy. To be frank, I don't think we would suit each other."

"We could have good times, Libby."

"Ah, but we might differ on what constituted good times. I think we'll do best to remain friends and not try to make more of it than that."

He swore softly, and she stepped back.

"You'd best go home. I expect your daughter will have supper waiting when you get there. Good night." She shut the door quickly and once more shot the bolt. Cyrus raised his hands to the door frame and peered in at her. "Good night," she said again and plopped the bar into place. She turned away and hurried up the stairs to her apartment.

As she took out bread, preserves, and cheese for a cold supper, she shook her head. "Drinking, this early. He never did that when Mary was alive." She wondered how his daughter, Isabel, liked that. Isabel taught the village school. A thin, colorless young woman, she'd always kept to herself. Libby had made a point of drawing her out. She'd known Isabel's mother and felt a nebulous duty to make sure Isabel wasn't forgotten and isolated after her mother's death. For the last year, Isabel had taken part in the Ladies' Shooting Club against her father's wishes. Cyrus had declared the club a menace to the town, but he'd backed off somewhat when the ladies' organization had proved its worth. He still wasn't keen on it—which was one more difference between her and Cyrus. Libby loved the shooting club and saw it as a benefit to the members and an asset to the town.

She took her plate to the parlor and sat down on the French settee Isaac had imported for her. She ought to entertain more. What good was all this fancy furniture with no one else to enjoy it? But she was always too tired in the evening. She did well to carve out time for shooting practice.

Cyrus's renewed interest surprised her. She'd assumed he'd given up the notion of wooing her. A couple of years ago, she'd made it clear—or so she thought—that she didn't want a new husband, even if he was the richest man in Fergus and a member of the town council.

She bent over and unlaced her shoes, then kicked them off and leaned back on the cushions. For a moment, she allowed herself to imagine life at the Fennel ranch. Cyrus would ride into town every morning to run the stagecoach line. Isabel would go to the schoolhouse. And Libby—Libby would clean the house and bake and sew, she supposed. Maybe tend the hens and a vegetable garden. She'd probably not see another soul all day, except perhaps a ranch hand or two. None of the bright visits she enjoyed now with her customers. It struck her that, as owner of the emporium, she was privileged to see nearly every resident of the town at least once a month. Who else could claim that?

She tried to conjure up a picture of Cyrus as a loving husband. She'd counted Mary Fennel as a friend, but Libby suspected she'd harbored a deep unhappiness. Without tangible proof, she held the keen memory of a night twelve years ago when she'd been called with Annie Harper to Mary's bedside. Mrs. Fennel had miscarried a baby that night, and she'd wept long afterward.

Libby, in her own awkwardness, had tried to soothe Mary, but she would not be comforted. In a moment alone, when Annie had gone to the kitchen, Libby had patted Mary's shoulder and said, "There, now. You have Isabel. She's a good girl, and perhaps the Lord will give you another child yet."

"No," Mary wailed. "He's punishing me. Cyrus wanted a child of his own, but it's never to be. God won't let me give him that."

Shocked into silence, Libby had listened to her weeping for hours. She had never told anyone of Mary's words, but many times she had pondered them. Her own barrenness had brought on deep sorrow and feelings of inadequacy from which she'd never recovered. But Mary. . .something odd lay behind those words. Though she and Mary visited many more times, Libby had sealed her lips and never brought it up again.

Now Cyrus had come to her door and invited her to dinner—offering much more than that. She shivered. If God had another husband for her, she would consider it. But not Cyrus. Never would she tie herself to that unhappy family.

★ CHAPTER 2 ★

Isabel Fennel brushed back a wisp of light brown hair that clung to her damp forehead. A cloud of steam engulfed her as she drained the water off the pan of green beans she'd cooked for supper.

The spring term of school was drawing to a close, and she looked forward to the coming break. She found teaching exhilarating—except when Willie Ingram started cutting up. But coming home to her sullen father's dark moods and having to prepare supper for the two of them tired her out. She found it nearly as exhausting as running the boardinghouse on Main Street, as she had for a few weeks last summer between school terms.

She set the bowl of beans on the table and opened the oven to spear the baked potatoes. When everything was on the table, she went to the hallway that ran the length of the ranch house. Her father had come in twenty minutes before and settled in the parlor to read.

"Papa?"

"Here!" His muffled voice and the rattle of newspaper reached her from the front of the house.

"Supper."

She heard his chair creak as he rose. She'd begun to turn back to the kitchen when a peremptory knock sounded on the front door. Likely one of the ranch hands, though they usually came around back. She glanced at the kitchen table, laden with steaming dishes, and hoped whoever it was wouldn't keep Papa talking long. A sudden reminder that most of the ranch hands were off on spring roundup sent her to the doorway to peer down the hall.

Her father shuffled out of the front room, glanced her way, then went to the door and opened it. "Yes?"

She couldn't see past her tall father's form, but she heard a deep male voice say, "Cyrus? Is that you? My, you've aged, h'aint you?"

She frowned and cocked her head so she could hear her father's reply better.

"I. . .do I. . . ?"

"It's me," the other man crowed. "Kenton."

"No! Kenton? It can't be."

Isabel shook her head, thinking, *Well Papa, obviously it* can *be, whoever Kenton is.* She racked her brain for the name and came up dry.

"Come in." Her father ushered the man inside and steered him into the front room. Isabel barely caught a glimpse of him, but she had the impression of a limping man about her father's age or older. Cyrus Fennel was in his midfifties. This visitor must be someone he'd known many years ago, perhaps from his gold-mining days.

She heard their muffled voices but could no longer make out their words. Wondering what to do, she lingered. After a couple of minutes, with no one advising her and the voices still rumbling in the far room, she scurried about to cover the hot dishes with linen towels, hoping to save a little of their warmth. At least she'd baked a couple of extra potatoes, thinking she'd use them in a hash for tomorrow's breakfast.

If she was expected to put on a company meal, some drop biscuits might be a good addition to the menu. She quickly stirred them up and popped a pan in the oven, hoping it was still hot enough to brown them. The kitchen was so warm, she didn't want to add more fuel to the cook fire.

Ten minutes later, she decided the biscuits were as done as they'd ever be and was placing them in a basket when her father entered the kitchen with a grizzled man limping behind him.

"Isabel, I'd like to introduce you to your uncle Kenton."

Isabel nearly dropped the biscuits. "My uncle?" She stared at the man. His wrinkled face and small, dark eyes held nothing familiar and showed no resemblance that she could see to either side of her family. His dark hair was liberally sprinkled with gray, and his spotty beard reminded her of the old coyote's pelt one of their ranch hands had nailed to the bunkhouse door last winter. His shirt, none too clean, sported frayed cuffs and collar, and his scuffed boots had seen better days.

"Yes dear. This is your mother's brother, Kenton Smith. He's come all the way from back East, and he wanted to meet you."

Isabel felt her face flush. If her mother had a brother named Kenton, she certainly had never heard about him. The whole scene made little sense to her, but she hastened to untie her apron and fling it over the back of her chair. Hesitantly, she approached the man and held out her hand.

"Mr. Smith."

"Oh please, just call me Uncle Kenton." He grinned, exposing a row of crooked teeth and a gap where one should have been on the bottom left side.

"U–uncle Kenton," Isabel managed.

"My, what a fine young lady Mary's little girl grew to be."

His overly enthusiastic smile sickened Isabel, and she turned away. Snatching her apron from the chair, she crossed to her peg rack and hung it up.

"I've invited Kenton to take supper with us," her father said jovially, but his mirth didn't make it as far as his steely eyes.

Isabel walked to her cupboard and took down an extra plate, cup, and saucer.

"There you go, sir." She turned to fetch his silverware, but he held up one finger.

"Uh-uh-uh. Uncle Kenton." Again the sugary smile showed his neglected teeth.

"Uh, yes." She threw him a fleeting smile and scurried to the chest of drawers near the door, where she kept linens. She took her time choosing a napkin for him and sliding it through a pewter ring. When she turned back to the table, Kenton and her father were waiting beside their chairs. She handed Kenton the napkin.

"Thank you, niece."

Her father pulled out her chair, something he almost never did. Was he trying to impress her uncle?

She sat down and looked to her father expectantly. He bowed

his head, and so did she. Though she didn't peek to see if Uncle Kenton imitated them, she had the feeling he did not. Instead, she had the distinct impression that his gaze bored into her all during her father's brief blessing.

"Amen," she said on the heels of her father's. She shook out her napkin and spread it in her lap. "So, Mr.—Uncle Kenton, why is it that I've never met you before or even known of your existence?"

Her father cleared his throat, but Kenton gave a low chuckle.

"I expect I can explain that. Your parents left the area where I lived before you were born, and I've never come to Idaho before. I did try to keep up a correspondence with my. . .sister, but I'm afraid we let it lapse over the years. My fault, really. I never was much of a one to write letters."

"Mary did speak of you now and then, I think," Cyrus said vaguely as he served himself some meat and handed the dish to Kenton.

"Oh, this looks mighty fine." Kenton took a large slice of beef and passed the platter to Isabel. "Have you been keeping house for your pa since your mama died?"

"Yes, she has," Cyrus said.

"I also teach school," Isabel put in, aggravated that her father had neglected to mention it.

"You don't mean it!" Uncle Kenton seemed tickled beyond expectation. "Little Isabel, a teacher. Now ain't that something?" He accepted the dish of green beans from Pa and heaped most of its contents on his plate.

Throughout the meal, Isabel watched the man. Something didn't add up. Her mother had been dead three years, but Isabel had enjoyed her company for nearly thirty, and certainly she would recall if Mama had ever mentioned a brother. Instead, Isabel was certain that Mary Smith Fennel had told her on several occasions that she had no brothers whatsoever, not even a half brother or a stepbrother. She had mentioned an older sister many times. The sister had died of diphtheria at the age of fifteen, when Mary was but nine, and she grieved over dear Leola all her life. But brothers? Nary a one.

"So you lived with Mama and her parents on the farm back in Waterville?" she asked as she cleared their plates and brought the coffeepot.

"Waterford, my dear," her father said quickly, spoiling her attempt to trip up the guest. She'd thought it a clever ploy, but not with Papa there to catch it before the alleged uncle had time to open his mouth.

"Oh yes, of course." Isabel turned a smile on the stranger. "You'll have to forgive me, sir. I was born after my parents came west, so I don't remember that place at all."

"Think nothing of it." Uncle Kenton picked up his cup and sipped his coffee, giving no indication that he intended to answer the question.

"Er. . .so you were Mama's older brother?"

"By a few years."

"Oh." Isabel was certain that her mother would have extolled a brother who fell between her and Leola in age—as certain as she was that the Ladies' Shooting Club met on Monday and Thursday afternoons. Possibly more so, since the club occasionally adjusted their schedule to accommodate funerals, butchering days, and the club president's recent catarrh.

While the guest continued to sip his coffee, Papa scowled at her, his eyebrows nearly meeting in the middle of his brow to form a miniature windbreak. His hard, gray eyes sent such a chilly look her way that Isabel shivered. She turned quickly away and set the coffeepot on the stove. After taking a moment to collect herself, she returned to the table, bearing half a mince pie.

"Would you gentlemen like dessert?"

"Oh, now that looks fine. Pert' near scrumptious." Kenton's lips spread in a wolflike grin.

"Yes, thank you," said Papa.

She cut generous slices for them both but none for herself. She sat down again and stirred her coffee, which didn't need it, and pondered the situation. When the men's cups reached half empty, she jumped up and refilled them.

"Well!" Papa wiped his mouth with his napkin and threaded it through his napkin ring again. "Kenton, what do you say we go into my office and talk things over? Bring your coffee along."

"Certainly." Uncle Kenton rose, nodded to Isabel, and followed her father into the hall.

Isabel sat still at the table, her mind and heart racing. The men walked down the hallway to the small room Papa called his office, and the door closed. Of course, Papa had a larger office in town, where he used to have his assay business and where he now sold tickets for the Wells Fargo line. But he kept a room at the ranch house for himself—a place where he could smoke a cigar, or read, or go over the accounts for the ranch or for one of his businesses in town.

What was the man doing here? Had he truly come to meet his niece? Then why closet himself with Papa? And why had he evaded her questions?

She rose and put away the leftover food, washed and dried the dishes, swept the floor, and filled the water reservoir on the cookstove, but the two men did not emerge from the office.

At a gentle tapping sound, she hurried to the back door. One of the ranch hands stood there with an armload of kindling and stove wood. Five of their six hired men had ridden out that morning for the roundup, leaving only Brady behind to tend to chores at the ranch house.

"Come in, Brady. Thank you." Isabel swung the door wide. Brady had been with them since before Mama died. Older than most of the other hands, he usually hauled firewood and water for Isabel each evening, as he had for her mother. She appreciated that.

Brady walked to the wood box and dumped his load of sticks.

"Saw a horse out front. Your pa got company?"

"Yes."

Brady lingered, and she knew he expected more. He wasn't being nosy, exactly. After all, the ranch's business was his business. Isabel wondered if he wished he was out on the roundup with the others, or if the middle-aged man was glad he didn't have to sleep on the cold ground tonight. Regardless, she could see that he wanted an explanation.

"My uncle is visiting. They're. . .they're talking in Papa's office."

"That right?" Brady frowned but said no more about it. "Thought I'd butcher a couple of hens tomorrow, since we're about out of fresh meat."

Isabel trusted Brady's judgment on such things. Judah, the

cook, was off with the other hands to prepare their meals on the roundup, and he usually supervised the butchering. But with the warmer spring weather upon them, they'd used all the frozen meat and all the smoked hams and fish. Only a side or two of bacon remained in the smokehouse. But Brady would keep her in small lots of meat until the other men came home and Judah butchered again.

"Fine. I'll be at school all day, but you can leave them in the lean-to. I'll cook them when I come home."

Brady would hang the chickens where no dogs or other critters could get at them. He nodded and picked up the empty water pail from beside the stove. "I'll get you some more water and coal, Miss Isabel."

When he'd gone out, she went to the hall door and listened. Papa's voice and Uncle Kenton's rose and fell. She wondered if she could distinguish what they said if she were, say, three yards farther down the hallway.

As she turned this over in her mind, Brady entered again through the back door and set the full bucket of water beside the stove. He dumped the coal into the scuttle by the wood box. Isabel was thankful that her father was blessed with enough resources to buy coal. The town of Fergus had long mourned its dashed hopes of getting a railroad spur. Coal must be hauled in by freighters and cost more than some of the town's one hundred or so residents could afford. Firewood was hard to come by, but some scoured the mountains for it in the dead of winter. Old-timers told of when dried buffalo chips were available on the prairie a few miles distant, but that era had long since closed.

"Is the gentleman staying over?"

Isabel stared at him, dismayed at the thought. "Oh, I. . .I think not." But where *would* Uncle Kenton stay the night? She supposed Papa might send him a mile to the boardinghouse, but was that polite, to shuffle a relative off like that? She certainly hoped Papa wouldn't invite him to stay at the ranch.

"Anything else you need tonight, Miss Isabel?"

"No, thank you."

"I was going to ask the boss if I could ride into town for a bit."

Isabel looked away. Of course Brady would want to stop in

★THE GUNSMITH'S GALLANTRY★

at the Nugget saloon. She hated the place, but her own father patronized it. He let his hands go to town on paydays. She knew Papa would say yes tonight if Brady asked him, since it was a quiet evening. The seasoned cowboy rarely overindulged, but he liked a glass or two and some company.

"I hate to disturb them." She nodded and met his gaze. "I'm sure it's all right, Brady."

"Thanks. I won't be gone but an hour."

The cowboy touched his hat brim and disappeared, shutting the door behind him. Isabel shivered. The kitchen was no longer overly warm. No doubt the temperature would drop even farther tonight. Spring took its time settling into these mountains, and they still had to keep a fire all night. Her father, being the richest man in Fergus, wouldn't feel the bite of cold.

Kenton Smith, she reflected, looked less prosperous than his brother-in-law. A thought oozed into her mind that he might have come looking for a job or a leg up in the world. Kin was kin, and one didn't turn family away.

She looked at the clock. Quarter to eight. Should she wait to see if the men came out and joined her for further conversation? She didn't want to spend any more time with Uncle Kenton. He had none of her mother's sweetness and charm. He didn't even look like Mama. And if Mama had been proud of him, she'd have told her daughter about him.

Maybe she could quietly retire and avoid seeing him again. But just in case, she'd better check the linens in the spare room. She blew out the lamp on the table.

As she tiptoed down the dusky hallway, she heard Uncle Kenton's voice rise in pitch to rival Bertha Runnels' soprano.

"No, you listen to me!"

Isabel gasped and backed up against the wall across from the closed office door, her pulse throbbing. Her father's voice came, calmer and firm.

"Sit down, Kenton. We can work this out."

Isabel didn't want to hear any more. Papa said people in town were always asking him for money for one thing or another. Probably this no-account uncle she'd never heard of wanted some, too. Come to think of it, that might explain why she'd never heard

339

of Uncle Kenton. Maybe he was a leech, and Mama hadn't wanted him to find them and beg for a handout.

She wrapped her arms around herself and hurried toward her room, passing the door to the spare room. Better take a look.

A quick glance told her the chamber was ready if her father decided to put her uncle in there, but she hoped he wouldn't. Feeling a bit selfish and uncharitable, she sent up a quick prayer. *Lord, if Thou carest about my comfort, please do not let that man stay the night in this house.*

Guilt crept over her, and she stopped praying as she walked to her own room. He was her mother's brother, after all. She set her spectacles on the dresser and took her time brushing her long, light brown hair and thinking about tomorrow's lessons. The fourth graders would multiply fractions, and she had no doubt Will Ingram would have trouble with the concept. In the end, he would probably *make* trouble to distract her from the arithmetic lesson.

No sound of the stranger's leaving had reached her. Not for the first time, she wished she could see the front dooryard from her window, but her room was on the back side of the house. Finally, she drew the curtains and undressed. If Papa came out of his office this late and expected her to play hostess, shame on him.

She cracked the window open, turned out her lamp, and crawled under the quilts. Once or twice, she heard their voices, but when she raised her head, the tones had dropped again. After a long lull, she drifted into near sleep, but suddenly she opened her eyes. A regular crunching sound came to her, not from down the hall, but from outside. Hoofbeats?

Isabel sat up in the dark.

The sound continued but got no fainter or louder. She rose and went to her window. It seemed to come from the direction of the barn. She stuck her feet into her shoes and grabbed a big shawl. Wrapping it around her, she crossed the room, opened the door, and stood listening. She heard nothing from within the house. A faint glow showed that a lamp still burned somewhere at the front of the dwelling. She walked down the hall, her shoes clumping a little since she hadn't buttoned them all the way up.

The front room was empty, and the table lamp burned low.

"Papa?"

No one answered.

She stole to the kitchen and opened the back door an inch. Again she heard the *crunch-crunch*, with a bit of a metallic clang to it.

After a quick look around, she gathered the heavy flannel skirt of her nightdress and tiptoed across the yard between the house and the barn. A pause in the noise made her flatten herself against the rough boards of the barn siding. Her breath came in deep gulps. She made herself exhale slowly and quietly, though her heart raced. A clack came from behind the barn, and then a moment's stillness. Measuring the distance from her position to the kitchen door, she wondered just how foolish she was.

The crunching began again, and she edged toward the back corner of the barn. A glow brighter than starlight and lower than the heavens spilled around the edge of the wall. She sneaked one step closer and another, until her icy fingers touched the boards at the back corner.

Crunch-splat. Crunch-splat.

She knew what made that sound. To confirm her inkling, she peeked around the corner.

A kerosene lantern sat on the ground near a small heap of dirt. Her father, tall and broad-shouldered, cast a huge shadow against the back wall of the barn as he wielded a spade.

Isabel pulled back around the edge and leaned against the boards with her eyes shut. What did it mean? Her father was digging a hole in the night. . .for what? And where was Uncle Kenton? Maybe he was there, too, and she hadn't seen him in the shadows.

Slowly, she leaned forward, until one eye passed the corner. No Uncle Kenton. Her father scooped up another spadeful of dirt. A cold breeze caught the fringe of Isabel's shawl and her loose hair. She drew back, not wanting to think about the scene. She gathered her nightdress and sidled along to the front of the barn wall. As quietly as she could, she fled across the barnyard to the kitchen door. Once inside, she ran down the hall to her room and closed the door behind her. She sat down on her bed, panting. There was no doubt.

Her father was not opening the hole; he was filling it in.

★ CHAPTER 3 ★

"Are you going to Boise to fetch Rose?" Ethan asked as he shuffled two biscuits from the serving plate to his own.

Hiram shook his head. He'd thought about Rose's telegram for the last two hours, and the more he considered its implications, the more they troubled him.

As she often did, his sister spoke for him. "She's taking the stagecoach tomorrow."

"That road has been open only a few days." Ethan frowned as he buttered his biscuit. "The stage had trouble getting through from Reynolds yesterday."

"Well, if the stage can't get through, chances are a wagon couldn't either," Trudy said.

"True." Ethan shot a troubled glance at Hiram. "What'll you do? Will she stay here with you?"

"I don't suppose we could send her to the boardinghouse." Trudy frowned.

The idea of boarding Rose elsewhere hadn't occurred to Hiram, and he looked eagerly to Trudy.

"Don't look so hopeful. We couldn't do that, and you know it."

Hiram shrugged and put his knife to his venison steak.

"She's family." Trudy nodded as though that settled it. She picked up half her biscuit and smeared it with butter. "It's just plain rude to expect kinfolk to pay for their lodging."

Hiram eyed her sidelong. He and Trudy had been alone too long. She had an uncanny way of reading his unvoiced thoughts.

"Not even if we paid for it," she added.

342

Hiram drooped in his chair and turned his attention back to his food. His little sister was a good cook, and he would miss that if she married Ethan and moved out of the house. For eight years—no, nine—she'd been his cook, housekeeper, and nearest companion. She understood him. She let him grieve when he got in the sorrowful mood over Violet's passing, and she left him alone when he needed it. She even helped him in his business, testing people's guns after he'd fixed them.

She'd started that shortly after she came. Folks had brought Hiram a passel of work in some misguided attempt to keep him too busy to think of how Violet and their baby boy had died. Hiram had worked on those guns day and night. And as they piled up, repaired, Trudy had asked him if she should take them back to their owners.

"I'll need to fire them first," he'd said.

"I could do that for you. Just make sure they shoot okay?"

She'd taken on the job from that day, and her frequent practice had made an excellent shot out of her. So good that other women came to her now for lessons.

Ethan cleaned his plate before he addressed Trudy again. "So, you expect her on tomorrow's noon stagecoach?"

"Probably. I'm getting the front bedroom ready."

Hiram cast a worried glance toward the parlor, where the stairs went up. He was glad he'd be down here in his bedroom and Rose would stay in the bedroom upstairs. The front room was nicer than his sister's little room at the back, but Trudy didn't like the noise from the street and the saloon at night, so she used the snug room under the eaves, above the kitchen.

"How long is she staying?" Ethan asked.

Good question, Hiram thought—one he'd like answered, too.

"We don't know yet," Trudy said. A little frown settled between her eyebrows. The unspoken implication hung in the air. Like Hiram, she hoped Rose wouldn't extend her visit beyond a few weeks.

"Well, if there's anything I can do, let me know." Ethan's gaze left Trudy's face long enough to include Hiram, and he nodded his thanks.

After a cup of coffee and two pieces of pie, Hiram sat back

with a sigh. He surely would miss Trudy's presence, and not just in the kitchen. That was, if the sheriff ever got around to popping the question. The two walked out in the evenings and had made eyes at each other for nearly a year now. Even though it meant giving up his housekeeper, Hiram thought the time had come. Of course, he'd never say as much. Like him, Ethan took his time to come to a decision and even longer to act on it. But from the way those two looked at each other, everyone in town could tell the decision was as good as made. The only thing lacking was the formal proposal.

"Well, I'm glad Rose gave us a day's warning and didn't show up unannounced." Trudy had a faraway look, and Hiram figured she was ticking off the cleaning chores she'd do before Rose arrived. She stood. "More coffee?"

Hiram shook his head.

"No, thanks," Ethan said. "Want to walk tonight?"

"It's a little windy."

Ethan nodded reluctantly. "It's chilly." He waited, watching her, obviously hoping she'd brave the cold and the gale for him.

"I'd make a fire in the parlor," Hiram offered.

Ethan flicked a surprised glance at him. Hiram wished he'd stayed quiet, as usual. But if Trudy didn't want to go out into the cold. . .

"Thanks, Hi, but I'll wear my cloak and bonnet. Let me wash up these dishes first."

"I'll dry." Ethan started carrying plates from the table to the dishpan on the sideboard.

Hiram stood and gathered his own dishes. Trudy poured hot water into her dishpan and added soap. Hiram made a silent exit into the front room, where he had a half-finished gunstock waiting for him. If Ethan needed more time alone with Trudy to get his proposal out, Hiram would do all he could to provide it. He took a last glance back through the doorway into the kitchen and saw Trudy laughing as she tied an apron around the sheriff's waist. Hiram smiled and went to his comfortable chair.

A few minutes later, Trudy came to the doorway.

"We're going to walk down toward the river and back."

Hiram lifted a hand in salute. He wouldn't worry about her

in Ethan's care. Besides, it was too chilly for them to stay out late.

The back door shut on the laughing pair, and he sat in the comfortable quiet of the house, sanding the wood he held. He was happy for Trudy. She'd come as a gangly sixteen-year-old girl, powerless to help him in his fresh grief. Over the last nine years, she'd grown into a beautiful woman. She'd held off potential suitors until Hiram had wondered if she would remain a spinster for his sake.

Then he'd realized she was waiting for Ethan. For a long time, Ethan Chapman had glided along in self-made isolation, ignoring everything but his own hurt. Last summer the town council had thrust sheriffhood upon him. And he'd finally sat up and taken note of the town and Gertrude Dooley.

Hiram's contented smiled soured when he remembered the telegram. Rose Caplinger was as unlike her younger sister, Violet, as a buzzard was unlike a swallow. She might be handsome—Hiram couldn't really remember—but she had the sharpest tongue in Boothbay Harbor, Maine. That he recalled quite clearly. More than once, she'd been informally censured in the neighborhood for gossip. She had none of Violet's gentle spirit and always sought the limelight for herself. If Rose wasn't the center of attention, then the day was not worth living.

He looked about the room once more, regretting the extra work her visit would cause Trudy and the intrusion into their happy existence. What would happen to his peace when Rose arrived?

Isabel had the coffee scalding hot and the eggs nearly set in the pan before her father came to the kitchen. As he did every weekday morning, he appeared for breakfast fully dressed in the clothes he would wear to town. He was a somewhat snappy dresser, as men's fashions went in Fergus. With the Reverend Phineas Benton and Dr. James Kincaid, he completed the roster of men who wore a coat and tie every day.

He pulled a watch from his trouser pocket and consulted it before taking his seat. "Seven-oh-four."

"Are you sending out both coaches today?"

"Yes indeed. Winter's back is broken, and the line is open for business in both directions." He flapped his napkin out and laid it in his lap.

Isabel filled a plate with eggs, two leftover biscuits, and two sausage patties, and placed it before him.

"Papa?"

"Yes? That looks good."

"Thank you. Papa?"

"Yes?"

"Tell me about Uncle Kenton."

"Kenton?" Her father looked up at her briefly with a small frown. He picked up his fork. "What about him?"

"Well. . .where is he?"

"He left last evening."

"Obviously, but where did he go?" Isabel turned to get him a mug of coffee.

"Oh, I believe he's traveling about. He said he may come back again after a bit. You'll see him again, I'll warrant."

She set the steaming mug beside his plate and took her seat opposite him.

"Papa?"

"Hmm?"

She waited until he looked into her eyes.

"Why have I never heard of Uncle Kenton until last night? Mama told me many times that she never had a brother—only her and Leola."

Her father coughed and covered his face with his napkin for a moment. When he revealed it again, he looked rather blotchy and uncomfortable.

"My dear, I can only tell you the truth."

"Please do."

He sighed and returned the napkin to his lap. "You're grown up, and you deserve to know it. The fact is, I advised Mary to tell you years ago—certainly by the time you turned twenty-one. But no, she wanted to protect you."

"Protect me? From her brother?"

Papa cleared his throat and toyed with his fork. "Yes, actually. She didn't want you to ever know about his. . .his past. And she thought that as long as we were in the West and he was in the East, you would

346

never know about him and the disgrace he brought on her family."

Isabel stared at him. Her mother had never hinted at disgrace or regret concerning the Smith family. She'd spoken with longing about her parents and her childhood home, the happy days with her sister until the frail Leola sickened.

"I. . .don't understand."

Her father gave a big sigh and reached across the table for her hand. "It pains me to tell you this, my dear, but your Uncle Kenton spent several years in prison."

Isabel swallowed hard and wished she'd poured herself some coffee. "What for?"

"It's just as well if you don't know the details. Your mother was mortified by the scandal, and her family rarely talked about Kenton. She figured you'd be happier not knowing he existed." Papa ate his eggs, and Isabel watched him, unsatisfied.

After a moment's silence, she got up and fixed her own plate, though she didn't feel like eating. The memories badgered her as she sat down again and nibbled at her food. She didn't recall much about her early years, though there had been a farm in Nebraska. When she was seven, Papa left her and Mama there and came ahead of them to Idaho Territory, prospecting for gold. A year later, he'd sent for them, and they'd ridden the train as far as they could. Papa had met them in Salt Lake City and brought them to the boom town of Fergus, where by then, he ran the assay office.

Isabel ruminated on her father's words. She had a criminal for a relative: a man who'd done something so dire her father wouldn't even name the deed. What else did she not know about her family?

Her father took a second watch from his vest pocket and opened the case.

"Would you like more coffee?" she asked.

"No, I think I'll leave now and stop at the sheriff's before I open the stagecoach office." He stood and reached for his hat. "Want me to drop you at the schoolhouse?"

It was early yet. Though she could use some extra time to prepare in the classroom, Isabel had her domestic chores to think of, too. "Thank you, but I'll stay and do the dishes first. Oh, and Papa, I'll be going to the shooting club after school."

Her father scowled. Any mention of the Ladies' Shooting Club of Fergus put him in a foul mood. It was Isabel's one rebellion, and she stuck to it with a bit of pluck that surprised her.

"I thought they met during school hours."

"They do, but Trudy and the others agreed to meet at three now that the sun sets later. I appreciate their doing that for me."

He said nothing but clapped his hat to his light brown hair. She thought him quite handsome with the touches of gray at his temples. Not for the first time, she wondered if he'd thought of remarrying. Of course, he had a built-in cook and housekeeper. Should she ever leave him, he had the means to hire someone to do for him, as he had hired the Thistles to run the boardinghouse and the cowboys to do the ranch work. Did he ever long for companionship beyond what he got from her and his male friends in town? Once she'd thought he'd eyed Libby Adams wistfully, but she didn't know if he'd ever approached the beautiful storekeeper.

"I'll be here for supper," she said as he stepped toward the door. "You'll be home to eat, won't you?" It wasn't the question she wanted to ask, but she needed what information he was willing to give. The other would have to wait, perhaps forever. She would not dare ask.

"I'm not sure."

She sighed as his footsteps echoed down the hall and the front door closed. Would he linger in town and visit the Nugget before he came home? She'd have to prepare supper and have it waiting in case he did show up to eat it.

The question she'd stifled several times during their conversation overcame all other thoughts and reared up, dark and threatening. In the darkness of the night, what had Papa buried behind the barn?

★ CHAPTER 4 ★

Ethan Chapman entered the jailhouse whistling. No prisoners, which meant he'd slept in his own bed and had a good breakfast with his two ranch hands, brothers Spin and Johnny McDade. The sun shone on Fergus, though a cool wind blew down from the mountain passes. The river ran high from snow melt on the summits. And Trudy was in her kitchen—he could smell her baking from next door. Gingerbread. With the wind out of the south, he was pretty sure he knew what he'd have for dessert at noontime.

The office, cell, and back room retained the same neat condition he'd left them in yesterday. Not much call to stick around this morning. When he wasn't needed at the jailhouse, Ethan liked to walk about town to let himself be seen. His visits with the business owners reassured them that Fergus would remain peaceful. They hadn't had a serious crime since last summer, when the Penny Man had kept them all on edge for a few weeks.

He turned northward first and strolled past the boardinghouse. Mr. Thistle, a one-armed Civil War veteran, worked at washing the windows fronting on Main Street.

"Morning, Sheriff."

"Good morning, Mr. Thistle. How's business?"

"Pretty good since the stage started running again. We expect some guests to come in today. Rilla's fixing lamb stew for luncheon if you're interested."

"Thank you. We'll see." Ethan watched him adroitly wring out his rag with one hand, then ambled on past one of Cy Fennel's vacant buildings left over from the town's boom period and past the Nugget. The saloon was quiet now, but in twelve hours or so, things would heat up. Ethan would return then, with his damping influence on the party atmosphere. He could hear a rhythmic ringing from the smithy and crossed Main Street, since the Nugget was the last business on the west side of that end. As he stepped into the smithy, his friend Griffin Bane glanced up from his work and nodded.

"Ethan."

"Howdy, Griff."

The blacksmith hammered fussily at the edge of the hoe blade he was shaping, then plunged it into a tub of water. The sizzle and sharp-smelling cloud of steam comforted Ethan. Everything was right in Fergus.

"Livery busy these days?" he asked.

"Tolerable." With his tongs, Griffin seized a new piece of bar stock and stuck it into the forge. "We've got two coach teams to switch out today."

"So I've heard. That's good." When he went outside again, Ethan looked toward the livery stable, which Griffin also owned. The towering smith had bought it when the original owner moved on to a more prosperous town. For now, things looked quiet. The six-mule replacement teams for the stagecoaches were probably grazing out back.

Ethan wandered down the board sidewalk on the east side of Main. Beyond a vacant building was Charles Walker's feed store. He stepped inside, hoping to see Walker, but an employee was there alone, counting bags of oats. Ethan said a quick 'Good morning' and went out again.

Next came the stagecoach line's office. Cy Fennel was unlocking the door.

"Oh Sheriff, I was thinking of walking over to see you this morning."

"You're in town early, Mr. Fennel."

"Yes, well, things are picking up now, and I have some bookwork to go over. But I wanted to ask you something. Step in for a minute, won't you?"

Ethan followed him into the small office where Cyrus sold stagecoach tickets. He avoided looking at the discoloration on the board floor near the stove, which marked the spot where a corpse had once lain. He didn't like remembering that.

Cyrus sat down behind his desk and laid his keys and a ledger on the surface.

"What is it?" Ethan asked.

"I wondered if you know who owns the Peart place now."

Ethan raised his eyebrows, which made his hat ride up a little. "Frank and Milzie Peart's land?"

"That's right. Who's the owner?"

"Well, I don't rightly know."

"Didn't you have to contact the heirs when Milzie died?"

Ethan shook his head. "I reported it to the marshal and took an inventory, but I'm no lawyer."

Cyrus stroked his chin. "Maybe I'll take a look next time I'm in Boise. There must be an heir."

"My understanding is that they had no will and no surviving children. When I went through Mrs. Peart's belongings, I didn't find any evidence that she had living relatives. No letters or anything like that."

Cyrus shrugged. "Well, now that we've got us a preacher and a doctor, maybe we should try to entice a lawyer to come to Fergus."

The idea startled Ethan. His pa had always said lawyers were more trouble than they were worth. And he wasn't sure he wanted Cyrus poking into the Peart estate. Cyrus had already bought up more property in and around town than any one man ought to own. He cleared his throat. "I guess I could look into it a little more. Write some letters, maybe."

Cyrus stood and hung up his hat. "Good. Let me know if you find out anything, Sheriff."

Ethan was dismissed, no question. He turned and went out, but his complacency had wilted. Cyrus had that effect on people. And he usually got them to do what he wanted.

Across the street, smoke rose from the Dooleys' chimney, reminding him of the gingerbread. Of course. Trudy. She and her friends would rise to the challenge. He would invite the Ladies' Shooting Club to help him discover Milzie Peart's heir.

★ CHAPTER 5 ★

Hiram removed his hat as he entered the emporium with his sister shortly before noon. The smells of cinnamon, soap, leather, and vinegar hit his nostrils with a not unpleasant mix. Libby Adams kept the store tidy, and people tended to gravitate there to have a chat with neighbors and get the latest news.

Hiram hung back as Trudy approached the counter. His stomach rumbled because they'd put off lunch until after Rose's arrival on the stagecoach, and he wouldn't want the lovely Mrs. Adams to hear such an embarrassing sound. But he could watch with appreciation as she measured out a pound of coffee for Bertha Runnels. When Mrs. Runnels had paid for her purchase and turned away, Libby greeted Trudy with a broad smile, and Hiram inhaled carefully. Seeing Libby smile was as good as watching the sun rise from the top of War Eagle Mountain.

After a moment, he looked away and found some hardware to study, lest people notice him watching Mrs. Adams for an inordinate length of time. Couldn't have folks drawing unwarranted conclusions, and Hiram was not one to go about staring at women.

"How may I help you today?" Libby asked his sister.

After Mrs. Runnels was out the door, Hiram sneaked another glance. Libby's rose-colored dress set off her golden hair and blue eyes. She had to be at least his age, maybe a year or two older, but she was still the beauty of Fergus. Looking at her gave him the same lightheaded appreciation as when he'd first handled a .44-caliber six-shooter.

"I need some extra ammunition for this afternoon," Trudy

told her. "Don't forget we're meeting an hour later than usual so Isabel can join us after school lets out."

"Of course. I'll remind any of the ladies who come in this morning." Libby took a small box from beneath the counter and set it down. "Anything else for you or Hiram?" Her gaze beamed across the room and caught him looking. Hiram gave a quick nod and turned to examine the hammers and pry bars on the display behind him.

"I'm sure there's something I should be getting," Trudy said. "Hi's sister-in-law is coming in on the Boise stagecoach, and there's bound to be something we'll need during her visit."

"Oh? You didn't mention that you expected a visitor."

Trudy gave a dry chuckle. "That's because we didn't know. She sent a telegram yesterday afternoon from Boise."

"Oh my."

"Yes." Hiram looked over his shoulder in time to see his sister grimace. "I expect we'll get by. Let's see. . . . Maybe I'll take some tea and extra sugar. Rose might not like to drink coffee."

Libby fetched the items. "Do you have plenty of cream?"

Trudy frowned. "I'll have to ask Annie Harper to send some with the milk tomorrow morning. Unless you have some. . ."

"I have a can in the icebox." Once again Libby obliged and poured a pint into a glass bottle.

"I guess that's all." Trudy turned and beckoned to her brother. "Can you carry these things for me, Hi? I didn't bring a basket."

"Take one of mine," Libby said. "You can return it later."

Before either of the Dooleys could speak, she had placed Trudy's purchases in a light carrying basket woven of willow sprouts.

"Thank you. That's a lot like my market basket," Trudy said. "Well, it was Violet's, but I've used it ever since I came."

The mention of his deceased wife reminded Hiram of Rose's imminent arrival, and he glanced toward the front window. No sign of the stagecoach yet.

Trudy picked up on his anxiety. "We'd best get over to the stage stop. Thank you, Libby."

"Will you bring your guest to the shooting club?" Libby asked.

Trudy's eyes darkened. "I'm not sure yet. Though what we'll do with her if she doesn't care to go, I'm sure I can't imagine."

Libby's gentle smile eased Hiram's own misgivings on that

very topic. He didn't like the idea of sitting home with Rose while Trudy had fun with the club members. Unfortunately, gentlemen were not welcome at the club meetings.

"I'm sure things will work out."

Trudy nodded. "I expect so. I've been praying ever since Hi brought that telegram home."

Another customer came to the counter and stood behind them. Hiram glanced her way and nodded. Mrs. Storrey, her arms full of yard goods and notions, nodded back. Hiram reached for the basket.

"I'll see you this afternoon," Trudy said to Libby, and Hiram followed her out the door. He put his hat on as they gained the boardwalk and strolled beside Trudy toward the Wells Fargo office with the basket dangling from his hand.

Cyrus Fennel stood just outside his office door, looking anxiously northward, past the Nugget and the smithy, toward Boise.

"Good day, Dooleys." Cyrus barely looked at them as he eyed the road and then his pocket watch. To Hiram's amusement, he pulled out a second watch and compared it with the first.

"Stagecoach late?" Trudy asked.

"Not yet." Cyrus's lips thinned to a grim line. "That Bill Stout had better get the coach here in one piece. Folks have been waiting months for regular service to Boise to resume."

"Still snow in the passes." Hiram gazed off toward Boise, too, but he couldn't see farther than the mountains beyond the end of Main Street.

"They got through on Tuesday."

The only traffic on the north end of the street consisted of Ted Hire walking from the smithy to the Nugget, where he worked. Hiram set down the basket.

Cyrus eyed them with sudden interest. "Do you folks expect someone coming in today?"

"Yes sir," said Trudy. "We look for Mrs. Caplinger of the state of Maine."

Cyrus whistled. "She's had a long trip. Relative of yours?"

Trudy glanced at Hiram, and he shrugged. It would get around town soon enough, anyway. They'd already told Libby, who was not a gossip but definitely a link in the Fergus news chain.

"Our sister-in-law," Trudy said.

Cyrus's eyebrows flew up. "Oh? That would be the late Mrs. Dooley's sister?"

"Yes." Trudy's face brightened. "Oh look. Here comes the sheriff."

Hiram exhaled, feeling extra friendship for Ethan for arriving in time to curb an awkward conversation. The sheriff emerged from Gold Lane, the dusty little side street that sprouted westward between the jail and the boardinghouse. He caught sight of them and smiled, veering across Main Street to join them. Hiram wondered if he'd planned to go to their back door and beg some lunch. A glint of sun caught Ethan's badge on the front of his jacket. The tall, broad-shouldered young man did make an impressive figure of a lawman, and it was no wonder Trudy admired him so—though Trudy had lost her heart to Ethan long before he began wearing the star.

"Howdy," Ethan said, mainly in Trudy's direction, but swinging his head enough to include the men. A wagon rolled up the street, and rancher Arthur Tinen Jr. and his wife, Starr, stopped in front of the emporium.

"Hello," Starr called, waving as her husband reached to help her down from the wagon. Trudy, Ethan, and Hiram waved back, and the Tinens entered the store.

"You got the time, Chapman?" Cyrus asked.

"Nope, 'fraid not."

Hiram looked up at the sun, where it hovered on the edge of a noncommittal cloud. Cyrus wouldn't bother to ask him if he had a watch.

"They're late." Cyrus snapped the case of one watch shut and stuffed it into his vest pocket. "If Ned Harmon and Bill Stout were out drinking last night, I'll fire them both."

Trudy gritted her teeth, her eyes smoky gray. Cyrus chafed Hiram's sensibilities, too. He arched his eyebrows at his sister in a silent signal. Someday he might do battle with the mighty Fennel, but today's snappishness wasn't worth fussing over.

Ethan stepped closer to Trudy. "Say, would the ladies of the club be willing to help me out? Mr. Fennel was asking me this morning about the Peart place. I may need to write several letters to get information. Do you think the ladies would be interested?"

"I know they would," Trudy said.

She and Bitsy Shepard, owner of the Spur & Saddle saloon, which rivaled the Nugget, had served as temporary sheriff's deputies for a brief time last summer, and the ladies took their duty to the town seriously. Ethan's expression cleared at her ready acceptance, and he shot a satisfied glance at Fennel. Sometimes Cyrus wanted more than folks could give him, and Hiram knew some of the wrangling Ethan had gone through with the stubborn man. But if the shooting club helped, Ethan could rest easy. A heap of work would be accomplished, whether the ladies got the information he wanted or not.

But the fact that Fennel wanted someone to investigate the ownership of poor old Milzie Peart's land troubled Hiram. He caught Ethan's eye. Ethan nodded unhappily, but by unspoken agreement, they said no more in front of Cyrus.

Trudy pushed back a strand of her light hair. "I'm sure we can help if it's a letter-writing campaign you need. I'll mention it at this afternoon's meeting."

"Thank you kindly," Ethan said.

A drumming of hoofbeats and a rattle of wheels pulled their attention to the north end of the street once more. Hiram exhaled. The stagecoach. He squared his shoulders and drew Trudy back from the edge of the boardwalk. She was apt to be so busy casting sweet glances at Ethan that she wouldn't think to corral her skirts and get out of the way.

The coach had advanced up the street at a good clip and was nearly upon them. Cyrus stepped forward, still holding one watch open and glaring at the driver.

"Whoa!" Bill Stout pulled the horses up so that the coach door sat even with his boss. The leather straps creaked, and the coach swayed. The horses panted and shook their heads.

"You're ten minutes late." Cyrus's harsh tone cut through the cool air.

Bill sighed and shook his head. "It's heavy going through the passes, Mr. Fennel. I told you that day before yesterday."

"I expect you to maintain the schedule."

"When humanly possible," Bill said evenly. "I hope we've got mules for the next leg."

By this time, Ned, the shotgun messenger, had stowed his weapon and leaped down from the box to open the door for the passengers.

The first person to fill the doorway, in a flurry of lavender skirts, pleats, soutache braid, and covered buttons, was Rose Caplinger. The woman's dark hair was swept up beneath a large hat, and her snapping brown eyes critically surveyed what she could see of Main Street. Cyrus stepped forward quickly, but Ned already had extended a hand to her.

"Watch your step, ma'am," Ned said.

When Rose's dainty feet in patent leather shoes hit the boardwalk, Cyrus edged Ned aside.

"Welcome to Fergus. I'm Cyrus Fennel. I trust you had a pleasant journey with the Wells Fargo line?"

"Pleasant?" Rose blinked up at him. "Not unless your idea of *pleasant* is bouncing over every rock in Idaho Territory at high speed and being jostled by a drummer and a herdsman stinking of sheep, while a quartet of Chinese miners stares at you from across the coach."

Said drummer and shepherd were staggering out of the coach while the miners hung back; whether out of courtesy or intimidation, Hiram couldn't tell. But the time had come when he must step up and rescue Rose from Cyrus's arrogance—or perhaps rescue Cyrus from Rose's ill temper. At any rate, he forced one leg forward, then the other, until he stood next to Cyrus.

Rose's gaze lit on him, and the sour cast fled from her face. Her eyes softened. Her lips trembled.

"Hiram Dooley!" With only this brief warning, she flung herself at him.

⭐ CHAPTER 6 ⭐

My dear, dear brother-in-law." Rose entangled her arms about Hiram's neck, pushing him back three steps so that Trudy had to jump aside, nearly upsetting the willow basket. Rose placed a heartfelt smack on Hiram's jaw. It probably would have landed higher if Hiram hadn't had the presence of mind to raise his chin as her puckered lips reached toward him. Trudy felt her face flush in sympathy for her brother.

"Uh, good day, Rose." Hiram's voice sounded somewhat constricted. He held his hands inches from Rose's back, obviously trying to avoid placing them on her person, darting desperate glances toward Trudy and Ethan.

Not one to neglect her duty, Trudy came to the rescue.

"Rose, how lovely to have you here." She touched Rose's shoulder, and the newly arrived lady gave a reluctant sigh and released Hiram.

"Gert." Rose turned and eyed her from head to toe. "My, how you've grown."

Trudy's strained smile congealed on her face. "I go by Trudy now, if you don't mind."

"What? Oh." Rose's gaze had already strayed to Ethan, who stood comfortingly close to Trudy. "And who is this dashing gentleman? A lawman, I see."

Trudy's heart beat faster. Flirting was not the norm in Fergus. Fluttering lashes and coy smiles tended to occur behind the doors of the Nugget or the Spur & Saddle. She felt like taking Ethan's arm and staking her claim. Ethan, however, seemed not to mind the pretty woman's admiration.

"Hello. You must be Violet's sister." He held out his hand, and Rose took it eagerly.

"Yes, I am."

"Rose Caplinger, this is our sheriff, Ethan Chapman," Trudy said dryly. "Ethan, Mrs. Caplinger."

"How *do* you do?" Rose's eyes flicked back and forth between Ethan and Hiram. "My, I can see that this town is the place to find handsome gentlemen."

At that moment, Ned Harmon plopped a large valise and a carpet bag onto the boardwalk beside them. He pushed back his wide-brimmed hat. "Where do you want your trunk, ma'am?"

"Trunk?" Trudy squeaked. She looked at the roof of the stagecoach, where a huge black steamer trunk was roped down.

"Oh anywhere, thank you," Rose said with a smile. "I'm sure my brother-in-law has a conveyance nearby."

"Uh, no, actually, we live just across the street and down a bit." Trudy fixed Ned with a meaningful frown. "I don't suppose you and Bill could drop it over there for us?"

"Well. . ."

Hiram slid a coin into Ned's hand.

"Surely." Ned tipped his hat to the ladies, nodded at Hiram, and turned to the clutch of men waiting for their bags.

"Well then," Trudy said, "Let's get you over to the house. You must be famished, and I have luncheon ready."

Ethan helped Hiram with the luggage, and Trudy picked up the basket. By the time they'd walked to the Dooleys' house, Bill Stout had brought the coach down the street. Hiram dropped Rose's valise on the tender grass beside the path and hurried to help Ned lower the trunk to earth. The question of just how long Rose intended to stay niggled at Trudy's mind, but she said nothing.

Ethan scooped up the valise, which more than counterbalanced the big carpet bag he already carried, and followed the two women around to the back door.

As they wound around the rear corner of the cozy little house, Rose gazed about, and her nose crinkled. "Oh, you have livestock."

"Just a few hens and two horses." Trudy opened the kitchen

door and held it for Rose. Ethan had to turn sideways to get in with the luggage. He looked questioningly at her, and Trudy said, "In the front room, if you please."

Rose removed her hat and looked about for a place to settle it. "Oh, my hatboxes. I must have left them in the coach."

"Here, let me take that." Trudy took the hat, a feathery, red velvet creation that was more stylish than even Libby Adams would wear, and placed it on the rack near the door. It hung there next to Trudy's second best cotton sunbonnet and Hiram's battered "barn hat," appearing so flamboyant beside them that in Trudy's mind it walked a narrow line between elegant and tawdry, barely coming down on the fashionable side. She couldn't help being reminded of one of Bitsy Shepard's hats.

Ethan edged into the kitchen from the parlor minus the bags.

"Would you mind going out and asking Ned to see if Mrs. Caplinger's hatboxes are still in the coach?" Trudy asked.

"Don't mind if I do." Ethan bolted out the door so fast neither woman had time to thank him.

Rose turned to Trudy instead. "Thank you, Gert. I can't do without my hats."

"I go by Trudy now."

"What a quaint kitchen. Don't you have electricity?"

"No, we don't. It will probably be a long time before they bring electric lines up these mountains."

"But you have telegraph wires." Rose arched her shapely dark brows. "You did get my message?"

"We did. But we still don't have electricity."

Rose nodded and gazed toward the work counter and woodstove. "And no pump?"

"It's out back."

"Oh my dear. You still have to haul all your water?"

Trudy shrugged. "It's not so bad."

"But on wash day. And to think of all the trouble when one wants a bath...." Rose looked hopelessly down at her dust-coated clothing. "Oh my."

Trudy pulled in a deep breath. "I'm sure you'd like to freshen up before we eat lunch. I put a pitcher of water in your room upstairs. Let me take you up. Hiram will bring your luggage up, and. . ." She hesitated, but duty took precedence over personal comfort. "I thought we could heat water this evening so you could have a bath if you'd like."

"Ah. And wash day is. . . ?"

"Monday. Unless you need something right away."

"No, I think I can get by until then."

Trudy mounted the stairs before her sister-in-law and showed her into the front bedroom.

"Well, this isn't so bad."

Trudy tried to view the room through Rose's eyes. She'd given her the flying geese quilt that Violet had stitched ten years ago. A small box stove stood under the eaves, with a stovepipe flue poking out through the ceiling. A chair, washstand, and small chest of drawers completed the furnishings. Plain white curtains edged the window.

"Aunt Sal warned me to expect rustic conditions," Rose said.

"You spoke to Mama before you left home?" Trudy couldn't hold back the eagerness in her voice.

"Yes. Actually, she tried to discourage me from coming, but I was ready for new vistas." Her face puckered up. "It was so dreary after my Albert died. I needed a change of scenery. So I thought, what better than a visit to my brother-in-law in the West?"

"Indeed." Trudy could hear Hiram thumping slowly up the narrow stairs with some of Rose's luggage.

"I had no idea how vast the West is," Rose proclaimed as he appeared in the doorway, laden with the valise, the carpet bag, and a hatbox under each arm. "Oh, thank you so much, Hiram. Right there, near the dresser." She glanced about. "I suppose there's no closet."

"No, but we have hooks." Trudy nodded to the peg rack.

"I see."

"Did you want that big trunk up here?" Hiram asked doubtfully.

"If it's not too much trouble."

He winced. "Ethan stayed in case you wanted it. . . ." He cast a pleading glance at his sister.

"It might be easier for you to unpack it in the parlor and carry small lots up here," Trudy said with a determined smile.

Rose tapped her chin and looked about. "No, I think I'll put it right there under the window so that I can sit on it if I wish and look out." She walked over and pushed the curtains back. "Oh."

Trudy and Hiram exchanged a troubled glance. "Is everything all right?" Trudy asked.

"This window fronts on the street."

"Well yes. But it's by far the larger of the two bedrooms up here."

"May I see the other?"

Trudy swallowed hard. "The other one is my room, and as I said, it's not nearly so spacious as this one."

"Nevertheless, I'm afraid the dust from the street will affect my sinuses. I do have delicate sinuses, you know."

Trudy looked down at the rag rug and mustered her dignity. If Mama were here, she would do the ladylike thing.

Hiram surprised her by speaking up. "I don't think you should ask Trudy to give up her room."

"It's all right, Hi." Trudy smiled out of affection for him and appreciation of his small gesture of chivalry. "If Rose prefers it, we can switch."

She led Rose across the landing and swung open the door to her room. Rose entered and looked about the cozy but small chamber. The eaves came down on both sides, making slanted walls to within a yard of the floor. The one windowsill at the back was only inches above the floor. Yellow wallpaper with nosegays of darker yellow and orange flowers brightened the room.

Trudy's bed was narrower than the one in the front room, but she preferred this room to the bigger one Hiram and Violet had shared. Hiram, too, seemed unable to sleep there and had moved downstairs before Trudy arrived nearly nine years ago. They never discussed it, but the front bedroom remained vacant except for the rare occasions when they entertained a guest. Trudy could count those on one hand.

Rose cleared her throat. "Perhaps you're right, dear. I can see that you're comfortable in here. I'll manage across the hall, I'm sure."

"If you need anything, just let me know," Trudy said.

Hiram gazed at her, his eyebrows hiked up under the hair that spilled over his forehead.

"What is it?" Trudy asked.

"Ethan's still waiting."

"Isn't he staying to lunch?"

Hiram raised his hands and shoulders and cast a glance after Rose, but she had already stridden across the landing, and the sound of drawers being opened reached them.

Trudy stepped closer to her brother. "What do you think?"

He gulped audibly, and she would have laughed had she not felt like doing the same. He said softly, "Ask me again after she unpacks that trunk and plants a garden."

Trudy drew in a quick breath. "You don't think she'll stay all summer?"

"Well. . .she sure brought a heap of stuff."

"Hiram, you don't think. . . ?"

His face drooped into a forlorn mask.

"Come," Trudy said. "We've got to convince Ethan to stay and eat with us."

"And you'll take her with you this afternoon?" His hangdog expression gave her a maternal pang. Sometimes it was hard to remember that Hiram was nine years older than she.

"We'll see. She may want to rest from her trip."

"If she does, I'm heading over to the livery to keep Griff company."

"Good plan." Trudy walked out to the head of the stairs and called, "Rose, I'll have lunch on the table in five minutes."

"I'll be right there," came the muffled reply.

Ethan sprang up from a chair when Trudy and Hiram entered the kitchen. "What's the word on that trunk?"

Trudy glanced at her brother, but he was no help. "Let's leave it in the front room for now. If she insists on having it upstairs, I'll ask her to take the heavy stuff out first."

Both men sighed, and she chuckled. "Come on, fellows, you must be hungry."

"Starved," Ethan admitted. "Are you sure you want me, though, with your company and all? 'Cause I could go over to the boardinghouse."

"Would I have set four places at the table if we didn't?" She looked pointedly toward the extra place setting. As much as she loved him, sometimes Ethan needed things spelled out for him.

He smiled and sank back into the chair. "Thanks."

A few minutes later, Rose came down and joined them. She'd brushed her dress off and combed her hair. Hiram held a chair for her, and Ethan held Trudy's. When all were seated, Hiram nodded at Ethan.

His friend, having known Hiram's quiet ways for years, bowed his head and began to pray.

After the blessing, Rose smiled brightly at Ethan. "Sheriff, I didn't realize you were joining us for the meal. How delightful."

"Thank you, ma'am." The tips of Ethan's ears turned pink.

"Are you a particular friend of Hiram's?"

"You might say that." Ethan's gaze darted to Trudy's, and she imagined she read apology there.

It's all right, Trudy thought. *I know you care for me.* She held his look and tried to communicate that thought to him. Ethan's ears became red.

"Uh, how long can we expect to enjoy your company, Mrs. Caplinger?" He tore his gaze from Trudy's and looked back to the visitor.

"I haven't decided yet. If I like Fergus and dear Hiram thinks it's a good idea"—Rose turned her beaming face toward her stunned brother-in-law—"I may decide to make this my new home."

Hiram dropped his fork. It clattered off his ironstone plate onto the floor. The others all stared at him. Hiram's face went three shades redder than Ethan's.

★ CHAPTER 7 ★

Libby and her clerk, Florence Nash, dashed out of the emporium at half past two.

Annie Harper and her daughter, Myra, were just driving out of Harper Lane, where their farm lay. Annie's husband, Zachary, one of the town council members and occasional deputy for Ethan, allowed her to take the wagon to shooting club meetings and carry several of the other women who lived within the town limits. They usually drove out to a ranch near Ethan's to practice their marksmanship.

Trudy came from her house, carrying her brother's Sharps rifle, and Apphia Benton, the minister's wife, bustled up the sidewalk from Gold Lane, where she and her husband rented a little cottage from Cyrus Fennel. From the Spur & Saddle, at the south end of Main, came the owner, Bitsy Shepard, and two of her saloon girls.

Each woman carried her weapon of choice to the practice sessions, or whatever she was able to lay hands on, ranging from Bitsy's tiny Deringer pistol to prewar muskets used by some of the outlying ranchers' wives. Libby had begun selling a variety of firearms the summer before, and several ladies had purchased pistols that would fit into their handbags.

Annie stopped the wagon and waited for the various club members to climb in at the back. Libby placed her handbag in the wagon bed, carefully lifted her skirts, turned, and gave a little hop onto the edge. Florence's mother, Ellie Nash, ran down the steps of her house, where her husband kept the post office, her skirts hiked up above her ankles.

"We'll wait for you, Mama," Florence called. "Don't get all in a dither."

"Isn't your sister-in-law coming?" Libby asked as Trudy settled beside her and smoothed her skirts over her ankles.

Trudy shook her head. "She wanted to take a nap, and I can't say I blame her. She's had more than a week's travel by train and stagecoach."

"Poor thing must be exhausted," Libby said.

"Your sister-in-law?" Florence asked. "I didn't know you had one."

"She's come to visit us from Maine." Trudy's strained smile told Libby she would rather not discuss it—indeed, would probably rather not be hosting the woman. But in a small town like Fergus, news of a newcomer always interested folks.

"Is she your brother's kin?" Annie asked, looking over her shoulder at Trudy.

"That's right. Rose is the sister of Hiram's wife, Violet."

"Poor dear," Annie murmured.

Trudy's lips tightened, and she busied herself with resting the Sharps so that it wouldn't jostle on the ride. Libby considered Trudy her best friend. Their experiences of the past year had bound them together in spirit, though Trudy was younger by a decade, and Libby could read her friend quite well by now.

"I remember Violet," said Bitsy. "She was a dainty thing, comely and pert." Bitsy was a shrewd business owner, and she made up for her diminutive size by wearing bright colors, startling makeup, and when she felt the occasion warranted it, shocking fashions. For the moment, she wore her bright red bloomer costume, which, where Bitsy was concerned, exhibited the height of modesty.

Her two girls were also apt to show up sporting what some ladies would deem inappropriate clothing. This time their skirts hung short enough to reveal their shoe tops and sheer, clocked stockings with a suggestion of ruffled satin petticoats—a sharp contrast to Mrs. Benton's proper two-piece, black bombazine dress. But the club members had welcomed them into their ranks and their hearts. Their friendship and prayers had borne fruit, and Goldie and Vashti now regularly attended the Reverend Mr.

Benton's church services. Bitsy, however, had come to church only once. Libby had not given up praying for her.

"I wish I could have known Violet," said Apphia, the newest arrival among them. "I've heard she was lovely in spirit as well as in form."

"I sort of remember her, but I was only a tyke when she passed on," Myra said as Annie clucked to the horses. "Is her sister as pretty as Violet was?"

"Rose is. . ." Trudy cleared her throat and shot a glance at Libby. "Yes, she's very pretty."

Libby determined to have a moment alone with Trudy before the day was over. Something had clearly gone wrong with the visit, and the young woman's insecurities had resurfaced.

"And what's Hiram up to this afternoon?" Apphia asked gently, but Libby had to wonder if she asked to make sure that Hiram had not stayed home alone with Rose. That wouldn't be proper, though most of the people in Fergus wouldn't give a hoot.

"He's gone over to the livery to help Griffin Bane," Trudy said. The wagon was now nearly even with the smithy on the right, and beyond it lay Bane's livery stable. All the ladies gazed toward it.

"Mrs. Harper!" A high female voice reached them from the other side, and all those in the wagon swung around and looked toward the Nugget saloon. Opal, one of the employees at that establishment, hurried out the door and ran toward them carrying a shotgun. "Do you have room for me?"

"Surely. Pile in at the back." Annie stopped the horse and waited for Opal to climb in. She handled the shotgun with utmost care. One of the first things Trudy taught each new club member was gun safety, and carrying loaded guns in wagons was forbidden.

"Miz Adams, I'll need more shells for this when we're done," Opal said when she'd caught her breath.

"Save your empty shells for me, and I'll give you a discount." Libby had recently made a practice of buying back used shotgun shells and spent brass casings from the women.

"Ted doesn't like me taking it, but he said if I buy my own ammunition, it's all right. I'm saving up for a pistol like yours."

"Take your time," Libby said. "And be sure to thank Mr. Hire for letting you use his shotgun."

367

" 'Tisn't his, really." Opal shook her head as though nothing made sense anymore. "Since Mr. Morrell was—" She broke off and cast an uneasy glance at Trudy. "Well, since he died, Ted's just kind of taken over the Nugget. I don't think he really owns it."

"I'm told he has rights," Trudy said. "I asked the sheriff about it myself. He said Ted Hire has contacted Jamin Morrell's kin. Morrell has two sisters in Philadelphia, and Ted is negotiating with them to buy the business. He's putting aside a percentage of the income from the Nugget in an account for the family."

Libby wondered if Ted kept honest records for the ill-fated saloon owner's sisters, but that was none of her business. Ted seemed decent enough—he always kept short accounts with her at the emporium. But he was shrewd. He'd managed to keep undisputed control of the Nugget when the owner died. And he never came to church, unlike Augie Moore. The big man who tended the bar at Bitsy's saloon attended services faithfully and even carried his own Bible. Funny, Libby thought. If she needed help and had only the rival saloons' men to give it, she'd pick big, muscular Augie any day over cold-eyed Ted.

"I'm glad the snow's off and we can shoot out to Thalens' ranch again," Florence said. "It was all right meeting out behind your place now and then in the winter, Trudy, but it's so much nicer to get out away from town."

"And to be able to shoot without your gloves on," her friend Myra added.

"Yes," said Ellie, "and to be back on the twice-a-week schedule. My aim suffered over the winter."

When they arrived at the ravine where they practiced in good weather, four ranchers' wives awaited them, and Isabel Fennel was walking over the hill from the schoolhouse.

As the other riders climbed down, Trudy waited, standing in the wagon bed.

"Ladies," she called, and they all gathered around and looked up at her. "Sheriff Chapman has requested help from our membership. It's not a dangerous task, and it's one that any of you could take part in if you have the time and the desire."

The women's eyes glinted with interest. After the quiet winter in Fergus, they were ready for some action.

Trudy cleared her throat. "You all remember our dear, departed member, Millicent Peart."

The ladies murmured, "Oh yes" and "We surely do." Tears sprang into Libby's eyes just thinking about the old woman.

Trudy nodded. "Of course you do. We all do. Well, it's been brought to the sheriff's attention that Millicent had no will, and no one in town seems to know whether the Pearts had an heir who can claim their property."

"How can we help?" asked Starr Tinen.

Trudy nodded at her. "Afternoon, Starr. The sheriff asked if some of our members could help write letters. He'd like to inquire of town officials and law officers back East, in the area where the Pearts came from, to see if we can find a trace of any relatives back there."

"I'll help," said Emmaline Landry. Several other women raised their hands.

"Wonderful," Trudy said.

Libby rummaged in her bag. "Would you like me to take names?"

"I'm not sure we need to." Trudy raised her voice. "Any of those willing and able may gather this evening at my house. Come after supper—six thirty or so. Bring your pen and ink. If you can spare an envelope and a sheet of writing paper, bring those, too. The sheriff is asking around town for information about Frank and Milzie Peart's background. He'll come by tonight and tell us what he knows so that we can begin our task."

"Maybe we could send some telegrams," Bitsy said. "It would be faster."

"But explaining the situation may take quite a few words."

Ellie frowned. "That could get expensive."

"Yes, I think it's best if we write letters," Trudy said. "There's no big hurry, and Sheriff Chapman can help us word our inquiries discreetly." She looked over the club members. Isabel nodded soberly, and Trudy hoped the schoolteacher would come to the gathering, though she lived outside town. "All right, then. If there's no other business, let's get started. Mrs. Benton, would you open our meeting in prayer, please?"

After the prayer, Libby went to the back of the wagon to

offer Trudy a steadying hand as she climbed down. "I can't come tonight, but I'll send a dozen envelopes over with Florence."

"Thank you." Trudy brushed off her skirt and straightened.

Libby shrugged. "It's not much." She wished she could go. She always enjoyed visiting with Trudy and her brother. The other ladies would liven up the evening for sure. But she kept the emporium open until six every night, and afterward she straightened the store and worked on her bookkeeping. Like Bitsy and the saloon girls, she would have to bypass the gathering. "I wonder why anyone cares about that place. The Pearts' cabin burned flat, and the mine never paid much. The land is practically vertical."

"I know, but. . ." Trudy's brow wrinkled above her blue gray eyes. "Ethan told me Cy Fennel was the one who asked about the property."

Libby looked over her shoulder to see if Cyrus's daughter was within earshot, but Isabel had already gone to her shooting station. "He's already bought up every parcel available. Doesn't he own enough land?"

"Apparently not."

★ CHAPTER 8 ★

Ethan made his rounds that evening at a measured pace. He'd just come from an enjoyable half hour in Trudy's kitchen, instructing the ladies on how to frame their inquiries about the Pearts. Some of the old-timers of Fergus had given him a few scraps of information. Several folks had recalled that Frank Peart was from New Jersey, and Ethan had probed the memories of those who had been in town the longest.

Charles Walker, the former mayor of Fergus, remembered the name of a town Frank had talked about. Ethan had borrowed a geography book from Isabel during the school's lunch hour and found that the town was just outside Elizabeth, a fair-sized city. He'd decided to inquire of the city clerk as well, in case some of the Peart family records were filed there. A wire to the U.S. marshal in Boise might turn up something, and he'd passed the name of an attorney in the territorial capital to Trudy. She would write to the lawyer and explain the situation, asking for any advice the man could give the sheriff. Ethan was confident that within a few weeks they would learn something.

He mounted the steps to the Spur & Saddle. Nine months ago, he'd cringed to enter the saloons. Now it didn't bother him. It was a regular part of his job. Bitsy's place wasn't bad, anyway. Inside, it looked like a swanky hotel lobby. Bitsy'd had the piano and two velvet-covered settees hauled all the way up here by mule train. She did all right. Lots of regular patrons came here once a week or more.

Now, the Nugget, at the other end of Main Street, sang a

371

different tune. The plain, square building held a few tables, a rustic bar, and short benches. Men didn't go in there for the atmosphere. The former owner had made plans to improve the place, but right now, Ted Hire was running the Nugget. He seemed to be doing all right, but who could really say? Maybe Oscar Runnels, who freighted in the liquor for him. But Ted kept his business affairs to himself.

Ethan took only a few steps into the Spur & Saddle. On a Thursday evening, things weren't too lively. About ten men sat in the cushioned chairs or on the settees with their drinks in their hands. Three played a quiet poker game. The rest conversed with each other or the ladies serving drinks. Funny how he thought of Bitsy, Goldie, and Vashti as ladies now. A year ago, he'd have blushed scarlet to think about the saloon women. Now he considered Bitsy a friend and ally, if an eccentric one, and he knew Trudy cared about Bitsy and her girls as well.

Augie stood behind the bar and waved. Ethan nodded to him. Bitsy sat at a table, engaged in conversation with a gentleman Ethan didn't recognize, but he had the look of a salesman. Probably staying overnight at the Fennel House, the boardinghouse owned by the number-one landlord of Fergus, good old Cyrus.

Vashti, the dark-haired girl, caught his eye as she sashayed across from the bar to the poker players, balancing a tray with three glasses on it. She smiled broadly, and Ethan had to admit the girl had a pleasant face. He turned away before he could form any impressions of the rest of her. Augie and the ladies had everything under control. He rarely had to take action at the Spur & Saddle.

He strolled across the street and passed the end of Harper Lane and the Walkers' house. Lamplight streamed from the parlor windows of the yellow house. Ethan thought of stopping in to see how the former mayor was doing, but he shrank from the almost certainly sour reception Orissa Walker would give him. Charles hadn't fully recovered after being shot last summer, and he'd had to give up his position as mayor. Just couldn't keep up with things anymore. Orissa seemed to take it personally that she was no longer the mayor's wife, but no way could she keep that position when her husband couldn't serve.

After the shooting, Ethan had wondered if Cyrus Fennel

would manage to get himself named mayor, but the folks had demanded a vote. They'd elected a man everyone truly liked: postmaster Peter Nash, Walker's next-door neighbor. Things had been quiet since, to Ethan's relief. He'd spent a quiet winter on the ranch, riding into town most days and taking his time courting Trudy. Life in Fergus was good these days. Good and peaceful.

He sauntered on, checking locked storefronts and peering into vacant buildings left over from the Gold Rush of twenty years ago. He even moseyed along the side streets. Quiet. Absolutely, pin-droppingly quiet.

Outside the livery, he found Griffin and Hiram sitting on a couple of hay bales shooting the breeze.

"What are you doing out here, Hi?" Ethan asked.

Hiram rolled his eyes heavenward.

Griffin laughed. "He's got a kitchen full of women, and he says it's your fault."

"Oh yeah." Ethan leaned against the wall and guffawed. "I expect the ladies will be finished before long."

The big blacksmith ran a hand through his beard. "He don't like being booted out of his own house. Can't say as I blame him."

"That so?" Ethan eyed Hiram, but he only grimaced and looked skyward. "Tell Trudy. Maybe next time they can meet at Preacher Benton's house."

"Yeah," said Griffin, "or how about Bitsy's place? She's got plenty of room."

Hiram sat up and glared at Griffin.

"Take it easy, now." Ethan clamped his hand on Hiram's shoulder. "You know he's just teasing. We wouldn't want our womenfolk meeting in a saloon, would we, Griff?"

"Oh, I dunno. Bitsy's all right. And her bar girls come to church now. I can't see why it would matter if they had a meeting at the Spur & Saddle."

"Well, I can."

Hiram spoke so rarely that both his friends stared at him in surprise.

"Okay," Griff said. "I won't suggest it."

"But I will suggest to Trudy that they might want to meet at someone else's house next time," Ethan said. "They can spread the fellowship around. And you know they're doing this for a good cause."

"What? So Cyrus can buy up more land?" Hiram shook his head and shoved his hands into his pockets.

Another touchy subject, Ethan realized. Ten years ago, Cyrus had bought the ranch Hiram had had his eye on.

Ethan looked toward the rising moon. "Think the ladies are done writing their letters?"

Hiram shrugged and kicked at a pebble on the ground.

"What about that sister-in-law of yours?" Griffin asked. "She writing letters, too?"

Hiram looked uneasy. "She came in the parlor as soon as Ethan left, so I slipped out."

"Maybe she's not the sharpshooter type," Griff suggested.

"Come on," Ethan said. "It's getting dark. Let's go around to your place, Hiram. I've a mind to take Trudy walking tonight."

Griffin chuckled. "I'll see you boys around."

The two friends walked in silence past the smithy and across the street. Lamplight shone from the windows of the Nugget. Several horses rubbed stirrups at the hitching rail. The men headed up the boardwalk. As they passed the jail, Ethan threw a cursory glance toward his office. Quiet and dark, just the way he liked it.

Annie Harper and her daughter, Myra, emerged from the path that led to the Dooleys' back door.

"Evening, ladies," Ethan called, and Hiram tipped his hat in silence. "Are you finished with your meeting?"

"Hello again, Sheriff," Annie said. "Yes, we're the last to leave. Gert—I mean, Trudy—has all the letters ready to be mailed."

"That's fine. I appreciate your help." Ethan smiled and watched them cross the street. Myra looked back over her shoulder and gave a coy wave.

"Ha! She's waving at you, Hiram."

"Not me."

"Well, surely not me. She knows who I'm sweet on, and I'm not ashamed to say so."

"Yeah, you been sweet on Trudy for a long time."

"So?"

Hiram shrugged. "You coming in?"

They ambled around to the back. Hiram mounted the stoop first and opened the kitchen door.

"Oh, you're back," Trudy said when her brother entered. "You want coffee? We've got some cookies, too. Ellie Nash brought them, and there are some left over." She looked past Hiram and met Ethan's gaze. Her voice dropped a pitch. "Hello, Ethan."

"Trudy."

They stood looking at each other for a long moment. Hiram plopped his hat on its peg and walked to the woodstove. He opened the coffeepot and peered into it. After a moment, he held it out toward Ethan, his eyebrows arched.

"Thanks," Ethan said, "but if Trudy wants to go walking. . ."

"Surely." She turned her gaze to Hiram. "Go ahead and drink that. I'll put on more so that Ethan can have a fresh cup with you when we get back."

From the next room, the sound of footsteps on the stairs reached them. Hiram caught his breath, his face freezing in a panicky mask.

"She won't kill you," Trudy hissed. "We'll be back in half an hour. Right, Ethan?"

"No more than that."

Hiram shook his head violently.

"Twenty minutes," Trudy amended.

Ethan gritted his teeth. How was a fellow supposed to court a girl in twenty-minute increments? But anyone could see Hiram did not want to be left alone with his sister-in-law. Light footsteps crossed the parlor toward them.

"Well, let's head out." Ethan hoped they could leave before—

"Why, Sheriff! I didn't expect to see you again tonight."

Too late.

"Uh. . ." Ethan shot a glance at Trudy and back at the elegant brunette framed in the doorway. She wore a different dress than she had this afternoon, pink and frothy, and her hair was neatly coiffed. "Trudy and I were just going to take a stroll."

"Yes," Trudy said. "We'll be back shortly. Help yourself to coffee if you want some."

"Oh, I'd love to see the town by moonlight," Rose said with

a broad smile. She walked over to Ethan and laid a hand on his forearm. "Maybe you could point out the sights to me."

"Uh..."

"Ethan's courting Trudy," Hiram said testily.

They all turned and stared at him. He still stood in front of the stove with the coffeepot in his hands.

Rose's jaw dropped. "Well, I never! How...exciting. Perhaps Hiram and I should go along as chaperones."

"They don't need no chaperone," Hiram said.

Ethan was surprised Trudy hadn't spoken up and given Rose what for. Hiram's outburst must have shocked her into silence. He cleared his throat, not sure what Trudy's reaction would be, but knowing what his mother would have demanded that he do. "Mrs. Caplinger, I'm sure we'd be happy to have you accompany us if you'd care to come along."

Rose smiled sweetly at him. "Thank you. That's very kind of you. But since Hiram says it's all right, I'm sure you have an understanding with him. And with Gert, of course. I think I'll stay here and keep my brother-in-law company. We haven't had a chance to discuss the folks back home. I need to catch him up on all the doings in his old neighborhood."

Trudy opened her mouth and closed it.

Ethan said, "Well then, if you're sure you don't mind, we'll be going. Trudy, do you want your shawl and bonnet? It's a little cool out tonight."

While she gathered her wrap and put on her bonnet, Ethan looked over Rose's shoulder at Hiram. His friend's face was gray.

"We'll see you in half an hour," Ethan said. Hiram scowled. "Or less."

"Take your time," Rose said. She took down one of Trudy's teacups. "We'll be right here when you return. Won't we, Hiram?"

Hiram's shoulders drooped. He walked to the table, poured Rose's teacup full of coffee, and took a mug for himself from the cupboard. A small stream of coffee trickled from the pot, then gave out. Hiram gazed at it mournfully.

If Trudy noticed, she would stop to start a new pot. Ethan scooted her out the back door and pulled it closed behind them. "Guess it'll be a short stroll this evening." He put his hat on.

"It had better be." She frowned up at him. "I feel guilty leaving them together."

"Hiram does seem a little on edge around her."

"You heard her this noon. She's talking about staying here permanently. Hiram's petrified. He thinks that somehow he fits into her future plans."

Ethan reached for her hand. "Let's not think about that now. What do you say we walk down to the river?"

"No, that would take too long. I'm sorry, Ethan, but I'm worked up myself. If I thought I could get away with it, I'd ask her to stay at the boardinghouse. She's making Hiram very uncomfortable. But if I did that, she'd wire her mother, and her mother would tell my mother, and then I'd be in trouble. No, we've got to be good hosts. But somehow we've got to disabuse her of the notion that we want her to live with us."

Ethan squeezed her hand. "I'm sure it will work out. Do you want to walk out Harper Lane?"

Trudy stopped on the boardwalk. "No. No, I don't. I don't know why I'm even out here with you. I should be back there with them. We may not need a chaperone, but Hiram does."

"Aw, that's a little extreme, don't you think? Twenty minutes. . ."

She put her hand up to his cheek, warm and gentle, and Ethan's hopes rose. For about three seconds.

"I'm sorry, Ethan. Any other time, I'd love to be out here walking with you. But my brother needs me. Please, let's go back."

★ CHAPTER 9 ★

Rain began after midnight and fell incessantly through dawn. Isabel's father drove her to school in the wagon. The schoolroom was cold, and she decided to keep her cloak on for a while. When it was too chilly, the children couldn't concentrate on their lessons. They never worked sums quickly if their hands were cold.

The door crashed open behind her, and Will Ingram bounced in.

"Morning, Teacher."

"Good morning, William. Please close the door more gently than you opened it."

"Yes ma'am. My ma said to come early and see if you wanted a fire built in the stove this morning."

"Yes, please. I was just going to do that, but you may have the task." She went to her desk and arranged her books and lesson notes.

Will puttered about at the stove and went out for a minute to bring in an armful of wood from the shed.

"Not much wood left," he said when he came in. Water dripped off his clothes, and he left wet footprints from the door to the potbellied stove halfway along one wall of the large room.

"Thank you. I'll inform the school board. I expect they thought we were done needing a fire this spring."

The other children filtered in by twos and threes. Most days they stayed outside until she rang her bell, but on days of rain or extreme cold, they were allowed to enter the schoolroom as soon as they arrived. All knew the rule, however, that they must remain quiet.

At precisely eight o'clock, Isabel stood and rang her handbell softly. "Good morning, students."

"Good morning, Miss Fennel," they chorused.

She opened the school day by taking the roll, offering prayer, and reading a psalm. Then began the round of arithmetic classes. At the blackboard, she set problems for the older children to work while she drilled addition and subtraction up to tens with the two first graders. No second graders attended the Fergus school this year, and the third and fourth grades had only one pupil each. She generally called them together for their arithmetic.

She erased the older children's problems from the chalkboard and began to write two examples each for Julie Harper and Paul Storrey. Behind her, the stove door creaked open. Will must be adding fuel to the fire, though the classroom had warmed up nicely. She thought she heard a whisper. Isabel turned around with a stick of chalk in one hand and her open arithmetic book in the other. Will was sliding into his seat beside Nathan Landry.

Pow! Bang!

Girls screamed and jumped up, knocking books and slates from their desks. Isabel's chalk flew from her hand, and the book tumbled to the floor. Children scrambled in a tangle of pantalets and fallen benches away from the stove.

Pow!

The older boys had remained in their seats. Will held one hand across his mouth, Isabel's brief impression of his expression was not horror, but rather an ill-hidden smirk. The girls continued to shriek. Six-year-old Millie Pooler wailed. Her classmate Ben Rollins, whose seat was near the stove, appeared to have wet his pants.

"Children! Calm yourselves."

The room stilled. Julie Harper caught a prolonged sob and hiccupped.

Isabel glared at Will. His gaze met hers, and he dropped his hand to his side and sobered. "Want me to check the stove, ma'am?"

"No William. I think you've done enough for today. You will go straight home and tell your father what you've done." She looked at the watch pinned to her bodice. "I shall come around to see your parents this afternoon, and I shall ask them what time you reached home. If you have not arrived there by nine-twenty, I shall ask them to increase whatever punishment they have meted out for this act of yours."

"But—"

"Go. Now. Anything you wish to say to me may be said this afternoon at your home."

He held her gaze only a moment longer then lowered his chin. "Yes ma'am." He walked slowly toward the cloakroom, and a few seconds later the outer door slammed behind him.

Isabel surveyed her class. "Children, pick up the mess and resume your seats, please." She walked to Ben and touched his shoulder. "Ben, you may be excused. Tell your mother I said you may return to school after you change your clothes."

Ben hung his head. His eyes full of tears, he murmured, "Yes ma'am," and headed for the door.

Before going back to the blackboard, Isabel eyed the stove. When it cooled off, she would examine the contents, but she thought she knew what she would find.

"No one is to go near the stove," she said firmly. Stooping, she retrieved her arithmetic book.

"Here's the man you want to ask," Libby said, nodding toward the door. Hiram Dooley had just entered the emporium, letting in a chilly draft. He stopped on the rag mat and wiped his boots, but rainwater dripped off his hat brim onto the floor as he looked downward.

"Yes, a good idea," Isabel said.

"Mr. Dooley, may we have a word with you?" Libby called.

Hiram looked up with widened eyes as though shocked that a woman would speak to him. He glanced down at the small puddle on the floor, as if he suspected that prompted the attention they gave him.

"Don't worry about that, Hiram. Folks have been tracking in mud all day, and a little more water won't hurt. I intend to mop the whole floor this evening after closing."

He slid out of his slicker and hung it on one of the hooks near the door, then walked toward the counter, eyeing Libby and the schoolmarm cautiously.

"What can I do for you ladies?"

Libby smiled, hoping to put him at ease. A quiet man who always seemed a little on edge around women other than his sister, Hiram had become one of her favorite neighbors. Since the start of the shooting club, she'd furthered her acquaintance with both Dooleys, and she liked what she found beneath his self-effacing exterior.

"Miss Fennel was just telling me about a prank one of her students pulled today. It seems while she had her back turned, one of the boys tossed a few cartridges into the school stove."

Hiram frowned. "The boy ought to know better."

Isabel nodded, her pale blue eyes snapping. "So I told his father twenty minutes ago. Mr. Ingram assured me he will deal with the boy, but he also said something I had to wonder about. Mr. Dooley, is it true that putting a bullet in a stove is not dangerous? Mr. Ingram seemed to think it was a harmless joke his son played."

Hiram rubbed the side of his neck thoughtfully. "Well now, I expect it set off the powder charge and made a pretty big bang, depending on what caliber shells you're talking about."

Isabel winced. "I confess it frightened me. It scared us all and put the classroom in an uproar."

"Which is just what Will Ingram wanted," Libby said.

"I suppose so."

"Well ma'am, it's like this," Hiram said. "The powder would make a big boom, for certain, and the cartridge case would move, but it would stop when it hit the side of the stove's firebox. Not being confined in the chamber of a gun, it wouldn't shoot off so hard or go in a particular direction. I reckon the blast was a lot of noise without much force behind it, and the lead bullet pretty much stayed put inside the stove."

"I suppose that's a good thing," Isabel said gravely. "I'm glad to know there wasn't as much danger to the children as I at first feared. But it certainly disrupted the class."

"It's a bad trick to pull," Hiram said. "And you never know. If the stove door weren't shut tight. . .well, we could imagine circumstances where it could result in tragedy."

"Yes," Libby said. "If another child went over and opened the stove door, for instance, just before the powder caught."

"True." Hiram set his lips together in a tight line.

"Mr. Ingram will probably tan his backside," Libby said.

"I hope he does." Isabel colored slightly. "Perhaps as his teacher, I shouldn't admit that, but Will has been a handful this spring. It took an extreme situation like this for me to go directly to his father. And I'm not sure yet that one of the other boys didn't supply the bullets. Mr. Ingram agreed to get the entire story out of him. But I'm glad to know there was little danger to the other children. Thank you, Mr. Dooley."

He nodded.

Libby had been keeping an eye on the other customers browsing throughout the store. Laura Storrey looked her way from the section where kitchen utensils hung on a pegboard. Libby glanced at Isabel and Hiram. "Can I get either of you anything? I see Mrs. Storrey looking my way as though she'd like assistance."

"I just came for a can of cinnamon for Trudy, but I can find it, thank you." Hiram gave the cinnamon the same sober nod other people would give a coffin, but Libby remembered when he had been more lighthearted. She was sure that the gentle gunsmith needed only the right circumstances to banish his gloomy aspect. Of course, the arrival of the widowed sister-in-law he so disliked hadn't helped. As she hurried to assist Mrs. Storrey, she resolved to add his name to her prayer list. It might seem frivolous to some, but to Libby it made perfect sense to pray that another person's dejected spirits be lifted.

★

The rough benches in the old haberdashery building filled quickly on Sunday morning. More than half of Fergus's one hundred–plus residents had signed the church's new constitution and become members. The holdouts lay low on Sundays, and some slunk into the saloons after sundown.

Hiram looked about with satisfaction while Rose engaged Trudy in a whispered conversation. He hoped they'd build a proper church this summer. Mayor Nash had already spoken to him about leading the building crew.

Libby had stopped halfway up the center aisle to speak

to Vashti and Goldie, the two girls who worked at the Spur &
Saddle. He found it hard to take his eyes off Libby. Her golden
hair picked up rays of sunlight that reached in through the front
windows. She always radiated a sweet spirit, and he couldn't think
of a kinder, more competent woman. She'd done a lot for Trudy
this past year by befriending her and prompting her to organize
the shooting club for the women.

As he gazed at Libby, she straightened and glanced his way.
Hiram's chest tightened as he realized she'd caught him staring.
But she only smiled, that gentle, thoughtful smile he'd come to
admire. He allowed himself to answer it and give a half nod,
remembering his conversation with her and Isabel just a few days
ago. He'd managed to keep from making a fool of himself then,
largely due to the serious topic and Isabel's presence. Libby turned
to find her seat, and he lowered his gaze to his hands, thankful
that Rose hadn't noticed the silent exchange.

All the men Hiram considered friends sat in the benches facing
the podium—Ethan, Griff, Peter, Josiah Runnels, and many others
besides. He could only think of two women in town who weren't
at church, aside from outlying ranchers' wives. That would be Bitsy
Shepard and the new girl at the Nugget. He didn't even know
her name, but her arrival on the stagecoach had drawn everyone's
attention. She wore a fur stole over a dress with no shoulders. Or
at least that's what Griff had told him. Hiram hadn't gone over to
the stage stop to get a peek. But Ted Hire hadn't wasted much time
replacing the bar girl who'd been arrested last summer; that was
certain.

Rose, who sat between Hiram and Trudy, chose that moment
to leap to her feet. "Oh, Mr. Fennel. So nice to see you again."

Hiram automatically rose. He'd been taught since childhood
to stand when a lady stood. Cyrus had paused at the end of the
bench, beyond Trudy. Rose gushed like a schoolgirl and allowed
him to shake her hand.

"I trust you've recovered from your arduous journey, Mrs.
Caplinger."

"Yes, I believe I have. This mountain air is quite invigorating."

Cyrus smiled at her. Hiram didn't like the way his gaze darted
to Rose's figure. He felt the blood infuse his cheeks and wondered

for an instant whether a man could be embarrassed for another when the other man should be ashamed and wasn't. It was an interesting train of thought, but a flash of color as the door opened again distracted him from it.

He wished he were standing beside Trudy, without Rose and her poufy dress between them. He'd have nudged Trudy to be certain she noticed the new arrivals.

Augie Moore, the bartender (and some said the cook for the Sunday chicken dinner) at the Spur & Saddle had just entered, which was not unusual. In the crook of his left arm, he cradled his black leather Bible. In the crook of his right arm lay Bitsy Shepard's bejeweled hand.

Bitsy hung back a little, but Augie tugged her gently forward. The dyed feathers on her cobalt blue hat bobbed. At the next-to-last bench, Augie stepped aside and let her enter the row ahead of him. They sat down next to Ralph and Laura Storrey. Bitsy kept her chin down, but Hiram could see her dark eyes flicking back and forth beneath the net veil of her hat. Her dress, black with touches of bright blue on the sleeves and bodice, would have been as modest as Trudy's if it had contained about a half yard more fabric. Still, for Bitsy, it was quite ladylike.

The real shock was her presence in a church meeting. Trudy and the other shooting club members had invited Bitsy for months, but except for one time last summer, she'd always said no. What had changed her mind?

Pastor Benton stepped up to the pulpit, and Cyrus moved quickly down the aisle to his seat beside Isabel. As their guest settled her skirts about her, Hiram met Trudy's gaze over Rose's head. Trudy's grayish eyes sparkled with the reflected blue of her Sunday dress. Hiram could tell from her suppressed energy that she'd seen Bitsy come in. Months of prayers answered—that's what Trudy's look said. He nodded and resumed his seat. Now maybe they could turn their prayers to the family problem and seek guidance for what they should do with Rose.

She leaned toward him and murmured near his ear, "I declare, some folks' mothers never taught them how to dress appropriately for church services, did they?"

Hiram pretended he hadn't heard and hoped no one else had.

★ CHAPTER 10 ★

On Monday afternoon, Libby noticed that Isabel looked a little peaked at shooting practice. She drew her aside while others were firing their rounds and invited her to tea after the meeting ended.

"Won't you have to go right back to your store?" Isabel's eyes held a flicker of hope, though her tone was doubtful.

"Some days I make time for a tea break. Florence can take over the store for half an hour. . .if you'd like to talk, that is."

"Yes, I think I would."

The schoolmarm rode back to town with the rest in Annie's wagon, and she got out with Libby and Florence at the Paragon Emporium. Josiah Runnels reported that business had been spotty, which was normal during shooting club hours. Half the town's women had been improving their marksmanship.

"Florence, you'll be all right for a short while?" Libby asked as she removed her bonnet.

"Yes ma'am."

Libby smiled and led Isabel up the stairs to her private quarters. She quickly built up the fire in her cookstove and set the kettle on. While they waited for it to heat, she took out delicate pink and white china cups and silver teaspoons. Snowy linen napkins and a cut glass plate followed. Isabel watched so avidly that Libby wondered whether the young woman was starved for beauty. Libby loaded the plate with small shortbread cookies, dried figs, and chocolate-dipped wafers. Not homemade, but she supposed Isabel would understand.

"I don't have much time to cook, so I let the store keep me in refreshments for my few guests."

"You needn't apologize. Those look heavenly." Isabel carried the plate to a drop-leaf table while Libby poured the hot water into a teapot that matched the cups. She brought it to the table and sat down.

"How have you been, Isabel?" she asked. "School is nearly out, isn't it? You must be ready for a break."

"I am. And I hope I'll be able to rest a bit. Not like last summer." Isabel scrunched up her face.

"Ah yes, the boardinghouse."

"It's a good venture on Papa's part," Isabel said quickly. "The Fennel House was profitable last fall, but I'm glad Papa hired the Thistles to take it over."

"Yes. It was too much for you when school resumed." Libby carefully filled their teacups.

"Of course, they barely had any boarders all winter, but now that the stage line is running again, the drivers bunk there, and passengers go there for dinners. We had quite a few wanting overnight accommodations last summer and fall."

Libby nodded with a smile and wondered how long it would take Isabel to get around to the real issue. "Are you getting enough rest now?" she asked.

"Oh yes, I suppose so. The end of a school term is always hectic. But we'll have the final program and recitations in a few weeks, and then we'll have six weeks off. I do look forward to it." The lines on Isabel's forehead didn't smooth out as she took a sip of her tea.

"I'm glad you get some time off. Of course, I imagine you'll have a garden to tend and a lot of other things to catch up on."

"Yes, I always have projects I've put off during school, but a change is as good as a rest, they say."

Libby reached for a cookie. "Please help yourself, my dear. I'm glad you were able to rejoin the shooting club this spring. It always refreshes me to get out of the store and have a chance to talk to other women."

Isabel nodded hesitantly. Until she'd joined the club, she hadn't mixed much with other women in town. Lately Libby had begun to know Isabel a little better. Beneath the prim, correct exterior, she found a lonely woman grieving the loss of her mother.

"Mrs. Adams—"

"Yes?"

Isabel's gaze fell. "Nothing. It's just. . ."

"You can speak freely."

Isabel swallowed and looked up at her. "I've worried about Papa lately."

"Have you? Is his health declining?"

"No, it's not that." Isabel picked up her teaspoon and laid it down again. "May I confide in you, Mrs. Adams?"

"Of course, but please call me Libby."

"Thank you. You knew my mother."

The turn of conversation took Libby by surprise, but she nodded and smiled. Better to discuss Mary than Cyrus. "Of course. Mary was a lovely lady."

"Did she ever talk to you about her family back East?"

"Maybe now and then." Libby frowned, trying to remember. "She was from Massachusetts, wasn't she?"

"Yes. Waterford. And she had an older sister, who died at the age of fifteen. Consumption."

"Oh, I'm sorry." Libby waited, sensing that there must be more to come.

Isabel sighed. "Yes, Mama grieved for her sister to her dying day. I was always told it was just the two girls in the family. But. . ." Her face tightened, and she caught her breath.

"But what, my dear?" Libby asked gently.

"A man came to call last Wednesday evening. He said he was her brother."

"Oh my." Libby sat back and studied her guest. "Was your father at home?"

"Yes, for which I was thankful. But. . .but Papa talked to him for a long time in his study. The man stayed for dinner, and he seemed glad to meet me. But you'd think I'd have known I had an uncle, wouldn't you?"

"Yes, it does seem odd. Did you speak to your father about this?"

"The next morning I asked him point-blank why I'd never heard of Uncle Kenton before." Isabel lifted her teacup with trembling hands and took a sip.

"What was his explanation?" Libby asked.

"He told me Kenton had been to prison, and my mother was ashamed of him."

Libby pondered that. "Perhaps it's true."

"Perhaps. But it seems odd that my parents kept up this rather elaborate lie for nearly thirty years. Mother even told me once she wished she'd had more siblings. It was always her and Leola in the stories she told, never any boys. This Kenton said he was a few years older than Mother, and by the look of him, it fits, but. . ." Isabel shook her head. "I'm confused. Papa said he wanted to tell me when I reached my majority, but Mama discouraged him, so he kept it quiet."

Libby reached across the table and patted her hand. "I'm sorry you found out so abruptly. I'm sure your father didn't mean to shock you."

"I suppose not."

"Many people come out West to make a new start, hoping no one will ever learn of their somewhat checkered past."

"That's true, but when I was younger, we got letters now and then from my grandparents in Massachusetts. They never spoke of Kenton. It's strange."

"Yes, it is." Libby considered all she knew about Cyrus Fennel and the way he treated people. She suspected Isabel had not experienced the closeness of a doting father. Mary's cryptic words after her miscarriage came to mind, but this was not the time to bring up that sad memory. "I'm sure he felt it was in your best interest not to know about this unsavory uncle, and that you would be happier not knowing."

"Perhaps."

"And if you decided to marry someday and have children of your own, you wouldn't feel burdened to pass on the family's dark secret."

Isabel huffed out a bitter chuckle. "Not much chance of that happening."

"Oh, come now." Libby smiled, hoping to draw her guest into a lighter frame of mind. "Women your age, and even mine, have been known to find husbands."

"Do you mean you would consider marrying again?" Isabel stared at her with huge eyes.

Libby smiled and gave a delicate shrug. "I haven't ruled out the possibility. If the right man should take notice."

"I know what you mean."

"Do you?" Libby suspected she knew the man Isabel longed to have notice her. The schoolteacher had cast yearning glances at Griffin Bane for years, but the blacksmith had never seemed to take the hint. "There are several good men in Fergus who are eligible, and it's more than two years since my Isaac died."

"You don't have someone in mind, do you? Oh, forgive me." Isabel blushed a becoming pink. "That was too nosy of me."

"Not at all. I'll confide in you as well. There is one man in town who interests me. Perhaps one day both of us will find romance."

Isabel smiled for the first time all afternoon. "I hope so for your sake. I fear it's not in my future. But now I'm wondering. . . ."

"Yes?" Libby prepared for a direct question as to where her heart lay. She wasn't ready to reveal that, though it might set Isabel at ease to know they were not both attracted to the same man.

Instead, Isabel looked up, the strain showing in her thin face. "There's something else."

"Concerning your father?"

"Yes."

Libby took a sip of her tea and braced herself for a mention of Cyrus's drinking habits. What on earth would she say?

Isabel inhaled deeply and met her gaze. "I wasn't going to say anything about this part, but. . ."

"What you say will go no further than this room," Libby said.

"Thank you. I fell asleep Wednesday evening. Uncle Kenton was still in Papa's study with him. I'd overheard what sounded like an argument, but I couldn't make sense of it. I was afraid Papa would invite him to spend the night, and I didn't want to face him again, so I went to bed. Some time later, I awoke to a strange noise."

"What sort of noise?"

"Digging."

"Digging?"

Isabel nodded. "I couldn't imagine at first what it was, but I went outside. All of our ranch hands were away. I was terrified."

Libby knew well the shiver of fear that could come over a woman alone, especially at night. "What happened?"

"You mustn't tell anyone."

"Of course not."

"I. . .I went out around the barn, and I saw my father burying something."

Libby sat back quickly and thought about that. "What was it?"

"I have no idea."

The silence hung between them. Libby didn't like where her thoughts led her.

"Was your uncle with him?" she asked at last.

"No, he wasn't. I hadn't heard him leave, but as I said, I'd fallen asleep."

Libby reached for her cup. "Let's think about this logically, my dear. Did the man arrive on horseback?"

"I don't know."

"And you haven't seen him since?"

"No. I asked Papa about him the next morning. He said Uncle Kenton would stay in the area and might visit us again, but he hasn't so far."

"It's been less than a week," Libby noted. "Still. . ."

"Yes," said Isabel. They sat looking at each other. Finally, she picked up her cup.

"Let me freshen that for you," Libby said.

"No, thank you. I should let you get back to work. But thank you for listening."

"Isabel, you can't think. . ." Libby stopped, not wanting to put it into words.

"That my uncle is in the hole behind the barn?" Isabel grimaced. "I'm trying not to think it. I expect I'm being silly. But I haven't dared ask Papa about that hole."

Libby reached for her hand. "Let me go with you to your father's office. We'll confront him together, and he'll tell you this is a huge mistake. There must be a sensible explanation."

Isabel bit her lip and shook her head quickly. "I daren't, Libby. He would be angry with me for suggesting something so foolish, don't you see? That might—probably would—be worse than the truth we would learn."

Libby sighed and drew back her hand. "I'm sorry. Do you think. . . ?"

"What?"

"I don't know. Perhaps we should tell someone. Sheriff Chapman, for instance."

"Oh no!" Isabel's cheeks grew rosy. "I'm risking Papa's anger just by telling you. You mustn't let anyone else know what I saw, Libby. You promised."

"Yes, I did," she said reluctantly. "I'll keep my word. But you must make me a promise."

"What?"

"That if you're ever afraid, you will come to me. Or go straight to Ethan Chapman. His ranch is close to yours."

"Oh, I couldn't—"

"Now you're being silly. My dear, if you ever think there's a remote possibility that you're in physical danger, you must act. Come here anytime, day or night. Give me your word."

"All right." Isabel inhaled deeply and let out a shaky breath. "I know it can't be true. . .what we're both thinking. But even if it's not, I can't help wondering where Uncle Kenton is and what is buried out back, and. . .Libby, what else has my father not told me?"

★ CHAPTER 11 ★

Hiram slid his checker forward with one finger. He looked up into Ethan's eyes and chuckled. Ethan scowled but crowned his playing piece with another checker.

Hiram sat back and waited for his friend to consider his next move. One good thing about Ethan: He was there when you needed him. The Dooley house had gotten a little too congested for Hiram during the past week. Females in and out all the time, what with the welcome tea the preacher's wife had helped Trudy host for Rose, and the shooting club ladies coming to consult Trudy on everything from guns to quilting bees these days.

The jailhouse had become his hideaway, and Ethan didn't seem to mind. After all, the sheriff had spent enough evenings in Hiram and Trudy's kitchen. The way Hiram saw it, he'd called the loan, and Ethan was paying him back by giving him a quiet place to get away from the petticoats.

Scrambling footsteps on the walk jostled them both from their reverie. Ethan stood as they looked toward the door.

"Sheriff! Come quick!" The dark-haired saloon girl, Vashti, stood panting in the doorway.

"What is it?" Ethan reached for his hat as he spoke.

"A bunch of tough cowpokes are likely to tear up Miss Bitsy's place. She told me to get you pronto."

"Where they from?"

"I never seen 'em before. Augie went for his shotgun, but the leader drew on him before he could get to it."

Ethan touched his sidearm as though making sure it was there and strode to the door. "Stay here, Miss Vashti, or go to Dooleys' and stay with Trudy."

Hiram followed him down the path toward the street. No way was he staying behind with the flashy bar girl.

Ethan dashed up the boardwalk, and Hiram stuck to his heels. Not that he wanted to get involved in a brawl, but if Ethan was headed for trouble, he might need someone he trusted at his back. He couldn't let Trudy's suitor get shot up before he'd gotten around to proposing either. What would he tell his sister?

Hiram had never been into the Spur & Saddle, not even for the Sunday chicken dinner. But he knew from what people told him that the place mostly stayed quiet and orderly compared to the Nugget. Miners and ranch hands favored the noisier, roughneck place. Tonight was only Friday, in any case. Saturday night was when most cowpokes cut loose.

A gunshot rang through the cool evening air. Ethan picked up speed, and so did Hiram. Bitsy had invested a lot in her business. Even though it was a saloon, everyone would hate to see anyone hurt or the only piano in town get damaged.

Nearly a dozen horses were tied outside the Spur & Saddle, and sharp voices burst from inside. A rancher tore out the door and nearly collided with Ethan.

"What's going on in there?" Ethan grabbed Micah Landry's jacket to steady them both.

"Sheriff! Good thing you're here. Bunch of toughs giving Bitsy a hard time. Wanting more drink and getting personal with the girls. She told them to take it to the Nugget, but they won't leave."

"Who fired the shot?"

"One of them. Augie went for his piece, but he wasn't fast enough."

Ethan pulled his .45. "How many customers inside?"

"Maybe ten or a dozen."

Bitsy's strident voice came from within. "Leave her alone. You all just get out of here. You're not welcome anymore."

"Get away, Micah." Ethan mounted the steps and cautiously peered through the half-open door.

Micah stared after him then looked at Hiram. "You're going in with him?"

Hiram shrugged and climbed the steps to stand behind Ethan. He wished he had a gun.

From inside, a man snarled, "We don't leave till I say we leave. And you, Mr. Bartender—you can just step away from where your gun is and pour the whiskey. Me an' the boys want another drink."

Hiram caught a deep breath and shot off something like a prayer as he peered over Ethan's shoulder. The well-lit room seemed full of people. It took him a moment to realize half of them were reflected in the mirror behind the bar. That must be the one Oscar Runnels had packed all the way up here by mule train ten years or more ago.

A big cowboy seemed to be the one speaking. He faced away from them and toward Augie, whose fists were clenched on the surface of the bar. So far the leader hadn't noticed Ethan and Hiram in the mirror.

Three other men stood near the interloper with their hands hovering over their holsters. One of them held Goldie, the blond bar girl, close to him, with his arm clamped about her waist. Hiram didn't let his gaze linger on that travesty. The poor girl must be terrified. Bitsy stood to one side, next to a table full of regulars—two town councilmen and a stagecoach driver.

Ethan stepped into the room. Before he could reason himself out of it, Hiram followed. He sensed someone close behind him and flicked a glance rearward. Micah had changed his mind. The odds felt better.

"All right, folks," Ethan said, "Let's settle down and put the firearms away."

The big cowboy spun toward him with a heavy Colt Dragoon pistol in his hand.

"Well now, it's the law." The man's teeth gleamed white in the lamplight. He held the pistol loosely in his hand, as though he'd forgotten it was there, but the muzzle pointing toward Ethan didn't waver. The sounds Hiram expected in a saloon—clinking glass, soulful music, and friendly laughter—all were absent.

"Put it away," Ethan said. Everyone in the room stood still. Ethan held the cowboy's stare. "Unless you want to spend the night in jail, be quick about it."

At the extreme range of his vision, Hiram caught movement.

Zach Harper was scooting around the edge of the room toward the door. Now that the attention was off him, Augie cautiously stooped and slid his hands beneath the bar.

"You heard the sheriff." Bitsy stepped forward in all her shimmering evening finery. The jeweled choker about her snowy neck caught the lamplight. "Drop the gun."

The big man made as if to lay his pistol on the nearest table then whipped it toward Ethan. At the same moment, one of the other roughnecks leaped toward Hiram with his fists raised.

A pistol roared. Hiram didn't pause to think about it. He ducked, avoiding the cowboy's swing, and landed a solid blow in the assailant's midsection. The cowboy grunted and swayed. Hiram took the opportunity and threw his weight behind the next punch. He hit the man square on the jaw.

Shouts and screams erupted around him. Chairs scraped the floor. Hiram was aware only of the man he'd punched sagging backward and spreading his arms as he hit the floor.

Another shot rang close behind him, and Ethan yelled. "That's it, folks. We're done."

Hiram sucked in a breath and pulled his throbbing knuckles to his mouth. When he was a kid, it never hurt like that to hit someone.

Ethan continued to speak in a firm but soothing tone. "Easy now. You fellows just keep your hands high."

Hiram turned slowly. Acrid smoke hung in the air. Ethan covered the two remaining strangers with his pistol. The one who'd started the trouble lay sprawled on the floor near a tipped chair, bleeding on Bitsy's nice oak floor. Goldie had escaped the men and huddled at the end of the bar near Augie, who now held his shotgun up where all could see it.

Didn't Ethan look fine? Too bad Trudy couldn't see him, with his dark hair falling down over his forehead and his eyes blazing. Their sheriff had proved his mettle tonight. The two unscathed cowpokes shook in their boots at the sight of him.

Bitsy stepped forward. "Want I should disarm them, Sheriff?"

"Thank you, ma'am." Ethan held his ground with his gun trained on the cowboys.

Bitsy stepped toward the first one, staying as far away as she could and still ease his pistol out of his holster. When she had both the men's sidearms, she laid them on the bar.

"All, right, you two," Ethan said, "you didn't draw your weapons, so go on. Get out of here, and don't come back."

"What about Eli and Sandy?" one of them asked. He looked toward the man Ethan had shot and shuddered.

"I don't expect that one is going anywhere. As to the other fella, he'll spend the night in the jailhouse." Ethan nodded toward the man Hiram had laid out on the floor.

"Wait a minute, Sheriff." Bitsy strode toward the man who had spoken. She glared at him for a moment, drew back her hand, and slapped him. "That's for Goldie. She ain't that kind of girl." She turned her back and walked over to embrace Goldie. "It's okay, honey."

Ethan looked at the cowpokes and nodded toward the door. "Go on. Tell your boss he can come bail that one fella out if he wants him back."

The two glanced toward their six-guns.

"You can pick those up tomorrow at the jail, provided you're sober."

The men walked meekly out the door. Ethan exhaled and closed his eyes for a second.

Micah clapped him on the back. "Good job, Ethan."

The men who had been playing poker before the incident started clapping. Bitsy, Goldie, Augie, and the other patrons joined the applause.

Hiram grinned at Ethan. "Want me to fetch Doc Kincaid?"

Ethan caught his breath. "Yes, get him quick. There may be help for that fella."

Augie was already bending over the wounded man. The one Hiram had hit stirred and moaned. He raised his hand to his jaw.

"Hiram Dooley, you surprised me!"

Hiram turned and found Zack Harper beside him.

"You sure conked that no-account. I wouldn't have believed it if I hadn't seen it."

"Yeah, Hi, where'd that punch come from?" Micah asked. "You weren't a boxer in your salad days, were you?"

Bitsy walked over and squeezed his arm. "I never thought of

you as pugilistic, Hiram. Goes to show you never know a person as well as you think. And I thank you for assisting the sheriff."

Hiram opened his mouth to speak and closed it again. Truth was, he felt a little shaky.

Ethan was conferring in low tones with Augie, but he turned to the second cowboy, who had rolled over and pushed himself up on his knees.

"Okay, mister, get up nice and slow. Put your hands out where I can see 'em." Within seconds, Ethan had the cowboy's wrists tied with a short length of twine supplied by Augie. "No need for the doctor, Hi."

Hiram nodded and looked again at the dead cowboy as Ethan herded his prisoner toward the door.

"Death certificate?"

"That's right," Bitsy said. "Now that we have a doctor, we should get him to look at all the dead bodies and write out death certificates."

The others stared at her.

"That came out wrong," she said. "You know what I mean. We went a long time with no doc to make it official."

Hiram nodded with the rest. They all remembered deaths in Fergus that had gone unrecorded.

"I'll fetch him." Hiram hurried out the door in spite of his wobbly knees. The fresh air revived him. He ran along the boardwalk ahead of Ethan and the prisoner, past the jail to the boardinghouse. Dr. Kincaid sat in the parlor, reading by lamplight.

"Can you come to the Spur & Saddle, Doc?"

Kincaid rose, his lithe, athletic form seeming out of place among the fussy cushions and doilies of Mrs. Thistle's parlor. "I'll get my bag."

"You won't need it," Hiram said.

"Oh?" Kincaid arched his eyebrows.

"The fella's dead. Sheriff Chapman shot him."

"I see."

"We need you to. . .well, look at him."

"I'll go right along. Anyone else hurt?"

"Well. . .one fella got a little bruised up, and. . ." Hiram realized he was kneading the knuckles of his right hand. He held it out sheepishly. "Looks like he's not the only one."

Kincaid reached for Hiram's hand and drew him closer to the lamp. He probed the joints. "Does that hurt?"

"Yes sir."

The doctor studied the hand for a moment longer, feeling it gently. "Flex your fingers, please." After Hiram complied, he nodded. "You'll be sore for a week or two. It's swelling. Soak it in Epsom salts. Sometimes wrapping it helps. And a nip of whiskey—"

"Oh, I can't have whiskey."

Kincaid nodded. "Well then, willow bark tea may ease the pain if it's bad enough for you to want something. Tell your sister."

"Yes sir. Thank you."

"All right, I'll go along to the Spur & Saddle. Where do they want the body?"

"Griff Bane can lay him out at the livery."

"Who is it, anyway?"

Hiram puzzled for a moment. "I don't rightly know. There were four of them. Cowboys, not miners. They were wearing spurs. But they never said what outfit they work for."

"I'll ask the sheriff." Kincaid headed for the stairs.

Mrs. Thistle stood in the doorway between the parlor and the dining room. "What happened, Mr. Dooley?"

"Just a little fracas at the saloon, ma'am."

"Thank heaven it was the one down the street for a change."

"Yes ma'am."

"Did I hear you say you hurt your hand?"

"Oh, it's nothing." He shoved his hand into his trouser pocket and tried not to wince. He was eager to get home and try that willow bark tea and Epsom salts.

"Well, between your sister and Mrs. Caplinger, the womenfolk will know what to do, like Dr. Jim said."

Hiram gulped. The last person he wanted hovering and fussing over him was Rose.

★ CHAPTER 12 ★

Libby totaled the order for Annie Harper. Coffee, sugar, saleratus, and a length of dress goods.

"Let's see, now. I believe that with the eggs and milk you've been supplying me, you haven't used all your credit, Annie."

"That's wonderful. Zack's been a little short on cash lately. Say, did you hear about the dustup at Bitsy's place last night?"

"No. What happened?" Libby reached under the counter for a roll of brown paper. "Let me wrap your material for you."

"Thank you. Seems Sheriff Chapman and Hiram Dooley stood off a half dozen gunfighters."

Libby let the roll of paper thump onto the counter. "They *what*?"

"My husband saw the whole thing. He said a bunch of strangers rode in and were drinking too hard. They started tearing up the saloon. Ethan marched in there and shot the leader dead, and Hiram got into fisticuffs with one of the others. Laid him out cold on the floor."

Aware that her lower jaw was hanging, Libby snapped it shut. She could scarcely credit what she was hearing, but still. . .Zack Harper wouldn't lie about something like that. Though he might exaggerate.

"I thought I heard a gunshot or two, but when I opened my window, I didn't hear anything more," she said. "Is. . .is the sheriff all right?"

"I expect so. Zachary said he was right as rain when he left the saloon last night, and I haven't heard otherwise."

Libby finished wrapping the parcel, and Annie went on her way. Only a few customers had come early to the emporium. Libby took off her apron and beckoned Florence to the counter.

"I need to step over to Trudy's for a minute. Will you be all right?"

"Yes ma'am." Florence, at nineteen, was one of the beauties of Fergus. Her red hair and green eyes drew all the young men's attention, and she sometimes had to choose whom to allow to sit beside her at church. She was a good girl and a steady worker, and Libby had trained her well over the past two years.

"Say, did your father mention anything this morning about some unpleasantness at the Spur & Saddle last night?"

"No, but Mr. Harper and Mr. Bane came to see him as I was leaving to come to work. Papa was still at breakfast."

So, the council members were making sure Peter Nash, the mayor, knew about the latest doings. "I won't be long." Libby grabbed her bonnet and shawl and hustled out the door. She dashed across Main Street and down the boardwalk to the path beside the Dooleys' house. When she knocked, Rose opened the back door.

"Oh, Mrs. Caplinger." Libby paused to catch her breath and consider how to word her inquiry. "Is Trudy about this morning?"

Rose's pretty nose wrinkled. "She's feeding the livestock. Mr. Dooley injured his hand, and his sister felt obliged to do the chores for him."

"Oh my. It's not serious, I hope."

Rose lowered her thick, dark eyelashes and sighed. "The doctor examined him, and he assured Mr. Dooley that he would recover in a few weeks."

"Weeks?" Libby caught herself. She'd save the questions for Trudy. "Well, I hope this won't keep him from his work. I'll just step over and..." She turned as a door creaked across the barnyard. Trudy was just coming from the barn, carrying a basin of chicken feed.

"Hello, Libby! What are you doing here?" she called.

Libby gathered her skirts. "Thank you, Mrs. Caplinger." She turned and hurried toward Trudy. "I came to ask you a question." She lowered her voice and looked back toward the kitchen, but

Rose had already withdrawn and closed the door. "Is. . .is the sheriff all right? I just heard about the brawl at Bitsy's."

Trudy gave a rueful smile. "Ethan's fine. He's taking it hard that he killed a man. But I wish I'd been there to see it when he stood up to those fellows. Hiram, too."

"Yes. Your sister-in-law said Hiram was injured."

Trudy shrugged and opened the gate to the poultry yard. "He'll be all right. But next time I expect he'll think a little longer before he lambastes a tough cowpoke."

Libby gasped. "His hand. . . ?"

"Bruised pretty good. All colors of the rainbow this morning."

"Will he be able to work?"

"It may be a few days before he does fine work. I'm tending the horses this morning only because Rose insisted he shouldn't carry a pail of water from the pump to the trough. As if he couldn't lug it with his left hand. But I don't mind. Hiram's done a lot of chores for me." Trudy flung handfuls of cracked corn to the dozen chickens in the yard, and they scrambled about her feet to get it.

Libby noted that Rose's mothering of Hiram stopped short of offering to do the work herself. "Well. I'm glad he's all right. If you need anything. . ."

"Doc Kincaid said to soak it in Epsom salts, and we did that last night. I may need another package, though."

"I'll bring it over this afternoon. No charge."

Trudy's eyes widened. "Why, thank you, but there's no need to bankrupt yourself on our account."

"You said your brother may be unable to do close work for a while, so he'll lose some income. Besides, a man who defends our town ought to be treated special, don't you think?"

Trudy lowered her empty basin and grasped Libby's sleeve, her eyes gleaming. "Libby, you know Hiram wouldn't want anyone to fuss over him—he'd be so embarrassed—but I've got to tell you, from what Ethan says, Hi is a real hero. He jumped right into the fray to support Ethan. Those men would have ruined Bitsy's place and maybe killed some innocent people if Ethan and Hi hadn't stepped in." Her grave expression smoothed out, and she gave a conspiratorial smile. "Rose asked Hiram whatever ailed him to walk into danger like that. Know what he said?"

Libby shook her head, amazed at how eager she was to hear the answer.

"He said he'd heard Miss Bitsy had a great big mirror and lots of pretty furniture in there, and when he saw it was true, he couldn't bear to let those rowdies stave it up."

Libby blinked at her. "That doesn't sound like Hiram."

Trudy laughed. "I think he was trying to get Rose to ease up. She practically swooned when she saw what he did to his hand. I think he was afraid Ethan was going to get himself killed. He went in there for his friend's sake. Well, and maybe a little for Bitsy, too, since she was so good about helping defend the town when we needed it. Hiram and I pray every day that she'll come to know the Lord."

"So do I." Libby felt tears spring into her eyes. She'd known Hiram was a praying man, but it touched her deeply to hear of his faithful pleas for the saloon owner. "Do you and Hiram pray together? He's so quiet."

"Usually I pray, and he just says, 'amen.' But I know he prays inside." Trudy frowned. "Since Rose came, we've quit reading scripture together. Used to do it after breakfast every morning, but now. . ." Trudy sighed. "Rose being here sort of puts us off kilter. She makes Hi nervous as a cat."

"I'm sorry about that. Any indication of how long her visit will last?"

"Not yet." Trudy fastened the gate to the chicken yard. "She made gingerbread yesterday because she remembered he used to like it, and she's talking about piecing a wedding ring quilt, of all things."

It was a bit blatant, but Libby couldn't bring herself to comment on Rose's choice of quilt patterns.

"Now that she sees my brother as a wounded hero, who knows?" Trudy asked. "If she had her way, I think she'd make mollycoddling him her life's mission, if you know what I mean."

Libby knew all too well what she meant.

★ CHAPTER 13 ★

Ethan slid his prisoner's breakfast through the slot at the bottom of the cell wall. It was a little late, but the Thistles had fed their roomers first before bringing flapjacks and bacon for two to the jailhouse. He poured himself a mug of coffee, set the pot back on the small woodstove, and went to his desk to eat his own meal from the tray. He'd left the door of his office open, since the stove had heated things up all too well.

He'd just finished the stack of flapjacks and wished there were more when the prisoner decided to talk.

"You gonna keep me here all day?"

"Maybe." Ethan shoved the tray aside and tilted his chair back, resting his boots on the desktop. He sipped his coffee. "How's the headache this mornin'?"

"Tolerable."

Ethan grunted and drank more coffee. So far all he'd gotten out of the prisoner was his name—Eli Button. Didn't sound like a real name to Ethan. Probably made it up, though he'd met some folks with strange names. But none of the current wanted posters had a name like that.

When he'd drained his mug, he lowered his feet to the floor with a thump and stood. "You want more coffee, Button?"

"Much obliged."

"Slide your cup out here."

When the prisoner had stood back from the bars again, Ethan picked up the tin cup he allowed inmates and took it with his ironstone mug to the stove. He poured Button's drink first and

403

took it back to the cell. "There you go." When he had his own refilled mug in hand, he went back to his desk. "I can't let you go until I know who you work for. I need to notify your boss about your dead partner."

Button scowled. "I'm sure the other boys told him."

"We'll see." Ethan settled his boots on the desktop again. "I'm not letting you go until I see your ranch foreman in here." He hadn't voiced the thought that perhaps Button wasn't really employed at a local ranch at all. He'd never seen any of the men who'd caused trouble at Bitsy's last night. Odd for a rancher to hire an all-new crew, and even odder for the folks in town not to hear about it.

"We h'aint been here long." Button's voice bordered on whiny. "The fella that owns the ranch is named Fennel."

Ethan froze with his mug an inch from his lips. After a moment, he set it down. "Cyrus Fennel."

"That's right."

"You don't work on Fennel's main ranch, though." Fennel was a close neighbor of Ethan's, and they saw each other almost daily on the road or in town. Ethan couldn't believe he wouldn't know if Cyrus had doubled his crew overnight.

"Naw, it's about ten miles from here. But he owns it."

"Who's the foreman?"

"Eastern fella, name of Smith."

Ethan let out a short puff of air, just short of a snort. Smith sounded even more bogus than Button.

The doorway darkened, and he looked up. Griffin Bane, the big blacksmith, filled the space.

"I can stay for an hour. No more."

"Shouldn't take that long." Ethan swung his long legs down off the desk. "I don't expect trouble, but it's possible someone from the ranch where this hothead works will come by to bail him out."

"Where you going to be if I need you?"

Ethan stood and reached for his hat. "Over to Mayor Nash's house. The council's meeting. I don't know why they need me there." He gritted his teeth, hoping they weren't going to give him any grief over last night's shooting.

"Glad I'm not on the council this year." Griff plopped down

in Ethan's chair and eyed his mug speculatively. "You done with this coffee?"

"Yeah. Help yourself to more. See you shortly."

Ethan hoofed it for the Nashes' home, where Peter kept the post office on the boarded-in front porch. He'd hoped to catch Cyrus as he left his office, but the Wells Fargo station was empty when Ethan passed.

He walked into the post office—you never knocked on the outer door—and rapped on the door to the house. Ellie Nash opened it.

"Good morning, Sheriff. The council is all here, I believe. They're in the parlor. Can I bring you coffee?"

"Just had some, thank you, ma'am." Ethan pulled off his hat and entered the small parlor. Though it wasn't so fine as the Walkers', it felt cozier. Meetings here always seemed more cordial than the ones last year, when Charles Walker had presided.

Ethan nodded at Libby Adams, the newest member. Folks had debated long and hard last fall over letting a woman sit on the town council. Since they hadn't achieved statehood yet, the town pretty much made its own rules. The Ladies' Shooting Club of Fergus had strong opinions that they lobbied for, one of them being that women should be able to hold town offices and vote on local questions.

A lot of men had protested, but in the end, the ladies and the minority of men supporting them had won. Bitsy had pointed out that widows and unmarried women who owned property were already allowed to vote on special property-tax issues in the territory. It was only a small step, she declared, until they gained equal suffrage with men. Throughout the territory, the push for women's voting rights was strong.

Personally, Ethan was glad they had a female council member. It kept Cyrus, Oscar, and Zack from swearing and smoking those infernal cigars they liked so much.

"Welcome, Sheriff," Peter said. "Take a seat. We have several items to discuss, but we'll put the one that concerns you first so you can get back to your duties."

"Thank you." Ethan tried to ignore the tickle in his chest. How bad could it be?

"First of all, as the current leaders of the town, we would like to thank you for the boldness you exhibited last night in protecting the lives and virtue of our citizens and the property of one of our leading business owners."

Ethan looked down and adjusted his position in the chair. What other town would commend a man for defending a saloon? "It's part of the job, I reckon."

"Nevertheless, we extend our gratitude to you as sheriff. This council is in agreement that we ought to raise your pay a dollar a week."

Ethan jerked his chin up and met Peter's gaze. A dollar a week would go a long ways. Because of all the time he spent in town fulfilling his duties, he'd had to keep his ranch hands longer in the fall and hire them back earlier this spring.

"Why, thank you very much. I appreciate your confidence."

Libby said, "And we appreciate your valiance."

Oscar frowned as if puzzling over that word.

"Thank you, ma'am," Ethan said.

"Did you find out who the fella you plugged is?" Zack asked.

Libby winced, and Ethan felt his face flush in sympathy.

"Not yet. The prisoner's pretty tight-lipped, but"—he glanced at Cyrus—"Mr. Fennel, if I might have a word with you when you're finished here, I'd appreciate it."

Cyrus cleared his throat. "Are you implying that I had something to do with last night's shootout? Because I haven't set foot in the Spur & Saddle since—"

Ethan held out one hand. "No sir, not at all. It's just. . ." He looked around, wondering how much he should spill in front of the others.

"Spit it out." Cyrus glared at him.

"All right. The prisoner—that is, the man Hiram Dooley knocked out during the fracas—says he and the other troublemakers work on one of your ranches."

"What—" Cyrus stopped abruptly and clamped his lips shut in a bitter frown. "I see."

"Do you? Because I don't, Mr. Fennel."

Cyrus harrumphed and took a gulp from his cup.

Peter looked around at the others, and his gaze came back

to Cyrus. "If you can shed any light on this situation, Cy, we'd appreciate it. Zack said the four roughnecks were all strangers, but if you know them. . ."

"I don't know them." Cyrus shot Ethan a dark glance then heaved a sigh. "I suppose they're out to the old Martin ranch."

"You don't know?" Oscar sat up and poked a stubby, accusing finger toward him. "You mean to tell me you don't know who's living on your property? That don't sound like you, Cyrus."

Fennel rubbed the back of his neck and met Peter's gaze. "The truth is, I have a tenant out there now. Didn't know he would hire a bunch of rabble-rousers. I had no idea until this minute that those men came from out there." He turned toward Ethan. "You sure that's where they're from?"

"No sir, but the prisoner says it's about ten miles from here."

Cyrus nodded reluctantly. "That's about how far it is to the old Martin place. My most remote property." He sighed again and slumped in the armchair. "I haven't been able to do anything with the place. A fellow came along wanting to lease with an option to buy. He seemed like a decent man, and I agreed to let him live out there. He said he'd run some beef on the land."

"What's his name?" Libby eyed him keenly.

"Uh. . .Smith."

Ethan wondered at the little frown that puckered Libby's smooth brow.

"I don't know where he got his hands. Maybe some fellows who had worked for him someplace else. Anyway, I'll ride out there this afternoon after the stagecoach comes in. You can be sure this won't happen again."

"I should hope not," Peter said.

"I'll lay down the law to him." Cyrus reached for his coffee.

"You want me to let the prisoner go?" Ethan asked.

Zack let out a whoop of laughter. "Still can't believe Hiram Dooley put out his lights. Never would have expected him to do that, him being such a quiet man."

"Does the prisoner owe anything?" Cyrus asked, ignoring Zack.

Ethan shrugged. "I generally charge a buck a night, to save the town from paying their expenses. He had a couple of dollars on him. I can take it out of that if you want and pay the Thistles for his meals. But someone ought to pay for the damage at Bitsy's."

"How bad was it?" Oscar asked.

"Not much. I had her give me a list this morning. She says they broke one chair and three glasses, and the man that fired the gun made a hole in the wall. A couple of dollars ought to cover everything."

"I'll stop by the jailhouse later and pay you," Cyrus said. "And I'll speak to my tenant about making sure his hands stay out of trouble."

"Oh, and the other two—the ones I let go—I've got their six-shooters over at the jailhouse. You could return them, I guess, if you get a pledge they won't come fixing to bust up the town again."

"All right. I'll see you after lunch."

Ethan nodded. "We done?"

"I guess so," Peter said, glancing around at the other council members. "And again, Sheriff, we thank you for your excellent service."

Ethan left the house, wondering if Cyrus would be able to control his tenant's hired hands. He didn't want to walk into another gunfight anytime soon.

★ CHAPTER 14 ★

Late Saturday afternoon, the Ladies' Shooting Club met at its customary practice range. Libby almost skipped the extra practice session, but knowing her store could be the next place targeted by ne'er-do-wells spurred her to ask Josiah Runnels to take charge while she and Florence attended.

"This is awfully good of you," Bitsy said to her as they climbed down from Annie's wagon. "I know it's hard to leave off during business hours."

Libby put her arm around Bitsy's shoulders and gave her a squeeze. "The ladies rallied around me last year when I needed help. I think it behooves us all to be ready."

"I admit I was a little on edge last night. When Trudy said we ought to hold an extra meeting and show we can't be scared by a bunch of tough cowpokes, well, it seemed the right thing to do."

"I agree," Libby said. "It makes me feel stronger when we get together to shoot."

"Shooting is a skill every woman should learn, like plucking a chicken or making soap." Bitsy picked up the handful of bright rags they had brought along. The orange wool Annie had donated clashed with her red bloomer costume. "Don't like men messing up my place, though. Sometimes I wonder if I'm in the wrong business." She gave Libby a rueful smile.

"Shall we set up the targets?"

While Trudy gathered the other women for a safety review, Libby and Bitsy walked across the new green grass to fasten bits of cloth to sticks for the ladies to use as practice targets. Libby's mind roiled with possible comments. *Of course you're in the wrong business,* she wanted to scream. But that wouldn't help Bitsy or their tenuous friendship.

As Bitsy worked a scrap of orange fabric into the end of a split stick, Libby said cautiously, "You're such a good businesswoman. You've been on your own a long time, and you've made a success of it."

"Yes, I have." Bitsy pushed the other end of the stick into the soft earth. "Twenty years and more I've had my own place. Yes, twenty-three now. I came here at the height of the boom in these parts."

"About the time my Isaac came."

"True enough."

They walked a few yards to the spot where the next team would aim. Libby stood up the fallen stick they'd used to hold a rag on Thursday. "Do you ever think of doing something else?" she asked.

"Not really. What else could I do? I know liquor, and I know men. Oh, I know how to turn a dollar all right. But what else could I do now? Everyone knows I'm a saloon keeper."

"You could carry the same success into a new venture." Libby swallowed her jitters and went on. "I was glad to see you in church Sunday."

"Augie and the girls have been pestering me to go for months." Bitsy shrugged. "I still don't think I belong there."

"Why not? God welcomes anyone who comes." Libby expected a sharp rebuff, but Bitsy's expression softened.

"Maybe I'll go again. But if I go tomorrow, folks will expect me to be there every Sunday morning, and then who will set up the dining room? We were barely ready to serve dinner on time last week, and then only because Augie got up an hour early to bake his pies and biscuits."

Libby smiled. "I'm going to come over there for dinner one of these Sundays if I can get a handsome man to escort me."

"Naw! You wouldn't."

"Why wouldn't I?"

"You know why."

A flush tingled Libby's cheeks. It was true, she and a few others avoided the saloon, even though the chicken dinner was served without alcoholic beverages on Sunday. Many families went. She'd heard the meal complimented by her customers. But the Sunday dinner had been instituted at the Spur & Saddle after Isaac died. Libby had never felt it proper, as a single woman, to be seen there.

"I wouldn't be embarrassed to come into your place for a meal. As I said, I'll just have to find someone. . ." She eyed Bitsy thoughtfully. "I don't suppose you've ever thought of going into the restaurant business?"

Bitsy waved a hand in dismissal. "There ain't enough folks in Fergus to support another eatery. Miz Thistle serves three meals a day now at the boardinghouse. I think she kinda resents us offering dinner on Sunday."

"Well you were here before she was." Libby smiled. "Come on. One more target."

As they set up the last one, Bitsy frowned in concentration. "You know, you're not the first to suggest I clean up my act, so to speak, though if I do say so, my place is always clean as a whistle."

"I'm sure it is." Libby waited, hoping she'd continue.

Bitsy straightened and brushed her hands together. "There. All set. I think Augie would like it if I switched to another line of work. He's not a jealous man, but he doesn't like it when drunks come in and point guns at him."

Libby arched her eyebrows. "You surprise me. I mean. . .I didn't know."

"About me an' Augie?" Bitsy shrugged. "He's been with me eight years and trying to get me to marry him for seven."

"Really!"

"Yup." Bitsy winked at her. "Didn't know I could keep a secret so good, did ya?"

"Well, no, I didn't." Libby opened her mouth again and then closed it. She was dying to ask Bitsy why she didn't marry Augie if he was so keen on it. The muscular, bald bartender seemed like a reliable man, and he'd shown more than once that he would protect Bitsy and work hard to help her succeed. Libby had always figured he was a loyal employee whom Bitsy paid well to tend bar and run out rowdies. No more. Now she'd discovered that he cooked the succulent meals people raved about and secretly wooed his boss. Quite a character, Augie Moore.

Bitsy smiled. "Looks like the teams are ready to shoot, Miz Adams. Let's git on over there. And you come by any Sunday. I promise you won't be embarrassed."

"I'm sure I won't, Bitsy."

"Nope. No risky paintings in my place. And my girls are good girls."

★

"Papa, I heard something today that disturbs me." Isabel set the platter of pork roast down on the table and faced her father, determined not to let him evade her questions.

"What was that?" He spread his napkin in his lap and waited for her to take her seat.

"That those wild cowboys who started trouble at the Spur & Saddle last Friday evening live on your property. People are saying it was one of your tenants that Sheriff Chapman shot."

Her father speared a baked potato and put it on his plate, then reached for the dish of mashed squash.

"Is it true, Papa?" She sat down and cut slices of meat for both of them.

Papa cut his potato open and smeared a generous slab of butter over the steaming pulp. "The men in the saloon weren't tenants. They were employees of a tenant."

She watched him cut his meat, certain there was more to the story than he revealed.

He stopped chewing and fixed his gaze on her. "Who are these people that you gossip so much with, anyway?"

Heat climbed from her collar to her hairline. "It seems everyone in town is talking about it."

"Yes, but it's those shooting club women you got it from, isn't it? I tried to tell Charles Walker last year that it meant trouble, letting women get together and shoot guns instead of tending their families like they'd ought."

"Well, Mayor Walker would be dead if it weren't for the shooting club. And maybe you, too."

Her father's whole face drooped. She felt a pang of guilt, reminding him that his friend had been injured so badly he'd had to step down as mayor last summer. Walker had only recently resumed his activity at the feed store. But the truth could not be denied—without the patrols taken on by the women in time of crisis, the town of Fergus would have seen more murders.

They ate supper in gloomy silence. Isabel wondered how long she could endure this dreary existence. Uncle Kenton's appearance had brought new anxiety, and she had not forgotten about the hole behind the barn.

Since her mother's death, life at the ranch had become nearly unbearable. Only her teaching position and the new friendships she'd made through the shooting club kept her going. She'd nearly given up her girlhood dreams of marriage and a family of her own. She blamed that on her plain looks and living outside town, where she didn't get to know the other young people. Fergus hadn't even had a minister or regular church services until last July.

No suitors had ever approached her father for permission to court her. There'd been a day when she longed only for one man, but she'd never told anyone. Griffin Bane, the big, bearded blacksmith, though not as educated and refined as might be desired, had captured her heart long ago. If only he knew it. But she didn't expect him ever to ride out to the ranch to call on her.

"What's the matter now?" Her father stared at her with those cold gray eyes.

She realized she had let out a plaintive sigh. "Nothing, Papa. Would you like more pork?"

★ CHAPTER 15 ★

On Thursday afternoon, Trudy and Libby rode on horseback to the shooting club site. They'd started out early so they could set up new targets as a surprise for the women—animal shapes that Myra Harper had painted on muslin. Trudy had sewn them into bags and stuffed them with hay, so now the ladies would be able to shoot at a hare or a coyote or even a pronghorn for practice.

When they arrived, they ground tied Trudy's horse, Crinkles, and Hiram's laconic gelding, Hoss, who suffered Libby to ride him on occasion. Each horse was burdened with two of the bulky new targets, and they stood still while the women removed them.

"I'm glad I was able to get four done," Trudy said. "Each team will have one this way."

"The ladies will be so pleased." Libby helped her prop the first one up with sticks. "What's Rose up to these days?"

"Working on her quilt and cooking everything she thinks Hiram will like."

"Oh dear. At least it saves you some work if she does the cooking."

"Ha. Did I say she does the dishes afterward?" Trudy scowled as she prepared to hammer the stick into the ground. "That woman can dirty more dishes making a cake than the folks at the boardinghouse use in a week. Why, I might have to come over to the emporium and buy more dishes just so she can have enough to make an apple pandowdy."

Libby smiled, but she didn't feel any jollity. "She still won't come to the club?"

"Nope. Too mannish, she says. She thinks all the men in town are going to swarm around her because she's too delicate to pick up a gun."

"Oh." Libby swallowed hard as Trudy pounded in the stake. "I...thought she was only interested in Hiram."

"That doesn't keep her from harping on what a bad example I am and how uncouth western women have become. She's sure the men of Fergus would like their women to act feminine for a change." Trudy shrugged. "Between her nagging and Hiram's complaining, I don't much enjoy sticking to home these days."

"Hiram's..."

"He thinks I ought to be able to get Rose to leave him alone. Don't ask me how. She's got him running as scared as a rabbit that stumbled on a timber wolf rendezvous."

"Really?" Libby couldn't explain the warm feeling that washed over her, but she smiled as they carried the remaining targets to the next spot.

"She keeps wanting to change things in the house. She asked him if he wouldn't like Violet's sampler better between the windows instead of beside the door. Or if he wouldn't like her to make him a new blue shirt for Sundays, to bring out the blue in his eyes. Yesterday she went up in the attic and got into the trunk full of Violet's things. She said at the supper table she wanted to shorten one of Violet's skirts for herself."

"What did Hiram say?"

"He wasn't happy. But Rose said that since I hadn't made use of her sister's things in ten years, why shouldn't she? And Hiram gave in."

"Did you want the skirt?"

"No. It's taffeta, and I'm not a taffeta-wearing woman."

Libby smiled. "You would look lovely in the right taffeta dress. Though I can't for the life of me think where you'd wear it in Fergus. How is Hiram's hand?"

"Better, I think. He was working on Lyman Robinson's musket last evening." Trudy slipped a stick inside the cloth bag of a coyote target and stood it up. "Pound that in m'dear. But be ladylike about it."

Libby laughed and raised the hammer. "I'll be delicate, I

promise. Watch your thumbs, though."

When they finished situating the last target, Trudy wiped her brow. "It's getting right warm today."

"Summer will be here before you know it." Libby eyed her cautiously. "So what does your brother do when you're here at the club?"

"Goes wandering all over town to keep out of Rose's range."

"Ha!" Libby clapped her hand over her mouth after her unmannerly laugh. "Oh dear, forgive me."

"What is there to forgive? Hiram actually asked me this afternoon if there wasn't some way I could steer her off toward some other gent so she'd leave him alone."

"Say, that might not be a bad idea," Libby said. The more she considered it, the better she liked it. She studied Trudy. "I mean, if Hiram doesn't see the need to marry, why should he let a woman pester him?"

"Hiram's not against marriage. He wouldn't have married Violet in the first place if he were." Trudy's eyebrows drew together. "I think it's more that he doesn't want someone else deciding for him when he'll like a woman—or which woman he'll like."

Libby nodded. "Yes. Do you think. . ."

"What?"

"That he's finished his grieving? I know I still ache sometimes when I think of Isaac. And if someone else came along and told me it was time to be done with it and move on, I might resent their interference."

Trudy's face grew somber. "Hiram's grieved long and hard. I can't really say whether he's done or not."

Libby looked off toward the mountains. "I didn't mean to suggest he'd ever forget about Violet, but I think there does come a time for most folks when they realize. . .well, that God's left them here after their loved one went, and there's probably a reason for that. It makes you ready to open your eyes a little wider and try something new. Not a new marriage, necessarily, but *something*."

"Yes. But Rose won't be that something for Hi. So a distraction for Rose might be just the thing."

"Do you think so?"

"Well, he's the one who said it first." Trudy tugged at her

bonnet strings. "Maybe the shooting club could come up with a plan that would set her off in a different direction."

"It wouldn't surprise me a bit. We have some very imaginative ladies in the club. Surely if we put our heads together..."

"Well, I don't know. Hiram probably wouldn't like it if every woman in town was in on it. He doesn't like everybody else knowing his business, you know?"

"Hmm. What if you and I and one or two others attacked the problem?"

Trudy nodded slowly. "But not Mrs. Benton."

"Oh?"

"Not that there's anything wrong with the plan, but the preacher's wife might see it as..."

"Underhanded?"

"Well, do you think it's wrong to try to do a little matchmaking for the sake of someone you love?" Trudy studied her with somber blue gray eyes.

"Not wrong, but perhaps it would be best to keep Apphia out of it. That way, if anything backfires, she can tell her husband honestly that she knew nothing about it. How about Bitsy?"

"Bitsy's idea of the right man for Rose might not measure up to ours."

"True." Libby looked up at the sound of hoofbeats. "Here comes Starr. Looks like she's alone today."

The young woman cantered up on her husband's pinto with her dark hair tumbling down her back below her sunbonnet.

"Hello!" Starr pulled the mare to a halt near Crinkles and Hoss and leaped down. "Am I early?"

"The others will be here soon," Libby said.

"Where's Jessie?" Trudy asked.

"Oh, she's staying home with Hester today. I think our little gal's got the croup."

"That's too bad. But it was nice of your mother-in-law to stay with her and let you get out." Trudy looked over at Libby and raised her eyebrows.

"Oh, look! Are we going to shoot at those?" Starr had spotted the animal targets and strode toward them.

"Aren't they delightful?" Libby asked, walking after her. "Myra painted them, and Trudy stitched and stuffed them."

"I think they're absolutely darling. May my team shoot the bear?"

Trudy smiled. "I don't see why not."

Libby halted beside the young woman as she examined Myra's handiwork. "Starr, since we have a few moments alone, Trudy and I wanted to get your opinion on a matter."

"Oh?" Starr turned toward her eagerly. "I'll do anything for the club, if it's not too time-consuming. Arthur doesn't like me to be gone from the ranch for hours and hours."

"We just need to ask you something," Libby said.

"Yes," Trudy added. "It concerns my brother."

Starr looked from her to Libby, clearly intrigued. "I can't imagine what it could be, so you'll have to tell me."

Trudy cleared her throat. "Well, as you know, my sister-in-law has been visiting us for the past couple of weeks. Her visit has presented a. . ."

"An interesting challenge," Libby said quickly.

"If you mean how she follows Mr. Dooley around all the time and stares at him in church—" Starr laughed at Trudy's abashed expression.

"That's exactly what we're talking about," Libby admitted. "Is it that obvious?"

"About as obvious as the new red and gold sign at the Nugget."

Trudy expelled her breath and shook her head.

"Why'n't they put some clothes on that woman?" Starr asked.

"I'll inform the town council that a resident raised an objection to the Nugget's new sign," Libby said. She knew it was too early to give up on the plan to help Hiram, and she refused to be sidetracked by the Nugget's lurid sign, though she'd already complained privately about it to Mayor Nash. "Perhaps it's just as obvious to you that Mr. Dooley does not return Mrs. Caplinger's regard. Not that he disdains her, you understand, but he's just not. . .not in the same frame of mind she seems to be in."

"He doesn't want to marry her."

"Er, yes." Libby glanced at Trudy to see if Starr's bluntness had upset her. Trudy's mouth sagged, and she kicked at a clump of grass.

"So what do you want to ask me?" Starr's brown eyes twinkled.

"We had a thought." Libby smiled gently. "Not that we generally try to manipulate people's lives, of course..."

"Of course not." Starr waited, obviously enjoying the conversation.

"It occurred to us that if Rose were distracted, that is, if her attention were deflected onto another gentleman—one on whom she could fix her affections..."

"And one who doesn't mind," Trudy said with a scowl. "One who doesn't feel like running and hiding every time he sees her coming, which is pretty often if she's staying at your house."

"I see." Starr blinked and inhaled. "Let me contemplate the problem."

"Oh dear, I'm afraid Annie and the others are here." Libby looked toward the road, where the Harpers' team was approaching with the wagon full of petticoats and firearms.

"Maybe we can talk about this later," Trudy said. "My brother doesn't want to be the object of gossip."

"Griffin Bane," Starr said.

Libby and Trudy both stared at her.

"Of course!" Libby grinned at Trudy, though she felt a flicker of protest on Isabel's behalf.

"Griff is the perfect man for the job," Starr insisted.

"I don't know." Trudy scrunched up her face. "If he hasn't found a wife all these years, what makes you think we can wish one on him?"

"My dear, you make him sound ancient." Libby pressed her arm as the wagon drew nearer. "He's my age, which isn't much beyond Rose's years. And trust me, he's lonely."

"That's the important thing," Starr said. "Trudy, if you get Ethan to whisper a hint in his ear, and if Libby mentions his manly good looks to Rose and tells her what a thrifty and diligent businessman he is..."

"Yes," said Libby. "If we do that, I'll warrant we'll soon see some stares beaming in a different direction during church."

Starr giggled. "I think it would work!"

★ CHAPTER 16 ★

Isabel dragged her feet as she walked toward the ravine. She wasn't sure she wanted to face the other women today. Usually a shooting club meeting buoyed her. They were all so nice. But she'd had a trying day at school, and her family situation wasn't helping any. She felt more like going home, crawling into bed, and covering her head with Mama's tumbling-blocks quilt. The boys in her class refused to learn their lines for the closing program. And Papa drove her insane some days, though she loved him. Ever since he'd dug that mysterious hole behind the barn in the middle of the night, their relationship had carried a strain, like barbed wired stretched tight between two posts and ready to shear off and hit someone. More than ever, she wanted to get away from him.

But what chance did she have of that?

She might be able to get a school in another township for next winter. But then she'd probably have to live with a strange family. She'd certainly have to get used to a new town, new students, and a new school board that might want things done differently than she'd done for the past decade in the little school at Fergus. Could she adapt so readily? She wasn't sure.

The only other acceptable option was marriage, and that seemed unattainable. A plain spinster with a domineering father didn't command a lot of attention from bachelors. And if a man did come forward by some miracle, marriage would demand even more changes than a new school would. Maybe it was best she didn't have the opportunity.

The other women had already gathered, and the teams

were forming up to shoot the first round when she joined them. Starr Tinen was Isabel's group's leader. As usual, she looked as pretty and wholesome as a ripe peach. Everyone liked her, with her friendliness and a dash of derring-do. But on days like this, surrounding herself with beautiful, clever women only dampened Isabel's spirits. She sighed and rested her handbag on the tailgate of Annie's wagon while she rummaged for her pistol and box of ammunition.

"Bad day?" Starr came to stand beside her, smiling sympathetically.

"Sort of. The children are eager for school to let out for the summer break. I'm not sure Will Ingram and Paul Storrey will last another two weeks."

"That's rough. Are you ready to practice? We have new targets."

Isabel looked toward their shooting range. "Ah. Those are clever."

"Aren't they? I adore them." Starr giggled. "Trudy told me that they'll keep her from sinning."

"Oh?" The idea startled Isabel. "How so?"

"She says she usually pretends she's shooting at someone she doesn't like, and that's how she aims so well."

Isabel caught her breath, a bit startled. "Really?" Trudy was such a pleasant, friendly young woman.

Starr's shoulders quaked. "Not seriously. I expect her idea of someone unlikable is John Wilkes Booth or the porcupine that gnawed into her grain bin."

"Of course."

"Well, Trudy's got other things to think about right now, anyway."

"Oh?"

Starr nodded. "The big thing is her sister-in-law. That Rose Caplinger appears to have set her cap at Hiram, and Trudy says he wants none of it. She's cooking up a scheme to save her brother."

"What sort of scheme?" Isabel managed a sketchy smile, but she didn't feel the spirit of the plan or quite see the humor of it.

"She's going to try to match Rose up with the blacksmith. Get her out of Hiram's hair."

Susan Page Davis

Isabel's mouth went dry. She could see her second nonoption evaporating into thin air over the distant peak of War Eagle Mountain.

Starr grinned. "Come on, let's get you set up to shoot."

Isabel supposed she could pretend the pronghorn painted on her target was Rose Caplinger. The very thought shocked her, and she quickly offered a silent prayer of repentance. She fired her rounds and squinted through the haze to see if she'd aimed well. The acrid smoke of the pistol she'd bought against Papa's wishes left a bitter taste that lingered on her tongue.

When she left the practice an hour later, Isabel couldn't stop thinking about what Starr Tinen had told her. The women of the shooting club, whom she had actually begun to think of as friends, planned to do their utmost to marry off the man she loved to Hiram Dooley's shrewish sister-in-law. She couldn't bear it. For years she had carried a secret adoration of the big, brawny smith. Griffin Bane was all that she imagined in a good husband. Unlike her father, he was forthright and plainspoken. No devious schemes for Griffin. He lived a simple life, open for all to read. Honest, hardworking, not to mention handsome. And he'd proved faithful in church, too, since they'd begun having church.

She marched home and straight to her bedroom. Papa wouldn't be home for another couple of hours, provided he didn't stop at the Nugget first. In that case, who knew?

She sat down on the edge of her bed. Her heart felt heavy in her chest. Had she made a fatal mistake in never revealing her feelings for Griffin? No one knew except her mother, and she'd taken the secret to her grave. Isabel had dreaded anyone finding out. If Griffin learned of her love and rejected her, she wouldn't be able to stand the sorrow. It was better that he didn't suspect. Yet she'd said nothing all this time, and now she stood a good chance of losing him forever. If she didn't act swiftly, Starr and Trudy would throw Rose Caplinger at him. But if she let the facts be known?

The very idea terrified her.

She'd nearly told Libby a week ago when they'd talked about her father. If she had, would Libby have put a stop to this wild plan?

422

Tears streamed down Isabel's cheeks. When she reached for a handkerchief, her hands shook. She gave in to her sorrow and buried her face in her pillow. She'd never really thought Griffin would come courting. But the notion that he couldn't—ever—if Trudy Dooley's plan went forward, opened a black chasm inside her. She sobbed with abandon. The knowledge that no one would hear her only magnified her loneliness. She cried harder.

Twenty minutes later, she sat up and dried her eyes. If Papa discovered she'd cried over a man who barely knew she existed, he'd tell her she was foolish, and perhaps he'd be right.

"Are you just going to let this happen?" she asked aloud.

Continuing to live unloved and unacknowledged suddenly loomed a larger danger than the humiliation she might suffer if she took action.

Before she could change her mind, she washed her face and grabbed her shawl and bonnet. She walked quickly the half mile to town, hoping the cool breeze would even out her blotchy complexion and repair the mottling her weeping session had caused. Instead of dissipating with the exercise, her indignation grew. When the livery stable came into view, she headed straight for it, not allowing herself to think about whether anyone else saw her. The townsfolk would assume she went on business for her father, anyway. No one would ever imagine her walking into a man's place of business on a personal errand.

Smoke poured from the stovepipe on top of the smithy next to the stable, and she veered toward it. The sun would set soon, and Griffin would stop his work. She was glad she'd caught him before he left for the evening. The ringing of steel on steel beckoned her.

When she shoved the door open, he looked up from his anvil, where he was shaping a horseshoe. Despite the chilly May air outside, the smithy was warm, and Griffin stood near the forge wearing his denim trousers, leather apron, and one of the men's cotton loomed undervests that Libby sold in the ready-mades section at the emporium. His suspenders hung in loops from his belt, and perspiration glistened on his noble brow. Isabel's knees wobbled suddenly. She grasped the doorjamb and hauled in a deep breath to stave off a swoon.

"Miss Fennel. What can I do for you?" Her sudden appearance in the doorway of the smithy startled Griffin.

"What can you do for me?" Isabel's voice shook.

"Does your father need something?" Cyrus had already been over here twice today to grouse about the quality of the new team Bill Stout had brought in for tomorrow's stage run. Griffin had stood the man's griping only so long. Then he'd told Cyrus it wasn't his fault if someone had bought inferior livestock for the stage line, and maybe the division agent—Cyrus himself—ought to take over the task of buying the replacement horses. Then Griffin had politely but firmly asked him to clear out so *some* people could get their work done. And now Cyrus was sending his daughter over to bother him? He lowered the hot horseshoe into the tub of water by the forge.

The steam plumed up between them. Isabel stared at him with her pale eyes. She seemed colorless, standing there in her dress the hue of dust. Any tints her clothing caught came from the glowing coals in his forge.

"Mr. Bane. . ."

She swallowed hard, and his heart tripped. Was she bringing bad news? Her visit was unprecedented, and she wore an expression that bespoke resignation. Maybe someone had died. He almost turned to look at his friend, who sat in the shadowy corner to her left, but she began speaking again.

"I'll tell you what you can do for me." She squared her shoulders. "At the very least, you can notice I'm alive."

Griff straightened with the three-pound rounding hammer in his hands and cocked his head to one side. "I beg your pardon?"

"Griffin Bane, we've been acquainted more than ten years, and I don't think you've ever once noticed me."

He tried to get out an answer to that, but no sound was capable of passing his constricted windpipe.

Isabel balled her hands into fists. "I'm a good cook and a woman of faith. Do I need to remind you that I'm also intelligent, or that my father owns a great deal of property? When he passes on, I shall inherit it all. Every acre. I may not be the handsomest woman in Fergus, but I daresay I'm among the most eligible."

He cleared his throat. "Yes ma'am, I expect so."

"Do you? Well then, do something about it. Or do you prefer to be sacrificed to *that woman*, so that Hiram Dooley doesn't have to think about getting married?"

A sudden movement in the corner drew a startled gasp from her. Hiram leaped from his perch as Isabel whirled and stared at him. She lifted one thin hand to her lips and sobbed. Lifting her skirt, she turned and ran.

Hiram raised one hand as though to stop her, but she was gone. He looked around at Griffin. For a long moment they stared at each other. Hiram shrugged.

The quiet gunsmith's bewilderment reflected his own, and Griffin began to shake. A huge laugh worked its way up from his belly to his chest. Unable to stop, he let it out in a whoop. Hiram's eyes flared, but he soon chortled sheepishly. Griffin laughed until tears rolled down his cheeks and sputtered on the coals in the forge.

At last he pulled his bandanna from his back pocket and wiped his eyes. "I ask you, what on earth was that all about?"

Hiram gulped. "I have no idea. But her eyes were kinda wild and scary looking."

Griffin rubbed the back of his neck and lowered his eyebrows. "I don't know what got into her. It was like. . .like a mare that's been in the loco weed."

Hiram looked toward the doorway and shook his head. "Don't think she even knew I was here, at first."

"Me neither," Griffin said. "But what do you suppose she meant, me being sacrificed at your weddin'?"

Hiram's face froze. "She didn't say that."

"What *did* she say? Some babble about how I'd ought to respect her pa's money. Do you think she wants me to take on shopping for a new team for him? Because I told him I don't have time to go to the horse auction in Boise."

"That's. . .not the impression I got." Hiram hesitated. "I can't say for certain, but it sounds to me like she thinks one of us ought to marry her."

Griffin's hand went slack, and the hammer clattered to the

floor. "Ow!" He grabbed the toe of his boot and hopped about the smithy on one foot. When he at last stood still again and gingerly tested his weight on his injured foot, Hiram's face had gone all sad, the way he'd looked most of the time since Violet died.

"Griff?"

"Yeah?"

"Seems to me there's an awful lot of nuptial thinking going on in this town."

Griffin gulped. "You think she was serious? Maybe we ought to do something about it."

"Like what?"

"Maybe ask the sheriff to put a moratorium on weddings?"

Hiram frowned. "Ethan can't do that."

"Well then, the preacher maybe?"

★ CHAPTER 17 ★

Libby knocked on the door of the small house and looked around appreciatively. Lilies bloomed below the front windows, and the fresh white paint on the board siding made the dwelling stand out from the weather-beaten gray buildings on either side.

The Bentons had come to town less than a year ago, but they'd made a lot of improvements in the little rental. The pastor had purchased paint, nails, and various other items at the emporium, and Libby wondered if the landlord—Cyrus Fennel—had reimbursed the couple for enhancing his property. She also wondered if he'd followed through on his original promise to let them buy the house if they wanted to, after the six months' free rent he'd grudgingly given them had expired. On the Reverend Mr. Benton's small salary, she doubted they could afford it. Perhaps she should bring the matter up at the next town council meeting.

Bitsy cleared her throat, and Libby glanced over at her. Her companion eyed the door through narrowed eyes and twisted the chain handle of her mesh reticule between her hands.

Before Libby could assure her there was no need for nervousness, Apphia opened the door, her face glowing with pleasure.

"Ladies! Do come in. I'm so happy to see you both."

"I hope we're not interrupting your supper," Libby said.

"Not at all. We just finished. Are you here to consult my husband or to visit with me?"

Bitsy jerked her shoulders back and shot a panicky glance at Libby.

"You, please," Libby said, and Bitsy huffed out a quiet sigh.

427

"Delightful. Won't you come and sit in the parlor?"

Libby stood aside, beckoning for Bitsy to precede her. Her friend hesitated then mounted the steps and followed Apphia, pulling her shawl across the deep neckline of her bright yellow satin dress. Libby came last, closing the door.

The tiny house had no entry hall, and the front door opened on what the hostess had so glibly called a parlor. The cramped room held two chairs and a cushioned bench, a small table bearing a kerosene lamp, and a bookshelf consisting of rough boards stacked on large tin cans painted a jaunty red. Two potted plants and a framed miniature sat atop the shelves, and one wall held a sampler portraying a cross wreathed in roses and silk-floss letters, reading: BUT MY GOD SHALL SUPPLY ALL YOUR NEED ACCORDING TO HIS RICHES IN GLORY BY CHRIST JESUS.—PHILIPPIANS 4:19.

Mr. Benton peered in a doorway at the back, which Libby knew from previous visits led to the kitchen.

"Good evening, ladies."

"Hello, Pastor."

"May I serve you three ladies something?"

"No, thank you," Libby said quickly, and Bitsy shook her head, not meeting the preacher's gaze.

"That's kind of you, Phineas, but we seem to be content." Apphia nodded to her husband with a smile, and he withdrew. "Please sit down." She indicated the two chairs and took a seat on the bench.

"I do hope we're not intruding," Libby said.

Bitsy seemed more on edge than before. She wriggled in her chair, arranging her skirt and shawl to expose as little of her flesh as possible.

"Not at all. I didn't get a chance to congratulate you this afternoon on your fine shooting," Apphia said to Bitsy. "Earning the 'personal best' ribbon is an honor."

"It surely is." Bitsy touched the bit of sky blue ribbon pinned to her bodice. "I think I hold this more valuable than my onyx eardrops."

"The shooting club has helped us all to grow inwardly, I think."

Libby nodded, and silence descended on them. Apphia obviously waited for a cue from her as to the nature of their visit.

The pastor's wife wouldn't want to make presumptions, yet she mustn't enjoy seeing Bitsy so uncomfortable in the parsonage.

"Bitsy and I were talking today, and she had some questions that I couldn't answer concerning spiritual matters. Do you mind if we present her inquiries to you?"

"Of course not—unless you'd prefer to speak to Mr. Benton. He is much more knowledgeable than I am."

Bitsy's eyes darted toward the door. Perspiration beaded on her powdered brow.

"I think we'd prefer you for this errand," Libby said.

"Of course." Apphia waited, an expectant smile hovering at her lips. "Bitsy, let me say again how glad I am to have you here."

"Oh, I . . ." Bitsy cleared her throat and studied the crocheted doily beneath the lamp. Libby wondered how many invitations from Apphia the saloon owner had turned down in the past year. But she was here now, and that was what counted.

"Bitsy is very interested in the scriptures, and more pointedly, the matter of salvation."

Bitsy drew in a deep breath. "I'm convinced now that God can save me. Didn't know for sure, but Libby's shown me lots of places in the Bible where it says He can."

"Oh yes, most assuredly He can," Apphia said.

After a quick nod, Bitsy plunged on. "Well, here's the thing. If I got saved, would God make me close the saloon?"

Apphia blinked twice. "To be honest, I'm not sure. But I believe the Lord *is* going to save you, my dear, and I also believe that if you come to Him, you'll want to do whatever will please Him."

Libby let out a pent-up breath. She'd known there was a better answer than her poor brain had come up with.

"But how will I know what He expects me to do?" Bitsy leaned forward in her earnestness, letting the edges of her shawl slip.

"He makes that very clear in His Word." Apphia reached to the bookcase and took out a black-covered Bible. "Let me show you some verses."

Libby watched quietly as Apphia turned to Acts 16:31. " 'Believe on the Lord Jesus Christ, and thou shalt be saved.' "

"Hmm." Bitsy bit her bottom lip. "I thought He expected us to do good deeds."

"That comes after," Apphia said. "If you believe Jesus died to pay for your sins, you'll want to do things that please Him. But that's not what will save you and get you into heaven."

Bitsy frowned. "Funny. I always heard that it did. When someone died, folks would say, 'He's surely in heaven, he was such a good person.' But you're telling me different."

Apphia smiled. "If there's one thing I want you to understand, Bitsy, it's that all the good deeds in the world won't amount to a thing if you don't trust in Jesus. The first and most important thing is that you believe on Him. Doing good doesn't save you. But after you are saved, you will want to do good to please Him."

Bitsy's frown deepened, and she shook her head. "See, that's what I was afraid of. If I listen to this, I'll have to change my entire life and start being good."

Libby smiled involuntarily. "Bitsy, you already do good deeds. I don't know many people as generous as you."

"But my business. How would I live?" Bitsy shook her head. "I'll have to give it some thought."

Apphia said gently, "If God is calling you, then you won't be able to resist. But you needn't be afraid. He wants only what is good for you."

"That's what Augie says."

Apphia said nothing but shot a surprised look Libby's way. "Let me share another scripture with you. It tells a little bit of what God expects from us after we believe in Him."

"Yes, I'd like to hear that." Bitsy settled back and waited while Apphia turned the pages.

"Here. This is in Micah 6:8. 'He hath shewed thee, O man, what is good; and what doth the Lord require of thee, but to do justly, and to love mercy, and to walk humbly with thy God?' You see? God wants us to walk with Him. He wants us to do kindnesses to others and to be merciful."

"I expect I could work on it," Bitsy said doubtfully.

"That's one of the best parts," Libby told her. "God will help you know what's right through reading the Bible. And He'll give you the strength to do it."

"That's right." Apphia began turning pages again.

At that moment, male voices could be heard outside the front door, and a firm knock resounded throughout the house.

"Excuse me." Apphia laid her Bible aside and hopped up to answer it.

"Hello, ma'am." Griffin Bane's deep voice was filled with humility. "We're sorry to disturb you this evening, but Mr. Dooley and I wondered if we could have a word with the parson. If he's not too busy, that is."

At the mention of Hiram's name, Libby tuned her ears to the conversation. She leaned over to try to get a look, but Griffin's large figure completely cut off her view of anyone accompanying him.

"Certainly, Mr. Bane. Won't you both go on through to the kitchen? I believe my husband is out there studying his sermon."

"Oh, we don't want to bother him," Griffin said.

"It's no trouble. He's here to serve you in any way he can." Apphia stood back, and he ducked and entered the room, which seemed instantly to grow smaller.

As Griffin cleared the doorway, Hiram appeared behind him, hat in hand. Standing next to the huge smith, Hiram looked almost scrawny, though Libby knew he was several inches taller than she was. Her past surreptitious scrutiny had told her he didn't want for muscles, though he didn't have Griffin's brawn. Griffin looked toward the women and hesitated.

"I'm entertaining a couple of my dearest friends," Apphia said.

"Good evening, ladies," said Griffin.

To Libby's surprise, Hiram spoke. "Nice to see you, Bitsy. Libby." His gaze lingered on her, and Libby felt her cheeks color.

"How do you do, gentlemen?" she asked.

"Howdy," said Bitsy at the same time.

"We're good." Griffin looked expectantly at Apphia.

"Right this way," she said.

Mr. Benton came to the kitchen doorway. "Well, look who's here. I thought I heard more company. Gentlemen, will you join me for some coffee?"

"Thank you, sir," Hiram said.

"Since you two are having some, why not?" Griffin's loud voice echoed off the walls and low ceiling.

The three men shuffled into the kitchen. Apphia waited until all were well out of the parlor then shut the door between the rooms.

"There, now. This seems to be a busy place tonight."

"I ought to get going," Bitsy said. "Thursday nights can get busy. You just never know. But. . ." She looked wistfully to Apphia. "I hope we can talk about this again sometime."

"Of course we can," Apphia said. "Come anytime. If you have mornings free, drop by whenever it suits you. I'm usually here."

Bitsy nodded soberly and stood. "Thank you. I need to think some on what you told me. And. . .could you write down those scriptures you read? I think Augie could find them in his Bible for me. I mean, all Bibles are the same, aren't they?"

Libby's heart bubbled with joy as she watched Apphia write the references for Bitsy on a scrap of paper. They had made it to the door and were saying their good-byes to Mrs. Benton when the parson emerged from the kitchen.

"Ladies! I'm glad I caught you."

Libby turned toward him, curious about why he had detained them.

"My two guests just departed out the back door," the pastor said, "but they came to me on an odd errand. I wondered, Mrs. Adams, if you could possibly shed any light on it."

"If I'm able, I'll be most willing."

"Mr. Bane told me a strange tale." He eyed Libby and Bitsy sternly. "Now, this is not for distribution. I'm sure you understand that we must keep it confidential. But since you ladies are friends of Isabel Fennel's—"

"Isabel's?" Bitsy jerked her chin back. "They came to discuss Isabel with you?"

"Er. . .well, it's a delicate matter." Phineas Benton glanced uncertainly at his wife.

"I'm sure these ladies will practice utmost discretion," Apphia said.

"Yes. Well, it seems Miss Fennel entered the smithy earlier this evening in high dudgeon and let loose at Mr. Bane. Something about Mr. Dooley not wanting to get married again. Mr. Dooley overheard it all, and both men were puzzled by what she meant. Remembering that the shooting club met late this afternoon, I wondered if perhaps an incident had occurred during that meeting which upset Miss Fennel."

"Hiram getting married?" Bitsy scowled. "First I heard of it."

"That's just it," said the pastor. "He didn't know about it either. I. . .understand Miss Fennel wasn't completely intelligible. Something about Mr. Fennel's financial situation as well, but the one thing that stood out to both men was that she clearly said Mr. Dooley didn't want to get married, and that Mr. Bane ought to do something about it."

Libby again felt color infuse her face. "Oh dear."

"What is it?" Apphia asked.

"This afternoon, before you all arrived from town, Trudy and I had a conversation about her brother. I'm afraid. . ." Libby glanced quickly at the other three. "As you say, sir, we must all be the soul of discretion. Trudy is concerned that her sister-in-law, Mrs. Caplinger, is determined to marry Hiram, but Hiram wants no such alliance. We remarked on how it would be nice if Rose would look elsewhere. Starr Tinen arrived, and she rather glibly suggested that we somehow redirect Mrs. Caplinger's affections to Mr. Bane, giving Hiram an avenue of escape. It began as somewhat of jest, and I thought it ended when the other ladies arrived to shoot. I've no idea how Isabel heard of it."

"Obviously she did from either Trudy or Starr." Apphia laid a sympathetic hand on Libby's arm.

"Well, I didn't hear anything about it," Bitsy said, "but if you ask me, I think it's a good plan. That Rose Caplinger is an overbearing, hoity-toity—"

The pastor cleared his throat, and Bitsy broke off with a shrug.

"I take it Mr. Bane isn't interested in matrimony either?" Apphia asked.

The pastor smiled ruefully. "I'm afraid Mrs. Caplinger didn't enter their heads. They thought Isabel was implying that one of them should offer for *her* hand."

"For Isabel's?" Bitsy snorted. "As if either one of them would want Cy Fennel for a father-in-law."

"Er. . .yes."

"I regret my part in this." Libby's heart ached as she thought back over her conversation with Trudy and Starr. How eagerly she'd pounced on the suggestion that Hiram would like it if Rose found some other outlet for her machinations. She'd been only too happy to participate in the plan to get Rose to stop cosseting him.

"Well, I told the young gentlemen to keep quiet about it so that Isabel isn't publicly embarrassed by her outburst. Perhaps it's one of those things that will be soon forgotten."

"I think I shall visit Isabel tomorrow," Libby said. "It was never my intent—or Trudy's or Starr's for that matter—to bring pain or sorrow to anyone."

Bitsy jutted out her chin. "Might be better to just leave it alone, like the preacher says."

"But if she harbors feelings for. . .for a certain gentlemen, and we who are supposed to be her friends scheme to match him with another lady, she must feel betrayed."

"My dear, you cannot force the man to return the lady's sentiments." As usual, Apphia's gentle observation made sense.

"But still, Isabel has confided in me lately, and I should have foreseen trouble with the course we so lightly planned. Whether we would actually have tried to carry it out or not, I cannot say, but I confess it tempted me."

"It bothers you to see Hiram annoyed and afflicted by Mrs. Caplinger's unwanted attentions," Apphia said.

"Yes." Libby looked earnestly at the minister and his wife. "Please pray about this situation. I do feel I should apologize to Isabel for my part in it, though she may not know of it yet."

She left the Bentons' house with Bitsy. "I think I might stop in at Trudy's," she said as they neared the Dooleys' home. "She can't have any idea what has happened unless her brother told her." Libby wished she could undo the afternoon's events. The least she could do was warn her friend of the flurry they'd caused.

"I doubt Hiram would string so many words together," Bitsy said. "But it might be best to talk to her, especially since the trouble began at shooting practice. She'll wonder if Isabel stops coming or won't speak to her civilly."

"I'll explain it to her," Libby assured her. Bitsy's suggestion dragged her spirits even lower. Had she helped cause a rift in the close-knit shooting society?

★ CHAPTER 18 ★

"To Him be the glory, both now and forever. Amen."

Trudy opened her eyes. The Reverend Mr. Benton lowered his hands after the benediction but remained at the pulpit.

"If you would please be seated, I have an announcement."

Trudy resumed her seat on the bench between Rose and Ethan. She smoothed down her blue skirt and waited. Like everyone else, she kept her eyes on the pastor. He presented most announcements during the worship service. But now his eyes twinkled and his lips twitched as though itching to stretch into a smile.

"Ladies and gentlemen, I've been asked to issue an invitation to you all. It gives me immeasurable delight to announce a wedding to be held next Sunday immediately after our worship service. All residents of Fergus are invited."

To her dismay, Trudy felt the eyes of many people on her. Beside her, Ethan stirred. They looked at each other. Ethan gave the slightest of shrugs, as if to say, *Don't know why on earth they're looking our way.* She felt her cheeks go scarlet. It might be more humiliating *not* to be the object of speculation at a time like this, but she doubted that.

A murmur spread through the congregation, and Mr. Benton raised his hands once more. "Let me read this, to be sure I get it right." He picked up a sheet of paper and squinted at it. " 'The pleasure of your presence is requested at the marriage of Miss Elizabeth Molly Shepard and Mr. Augustus Moore'"—a choral gasp resounded across the room—" 'at half after twelve in the afternoon, Sunday, May 23rd, in the year of Our Lord 1886, in the dining room of the Spur & Saddle. Luncheon will be served afterward to all guests.' "

The pastor laid down the paper and smiled at the audience. "I understand it's been some time since a wedding was performed in Fergus. It's my pleasure to be the one officiating. I'm sure you'll all want to offer your best wishes to Bitsy and Augie. I asked them to stand with me at the door to shake hands today, but they both declined, as it's their custom to hurry home and prepare the chicken dinner they'll serve today. So I guess if you want to congratulate them, you'll either have to wait until the wedding or go around for the chicken dinner. You are dismissed."

Mr. Benton picked up his Bible and strode down the aisle, smiling. Bitsy and Augie were among the first to scoot out the door.

"Well," Ethan said. "I guess the chicken dinner will be sold out today."

Trudy couldn't help feeling just a smidgen disappointed—not that Bitsy was getting married. That was wonderful. But she'd imagined somehow that she would be the first bride Mr. Benton married in Fergus.

"A wedding in a tavern?" Rose sniffed. "I should think not."

"She's being married at her home," Trudy said. "You were married at your home. What's wrong with it?"

"You know what's wrong with it. Although I can see why the minister didn't want to perform the ceremony here in the church. If you call it a church."

"I beg your pardon." Trudy's patience had worn thinner than the knees of Hiram's gardening trousers.

"All you have is an old store building and a slew of benches. Not a proper church."

"The church is not built with human hands," Ethan said.

Trudy threw him a grateful look.

"Humph. I'm surprised he'll even conduct the wedding." Rose stood and arranged her shawl, fan, and reticule.

"Careful," Hiram said.

She smiled at him with an air of superiority. "Careful of what? She's a woman of ill repute. Why is she even bothering with a wedding?"

Hiram eyed her for a long moment then turned and pushed into the aisle at his end of the bench. He didn't look back.

"Bitsy is not a loose woman," Trudy said between her teeth.

"Hmm. If you say so. But still, being married in *that place*."

"It's a saloon. That's all." Even Ethan sounded ready to snap.

Rose watched Hiram's progress toward the door and shook her head. "Sometimes, Gert, I don't think your brother likes me."

Trudy hesitated. Their eyes met. "I go by Trudy now."

Rose flipped one end of her shawl across her shoulder, and the fringe hit Trudy in the face. "So I've been told."

She entered the aisle. Trudy stood still, fighting back tears. Ethan's hand settled on her arm. She could feel the warmth of his fingers through the fabric of her dress.

"I have a thought, sweet Trudy."

"What?"

"How'd you like to sample the chicken dinner today?"

She reached for the lace edge of the handkerchief she always kept up her sleeve on Sunday, in case Mr. Benton's sermon illustrations got too heart-wrenching. She shook it out and dabbed at her eyes. Turning to Ethan, she smiled, trying to keep her lips from quivering.

"If I hadn't cooked a big roast last night...besides, we can't run out on Hiram."

"I expect you're right." He picked up his hat and stepped into the aisle.

All the way to the door, Trudy felt his fingertips, warm and feather-light, at her back. They shook hands with Apphia and Phineas Benton. When they reached the boardwalk outside, Trudy automatically headed for home.

Ethan nudged her. "Hey, look."

She turned and followed his gaze. Her brother was walking slowly down the street in the wrong direction, letting other people pass him. She glanced up at Ethan then hurried after Hiram. She didn't speak until she was at his side, a little out of breath.

"Where are you going? Ethan's coming over for lunch."

Hiram stopped walking. Ethan caught up to Trudy and stood beside her. Hiram pulled in a deep breath and cocked one eyebrow southward, along the street.

"You two go on home and eat with Rose, if that's what's proper. I thought it was time I tried the chicken dinner."

Rose's presence at the wedding the next Sunday surprised Libby to no end. She had fully expected the eastern lady to boycott the event. Instead, she'd shown up wearing a watered silk gown of palest pink and a confection of a hat that Libby would have given a week's profit for.

After the simple ceremony, which the pastor performed before the bar without apparent qualms, Rose attached herself to the Runnels family. She went through the refreshment line laughing with Josiah, who was at least five years younger than she was. Libby told herself it was none of her business and she didn't care, so long as Rose's claws weren't poised over Hiram.

Trudy insisted that Libby join the Dooleys at their table to enjoy their luncheon, though she'd sat with the Harpers during the wedding. The saloon girls had transformed into bridesmaids, and the bridal couple had hired Terrence and Rilla Thistle, along with Ezra Dyer, to serve up the roast beef, mashed turnips, biscuits, and gravy.

"Don't Vashti and Goldie look sweet?" Trudy asked as they walked to one of the round tables near the bar.

Libby noted that no bottles of liquor were displayed on the shelves. Snowy linen tablecloths covered the bar, where the wedding cake and punch bowl were set out in splendor. She glanced at the huge mirror and moved toward another chair.

"Want to see your reflection while you eat?" Hiram asked, shaking his head.

"No, I want to watch everyone else without them knowing it."

He laughed silently. Their eyes met, and the warmth of the connection startled her. Feelings Libby hadn't known since early in her marriage to Isaac surged through her.

Ethan held Trudy's chair. Glad for the distraction, Libby smiled at them. They made a lovely couple. Perhaps observing today's wedding would help Ethan get past whatever kept him from making their engagement official.

She realized with a start that Hiram was holding her chair. "Oh, thank you." She sat down and avoided looking directly at him for fear she would blush scarlet. She gazed across the room to where Vashti and Goldie sat with the bride and groom. "You're right, Trudy. The girls do look fine today."

Vashti had asked Annie Harper to help her and Goldie stitch lace inserts into the necklines of their best dresses. Flounces of Viennese lace from Libby's most expensive yard goods had given the gowns a respectable "formal" length.

The bride had come to Libby for help in finding a suitable dress on short notice. Two telegrams to Boise had performed a near miracle—an elegant ivory gown had arrived by stagecoach on Wednesday, and Annie had spent all day Thursday altering it to Bitsy's form. Anyone would deem today's bride lovely and well-gowned, Libby was certain—even Rose Caplinger's snooty New England friends.

Augie had arrived at the wedding carrying a top hat, which Libby suspected was too small for him to actually wear. She recognized it as one belonging to former mayor Charles Walker—the only top hat in town, so far as she knew. Augie's plain black coat and pants, with a new white shirt and black ribbon tie, were complemented by a gold-embroidered waistcoat.

"Everyone looks well-turned-out today." Ethan gazed at Trudy as he spoke.

Griffin Bane, who had served as Augie's best man, rose and tapped on his glass with a spoon. The chatter ceased, and all eyes homed in on him.

"Folks, we're gathered for this happy occasion, and Augie asked me to tell ya all that he and the missus appreciate your friendship."

The men began to clap and whistle, but Griffin held up one hand.

"All right, thanks, but I got something else to say. That is, Bitsy and Augie have something else to say."

Bitsy stood, and Augie shoved back his chair and stood beside her behind the flower-decked table. She looked up at him, and Augie nodded and slipped his arm around her.

"Friends," Bitsy said, "we thank you all for coming. I know it's the first time some of you've been in this building, and I appreciate your being here with us today. I hope you'll consider this our home and come back often." She paused and cleared her throat. "You all know I've never served liquor in this building on Sunday for all the twenty-three years I've lived here."

"You gonna start now, Bitsy?" yelled Parnell Oxley, one of the cowhands from the Landry ranch.

"Yeah, let's have something to help celebrate," said stagecoach driver Nick Telford.

"Nope, I ain't going to do it. And furthermore, if you and the other boys come around here Saturday night, you'll be disappointed again. Folks, the Spur & Saddle is hereby closing its bar. Last night we did a good business, and I hope the fellas all enjoyed it, because that was my last evening as the owner of a saloon. Augie and I decided together that we want to get out of the business."

The room was so quiet, Trudy could hear Rose's fan flap from two tables away.

Pastor Benton rose, and all heads turned his way. "Bitsy, Augie. . ." He turned to look over the room full of people. "You've made a courageous decision, and one I'm sure the Lord will honor. I know the people of this town will support you in your new endeavors."

Augie grinned and squeezed Bitsy. "Thank you, Preacher. This decision was a long time coming, just like my darlin's decision to tie the knot."

A subdued laugh rippled across the dining room.

"Let's just say the Lord and Augie were both patient with me," Bitsy said. "As of tomorrow morning, the Spur & Saddle will serve meals, coffee, sarsaparilla, lemonade, and sweet cider."

"Amen!" Pastor Benton clapped his hands, and Libby hastened to join in. Pride welled up in her. Soon at least half the people applauded. Some of the men sat thunderstruck, their mouths set in disappointed lines.

"Good for them," Ethan said as he clapped enthusiastically.

Trudy nodded. "We'll have to come in often."

Libby smiled as she watched the newlyweds accept the unaccustomed encouragement. Bitsy's spiritual struggle had involved several more conversations with the Bentons, and after last week's announcement of the impending wedding, she'd confided to Libby that she'd believed in Christ and surrendered her heart to Him. Libby hadn't pressed her about her earlier question concerning the saloon, but she'd wondered.

Trudy leaned toward her and whispered, "What do you suppose they did with their leftover inventory of spirits?"

Libby just shrugged. She glanced at Hiram and found he was watching her. He looked away but then looked back with a sheepish smile. She hadn't felt so lighthearted in years.

When the applause petered out, Bitsy gave a decisive nod. "Well then, I hope you enjoy the cake. Augie spent the better part of the last two days working on that thing, so eat up."

"It's a work of art," Bertha Runnels called out. "Bitsy, you oughta frame that cake and hang it on the wall."

Everyone laughed, and soon Goldie and Vashti were darting between the tables, distributing slices of Augie's masterpiece. Libby got a piece with a sugar bell on it. She had to agree with Bertha, it was almost too pretty to eat.

When Vashti handed a plate to Cyrus Fennel, who sat at a nearby table with Isabel and the Walkers, he grinned up at the girl. "You sure there's nothing with a kick to wash that down with?"

"It's lemonade from here on in, Mr. Fennel."

"Bitsy can't be serious about that."

"Oh yes sir, she is."

"What will you and Goldie do for a living?" Cyrus asked. Libby didn't like to eavesdrop, but she, too, was curious.

"For now, we're staying on here to board. Miss Bitsy says we can try waiting on the customers who come to eat here and wash the dishes. Goldie's going to keep playing the piano when people want her to."

"Are you happy about the change?" Isabel asked.

"Yes ma'am. Mostly. Augie says they won't make as much money as they have been, and if business drops off, they might have to pay us less. We'll see."

Cyrus frowned as the girl moved on to the next table. Libby could almost see the gears turning in his head, like a windup music box. This place would transform nicely into an elegant restaurant, and Augie's cooking far outstripped Mrs. Thistle's. Competition for the boardinghouse. If Bitsy decided to open rooms for rent as well, she might just put the Fennel House out of business.

"Cyrus doesn't look too happy," Hiram said.

"No he doesn't." Libby decided it was time to bring up an idea she'd considered for several weeks. "Hiram, I've been thinking. You know we ladies go through a lot of ammunition at our shooting practice."

He chuckled. "Trudy's fired more rounds this spring than I've shot in my whole life."

"That's not true, and you know it." His sister scowled at him. "You used to shoot all day, seemed like, for the fun of it. You're a much better shot than I am."

Ethan leaned back and eyed her skeptically. "Everybody knows you're the best shot in Fergus."

"They *think* they know." Trudy took a bite of the wedding cake.

"So, what about the ammunition?" Hiram asked.

Libby hesitated. She'd intended for this conversation with Hiram to be private, in case he wasn't agreeable, but the others at the table had obviously heard her opening, and she couldn't back down now. "Well, I've always told the girls to gather up their empty shells. I give them a small discount on the next box when they bring me their brass or shotgun shells."

Hiram nodded. He'd often bought used shells from her to reload, as did many of the other townspeople.

"So, I wondered, would you be interested in a business arrangement with me where you reload them for me? I could resell them as reloaded ammunition, not just as empty shells. Of course, I'd supply the powder and lead as well. And if you didn't have molds for certain sizes, I'd order them for you."

His eyes took on an appreciative gleam as she spoke, and by the time she finished, his crooked, shy smile shone through. "That sounds like a good idea. I could work on them when my gun business is slow."

"I could pay you half a cent each, I think."

"That could be good for both of you," Ethan said.

Hiram nodded. "A sound business idea."

Later Libby barely remembered the rest of the afternoon. Goldie's sweet piano rendition of "Sweet Genevieve," when Augie had led Bitsy around the small piece of open floor in a waltz, had shocked those who didn't believe in dancing, and those who didn't believe in worldly entertainments on Sunday even worse. But for Libby, the most memorable moment of the day was when the quiet gunsmith gazed at her with his calm gray eyes and praised her business acumen.

★ CHAPTER 19 ★

School was finally out, and Isabel reveled in her freedom. On the Monday after the closing program, she rode into town with her father. She asked him to let her out before he turned off Main Street to leave the wagon at the livery stable. She was determined to avoid a face-to-face meeting with Griffin Bane at all costs.

Since her regrettable outburst at the smithy, she'd only seen him across the room at church and at Bitsy's wedding. He hadn't acknowledged her presence, and she'd done all she could to stay out of his line of vision. As far as she could tell, word of the incident had not reached her father, but she still held her breath every time he came home from town.

She walked to the emporium and entered. Libby looked up from arranging new merchandise in the linens section. "Good morning. It's a pleasure to see you in here on a weekday."

Isabel approached her, smiling. "Thank you. Since I've six weeks until the summer term begins, I thought I'd pick up some sewing notions. I want to make over a couple of Mama's summer dresses."

"A bittersweet task." Libby walked with her to the fabric section. "New items for your wardrobe, but constant reminders of your departed loved one."

The door opened, and Ralph Storrey came in.

"Excuse me," Libby said. "If you need any help, I shan't be far." She turned to greet Ralph. "What can I do for you today, sir?"

"Did you get any more barbed wire?" the rancher asked. "I've strung all I had, and I'm a thousand feet short."

"Yes, I did. It's on the back porch, where Josiah unloaded it for me. Do you want to drive your wagon around back, and I'll meet you out there?"

Ten minutes later, she returned to the store through the back room and jotted something in her ledger. Several other customers had come in while she was gone. Florence was weighing out dry beans for Bertha Runnels. Isabel had found all the items on her list and had stopped to examine the selection of buttons.

Libby made her way between the tables and shelves of merchandise. Isabel looked up as she approached.

"I think I've found what I need, but these darling silver buttons caught my eye."

"They can make an older dress look new."

"That's what I was thinking." Isabel slid them into her basket. "There. I suppose I'm finished, except for a pound of coffee for Papa."

She waited while Libby measured it for her.

"Any more word about your uncle?" Libby asked.

"No." Isabel glanced around at the other shoppers and back to Libby. "I haven't heard a word since that one visit. Papa doesn't talk about him. Our dinner conversation is rather strained." She had tried to put Uncle Kenton out of her mind these past few weeks, and her father hadn't spoken his name once. The entire connection with the ex-convict had a sordid feel, and she wished she could erase the memory of the night he'd come to the ranch.

"I'm sorry to hear that," Libby said. "Do you want this on your father's account?"

Isabel hesitated. "The coffee only. I'll pay for the notions." She wished she could talk to Libby again. They hadn't had much of a conversation since Libby had come to the schoolhouse to apologize for encouraging Starr and Trudy to match up Rose Caplinger and Griffin. When Libby had explained how it came about and assured her they meant no harm, Isabel was able to forgive the three ladies.

Rose swept into the emporium, followed by Trudy.

"Ladies," Libby said in greeting. Rose smiled cordially, but Trudy wore a downcast expression.

Isabel accepted her change from Libby and picked up her

market basket. "Good day, ladies." She didn't think she could remain long in the same room with Rose and not feel the pangs of jealousy rise again. The young widow was an outsider who would never understand Griffin, a man who'd grown up in the West. So far Isabel had seen no evidence that Rose had looked Griffin's way any more intently than she looked at other men. Apparently the plan had fizzled. But she still didn't want to be around the woman.

"I'll see you this afternoon," Trudy called after her.

Isabel stepped onto the boardwalk then flattened herself against the emporium's door. A short way up the street, Griffin was leaving her father's office. She stood still, her heart pounding, until he turned northward toward the livery stable without seeing her.

She felt the irony of the situation. Ten days ago, she'd longed for him to notice her. Now her cheeks burned in shame at the thought, and she was glad he'd gone the other way.

"How may I help you, Mrs. Caplinger?" Libby asked.

"Do you have any dye?"

"Yes, I have a good selection of colors." Libby led her down the room. "The newer line from the Fossett Company seems to hold better than the old ones. Emmaline Landry dyed a set of curtains with the scarlet, and she said they came out beautifully."

"Colorfastness is especially crucial in apparel," Rose said.

"Oh, are you dyeing some clothing?"

"Feathers," Trudy said with a woeful grimace. "She's going to make hats."

Libby looked at Rose and smiled. "This town could use a few more hats, and some of yours are delectable."

"Why, thank you. I've decided it's my calling."

"Oh? Are you saying you make your own hats? The pink one you wore to the wedding was exquisite."

"Thank you. Yes, I have a natural talent for it. And I've decided to stay here in Fergus and ply my skill as a trade," Rose said.

Libby looked anxiously at Trudy, who shrugged, a perfect imitation of Hiram's favorite gesture.

"No slight to your merchandise," Rose went on, "but I think this town needs a decent millinery shop."

Libby's love of fashion struggled against her loyalty to the Dooleys. "What a lovely idea. Of course, I have to stock a wide variety of merchandise, and I only carry a limited selection of ladies' hats and bonnets. But. . .do you think there are enough ladies with spending money in this town to support such a shop?"

"I believe women are willing to pay for the best. When they find superior items that flatter their looks, they're happy to turn over their savings."

"Well, you may be right."

"I've mailed an order for supplies." Rose picked up a roll of lace edging and peered at it. Her lip curled, and she laid it down. "Feathers, netting, and embellishments."

"I wish you success," Libby said.

Trudy brought a one-pound bag of salt and laid it on the counter. She turned away, toward the spice shelves.

"I perceive that in this town, widows are required to support themselves," Rose said.

Libby felt her face color. "I would rather say that in this town, women of any marital status are able to support themselves if they so choose and if they are willing to work hard."

"Well, it seems my brother-in-law does not look for a closer relationship." Rose frowned. "No matter."

Indeed, Libby thought. To an untrained eye, she supposed Fergus might look like a fertile hunting ground for husbands. Several solvent widowers and bachelors made their home here. Without even trying, she could name a dozen, from Cyrus Fennel and Dr. Kincaid to the ranch hands and miners who populated the valley.

Rose probably considered her prospects quite good, even though Hiram wasn't interested. At least she'd finally deciphered that message. She'd been blessed with a pretty face and figure, and she could be charming when she wished. Unfortunately, a lot of the men in town already knew she could also be a harridan. Libby expected most of them to avoid Rose, if only out of sympathy for Hiram. But some gentleman might place more value on her looks than her personality and offer for her in spite of her acid tongue. And God could work the impossible, after all. Rose might, with divine intervention, change her ways.

Libby's pity collided with the knowledge that she hadn't prayed faithfully for Rose. Guilt seeped through her. The woman needed her friendship and her prayers. Instead, she had schooled her features to neutrality whenever Rose was around and had harbored her private dislike of the interloper.

On impulse, she smiled and leaned toward Rose. "Mrs. Caplinger, I know Trudy has invited you to our shooting circle, but I want to extend my invitation, as well. We'd love to have you join us on Mondays and Thursdays if it suits you."

"Hmm." Rose eyed her suspiciously. "I'm not sure that it would suit me. But I've heard so much about it, I might try it once. We shall see."

Trudy paid for her salt. Rose didn't buy so much as a spool of thread. Libby wasn't sure whether she should feel insulted. Apparently Rose planned to order her supplies for her millinery venture directly from the manufacturers and bypass the emporium. Fair enough. A dozen questions leaped to her mind. Where would Rose set up shop? Would she continue to live with the Dooleys? She decided to let the questions go until she had a private audience with Trudy. As the two women left her store, Libby thanked God for apparently solving Hiram's problem without the Ladies' Shooting Club's involvement.

Ethan hurried across the street toward the post office. Peter Nash never sent for him without reason. The summons had come by way of Peter's son, who'd popped in at the jailhouse and said, "Sheriff, my pa wants to talk to you," and left.

When he mounted the steps to the Nashes' front porch and opened the post office door, Ethan saw that Peter was deep in conversation with a stranger.

"Oh Sheriff, you're here. Thanks for coming." Peter gestured to the man, who wore spurs, work pants, and a cotton shirt. A wide leather belt slung around his waist carried a holstered gun and dozens of rounds of ammunition.

"This here's Wilfred Sterling," Peter continued. "He says he's Frank Peart's nephew."

Ethan stepped forward, scrutinizing the man. He hadn't

removed his hat, but even so, Ethan recognized him.

"Sterling?" Ethan studied him carefully.

"That's right." The man made no offer to shake his hand.

"If you're Frank Peart's kin, why didn't you say so earlier? Oh, and don't think I don't know you. You're one of the rascals I ran out of the Spur & Saddle a couple of weeks ago."

"Just been getting settled in at my new job."

Ethan noted that he had his pistol back—Cyrus had taken the two cowpokes' guns away with him when he'd paid for the damage at Bitsy's. "At the old Martin ranch."

Sterling returned Ethan's gaze from beneath long lashes. "That's right."

"I've been inquiring all over the country, with some help of other folks here in town. Everything we've gotten back says Frank Peart has no living family."

"Guess they missed me."

Ethan nodded, more skeptical than ever. "And exactly how are you related to Frank?"

"My ma was his sister. She married and moved upstate. Hadn't seen her brother for nigh on thirty years."

"Uh-huh. And she's deceased now?"

"That's correct."

Ethan scratched the back of his head. He'd received replies from New Jersey indicating Frank Peart had indeed had a couple of sisters, but both were deceased.

"I'm not sure you have a legal claim to Frank and Milzie's land. But you'll have to go to Boise and do a lot of paperwork if you plan to try to inherit it. They'll expect you to prove your relationship to Frank. Can you do it?"

Sterling's eyebrows lowered and his mouth tightened. "How'm I supposed to do that?"

"I don't know. I'm not an attorney. But I'll tell you right now, you can't just squat on the Pearts' land and call it yours." Ethan wasn't sure what would happen to the land, but he had an impression the government was going to take it back. Not that the old mine was worth anything. But as sheriff of Fergus, he wouldn't let just anyone waltz in and lay claim to it. Especially someone he suspected of lying.

Susan Page Davis

"We'll see about that." Sterling stomped out, his spurs scraping the porch steps.

Ethan closed the door the cowboy had left open. "So, Mr. Nash, was he here to pick up some mail?"

Peter shook his head. "Sending some."

"Where to, if I may be so bold as to ask?"

"Well, since you're the law. . ." Peter produced two envelopes and laid them on the counter. "Can't let you take them, but you can see them, I guess."

Ethan looked down at the letters. "Hmm. Written by two different people, I'd say."

"He told me one was from his boss."

Ethan bent down to decipher the addresses. "Pennsylvania. And Massachusetts."

"That's right," Peter said.

"Reckon I'll send some wires to the authorities in those towns, if Fergus can stand the expense, Mayor."

"Feel free, Ethan. I don't like that fellow." Peter scooped up the letters.

"Right. Thanks for sending your boy over for me."

Ethan stepped outside. Cyrus Fennel must be in his office now. Time for another parley.

He waited on the boardwalk while Cyrus sold a stagecoach ticket to a salesman who'd stopped overnight at the Fennel House. The man talked on and on about his recent travels. At last he came out and headed across the street toward the boardinghouse.

Ethan stepped into the office. "Morning, Mr. Fennel."

Cyrus had begun to rise from the chair behind his desk but sank back into it.

"Sheriff. What can I do for you?"

"You expressed an interest in buying the Peart place. I just wanted you to know there's a fellow in the area who claims to be Frank's heir."

"Really?" Cyrus shrugged. "Thanks, but I'm not so much interested anymore."

"That right?"

Cyrus opened a wooden box on his desk and took out a cigar. "As a matter of fact, I'm thinking of selling off some of my

450

property outside of town."

Ethan watched him in surprise. Cyrus usually held on to real estate like it was his life's blood. If he ever sold a piece, he made sure he took a very good profit.

Cyrus lit the cigar and took a couple of puffs. "I'm having a little cash flow problem." He grimaced. "Had some family needing a little help. So I can't buy any more land just now. But thanks for letting me know."

"All right." Ethan turned back outside into the brilliant sunshine. Odd. Very odd. And the coincidence of one of the hands at a ranch Cyrus owned claiming to be Frank's nephew—that was even odder.

★ CHAPTER 20 ★

Hiram welcomed Ethan for supper on Wednesday evening. Meals at the Dooley home had become monologues from Rose. Neither he nor Trudy had the energy to wrest the conversation from her anymore.

"Mr. Fennel showed me three buildings today. As soon as I decide which one I like best and find someone to help me clean it, I shall open my business." Rose gazed pointedly across the table at Trudy but elicited no reaction.

Trudy looked wrung out, Hiram realized. As exhausted as he felt.

Ethan smiled cordially and passed the dish of dandelion greens to Rose. "And will you continue living here when you've established your shop?"

Frown lines appeared between Rose's eyebrows. "I'm sure I've enjoyed visiting with my kin, and we have a pleasant household here. But truthfully, I'm considering another arrangement."

"Oh?"

To give him credit, Ethan hid the glee that statement must have fanned in his heart. Hiram accepted the dish of greens from Rose and nodded his silent thanks.

"Yes, I wouldn't want to impose on my brother-in-law and Gertrude. After all, this is their home. I had thoughts at one time that we might all continue as a unit, but..." Rose shook her head. "I've decided to become an independent businesswoman. This town seems to foster such enterprises, and I'd like to try."

"I wish you success," Ethan said. He looked over at Hiram. "I heard back from the governor this afternoon."

"About the Peart property?" Hiram asked.

"Yes. Since Milzie inherited from Frank, and then she died without a will, if no next of kin is found, the government will take possession of the property."

"But you said this Sterling fellow claims to be Frank's kin," Trudy said.

"But Milzie was the last owner of the property. Sterling's not blood kin to her. I'm not sure that matters." Ethan shook his head as he picked up his fork. "I don't pretend to understand it all. There's another complication, though. Milzie didn't pay taxes on the land for the last ten years, so it may be sold for back taxes."

"Wouldn't that be something?" Trudy rose and went to the stove for the coffeepot. "And you said Sterling hasn't proved his relationship to Frank."

"I doubt he can." Ethan held his mug up for some coffee.

Rose tossed her head when Trudy approached her. "I'll have tea, please."

Trudy said nothing but came around the table and filled Hiram's mug and her own. After replacing the coffeepot on the stove, she took down a china cup and saucer. Rose had made it clear the first day of her visit that it wasn't right to drink tea from a mug. One needed the saucer to partake properly. Lately Trudy had been waiting on Rose less and prompting her to take care of herself. Hiram wondered if her hints at moving out sprang from this. Though they'd tried to remain courteous, she must feel their reluctance to have her stay much longer.

"Well, you've got to do right by Milzie," Trudy said as she measured out tea leaves. "You can't let anyone take her land."

"I agree," Ethan said.

Hiram sipped his coffee and set the mug down. "Seems to me the law is in place, but whether Boise will bother to see that it's enforced is another question."

Trudy's eyebrows drew together. "That might fall to you, Eth."

Ethan nodded, but he didn't look happy. Hiram hated for his friend to feel pressure from the territorial officials as well as the townspeople and folks who skirted the edge of the law. But better

Ethan than him. Give him a good piece of cherry wood and some sandpaper, and Hiram would be happy to stay out of public doings.

Ethan ate the last bite of pumpkin pudding with cream and pushed back his chair. Trudy was a powerful good cook. But Rose had stopped her flurry of baking since the Sunday Hiram made it clear he wasn't interested in marrying her. And when Trudy rose to clear the table, Rose made no offer to help.

"You folks go on into the parlor," Trudy said with a tight smile.

"Why don't you gentlemen bring your coffee, if you'd like." Rose's bright comment included them both, though Ethan had emptied his mug. "Oh Trudy, the sheriff needs a refill."

"No, I'm fine, thanks." Ethan stood. "I'll just help put these dishes through the dishpan."

"Nonsense." Rose smiled beguilingly. "You've worked hard all day. You need a chance to relax."

Ethan chuckled. "I haven't done much strenuous work today, ma'am, and I expect Trudy's done a heap more in that line than I have." He picked up his dishes and carried them to the work counter. Trudy set out her dishpan and started to walk around him, to the hot water reservoir on the stove. He touched her sleeve. "Let me get that for you."

"Thank you." Her smile was genuine now, if fatigued.

Hiram also carried his dishes over and set them in the dishpan. "How about I wash and Ethan dries? You go take a load off and visit with Rose."

Apparently that prospect didn't appeal to Trudy either. "If we all work at it, the chores will be done sooner."

"All right," Hiram said. "What would you like me to do? Whatever will help you most."

"You could sweep the floor and take the table scraps out to the chicken yard."

Rose stood uncertainly in the doorway to the parlor. "Aren't you coming, Hiram?"

"Might as well help clean up. I did my share of eating."

"You could wipe the table," Trudy suggested.

Rose's eyes narrowed. "I believe I'll work on my hat models."

She disappeared into the parlor.

Ethan glanced at the Dooleys and lowered his voice. "Now that I've got you two alone, you might be interested to know that I heard back from a police chief in Massachusetts—the town where Kenton Smith sent his letter. He's never heard of anyone by that name."

"Well, you tried." Trudy finished loading the dishpan. Fifteen minutes later, the dishes were done and the kitchen back in order.

"I think I'll go 'round and see Doc Kincaid," Hiram said. "He mentioned the other day that he likes to read, and I told him he could borrow that book you gave me last Christmas."

"All right," Trudy said. "I hope he's not out on a professional call."

Hiram took his hat and slipped out the back door.

"Feel up to a stroll?" Ethan asked. "There's a near-full moon tonight."

"Yes, I'd like that." Trudy stepped to the parlor doorway. "Rose, I'm stepping out with Ethan for a little while."

"Oh. Is Hiram going?"

"He's visiting Dr. Kincaid."

"I thought his hand was healed."

"It is, pretty much. I think this is a social visit."

"Oh. I see."

Ethan took Trudy's shawl from its hook and held it for her. When she turned into it, he wrapped it around her shoulders and squeezed them. She smiled up at him.

"I expect you'll want a bonnet, too. It's still cool out evenings."

Soon they left and walked the short distance to Gold Lane. Ethan hoped she'd go with him as far as the river this time. It was quiet there and secluded. Late in summer, the river would be little more than a trickle, but now, in mid-June, it flowed fast over the rocky streambed. The sound of it reached them as they ambled past the last houses in town and down the slope toward the water. The moon peeked between the mountain summits to the east. He reached for Trudy's hand.

"What can you do about that cowboy claiming Milzie's land?" she asked.

"I expect I ought to go out and talk to him. Maybe I'll ride out in the morning. I'll tell him again that unless he can prove his kinship to Frank Peart, he can't inherit the land, and maybe not even then. He really needs to talk to a lawyer who knows the territorial statutes if he wants to pursue it."

"What will happen if he can't claim it? None of those letters we wrote have been answered yet."

"It'll sit for a while, and then it will probably be sold at auction for back taxes."

"Cyrus will buy it."

"Well, I dunno about that. Cy seems to have changed his mind about wanting it. Says he's having a cash flow problem."

"What's that?"

"Reckon it's like the river in August. Not enough liquid to keep things flowing."

"He's short on money?" She looked up at him in the moonlight.

Ethan stopped walking. "Something like that." He tugged her toward him, and she floated into his arms.

"Trudy."

"Mmm?"

He kissed her.

Trudy hurried around to the back door on Thursday afternoon. She'd stayed longer than usual at the shooting practice to help one of the ranchers' wives steady her aim. Now she'd be late putting supper on the table.

The warm, rich smell of baking hit her as she crossed the threshold. Rose turned from the stove with a sheet of hot cookies in her hand.

"That smells delicious." Trudy smiled at her. "Thank you for baking today. I'm sure the men will appreciate it." Ethan's presence at the supper table was a forgone conclusion.

But Rose turned away a bit flustered. "Oh, these aren't for supper, actually."

"What are they for?" Trudy hung up her bonnet and shawl and tied on her apron.

"I thought I'd take a basket around to Dr. Kincaid tomorrow, to thank him for the excellent job he did on Hiram's hand."

Trudy stood still with her hands behind her, on the apron strings. "He hardly did a thing."

Rose shrugged and began removing her golden oatmeal cookies from the baking sheet with a spatula.

"Wait a minute." Trudy marched around until she was in Rose's line of sight. "I thought you'd decided you liked Griffin Bane."

Rose's nose wrinkled. "I'm sure he's a nice enough man, but he smells like the stable all the time. And his voice is so loud he startles me when he speaks."

"Oh." Trudy hadn't given it much thought. A livery owner ought to smell like the stable, and a man as large as Griff was bound to have a stentorian voice. She eyed the plates of cooling cookies. Dr. Kincaid certainly would have plenty, and so far as she knew, the ingredients came from her supplies.

"Where's Hiram?"

"I'm not sure. I think I heard him out near the barn."

Trudy quickly put a pan of potatoes on to boil. "I guess we'll use the leftover chicken. I'll go out to the root cellar and see if there aren't a few carrots left."

As she crossed the backyard, Hiram came to the barn door and waved. She veered toward him.

"Did you know Rose was baking cookies for the doctor?"

He raised his eyebrows. "Smelled something good."

"Well, she's given up on Griffin. Says he smells like the barn. Now she's after Doc Kincaid."

"Maybe we should warn him."

Trudy cracked a smile. "Do we want to? Maybe she'll have a better chance with him. Griffin's too down-to-earth for her. He sees through hypocrisy every time."

Hiram sighed. "I was hoping to get a few of those cookies without any obligations attached."

"I doubt you will. Though she's baked a pile of them."

"Maybe she'll give them to more than one fella and see who comes back for more."

They both laughed.

Trudy cocked her head to one side. "How are you doing? Really?"

"All right. I feel a mite guilty."

"Whatever for?"

He shrugged. "Seems like a gentleman ought to offer her his protection."

"Oh Hiram. That's no reason to get married. Not when she's perfectly capable of taking care of herself."

"Well, I hope she snares a man soon and moves out of our house. Can't help it. I feel all kinds of sinful to think it—especially since Griff and the doctor are both nice people."

Trudy had to admit she also felt twinges of remorse for her ill feelings toward Rose. "I'm surprised she came all the way out here looking for a husband. Wasn't there anyone back home she could have married?"

"Don't know. She doesn't talk about Albert much."

They stood in silence for a moment. Trudy wondered about Rose's dead husband. Neither she nor Hiram had ever met him, but Trudy couldn't imagine he'd had any backbone.

"Why are we trying to push her off on our friends?" Hiram asked.

"So she'll leave you alone."

"Yes, but. . .isn't it wrong of us to wish her on someone else?"

"Maybe so." Trudy sighed. "You know, she can cook and keep house when she wants to. Maybe you ought to consider keeping her on as your housekeeper."

"You mean when you and Ethan get married?"

She could see that her brother was troubled. Hiram hated change. But if she did marry Ethan, he'd have to deal with it.

"I'd rather live alone than with Rose," he said. "Besides, that wouldn't be proper. I'm sorry if it's a sin to dislike her so much. I've been praying for her and that God will change my feelings if He wants me to marry her."

She stared at him in horror. "You mean you've actually thought about it?"

"Only as a—what would Pastor call it? A spiritual exercise."

"I see."

"Have you?"

"Not really. But I should probably be praying, too. She's nothing at all like her sister was, though she bears a passing resemblance to her. Violet was sweet and kind. Whenever Rose says something mean, it makes me so mad I could slap her."

"I don't think I could stand to live alone with her, and that's the truth."

Trudy nodded. She could easily gauge his agitation by the amount he had spoken that evening. He never talked more than was needful.

"I'm sorry you're in this situation. And I don't think God will blame you for not wanting to marry her. It'd be different if her heart was softer."

"She so talkative." His eyes pleaded with her to forgive him.

Trudy lifted her arms and hugged him. "I know she's not right for you. It's obvious. And it's all right. You don't need to feel bad. If you ever do want to get married again, I know you'll choose a quiet, genteel woman."

Hiram exhaled heavily and gave her a squeeze before backing away. She wondered if he would ever get to the point where he'd consider taking a wife again. There had been fleeting moments when she'd wondered, like the short time they'd sat together with Ethan and Libby after Bitsy's wedding. Hiram and Libby had talked and smiled and seemed to get along perfectly. Yet she couldn't imagine him going courting. If she knew her brother as well as she thought she did, he viewed himself as beneath Libby socially and perhaps intellectually, which was too bad. Hiram was a smart man. A near genius where mechanical things were concerned.

She patted his shoulder. "I'm going to the root cellar for carrots."

"I can get 'em for you."

"Thanks. I hope there's enough for supper. I know they're 'most gone."

"Trudy. . ."

"Yes?"

He looked away for a second. "You know I think a lot of you. I'm glad you've been here with me all this time."

Her heart warmed. "Thank you for saying that. I'll miss you if. . .well, if Ethan ever proves up."

He nodded. As usual, she felt they understood one another perfectly.

★ CHAPTER 21 ★

Libby smiled as Bitsy and Augie entered the mayor's parlor on Friday afternoon. She patted the settee beside her. Bitsy glanced at the men who made up the rest of the gathering and took the seat next to Libby. Augie settled in the chair beside the settee.

"Good afternoon, Mr. and Mrs. Moore," Peter Nash said. "We're pleased that you could join us today. As you can see, we've invited all the town's leading business owners to help the council decide on a matter that's been hanging for nearly a year now— that of Dr. Kincaid's situation."

Charles Walker, Maitland Dostie, Ethan, Griffin, the Reverend Mr. Benton, and Ted Hire, along with council members Libby, Cyrus, Oscar Runnels, and Zachary Harper, completed the group. Ellie Nash entered bearing a tray of mismatched mugs and teacups. She circulated, allowing each guest to choose coffee or tea.

Libby accepted a pretty, violet-sprigged cup of black tea, and Bitsy followed her lead, still darting nervous glances at various members of the gathering.

"Dr. Kincaid will join us in about a half hour," the mayor went on. "That is, provided he doesn't get an emergency call. I thought that would give us time to discuss a few things before he gets here."

"Is there a problem?" asked Maitland, the telegraph operator.

"The doc isn't happy with his living situation," Peter said.

"He's perfectly comfortable at the Fennel House."

Cyrus's defensive comment drew a sigh from Bitsy. Libby half-expected her to speak up, but for once she withheld her usually frank opinion.

"I'm sure he is, but he'd like a more permanent arrangement." Peter looked around at the others. "What happened is this: A citizen of our town, who is now deceased, invited Dr. Kincaid to come and practice in Fergus. We're glad he did, but the promises Mr. Morrell made to the doctor had not been approved by the town council, and we found them to be a bit extravagant."

"Just what did he promise?" Oscar asked. He reached into his inner pocket and pulled out a cigar. He glanced over at the ladies, as though suddenly remembering their presence. Libby frowned at him, and for once, Oscar took the hint and put his cigar back without lighting it.

Peter lifted a sheet of paper. "The doctor was kind enough to loan me the actual letter he received. In it, Morrell promised him a house, rent-free, in town, along with a horse and buggy to be maintained gratis at the livery stable"—at this, Griffin scowled fiercely—"and medical supplies to be shipped in regularly from Boise at no charge to the doctor."

"The town can't afford all that." Charles Walker spoke for the first time, his voice higher and thinner even than it had been before his grave injury the summer before.

"No, we can't, and it's not reasonable." Peter folded the letter and laid it aside. "No other physician would expect such benefits. I've discussed this with Dr. Kincaid, and he understands. However, he doesn't feel he can open an office and stock the supplies he'll need without some help from the town. So far he's been operating from the boardinghouse, going to his patients whenever he's called upon."

"But we're paying his board and room for him," Bitsy said.

Cyrus leaned forward. "Correction. The town is paying for his board. He's getting his room at the Fennel House free, which doesn't help me much in paying the couple who are running the place."

"But surely it's good advertising," Libby said. "Folks must feel safer staying there with a doctor in the house."

"Yes," said Ethan. "I expect the doc lends the place an air of respectability."

No one mentioned the boardinghouse's proximity to the Nugget saloon, but Ted Hire, who currently managed the place, sank a little lower in his chair.

The minister cleared his throat. "If I might make a suggestion, Mr. Mayor."

"Of course, Reverend."

"There are several vacant buildings on Main Street and Gold Lane, mostly owned by Mr. Fennel." He nodded deferentially at Cyrus. "Mr. Fennel made my wife and me an offer last year. We lived rent free in one of his houses for six months. During that time, the church began to pay me a salary. Apphia and I sought the Lord's direction. At the end of the six months, we approached Mr. Fennel about buying the house. We reached a satisfactory agreement with payments we can afford. Perhaps he would like to extend a similar offer to the doctor."

"I don't know how much income he has," Libby said. "Some folks pay him in foodstuffs." She didn't reveal how Kincaid had come to her asking if she could take two bushels of dried corn off his hands and apply the value to the account he'd run up at the emporium for medical supplies and sundries.

"And besides," Cyrus added, "I've already given him ten months' free rent at the Fennel House. I can't see extending it any longer."

"Hmm." Peter looked around at all of them. "Perhaps the town could afford to pay Mr. Fennel a reasonable rent on a house for the doctor. Then he could set up his office and take patients there, as well as have more private living quarters. I'm afraid we'll lose him if we don't resolve the issue soon."

"I'm sure the church members would help fix up the house, as they helped us with ours," Mr. Benton said.

Griffin straightened his shoulders. "I can let him use one of my wagons, and I can make him a good deal on a horse if he wants to buy one. Can't just give him one. I mean, they cost money. So does feed. But if he wants to arrange payments or something, I'll work with him. He's a good doctor, and I think we should do all we can to keep him here."

"I agree," Bitsy said. "Augie and I can pitch in a few extra dollars, can't we?" She looked to her new husband.

He nodded. "Guess so."

"Donations would help," Peter said, "but if it's to be a regular thing, we really ought to make it part of the town's budget."

Oscar laughed. "What's that? We've never had a budget."

"Certainly we have." Zack shook a finger toward his neighbor. "Just because we never wrote it down, don't mean we don't have one. We always collect taxes for the sheriff's pay and things like that. So, we add a dollar or two to each family's yearly bill to help the doctor out until his practice becomes more profitable."

Libby stirred. "Mr. Mayor, I think Mr. Runnels has a point. The town council hasn't kept the best records of its meetings, and we generally collect money until we have enough to pay our bills, but it really should be better organized."

"Are you volunteering, ma'am?" Peter's eyes twinkled as he spoke.

Libby smiled with gritted teeth. "I'll take part of the responsibility, but not all. I could keep official minutes at the meetings, for instance. But we really should keep precise records on how much is collected from whom and how it is spent."

"I've been saying that for years," Cyrus said.

"Well then, Mr. Fennel, would you set up a ledger for the town's local tax collection and distribution?"

"I wasn't volunteering."

Everyone stared at Cyrus.

"Oh all right." He shrugged. "Someone's got to do it, I suppose. Perhaps Mrs. Adams will assist me, to make certain I set the accounts up properly."

His suggestion surprised Libby. She'd thought she'd successfully discouraged his advances, and she had no desire to spend time alone with him. "Really, you ought to be able to do it without my help. You ran the assay office for some time, and now you run the stagecoach line. You must keep books for that and report to Wells Fargo."

Cyrus didn't look happy, but in the end, he agreed to set up the town's ledger.

Peter nodded at him. "That's the way, Mr. Fennel. Your labor in this matter will be greatly appreciated." He took out his pocket watch. "The doctor should be here soon, and we'll present this plan to him. Any other business to discuss while we wait?"

"Mr. Fennel," said the minister, "yesterday I rode out to that ranch you have northeast of town."

Cyrus's eyes flared, and he waited in silence.

"I met Mr. Smith, your tenant."

"Oh?"

"Yes, I'd heard you had a gentleman living out there and working the ranch. I invited him and his employees to the church services."

"What did he say?" Cyrus asked.

"He said he might come, but truthfully, he didn't sound committed to the idea. He also warned me not to expect his men, as they're busy stringing fence."

Libby listened with interest. That must be where the rolls of barbed wire Cyrus had ordered went.

"We have a lot of newcomers in town," Griffin noted.

"Yes, we do." Mr. Benton smiled. "My wife suggested we have a social event to bring folks together. A box social, perhaps."

"That sounds like fun," Libby said. "I'm sure the Ladies' Shooting Club would support the event."

"Thank you, Mrs. Adams. I'll ask Apphia to speak with you about it." The minister beamed at her. "Social gatherings now and then can draw the community together."

Bitsy looked askance at Libby. "I'm not sure you'd want Mr. Smith's cowhands to go to it. They might make a ruckus."

Ethan frowned. "So long as we make sure no alcohol is served, the whole town could enjoy a holiday. We could stipulate that it's a dry party when we announce it."

"We'd lose a workday," Zack noted.

"Yes, but we'd get to know some of these new people." Mr. Benton's face lit as he named them off. "There's Dr. Kincaid and Mrs. Caplinger, who tells me she's thinking of locating here permanently, and a new couple out on the Colburn place and Mr. Smith and his men. There may be others I'm forgetting."

"The Thistles," Libby said. "They came last summer."

"Yes, and we don't have many social occasions when it comes down to it," Peter said. "Folks enjoyed the Moores' wedding so much, I think they'd welcome another chance to get together without waiting for a funeral."

Bitsy's cheeks reddened deeper than her rouge accounted for.

"I'll help Miz Adams and the other women, Mayor. Just tell us what you want, and we'll arrange the refreshments and such."

A sudden thought came to Libby. "Say, what if we made this into a fund-raiser to help support Dr. Kincaid?"

After a moment's silence, Peter said, "Mrs. Adams, that's brilliant."

Ethan grinned at him. "Mayor, if you want someone to be sure everyone in town gets an invitation, I highly recommend the Ladies' Shooting Club. They helped me write some letters about the Peart property a couple of weeks ago."

"What did you find out about that?" Griffin asked.

"Nothing much yet."

Ellie Nash opened the parlor door. "Excuse me, folks. The doctor's here. Are you ready for him?"

Dr. Kincaid entered, and the discussion returned to his living quarters. By that time, Cyrus had accepted the idea of putting the physician in one of his vacant houses, even if he received a miniscule rent. *Better than nothing,* Libby thought. *He can always raise the rent when the doctor's practice prospers.*

Isabel opened the oven to check on the chicken. Papa was late for supper. He'd had that meeting with the council and business owners this afternoon, but surely that was finished by now. She poured a little water in the roasting pan to keep the chicken from drying out.

A knock at the front door startled her. She doffed her apron and hurried down the hall. She pulled the door open and stared into feral dark eyes. If asked, she'd have said Kenton Smith was the one person she least wanted to see, yet she couldn't deny the relief that washed over her when she found him waiting on the stoop.

"Oh, Mr. . . . Uncle Kenton."

"Isabel. Is your father home?"

"Uh. . ." The plaid shirt he wore was in better condition than the one she'd first seen him in, and his beard had filled in, but it did nothing to enhance his pinched face and crooked teeth. His eyelids lowered at her hesitation, making slits of the critical orbs.

She quickly cataloged how many of the hired hands were about the place and how loudly she would have to scream for one of them to hear her. "I expect him any minute. Could I...could I get you some coffee?"

"That'd be nice, thank you. And can one of your boys tend to my horse? He's mighty dry, too, after that long ride."

"Certainly. Would you like to sit here on the porch or in the parlor?"

"Oh, what's wrong with your pa's study?"

Her lungs contracted, and her breath whooshed out. Papa would never want anyone in there when he wasn't present. "I'm sorry, I haven't straightened the room today. Let me show you to the parlor."

Hoofbeats sounded on the dirt road leading to the ranch house, and she peered over her uncle's shoulder toward the sound.

"Ah, there's Papa now."

"Good. I'll go and meet him."

Papa rode his big roan gelding toward the corral near the barn. Kenton limped across the yard after him. Brady came from the barn to take Papa's horse. Isabel sighed and allowed herself to relax for a moment. Then she scurried back to the kitchen. No doubt Uncle Kenton would expect a meal. She set another place at the table then sank into her chair. She could hardly believe he was alive and well. He had indeed stayed in the area and come around to visit again. She closed her eyes. *Thank You, Lord.* It felt so good to let go of that worry. *And forgive me for thinking such an awful thing about Papa.*

Libby. She would have to tell Libby as soon as possible that her fears were unfounded. How silly she had been to think. . .

She refused to wonder about the hole Papa had dug. There must be some simple, mundane explanation. Shameful that she had thought otherwise.

She rose, tiptoed to the back door, and opened it a crack so that she could peek out at the barnyard without being observed.

Her father and Kenton stood by the corral fence. The sound of their voices carried to her. Papa didn't seem to care that all the hands could hear, let alone his daughter in the house.

"I told you I can't do it."

"And I say you'd better."

Kenton's tone shocked Isabel. No one spoke to her father that way. He'd fire any cowboy who dared. He glared at the shorter man with a look of authoritative dislike that she'd seen him use only twice before—once when he'd caught a ranch hand pilfering from his desk and again when he'd discovered a prairie rattler under the back stoop.

"Get out of here." She could almost see sparks fly from Papa's flinty eyes.

"You'll regret this."

"Maybe so."

Uncle Kenton whirled and strode toward the front of the house. Isabel quickly closed the door. She stood shaking for a moment, breathing in shallow gulps. Her hands shook, and she clasped them together. When they'd stopped trembling, she took the extra plate and silverware off the table.

Her father came in a few minutes later. "Supper ready?"

"Yes."

He washed his hands while Isabel took the chicken from the oven. They both sat down. Papa offered a rather curt blessing for the food.

Isabel started to speak several times but swallowed her words. As she handed him the potatoes, he squinted at her.

"Why are you staring?"

"I. . .I'm sorry. I wondered what Uncle Kenton wanted."

"Nothing."

"But he said he'd ridden a long way to see you."

Her father took a large bite of chicken and chewed it, all the while scowling and avoiding her gaze.

"Not that far," he said at last. "You may as well know, I let him move into the old Martin place. Wish I hadn't now."

Isabel's bite of potato refused to go down. She coughed and took a drink of water. "Isn't that where those awful men came from? The ones who made such a commotion in the saloon?"

"Yes, they were his hands."

"But you made it sound like you didn't know where he would be! It seems he's been out on the old Martin ranch ever since he was last here. Why didn't you tell me?"

His mouth slid into a crooked gash. "Isabel, if there are things you need to know, I will tell you. And things change. Just because Kenton is now at the Martin place doesn't mean he was the day you asked me."

She closed her mouth and sliced off a bite of her chicken. She hated it when Papa treated her this way. She was not a child.

They ate in silence for a few minutes. When Papa's plate was empty, instead of taking seconds, he sighed and pushed his chair back. "I'm going back into town. Don't wait up for me."

"But Papa, you haven't had your coffee."

She leaped up, but he was already gone. His heavy footsteps receded down the hallway, and the front door opened and closed. She began to clear the table mechanically. A few minutes later, she heard hoofbeats as a horse left the ranch at high speed.

The coffeepot was still full. She poured herself a mug and added milk, then sat down again. Papa certainly had a lot of secrets, and he wasn't about to enlighten her on Uncle Kenton's situation or the demands the man had made this evening. Could the hole behind the barn somehow be related to Kenton Smith's appearance? Or was it just the spot where Papa had buried a dead animal? He kept the spade in the barn. Should she. . .

She shuddered.

No, she absolutely should not.

★ CHAPTER 22 ★

W hat should I do? Do you think I should talk to the sheriff?"

Libby sat opposite Isabel in her lovely parlor and pondered. It was difficult to imagine herself in her guest's position. She had come to care for Isabel, and the young woman's plight made her heart ache.

"I'm not sure there's any need for that," Libby said. "After all, now that you're certain your uncle is well, you've less reason to think a crime has been committed—other than the disorderly conduct of his ranch hands, of course, but Sheriff Chapman has dealt with that." She tried not to think about the dead cowboy out in the cemetery near the schoolhouse. Apphia Benton had described the bleak little burial service to Libby: Only the Reverend and Mrs. Benton, the sheriff, and the two men who'd dug the grave— Griff Bane and Hiram Dooley—had attended.

"But Papa. . ." Isabel wiped her streaming eyes again with her muslin handkerchief.

"I know, my dear, but you've said last night's behavior was an aberration."

"True. Papa rarely drinks to the point of. . ." Isabel trailed off, but Libby had already heard how he'd come home after midnight and two of their trusted cowpunchers had carried him in and put him to bed, shushing each other as they tripped over chairs and banged into the bedstead, trying not to awaken her. "He often has a couple of drinks in the evening. I know this. Sometimes it makes him. . .less cordial than he would otherwise be. But last night. . ."

"He was still asleep when you left home, you said."

"Yes. When he was an hour late, I tried to wake him, but he..."

Libby leaned forward and patted her hand. "I'm sorry, dear. You did right to go to Mr. Bane and tell him your father was indisposed today. I'm sure Griffin will do fine with meeting the stagecoach and taking care of any passengers' needs."

"Yes. He..." Isabel licked her chapped lips. "He assured me he would see to things, and he had me letter a sign to hang on the office door: 'For tickets and other stage line business, see G. Bane at the livery today.' And he's a man of his word."

"Indeed." Libby rose. "Let me freshen your tea."

"Oh no. I'm keeping you from your work." Isabel rose, spilling her cotton bag and gloves to the floor.

Libby bent to help her retrieve them. "You mustn't fret about that. Florence is doing a good job. I'm actually thinking of training another clerk to give me more time away from the store."

"Business has been good lately?" Isabel asked.

"Yes, and I see it as a way to help one more woman in Fergus become independent."

"Oh? Of whom are you thinking? If it's not a private matter."

"I haven't settled my mind on one person yet, but I'm watching the Spur & Saddle. I thought that if Bitsy and Augie have a slack time when they can't afford to keep both Vashti and Goldie on, I might take one of them under my wing." Libby eyed her anxiously, but no censure met her in Isabel's face. There was a time when the schoolmarm would have been horrified and boycotted the emporium if Libby hired a former saloon girl. Now the moral judgments were left to Rose Caplinger and a few of the town's older women, Libby thought wryly. "There's Myra Harper, too. She hasn't expressed interest, but I think she might be a good candidate."

"I guess there are plenty of women in this town who'd like a chance to earn some money at a respectable establishment." Isabel drew on her gloves. "Thank you for your advice. You are a good friend."

"You're welcome," Libby said. "Speak softly to your father, and I'm sure this time of turbulence will pass. And as to that hole he dug behind the barn..."

"It's probably nothing."

"Probably." They looked at each other for a moment. Libby hoped they were right, but she couldn't see an advantage to stirring up more suspicion and anger between Isabel and her father. Cyrus was a proud, opinionated man. Best to ignore his occasional lapses. "Now don't forget the box social next Saturday."

Isabel ducked her head. "I don't think I'll put a box in the auction."

"You must!" Libby squeezed her arm. "My dear, there will be dozens of bachelors bidding on the box lunches. It's a civic duty of all the single women to enter."

That drew a wan smile. "Do you think so, or are you in jest?"

Libby lifted her eyebrows. "I am entering."

Isabel's skeptical face made her burst out in laughter.

"I am, truly. So you must enter, too."

"What if we end up with a couple of crude miners?"

"Then we'll insist on eating together to keep one another safe, and rejoice in the amount of money we raised toward outfitting Dr. Kincaid's new office. But I shall pray that two nice gentlemen buy our lunches. And you must enter the pie contest, too. I happen to know you make the best lemon meringue pie in the territory."

Isabel smiled and drew Libby into an awkward hug. "Thank you so much. I've not had anyone to talk with this way since Mama died."

Tears filled Libby's eyes. "Come again soon. And if your father is cross with you tonight, ride into town and stay with me. I mean it."

Isabel opened her mouth as though to protest, then closed her lips and nodded. "Thank you, then."

She exited through the kitchen door. Libby watched over the rail until Isabel was safely down the stairs and on the back porch that served as her freight platform.

She carried their dishes to the dry sink and tidied the apartment. As she walked down the inside stairs into the emporium, she assured herself that hushing up the matter was best. What good would it do to report Cyrus's drunken spree—of which Ethan might already be aware? But it bothered her that Cyrus had set up his brother-in-law as a rancher when he'd had no contact with him for more than twenty years and didn't seem to like him much. Smith had been in prison before, and he'd hired a crew of unsavory characters.

The whole matter puzzled Libby. Cyrus was a shrewd businessman, known for running a tight ship. He wouldn't put up with laziness or drunkenness and had been known to fire stagecoach drivers for tardiness.

A vague uneasiness hovered in her chest. Kenton Smith's reappearance had not eased Isabel's fears; instead, it had substituted new ones for the old. How long could her friend continue living in dread?

✦

The day of the social dawned bright and clear. Ethan and his two ranch hands hurried to complete morning chores so they all could attend the gathering at the schoolhouse. Spin and Johnny eagerly accepted their pay from Ethan.

"I sure hope Florence Nash tells me which basket is hers." Spin riffled the bills Ethan had handed him.

"Don't spend your whole week's pay on a lunch." Johnny shook his head at his brother's enthusiasm. "That little redhead's got you in a tizzy."

"Ain't no shame in likin' a girl. Right, Sheriff?" Spin wiggled his eyebrows at Ethan.

"No Marcus. No shame a'tall."

Spin scowled at Ethan's use of his proper name. "Hey! You better not call me that in town."

"Watch it," Johnny said. "He's the boss, remember?"

Ethan grinned. "I expect you'll be eyeing the females soon, too. I suggest you take a hard look at the Harper sisters. They're good girls."

Spin pushed his hat back and frowned. "Myra's too old for him."

"Who says? Anyway, Alice isn't. And she's not homely either." Ethan took off his work gloves. "All right, let's get breakfast and clean up. Folks will start gathering by ten o'clock."

"Are you cookin' breakfast?" Spin's eyes gleamed with hope.

"No, you are. Call me when it's ready." Ethan slapped his shoulder with his leather gloves and strode toward the house.

An hour and a half later, he and the McDade boys saddled up and rode to the schoolhouse. The school yard was already thronged. Rough tables covered with dishes stretched along one side of the meadow where the scholars played during recesses. Food for those who would not be dining on auctioned box lunches filled the plank surfaces.

Ethan tied Scout to the fence between the schoolhouse and the graveyard and ambled about the grounds speaking to the townspeople. Seemed every rancher and miner within the Owyhee Valley had gotten the word and come to join in the gala.

"Hello, Lyman," he called to a gray-haired rancher who lived five miles outside town. He hadn't seen Lyman and Ruth Robinson for at least eight months. "How'd you fare last winter?"

"We got by."

Ethan lingered a moment with the couple and strolled on. Dr. Kincaid hailed him and excused himself from a knot of gaily gowned ladies.

"Well Doc, seems you've got some admirers." Ethan extended his hand, and Kincaid shook it heartily.

"For some reason, all the single ladies seem to be competing to get my attention. It's rather distracting. Does that happen to you, Sheriff?"

Ethan chuckled. "Not since I started stepping out with Trudy."

"Ah, so that's the key. A steady girl."

"Maybe so. Have any of them told you which is their box lunch yet, to be sure you'll bid on it?"

Enlightenment brightened Kincaid's face. "Oh, so *that's* what Miss Edwards meant when she said she hoped I liked pink and green ribbons. Mumbo jumbo, I thought."

"Far from it. She's gunning for you, that's sure."

"Aha. And has the fair Miss Dooley told you which is hers?"

Ethan frowned. "No, she hasn't." Was Trudy really going to risk letting another man buy her lunch? He'd better find her soon and see if he could get a hint out of her.

"Oh, and the eldest Harper girl asked me if I like currant pie and said something about a red bow. . . ." The doctor looked anxiously toward the table set aside for the mystery lunches.

"You'd best decide which one you want and put your money on it, Doc." Ethan clapped him on the shoulder. He'd just spotted Hiram and Trudy walking into the school yard with Rose, Libby, and the Nash family.

The ladies carried large baskets with bright cloths covering the contents.

Ethan greeted them and fell into step beside Trudy.

"May I carry that for you?"

She laughed. "Oh no. No man is going to get his hands on our baskets before we deliver our boxes for the auction. Right, Libby?"

"Absolutely." Libby smiled at him. "I hope you intend to participate in the auction, Sheriff."

"Of course. But it will be difficult to remain impartial. If I only had an inkling of what to bid on. . ."

"You may carry my basket, Sheriff," Rose called.

Ethan broke stride. "Oh. . .of course. Where would you like it?"

"Just follow me, sir. You'll need to exercise discretion, however. Mustn't tell any of the other fellows which box is mine." Rose giggled and wiggled a finger, beckoning him toward the auction table.

Ethan cast a helpless glance at Trudy. She shrugged as though to say, "You got yourself into it."

Orissa Walker and Annie Harper accepted the single women's offerings under cover of a strategically hung tablecloth.

"Go on and enjoy yourselves, gals," Annie told Trudy and Libby. "We'll get a batch of six or eight before we add them to the ones on the table. That way, if the gents are watching, they still won't know whose is whose."

"What have we here?" Orissa asked as Ethan and Rose stopped before her.

"Why, it's my lunch for auction." Rose smiled prettily and lifted the linen towel draped over her box. Ethan couldn't help seeing the curled lavender ribbons and paper pansies that decorated the top of the box. "Now, Sheriff, remember, mum's the word." She winked at him, and Ethan felt the blood rush to his cheeks. Was she hinting that he should bid on her box? Or perhaps that he should tell the other men to bid on it? If he whispered about which was hers, would that in reality drive away bidders?

"I'll see you later, I'm sure, Mrs. Caplinger."

"All right, Sheriff. And thank you for your assistance."

Hiram sidled up to him. "Can you help lug out benches from the schoolroom so people can sit while they watch the shooting contest?"

"Sure. When's that going to be held?" Ethan glanced around

as they walked, wondering where Trudy had gotten to. He spotted her and Libby talking with Starr and Jessie Tinen near a table covered with pies.

"After lunch," Hiram said. "The judges sample the pies and announce the winners of the pie contest, and then the shooting match will start."

"The horse race is the last event of the day?" Ethan asked.

Hiram nodded.

"You entering anything?"

Hiram shook his head.

"What's the matter? Old Hoss getting slow?" Ethan chuckled at Hiram's expression.

"You taking Scout in the race?"

"Naw, I'm just going to watch and make sure things stay peaceful."

"Hey." Hiram jerked his chin toward the road.

Ethan turned and saw several riders cantering into the schoolyard in a swirl of dust. He studied them closely and caught his breath. Eli Button, Wilfred Sterling, and the other man he'd let go after the Spur & Saddle incident had arrived, accompanied by three more men. So. Someone had extended the invitation to them, and they'd left the Martin ranch en masse for the social. He'd better speak to them immediately to be sure they hadn't brought along any liquor.

Before he could approach them, Cyrus detached himself from a knot of men and walked over to the newcomers. The oldest of the riders dismounted and fell into conversation with him.

"That must be Mr. Fennel's brother-in-law," Ethan said.

"You go ahead," Hiram said. "I'll get Griff to help me."

"All right. Oh, say, Hiram. Wait a sec." He grabbed the gunsmith's sleeve and drew him closer.

Hiram raised his eyebrows.

"Don't bid on anything with lavender ribbons and pansies," Ethan whispered.

Light dawned in Hiram's eyes, and he nodded. He smiled and slapped Ethan's shoulder before he walked away toward where Griff Bane towered over a cluster of men preparing to start a horseshoe game.

Ethan sauntered toward Cyrus and the stranger. The cowboys had dismounted and led their horses to the side of the schoolyard and tethered them near the townsfolks' mounts.

"Good day, Mr. Fennel." Ethan smiled and tried to sound friendly.

"Well Sheriff. How are you doing?" Cyrus's smile looked a little strained. "I s'pose you'd like to meet my brother-in-law, Kenton Smith."

Ethan held out his hand to the graying man. "You're the tenant on the Martin ranch."

"That's right." Smith clasped his hand briefly.

"Welcome to Fergus, Mr. Smith. Just make sure your boys behave themselves."

The older man's eyes narrowed. "Oh they will. They're good boys. They just get a little rambunctious now and then. I'm sorry about what happened earlier, but saloons have to expect a bit of action now and then."

"I don't see it that way. Were you informed that there's to be no alcohol at this picnic?"

"We got the word," Smith said.

Ethan nodded. "I hope you and your boys enjoy the day."

He walked away feeling Smith and Fennel watching him. He wondered if they had contacted the dead cowboy's family, as Cyrus had promised, but he wasn't going to ask. And he was going to do his best to find out what Trudy's box looked like. He didn't want her to wind up eating lunch with the likes of Eli Button.

★ CHAPTER 23 ★

Y ou've got to know what she put on it. Come on, Hi. I can't let some other man buy my sweetheart's box lunch."

Hiram scowled and shook his head. His sister hadn't let him see her creation. She had taken great pains to hide it from both him and Rose. If Ethan wanted to wheedle the information out of Trudy, he should do it himself.

"They're about to start the bidding." Ethan looked anxiously toward where Peter Nash was preparing to auction off the ladies' lunches.

"Folks, and especially gentlemen, gather 'round. The single ladies have put their best efforts into preparing lunches for your gustatory pleasure. We have fourteen box lunches for our auction. Mrs. Nash is going to bring me the first one, and it's up to you fellows how much money we raise here today, but I'm telling you, if you don't bid on these boxes, you're missing out on a good thing."

Ellie smiled and carried a box wrapped in plaid flannel to her husband. "Looks like the lady who made this lunch wrapped it up in a tablecloth."

Peter took the bundle and held it up. "There you go, gentlemen. Isn't that an inviting parcel? Why, Parnell, this would go nicely with your shirt."

Parnell Oxley, one of the cowboys from the Landry ranch, guffawed. "All right, Mayor, you talked me into it. I'll bid two bits."

The other men edged closer and the bids began to fly. When they lagged at two dollars, Peter let his gavel fall. "Sold to Mr. Runnels for two dollars."

Josiah Runnels walked forward to accept the package amid applause and catcalls.

"Would the lady who made the lunch please come forward?" Peter asked.

Myra Harper came from the edge of the crowd, flushing as she peeled off her apron and tossed it to her mother. She strolled over to Josiah and looked up at him. "Disappointed it's your next-door neighbor's box, Josiah?"

"Nah. I hope you made fried chicken."

Everyone laughed.

Hiram eyed Ethan. "Whyn't you bid?"

"It didn't look like what I thought Trudy would pack."

"Huh."

They stood shoulder to shoulder while Ellie took the next box to Peter. The plain white pasteboard box was tied with a wide green ribbon. Hiram wondered whose it was. What if it was Libby's and someone like Ted Hire or one of those rough cowpokes bought it? That was scary.

Spin McDade leaped into the bidding early, and Ethan sighed. "Must be Florence's box, and she told him."

"Think so?" Hiram felt a little better. Sure enough, when the others dropped out and Spin plunked down a dollar and four bits, Florence minced toward him, her face a brilliant red that clashed with her carroty hair.

The box with pansies and lavender ribbons came up next. Hiram stood perfectly still, not moving a muscle. Ethan also stayed silent, but several men began bidding. The gavel fell at two dollars and a quarter.

Rose swept forward.

"Mrs. Caplinger, thank you for a lovely entry that raised a good amount for our cause," Peter said.

Dr. Kincaid accepted his purchase with aplomb and offered his arm to Rose. She slid her hand through the crook of his elbow with a satisfied smile.

"He almost looks happy," Ethan said.

"Think he knew?" Hiram asked.

"Oh yeah, he knew. I wouldn't be surprised if every man here knew."

The next box was wrapped in plain brown paper and tied with a black ribbon like a man's necktie.

"That's an odd one," Ethan said.

Hiram felt a strange prickle at the back of his neck. He reached to scratch it.

"Ah, this is an interesting package." Peter held it up for all to see. He tipped the top slightly toward the crowd. Fastened near the bow was a packet of primers.

Peter grinned at them. "Something tells me this box was prepared by one of the members of the Ladies' Shooting Club."

Four hands shot up, and men began flinging bids at the mayor.

Ethan leaned close to Hiram's ear. "You think that's Trudy's?"

Hiram shook his head. The brown paper was what Libby used to wrap customers' packages every day, and he'd gone into the emporium only yesterday and bought a packet of primers. Trouble was, every man in town was interested. He stuck his hands into his pockets and fingered the coins in the right one.

"Two-seventy-five," Peter called before the bidding slowed down. "And now three dollars. Who'll bid three dollars?"

Hiram reached up and lifted his hat. Peter looked his way, and Hiram nodded.

"Three dollars," Peter said. "I have three dollars from a man who knows a good thing when he sees it. Who'll bid three bucks and two bits?"

Griffin roared, "Right here, Mayor."

"Three-twenty-five. Who'll make it three and a half?" He glanced at Hiram.

How could he afford it? He had only three silver dollars in his pocket. Griff Bane would win. Hiram shook his head slightly.

"Three and a half," Peter said. "Who'll bid three-fifty?" He paused, holding up his gavel. "Going once..."

"Three-fifty." Everyone turned and stared at the cowboy who'd bid. Hiram sucked in a deep breath. It was Eli Button, the man he'd walloped at Bitsy's place.

Ethan looked askance at him. "Can't let that fella get it."

Hiram grimaced.

Ethan looked at the mayor, who was saying, "Going twice..."

"Four dollars!"

Everyone turned to stare at Ethan.

"The sheriff is in the game with a bid of four dollars." Peter grinned at him. "Do I hear four-twenty-five?"

Button shook his head and walked away.

"Well Ethan, looks like you bought yourself a lunch." Peter brought the gavel down.

Hiram exhaled and watched as Libby stepped forward. She took the box from Peter and walked toward the sheriff, smiling.

"Thanks for buying my box, Ethan. I hope you enjoy what I've packed." Her gaze slid toward Hiram. "I thought for a minute you'd be my dining partner, Mr. Dooley."

He felt his face going red. "Well I. . ." He looked down at the ground.

"Guess I'd better go pay for it." Ethan looked at Libby and then at Hiram. "Hi, why don't you join us, whether you snag a box or not."

"Oh, I don't know. . ."

"Yes, do," Libby said. "There's plenty. And I have a quilt yonder. We can spread it in the shade of the schoolhouse."

"Sounds good," Ethan said. "I'll be there in just a minute." He turned and headed for the small table where Emmaline Landry was collecting the fees from the bidders.

Libby leaned toward Hiram. "Interested in buying your sister's lunch for Ethan?"

He jerked his chin up. Her beautiful blue eyes twinkled at him. He nodded.

"A nosegay of buttercups," Libby whispered. "Yellow grosgrain ribbon."

He glanced quickly at Peter, but the box the mayor now held was trimmed with blue and red rickrack.

"Meet us over there." Libby nodded toward the side of the school building, where a narrow strip of shade would give the barest relief from the sun.

Parnell Oxley walked off with the current offering, and to Hiram's surprise, Isabel went with him. He hadn't supposed Isabel would loosen up enough to participate in the event. She'd changed a lot since she'd begun going to the shooting club.

The next box sported gaudy red, pink, and orange paper. It

looked as though a child had thrown blobs of paint at it. A glittery gold cord decorated it, with several unnaturally red feathers fluttering from the knot on top.

Hiram looked about and studied the remaining widows and single women in the crowd. The two saloon girls from the Nugget giggled and nudged each other. Several men joined the bidding, and one of the cowboys won the prize of lunch with Opal Knoff, the blond from the Nugget. Another box went to Kenton Smith, and he graciously escorted the widow Daniels—whose husband had died in a wagon accident last winter—to a spot on the grass. Two cowboys and Cyrus Fennel bought boxes, and at last the one with the yellow ribbon and drooping buttercups came up for sale. The bidding slowed at two dollars.

"Come on, fellas," Peter called. "Only a few boxes left. Don't you have any cash on ya?"

Hiram looked around for Trudy, but she was keeping busy with Mrs. Storrey and Mrs. Tinen at the food tables, not paying any attention.

"Going once, going twice…sold to Mr. Hiram Dooley for two dollars."

Hiram accepted the box and walked over to Mrs. Landry's table.

"Who's the cook?" someone shouted.

Trudy looked up and clapped a hand to her mouth. She hurried around the tables toward Hiram. "Guess you're stuck with me."

The crowd laughed.

"He bought his sister's box," Hiram heard Cy Fennel tell someone else.

"Hey, Dooley, I'll buy it from you for two-ten," called stagecoach driver Nick Telford.

Hiram smiled and shook his head.

"You missed your chance," Emmaline yelled. "Bid on the next one." She smiled up at Hiram and held out her hand for the two silver dollars. "Thank you, sir."

He turned and found Trudy at his elbow.

"Sorry," she said.

"What for? It'll be good, I know that."

She smiled and walked beside him with her head high.

"Did you know it was hers?" Augie called.

Hiram just smiled and gave a little shrug. The crowd turned its attention back to the auction. Griffin and Nick began a battle for the next box. Hiram led his sister straight to the quilt in the shade, where Libby and Ethan were unpacking Libby's box.

★ CHAPTER 24 ★

Nearly one hundred people thronged around the pie table as the judges—Charles Walker, Bertha Runnels, and Micah Landry—sampled the entries. Much fidgeting and whispering ensued while the three conferred.

At last Charles Walker stepped forward and held up his hands. "Folks, it's a tough decision, but we've decided on the winners. The grand prize, which is that magnificent new set of bakeware over yonder donated by the Paragon Emporium, goes to Augie Moore for his pecan pie."

Everyone cheered. Augie and Bitsy stood near Ethan, and he grinned at the new restaurateurs.

"Congratulations, Augie."

The bald, muscular man blushed to the tips of his ears. "Thanks, Sheriff." He walked up to shake the judges' hands.

"Folks, the rest of Augie's pie will be sold by the slice when we're finished," Walker said. "Now, as to the best fruit pie, that was very difficult, but we've decided on a fresh rhubarb and strawberry pie by Rilla Thistle."

Again the people cheered and applauded. Mrs. Thistle, her face pink with pleasure, accepted the gift of a new apron, pieced by Orissa Walker.

"And in the cream pie division," Walker called out, "the judges are unanimous. The set of linen napkins embroidered by Ruth Robinson goes to our very own schoolteacher, Miss Isabel Fennel, for her lemon meringue."

Isabel gasped and left her father's side to retrieve her prize.

"Now, folks," Walker continued, "you know these three are mighty fine cooks. Some of the best eating in town is to be found at the Spur & Saddle and the Fennel House. And Miss Isabel showed her skills, as well, last summer during the opening of the boardinghouse. So you know you're getting your money's worth when you pay two bits for a slice of one of these winning pies. The other pies can be had for ten cents a slice. All the proceeds will go toward furnishing and equipping Dr. Kincaid's new office. So eat up and pay up."

The doctor stepped up beside Walker for a moment, and the laughter and murmuring stilled.

"Folks, I just want you to know how much I appreciate all you're doing. The town council has worked with me to help me give you the finest medical care I can. But I didn't expect the entire town to turn out and support the effort like this. All I can say is thank you, and I'll be there for you when you need medical attention."

Everyone clapped as Dr. Kincaid beamed and nodded.

"That's great," Walker said. "The ladies will serve the pies now, and I believe Miss Dooley and her helpers will be setting up for the shooting contest while that's going on." He pulled out his pocket watch. "Let's say the first round of the shooting match will begin in thirty minutes." He looked questioningly at Trudy, and she nodded.

Cowboys, miners, and townspeople lined up for pie. Ethan noted that Kenton Smith and a couple of his men were among them. He could relax as long as they kept busy. If they started getting bored, things might heat up.

He strolled toward the fence that served as a hitching rail, where a dozen wagons stood and thirty or more horses and mules switched their tails at flies. Wouldn't hurt to make sure nobody was poking around the wagons and sneaking flasks out of saddlebags. He greeted a couple of ranchers feeding their animals and ambled around the perimeter of the yard where others had hobbled their teams. Griffin and Parnell had cans of flour and were sprinkling it in a line across the road.

"You getting ready for the horse race?" Ethan asked.

"Yup." Griffin frowned as he shook the can gently. "This is the starting and finishing line. They'll ride into town, grab a flag from Ted Hire at the Nugget, and come back here. First one to cross the finish holding his flag wins."

Ethan nodded. Sounded simple enough.

Goldie and Vashti had teamed with Myra and Florence to organize games for the schoolchildren. Ethan stood for a few minutes watching the girls hand out feed sacks for the sack race. Parents and cowboys alike mingled to cheer the youngsters on. Will Ingram collected the prize of a peppermint stick. Myra announced that for the next event, the children would divide into teams for an egg-and-spoon relay. Ethan walked on to the back of the schoolhouse. Behind the building, Trudy, Libby, and Starr had set up four targets, with the shooting range facing the open prairie and the distant mountains.

Trudy came to meet him in the knee-high grass. "Ethan, we can't decide how to set up the divisions. We had planned to just let anyone enter who wanted to and not split up the contestants, but nearly thirty people have signed up. Some say we ought to separate the men and the ladies. But some of the ladies from the club want to try their skills against the men."

"How many prizes do you have?"

"Three. The grand prize, a free dinner at the Spur & Saddle for second place, and a box of ammunition for third."

Ethan nodded, thinking about the possibilities. "That Colt pistol for the grand prize is something. If I thought I had a chance, I'd enter myself."

"Libby talked the town council into buying it wholesale out of the proceeds of the day. They decided it would be a good draw for the contests, and it seems as though it worked. It's only two bits to enter, and it's for a good cause."

Ethan chuckled. "Well, in my case, it would be money thrown away, because I happen to know several ladies who can outshoot me. Probably a lot of the men can, too, but I don't think I'll stand up today and let the whole town know. If you need people who aren't competing to be judges or help change the targets, I'm willing."

"Thank you."

Libby and Starr came to join them.

"So, what do you think, Sheriff?" Starr pointed to the four

identical bull's-eye targets they'd set up. "We decided that to be really fair, we'll have to change the targets for each shooter."

"It's a good thing we brought the paper and paint," Libby said. "Twelve more people have signed up since this morning. We've got Opal and Bitsy working on more targets."

"They look good." Ethan surveyed the shooting range. "Will you be ready on time?"

Trudy's brow wrinkled. "I think so."

"Some of the men were muttering at lunchtime," Starr said. "They don't think we should let the ladies compete against them."

Libby waved one hand in dismissal. "What you mean is they don't think we ought to make them compete against us ladies."

Starr nodded with a smirk. "Guess you're right. They're afraid we'll outshoot them."

"And everybody will see," Trudy said.

Ethan raised his hands palms up, smiling. "It's up to you, but shooting's one skill that doesn't favor men or women, so far as I can see. Some have put in more practice than others, and there's always folks who have a natural talent for it."

"That's right." Starr scowled at Trudy. "Why shouldn't we be allowed to go against them?"

"Well, uh. . ." Trudy glanced at Libby. "Sometimes men get all. . ."

"Humiliated?" Libby suggested.

"Well yes. We don't want to embarrass the men that badly, do we?"

Starr let out a whoop. "Of course we do! We've been working for nigh on a year now to become good shots."

"Yes, but our purpose was to protect our families and property, not to outdo our fellow citizens." Libby arched her brows. The three ladies waited, obviously expecting Ethan to settle the matter.

"Well, if you have a first round where all the contestants shoot their rounds, then narrow it down for the next round. . . And if some of them are ladies, who can argue?"

Trudy nodded. "That's the way we were figuring to do it. If we have thirty in the first round, then we can let the ten best move on to the second round, and three for the final. Or four if it's close. We'll use fresh targets for the final go. I think we'll have enough."

"We can circle their shots on the targets from the first round and reuse them in the second round," Libby said.

Starr grinned. "Yes, and if some of them miss the target completely, we can certainly reuse those."

"Oh my, you ladies don't think much of the competition, do you?" Ethan laughed. "Are you all entering?"

"I don't know as we should," Trudy said. "We're setting up the range, after all."

"Ah, that's nothing. I'd like to see you gals shoot. I think a lot of people would. Let us see the fruits of your hard labor."

Trudy chewed her bottom lip. "Cyrus is entered."

"Is he, now?" Ethan asked.

"Yes," Starr said. "All those new cowpokes, too, and Augie and Griff and Doc Kincaid. Half the town's going to shoot this afternoon."

"Trudy, you have to enter." Libby laid a hand on her friend's sleeve, her blue eyes coaxing.

Trudy inhaled deeply and eyed the far targets. "I will if you will."

"Done!" Libby hugged her.

"We'll have to borrow a rifle." Trudy seemed to have forgotten her hesitation. "This contest is for long guns."

"You know I haven't shot much with a rifle." Libby frowned. "Hiram's is the only one I've practiced with."

"He'll let us both use it." Trudy turned eagerly to Ethan. "Do you know where he is? One of us will have to run home and get it."

"I could ride into town on Scout. I'd be back in fifteen minutes."

"Would you?" Trudy's eyes lit, and he was glad he'd offered.

"Sure. I'll find Hiram and speak to him first. I'll be back in twenty minutes, no more, I promise."

"Good," Trudy said. "Libby and I will go sign up and pay our two bits each."

"I wish we had time to get a few practice shots in." Libby looked along the barrel of Hiram's Sharps repeating rifle and squinted at the sights.

"You'll do great," Trudy said.

"I don't know. It doesn't handle like my pistol." Libby lowered the rifle.

"Here comes Mayor Nash." Trudy took the Sharps and rested it on her shoulder, pointing skyward. She and Libby walked toward the shooting line and met Peter just beyond it.

"Are you ladies all set?" He looked out over the range. "Looks good. Four shooters at a time?"

"That's right," Trudy said. "We have the list of names. And Sheriff Chapman has offered to help with the scoring and such. If he and Mrs. Runnels and Mrs. Walker handle it, we reckon it'll be all right for the members of the Ladies' Shooting Club to enter."

Peter nodded slowly. "Hadn't thought about it much, but I know my Florence wants to shoot."

Myra hurried toward them waving a sheaf of papers. "Trudy! Look! More people have signed up. We have forty-two entries now."

"That's ten dollars and a half in entry fees." Libby stared at the young woman. "I can hardly believe it."

Myra laughed and handed her the papers. "You can believe it, all right. And eighteen of them are ladies."

Trudy cleared her throat. "Mr. Mayor, we women would like to compete against the men. That is, we don't want a separate division for the women."

"I see."

"Do you?"

Peter threw back his head and laughed. "Oh yes, I think I do. Fine, ladies. When folks gather over here, I'll announce it."

Trudy nodded and scanned the papers. "For the first round, you can just read off the names four at a time, I guess. The judges will decide who moves on to the next round."

"We're setting up a table," Peter said. "Mrs. Runnels and Mrs. Walker will let the contestants draw numbers for their shooting order."

Libby nodded with approval. "That's a good idea. Then no one can complain."

Bitsy and Opal approached with Augie helping carry stacks of large paper targets.

"These things are barely dry," Bitsy called, swishing along in her red bloomers, "but I think we've got plenty now."

Libby grabbed Trudy's arm and pulled her aside. "Do you think we're doing the right thing?"

"Sure. Why not?"

"I really don't want to intimidate the men. Some of them are our friends."

Trudy frowned and placed her free hand on her hip. "Libby, if you don't want to shoot, that's fine. Just go cross your name off the list. But I've worked hard for the club, and I've taken a lot of grousing from the men of this town. I'm going to shoot today."

Libby glanced toward where Hiram and Ethan were helping the mayor set up seats for the judges. "All right. I guess." She bit her bottom lip. "Is your brother shooting?"

"Don't think so."

"Why not?"

Trudy shrugged. "Hiram hates to call attention to himself."

"Well. . .so do I. And if Hiram can be modest, so can I."

"Aw, Libby, no."

She felt the annoying blush begin under her lacy collar. "I don't think I want all those cowboys watching me shoot. And what if I miss completely?"

"Then you'll be out after the first round, and no one will stare at you any longer. Come on, Libby. Please? You're just nervous. Hi will be disappointed if you don't do it."

"You're just saying that." Libby couldn't help sneaking a glance toward the cluster of men. Hiram met her gaze from twenty yards away and smiled gently.

"I'm serious. When he came back with Ethan, carrying this rifle, he said to me, 'Libby's going to give it a try, isn't she?' I told him you were, and he grinned like a little kid with a nickel in his pocket. He wants to see you shoot his rifle."

"That's silly." Libby felt her face go a shade deeper.

"No, it's not. He's been more supportive of our club than anyone else in town. He wants to see us beat those men."

Libby flicked another glance. Hiram was moving benches and didn't see her this time. "I'll lose."

"So what? You'll be the most beautiful contestant of the day." Trudy turned toward the starting line. "Oh look! Bertha and Orissa have set up a table and are giving out the numbers. Let's get ours."

She took Libby's arm and propelled her toward the judges' table.

"Hello, ladies." Bertha's wide frame dwarfed the chair the men had brought out from the schoolhouse. "Would you like to pick your numbers?"

"Yes, we would." Trudy shot a hard glance at Libby. "Both of us." She stuck her hand into the flour sack Orissa held. "Twenty-seven. Could be worse."

"Hey."

The soft voice in her ear sent tingles down Libby's spine. She whirled and faced Hiram.

"You gonna shoot my Sharps?" he asked.

"Well. . ."

Hiram shoved his hat back and smiled. "It's a sight I'm looking forward to."

She swallowed down the lump in the back of her throat. "It seems so silly."

He shook his head. "No. This town needs some good, whole-some entertainment now and then."

Ethan stood beside him, smiling broadly. "It would be dishonest if you ladies didn't shoot. You wouldn't let some half-baked cowpoke take the prize, would you, when you could shoot circles around him?"

"Come on, Libby, pick your number." Trudy's blue gray eyes coaxed her. "Those cowboys that caused the trouble at Bitsy's place are bragging how they're going to win the pistol."

Hiram's eyes perfectly matched his sister's and had a powerful effect on Libby. Sometimes she thought his eyes spoke when he kept quiet. But today he actually voiced his opinion. "You can do it. We all want to see you put those loudmouthed hands from the Martin ranch in their place."

Her cheeks grew warm. "Oh, I couldn't do that. Maybe Trudy could."

Hiram nodded. "Sure. Let Trudy dig their grave with her shooting. Then you come along and push 'em in."

Libby had to laugh. "All right, I'll take my turn. But I don't expect to be in the final round." She stepped forward, her pulse pounding. It still felt boastful to set herself up to shoot against half the men in town, but how could she refuse Hiram's gentle prodding?

She thrust her hand into Orissa's flour sack and pulled it out. "Oh no."

Hiram grinned. "Number one. You'll show them how it's done."

She found herself smiling but blushing as she shook her head in protest.

A scant fifteen minutes later, Peter called, "Ladies and gentlemen, the first four contestants in our shooting match: Mrs. Elizabeth Adams, Miss Vashti Edwards, Mr. Augie Moore, and Mr. Arthur Tinen Jr."

The four walked to the shooting line carrying their weapons. Everyone in town crowded the edges of the line. Libby shoved her bonnet off her forehead and let it fall down her back.

"You will fire five rounds at your targets," Peter said. Stillness fell over the crowd.

"Ladies and gentlemen, on your marks. Get ready. Fire at will."

Libby's hands shook as she raised the Sharps. Hiram's rifle. And he was watching. Three guns cracked, and she hadn't fired with them. She inhaled and held her breath then pulled the trigger. She was sure she'd missed the target clean.

"Come on, Miz Adams!" Florence yelled from the side. Of course, Starr would root for Arthur, but the rest of the ladies would want Libby and Vashti to shine.

Then she heard it. Low and quiet, just before the others fired again, Hiram's voice reached her.

"You can do it, Libby."

She gritted her teeth and focused on the target.

"I'll now announce the names of the ten shooters who will advance to the second round," Peter shouted. "Let me say that it was a difficult choice."

Ethan looked over at Ted Hire, who had joined him, Bertha, and Orissa in examining the targets and judging the scores.

"*Really* difficult," Ted muttered. "Hope no one holds it against me."

Ethan smiled. He scanned the crowd and located Trudy and Libby standing near the other club members who had entered the contest.

Peter coughed and held up the sheet of paper Orissa had delivered to him. "I'll read the names in order of score, with the highest score first. These ten will start with a clean slate in round two. They are: Miss Gertrude Dooley."

The crowd erupted in cheers and applause. Ethan grinned as the enthusiastic shooting club women surged around Trudy for hugs.

Peter waited for the rumble of voices to subside. "Second, Mr. Cyrus Fennel."

Less ardent applause sounded.

"Mr. Augie Moore. And *Mrs.* Augie Moore."

Everyone laughed and called their congratulations to Bitsy and her husband.

"Dr. James Kincaid."

"Ooh, I *knew* it." Rose squealed and catapulted into the doctor's reluctant embrace.

"That's five." Peter paused, looking over the people. "Mrs. Arthur Tinen Jr."

"Congratulations, Starr!" Her husband good-naturedly slapped her on the back.

"Mr. Ned Harmon."

The stagecoach messenger grinned and accepted the praise of his friends.

"Miss Vashti Edwards."

The saloon girl, lately become a waitress and dishwasher, hugged Bitsy, Goldie, and the other members of the club. Peter waited until everyone was quiet again.

"I have two more names. If you're not among 'em, I'm sorry. We're going by where the lead hit the targets. So if you didn't pass muster, why maybe you should go practice more often." He nodded and looked down at the paper. "Mr. Wilfred Sterling."

The young cowboy swaggered about, shaking hands with the other ranch hands.

"And the tenth person moving on to the next round. . ."

All eyes were on Peter.

"This person missed one shot completely, but the other four shots were good enough to secure her a place in the next round."

The men exhaled, realizing a fifth woman had made the grade. Peter smiled. "I'm happy to say it's another of our town council members, Mrs. Elizabeth Adams."

★ CHAPTER 25 ★

Hiram was so proud he thought he might need a bigger hat. His own little sister had outshot the whole town in the first round. That hadn't shocked him, but Libby—lovely, fine-boned, soft-spoken Libby—had also made the final ten.

True, she'd just squeaked into the elite ranks, but it was enough.

The saloon girls in their satin gowns and the ranchers' wives in cotton dresses milled about the five women who'd qualified, squeezing them and kissing their cheeks. Hiram stayed clear for a good ten minutes. It was only when Peter gave the call for the first four of the ten to come forward and shoot again that he edged close to Libby.

"Good shooting."

She spun and looked into his face, her china blue eyes dancing. "Thank you."

He nodded, still looking into those fascinating eyes. Her cheeks already bore a becoming flush. A few strands of her golden hair had escaped her bun and cascaded down along her smooth neck.

He inhaled slowly. "Mighty good."

"Thank you." Her eyes widened suddenly, as though she realized she'd repeated herself. "Oh. I—"

They stood for a moment, gazing at each other.

"Fire at will," Peter shouted, and four rifles cracked.

Libby leaned toward Hiram. "I froze up at first."

He nodded. "Take your time. Remember all the things you've

494

practiced. That's a good gun. It'll be kind to you if you keep steady."

"I'll try to remember that." She looked over her shoulder. "Oh, Trudy's shooting."

They both turned and stood, shoulder to shoulder, watching the contestants fire off the rest of their rounds.

When all the shooters rested their gunstocks on the ground, Ethan and Ted went to gather in the targets and replace them with new ones.

"The next four will shoot now." Peter called the names.

"Looks like you'll shoot last, against that cowboy." Hiram frowned as he looked at her.

"It's all right," Libby said. "I know I won't make the final. I'll just do my best and be done with it."

"Well, I'm proud of you."

"Are you?"

Her tone nearly knocked him over. Was Libby flirting with him? He smiled without meaning to. "Oh yes I am."

It seemed as though she'd leaned a little closer, and her shoulder touched his arm as they watched Doc, Starr, Ned, and Vashti prepare to fire.

Hiram reached up with his free hand and settled his hat so that the brim shaded his eyes a little better. Then he stood perfectly still, feeling the warmth of Libby's arm through the cotton sleeve of his shirt and watching the contest.

All too soon it was Libby's turn to shoot against Sterling.

"Good luck," Hiram said as Trudy handed her the rifle.

Libby looked up at him and nodded before she strode to the line.

Hiram glanced at Trudy. "How'd you do?"

"Don't know yet."

He nodded, but he knew. Even from a distance, he'd seen how close her second group lay on the target. She must know it, too, but she wouldn't say so. He sent up a silent prayer for Libby, that she wouldn't be nervous.

"Hey, Wilfred," one of Kenton Smith's men shouted, "you can't get beat by a woman. Let's see some good shootin'."

"Don't worry," Sterling replied. "I ain't never been whupped by anything in skirts, and I don't intend to commence now."

"Ladies and gentlemen, the scores in this round are very close, so we'll have four people advancing."

Libby held her breath. To her surprise, she wanted to be in that final group.

Peter consulted his notes and called out, "Those shooting in our final round will be Miss Gertrude Dooley, Mrs. Elizabeth Adams, Mr. Wilfred Sterling, and Dr. James Kincaid."

Libby clapped her hands to her face. Trudy patted her back, laughing.

"Congratulations! I knew you could do it."

"Unbelievable," Libby whispered.

"The finalists will have a few more minutes to prepare while we change the targets," the mayor said.

Ethan was busy setting up the final targets, but Hiram hovered at his sister's side.

"Can I get you ladies a drink of lemonade before the next round?"

Trudy smiled at him and leaned on the rifle with the stock on the ground. "Thanks. That would be nice."

He hurried off before Libby could even fathom his offer.

"I'm so nervous."

"Just take your time with each shot, but don't overthink it," Trudy said.

Libby wondered how she could do both. The other women clustered around them.

"Miss Trudy, I'm so proud of you." Goldie hugged Trudy, and Vashti moved in on Libby.

"You did great, Miz Adams."

Bitsy, Starr, Jessie, Florence, and half a dozen other women surrounded them, giving advice and wishing them luck.

"Pardon, ladies." Hiram's quiet voice was enough to part the waters, and a path opened for him. He handed a tin cup of lemonade to Libby and another to Trudy.

"Thank you," Libby murmured.

"Miss Dooley, do you want me to check your gun and make sure it's ready?" Vashti asked.

Trudy's eyes widened. "How can we both shoot in the same round? We're using the same rifle."

Bitsy put an arm across her shoulders. "There, now, dearie, don't fret. One of you can use Augie's rifle."

Trudy's face cleared. "Thank you, Bitsy. I'll use it, and Libby can take this one." She held the Sharps out to Libby.

"Oh no. I wouldn't think of taking your gun. I'll accept Bitsy's offer."

"But you've never shot any other rifle," Trudy said.

Libby shook her head adamantly. "You're the best shot in Fergus, and we women all know it. It would be tragic if you lost because you had to shoot the final round with a gun you weren't acquainted with. It won't matter if I do poorly, but you've led this whole contest. I insist." She reached to take the Winchester Augie had brought over.

"Oh now—"

"Hush, Trudy." Libby glared at her. "I'm putting my foot down on this. You're representing all of us."

"She's right," Starr said. "We all want to see you win, Trudy."

"We *need* to see you win," Goldie added.

Bitsy pushed the Sharps back against Trudy's chest. "Libby will be fine with Augie's gun. Don't you let that nasty cowboy take the prize, now, will ya?"

Peter Nash stood on the bench near the judges' table. "Will the finalists please take their places?"

Trudy squared her shoulders. "If you really feel that way. . ."

"We do." Libby hugged her, rifle and all. "I'm tickled to be standing up there with you. Now, do us proud."

Dr. Kincaid and Sterling already waited at the shooting line. Libby and Trudy carried their weapons over and stood beside them.

"Everyone satisfied with his or her target?" Peter asked.

Libby, Trudy, and the doctor nodded.

Sterling squinted down the range. "I had an end target last time."

"By all means, switch with me, sir." Libby sidled around him to stand between the two men.

Peter looked them all over. "Anyone object to the new positions?"

"Fine with me," Trudy said.

The others nodded.

"Then get ready." Peter paused while they took their shooting stances and raised their rifles.

"Fire at will."

Libby squeezed off her five rounds quickly. The smoke hung thick around them, putting a bitter taste on her tongue. The others finished shooting.

"Check your weapons for safety, please," Peter said.

Libby opened the breach on Augie's gun and made sure no cartridges were left in the chamber or the magazine.

"The judges will now inspect the targets."

Ethan, Ted, and Orissa walked across the field. Tension hung over the crowd, along with the dissipating smoke. Libby walked slowly over to Bitsy and Augie and held out the gun.

"Thank you very much."

"My pleasure." Augie accepted the Winchester and held it in his beefy hands.

Libby sensed someone close behind her. She looked over her shoulder. Hiram and Trudy had followed her. Hiram smiled reassuringly. Trudy kept her eyes on the field and sucked her bottom lip.

"I'm not sure about my third shot," she muttered.

Everyone watched the three judges walk from one target to another. At last, Ethan detached them from the stands, and they ambled back toward Peter, talking in low tones.

With the mayor, the judges formed a huddle.

Griff Bane came to stand near the Dooleys and Libby.

"Ethan will give you first place no matter what."

Trudy whirled. Her eyes shot daggers at him. "You take that back."

Hiram stared up into the blacksmith's dark eyes. "You know Ethan wouldn't throw the match. He's an honest man."

Griffin smiled. "Reckon he is. I was just teasing, but your sister's got a feisty temper, ain't she?"

Peter climbed up on the bench again. His smile drooped a little.

"Folks, it's hot, and we're all eager to get the horse race

started, but the judges have decided we need one last round. Miss Gertrude Dooley and Dr. James Kincaid will shoot again if they're willing, to determine the winner. Oh, and third place goes to Mrs. Elizabeth Adams."

Libby staggered. She felt as though one of Oscar's freighting mules had kicked her. Hiram reached and took her elbow.

"You all right, Miz Adams?"

She managed to breathe. "I. . .I think so."

The next few minutes blurred into a noisy clutch of women hugging, patting, and congratulating her. From the corner of her eye, Libby saw Wilfred Sterling stalk off toward the hitching rail.

"Hey, you won the box of cartridges." Goldie grinned at her.

"I guess I did. I'd rather have won the free dinner."

Hiram caught her eye. Libby had never seen him smile so thoroughly. With his long sorrow lifted momentarily from his shoulders, he looked as handsome and debonair as the doctor. Or even handsomer.

"Will the finalists please step forward."

Trudy and Dr. Kincaid went to the line.

"Come on, Trudy," Myra Harper called. "Make us proud."

"May the best *man* win," Micah Landry shouted. His wife elbowed him.

Rose, who had shared her box lunch with the doctor, stood at the edge of the crowd, breathlessly waving a lacy handkerchief.

"On your mark," Peter called.

Trudy and Doc squared up, facing the targets.

"Get ready."

They raised their rifles.

"Fire at will."

The ten shots rang out quickly, and the crowd exhaled. The contestants broke their rifles open, and Ethan and Orissa again made the trek to the targets. Bertha, who carried extra weight, sat at the judges' table fanning herself; and Ted had headed back into town to set up the flags for the horse race. Ethan and Orissa fetched the targets back to Bertha and laid them out on the table. All three judges leaned over them and consulted for a moment. Ethan straightened and walked over to Peter, who hadn't bothered to climb down from his perch.

The mayor held up both hands. "Ladies and gentlemen, the judges are unanimous. The best shot in Fergus, and the winner of the Colt pistol, is Miss Gertrude Dooley."

The women and most of the men erupted in cheers. A few sore losers shot off disparaging remarks and went in search of lemonade or something stronger. Ellie carried the wooden box with the prize to Peter, and he called Trudy over.

"Miss Dooley, it gives me great pleasure to present you with this pistol. Congratulations. I know you'll use it well."

Trudy's scarlet face beamed as she accepted the prize.

"She deserves it," Libby said.

Hiram nodded. "She's never had a gun of her own. She was hankering to win that, but she never said so. This means a lot to her."

Libby's insides warmed, and not just from the sun. She was glad she'd chosen the latest Colt model when the council had told her to pick out a pistol for the prize, and glad Trudy had won it. She hadn't thought of how the young woman always used her brother's rifle. But Trudy gave generously of her time to help other women learn to shoot safely and accurately. She'd fired nearly every gun in town as part of her aid to her brother's business or the shooting club, but she'd never had her own weapon.

Trudy hurried to them amid the applause. She held out the box, and Hiram steadied it while she lifted the cover. Her face settled into lines of deep satisfaction, and she sighed.

"It's a beaut, isn't it?"

Hiram held the box and leaned over to kiss her cheek. "You did fine today."

Libby squeezed Trudy's shoulders. "You surely did." The day seemed nearly perfect. Her pleasure at having come in third in the contest increased when she saw Trudy's delight and her friends clustering around her. But perhaps the one element that tipped her toward giddiness was Hiram's subtle attention throughout the day.

People crowded around Trudy and Dr. Kincaid, offering their felicitations. Isabel, Rose, Myra, and the saloon girls gathered so thickly about the doctor that all Libby could see was his gleaming blond hair as he bent to receive their praise. Truthfully, the man was well-favored, but she couldn't see that he was any handsomer than. . .

   She felt her cheeks flush once more as she looked toward Hiram and caught his smile again. Was the shy gunsmith coming out of his mournful shell at last?

The horse race ended with Arthur Tinen Jr. scooping up the prize of a new bridle. Ethan was glad the official doings of the day had ended. Everyone had enjoyed the contests and time of relaxation, but some of the cowboys had relaxed a little too much, in his opinion.

Smith's men left their places near the finish line, where they'd cheered on Eli Button, and headed for where their own mounts were tied. Button had claimed second place in the race, but his bay gelding wasn't fast enough to outdo Arthur's pinto. The cowboys assured Button he should have won. Ethan watched them as they neared the hitching rail. Wilfred Sterling took a bottle out of his saddlebag, tipped it up for a swallow, and handed it to one of his comrades. From their boisterous conduct during the race, Ethan guessed they'd imbibed some earlier while he was busy helping judge the shooting contest.

He hesitated. Maybe he should get a couple of friends before he confronted them. This sheriffing job held challenges he'd never imagined. But he couldn't rely on his friends all the time or he'd soon become known as the sissy sheriff. He squared his shoulders and approached the cowboys.

"Say, fellas, the town asked that no liquor be taken on the school premises today."

The four cowboys swung around and frowned at him.

Button took a step back, but the others held their ground. Wilfred Sterling especially took on a belligerent air. He passed the bottle to another man.

"You wanna make something of it, Sheriff?"

"We was just leaving." The third man hastily shoved the bottle into the saddlebag on the nearest horse. "Weren't we, Eli?"

Button had begun to untie his horse, but he shot a look over his shoulder. "That's right. The boss told us to stay out of trouble, and we're going to. Thanks for the good time, Sheriff."

Ethan nodded. "Congrats on your second-place finish in the race, Button."

Eli put his fingers to his hat brim. "Hey, a silver dollar's better'n nothing. Me and the boys thought we'd go spend it at the Nugget."

"Well, take it easy," Ethan said. "I don't want you in my jail again tonight."

"No sir." Button walked his horse away from the rail and swung into the saddle. "Come on, Wilfred. Buck. You ready?"

The other cowboys mounted and headed toward the center of town. Ethan hoped Ted Hire was open for business and ready for them. It was early yet—only four in the afternoon—but since the Spur & Saddle stopped serving alcohol, Ted had hired an extra bartender and kept the Nugget open pretty near twenty-four hours a day. Ethan rubbed the back of his sunburned neck. He'd have to stop by the saloon later and make sure those cowpokes hadn't gotten out of hand again.

He strolled back across the schoolyard and found Hiram and Griffin helping take down the tables where the food had been set out. Trudy, Libby, and a dozen other women worked at packing up all the food, dishes, and tablecloths for their men to tote home.

"Are you coming by for supper tonight, Ethan?" Trudy asked as he walked past.

"Don't know as I'd ought to. You've been busy all day."

"It won't be anything fancy."

Her eyes held a longing that drew him. He knew he couldn't refuse when she wanted him at her side. "All right. I didn't see your horses. Did you and Hi walk out here?"

"Yes. Go ahead. You probably have things to do before we eat."

Ethan collected Scout and put the saddle and bridle on him. They trotted smartly into town, where he left the gelding at the livery stable. Griffin wasn't back from the schoolhouse yet. He always let Ethan keep his horse in the stable or corral for free as part of his contribution toward the sheriff's maintenance. A bucketful of water, a scoop of oats, and an armful of hay. What more could Scout want?

As Ethan left the livery, Ellie Nash drove by in the family's wagon.

"Where's the mayor?" Ethan called.

"He went home early to sort the mail that came in on the stagecoach today."

Ethan decided to make the post office his first stop and headed up the boardwalk, past the Wells Fargo office and the emporium.

Peter had two letters for him. Ethan stuck them in his vest pocket and crossed the street. Augie was unloading his wagon in front of the Spur & Saddle.

"You folks aren't serving supper tonight, are you?" Ethan asked.

"We sure are. Had a stew simmering all day and plenty of cobbler waiting. You coming in tonight, Sheriff?"

"Thanks," Ethan said, "but I've had an invitation elsewhere."

Augie grinned knowingly. "Sometime you've got to bring your sweetheart in."

"I will." Ethan carried his letters down the street to the jail. He hung up his hat, leaned his chair back against the wall, and lifted his boots to the desktop. The first letter was from a constable in New Jersey.

Sorry, but I've turned up very little information about the Peart family. Frank Peart went west more than twenty years ago. His parents died after that, and apparently both sisters moved away, but I don't know where.

Ethan tossed it aside, opened the second envelope, and perused the message. For several minutes he sat thinking.

The sun was waning. Probably time to get over to the Dooleys' for supper. He rocked his chair forward and stood, scooping the letters off the desk.

Trudy let him in the back door. Rose was setting the table for four.

"Oh, hello, Sheriff! Wasn't it a lovely day?" She smiled at him across the room and fluttered her lashes.

"Yes ma'am." Ethan let Trudy take his hat and hang it on the rack. "Am I early?"

"No, this is fine," Trudy said. "We just need to put a few more things on the table."

"Can I help?"

"Sure, you can fill the water bucket for me."

A few minutes later, Ethan settled down for supper with the two women and Hiram. Rose was still gushing about the picnic, what a gentleman Dr. Kincaid was, and her pride in his second-place finish in the shooting match. She said nothing of Trudy's win.

Ethan looked over at Trudy and winked.

She smiled faintly. "Ethan, would you please ask the blessing?"

After the prayer, Trudy jumped in with a question for Ethan and succeeded in wresting the conversation away from Rose.

"Was the judging really that hard?"

Ethan shrugged. "Most of the time the leaders were obvious. But Trudy and Doc were so close on the next-to-last round I was afraid we'd be run out of town unless we had a clear winner. Doc slipped a little in the final shootout, and there was no question. And how about Libby Adams' shooting? She did great."

"I'm glad Libby placed. She was sure she'd be out in the first round, but she's a very good shot."

"Where's your prize?" Ethan asked.

Hiram grinned. "She's got it on display in the parlor."

Trudy scowled at him. "I'm not displaying it. I just. . .like to look at it." She twisted her napkin in her hands.

Ethan reached over and patted her arm. "I don't blame you. It's a fine pistol. I'm tickled that you got it. By the way, I got a couple more answers to the inquiries you ladies sent out for me."

"Anything that will help?" she asked.

"One had nothing new, but the second one—I'll let you read it later. It gives me serious doubts that Sterling is telling the truth."

Hiram stopped in the act of buttering a biscuit. "What will you do?"

"I'm thinking of riding out to the ranch tomorrow and talking to him."

"Need company?"

Ethan nodded. "Thanks. Wouldn't mind it."

On Sunday afternoon, Hiram and Ethan saddled up and made the long ride out to the Martin ranch. The ranch house was a rough cabin built on the mountainside, and a pole barn lay beyond it. A handful of thin cattle grazed on the sparse vegetation in the pasture. To one side of the barn sat a soddy that apparently housed the hired men. Four of them spilled out as the riders approached. The hair on the back of Hiram's neck prickled. All of them wore sidearms. Had they made a smart move by coming out here alone?

"Howdy, boys," Ethan said.

The four cowboys watched him with narrowed eyes.

The door of the ranch house opened, and Kenton Smith stood at the top of the steps and looked them up and down.

"I just want a word with Wilfred Sterling," Ethan said. "Won't take but a minute."

Smith held his gaze for a long moment and then nodded.

Sterling detached himself from the group of cowhands and shuffled forward.

"Yeah?"

Ethan dismounted. Hiram felt better in the saddle. His friend took out the letter he'd received from Frank Peart's sister.

"This is a letter that came yesterday. It concerns your claim to the Peart property. I'll let you read it if you promise to behave like a gentleman."

One of the other cowboys guffawed. "That's a laugh, Sheriff. He can't read."

Sterling whirled around. "Shut up!"

The other cowboy held up his hands, smirking. "Maybe the sheriff will read it to you if you're extra nice."

"All right, I'll tell you what it says." Ethan handed Scout's reins to Hiram and took the letter from the envelope.

Hiram sat astride Hoss and waited, keeping one eye on the cluster of men near the soddy while Ethan read the short message. Smith lounged in the ranch house doorway.

"I, being the sister of Franklin Peart, can tell you that neither I nor my sister Margaret had any children. This man you say calls himself Sterling cannot be any relation that I know of. I don't know of any people by that name. As to the property, I am too old to come out and see it, but if it is sold, I'd appreciate having the money sent to this address. Sincerely, Agnes Peart." Ethan stopped reading and looked at Sterling. "You understand?"

The cowboy nodded.

"Good. Because according to this letter, you aren't who you claim to be. This Agnes Peart isn't claiming you as either a son or a nephew. Is Sterling your real name?"

"I resent that."

"Take it easy. I just want you to understand real well that you can't inherit a square inch of that land. And if I catch you or anybody else on it, I'll have to put you in jail."

Sterling glared at him.

"You got it?" Ethan asked.

He nodded.

"All right." Ethan walked to his horse and took the reins from Hiram. He swung into Scout's saddle and turned toward Smith. "Mr. Smith, I expect this man to respect the law and keep away from what's known as the old Peart place."

Smith nodded, retreated into his home, and shut the door.

"Odd bird," Ethan said as they trotted toward Fergus.

"Smith or Sterling?" Hiram asked.

"Both, but I was thinking of Smith."

"Uh-huh." Hiram relaxed as soon as they were out of sight of the ranch. They rode in silence for a couple of miles. Finally, on a fairly flat stretch, he urged Hoss to extend his stride and trot alongside Scout. "I got to ask you something."

"What's that?"

"How long do you intend to court my sister?"

Ethan glanced over at him then back at the road. "As long as she'll let me, I guess."

Hiram digested that. Half a mile later he said, "Well, I think it's time it ended."

Ethan hauled back on his reins, and Scout stopped in the path. Hiram stopped Hoss, too.

"What? You're against me courting Trudy?" Ethan's eyes held a spark of belligerence.

"Yes. Unless you intend to marry her."

Ethan's lower jaw dropped nearly fit to hit his chest. "Of course I intend to marry her."

Hiram inhaled through his nose and leaned with both wrists on the saddle horn. "Don't you think it's about time?"

Ethan scowled at him. "I wouldn't toy with Trudy's affections."

"Prove it."

The hurt in Ethan's dark eyes stabbed him. Ethan was a good guy. Hiram hated to get after him. He sighed and lifted his reins. Hoss and Scout started walking.

"I'm standing in for Trudy's pa. You know that."

"Well yeah, but Hi, you know me. I intend to do right by her."

"Folks in town are starting to talk."

"Talk how?"

"Like you don't need to marry her."

"I could bust your jaw for saying that."

"I expect you could."

They rode on until they hit the mountain road. "How do you know what they're saying?" Ethan asked.

"Augie told me. I rebuilt the back steps over there this week."

Ethan's jaw worked for a few seconds. "I was only waiting until I could put away a little more cash. The town raised my pay a dollar a couple of weeks back. I want to have things nice for her."

"She doesn't care about nice. Besides, your place is nicer than what she's been living in the last nine years."

"You think so?"

"Yup." A mile farther along, Hiram said, "So you're sure you want to get married?"

"Oh yeah. I do. It's just. . ." Ethan glanced over at him. "It's a little unnerving."

"You're not still tied in knots over the Indian wars and your part in them?"

"I talked that out with Trudy."

"And?"

Ethan nodded. "You were right. She's a very understanding woman."

"Glad you realized that. I'm right this time, too. Quit shilly-shallying."

"I'll certainly ruminate on that."

"Good. Now let's put some miles behind us."

Tuesday evening, Isabel heard her father come in at what used to be his regular time. She dashed about the kitchen. She'd more than half expected him to be late again.

He'd left his coat and hat in the entry. When he crossed the threshold, he looked sheepishly at her. "Supper ready?"

She nearly dropped the dish of boiled greens. The flesh beneath his left eye puffed out in a red and purple bruise. "Papa! What happened to your eye?"

"Relax, Isabel. It's just a shiner."

She gulped and set the dish on the table. "It. . .looks painful. Shouldn't you see Doc Kincaid?"

"For this?" He laughed bitterly. "I've had lots worse than this when there was no doctor within a hundred miles."

They ate in silence. When she rose to get the coffeepot and her back was turned to him, she dared to say, "I can fix you a cold cloth."

"I'll be fine."

"Did someone hit you?"

"Just leave it alone, Isabel."

"Sorry. I'm concerned about you, Papa, that's all." She poured his mug full, wishing he wouldn't be so stubborn.

"Well, I don't need your concern."

"But when Paul Storrey fell on the rocks and had a shiner, the doctor said it could permanently injure his eyesight. I could have one of the men hitch up the wagon, and we could drive into town. Just let Dr. Kincaid take a look at it, Papa, to be sure—"

"Oh that's it. You just want a chance to see Doc Kincaid again. I saw you staring at him at the picnic Saturday, wishing he'd bought your lunch basket instead of Oxley."

"Papa!" Isabel stared after him. Tears filled her eyes. "I wasn't ogling the doctor."

"Oh, of course not. Saw you eyeing him at church, too." He shoved his chair back and stood, then picked up his coffee. "I'll be just fine, so you don't need to be thinking about going calling on the doc. He wouldn't look at you, anyhow. Why should he?"

"Wh–what do you mean?" She could barely believe the meanness of his tone.

"You're a skinny old maid. Kincaid's got the pick of the widows and single gals in this town. He won't likely come calling here."

Isabel gasped and pulled her apron up to her face, burying her eyes in the folds of cotton. "I never—Oh Papa, how could you say such a thing?"

She turned and ran from the room, not sure to where she would run.

★ CHAPTER 27 ★

Libby locked the door of the emporium and pulled the shade.

"Good night, Florence."

"Good night, Miz Adams. I'll see you in the morning." Florence slipped through the storeroom and out the back door.

Libby lifted the ledgers off the counter and took them to her desk in the back room. Usually she spent an hour or so on the books after closing, but not tonight. Trudy had invited her to supper. It seemed her friend's latest way of coping with Rose's overbearing personality was to have company to diffuse the conversation. Trudy had offered to hold the meal later than their usual supper hour so that Libby could join them after she closed the store at six.

She went back for the cash box and opened the safe.

Wild pounding on the back door startled her. She shoved the ledgers and cash box into the safe and shut the door then straightened, her heart thumping.

"Libby?"

She exhaled and hurried to let Isabel in.

"What is it, dear? What's wrong?"

"It's Papa. He's been in a fight or something, but he won't tell me what happened." Isabel's tears had dried on her blotchy face, and her hair hung all aflutter from her displaced hairpins.

Libby pulled her into the dim storeroom and closed the door. "Come sit down and tell me all about it."

"I. . .I didn't want to bother you, but I didn't know what else to do. He insulted me. My own father. I can't bear to stay there, Libby. I just can't."

"Oh my dear." Libby drew her into a gentle embrace and patted the back of her serviceable gray cotton dress.

Isabel sobbed on her shoulder. "I'm sorry. I'm sure you have things to do."

"It's all right." Libby considered whether she should tell Isabel of her dinner plans. If she delayed much longer, Trudy would worry and come to check on her. But Ethan was also an invited dinner guest. In his capacity as sheriff, he might be able to suggest a course of action for Isabel. "My dear, please don't upset yourself so. I'm due at the Dooleys' for supper, and I'd like you to accompany me. I'm sure Trudy and Hiram won't mind one more guest, as we're already planning a party of five."

Isabel lifted her head. "Oh no, I couldn't."

"Of course you could. In fact, I'll take a quart of milk and some peanut brittle as our contribution." Libby turned toward the main room of the emporium. "Wait right here while I fetch the items."

Isabel continued to protest, but Libby prevailed, and a minute later, Isabel's coiffure repaired, they set out together across the street. Libby carried the small milk can and a box of shells for Trudy's new pistol, and Isabel brought the box of peanut brittle.

"I shouldn't have come to you at the dinner hour."

"Nonsense." Libby shifted the cool milk can to her other hand. "One must act when the crisis occurs. Now, what do you think really happened?"

"I don't know, but when I asked questions, Papa became angry and. . .I cannot call it anything short of abusive."

Libby tsked and waited for more information.

"I've been desolate these past few weeks, I'll admit. Papa doesn't seem to pay attention to me anymore. Of course, if I don't have his meals ready, he notices. But he takes nearly all of his lunches at the Fennel House now. I make breakfast in the morning and supper at night. But half the time he's late for supper—sometimes very late. And sometimes. . .sometimes he imbibes. More than he should." Isabel's blue eyes with their pale fringe of lashes blinked anxiously.

"There, dear. It's a rare man who doesn't do so now and then." Libby recalled her own Isaac spending the occasional evening at the Spur & Saddle, much to her consternation, but she'd grown used to his habits for lack of a means to change them. "We adapt, don't we?"

"Yes, I suppose you are right. We do what we must." Isabel let out a deep sigh. "I should be used to his ways by now, but since Mama died, he's treated me rather shabbily, I think. Tonight he... he commented on my single state and hinted that no man would ever look twice at me."

Libby shook her head, new animosity toward Cyrus rising in her breast. "It's unconscionable, my dear." To think it was one thing, she told herself, but for a father to say as much to his daughter, especially a daughter who had shown her diligence and devotion, kindled her ire. More than ever, she was glad she had rebuffed Cyrus's advances in the months following her husband's death. Isabel need never learn about that. "Does he know you have fixed your affections on a certain man?"

"Oh no! If he knew that, I expect he would ridicule me even more and tell me how unsuitable I am for the gentleman."

"You know that's not true. You would make any man a good wife."

Isabel pinched up her features and shook her head. "I would try if given the chance, but that's his point—I shall never have a chance unless a blind man comes to town."

Libby's heart wrenched. While not a beauty by any means, Isabel could not be called ugly either. Many women with fewer physical charms had found husbands. Still, she had a hard time picturing Isabel happily married to the rough blacksmith. Surely the teacher needed the companionship of a more educated man. Of course, that sort of man was rare in Fergus. They reached the path that led around to the back of the Dooleys' house, and Libby led her to the kitchen door.

She prepared to apologize to Trudy for being late but caught her breath when Hiram responded to her knock. He'd forsaken his usual flannel and wore a fresh cambric dress shirt, as he did on Sundays. His damp hair lay parted neatly to the side, and he met her gaze squarely, something he'd had trouble doing a few months ago. His frank smile sent a flutter through her stomach.

"Oh. Good evening, Hiram."

He nodded. "Hello. Glad you could come." His gaze slid past

her to Isabel. "Evening, Miss Fennel."

"I hope you don't mind," Libby said quickly. "I brought another guest without asking the hosts' permission."

"That's fine. Come on in, ladies." Hiram swung the door wide and called over his shoulder, "Can we throw another plate on, Trudy?"

His sister came toward them and held her hands out to Isabel. "Of course. Welcome, Isabel."

"I apologize for barging in with Libby. If it's too much—"

"Don't be silly. We're happy to see you."

"Thank you. Oh—" Isabel held out the box of peanut brittle. "Compliments of Mrs. Adams."

"I brought some milk, too," Libby said.

"Thank you very much."

"I'll take it to the root cellar." Hiram took the can from Libby's hands and slid out the back door.

Ethan leaned against the far wall, obviously feeling at home. He straightened and nodded at the newcomers.

Libby smiled at him. "Hello, Ethan."

"Evening, Libby. Good to see you again. Howdy, Miss Fennel."

"Oh please, it's Isabel." Her face again flushed, but she looked less haggard than she had on her arrival at the emporium.

"This is for you," Libby said, handing the ammunition to Trudy. "For your new gun."

"Oh thank you. You didn't need to do that."

"I know. I wanted to."

Trudy kissed her cheek then scurried about, fetching an extra plate and cup from the cupboard and silverware from the sideboard.

"Where's Rose this evening?" Libby asked.

Trudy shrugged and laid the flatware on the table. "She's gone out to eat with a gentleman."

"Indeed?" Libby glanced at Isabel and saw that her face had paled. Perhaps she feared Rose had snared the man she had her heart set on. It would be a shame if Griffin entangled himself with Mrs. Caplinger.

"Yes, we were a bit surprised." Trudy turned to the stove, her long, straw-colored braid swinging out behind her.

"Not Dr. Kincaid?" Libby hazarded. "Did Saturday's picnic take?"

Ethan chuckled. "No, she went to eat with someone else who was at the picnic."

Trudy opened the oven. As Hiram came through the back door, she lifted out a pan that held a plump, roasted chicken. "I never would have thought she'd patronize the Spur & Saddle."

Hiram said, "Ha. She doesn't seem to object when some man is paying for her dinner."

Trudy's brow furrowed. "There, now. Let's not fuss about Rose. She's an adult, and she can decide whom she wants to eat with and where."

Libby's curiosity prickled, but her manners prevailed. Instead of inquiring outright for the name of Rose's escort, she asked, "How can I help you, Trudy?"

"I think we're ready. Just bring that dish of squash over, would you?"

Libby found the steaming dish on the back of the cookstove and took it to the table.

"Here, Isabel. You sit next to me," Trudy said. "It's lovely to have you in town this evening."

Isabel looked bleakly at Libby. In the flurry of being seated, Libby had let go the reminder of Isabel's woes—especially when Hiram pulled out a chair for her kitty-corner from his own. But as soon as Ethan had asked the blessing, she deemed it time to explain her guest's presence.

Hiram picked up the fork and carving knife and sliced a piece from the chicken's breast. "Miss Fennel?"

Isabel's hands shook as she held her plate out toward the platter.

"Trudy, I insisted that Isabel come with me," Libby said, "because I thought it was time she made known her concerns about her father—at least to Ethan, and I know you and Hiram will be discreet if she consents to tell you, too."

"Of course. You're among friends here, Isabel." Trudy shot a look at her brother, and he nodded gravely.

Isabel set her plate down before her and stared at the chicken. "I. . .I don't want to burden anyone. You've all been kind to me. . . ."

Libby reached over and squeezed her hand. "My dear, you've undergone a long period of stress and ill treatment. I think the sheriff should know."

Isabel caught her breath and flicked a glance at Ethan then stared at her plate again. Her eyes shone with tears.

Ethan leaned forward and spoke softly. "Miss Fennel, you may speak to me as a friend or as an officer of the law, whichever you prefer. Whatever you say will not go beyond these walls. Unless, of course, it bears on a crime. In that case, I can't promise."

She nodded, and a single tear fell onto the linen napkin in her lap. "It's all so complicated and. . .sordid."

Trudy caught Libby's gaze, her eyes wide with alarm. Libby's lips twitched in a rueful smile. She kept her hold on Isabel's hand until the young woman began speaking again.

"My father. . .ever since Mama died, he's acted cold and aloof toward me. He's grieving, of course, and I overlooked much, knowing that."

Trudy made a sympathetic sound in her throat.

Isabel hauled in a breath. "It's been worse this spring, though. Since my Uncle Kenton came the first time."

"Your uncle?" Trudy asked. "You mean Mr. Smith?"

"Yes."

"I first saw him at the box social. Ethan said he was a relative of yours."

Isabel nodded her assent. "I hadn't known he existed, you see, until a few weeks ago."

Everyone was silent for a long moment. At last Libby said, "Isabel told me this some time ago, but I felt it was best to keep it to myself. This Kenton Smith showed up out of nowhere, claiming to be her mother's brother, and Cyrus accepted him as such. Isabel, however, was stunned, and her father broke the news to her that they'd never told her about him because he has a criminal past."

Trudy nodded slowly, staring at Libby, then switched her gaze to Ethan.

"I met him Saturday," the sheriff said. "Cyrus introduced him as his brother-in-law, and I knew he'd let Smith settle in at the old Martin ranch. But I didn't know he'd been in prison. May I ask what for?"

Isabel stared at him blankly. "I don't know. Papa wouldn't tell me. He wouldn't tell me anything. And Uncle Kenton went away, and I didn't know where he'd gone. You see, Papa didn't tell me he was out at the ranch either. He let me think Uncle Kenton had left the valley. And I wondered. . ." She faltered and glanced at Libby. "Anyway, he came again last week. I. . .he. . ."

Libby patted her shoulder. "There, dear, it's all right. You can tell the sheriff."

"He and Papa had words. And Uncle Kenton left again. I didn't see him again until the box social."

Ethan nodded and rubbed his chin. "Hiram and I saw him again briefly on Sunday afternoon. We rode out to tell Wilfred Sterling he can't claim Milzie Peart's estate."

"Oh?" Libby asked. "You got conclusive news?"

"Seems so to me. I telegraphed the territorial governor's office in Boise after I got the letter from Frank's sister. She's married but never had any children. And there was one more Peart sister, but she died before she was twenty. Mrs. Cochran, who wrote the letter, said that despite what this cowpoke Sterling told me, Frank didn't have any nephews."

"How about that." Libby nodded thoughtfully.

"Yes. Wilfred Sterling wasn't too happy. He still claims there's been a mistake, but I let him know I'd be watching to make sure no one tries to squat on the land or anything like that."

"I wonder how he came to work for my uncle," Isabel said.

"So do I." Ethan helped himself to one of Trudy's icicle pickles. "And now Mr. Smith is courting Mrs. Caplinger."

"*What?*" Isabel stared at him.

"I'm sorry," Ethan said. "I guess we didn't mention it. The man Rose is dining with tonight is your uncle."

★ CHAPTER 28 ★

Isabel couldn't breathe. She crumpled her napkin in her fist and pressed it to her chest. How could a woman as dainty as Rose Caplinger find Uncle Kenton attractive?

"Are you all right?" Libby asked, leaning so close that Isabel could see dark violet flecks in her blue eyes.

"I—yes—no." Isabel gasped and lunged for her cup of water. She inhaled instead of swallowing and began to cough.

Libby slapped her daintily on the back. Trudy was not so gentle. She slapped Isabel smartly between the shoulder blades.

She sucked in a deep breath and held up both hands. "I'm all right."

They all stared at her. True, their faces held concern, but still she felt like a sideshow exhibit.

"I. . .I thought she was interested in someone else."

"Who? Dr. Kincaid?" Trudy shook her head. "I daresay she likes him, but he's living on a shoestring just now. Rose wants someone who can support her. The rancher came a-calling, and she accepted his invitation. I can't think it's serious, though. Not yet."

Isabel looked frantically to Libby. She smiled and said quietly, "No dear, not the one you were thinking of."

"But. . .but Starr Tinen said. . ."

"I know." Libby bent to retrieve Isabel's napkin from the floor and tucked it into her slack hand. "That incident came to naught. I'm sorry you even heard of it, but I assure you, it was nothing."

Isabel still found it hard to believe. She had stormed the smithy and humiliated herself for nothing. And Hiram Dooley had witnessed it all. He knew where her interest lay. Had he told anyone how she'd ranted at Griffin? She didn't dare look across the table at him.

She opened her mouth then closed it.

"Miss Fennel."

She snapped her eyes toward him. He'd barely spoken since they sat down.

"Yes Mr. Dooley?"

"Please, it's Hiram. And it's all right, miss." He nodded gravely, and she looked into his eyes. His expression radiated the discretion Libby had claimed he possessed. Suddenly she realized Libby would know his character well. Because this was the man Libby loved. In that moment, Isabel trusted Hiram with her secret.

"Feeling better?" Trudy asked.

She nodded. In fact, she found herself thinking that perhaps Griff Bane wouldn't make the ideal husband she'd always imagined he would.

"In that case, would you like a baked potato?"

Isabel took the dish from Trudy. "Yes, thank you. But I wonder. . ."

"What is it?" Libby asked.

Isabel met her gaze. "Is Mrs. Caplinger safe with Uncle Kenton?"

Trudy winced. "If I'd known he'd been in prison, I'd have warned her. I'm sorry."

"Should we go fetch her, do you think?" Hiram asked.

Ethan shook his head slowly. "I doubt they'll come to grief having dinner at Bitsy and Augie's. They don't even serve liquor anymore."

"I should have told you about all this when Mrs. Adams first urged me to." Isabel stared down at her untouched dinner.

Libby caught her breath. "Well. . .in light of what we all know of Mr. Smith already and the behavior of his hired hands, I think it's time you told these dear friends all."

Isabel's pulse thundered. "You mean. . .everything?"

"Yes. Your father's relationship with your uncle, and the black eye he came home with tonight, and even the incident behind the barn."

Isabel's eyebrows shot up involuntarily. "I didn't really think Papa had killed him."

Ethan's jaw dropped. "I beg your pardon."

She laughed, though it wasn't funny. "It was silly, really. I saw Papa digging a hole behind the barn in the middle of the night. It was after Uncle Kenton left from that first visit. At least. . .I didn't see him leave, but he must have. And I heard digging, and I went out there, and I thought—oh, it's ludicrous. I can see that now. I'm so silly."

But no one else laughed.

After a moment of silence, Trudy said, "And why did he dig the hole that night?"

"I don't know. But when Uncle Kenton came to the ranch a second time, I was relieved and saw that I'd let my imagination run away with me. I'm sure there's an innocent explanation, but. . . I don't like to ask Papa."

"Mrs. Adams said your father has a black eye?" Ethan asked gently.

Isabel nodded and licked her lips. "He came home tonight looking as though he'd been engaging in fisticuffs. When I offered to tend to it, he got angry. I just don't understand his moods lately."

Ethan looked over at Hiram. "Maybe I'd ought to drop in at the Spur & Saddle after all."

"Oh, please don't run out in the middle of supper," Trudy said. "I made your favorite cake—oatmeal."

"Wouldn't want to miss that." Ethan grinned at her.

"Well then, eat up. Mr. Smith was here to get Rose not fifteen minutes before Libby and Isabel arrived. I'm sure they're over at Bitsy's enjoying their meal."

Isabel was grateful for Trudy's practical advice, but she still wondered what her father was up to. He'd probably eaten his dinner and left the dishes and leftover food all over the table. She ought to go home. But she didn't want to.

Ethan got the coffeepot and filled all their cups while Trudy cut the cake. "I suppose I ought to see Cyrus and ask him what this is all about."

"Isabel, I'd like you to stay with me tonight," Libby said.

Isabel started to protest but realized how much she dreaded going home. "I haven't anything with me."

Libby waved her hand. "Doesn't matter. I've anything you could need in my rooms or the emporium."

"Well. . ."

"That sounds like a good idea to me," Ethan said. "I'll try to see your father first thing in the morning."

Isabel blinked back tears. "Thank you. You're all so good to me." She smiled at Libby. "I shall accept your offer."

When they'd finished eating, Hiram rose and carried his dishes to Trudy's work counter and took an apron from the peg nearby.

"What's this?" Libby called. "I don't know if I've ever seen a man do dishes."

He smiled but said nothing.

"My brother is very good about it on special occasions," Trudy said. "Especially when he thinks I'd like to visit with my company."

"Well, your company will help as well." Libby rose, and Isabel followed her lead.

"I should say so. That was a delicious dinner, Trudy."

"Thank you, Isabel. Perhaps you can help me clear the table and Libby can dry whatever Hiram washes."

"I hate to be the slacker," Ethan said, "but I ought to check in on the Nugget, and then I'll stroll down to the Spur & Saddle. Won't be long, if you'd care to take a walk after." He waited hopefully for Trudy's answer.

She smiled and stacked the remaining plates. "I'll be ready."

Hiram nodded to Ethan and kept his back turned to the ladies as he set up his dishwashing operation. He was certain Trudy was on to his feelings. Dare he hope she saw reciprocation in Libby's attitude and threw them together on purpose? Libby's face was flushed and her eyes a bit twinkly when she joined him, putting on the ruffled apron Rose preferred.

His own cheeks felt warm, but he could blame that on the steam from the water he poured into the dishpan.

"Clean towels in the drawer yonder."

"Thank you." She opened the drawer in question and took out

a linen dish wiper. Trudy kept Isabel in conversation about the box social. Hiram didn't try to talk to Libby. He just enjoyed working beside her. He kept one ear tuned to what Trudy was saying about Saturday's event.

"So how did you enjoy having lunch with Parnell Oxley?"

Isabel sighed. "That man's manners could stand some improvement. But he appreciated my cooking, and overall it was not an unpleasant experience. I. . .don't often mix with gentlemen socially."

Hiram smiled at that, thinking, *If you could call Parnell a gentleman.* Not that the cowboy was a bad person, but he couldn't see Cyrus approving him as son-in-law material. No, the doctor might stand a better chance there—if he weren't so downright poor.

"How is the reloading coming?" Libby asked, and he snapped his head around. She stood there, cool and pretty as ever, watching him with a soft smile on her lips.

He realized he was staring at her delicate mouth and jerked his face back toward the dishpan. "Pretty well. I should have a couple of boxes for you by the end of the week."

"No rush."

"I'm glad to get the work. My gun business has been slow this spring." He scrubbed a plate and placed it in the pan of rinse water. He wasn't used to talking a lot, not even to Ethan and Trudy.

"I'm sure I can sell all you do." Libby used a fork to help her fish the plate from the rinse water.

The two conversations progressed quietly. Hiram gradually relaxed. He'd never supposed he could feel at ease with Libby, but somehow she chased away his nerves.

All too soon, the dishes were done. Trudy put them away quickly, and Libby and Isabel reached for their shawls.

"We enjoyed having you both," Trudy said.

Hiram looked at the floorboards. "Come again."

"Thank you so much." Libby hugged Trudy and extended her hand to Hiram. "This made for a very pleasant evening, in spite of the concerns we all share."

He clasped her hand, feeling all kinds of happy as he looked into her blue eyes. All these years Libby had been just across the street, but things had changed. Lately he felt drawn to the emporium on the slightest pretext. Where he would have dragged his feet, he now flew to fetch any item Trudy could express a desire for.

Isabel still carried a pinched, worried look, but she managed a ghost of a smile.

"I do feel better, knowing you and the sheriff know about. . . about Papa."

Trudy hugged her as she had Libby, and Isabel bent her stiff arms and tentatively returned the embrace.

Hiram released Libby's warm, smooth hand and waited to see if Isabel would also offer hers. She didn't, and the two were soon out the door.

As they went down the back steps, Ethan returned.

"Oh, Miss Fennel, I'm glad I caught you." He took his hat off and paused below the stoop. "Mr. Smith and Mrs. Caplinger are still at the Spur & Saddle, eating dessert and listening to Miss Goldie's piano concert. I expect everything's fine."

"Thank you, Sheriff."

Ethan hesitated. "I saw your pa, too, at the Nugget. Thought you'd want to know."

Isabel ducked her head. "Thank you."

"If you think he'll worry, ma'am, I could stop by there again and tell him you're staying at Mrs. Adams's."

Isabel shook her head. "He'll probably conclude that I've gone to bed when he goes home again. I doubt he'll realize I'm gone until he wants his breakfast."

Hiram wondered how much breakfast Cyrus would want if he was putting back the whiskey at the Nugget.

During this conversation, Trudy had hummed softly as she donned her shawl and bonnet. Ethan waited until Libby and Isabel had turned the corner of the path and then came into the kitchen.

"Well now, I see you're a woman of your word."

Trudy laughed up at him. "Yes, I am."

"You never keep me waiting," Ethan acknowledged.

Hiram's heart twisted just a little. Those two were so right for each other. Why on earth hadn't Ethan taken her to the preacher yet?

She turned and smiled at him. "I'll see you later."

They left, and Hiram wandered into the parlor and lit the lamp. On the mantel sat his reloading tools and bullet molds. He walked over and took one down. If he got busy, he'd have an excuse to see Libby again tomorrow.

The silent house comforted him after all the bustle and conversation. Days of hard work and long, quiet evenings had marked his life since. . .as long as he could recall. There had been a time, what seemed an eon ago, when he and Violet had looked forward to the noise and happy disturbance caused by a child. And Trudy had added some life to the house, but she had quickly adjusted to his melancholy mood and joined his detached existence without complaint.

What had happened this year to put unrest in his heart? To tell him it might not be harmful to venture out beyond the placid confines of his life?

He traced his new wistfulness back a year to the evening when Libby Adams had closed her store and come to shoot with Trudy. The old sheriff had been murdered, and Libby didn't feel safe alone in her apartment over the store. Somehow, since that day, his life had turned topsy-turvy. And a great deal of the frightening change was due to the beautiful widow.

Had the time come to alter his life in more significant ways? Trudy would leave him soon; he was sure of that. But Libby. . . he couldn't imagine her living in this weathered little house. His mind rebelled at the idea of himself living in her rooms over the emporium. Trudy had told him about Libby's elegant furnishings and expensive dishes and china. He wouldn't want her to give up the lifestyle that apparently suited her. But would he become a storekeeper? No, he could never stand behind a counter, waiting on people all day—he knew he couldn't. Neither could he let a wife run her thriving business and support him while he did. . .what? Fixed a gun now and then and reloaded spent shell casings?

For the past six months he'd made more income from carpentry odd jobs than he had at his gun business. Augie Moore had talked to him Sunday about possibly tearing the bar out of the Spur & Saddle and using the cherry wood as paneling. Hiram would like that job. His hands itched to touch the smooth, wide boards. But would Libby consider tying herself to an impoverished gunsmith and occasional cabinetmaker? Maybe she wasn't attracted to him at all, at least not in that way. Maybe she was just being friendly. She treated everyone in a pleasant, courteous manner.

But no, he was certain he'd seen something more in her expression tonight as they laughed together over the dishpan. Of all the places to further a romance. In the lamplight, he carefully measured out the black powder for the shells he was reloading, smiling and thinking all the while of Libby's blue eyes and creamy complexion.

A firm knock on the back door startled him.

Hiram laid aside his tools and stood. The knocking resounded again through the house.

He didn't pause to light a candle, but hurried through the dusky kitchen and opened the door.

"Hiram."

"Mr. Fennel?" Cyrus mounted the top step, so Hiram stood aside and let him enter. Whiskey fumes drove him back a step toward the table. "Here, let me get a light."

"Is it late?" As Hiram struck a match, Cyrus dipped into his vest pocket and hauled out a large gold watch on a chain.

"No, it's quite early," Hiram said. "I was working in the other room, so I didn't light the lamp here in the kitchen."

"Eight fifteen." Cyrus snapped the watch case shut.

"Uh. . .would you like some coffee?"

"No, I just came to tell you I've got a piece of land I'm willing to sell you."

"Me?" Hiram cocked his head to one side and tried to fathom his guest's intentions. Was Cyrus so drunk he didn't know what he was saying? He didn't sound that tipsy, but Hiram didn't have a lot of experience in gauging a man's relative sobriety. The way Cyrus was talking, and with a dark bruise shadowing his left eye and cheekbone, he might be halfway to insensible.

"You. I know you've always wanted a ranch of your own. You came here hoping to buy one, didn't you?"

"Well yes, but. . .that was a long time ago, sir."

Cyrus nodded as though he had it all figured out. "You wanted the ranch I'm living on."

Hiram cleared his throat. "You want to sell your home ranch? I'm sure I couldn't—"

"No no." Cyrus's mouth twisted in annoyance. He pulled off his hat and held it by the crown, waving it before him. "Not that one. I *live* there. It's the one out where the Logans used to live. Andy Logan sold out to me when he pulled up stakes five years or so ago. Quarter section. There's a well and a soddy."

Hiram shook his head. "I'm not interested. Sorry."

Cyrus blinked at him. His mouth drooped. "Oh. 'S all right."

For the first time, Hiram thought the man might be very drunk. "Uh. . .would you like me to drive you home, Mr. Fennel?"

"Why would I want that?" He drew himself up for a moment, tall and imposing. The fuzziness left his eyes, and they focused with anger. "Are you implying that I'm—"

"No sir, I'm not implying anything. It's just that it's getting late, and—"

"Late? You said it was early." Cyrus fumbled in his pants pocket. Hiram almost told him he was dredging the wrong pond when he pulled out another watch, this one silver. "Ha! Twenty past eight."

"Yes sir."

Cyrus nodded emphatically and shoved the watch back into his pocket. He fixed his gaze on Hiram. "You sure you don't want to buy some land? I'm short on cash. I'll give you a good deal."

Hiram shook his head. He didn't want to make enemies with Cyrus, but he certainly didn't have the wherewithal to buy a ranch, and if he did, the old Logan place wouldn't be his choice. "Maybe you could make Bitsy and Augie an offer. Or someone else with money. The Walkers, maybe."

Cyrus clapped his hat onto his head.

Hiram wondered if he ought to let him leave. And should he tell him that he'd find an empty house when he got home? Isabel had distinctly declined Ethan's offer to take the news to Cyrus. But he was right here. . . .

Hiram watched him walk to the door.

"Watch your step there."

Cyrus fumbled with the latch.

"Here, let me help you."

A moment later, Cyrus was gone. Hiram leaned against the doorjamb and gazed up at the three-quarter moon over the mountains. He hoped Ethan was making good use of that moon.

★ CHAPTER 29 ★

Ethan held Trudy's hand as they walked slowly along the riverbank.

"The water's low," she said. "Before we know it, that stream will be down to a trickle."

Ethan stopped and turned toward her. "Trudy. . ."

"Yes?"

"There's something. . ."

"What, Ethan?"

He hesitated, his heart racing. Just for a second, he wasn't sure he could do it. But the image of Hiram standing behind him with a pitchfork prodded him. *Quit that,* he told himself. *You know you want to do this.* He felt calmer then, because it was true. He did want to propose, and even more, he wanted to marry Trudy. That was all he needed to think about.

He held on to her hand and went down on one knee on the grass. "I love you so much."

She inhaled raggedly, staring down at him. Her eyes were almost luminous in the moonlight.

Ethan sucked in a lungful of air and blurted, "Marry me, Trudy. Please? I'll take good care of you."

She didn't say anything, but her face melted into sweetness so intense he feared she would cry.

"I didn't mean to make you wait. I've been saving for some things for the house, and thinking it would be nice to take you to Boise for a wedding trip, and—"

"I don't need any of that." She laid her free hand gently on his shoulder.

He gulped. "I never felt this way about anyone else. Will you. . . will you be my wife?"

"Yes."

As soon as he heard it, he sprang up and engulfed her in his arms. "Trudy, Trudy."

She raised her face to him, and he made himself calm down and lean slowly toward her to kiss her.

Ethan walked her to the kitchen door at quarter to nine. Trudy hated to let him leave, but his sweet good-night kisses would carry her through the next few hours.

She peered into the house. The kitchen was dark, but the lamp glowed in the parlor. Turning in the doorway, she let her bonnet slip down her back and slid her hands onto Ethan's shoulders. He stood on the step below her, bringing them close in height.

"Thanks so much," he whispered, drawing her into his arms.

"Tonight was lovely." She let him kiss her again, treasuring his sweet tenderness. It was new enough to set her a-tingle but familiar enough that she could nestle against his collar bone after and cling an extra moment with no fear he would think her too forward. He smelled of leather and soap and mountain wind.

He twirled a lock of her hair around one finger. "I love you, Trudy."

She smiled in the darkness and traced his badge with her fingertips. "I know. I'm glad." There was a lot more she wanted to say, but they had time. Years and years ahead. "I love you, too."

He kissed her again then pulled away. "Guess I'd better go 'round to the Nugget again. He touched the end of her nose. "I'll come by tomorrow."

"All right." She eased backward into the kitchen and watched him take the path around the corner. With a sigh, she closed the door. It was settled. She would be his wife. Soon.

She hung up her shawl and wandered into the softly lit parlor. Hiram sat near the lamp fitting a row of bullets into a small pasteboard box.

"Howdy," she said.

He glanced her way and nodded.

Susan Page Davis

"Is Rose home yet?" Trudy asked.

"Yes. She came in ten minutes ago and went upstairs."

"Did she say anything?"

He shrugged. "Just that she was surprised how well that little blond vixen could play the piano."

"She called Goldie that?"

"Coulda called her worse, I guess."

Trudy sat down on the window seat. "You might do yourself a favor and start looking for a likely woman to cook and keep house for you."

"That right?"

"Mm-hmm."

"Ethan pop the question?"

"What question would that be?" She kept her voice even, but she couldn't hold back her grin.

Hiram looked her way and stood. "Well now." He crossed the room and stooped to kiss her cheek.

"What do you think?" she asked.

"I think Ethan is a fine man and you couldn't do better. Congratulations." He went back to the table and closed the box of cartridges.

"When Rose hears, she might take it into her head again that she should be the one to do for you now."

Hiram shook his head. "That won't wash with me."

"I know. But if Ethan and I get married, the two of you can't stay here together."

Hiram scratched behind his ear. "Thought she was looking for other lodgings."

"I don't know. She goes out most days, and I have no idea where she goes."

"You going to tell her tonight?"

"I think I'll keep it to myself until morning. She'll want to know when the wedding will be, and I don't know yet. But soon."

"All right. And don't worry about me. I'll be fine. You and Ethan need to be together."

She stood and headed for the stairs. "You, Mr. Dooley, are a very observant man."

★ CHAPTER 30 ★

Isabel lay awake for a long time after she and Libby returned from the Dooleys' house. She couldn't help thinking about her future.

Did she really love Griffin Bane? Or did she only long for someone to help her escape from Papa's ranch? The burly blacksmith would never be her intellectual equal. He wasn't the smartest or the cleanest man in Fergus, though the other men respected him. He lived in a little room behind the smithy, which she suspected resembled a hovel inside. When he came to church, his clothes often smelled of sweat and horses. Did she really want a life with a man like him? Had she long ago given up finding a true soul mate and manufactured affections for one of the town's more prominent bachelors? When she made herself be honest, some of his habits and traits repelled her.

And what of Papa's accusation? Had he really caught her staring at Dr. Kincaid? The physician was handsome. In truth, she had never considered that he would find her attractive, but she might have looked regretfully his way a time or two. The doctor had the education, good manners, and refinement that Griffin lacked. Most likely, he would marry one of the town's prettier girls. Isabel wouldn't know what to do if a man like him looked her way.

Only when she turned her troubles over to God would her agitated mind stop racing from one concern to another. Her loneliness must matter very little in the Lord's eternal plan, yet she thanked Him for the friendships she had lately formed with Libby and the other women in town. If her destiny was to remain single, then she could survive that. Surely she and Papa could work toward congeniality. At last she drifted off to sleep with a whispered prayer on her lips.

On Wednesday morning, Libby loaned her a clean shirtwaist and stockings. Isabel dressed and gathered her things, prepared to leave for the ranch.

When she ventured out to the kitchen, Libby was making a pot of oatmeal.

"Breakfast is ready." Libby smiled cheerfully as she ladled the thick mush into two bowls. "The tea is brewing, and I've applesauce as well."

They chatted together like schoolgirls. Isabel told her hostess about the new literature books she hoped the school board would buy for her older students, and Libby mentioned the shipment of textiles and spices she expected Oscar Runnels to bring her later in the day. They went downstairs together after breakfast.

"Are you sure you want to go home now?" Libby asked. "You could stay a bit longer if you like. I could have Florence watch to see when your father opens his office."

"I'll have to face him sometime." Despite her brave words, a weight had settled on Isabel's chest. "I'll need to do some cleaning today and tend the garden. Best I get an early start."

"Yes." Libby stood uncertainly for a moment. "Would you like to go out the back?"

"It won't matter which door I use."

They walked to the front entrance together, and Libby turned the lock. She stood on tiptoe to undo a hook higher on the door frame, then turned to face her departing guest.

"Come anytime, my dear. I mean that. And not only of necessity—come whenever you wish for some company."

Isabel smiled and held out her hand. "Thank you. It comforts me to know there's a place I can retreat to, but I must work this out with Papa."

Libby clasped her hand and opened the door. "I'll be praying for you. Godspeed."

Isabel stepped out into the early morning coolness. A breeze from the valley swept up Main Street.

"Isabel!"

Her father's harsh shout spun her around toward the Wells

Fargo office. She gulped and stood her ground. He strode up the boardwalk toward her. She was glad that Libby had stopped in the act of closing the door and stood a couple of feet behind her.

"Where have you been?"

"I stayed with Mrs. Adams last night."

His steely eyes narrowed to slits. "I have never in my life known you to do something like this."

Isabel's heart thudded. She put her hand to her roiling midsection. "I'm sorry, Papa. I didn't suppose you would notice if I didn't return home."

"Not notice?" His voice rose, and Maitland Dostie, opening the telegraph office across the street, glanced their way. Cyrus looked past her and focused beyond. "Libby Adams, I wouldn't have thought you'd have a hand in this."

Libby stepped out onto the boardwalk beside Isabel. "In what, Cyrus? Having a friend over for a visit? I suggest that unless you want the entire town discussing why Isabel spent the night with me, you save your comments for later. You won't get much sympathy if you berate your daughter in public."

Isabel couldn't take her eyes off her father's face. It went from mottled gray to deep red. His lips twisted as he stared, and at last he blinked.

"I shall see you later," he barked at Isabel. "And I shall expect my supper on time." He stalked into his office and soundly shut the door.

Isabel swallowed hard.

Libby stepped closer and slipped an arm about her. "You're shaking, dear. Come inside. I'll fix you another cup of tea."

"No, I must go now. I don't want to give him another opportunity to dress me down here on Main Street."

"Then let me at least have Florence go with you. She'll be here any moment."

Isabel shook herself and gathered the edges of her shawl close. "No, I'll be fine. The walk will give me time to calm down." She reached deep and hoisted a smile for Libby. "I cannot thank you enough. I shall see you tomorrow afternoon at the shooting club."

She walked up Main Street without looking back. Folks were stirring. Charles Walker and one of his employees stood talking on the front porch of the feed store. Terrence Thistle was hanging the "vacancy" board on the bottom of the sign in front of the Fennel House. Isabel trudged past the smithy without looking toward it and continued on, out of town toward her father's ranch.

The road wound slightly uphill, and she took her time. About halfway home, she paused to admire the blue Jacob's ladder flowers growing on the slope. Probably the kitchen in the ranch house was a mess. Certainly Papa would not have cleaned up from her meal preparations last night. She doubted he'd called one of the men in to do it either.

Hoofbeats drummed in the distance. She shaded her eyes and looked northeast, in the direction she'd been walking. Between the hills, a cloud of dust sprang up, moving toward her as the sound increased. Over a rise in the road, several horsemen thundered. She stepped quickly off the way, into the grass. The five horses tore down the road, but as the leader came even to her, he pulled in his mount.

"Whoa!"

The others halted around him.

"You're the Fennel woman."

She opened her mouth and coughed at the dust hanging in the air. "I. . .yes." He looked slightly familiar.

"You're coming with us."

She stared at him and backed up a step. "I most certainly am not."

He nodded to one of the others. As the second man dismounted, she recognized him. He'd been at the box social.

She backed up again and tripped over a stone. The cowboy grabbed her arm as she stumbled and jerked her forward.

"Come on."

"No. Leave me alone."

A click drew her gaze back to the leader, and she froze. He had a pistol cocked and aimed at her.

"Do what we say, Miss Fennel."

"Where are you taking me?"

"You'll know soon enough."

The man holding her arms shoved her toward the leader's bay horse. The mounted man kicked off his near stirrup then leaned down and extended his hand.

"Hop up behind me."

"No, I—"

The man holding her slapped her so hard she recoiled and doubled over. He lifted her bodily and swung her up behind the leader. Her cheek stung, and she nearly tumbled over the far side of the horse. She grabbed for something to steady her and caught the back neck edge of the man's vest. The horse pranced beneath her, and she gasped.

"Take it easy, lady," the rider said. "This horse will be fine if you sit still."

Her skirts had hiked up nearly to her knee on the off side, and the other men were staring and smirking. She tugged with one hand but couldn't free up enough fabric to cover her calf.

"Sit still," the man in front of her said, more sharply.

She caught her breath and froze stiff, one hand still on his vest.

"That's better. Champ usually doesn't mind an extra load. How much do you weigh?"

"You insolent—"

"Stow it or we'll have to gag you." He returned his pistol to his holster.

The man who had lifted her climbed onto his horse. "She don't weigh much, Wilf. No meat on her bones."

Isabel tried to glare at him, but tears filled her eyes. Wilf. She was riding behind Wilfred Sterling, the man Libby had beaten out of third place in the shooting match.

And that other scoundrel, the one who had manhandled her—he was Button, the second-place winner from the horse race. Both Uncle Kenton's men. And Kenton was angry at Papa.

Sterling jerked his head and said to one of the others, "Go on, Chub. Make sure old Fennel gets the message."

The one he spoke to wheeled his dun cow pony and galloped toward Fergus. The other four horsemen headed up the road. A few minutes later, they passed the lane to the Fennel ranch. None of their hands were about. These ruffians must be taking her to the Martin ranch. Wonderful. A ten-mile canter behind Sterling's saddle. She looked down at the ground. The grass and stones flew by at a pace that made her feel dizzy. Staying on the horse seemed preferable to falling off and breaking her scrawny neck. But Uncle Kenton had better have a good explanation.

★ CHAPTER 31 ★

The Tinen ladies were among Libby's first customers of the day. Minutes after she opened shop, Starr and her mother-in-law, Jessie, entered the emporium, with five-year-old Hester hanging on to her grandmother's hand.

"Good morning. It's delightful to see you ladies." Libby stepped from behind the counter. "May I help you?"

Starr darted a glance at Jessie and smiled with a flush creeping up her face. "Arthur's over to Mr. Walker's buying oats, and we're here for flannel and such."

"Flannel?"

"That's right." Jessie grinned.

Libby turned toward the yard goods section. Florence, who was pricing a new shipment of tinned crackers, nodded and smiled at the Tinens as they passed her.

They reached the bolts of fabric, and Libby fanned out a red and gray plaid suitable for a man's shirt. "We just got this in."

Jessie held up a hand in protest. "Oh no. It's not for Arthur. Something for someone. . .er. . .younger." She cast a glance in Hester's direction.

"That's right," Starr said. "We're making a. . .a layette."

"Oh!" Libby hugged her. "How wonderful."

"Yes, isn't it?" Starr giggled. "Of course we haven't. . ." She jerked her head toward Hester, who walked slowly along the aisle, touching each bolt of cloth.

"She doesn't know yet," Jessie whispered loudly.

"Ah. Well, I'm very happy for you all." The little girl would be tickled to know she had a brother or sister coming, but some people waited to tell the siblings just before the new baby's birth. Libby had always thought that if she had children, she would tell them earlier so they could enjoy the anticipation with her. But that wasn't likely ever to happen. She shook off the thought and took a step to her left. "May I suggest this yellow print, or this new pale green plaid? Of course, it has a little pink stripe in it, but I think either. . .either could wear it."

Starr giggled. "Yes, I think so, too. I'll take a yard and a half of each."

"Oh look!" Jessie had opened the button drawer. "These little mother-of-pearl hearts are darling."

Libby's throat tightened as she carried the bolts of flannel to the counter. She didn't know why God hadn't seen fit to give her and Isaac children. They'd been married more than a decade, and she'd never lost hope until the day Isaac died, leaving her a widow of thirty-three years, childless, with a thriving business and an ache in her heart.

She measured out the flannel and folded each piece. As she jotted the amount on her slate, Florence and the Tinens approached.

"And I'll want some hooks and eyes," Starr said. "Hester was born in summer, so I expect I'll want a new woolen dress for winter this time around, or I'll have nothing to wear to church when it turns cold."

"Would you mind totting this up?" Libby asked Florence softly.

She succeeded in ducking into the back room before her tears spilled over. Why did this yearning hit her now? She'd thought she was beyond the sharp grief for Isaac, but lately she'd longed for the babies she'd never had. To hold an infant in her arms. Was it because she'd turned thirty-five this year and her chances had faded? Of course, Starr would let her hold her new baby. She pulled out her bleached muslin handkerchief and wiped her eyes. Perhaps she needed a drink of water.

Her sobbing overtook her as she reached the cupboard near her desk. She sank into the chair and buried her face in her arms to muffle the sound of her weeping. Florence came to her a minute later and touched her back lightly.

"Dear Mrs. Adams, what is it? Can I help?"

Libby raised her head and sniffed. "No, but thank you. And I'm sorry. Did anyone hear?"

"I don't think so. The Tinens left, and I came looking for you. I wanted to ask what price you want on the large biscuit tins."

Libby wiped her face. "Oh dear. I shall have to look it up. But first, I believe I'll run upstairs and wash my face."

"Take your time," Florence said with a sad smile.

Libby quickly crossed the store, avoiding the gazes of the few customers browsing her wares, and mounted the stairs to her empty rooms.

★

Ethan left the McDade brothers cleaning out the barn and rode in to town. He stopped to leave his horse with Griff at the livery and strolled over to the jail. After a quick look-in, he went to the Dooleys' back door. Hiram answered his knock.

"I've been thinking on it," Ethan said, "and I believe I ought to go and see Cyrus if he's sober now."

"He was here last night. After you and Trudy left."

"Do tell."

"Yup. Says he's short on cash and wants to sell the old Logan ranch." Hiram reached for his hat. "I'll go with you."

Trudy came to the parlor doorway. "Hello, Ethan."

His pulse picked up, but he reminded himself of his errand. "Hi's going with me over to the Wells Fargo for a bit. I want to sound Cyrus out about his brother-in-law and maybe this hole-behind-the-barn business, too."

"All right." Trudy glanced over her shoulder. "Rose hasn't come down yet. I was going to see if she'd talk about her outing with Smith, but I haven't had the chance yet. I'll put the coffeepot on, and maybe you'll get a chance to talk to her, too, when you come back."

Ethan and Hiram walked across the dusty street. A wagon was hitched before the feed store, and one of Oscar Runnels's mule teams trudged southward out of town. The OPEN sign hung in the emporium's window.

In front of the Wells Fargo office, Cyrus Fennel's big roan

was hitched to the rail. Ethan passed the horse and mounted the boardwalk. His boots thudded on the wood. The door was open, so he walked in.

"What do you want?" Cyrus sat at his desk with a ledger before him.

Ethan forced a smile. "How are you doing, Mr. Fennel?"

Cyrus frowned. "I'm busy."

Busy with a headache, Ethan thought. "Kenton Smith has begun to mix with the townsfolk, and I'd like you to tell me a little more about him."

"Like what?" Cyrus studied the ledger, moving the point of his fountain pen back and forth above the pages.

"Like where he was in prison, and what for."

That got him. Cyrus jerked his chin up and started to rise. "What do you—"

A crash of breaking glass drew their attention to the small back window of the office. It had shattered inward, throwing slivers all over the floor. A white object thunked on the pine floor.

Cyrus and Ethan stared at the rock wrapped in paper. Before Ethan could move, Hiram had slid from behind him and retrieved it. He placed it in Ethan's hand.

"Give me that!" Cyrus grabbed it and tore away the string that held the paper in place about the stone.

"That's a dangerous way to get mail," Ethan said.

Cyrus ignored him and smoothed the paper out on his desk. He bent over it, his bushy eyebrows pushed together like two colliding trains. After a moment, he shoved away from the desk and pushed past Ethan, grabbing his hat from its hook on the wall near the door.

Ethan stared after him. "Fennel!"

Cyrus untied his roan, leaped into the saddle, and galloped northward.

"Ethan."

He turned in the doorway. Hiram was studying the paper on the desk.

"It says, 'If you want to see your daughter alive again, repay your debt. Fast.'" Hiram looked up at him. "Sounds like someone's got Miss Isabel."

Ethan snatched the paper up, glanced at it, and headed for the door. "Come on. Get Hoss and meet me at the livery."

Hiram sprinted home and toward the barn behind the house. Trudy was inside the chicken yard and turned to stare at him. He dashed inside and grabbed Hoss's tack. When he headed for the barn door, Trudy blocked his path.

"What's going on?"

"Miss Fennel. Someone sent her papa a note. Sounds like she's been snatched, and they want money."

"Isabel? Kidnapped?" Trudy gaped at him.

"Lemme out."

She stepped aside, and he hurried to the corral gate and whistled. Hoss and Crinkles trotted eagerly toward him.

"Why would anyone do that?"

"It's 'cause her daddy's so rich. And he might owe someone money. He asked me last night if I wanted to buy a piece of land. Said he needed cash. And now he's got a threatening note asking for payment." As he puffed out the words, Hiram threw the saddle with its blanket on Hoss's back and reached under the horse's belly for the cinch. "Go get my rifle."

"If I do, I'm getting my pistol, too. You might need me."

"Ethan and I can handle it."

Trudy ran into the barn, not the house. Hiram shook his head and tied the cinch knot. He grabbed the bridle he'd draped over the top fence rail and fitted it over Hoss's ears. The gelding refused to open his mouth for a few seconds, and by the time Hiram pried it open with a finger tucked in at the side of Hoss's jaw, Trudy came flying from the barn with her saddle and bridle.

"By the time you get our guns, I'll have Crinkles saddled," she said.

"You're not—"

"Am, too."

"No, you're—"

"Hush! My Colt's in the pie safe."

He stared at her. She was already tightening her cinch. Hiram heaved out a big breath and trotted to the kitchen door. His rifle stood in the corner, but he knew for a fact that his sister had carried her new pistol up to her room each evening. Where she'd kept it during the day, he hadn't given much thought. Now he knew. She stashed it close by, where she could look at it anytime she wanted. He pulled it out of the pie safe and ran for the door.

She'd mounted and led Hoss to the back stoop. Hiram bounced into the saddle and handed her Colt across to her. He slipped his Sharps into the scabbard on the saddle and gathered the reins.

At the livery, Ethan sat astride Scout, ready to go. His eyes narrowed as they rode up.

"Trudy, you can't come."

"Can, too."

"Save your breath," Hiram warned him.

Ethan exhaled and shook his head slightly. He said no more but turned Scout toward the road and set out at a canter. Hoss and Crinkles managed to keep pace. When they'd nearly reached the lane to the Fennel ranch, Hiram spotted a couple of men working on the fence that bordered Fennel land.

Ethan trotted Scout over to the fence and stopped.

"Is Mr. Fennel here?"

"Nope," said the weather-beaten hand known as Brady. "He left for town this morning, same as always. Took his roan."

The horses fidgeted and shifted. Hoss tried to nip at Trudy's dun mare, and Hiram leaned forward to slap him. "Quit that."

"What about Miss Isabel?" Ethan asked.

"H'ain't seen her this morning," Brady said.

Ethan frowned and looked down the lane. "I'd like to go to the house and see if she's there."

Brady eyed him for a moment. "Help yourself."

"Something wrong?" asked the other cowboy.

"Maybe."

Brady spat in the grass and looked up at him. "I never seen Miss Isabel today, but we went down to work by the creek first thing. Just moved up here about a half hour ago. I reckon she's at the house, but I couldn't say for sure."

"Did anyone else come by here this morning?" Ethan asked. "Any riders?"

Brady scrunched up his mouth for a moment. "Seen a fella on a bay horse a while back, riding hard away from town. Nobody else."

"Mr. Fennel didn't come by, heading toward his house about ten minutes ago?"

"Nope."

Ethan looked around at Hiram. "What do you think?"

"The note said to pay his debt. That makes me think Smith is mixed up in it."

"Same here. He could have cut across country to save time getting to the Martin ranch."

Hiram hesitated then said softly, "Might be time to see what Cy's got stashed out back."

Ethan pushed his hat brim back. "Brady, I'm riding up to the house to see if Miss Fennel or her father's home."

"If they's anything we can help with, Sheriff. . ."

"Thanks. If I need you, I'll send word."

Brady looked at the other man and shrugged.

Ethan turned Scout toward the ranch, and Hiram and Trudy followed. They trotted into the silent barnyard. Ethan swung down and led Scout to the corral fence. "We'd better check the house, just to be sure."

Hiram pulled his rifle and dismounted. "You want to take the back door, and I'll take the front?"

Ethan nodded and pulled his revolver. "Trudy, you stay out here."

They met a minute later in the hallway outside Cyrus's den.

"Nobody in the kitchen, but it's a mess," Ethan said. "I checked the bedrooms back there."

Hiram lowered his gun and nodded back toward the way he'd come in. "Nobody in the parlor or those rooms yonder. I wonder where Cy keeps his shovel."

"You think we ought to look?"

Hiram shrugged. "It's a long ride out to the Martin place. I'm not against making it, but maybe we'd ought to check out Isabel's story first."

"Yeah. Might give us a better idea what we're up against."

"And whose side Cyrus is on."

Ethan's eyebrows shot up. "You think he's involved in something illegal?"

"I don't know what to think. But if we're going to end up shooting people, I'd like to get all the information I can before I decide who to shoot."

They walked out to the yard. Trudy stood near the horses. "Nobody's around," she said. "The men must all be out working. I looked in the barn. No horses in there, but there's half a dozen in the corral."

Ethan walked over to her. "Did you see a shovel in there?"

"Didn't think to look."

Hiram walked past them and entered the dark, cool barn. He squinted as he looked around. The loft was half full of hay, and the rows of stalls stood empty. Dust in the air tickled his nose, and he sneezed. Ethan came in behind him.

"Tools over there." Hiram pointed and walked toward the row of shovels, pitchforks, and dung forks hanging on the side wall. He chose the only spade and walked across the barn floor to a rear door and unhooked it. He stepped out and examined the earth.

Ethan came right behind him, and soon Trudy joined them. They walked along behind the barn, looking at the ground.

"Here," Trudy called.

The men walked toward her.

"Isabel said she came out the kitchen door and hid beside the barn and looked around the corner. That'd be over there." She pointed. "This here looks like loose dirt to me."

"As much as anything along here," Ethan agreed.

Hiram set the point of the spade to the earth and shoved the blade down with his foot. He dug swiftly, tossing the dirt aside.

"Want me to take over?" Ethan asked after a couple of minutes.

"No, I'm fine."

The spade struck metal with a clunk. Hiram's heart lurched. There really was something there. Carefully he dug around the rectangular object.

"It's a tin." He scraped dirt away from it and worked it out of the soil.

Ethan took it gingerly and set it on the ground nearby, then offered Hiram a hand and pulled him out of the shallow hole.

Trudy had already bent over the tin.

"Don't know if I can get the cover off," she said.

"Careful," Ethan said, and she handed it to him. He took out his pocket knife and pried the edge of the lid until it popped off. He looked into the container and reached inside. "A paper and this." He brought out a leather pouch and passed it to Trudy. "Careful. That's heavy."

She worked at the leather thong that held it shut. "Feels like coins." She straightened, and Hiram held out his cupped hands. She spilled the contents of the pouch into them.

Hiram whistled.

"Gold coins." Trudy looked at them with wide eyes.

"Count it," Ethan said as he reached into the metal box again. He pulled out a stiff roll of paper, folded in half and smashed to fit the container. "That's all there is."

Hiram dropped the coins one by one back into the pouch and nodded as Trudy closed it. "Got it." He turned to look at the paper Ethan held, and his friend handed it to him. Hiram carefully pulled it open like a scroll and stared into water-stained drawings of two faces. "It's a wanted poster, Eth."

Ethan held one corner, and they managed to hold it open so they could view the entire page. Trudy came to peer around Hiram's arm, still holding the pouch.

"The Kentons." Ethan frowned and huffed out a breath.

"That's Kenton Smith," Trudy said.

"Yes. A very young Kenton Smith, but the face is the same."

Hiram scanned the print silently, but Trudy read it off aloud.

"Wanted for robbery, John and Abigail Kenton. Reward $1,000. Last seen in Lexington, Massachusetts, June 1853."

Hiram stared hard at the drawings. Trudy continued to read.

"John Kenton, medium height, light brown hair, blue eyes. Abigail Kenton, slight of build, medium height, light hair, green eyes."

Hiram reached out and touched the woman's likeness. "I'm not sure, but. . ."

"I think so, too," Ethan said. "Mary Fennel."

"But she and Cyrus came here. . ." Trudy trailed off and looked at Ethan.

"Cy came right after gold was discovered in these parts, '62 or '63. Him and Charles Walker and Isaac Adams, remember?" Ethan glanced at both of them, his eyebrows raised, seeking confirmation.

Hiram nodded. "And Isabel's so-called uncle is going by Kenton Smith now."

"He's got to be John Kenton." Ethan took the poster back and rolled it up. "But the Fennels came here ten years after this poster was made."

Hiram took his hat off and scratched his head. "So what do we do?"

"How much money in the pouch?"

"Five hundred dollars even."

Ethan pressed his lips into a thin line. "I think it's time to ride out to the Martin place."

Trudy touched his sleeve. "Wait a minute. Isabel's mother died three years ago. She was a good woman."

Hiram didn't like the anxiety in his sister's eyes or the turmoil in his own stomach. Breakfast wasn't sitting very well. "She did seem like a nice lady. But Trudy, we don't know what she was like thirty years ago. She could have helped her brother rob a bank or something."

Trudy shook her head. "I can't believe that. And she was a Smith. She may look like this Abigail Kenton, but I'm not convinced it's her. You've got to show me more than this drawing. I'll bet there's a thousand women who look enough like that to match this poster."

Ethan blew out a deep breath. "It's true, drawings of wanted criminals are sometimes not very accurate. They're usually made from descriptions given by people who saw the subject only for a short time, under stressful circumstances."

"Maybe she had a sister named Abigail," Hiram suggested.

"She did have a sister," Trudy said grudgingly. "That wasn't the name, though. Isabel mentioned her aunt, but she said the aunt died young."

"Anyway," Ethan said, "the fact that this man showed up here calling himself Kenton, the name on the poster, and Smith, Mrs. Fennel's maiden name, makes me think we've got cause to go after him."

Hiram had to agree, but he surely didn't want to make a mistake. He looked Ethan in the eye. "He may be this robber, but he may also have done his time for his crimes. Cyrus said he'd been in jail. So maybe he's just trying to start over and get away from his past."

"True, but what about Isabel and the note demanding Cyrus pay his debt?"

Trudy straightened her shoulders. "I think we'd better bury this again and get to the Martin ranch as quick as we can."

★ CHAPTER 32 ★

The horses raced along the packed dirt road, throwing up clouds of dust. Ethan knew trying to persuade Trudy to go back to town was useless, so he headed straight for the Martin ranch.

About halfway there, they met Cyrus on his big red roan. The horse trotted along slowly with his head drooping and his sides streaked with sweat. Cyrus sat loose in the saddle, his face a study in displeasure.

He pulled the roan in when he reached them.

Ethan eyed him and decided to skip the small talk. "Did you find Isabel?"

"Kenton's got her." Cyrus's mouth twisted.

"It's time you told me everything, Mr. Fennel."

"That's what you think."

"No, it's the truth." Ethan pressed his leg against Scout's side to urge him closer to the roan. "Cyrus, I dug up your stash behind the barn. I saw the wanted poster."

"You *what*?" Cyrus's gray eyes lowered like thunderclouds. "Who gave you permission to snoop on my property?"

"Just calm down." Ethan sat back and rested both hands on his saddle horn. "Your daughter told me last night about you digging a hole out there. As soon as you got that note this morning and hightailed out of town, I rounded up a couple of friends and rode to your ranch. You weren't there, and neither was Isabel. I figured you'd come out here to see Smith, and I also figured it was time for some answers. Time you told the truth and let somebody help you."

"There's nothing you can do."

548

"How do you know?" Ethan held his gaze until Cyrus looked away and gathered his reins.

"Let me pass, Chapman."

Ethan leaned over and took hold of the near rein. "Mr. Fennel, if you don't cooperate, I'll have to lock you up."

"Lock me up? That's ridiculous!"

"Is it?" Ethan tried to muster the look he'd given the cowboy, Sandy, at the Spur & Saddle on the fateful night he and Hiram had stopped the brawl. Hiram had told him later he'd looked as fierce as a general with a brigade at his back. He needed that authority now. "Let me tell you something, mister. Everyone knows you've gone all over town trying to raise cash. You offered to sell Hiram some land. Charles Walker told me a few days ago you'd gone to him with the same offer, and Augie Moore told me—"

"All right." Cyrus let out a big sigh. "All right. I do need money. It's for my daughter's life. Do you understand? I have twelve hours to raise it."

"How much?"

"Fifteen thousand."

Ethan inhaled slowly and tried not to show his shock. "Suppose you start at the beginning and tell us what's going on."

"I don't have time."

"Make time."

Cyrus glared at him, but Ethan didn't budge. Trudy had sense enough to keep quiet, though her horse fidgeted.

Hiram's silence was usually a given, but now he nudged his bay gelding forward. "Cyrus, we're your neighbors. If you've got trouble, let us do something to help."

"All right," Cyrus said at last. "You can't help, but you want the truth. Here it is: Isabel's mother was really Abigail Kenton."

"I thought her maiden name was Smith," Ethan said.

"It was. She married John Kenton. When he came to my house a few weeks ago, I called him Kenton. He insisted I tell Isabel he was her uncle, so I renamed him Kenton Smith on the spot. He was my Mary's first husband."

Ethan swallowed hard as the implications hit him. "So, was she Mary, or was she Abigail?"

Cyrus sagged in the saddle. "Her real name was Abigail.

Abigail Smith, until she married Kenton. She got involved with him, but he was bad news. I was in love with Abigail, but she had an eye for the dark, dangerous type. She jilted me and married John Kenton. I learned afterward that he was a criminal. But when I went to Abigail about it, she got angry at *me*. Didn't want to hear anything against her husband." A tear seeped from the corner of Cyrus's eye and rolled down his cheek.

"What changed things?" Ethan asked softly.

"I went away. Didn't see her for several years. When I came back, she and Kenton were both wanted for armed robbery. I couldn't believe it, but I managed to see her alone one night. She told me he'd forced her to help him carry out several thefts. She'd stuck with him because she was afraid to leave him. I. . .tried to talk her into leaving him, but she refused. Said she'd chosen her course." Cyrus wiped his eyes with his sleeve. "Then John was captured and thrown in prison. I went to her and helped her escape the authorities. I guess that makes me a criminal, too."

Ethan said nothing. The words hung heavy in the air. Only the wind and the horses' movements rooted him in the present as he imagined Cyrus on the run with a young outlaw woman. The Mrs. Fennel he'd known had been quiet and. . .well, nice. Almost genteel, as far as miners' wives went. He considered whether Cyrus might have made up the story.

"We got away." Fennel's flat voice grated on Ethan's ears. "She agreed to go west with me because she knew the alternative would mean prison. Maybe hanging. We took a strongbox full of gold they'd accumulated. Loot from their robberies. And to keep people from recognizing her, she traveled as my wife. I called her Mary. Mary Fennel." He sighed. "Those first few weeks, I was happy, strange as that may seem. I had the woman I loved with me, even though she wasn't really my wife. Everyone thought she was." Cyrus glanced at Hiram and back to Ethan. "I treated her like royalty. Showed her that I would give her a better life than Kenton had. I wanted to make sure she didn't regret going with me."

"So. . .you just ran off together."

Cyrus sat taller in the saddle and glared at Ethan. "Even though she was wanted by the law and we had to live a lie, I was happy, you hear me?"

Ethan winced. "Yes sir. And that was a long time ago. More'n thirty years, I reckon."

"Yes." Cyrus held his reins loosely, and the big gelding put his head down, sniffing for grass. "Then everything changed."

"How's that?" Ethan asked.

"Mary told me she was pregnant."

Ethan didn't dare look at Trudy and Hiram, but his face heated up. Folks just didn't talk about those things in front of ladies. "You mean..."

"I mean she was expecting Kenton's child." Cyrus looked out toward the mountains, blinking rapidly. "I told her everything was all right. That the baby would be mine, no matter what. We stopped in St. Louis for three months, and she gave birth to Isabel there. We put my name on the birth certificate. Later we moved on to Nebraska, and I farmed for a while, but we lived hand to mouth. Didn't want to use up all the gold she'd brought, but we had to use some of it. I wanted to give Mary a better life. Her and my daughter. But we were always going behind and having to dip into that stash. After a few years, I heard about the gold strikes up here in Idaho territory. We sold the farm. I came up here ahead of Mary and Isabel and started mining."

Trudy moved Crinkles up beside Ethan and Scout. "Mr. Fennel, does Isabel know that you're not her real father?"

Cyrus jerked his head toward her. "*I* am her father. Legally, no one can prove otherwise. I've always considered her my daughter and treated her as such."

"So...she doesn't know."

After a long moment of silence, Cyrus shook his head. "I know we were wrong to lie to her, but at the time, I couldn't think of another way to save Abigail. We made the story become the truth. Abigail was Mary, my wife. Isabel was my child."

Trudy looked at Ethan, but he didn't know what to say. He didn't dare to bring up the matter of Cyrus and Mary Fennel not being legally married. That was way beyond where he wanted to go right now.

Trudy cocked her head to one side. "Mr. Fennel, it seems to me that Abigail should have turned herself in."

"If she'd done that, she would have been imprisoned. I couldn't bear the thought of her wasting away in jail and giving birth to her baby there."

"But you didn't know about Isabel until weeks after you'd run away."

Cyrus just shook his head. He pulled the roan's head up. "Can I go now? I have work to do."

"Is the gold that's in the buried tin stolen money?" Ethan asked.

"Probably. It's all we had left. I never asked Abigail for particulars, but we left Waterford with more than thirty thousand dollars. We used a little on the journey. Some went for the farm in Nebraska, more for our living expenses there. We had a couple of bad crops. . . . But we made out all right when we sold that. We spent most of what we had left here in Idaho, buying land and livestock."

"I thought you made your fortune mining," Trudy said.

"Not that much. I did come out ahead, and we lived off what I earned. But I used some of Abigail's money to buy up land after the boom was over. For Isabel. And. . .I always hoped we'd have a son. But that didn't happen, so I built up my holdings for her. When I got the contract for the stagecoach line to Boise and Silver City, we had a few thousand left in the can. I used it to buy livestock and coaches. That five hundred that's left in there is the last of it. Sort of an emergency stockpile. Cash if I really needed it."

"But now you need it, and it's not enough," Ethan said. "Kenton's out of prison, and he tracked you down."

Cyrus's lips twisted in a grimace. "He didn't seem to care what had happened to Abigail. He just wanted his share of the gold. I had fifteen hundred in that tin you found at that point. I dug it up after he came that first night and took out a thousand. I gave it to him the next day. I told him that was all I had. It was a lie, but I figured if things turned out badly, I ought not to leave Isabel with nothing. As long as there was a little money in that tin and no one else knew about it, she'd have enough to get away from here—or away from Kenton—if she needed to."

"Has he got her out to the Martin ranch?" Ethan asked.

Cyrus nodded. "I need to take him the other fourteen thousand by sundown. He's got half a dozen armed cowboys—'friends' he connected with in prison. They're ready to defend the place. He said if I brought you in on this, he'd kill her."

"What are we going to do?" Trudy asked. Her eyes were gray today, no blue tints of hope.

Ethan considered several options, none of them good. "Go back to town." She opened her mouth, but he said quickly, "Hear me out. I want you to raise a posse. Get every gun you can to come out to the Martin ranch. Hiram and I will head out there now with Mr. Fennel. We'll hang back where they can't see us and wait for more men." He reached out and touched her chin with his knuckles. "Raise the whole town if you can, sweetheart. But warn them to be cautious. I don't want anyone barging into trouble. One of us will meet them a mile down the road from the ranch and tell them what we've decided to do."

She nodded slowly. "What about the noon stagecoach?"

Cyrus inhaled sharply. "Perhaps you could ask Griff Bane to meet the coach."

"We need Griffin out here," Ethan said.

"Terry Thistle, then. And tell the driver he'll have to change the team himself. Bane will have the mules waiting in his paddock."

Trudy nodded. "What if someone wants to buy a ticket?"

Cyrus hesitated. "Tell Mr. Thistle to deal with it. I can't think about that right now."

"All right, sir. We'll handle it."

Hiram edged Hoss up even with their mounts. "You might ask Libby to bring some extra ammunition, and bring the two boxes on my bedroom shelf."

"All right." Trudy looked gravely at him and Ethan then turned Crinkles homeward and put her heels to his sides.

★ CHAPTER 33 ★

Trudy galloped Crinkles into town, straight to the livery stable.

"Griffin!"

The burly blacksmith came to the doorway, scratching his chin through his beard. "Hey, Gert. I mean, Trudy. Wha—"

"You've got to help me raise a posse. Men and women who can shoot. Ethan and Hi are out at the Martin ranch, where that no-good Kenton Smith is staying. They're holding Isabel Fennel for ransom. Ethan told Cyrus we'd raise the town. He wants anyone who can shoot to get out there. Can you help me?"

"Sure."

"Good. I'll get someone to change the stagecoach team for you. Start spreading the word."

She slapped Crinkles with the end of her reins and galloped over to the boardinghouse, where she dismounted and ran to the kitchen door. It stood open, and she called out as she ran up the steps, "Mrs. Thistle!"

The stout lady turned toward her, placing a hand over her heart. "You startled me, Miss Dooley. What's all the fuss?"

"Mr. Fennel asked me to get Mr. Thistle to meet the stagecoach today, in case he can't be there."

"Oh? Is he ill?"

Terrence Thistle entered from the dining room, and Trudy quickly gave him Cyrus's instructions about the stagecoach team and tickets. With his one good arm, Mr. Thistle pulled on a jacket. "I'd better go over to the livery and make sure I can find the right harnesses for the mule team."

"But isn't Mr. Bane there?" Mrs. Thistle's forehead wrinkled like a washboard. "Is something going on?"

"He's going to help the sheriff. I can't stay long enough to explain it all, but there's trouble out at the Martin ranch."

"Oh, those no-good cowpokes." Mrs. Thistle shook her head and went back to stirring her bowl of cake batter. "The night your brother came for the doctor, I knew no good would come out of that bunch."

"I really must go. Thank you both! Oh, and tell Dr. Kincaid if you see him." Trudy dashed out the door and scooped up Crinkles's reins. She was close to the Bentons' house, so she turned her mare down Gold Lane. Apphia was in the front yard, bent over her tiny flower bed.

"Trudy! What brings you out on horseback?" She stood and brushed at the stains on her skirt.

"The sheriff needs help. Is your husband home?"

"Yes. He's studying."

"Tell him I'm raising all the men and women I can. Isabel Fennel's been kidnapped by that awful man who calls himself her uncle. Ethan and Hiram are with Mr. Fennel out at the Martin ranch. Anyone who can help is to bring a weapon and meet them a mile down the road from the ranch house."

"We'll both come." Apphia hurried toward the house and called over her shoulder, "Don't wait! Go tell the Moores. Augie will get the word out."

Trudy turned Crinkles and cantered back to Main Street. She stopped at her own house only long enough to run inside and snatch the extra ammunition. Rose jumped up from her chair in the parlor and stared at her.

"Where are you going?"

"The sheriff needs everyone who can shoot out at the Martin ranch." She ran back out to her horse and stuffed the cartridge boxes into the saddlebag before she mounted. Already, word had spread up the street, and men were saddling their horses. She caught a glimpse of Griffin hurrying out of the feed store with Mr. Walker.

At the Spur & Saddle, she jumped down, threw the ends of the reins over the long hitching rail, and pounded up the steps.

"Augie! Bitsy!"

Bitsy and Goldie were working together in the dining room, setting the tables. They set down the dishes and napkins they held and came toward her. Augie popped out from the kitchen, wiping his hands on a linen towel.

"What is it, girl?" Bitsy asked.

"The sheriff needs you. All of you. Anyone who can shoot. Kenton Smith and his men have kidnapped Isabel and are demanding a ransom from her father. Ethan wants anyone who can help to ride out to the Martin ranch."

Goldie tore off her apron. "I'll run across the street and tell the Nashes, the Harpers, and anyone at the emporium. Miss Bitsy, bring my pistol, would you? And tell Vashti!"

Before Bitsy could reply, the girl was out the door. "I'll go down this side of the street and tell Dostie and—"

"I've been to the boardinghouse and the Bentons'. Anyone else you can reach. . ."

Augie grabbed his shotgun from behind the bar they now used as a serving counter. Bitsy ran to the bottom of the ornate staircase and shouted, "Vashti!"

"Yes'm?" came a muffled reply.

"Come down and bring your pistol and Goldie's. It's shooting club business."

Augie turned in the doorway. "You best be letting men into the club, then."

"The sheriff needs all of us," Trudy assured him.

Augie nodded and went out.

"Wait and ride back with us, Trudy. Do I have time to change into my bloomers?"

"I don't think so."

"Right." Bitsy planted her right foot on the seat of a chair and hiked her skirt up. Strapped to her garter was the tiny pistol she cherished. She drew it and checked the load then slipped it back into its diminutive holster. "That's good. Gotta get the rifle, too, though." She disappeared through the kitchen door.

Vashti scurried down the stairs, carrying her revolver and Goldie's, her long, dark hair floating about her shoulders.

"Do you ladies have horses?" Trudy asked.

556

"Augie's is over to the livery," Vashti said. "Maybe we can get a wagon." She peered out the front door. "Say, that looks like the Harpers. And Goldie's with them. We can catch a ride with them."

"Go," Trudy said. "Ask them to wait for Bitsy."

When Bitsy returned carrying the rifle, Trudy told her, "Hurry. Zach Harper's out there, and his wagon's nearly full."

They dashed outside. Down the street, Oscar Runnels and his son, Josiah, came from behind the feed store driving freight wagons. Each was pulled by a team of six sturdy mules.

"You shooting club ladies, pile in," Oscar yelled. Charles Walker, Pastor Benton, and a couple of other men climbed into the wagons, as well. Libby and Florence ran from the emporium carrying their weapons and hopped onto the back of Josiah's wagon.

Trudy mounted Crinkles and tore for the livery. Terrence Thistle bustled about, helping men find mounts and bridles. Doc Kincaid and Ted Hire quickly saddled their own horses.

"Just don't take the stagecoach mules," Thistle shouted to one of the freighters who ducked between the rails of the corral fence.

Kincaid mounted and rode over to Trudy. "I'm ready. Do you know the way, Miss Dooley?"

"I sure do. Let's go."

An hour later, Hiram lay on his stomach, looking over a knoll toward the ranch house. Ethan had given orders to the townspeople as they arrived, and now he ducked low and joined Hiram, sliding in next to him on his belly.

"If all goes well, we'll have the house surrounded in about fifteen minutes. Can you believe how many folks came?"

"Nope. It's almost like the day of the picnic." Hiram glanced over his shoulder. Rose sat on the tailgate of Josiah's wagon handing out cookies. "What'd she come for, anyhow?"

Ethan shook his head. "The entertainment?"

"I guess so."

"Maybe she cares about Smith. Kenton, that is."

"I don't think so. Trudy told me she said some mean things about him this morning—like how his teeth are all brown and how bad his grammar is."

"Well, why'd she go out to dinner with him last night?"

Hiram shrugged. "Bored?"

Ethan shook his head and slid up to where he could see the ranch house, barn, and corrals. "I guess the next thing is to try to talk to Kenton and demand that he release Isabel."

"I wondered."

Ethan sighed. "I'm not very good at this, Hiram."

"Been praying."

"Thanks." Ethan lifted his hat, wiped his brow with his sleeve, and settled it again. "It gives me the shivers to think one of our ladies could get shot. But I think we need numbers to make this fellow back down."

"He's been in prison before. Won't want to go back."

"That's the way I look at it. All right, I'll get Cyrus to go down with me. Maybe Griffin, too. Do you want to go?"

"What good would I do?"

"Some of those cowboys saw you lay Eli Button out. They probably think you're as tough as nails."

Hiram barked out a little laugh. "Likely." He slid back until he could stand without being seen over the mound. "Let's go."

He and Ethan rounded up Griffin. The three walked over to where Cyrus stood near his horse. Libby was talking to him, her back to them as they approached.

"We're all praying, Cyrus. The Lord can get her out of this."

Cyrus's face was gray as he looked down at her. "She got involved in that trouble last summer, and I vowed I'd see she had a good life. But. . .but lately I haven't been able to get along with her. Somehow we can't see eye to eye anymore. She started going to the shooting club—"

"No, Cyrus. Don't blame this on the shooting club. Things have been tense between you and Isabel since Mary died."

He hung his head. "I suppose you're right." He looked up as the others stepped forward. "Sheriff, when are you going to do something? We been here over an hour, just standing around waiting."

"We're going down there now," Ethan said. "You, me, Griffin, and Hiram. I want you to call out to Kenton and see if he'll parley."

"What if they shoot at us?"

Ethan scratched his chin. "Think we'd ought to carry a flag?"

"He told me not to bring you." Cyrus stood tall. "I think I should go down alone."

"Alone? No, come on, Mr. Fennel. We can't let you walk into a trap."

"All right, I'll take Dooley."

Hiram gulped.

"You'll what?" Ethan scowled at him.

"Kenton told me he'll kill Isabel if I bring in the law. All right, so I go down with a friend instead. I'll tell him Dooley's staking me the money."

Ethan frowned.

"I'll do it." Hiram was so startled at his own words that he jumped. He looked at the other three men to see if they'd heard him. Maybe he hadn't actually said the words aloud.

"Hiram, you must be cautious," Libby said, and he knew he'd blurted it out, all right.

"I will. We will. Won't we, Mr. Fennel?"

Cyrus nodded.

"We'll ask them to let us see Isabel," Hiram said.

"That's good." Ethan looked keenly into his eyes for a moment. "All right. But you've got to stall him. Tell him you're trying to raise the money but you don't think you can come up with the cash that fast."

"What's the point in that?" Cyrus asked.

"Get him talking and ask to see that Isabel's alive and well. If he's cooperative, maybe you can get a count of his men and see how their defenses look. Tell him you can't get the full amount, but maybe you can come up with less. See what he says—if he's willing to deal or not."

"And if he's not?"

Ethan's dark eyes narrowed to slits. "That's when you back off, and we show our hand. Forty guns trained on them."

Cyrus grabbed his hat from his head and threw it on the ground. "I knew I shouldn't have waited for you. They'll kill my daughter."

★ CHAPTER 34 ★

Here's your white flag." Trudy placed a long stick in her brother's hand. Fluttering from the top end was a white petticoat. He didn't want to know whose.

"Mr. Fennel, there's one more thing." Ethan looked around at Hiram, Trudy, and Cyrus. Griff Bane stood a few yards away, checking his saddle. The rest of the townsfolk had dispersed in a large cordon around the ranch. Libby had set up an ammunition station on the back of Josiah's wagon. Even Rose had stationed herself with the Harper ladies several yards away.

"What do you want?" Cyrus stood by his roan with the reins in his hands.

Ethan dropped his voice. "You said Isabel doesn't know Kenton is her father. Does Kenton know that she is his daughter?"

"No. So far as he knows, Isabel is mine and Abigail's."

Ethan let out his breath. "So he's not apt to spill the beans to her in there."

"No. I suppose he could tell her he was married to her mother." Cyrus's face twisted, and he looked away, toward the mountains.

Trudy touched his arm. "I'm sorry this is happening, Mr. Fennel. Do you think it would help the situation if Kenton did know that?" She looked at Ethan. "I mean, he might be less likely to hurt Isabel if he knew she was truly his kin."

"It's too risky," Ethan said. "If Isabel learns it from him, she might be overwrought. There's no telling what she would do."

Cyrus clenched his fists. "Besides, if Kenton knew, he might try to take Isabel away with him and force her to do things she

560

shouldn't. That's what he did with her mother thirty-five years ago. Why would he do any differently now?"

Ethan nodded reluctantly. "All right. We won't tell him. Just go in to where he can hear you and see if you can get him to release her."

Griffin walked over, leading his big gray gelding. "I'm going, too."

Cyrus hesitated then nodded. "All right then. The three of us."

Ethan looked at him, Hiram, and Griff. "Godspeed."

Hiram walked to Hoss. His stomach churned, but the docile bay gelding stood still for him while he mounted and shifted the flag to his other hand. He thought about taking his rifle from the scabbard and using it as a flag holder, but he might need his Sharps. And he couldn't ride in there with it drawn. Kenton might not think that was neighborly. He pried a spot for the end of the flag stick between his right boot and the stirrup.

Cyrus led the way, and Hiram followed, with Griff trotting along behind. The sun neared its zenith, and Hiram's cotton shirt stuck to his back. The breeze had died down. He could feel perspiration forming on his forehead along the sweatband of his hat.

The ranch house lay quiet, baking in the heat. The walls were built of logs, with only one small window on the front. Beyond the house lay the barn, corral, and the old soddy they used for a bunkhouse. Hiram remembered the Martins who had built the spread—two brothers. One of them had a skinny wife and two young'uns. They must have sold out to Cyrus and moved on five or six years ago. The isolated location was too far away from civilization for most women.

Cyrus's horse slowed to a walk, and Hoss broke stride as well. Hiram urged him up beside the roan. A magpie flew from under the barn eaves and swooped toward the corral. Griff closed in on Cyrus's other side, and they continued slowly toward the house, with the petticoat flag hanging limply over Hiram's head. A glint of metal caught his eye. Someone crouched behind the farm wagon near the corral fence.

He started to speak, but the door to the house opened.

"Don't come any closer."

They halted and stared at the door. It stood open only a couple of inches, and Hiram couldn't tell who had spoken. He saw a flicker of movement at the window to the left of the door frame as well.

"Tell Kenton I want to talk," Cyrus yelled.

The door opened wider, and Kenton Smith—or John Kenton—stood in the shadowed opening with a rifle in his hands.

"Why are those men with you? I told you to keep your trap shut. This is between you and me."

"Oh yeah?" Cyrus stood in the stirrups. "Then why have you got all your men guarding the house? Don't tell me you threw that rock through my office window personally."

Kenton shifted his gun so that the barrel pointed straight at them. "Have you got my money?"

"Not all of it. I told you—I can't raise that kind of cash that fast."

"Then go away until you've got it."

"Even if I had the resources, there's not that much hard money in Fergus. I'll have to send to Boise City. It'll take at least a couple of days."

"No deal. I've been waiting a long time, Fennel. I want my money now."

Cyrus's hard gray eyes narrowed. "Let Isabel go, and give me a few days. I promise I'll get the money."

"Why should I believe you? I told you not to tell anyone, and you've brought two men with you. Next thing I know, the sheriff will ride up."

"That's your own fault," Cyrus shouted. "I wasn't alone when the rock came through the window. Mighty hard to keep something like that secret when you've got folks in the room with you."

Another man appeared in the doorway behind Kenton, and they spoke in low tones.

"How much you got on you now?" Kenton yelled.

Cyrus hesitated. He looked askance at Hiram. "What do I say?"

"Ask to see Isabel."

Cyrus leaned over and unhooked a canteen from his saddle. He took his time uncorking it and tipping it up for a drink. Hiram could almost taste the water running down his dry throat, and he looked away. The second man had come out where he could be seen. Eli Button.

Cyrus cleared his throat. "Kenton, I'm not going anywhere until I see my daughter."

Kenton stared at him, his bushy eyebrows low. "What for?"

"To prove you've got her, for starters. And to see that she's all right."

Kenton turned his head and spoke to Button. The cowboy lumbered into the house, and they waited in tense silence.

After half a minute, Griffin said, "You think it's possible they don't have her?"

"It entered my mind." Cyrus started to put his canteen back and paused. "You boys want a drink?"

"Thanks. I was wishing I'd brought something." Griffin took the canteen and tipped it up for a swig. He passed it back to Cyrus, who relayed it to Hiram.

Hiram shook it. Half full. He took a mouthful and handed it back to Cyrus. "Thank you kindly. She wasn't in your house when we went there, sir. Your men said they hadn't seen her."

"Well, you just never know. She could still be over at Libby Adams's place. I'd hate to be doing this for nothing."

"No sir, Mrs. Adams came along with the other folks from town," Griffin pointed out. "She told us Miss Fennel left for home just before she opened the store this morning."

Near the corral, a cowboy stood up behind the wagon, showing himself openly. He rested a shotgun on the side of the wagon and stared insolently at them. Hiram caught a suggestion of movement again at the window of the house.

Isabel burst through the door of the ranch house in a flurry of gray skirts. Hiram caught his breath. Button held her around the waist with a revolver pointed at her right ear. Hair fluttered about her face in disarray. Her frantic, pale eyes focused on her father, and her mouth opened in a silent plea.

Kenton looked her over and turned toward the horsemen.

"All right, you seen her. How much you got on you?"

The creases at the corners of Cyrus's eyes deepened as he squinted. "About three dollars."

"What?" Kenton limped toward them, brandishing the rifle. "You get outta here right now and get me the money. You're a-wasting time! Be back by sundown, or Miss Isabel is a bye-bye. You get me?"

Hiram's heart pounded in his throat.

Cyrus's face went beet red. He stiffened in the saddle, and his horse pawed the ground.

"We'd best be going," Griffin said softly.

"Boss," yelled the cowboy near the corral.

Kenton turned his way. "Yeah?"

"They's men out there." The cowboy swept his arm in an arc, indicating the terrain toward the road and on each side.

"You double-crosser!" Kenton swung his rifle toward the horses and let off a charge.

★ CHAPTER 35 ★

We could pick off some of the men." Trudy jerked her bonnet back and let it slide down her back. She itched to do something. Studying the scene before them, she made a few mental calculations. "Dr. Kincaid and Libby and me. Bitsy, too. I'm sure we could get that one behind the wagon, and maybe the one peeking around the side of the house. There's got to be two or three more men in the house, though."

"Patience." Ethan kept his eyes on the three horsemen and the people standing before the ranch house below. From the length of the lane, he could make out the figures near the house but couldn't hear what was said.

Kenton whirled around, spoke to one of his men, then faced Cyrus and his friends and fired a bullet. Dust plumed near the horses' feet. All three horses jumped. Griffin's bucked and dumped the big blacksmith in a heap on the ground. Hiram's bay turned completely around and lunged a few steps away from Kenton, but Hiram quickly got him under control and brought him around to approach Griffin. Fennel's roan, meanwhile, turned and tore away from the gunman, straight toward where Ethan, Trudy, and Libby watched.

Cyrus never looked back until he reached them. He pulled the roan in and glared at Ethan. "He wants the money now. And he knows you're up here. The men saw you."

"If they know I'm here, I guess it won't matter if I go help Hiram." Ethan ran to his paint gelding and mounted.

Cyrus turned his horse and looked back, down the slight

decline toward the ranch house. Griffin slowly rose with Hiram supporting him and limped to where his horse stood, grabbing a mouthful of pale grass.

"What happened?" Cyrus asked.

Trudy scowled at him. Trust Cyrus to think of himself first and everyone else last. "Griff's horse dumped him when Kenton fired."

"He's not shot, is he?"

"How should we know? At least he's alive."

Dr. Kincaid came running from his post along the fence row. "Is Mr. Bane hurt?"

"Don't know," Trudy said. "Hiram's helping him get on his horse. Just wait here, and we'll see."

Ethan had reached the other two now and dismounted to help boost the huge blacksmith onto his horse. The gelding was skittish, but Hiram held his head firmly while Ethan loaned his shoulder and a shove. Griffin rose in the stirrup and swung his right leg gingerly over the saddle.

"Looks like his arm's hurt," Libby noted.

"Yes." Dr. Kincaid gritted his teeth. "Maybe I should go and meet them."

"No, wait here," Trudy said. "Let them come to you, out of range of those roughnecks."

Griffin's horse came toward them at a choppy walk, lifting each hoof high and fighting the bit. Griff held the reins in his right hand and let his left arm dangle at his side. His dark beard was coated in dust, and he held his mouth in a grimace as the horse's steps jostled him.

Hiram and Ethan mounted and trotted up on either side of the gray horse. After a moment, Ethan left Hiram and Griff behind and cantered toward the watchers.

He pulled his pinto in when he reached them and hopped to the ground. "Doc, Griff thinks his arm's broken."

Trudy exhaled heavily. "Didn't think Kenton shot him, but it was hard to tell from here."

"Hiram says Kenton fired to scare them, but it worked too well, and Griff's horse threw him."

"I'll tend to him." Doc looked around. "I'll have him lie down in the shade of that tree."

"Maybe you should take him back to town in one of the wagons," Ethan said.

Trudy shook her head. "Griff won't want to go."

Rose came running from her observation post, her pink and white skirts swaying. "Doctor, is there anything I can do to help?" She fluttered her lashes at him, but the gesture was lost on Dr. Kincaid as he strode toward his horse.

"Perhaps so, Mrs. Caplinger. I may be able to use an assistant."

Rose smiled triumphantly at Trudy and Libby before scurrying off after him.

Hiram and Griffin topped the rise, and Ethan and Cyrus went to help Griffin dismount.

"I'm sorry, Bane," Cyrus said as the big man slid from the saddle with a moan. "Didn't realize you'd gone down."

Trudy went to her brother's side. "You all right, Hi?"

He nodded.

Ethan stood close to Griffin so the bigger man could lean on him. "Where you want to sit, Griff?"

"Doc says to put him in the shade over there." Trudy pointed.

The men hobbled off together toward one of the few scrubby trees in the fencerow.

Libby stepped closer and eyed Hiram. She said nothing, but a glance passed between them that almost made Trudy blush. Her curiosity drew her gaze to Hiram's face.

He lifted his hat, wiped his brow with his cuff, and put his hat back. "I'm fine, ladies. Wish I could say the same about Griff and Miss Isabel. But I'm just fine."

"Is Isabel hurt?" Libby asked.

"Don't think so. But she looked like death."

Trudy reached for his elbow. "Maybe you should sit in the shade, too." She flicked a glance at Libby. "I'm sure Libby could find something for you to drink. I saw Annie passing a jug of water."

"No time," Hiram said. "We got to help Cy raise some cash. That or put some pressure on Kenton and his men."

Libby cleared her throat. "I wasn't in on the discussion when Cyrus told you about Mr. Smith's demands, but. . .I could lend him some money."

"Before sundown?" Trudy stared at her friend. "He needs fourteen thousand dollars."

Libby cleared her throat and shot a glance at Hiram. "Well, I don't have that much, of course, but I have"—she leaned toward them and dropped her voice—"about two thousand in my safe. I was planning to send most of it to the bank in Boise City by this afternoon's stagecoach."

Trudy tried not to let her eyes bug out. She'd always known Libby had a good income from the Paragon Emporium, but she would never have guessed she had that much cash on hand at any given time. How would this knowledge affect Hiram's feelings toward her?

Hiram cleared his throat. "If you want to offer that as a loan to Cyrus, it might help him some. And I'd be willing to escort you in to town to fetch it if you decide to do that."

Libby's sweet smile beamed for Hiram. "Thank you. That's kind of you. I would certainly want an escort I could count on."

Trudy saw that ardent look in Hiram's eyes—almost the same intent look Ethan had for her when he moved in to kiss her. She gulped.

"Why don't I fetch Cyrus so you can ask him if he thinks that would help?"

Isabel cowered against the wall farthest from the four men in the kitchen and rubbed her sore wrist. Eli Button had bruised her when he took her outside. Now he slouched against the front window frame, watching the lane. Kenton and two of the cowboys lolled at the table, playing cards.

"What if he don't bring you your money by suppertime?" asked the one they called Buck.

"He'd better." Kenton glanced her way. "Get on with the cooking, girl. We're powerful hungry."

"Yeah," said Eli. "We ain't had no woman's cooking for weeks and weeks."

She moved along the wall, keeping her distance, until she reached the work area. It consisted of a rough bench at waist height and a small heating stove with a flat top. No oven. No dry sink—just a dishpan and a bucket of water with a tin dipper floating in it. Dirty dishes lay strewn on every flat surface.

She rolled up her sleeves. *This is just like at home. Fixing dinner for Papa.*

Even as she thought it, she knew it was a lie. This was nothing like home, and these men had nothing in common with her father. She blinked back tears and looked about in vain for an apron. If only she could go back to the big, airy kitchen at home and clean up the dirty dishes she'd left last night. Could Papa ever forgive her for her outburst? His face had been like stone today as he'd gazed at her across the yard.

He'd come this morning and then gone away for an hour or two. Why hadn't he returned with the money Uncle Kenton wanted? Had he truly tried to raise it without success? Or didn't he intend to pay? Didn't he care about her?

And Griffin Bane had been with him, of all the odd things. He and Hiram Dooley had accompanied her father. She wasn't sure what to make of that. One of the ruffians had said they observed more men at a distance. So Griffin's appearance didn't necessarily mean he cared about her. She suspected the ladies of the shooting club harbored stronger feelings for her than the blacksmith did. For once, she didn't care.

She opened a crock that sat on the floor beneath the bench. Wheat flour. Another held rolled oats. Methodically, she surveyed the jars and tins on the bench. Nothing fancy, but she could make a bean soup and biscuits. She set a pan of dry beans to soak. Lifting the heavy kettle made her wrist ache.

Behind her the men began to bicker over the card game. She looked at them, and one of the cowboys caught her glance and grinned. He winked with a leering eye. She shuddered and turned away.

How could Papa owe Uncle Kenton so much money? He was asking for a fortune. Papa had a lot of property, and he never seemed to lack for cash, but surely he didn't have that much. Suppose Uncle Kenton was lying?

She went to the stove and opened the door. Ashes and charcoal filled the bottom of the firebox.

"You ain't going to light a fire, are you?" asked Buck. "It's hot enough in here already."

True, the day promised to be a scorcher. The gloomy log house offered some shelter, and Isabel had found it much cooler inside than out when Eli Button had pushed her back through the door.

She straightened and looked over at the card players. "How else do you expect me to cook?"

Uncle Kenton dealt the dog-eared cards rapidly. "Leave her alone. I'm hungry."

"Well, make it a little fire," Buck muttered, picking up his hand.

"Ain't there a fire ring out back where Sammy cooks sometimes?"

"Shut up, Red. I don't want her outside where they can see her." Uncle Kenton leaned back and studied his cards.

The man with carroty hair scowled but said no more on the matter. She found only a few sticks of wood in the box by the stove. No one offered to fetch her any kindling. She cleared her throat.

"Would there be more firewood about?"

"In the lean-to." Kenton nodded toward the door at the back of the room. "Eli, go with her."

"Thought you wanted me to keep guard."

Kenton swore and shoved his chair back, scraping the floor. Isabel's pulse pounded. She shrank toward the back door.

"Go on," he snarled. "I'm right behind you. Let's have some of that pie you served me and your daddy."

She gulped. "I'd need mincemeat. Do you have—"

"No, we ain't got mincemeat. I shoulda had the boys raid your larder when they grabbed you. Get moving." He nodded toward the door.

Isabel turned and walked the three steps to the door made of weathered boards. She swung it open and peered into the lean-to. A stack of firewood on one side of the door reached to her waist. Straight ahead was daylight. She could see part of the corral, and a ways from the house, where the land sloped sharply upward, a dilapidated outhouse.

"Quit lollygaggin'."

She chose an armful of sticks from the woodpile and carried

them past him, back into the kitchen. It would be a shame to heat up the place.

She dropped her load into the wood box and moved a crusty frying pan, a tin cup, a filthy towel, and a box of shotgun shells from the top of the stove to the workbench and knelt on the rough board floor. At least they had matches handy. When the kindling caught, she put a few sticks in and closed the stove door. The men ignored her as she bustled about to start a pot of coffee and get their dinner cooking.

At the back of the bench, she found a jug of molasses. A golden powder half filled a small, unmarked tin. When she sniffed it, her nose tickled. Ginger. She was halfway to a pan of gingerbread. Baking powder? Hmm. She poked about, setting dirty dishes into the dishpan. She'd probably have to wash those or the men wouldn't have plates enough to go around. She picked up the box of shotgun shells. Uncle Kenton apparently kept his supply of ammunition on a shelf beyond the table. If the boxes there were full, these men were prepared for a fight—or a siege.

"Hey, boss." Eli turned from the window. "Sammy's coming—"

The front door burst open. "Mr. Smith!"

"Right here, Sam." Uncle Kenton folded his cards and laid them facedown on the table. "What's the matter?"

"You know you told me and Chub to watch the hills out back?"

"Sure did. So why ain't you out there?"

"'Cause I seen people up there. With guns."

"Whyn't you come in the back door then?"

Sammy spit on the floor. "I didn't want to get shot at."

Uncle Kenton and the other two cowboys stood. "They's that close?" Red asked.

Sammy nodded. "Looked to me like they was sneaking closer. Wilfred's still out near the barn watching 'em, and Chub's out beside the wagon. I told them I'd come in and report to you."

"Those men out near the road are still there, too," Eli said from beside the window.

Kenton strode to his position and peered out. "You mean to tell me Cyrus ain't gone to get the money?"

"I don't know if he went or not," Eli said, "but there's somebody out there. I keep seein''em move."

Buck went to a corner and lifted his rifle. "Maybe the whole town is having another play party."

Isabel's heart leaped. Had the sheriff raised a posse to get her back? How many members of the Ladies' Shooting Club were out there right now, prepared to defend her? She surely would hate it if anyone got hurt helping her.

The men crowded around the one small window, all trying to get a better view. In the momentary silence, the fire in the stove crackled. Isabel jumped.

A stray thought took root in her mind. She glanced at the men with their backs to her. She reached across the workbench and opened the cartridge box. A half dozen shells stood inside it. She tucked them into the pocket of her skirt and closed the box.

"You think they've got us outgunned?" Eli sounded worried. Maybe he was thinking about the shooting match in the schoolyard.

Isabel tiptoed to the stove and opened the door. The men paid no attention. The fire had taken hold and had begun to burn down. She tossed a couple more sticks in.

"Uncle Kenton?"

"What do you want, girl?" He had a rifle in his hands now and was easing the front door open a crack.

"I need to use the necessary." She fingered the shells in her pocket and held her breath.

"What? Oh. Not now!"

Isabel swallowed hard. She thought of how little Millie Pooler's plaintive wail always got to her during school. "But I have to *go*, Uncle Kenton."

He turned and glared at her. "This ain't a good time, Isabel."

"I don't think I can wait." Her face flushed. Bad enough if it were true, but she'd never made a habit of lying.

"Sammy, take her out there. Watch yourself. And then resume your post."

Quickly, Isabel pulled out a handful of shotgun shells and tossed them into the firebox behind the cover of the stove door. She slammed it shut and stepped away.

"All right, let's move," Sammy said, waving his gun barrel toward the back door.

Gladly, Isabel scurried to the lean-to. When they'd left its cover and stepped into the open, she wondered if she'd done something wrong. Hiram Dooley had made it sound like you only had to drop the bullets into the stove and—

Behind them, gunfire erupted inside the house. Without looking back, Isabel lifted her skirt and ran for the outhouse.

★ CHAPTER 36 ★

Somebody's shooting! Let's go! Quick!" Ethan ducked low and ran toward the house with his rifle pointing at the front door. The stark terrain offered no cover. Footsteps thundered behind him as a dozen people followed. For a moment, it felt like his old army days, only now he was the officer leading the charge into battle.

Cyrus pounded past him on the lane.

"Mr. Fennel! Wait!"

"My daughter's in there!"

Fennel tore forward. Ethan was surprised the older man had such speed. Movement at the window distracted him, but someone behind him fired and broke the windowpane.

Cyrus slammed into the door and shoved on it, but it didn't open. He put his shoulder to it and rammed it again. The door flew open. Cyrus and Kenton stood face-to-face for an instant. Kenton raised his gun and fired. Cyrus let off a round as he staggered off the step. More shots came from within. Ethan leaped aside and flattened himself against the log wall beside the door.

Hiram and Doc Kincaid, with half a dozen other men behind them, stopped ten yards from the house and peppered it with bullets. Farther back, a cluster of women approached.

Hiram walked steadily forward, aiming his rifle at the front of the ranch house. They must be crazy, attacking like this. Didn't the British lose the whole country because they fought in the open and refused to skulk behind trees like Indians?

A few shots came from inside the house, but most of the gunfire came from his contingent. He looked around uneasily. What had happened to that cowpoke near the wagon? No one seemed to be crouched behind it now.

As the door opened and Cyrus went down, Hiram's hat flew off. He whirled toward the barn, his Sharps at his shoulder. Above them, through the cloud of gun smoke hovering over them, he saw a figure in the door of the hayloft. A heavyset man with a beard stood above the posse, taking aim at those below.

Hiram hated to use his rifle to harm another human being. He also hated to reveal his well-concealed shooting ability. But unless he acted quickly, one of his friends would likely be killed. They were sitting ducks for the sniper. He hesitated only an instant before he pulled the trigger. The man in the hayloft dropped his rifle. It fell to the ground below. He staggered back and disappeared into the dark loft.

Ethan held up his hands to stop the townsmen's shooting. Doc drew a bead and fired once more before he noticed the signal. The noise subsided. Cyrus lay still on the dirt at the bottom of the steps.

From a distance, Josiah Runnels shouted, "They're jumping out the back!" Several shots followed.

"Go ahead, Sheriff," Hiram called. "I'll cover the door."

Cautiously, Ethan took a quick peek around the doorjamb. Kenton Smith lay on his back just inside the door. Another man had crumpled beneath the window. Ethan couldn't see anyone else, but a thick haze of smoke obscured the room.

"Doc, tend to Cyrus." Ethan dove into the house, leading with his Colt. Eerie quiet buzzed around him.

From the doorway behind him, Hiram called, "All clear?"

"Reckon so." Ethan continued to scan the dim room.

"Art Tinen winged one of them that ran out the back door, and Doc says he hit one in here. The rest ran to their horses and got away clean."

Ethan jerked his head toward the man lying beneath the window. "That'd be Doc's target, I guess."

Hiram stepped over to the inert form and stooped to pick up the fallen man's weapon. "That's the fella I got into it with at Bitsy's."

"Yup. Eli Button." Ethan lifted his hat and wiped the sweat from his brow with his sleeve. "Where's Isabel? Did they take her?"

"Nobody's seen her. She wasn't with them when they ran."

Ethan stared at him. "That's crazy. We saw her an hour ago. She was in here with them."

"Maybe she's still in here."

Ethan looked around again. "Miss Fennel?"

No answer. The house appeared to have only one large room with a loft over part of it. He crossed to another door and opened it. The lean-to held a woodpile and a few tools. "All right, get a couple of people in here to search the loft. She could be tied up in a corner. You don't suppose she got away from them and ran?"

"Don't see how she could have," Hiram said. "We had the place surrounded."

Ethan called again, "Miss Fennel?" He stepped out into the lean-to. No one cowered behind the woodpile. Josiah, Augie, and several of the shooting club members had fanned out over the barnyard and corral. Ethan called to Augie, "Miss Fennel's not in here. Search that barn and the bunkhouse." He walked back through the house, stepped over Smith's body, and went out the front door.

Doc Kincaid and Bitsy knelt beside Cyrus, while Rose stood by, knotting her handkerchief. Ethan walked over to them.

"How is he, Doc?"

Kincaid glanced up at him. "I'm losing him."

Ethan grimaced. They were lucky no one else had been killed, the way things had erupted.

Augie came out of the barn and crossed the yard. "Funniest thing, Sheriff. I found a rifle lying on the ground in front of the barn, and up in the hayloft there's a dead cowpoke shot in the heart."

Ethan eyed the front of the barn. "Somebody must have shot him through that door to the loft."

"That's what I figure," Augie said. "Don't know who did it, though. Oh, and Art Tinen says he got a shot at that Sterling fella when he grabbed a horse out of the corral. Thinks he may have nicked him, but he got through our lines."

Ethan scratched the back of his neck. The sun beat down on them. "Go in and help Hiram tear this house apart. Isabel's got to be here someplace. We saw her less than an hour ago."

Kincaid sat back on his heels and looked soberly at Ethan. "He's gone, Sheriff."

Ethan let his shoulders sag. He'd handled everything wrong today. He should have let Cyrus scramble for the money and borrow what he could from Libby and the other business owners.

Josiah came tearing around the corner of the house. "Doc, there's a wounded man out back."

"One of Kenton's men?" Ethan asked.

"Yup. Looks like he fell off his horse and the others left him."

Dr. Kincaid stood and reached for his bag. "There's nothing more I can do here." He followed Josiah.

Ethan met Hiram's gaze and sank back against the wall. "Don't know what else we could have done when they started shooting in here."

Hiram's brow furrowed. He looked down at Kenton's body and over at Button. "That was an odd thing. All our people were holding back. Who started the shooting?"

Ethan shook his head slowly. "I thought some of our people got too close. Around back, you know? Where we couldn't see them."

Hiram shook his head. "Augie said they heard shooting here before they moved in. According to him, it sounded like the first shots were inside the house. The fellows around back thought you'd started something out front."

Ethan closed his eyes. Had he moved in too fast? Was it his fault that lives had been lost?

Lord, how could I have been so wrong? Now we've lost Cyrus and Isabel both. Those no-accounts must have gotten her out of here—don't ask me how. Show me what to do now, Lord, 'cause I'm not much good on my own.

No shots had sounded for a good ten minutes. Isabel had stopped shaking and had almost stopped noticing the stench of the privy.

Maybe it was safe to go out now. She reached for the rusty steel hook that held the outhouse door shut and pushed it out of the staple. Slowly she opened the door an inch and peered out.

Dr. Kincaid and Josiah Runnels were walking across the overgrown barnyard behind the ranch house. She opened the door farther, and the hinges creaked.

The men swung toward her, Josiah, bringing his gun around to point at her. The doctor's face changed from surprise to concern, and he hurried toward her.

"Miss Fennel? Is that you?"

She opened the door wider. "Yes. Is it safe to come out now?"

"Yes ma'am." He offered his hand as she stepped down from the little shack.

"Thank you." She stumbled a little, and he steadied her.

Josiah had lowered his gun but still stared at her. "Should I tell the folks you're all right, miss?"

Isabel managed a shaky smile. Josiah had been one of her students not so long ago. "Yes, please. I'm fine."

He turned without another word and ran toward the ranch house.

Isabel looked up into Dr. Kincaid's somber blue eyes. "Is my father all right? I heard a lot of shooting."

The doctor glanced uneasily back toward the house. "Ma'am, there was a big dustup, and. . ." He hesitated, and she studied his face. "I'm afraid the news is not good."

"Papa's been shot?"

"Yes."

"Then why aren't you with him? Is it serious?" The regret in his eyes told her more than she wanted to know. "Oh no. He's not—Tell me, Doctor. Is my father dead?"

Before he could speak, Josiah's whoop reached them. "She's found! Sheriff, Miss Fennel's found!"

Kincaid's quiet words sliced through her heart. "I'm afraid so, ma'am. I'm so very sorry."

Isabel reached for him, her head swimming. She clutched at his neat black vest as her knees buckled.

★ CHAPTER 37 ★

Hiram and Ethan met Josiah at the ranch house steps. Hiram had just spread a blanket over Cyrus's still body.

"Is she alive?" Ethan asked.

"Yeah, she's fine," Josiah said, his eyes glittering. "Doc and I walked out back and saw her coming out of the outhouse. Funniest thing—but she's right pert."

Ethan looked at Hiram. "She'll want to see her pa."

Hiram searched for his sister and saw her talking quietly with Libby, Bitsy, and Augie. "I'll get Trudy."

"Good. And Josiah. . ." Ethan turned back to the freighter's son. "Can you bring your wagon down here? We'll need to carry the bodies back to town. Tell your pa, too."

Hiram strode quickly to Trudy's side. "Miss Isabel might need you ladies when she finds out about her father."

Trudy and Libby took a hasty leave of the Moores. As they walked toward the steps, Dr. Kincaid rounded the corner of the house, carrying Isabel in his arms. Her gray skirts flapped about his legs as he bore her toward them, and her head lolled against his chest.

"Is she all right?" Trudy ran forward, and Hiram followed. Ethan and a dozen others joined them as they clustered around the doctor.

"She's had a shock. I need a place to put her down where she can rest." Kincaid caught Trudy's gaze. "Perhaps you could attend to her?"

"Yes, certainly. Mrs. Adams can help me."

"Should I take her inside?"

Ethan shook his head. "I don't think so, Doc. Why don't you lay her down here by the house? Josiah will bring a wagon down in a minute."

Kincaid stooped and lowered Isabel gently to earth.

"Can we get a blanket?" Libby asked. "What about a pillow?"

Ethan looked uneasily toward the house. They'd moved Cyrus off the steps, but Kenton's boots were visible through the doorway. "I'm not sure that's a good idea, ma'am."

"I'll get them." Hiram ran for the steps. He hopped over Kenton's body and looked around. On the bunk against the side wall he found one more musty wool blanket but no pillow. He carried it outside, shook it, and walked over to Libby. "This is all I could find."

"Thank you. We'll make do." She squinted at his battered hat. "Are you all right?"

"Yes ma'am. I'm fine."

She nodded soberly, and he wondered if she knew about the shooter in the barn.

"There's a hole in your hat brim," she said quietly.

He inhaled deeply. He'd noticed that hole when he retrieved his hat after the gunfire had ceased. Not much he could do about it. "Yes ma'am. I gave thanks to the Almighty."

"So did I," she said.

"Hey, Doc?" Arthur Tinen Jr. strode over to the knot of people, and Kincaid looked up at him.

"Yes?"

"That fella out back. . ."

Kincaid grimaced. "I confess I forgot about him. I'll come right away."

He started to stand, but Arthur put his hand on the doctor's shoulder. "No need."

Kincaid sighed. "I'm sorry."

Ethan stood. "It's all right, Doc. You need to see to Miss Fennel now. I'll go take a look at the cowpoke, and you can check him over later and do what you have to do."

Hiram looked from the huddle around Isabel to Ethan's retreating back and decided to tag after him. He followed Ethan

580

and Art behind the house and out to the far edge of the corral, where the ground sloped up sharply into the scrub pines.

Griffin Bane stood over the body, his face set in grim lines and his right arm cradled in a sling improvised from Annie Harper's paisley shawl.

"He's a goner, Ethan," Griff said as they approached. "Nothing you can do for him."

"Would it have helped if the doctor got to him?"

"Doubt it." Griffin looked down at the body. "I met this fella once, in the Nugget."

"Oh?" Ethan asked. "Does he have a name?"

"Red. On account of his hair, I reckon."

"Too bad we didn't catch any of them alive," Hiram said.

"Yeah." Ethan pushed his hat back. "We might have trouble identifying some of these fellas. We don't even know most of their names, and some of them we do know are false."

Hiram looked down at the dead man's face. "Guess you'll have to write some more letters before Doc can make out all the death certificates."

Ethan knelt and gingerly checked the man's pockets but found only a few extra cartridges, a nickel, and a pocketknife. "Hiram, would you ask Josiah to pick this one up after he gets Kenton and Button?"

"Sure. What about Cyrus?"

"He oughta ride in a different wagon from the others, I'd think."

"That's fittin'," Griff said.

Isabel moaned and put her hand to her aching temple. "What happened?"

"You swooned, dear," Libby said, "but you'll be all right. Dr. Kincaid has been attending you."

Dr. Kincaid. The privy. Papa.

Isabel struggled to sit up, and Trudy got her arm beneath her and gave her a boost. Her head ached. Isabel looked around and spotted a form lying by the steps that was covered with a dirty woolen blanket. Her stomach clenched. "That's Papa, isn't it?"

"Yes dear," Libby said. "I'm so sorry."

The men within earshot ducked their heads and removed their hats.

Libby reached both hands toward Isabel. "Come sit in the wagon and let Dr. Kincaid examine you."

"I want to see Papa." Tears gushed from Isabel's eyes, and she fumbled in her pocket for her handkerchief but found only a shotgun shell she'd missed when loading the stove. She stared down at it, her innards still swirling. Had her bid for freedom sparked a fatal shootout?

Libby put her arms around her. "There, now. Maybe you'd best wait until. . ." She glanced up at Hiram, who stood nearby. "Until the men take him home and. . .and clean him up, dear."

"No." Isabel found the hankie in her other pocket and held it to her eyes. "Please. Let me see him now."

With Dr. Kincaid on her left and Libby on her right, she tottered to the doorstep.

"Are you certain you're ready for this?" the doctor asked.

"I'm sure."

Kincaid looked toward Hiram. "Would you, Mr. Dooley?"

Hiram stepped forward, stooped, and grasped a corner of the blanket. He pulled it back a few inches, and Isabel could see her father's graying hair. Hiram shot a glance at the doctor. Kincaid arched his eyebrows and nodded, though he tightened his hold on Isabel's arm. Hiram laid the blanket back as far as her father's waist.

Blood drenched the front of Cyrus's clothing. His head was thrown back, his eyes shut. Isabel's lips trembled as she viewed him, so unnaturally still.

"Papa," she whispered. She plucked at her skirts and lifted them a few inches so she could kneel beside him. She glanced toward the open doorway of the house. A man's feet in worn boots lay just within. "Is that. . .Uncle Kenton?"

"Yes ma'am," the doctor said softly. "He's left this world as well."

She shivered.

Dr. Kincaid quickly wrapped his arm around her waist. A vague uneasiness swept over her. No man had ever touched her in so personal a manner. . .not until the vile cowboys, anyway. "Come, Miss Fennel. I think you've seen enough. You need to sit down and take some water. I want to check your pulse as well."

He pulled her gently toward the nearest wagon, and she let him guide her. He kept his arm about her, and the sensation was not unpleasant, though the back of her bodice was damp with perspiration where his arm encircled her. Josiah lowered the tailgate. Isabel wobbled a bit, and Dr. Kincaid braced her with his other arm.

"All right?"

She sized up the wagon bed. It seemed impossibly high. "I don't think I. . ."

"Allow me." Dr. Kincaid bent and lifted her, depositing her on the back of the wagon.

"Thank you." Isabel shut her eyes for a moment then opened them.

"I fear you've overtaxed yourself." The doctor took out his pocket watch and reached for her wrist.

"I shall be fine." Isabel looked over at her father as the doctor checked her pulse. Hiram had laid the blanket back over the body. She sucked in a breath and looked at the doctor instead. His blond hair gleamed in the brilliant sunlight.

Trudy moved in with an open canteen. "Here, Isabel. This is probably warm, but it will do you good."

Her hand shook as she took it and tipped it up. How many people had drunk from it before her? As she lowered the canteen, she eyed it critically. "This is Papa's."

"Is it?" Trudy asked.

"Yes." She took another swallow then handed it to her friend.

Kincaid looked around. "Where's Runnels? We need to put this wagon in the shade."

"I'll get him," Trudy said. "There's a strip of shade yonder, by the barn."

Libby climbed in over the wagon seat and came to sit beside Isabel. Dr. Kincaid looked into Isabel's eyes for a moment, frowning.

"Why don't you lie down and rest, Miss Fennel?" he asked as he put away his watch.

Isabel started to protest, but his suggestion made sense. From out of nowhere, Annie and Bitsy appeared beside the wagon and offered a shawl and a horse blanket. Libby arranged them so that Isabel could have a cushion for her head. She soaked a handkerchief in warm water from the canteen and dabbed at Isabel's forehead. It felt good, and Isabel closed her eyes.

"That's it," the doctor said in his melodious voice. "Try to rest. I have some other duties I must see to, but Mrs. Adams will stay with you. I'll come back and examine you again before you leave."

Leave? Where would she go? She pulled in a breath, fighting panic.

"What else you want done, Sheriff?"

Isabel's eyes flew open at the shout. That sounded like Micah Landry. When had he arrived? Was the entire town here? She must have slept, but she was roasting. The rays of sun seared through her cotton blouse. She wanted to be at home, in her cool, wallpapered bedroom, on the double feather bed. But then she'd have to listen to the empty house.

"They're going to move the wagon," Libby said. A few moments later, the wheels creaked, and they lurched several yards. Blessed shade crept over Isabel, and she shivered.

"Better?" asked Libby.

"Yes." She heard Ethan say something about the livestock. She would have to think of Papa's cattle, too. A little moan escaped her lips.

"It's all right, dear. You're going to be all right." Libby leaned over her.

"Papa. . ."

"Yes. He's gone."

Isabel puffed out a breath and shut her eyes again.

"I'll help you in any way I can," Libby said softly.

"It's so hot."

"We'll take you back to town soon."

"What happened?" Isabel asked. "Who killed him?"

After a short pause, Libby drew a deep breath. "Your father confronted Mr. Smith. It seems they shot each other." She blotted Isabel's brow again with the handkerchief.

"What will they do with him now?"

"Your father?" Libby touched her shoulder gently. "Shall we carry him into town, or do you wish to have him laid out at the ranch?"

Isabel shuddered. "I. . .don't know."

"If you'd like, the men can take him to the livery stable. Mr. Bane has offered to help care for him. Mr. Dooley will build a coffin, and they'll fix him up nicely for the funeral."

Isabel nodded. "I suppose that's best. Put him in here with me. I want to ride with him."

Libby squeezed her hand. "I'm so sorry, dear Isabel. So very sorry."

"Papa wasn't a bad man."

"No. No, he wasn't." Libby set her jaw and nodded firmly. "He came here to get you away from those evil men. He loved you very much."

"Our men at the ranch will want to see him."

"We'll pass by your home on the way to town. We can send a rider ahead to tell them. If they want, they can accompany the. . . the body to the livery stable."

"Good. I think they'd want to help get him ready." Isabel pressed her lips together. As dry as she felt, a new flood of tears sheeted down her cheeks.

Libby foraged in her pockets but came up empty.

"Will this help?"

At Hiram's soft inquiry, Libby turned. He stood beside the wagon offering a folded bandanna. She took it and held out the faded, soft square to Isabel.

"Th–thank you."

"The doctor's coming back," Hiram said.

Isabel sat up slowly. Libby reached to help her inch over to the tailgate. Trudy hovered on the other side and reached to help. Isabel let her feet hang over the edge of the wagon.

The physician had almost reached them when Rose ran out from a knot of people near the house, carrying her parasol.

"Doctor, my ears are still ringing from all that shooting."

Kincaid paused and eyed her pensively. "I'm sorry, Mrs. Caplinger. It will pass after a time."

Trudy rolled her eyes skyward and called, "Rose, Dr. Kincaid needs to tend to Miss Fennel."

"But I can barely hear you." Rose's face crumpled up. "Doctor, you don't think it could be permanent, do you?"

Kincaid shook his head. "I doubt it, ma'am. You weren't close to the gunfire. I expect you'll be fine by evening, if not before." He walked the last few yards to the wagon.

"I told her not to come," Trudy muttered. "But no, she heard about the posse and insisted on riding along."

Rose stood for a moment with her mouth pursed, but when the doctor paid her no more attention, she swung about and stalked back to the shade with the fringe on her shawl fluttering.

The doctor stood facing Isabel. "I'm glad to see you're feeling better, Miss Fennel. I couldn't see that you had any wounds."

"No. My wrist aches, but I think that's the only thing wrong." She shuddered, and Libby patted her shoulder again. So very much was wrong, after all.

"Let me see." Kincaid took her left hand gently.

Isabel winced. "It's quite tender. That Button man twisted it."

"I'm sorry. May I unfasten this cuff?"

Inexplicably, she found herself blushing. "I can do it." She fumbled with the button and extended her arm again.

He bent over her hand and pushed the sleeve up a few inches. "Mmm. I see the redness. A little swelling." He probed the wrist joint. "Turn your palm up, please. Uh-huh. Does that hurt?"

"No more than before."

"And when you make a fist?"

She tried it. "Yes, that hurts."

He felt the joint again. "I don't think anything is broken, but you should take it easy for a few days. It might help to wrap your wrist to support it for a day or two. Would you like me to bandage it for you?"

"No, thank you. I'm sure it will heal." She rubbed the sorest spot with her fingertips. "Doctor. . ."

"Yes?" Kincaid looked gravely into her eyes.

"Did you examine my father's body?"

"Yes ma'am."

"Could you please tell me. . .anything?"

Kincaid cleared his throat. "He died swiftly. One fatal wound to his heart."

She nodded. "He didn't suffer, then?"

"I think not. It was nearly instantaneous for both of them."

"Both—" Isabel glanced at Libby then back to the doctor. "You mean my uncle, don't you?"

He nodded. "The sheriff was right behind your father. As near as we can tell, Smith pulled the trigger as he opened the door, and your father returned fire. It was the last act for both of them."

"I heard someone say the rest of his men got away."

"Three were shot down. The others—three more, we think—escaped."

Isabel nodded, mentally counting the men she'd seen hulking about the ranch.

"Which ones?"

"One man was killed by a shot through the window. I believe he's the one who brought you outside when your father insisted on seeing you."

Kincaid avoided looking directly at her as he spoke. Isabel wondered if he'd taken part in the shootout, but she didn't ask. He was one of the best marksmen in town. Perhaps she would ask Libby sometime. Not now. It might be best if she didn't know who fired the fatal bullets.

"The other dead men are a large, heavy man with a beard and a red headed man."

"He was in the house when Papa and the others came. They were playing poker—Uncle Kenton, Red, and Buck—while Button kept watch at the window. I only saw the others from a distance."

"The one called Buck must have gotten away."

"Yes." Isabel gazed toward the ranch house and the mountains beyond.

"I think you should rest some more, ma'am," Kincaid said. "Is there anyone at home who can stay with you tonight?"

"No, I . . ."

"She can stay with me," Libby said. "Isabel stayed at my home last night, and I'd be delighted to have her again. We can stop briefly at her father's ranch on the way to town, and she can pick up a few things."

Isabel caught her breath. Did she want to do that? She certainly didn't want to stay alone at the ranch. She exhaled in a sigh. "Thank you. I believe I'd like that if it's not too much trouble."

"No trouble at all." Libby squeezed her shoulders gently. "You may stay as long as you like."

"Poor Papa." Isabel pushed back a loose wisp of her hair. "I wasn't there to fix his breakfast this morning."

★ CHAPTER 38 ★

The motley procession started for Fergus. The Harpers' wagon pulled out first, loaded with townspeople. Libby sat in the back of Josiah Runnels's wagon with Isabel and the Bentons. They'd persuaded Isabel to let Arthur Tinen Jr. transport her father's body in the wagon behind them. Libby was glad she didn't have to sit close to the corpse, but she would have if Isabel had insisted. Hiram and Trudy rode their horses alongside them. Ethan rode at the head of the procession with some of the other men. The wagon bearing Kenton and his dead ranch hands followed several yards behind.

Within a mile of the Fennel ranch, several riders galloped toward them. Cyrus's men paused to speak to the sheriff then rode on back and clustered their horses around the wagon in which Isabel rode.

The oldest of the cowboys lifted his hat and eyed her sorrowfully. "Is it true, Miss Isabel? Is your father dead?"

"Yes Brady. I'm having him laid out at the livery in town, where folks can stop in and see him before the funeral. I'll be stopping at home for a minute to pack a few things. I'm staying in town tonight with Mrs. Adams."

Brady touched the brim of his hat. "All right, miss. If you need anything, you let us know. The boys and I will go into town and make sure they tend to your papa right."

"Thank you."

Brady turned his horse and trotted back to the wagon behind them. He and the cowboys gazed into the bed then fell in behind.

At the lane to the Fennel ranch, Josiah turned in. His father and Arthur continued on, driving their grim burdens toward Fergus.

Ethan called to the freighter, "We'll be just a few minutes, Oscar. Head for the livery, and I'll be along before you get there."

Most of the townspeople went on, but Ethan and the Dooleys followed Josiah's wagon to the Fennel house.

Apphia Benton slid toward the back of the wagon. "My dear, I can go in with you and help you gather your things."

"Thank you." Isabel climbed down.

The pastor got out of the wagon, too. Libby stayed put and watched the three go into the house. Ethan and the Dooleys dismounted and walked their horses over close to the wagon.

Ethan said, "We thought maybe we'd ought to have a little discussion while Miss Isabel's inside."

"What about?" Libby asked.

"Her uncle Kenton."

"What about him?"

Ethan pushed his hat back and looked around at them. "Hiram, Trudy. . ." He glanced toward the wagon. "You know about this, too, Miz Adams."

Libby gathered her skirts and hopped to the ground. Josiah had climbed from the wagon seat and was checking his team's harness. Libby glanced at him and walked a few steps away with the others.

Ethan scratched his jaw. "The way I see it, we four are the only ones besides Isabel who know about that metal box her daddy buried behind the barn."

"Metal box?" Libby looked quickly from one face to another. "He buried a box?"

Trudy shrugged. "You knew he buried *something*. Isabel told you."

"Yes, of course, but I didn't realize you'd learned what it was."

"We went and dug it up this morning when Cyrus got the note and tore off," Trudy said. "When we got to his ranch, he wasn't here, so we decided to settle the question of what he'd buried."

"And you uncovered a can?" Libby asked.

Ethan nodded. "A tin like crackers and things come in. There's a pouch of coins in it and a wanted poster showing Kenton Smith and Mary Fennel—under different names."

Libby opened her mouth then closed it. Her brain whirled as she tried to make sense of that.

Trudy squeezed her arm. "Isabel's confided in you more than anyone else in town. You're probably her best friend right now. This morning we three rode out and met Cyrus and told him we'd dug up his secret. And he told us some shocking bits of family history."

"Isabel's not his daughter," Libby said with sudden certainty.

They all stared at her.

"How did you know that?" Trudy asked.

Libby puffed out a breath. "Something happened many years ago—it's not important what—but Mary Fennel said something to me I've never forgotten. She said Cyrus wanted a child of his own."

"That fits." Ethan gritted his teeth and looked toward the ranch house.

Hiram reached down and plucked a grass stem and stuck the end in his mouth.

"So do we all agree that it wouldn't do Isabel any good to know that?" Trudy asked. "Cyrus said Kenton didn't know she was his daughter."

"And Isabel certainly didn't know," Libby said. "It explains a lot of things, though. Why Cyrus has acted so strangely, and why he let Kenton stay on his land."

"Kenton was blackmailing him," Ethan said. "When he was arrested for robbery and put in prison, Mary took off with Cyrus—and the loot they'd collected from Kenton's robberies. Sounds like she may have helped him in some of those crimes. When Kenton was released, he tracked them out here. He wanted his share, and Cyrus didn't have it. That's why Kenton grabbed Isabel—to put pressure on Cyrus."

Libby's heart ached at the sordid sadness of it. "You mean. . . they weren't legally married."

Trudy winced and nodded.

"I never would have guessed Mary could take part in anything like that."

"Well, we've only Cy's word and an old wanted poster," Ethan said. "But why would he lie about something like that?"

Trudy straightened her shoulders. "Since Kenton and Cyrus are both dead, why not let this secret die, too? Why should we give Isabel more reason to grieve?"

Hiram nodded. He arched his eyebrows at Ethan.

"But if they were criminals. . ." Ethan looked around at his friends.

Trudy scowled at him. "All the criminals are dead, Ethan, except for the three cowpokes that escaped this morning. And we don't know that they did anything but follow their boss's orders."

Ethan sucked air in between his teeth. "I guess. But I'm supposed to uphold the law."

"And so you do, sweetheart." Trudy slipped her hand through the crook of his arm. "It's a shame about Cyrus, but I suspect the other men who were killed have a lot of dark deeds in their past."

"One of the others is hurting, thanks to you," Hiram said.

Ethan eyed him testily. "We should have gone after them."

"No," Libby said. "The most important thing was finding Isabel. By the time we knew she was safe, those cowpokes were halfway to Nampa."

"I expect you're right." Ethan sighed. "All right. I'll go along with you, though I'm not sure it's the best thing to do. But I'm telegraphing the authorities in Boise and Nampa when we get back to town."

"Not a bad idea," Hiram said.

"Libby, you okay with that?" Trudy looked to her friend with arched brows.

Libby spread her hands. "At this point, I'll do anything that will help Isabel, so long as we don't have to lie to her. She'll be more at peace burying Cyrus if she goes on believing he's her father."

Trudy gazed up into Ethan's face. "I feel the same way. At least. . .she'd be *less* at peace if she knew who her real papa was."

Ethan rubbed the back of his neck. "All right."

Hiram slapped him on the back. "There you go."

Trudy leaned close to her brother's face and said sternly, "But this is something none of us four can ever tell anyone, and we'd do best not even to talk about it amongst ourselves ever again. As far as we know, well. . .we don't. That is, we don't know anything."

"Agreed," Libby said quickly.

The door to the house opened, and Pastor Benton emerged carrying a valise.

"The ladies will be right out. Miss Fennel wanted to tend to a few things in the kitchen."

"Let me take that bag." Ethan took the valise and hefted it into Josiah's wagon.

As Libby turned to follow, she darted a glance at Hiram. Despite the day's grim events, he gave the appearance of a man at peace. He met her gaze, and just before he turned toward the hitching rail, she could have sworn he winked at her.

★ CHAPTER 39 ★

Ethan climbed the stairs at the back of the emporium building before seven the next morning and knocked on the door to Libby's apartment. In spite of the early hour, Libby greeted him pleasantly.

"Good morning, Sheriff! Can I help you?"

"I wondered if Miss Fennel is up. I'd like to speak to her about the time she was held hostage if she's feeling up to it."

"Why, yes." Libby stepped back to give him entry to her kitchen. "We just finished breakfast. I need to go downstairs and prepare to open the store, but perhaps you'd like to interview her here. There's some coffee on the stove, and it's quiet here. No one will bother you."

"Thank you. . .if you think. . ." He looked around cautiously. It felt a little odd, standing in an unmarried woman's home. Almost as awkward as the first time he went into the Nugget.

Libby smiled, and he suspected his ears had turned red. "I see nothing wrong with conducting official business in a friend's kitchen. And I'll be only a few yards away, after all."

He couldn't argue with that. He nodded, and she hastened into the next room.

Ten minutes later, he and Isabel sat across from each other at the little maple table. Sun streamed in through the eyelet curtains at the window on the back of the kitchen. The excellent coffee and the occasional quiet sounds of Libby moving about in the store below took away all Ethan's apprehension.

"You say the men talked some amongst themselves while you were their hostage. Can you tell me what they said?"

Isabel set her cup down and frowned. "Let me see. . . . I recall Uncle Kenton talking to the man they call Sterling. That was before Papa showed up the first time, when he came alone."

Ethan leaned forward. "What did they say?"

"It was something about a piece of land that they'd wanted to get for free. I wondered at the time if they were talking about the Peart property."

"Maybe so."

Isabel took a sip of her coffee. "Uncle Kenton said something like, 'Well, it's too bad that plan didn't work. That sheriff—' " She broke off and set the cup down, not meeting his gaze. "I'm sorry."

Ethan smiled. "It's all right, ma'am. I already know Smith didn't like me much, nor Wilfred Sterling either."

She shrugged and gave a little cough. "Well, if you must know, he said you might be smarter than he'd given you credit for."

"Do tell." Ethan sat back, rather pleased with her revelation.

"That was about the time I gathered they were demanding a ransom from my father." Her forehead wrinkled, and she picked up her spoon. "Why would my uncle demand a ransom? Did my father give you any idea?"

Ethan rose and got the coffeepot, though he didn't need more coffee. He poured a small amount into his cup. "Would you like more?"

"No, thank you."

He set the pot back on the stovetop and sat down again. "Miss Fennel, I was with your father when he first learned you'd been kidnapped."

"You were?"

"Yes. Hiram Dooley was there, too, at the Wells Fargo office. Someone tossed a rock wrapped in a note through the window. Your pa took off. Hiram and I read the note and rode off after him. But we had to stop and saddle up, and Trudy joined us."

She raised her pale eyebrows.

"We. . .uh. . .met him coming back from the Martin place. He'd been out there and talked to Mr. Smith."

"Yes, he came alone that first time, and Uncle Kenton told him to go and get some money and to come back with it by sundown." She shivered. "I confess I didn't take to my uncle when I first met

Susan Page Davis

him, but I had no inkling he would do violence to our family."

"You know he had been in prison, I believe."

"Papa told me. But still. . ."

Ethan sipped his coffee while thinking through what he knew and what he could reveal. "Well ma'am, I think it's obvious that when Mr. Smith was released from jail, he didn't give up his criminal ways. He may have pressured your father into giving him a place to live and then gathered some of the no-accounts he knew around him."

"His ranch hands? I suppose you're right. They could all be felons he met while in prison. And he might have seen Papa as an easy way to get some money, rather than earning it."

"Less risky than robbing a bank, or so it might seem. Of course, in the end. . ." Ethan shrugged.

"I wonder if he was jealous of Papa's success."

Ethan decided his best course was to avoid talking about money where Kenton and Cyrus were concerned, so he sipped his coffee without answering. A knock at the kitchen door startled him. Isabel caught her breath and looked to him expectantly. Ethan rose and walked to the door. He opened it and found Phineas Benton and his wife on the landing outside.

"Reverend."

"Sheriff. Mrs. Adams told us you were here. We wondered if Miss Fennel was up to discussing funeral arrangements for her father."

Ethan looked over his shoulder toward Isabel. "Ma'am, the parson and Mrs. Benton are here."

Isabel rose and came to the door. "Thank you for coming, Pastor."

The Bentons entered, and she accepted Apphia's embrace.

"Libby said we could sit up here with you and talk about your Papa's service if you're up to it." Apphia drew back and appraised Isabel. "Did you sleep last night, dear?"

"Not much. I did drop off toward dawn."

Ethan reached for his hat. "I'll get going, but please feel free to call on me if you need anything, Miss Fennel."

"Thank you, Sheriff."

He went out the door and down the back stairs. Isabel seemed

596

to accept his train of thought about her so-called uncle's motives, and he was glad she hadn't mentioned the hole behind the barn. At some point he'd have to retrieve the money for her, but that could come later. Maybe he could arrange it somehow so that she received it as part of Cyrus's estate, and its source could remain secret.

Isabel prepared a light luncheon for herself and Libby. It was the least she could do for her hostess. To her surprise, when they sat down together, she found her appetite had returned.

"That's a very good red flannel hash you've made," Libby said with a smile. "Thank you. I don't usually take time for a hot meal at noon."

"The air is cooler today, and I thought it might taste good. After all, you've done so much for me."

"Think nothing of it." Libby sliced off a bite of leftover chicken. "Did you have a good visit with the Bentons?"

"Yes, I. . .we've decided to hold the service in the church."

"I think that's wise," Libby said. "If it rains, or even if it doesn't—it's been so hot lately—it will be nice to be under cover."

Isabel detailed the plans they'd made for the service while they ate. When she'd finished, Libby stood.

"Forgive me for running out so soon, dear. I like to get back to the store quickly and let Florence go home for her dinner. Is there anything I can do for you before I leave you again?"

"No, I think I'll take a nap," Isabel said. "I fear I didn't sleep much last night."

"I'm sure it will do you good. Thank you for the delicious meal." Libby started to gather her dishes.

"Oh, just leave those. I'll take care of them."

Libby had hardly gone down the stairs when a knock came at the kitchen door. Isabel jumped and hurried to open the door. Dr. Kincaid stood on the landing, holding his black bag and smiling.

"It's good to see you looking so well, Miss Fennel. May I come in? Mrs. Adams said I would find you here."

"Why, yes, Doctor." Isabel stepped back and let him enter.

He removed his hat and stood looking at her expectantly.

"Oh, let me take that." As she reached for it, he smiled down at her, and Isabel felt suddenly at sea. She'd never been alone with such an attractive man. A hint of guilt buzzed about her mind, like a horsefly zipping in and leaving, only to return a moment later. Was it wrong to think a man pleasant to look at or listen to? She turned away and carefully placed his hat on a rack near the door.

"I shan't take long," Dr. Kincaid said. "I'd like to count your pulse and respirations if you don't mind, and ask you a few questions."

"Oh, of course." Isabel felt her cheeks flush. "Would you like to come into the parlor?" Now, why did she ask that? Surely the physician could listen to her heartbeat just as well in the kitchen.

"Thank you."

He didn't seem to think it odd, so she led him into Libby's parlor.

"Won't you sit down?" She took one of the straight chairs near the window.

He set his bag on the sofa and opened it. "I'll stand. How do you feel today?"

"Quite well, thank you."

"I'm sure yesterday was trying."

She nodded and lowered her gaze. "I met with Mr. and Mrs. Benton to plan Papa's funeral."

"Ah. And when is that to be?" He took a stethoscope from his bag and hung it about his neck.

"Tomorrow. The pastor thought it not wise to wait longer."

"I see."

She looked down at the carpet, feeling a bit queasy. Neither of them spoke of the heat that made the hasty service necessary. "I'm still. . .getting used to the idea that Papa is gone."

"Shall you stay here with Mrs. Adams?"

"For a while, I think. She's invited me to remain with her indefinitely, and I've decided to stay a few more days. I don't wish to impose on her, but—"

"I'm sure she finds your company stimulating." He took out his watch and approached her. "May I?"

She held up her wrist, and he took it gently, focusing on the timepiece.

"Your pulse is a bit rapid and thready. You haven't felt dizzy, have you?"

"No, but. . .when I think of all that happened yesterday. . ."

"Of course."

She didn't look at him. The touch of his warm hand contributed to the frantic pace of her heartbeat, she was sure.

He lowered her hand to her lap and stood back a bit. "Now, if you'll just breathe normally, I shall count your respiration."

Again she sought something else to look at. His compassionate blue eyes could make a woman think all sorts of things. Just the concept brought the flush to her cheeks again. *Oh dear, this will never do. He'll think I'm ill when I'm merely behaving like a schoolgirl—swooning over an attractive man. The idea!*

"Miss Fennel?"

She jumped. "Yes?"

"How was your sleep last night?"

"Fragmented, I fear."

"I'm a bit concerned. Do you have a strong constitution?"

"Certainly, under normal circumstances."

He nodded thoughtfully. "I'd like to prescribe a tonic for you."

She straightened her back, wondering whether she ought to protest that she was fine.

"I assure you it's mild, but it will help you sleep. Take it just at bedtime. And if you wish to lie down this afternoon, take a spoonful then, as well. I know it's difficult to keep the mind from racing when you've had a shock. The memory constantly replays the unfortunate events and the tragedy that ensued."

"Why, yes. That's exactly how it was." She looked into his eyes. They radiated a serene kindness.

"And how is your left wrist? Still sore?"

"A little, but it's much better today, thank you."

"I'm glad to hear it." Dr. Kincaid sat down on the sofa, sliding his bag over a few inches. "Do you plan to return to your teaching post?"

She blinked at him, surprised at the inquiry. "I hadn't considered not doing so."

"And when does the next term begin?"

"In about three weeks. We'll have a two-month summer term, then a break of three weeks during harvest, and then begin the fall term."

Susan Page Davis

"May I suggest that you take these next three weeks to rest? I know the temptation is there to busy yourself and forget about all of this—to prepare for school and perhaps overhaul the ranch house. But you need to build yourself up physically. You'll have your father's affairs to settle, too. He had a lot of business concerns, I understand."

"Well yes, there's the stagecoach line and the boardinghouse, in addition to the ranch. And he owned considerable property."

He leaned back on the sofa. "You'll have to think about those things, of course. But take time to rest your mind in between." He looked around at the pleasant room, and his gaze landed on Libby's cherry bookcases. "I see Mrs. Adams has quite a library."

"Yes. She has more books than anyone else in town. She's told me I may borrow any I like."

"That's good. It may seem frivolous right now, but if you can lose yourself in a novel for a few hours, it will help you stop thinking of your own troubles for a while."

"I thought I might try the latest one by Henry James, though Papa might. . ." She broke off and smiled in apology. "I was going to say, 'Papa might think it quite daring for a mountain schoolteacher.'"

Kincaid smiled. "I think you would enjoy it. I'm reading Turgenev's *Fathers and Sons* right now."

Isabel raised one hand. "Oh, those Nihilists!"

"You've read it?"

"Yes, but I'm not sure I understood it. I rather liked it, but I felt as though I shouldn't."

He chuckled. "We'll have to discuss it when I've finished it. That is, if you'd care to do so. . . ."

He must be lonely, Isabel thought. *That wistful look could mean nothing else.*

"I should be delighted." She swallowed hard and lowered her lashes. Papa's words had suddenly bounced back into her mind. *I saw you staring at him at the picnic. . .saw you eyeing him at church, too.* Should she say something to assure Dr. Kincaid that she wasn't pursuing him? No, if he hadn't thought such a thing, mentioning it might make him wary. And she would dearly love to discuss Turgenev with an intelligent person.

600

"Are you well?" He leaned toward her and reached for her wrist again.

"Why, yes. I only. . . . Oh, it's silly, but I was thinking of the books we might discuss. You've no idea how much I've longed to do that. My father isn't much—*wasn't* much of a reader for pleasure, and while I'm sure Mrs. Adams indulges, she is so busy that we rarely meet except at church or the shooting club."

"I should be delighted to engage in literary discussions." He fingered his stethoscope. "I was going to listen to your lungs—"

"I assure you, my breathing is fine. I shall recover soon from all of this." Her face must be as scarlet as a radish by now. There was no chance she would let him get any closer with that stethoscope without another female present. It would be too, too unsettling.

He took the instrument off and tucked it into his bag. "All right. Let me just write down the name of the tonic. Mrs. Adams stocks it in the emporium." He took a small pad and a pencil from his coat pocket and began to write.

"There you go. And if you don't mind, I'd like to come by and see you before the service tomorrow, just to be sure you're up to it."

"You may come, sir, but I shall be fine."

He nodded and stood. "In that case, I'll be off. I have a patient to visit at the Storrey ranch. But if you feel the need of my ministrations, send someone to the boardinghouse. I'll be back there in an hour or two."

"Thank you. I'll do that." Isabel looked down at the sheet of paper he'd handed her. They said doctors had terrible handwriting, but she could read his script perfectly. She rose and saw him to the door, trying to keep her breathing steady and willing her heart to stop hammering like a frenzied blacksmith.

The blacksmith. She paused with her hand on the doorknob. "Doctor, there is one thing that troubles me. I wonder if you might give me some advice on a financial matter."

"I'd be happy to, though I'm not an expert in that field."

"It's my father's business with the stagecoach company. He had a contract running through next spring. I suppose the logical thing is to ask Mr. Bane to see it through if he's willing. He already keeps the horses and changes the teams."

"He seems a good businessman. Didn't he start out with just the smithy?"

"Yes. He bought the livery when the former owner moved out of town."

"From everything I've seen of Mr. Bane, he's trustworthy. If he's not too busy to take it on, he would probably do well with the stage line."

Isabel nodded slowly, amazed that she could discuss Griffin Bane without becoming agitated.

"Do you know whom I should discuss it with if I were you?" Kincaid asked.

"No sir."

"Your friend Elizabeth Adams. She's the shrewdest woman I've ever met. And she's known Mr. Bane much longer than I have. She could tell you if he'd do well in the position."

"Yes, you're right." Isabel smiled as she swung the door open. "Thank you so much, Doctor. I shall put the matter to her this evening."

She closed the door behind him and stood for a moment, puzzling over the thoughts whirling through her mind. Dr. Kincaid would call again tomorrow. She must be ready to receive him graciously. But she mustn't throw herself at him. Indeed, she mustn't even think of pursuing him. How unladylike and vulgar that would be. Shades of Rose Caplinger and her mass distribution of cookies to the single men of the town. And Papa was surely right that the handsome doctor would never look her way. On the other hand, Dr. James Kincaid had expressed interest in discussing books with her.

She caught her breath. She'd better dust off that volume of Turgenev and refresh her memory of the story line and philosophy between its covers. Slowly she walked into Libby's parlor and stood gazing into the mirror between the windows. Papa was quite right. She was too thin, and her hair had always been a nondescript brown. Her pale eyes held none of the allure of Libby's sparkling blue ones. And yet... She strode toward the bookcase but stopped in the middle of the room.

First things first. She must fetch the tonic. Surely the doctor would inquire tomorrow whether she had followed his instructions.

★ CHAPTER 40 ★

On the Monday after Cyrus's funeral, Hiram plied his hoe in the corn patch behind his house. So much had changed in Fergus that he needed a few hours of solitude to sort it all out. His shirt stuck to his skin, wet with perspiration. He hoped this heat would break. As soon as Oscar hauled the lumber from the sawmill, Hiram and his crew would start on the new church building.

"Mr. Dooley?"

He looked up in surprise. Isabel made her way daintily across his garden, holding her skirt up as high as her shoe tops.

"Help you, ma'am?" He leaned on his hoe. The send-off they'd given her pa Saturday afternoon would have made Cyrus proud. Hiram hoped Cy had been able to look down and see them all honoring him at the haberdashery building and then out at the graveyard for the burial. He'd rest near the schoolhouse, where his daughter could walk over and visit the grave anytime she wanted.

"Mr. Dooley—Hiram—"

"Yes?"

Isabel's face, beneath the brim of her gray bonnet, seemed rather pinker than the warmth of the morning accounted for.

"I wonder if I might discuss a matter with you."

He waited, curious and a little on edge. Would this turn out like the evening she'd gone to the smithy? He pulled his bandanna from his back pocket and blotted his forehead so the sweat wouldn't trickle down his face while he talked to her.

She cleared her throat. "I've been staying with Mrs. Adams all week, and I find that I can't face moving back to the ranch, where

603

I lived so long with my father."

Hiram frowned, trying to fit her words with her nervous twisting of her reticule's strap.

"And so I wondered if it's possible—well, I happen to know that at one time you had considered buying the ranch where we lived. Before my father bought it, that is."

"Yes ma'am, I did."

"I. . .don't suppose. . ."

Hiram swallowed hard. Here it was again—the opportunity he'd wanted, and again he'd have to say no. "Miss Isabel, I don't have much money put by."

"Oh, I understand that."

A horrible thought suddenly came to him. She wasn't implying—was she?—that perhaps he'd consider marrying her and moving to the ranch with her? This had to be worse than that night at the smithy, when she approached Griffin. They'd all decided to ignore that outburst. But now she'd gotten desperate, since her father died.

"Ma'am, I. . ."

"I realize you've got your sister-in-law visiting and all, but with Trudy planning to get married. . ." Her eyes darted about as though seeking something less objectionable to gaze at than him. "Since the parson announced yesterday that Trudy and the sheriff will be married soon, I got to thinking you might rather live closer to them, and if you still want to try ranching, why maybe the solution would be for you to swap houses with me."

Hiram stared at her for a long half minute, remaining outwardly still while his heart pounded and leaped. Was she nuts? His little house in town with a couple of acres out back was worth far less than Cyrus's ranch. That fine, big ranch house outshone this little frame dwelling by far. And Cy had a big pole barn, and corrals and pastures, and a bunkhouse for his cowboys. And the cattle. What did she intend to do with all those beef steers? He certainly couldn't ante up for all the livestock, and what good was a ranch without cattle? But. . .swap houses?

"Well Miss Fennel, I don't know. . . ." He pushed his hat up in the back and scratched where the band had hugged his head. His hair was damp all around where the hat had rested. "Maybe you'd ought to wait a while before you decide something like that. Go through your pa's papers and such."

Isabel puffed out a breath and looked at the ground. It had been so dry lately, the grass was all brown and wilted. Cyrus's ranch bordered the river on the southwest. Hiram wondered how many cattle were running Cy's range right now.

"Maybe we could talk about it later." He wiped his forehead again. "After you know what's what with your pa's property."

"Papa had a lot of land." Her dull eyes shifted uneasily. "Honestly, I don't know what to do."

Hiram tucked the bandanna back into his pocket. He clasped his hands over the end of the hoe handle and leaned on it again. "I wonder if the sheriff and some of the town council members couldn't advise you a little."

She nodded. "They might. I've talked to Libby some. . . ."

"You must realize that your father's ranch is worth a lot more than my house."

"Well. . .I thought perhaps we could work it out somehow. I. . .don't want to live there anymore. I'm certain of that. I'd like to live in town, but I don't wish to impose on Libby much longer." Her head drooped.

Hiram couldn't help feeling a rush of sympathy for her, all alone in the world as she now found herself. "Say, don't you own the boardinghouse now? You could stay there for a while. Until you have time to make some decisions."

Her chin came up an inch. "Yes, I could."

"And your pa had some more empty houses in town."

"That's true. I could probably fit one up to live in. But even so, it's on my heart that you should have the ranch. Papa didn't do right when he bought it out from under you. I've heard people talk about it, and I think it's time you had the land you wanted."

Hiram pulled in a long, slow breath and looked down the rows of his garden. "Well now, that's kind of you to say so. The truth is, that dream has faded since my wife died. Violet and I, we thought we'd get us a ranch and work it together. Raise our family there. But without her, I'm not sure I could resurrect that vision."

They stood for a long moment in the hot sun, saying nothing. Hiram's thoughts spun off on a new dream's track. Would Libby consent to live on a ranch? The very idea enchanted him, but he couldn't picture her without the emporium. Libby, riding the range with him? Cooking up supper for a bunch of cowpokes? The idea began to grow on him. But could she be content living outside town, not seeing folks every day, away from other women? Not too far away, of course. Close enough to walk into town. And there was the shooting club. But what about the store?

Isabel sighed, and her shoulders sank again.

It occurred to him that her attitude might change if she found a husband. He eyed her uneasily. He'd about discounted the notion that she hoped he'd pop the question and marry her. But maybe this offer to swap property was an attempt to draw it out of him and make him think it was his idea.

"Miss Isabel, someday you might want that ranch. It's a good piece of land."

She shook her head. "It holds too many sorrowful memories. I shall never live there again. And I shall consider your advice about the boardinghouse. It might be a good place for me to stay while I consider my options."

"Didn't your pa have a lawyer or somebody like that to draw up papers and such?"

"Well yes." Her pale blue eyes brightened. "There is a man in Boise. I suppose I should telegraph him."

"Sure. He might be able to advise you on what to do about the property."

She nodded slowly. "And maybe—it just came into my mind that maybe you'd consider managing the ranch for me. You could still do your gun work. We could apply your wages to buying the property if you wanted."

Hiram frowned. It would take a ranch foreman a lifetime to save enough to buy that spread. And he was committed to overseeing the building of the new church.

She twisted the strap of her bag again. "I've so much to consider. There's the stagecoach line, for instance. I need to find someone who can fulfill Papa's contract."

"I expect Griff Bane might help you there."

"Do you? I don't like to ask him any favors."

Hiram shrugged. "If it's profitable for him, it won't be a favor."

"That's true." She gritted her teeth as though steeling her-self to do something unpleasant. "All right, I'll ask him. And will you think about the possibilities at the ranch? If you won't move out there, I'll have to sell it, and it seems property in Fergus is hard to sell just now."

That was true. Cy had tried to sell property just last week with little success. "I guess it can't hurt to think about it."

"Thank you." She turned and walked away, her shoulders slumped. She'd seemed almost handsome that night at the smithy when she'd raged at Griffin, but now she looked gray and tired. Hiram watched until she turned the corner of the house. The satisfaction he'd felt in the sunny day and the waist-high corn had fled. Why did he feel guilty?

The kitchen door opened, and Rose stood on the stoop staring toward him. He poked halfheartedly at a weed with the hoe.

"Hiram! Didn't I just see Miss Fennel go past the window?"

He sighed and turned toward the house, walking slowly through the rows. When he was ten feet from the back steps, he stopped and looked up at her. "Yes, she came to discuss some business with me."

"Business?"

"She has her father's estate to settle."

Rose's smooth, creamy brow wrinkled. "Why should she talk to you about that?"

Hiram drew in a deep breath, quickly running through and discarding possible answers. He gave up and shrugged.

"Ooo! You're so maddening! Why can't you speak like a normal man?" Rose gathered her skirts and stormed back into the house, shutting the door firmly behind her.

Hiram eyed the closed door helplessly. Yes, why couldn't he speak? Sometimes he kept quiet because he had nothing to say. When he was a boy, his father had often quoted Proverbs 17:28: *"Even a fool, when he holdeth his peace, is counted wise: and he that shutteth his lips is esteemed a man of understanding."* That made sense. Lincoln had put it another way: *"Better to remain silent and be thought a fool than to speak out and remove all doubt."*

There were other occasions when Hiram felt tongue-tied and fearful that what he said would be rejected—moments when he'd stood face-to-face with Libby came to mind. But you couldn't go all your life regretting what you never said. Perhaps it was time.

Griffin set the pritchel precisely where he wanted it on the branch of the red-hot horseshoe and hammered away. The jarring hurt his arm, but Doc had said it wasn't broken, so he gritted his teeth and kept at it. Three holes on each side of the horseshoe would do it. The metal cooled before he could do the last one. With his tongs, he lifted it from the anvil and stuck it back into the glowing forge.

"Mr. Bane?"

He jumped and looked toward the door of the smithy. Isabel stood there, much as she had that evening a few weeks back. He swallowed hard, trying to force back the sour taste in his mouth. He didn't even have Hiram here to deflect her anger today.

"Mr. Bane, I've come to talk to you about the stagecoach business. First of all, thank you for handling things for me the last few days."

"No problem." He turned and poked at the horseshoe. It glowed orange. He worked the bellows a few times.

She was still standing there. "I wondered if you could continue doing it—that is, if you would be in a position to fulfill my father's contract with Wells Fargo. He was to continue as division agent for this line until next May. I telegraphed the company the day after Papa died, and they've approved my finding a replacement for the duration of the contract. We're so far off the main line that I suppose they don't want to take the trouble to come all the way up here."

Griffin turned and eyed her suspiciously. "You want me to take on his duties as division agent?"

"That's right."

"I'm awful busy."

"Yes, I know, but I can't think of anyone else as qualified."

Griffin looked back at the forge. The side of the horseshoe he needed to work was white-hot now. He seized it with the tongs and carried it to the anvil. As he positioned the pritchel and picked up his hammer, he could feel her watching him.

A few blows did the job, and he plunged the shoe into the bucket of water at his feet. "We've got no one else in town who can run this smithy, ma'am. This and the livery keep me going all day."

"What if someone else could run the livery for you? Couldn't you hire an assistant?"

Griffin pulled the horseshoe from the water and squinted at it. "Maybe." Josiah Runnels came to mind immediately. He hated freighting with his father's mule teams. Griffin didn't say so, but he reckoned Josiah would jump at the chance. "Your pa did a good job of keeping the stages running on time."

"Yes, he did. You understand what's needed."

"What would you pay me?"

"You could collect Papa's salary. I would ask nothing of you other than fulfilling the contract in an efficient manner. The job would be yours."

Griffin stood for a long moment, thinking about that. How could he be sure she meant that? Nothing else required. Would she expect him to be grateful?

"I would also give you one of Papa's pocket watches to help you in the job."

He tossed the horseshoe into a bucket of finished shoes and scratched his chin through his beard. He'd never owned a watch but had never viewed it as necessary. "I dunno. It might work."

"You can think about it for a couple of days if you want. I'll continue at Mrs. Adams's lodgings a few more days. And can you see to the stage line until you give me your decision?"

"I s'pose I can. Maybe you could ask Josiah Runnels to sit in the office mornings and sell tickets? That way I can get my smithing and barn chores done."

"That's a good idea. Thank you. I'll ask him right away. Please let me know when you've made your decision."

Griffin stood ruminating after she'd gone. He still didn't want to hitch up with her, but if she was serious. . .

He had an inkling that Cyrus collected a hefty salary for running the branch line. He wouldn't have kept doing it year after year if he hadn't been making money.

Certainly he'd clear enough to hire a stable hand or two. He'd have to oversee the drivers and messengers. Probably would have to ride the line now and then and check out the other stops between Fergus and Boise to make sure things ran smoothly. If it worked out and he could get the contract on his own next year, he might even advertise to sell the smithy. And he'd be shoveling less manure. The more he thought about it, the better it sounded.

But he wouldn't rush over to the Paragon Emporium to tell Isabel. Not yet. He had a stagecoach team to switch out in an hour. And besides, he didn't want her to think he was too eager. She could get all sorts of notions.

★ CHAPTER 41 ★

The Paragon Emporium experienced a lull most afternoons. Patrons did their shopping early and stuck close to home during the heat of the day. Libby had ordered a thermometer from New York, and Josiah had posted it on the back porch, out of the direct sunlight. This afternoon it registered one hundred degrees. She'd sent Florence home at lunchtime and told her to take the rest of the day off. No sense having two of them in the store when only a handful of people would come in.

She'd thought about ordering a dozen of those mercury thermometers to sell in the emporium. But would people like to know how hot it really was, or would that just disturb them more? People like Hiram, who had a scientific turn of mind, would probably appreciate the device. Knowing how hot it was wouldn't keep him from working, but it would give him something to think about.

Bertha Runnels, on the other hand, often complained about the heat. Some days she declared that if it got any hotter she would surely die of heatstroke. So if she had a thermometer and it told her that the heat really had increased, would Bertha be more likely to keel over and die? The sobering thought kept Libby from stocking weather instruments. Maybe she would ask Dr. Kincaid his opinion. After all, he had a medical thermometer. Did he tell people when their fever was high enough to damage their organs? Or would that adversely affect the patient?

As she pondered the question, she sorted the nails that had fallen into the wrong buckets. The hardware section of the store took as much of her time as the yard goods. Isaac used to keep it organized, but now the chore fell to Libby—unless she delegated it to Florence.

After bending over the buckets for five minutes, she stood and stretched her arms and back. Some days she wished she hadn't married a storekeeper. She hardly got outside except for the shooting club. Not that she regretted coming out here in response to Isaac's plea, but it would be heavenly now to be out on the prairie away from town, where the breeze would reach her. If the good Lord ever gave her a chance for a different life, she'd choose to live out away from town. That and children. Of course, a thirty-five-year-old single woman was unlikely to see that opportunity.

The bell on the door jangled. She pasted a smile on her face before turning to greet the person brave enough to come out in this heat.

Hiram nodded soberly and closed the door behind him.

Libby's chest contracted, and she reached out to steady herself against the table of hinges and stovepipe. "Good day, Hiram. How is your garden taking this weather?"

"I'm hauling water."

"Of course." No one in Fergus would see a harvest this year without irrigating their crops. But wells were going dry. Going to the river to fill barrels and hauling them back to the fields took a lot of energy. "May I help you with something?"

He took two steps toward her then stopped. His eyes held hers, and he swallowed hard. "Would you. . ."

Her heart tripped. Instantly, she cautioned herself. *Don't assume anything, Libby. His next words might be, "Would you have any dung forks?"*

For a few breathless seconds, they stood eyeing each other. Libby refused to speak. Though she'd developed a fondness for Hiram, she would not go about completing his sentences for him and explaining his actions to other people, the way his sister did. Let him speak for himself.

"I. . .wondered if you'd. . .like to take dinner. . .with me."

He gritted his teeth and waited. Libby drew in a tight breath. In this moment, she could change their lives. If she declined and sent him away, he would never approach her again. But if she encouraged him—even if they only spent one evening together—her life would be different. Perhaps very different. Rockets of possibilities exploded in her mind. A new love. A new home. Trudy for a sister-in-law. A gentle husband. Children.

"I should be delighted."

He exhaled audibly. "I thought. . .maybe Bitsy and Augie's? Or the boardinghouse if you'd rather. . ."

"I've wanted to dine at the Spur & Saddle, but I hadn't the courage to go alone."

He nodded. "Tonight, then?"

Little pricks in the back of her throat made it hard for Libby to breathe, but she managed. "Yes. Thank you."

"Shall I come by after closing?"

She did some rapid calculations. She usually closed at six. "Would six thirty be too late?"

His rare smile came out like the sun sliding from behind a cloud. "No ma'am. That's perfect." He nodded and went out. The bell jangled as he shut the door.

Libby pulled in a deep breath, straightening her shoulders.

"I'm having dinner with a gentleman this evening." Saying it made her pulse throb even faster. And he was not only a gentleman, but a hero. She'd kept quiet and listened after the shootout at Kenton Smith's ranch, but Hiram had never owned up to shooting the man in the hayloft. If not for his quick action, at least one of their townsfolk might have been killed. The sheriff, perhaps. But Hiram didn't ask that anyone recognize his prowess. In fact, if anyone asked, he'd probably insist his sister was a better shot than he was. But Libby knew better.

She hurried to the apparel section and eyed the merchandise critically. Perhaps Rose was right and Fergus needed a milliner. She scooped up a pair of spotless white gloves with tiny seed pearls stitched in a floral design on the wrists. She would wear her best Sunday hat, though Hiram had seen it many times. At least she would have new gloves.

Hiram whistled as he loaded his tools and paintbrushes into a box. The heat no longer seemed oppressive. Clouds flirted with the sun, bringing welcome shade off and on.

As he headed out of the barn, carrying his toolbox, Griff Bane rounded the back corner of the house.

"Howdy, Griff."

"Hiram. Brought you something to work on. My rifle's jammed. Didn't want to do too much prodding for fear I'd blow my toe off, so I brought it to you."

"Fine. I'll look at it tomorrow if you don't mind. Got a little job to do for Augie and Bitsy this afternoon." Hiram set down the toolbox.

"Oh?" Griff handed him the gun.

"Yup. They want me to repaint the sign at their place."

"Huh. What's wrong with the old one?"

"It says, 'BEER & WHISKEY.'"

"Oh right." Griff shook his head. "Don't seem right with only one saloon in town. Main Street's not balanced anymore."

"Oh, somebody'll open up another watering hole soon. Wait and see." Hiram broke open the gun's breech and peered into the chamber. "Looks jammed, all right." He closed it and set the rifle inside the barn, leaning against the wall. "I'll get to it tomorrow, for sure."

Griffin frowned at him in silent study.

"What?" Hiram asked.

"I dunno. You just. . .you talk more than you used to."

Hiram chuckled and picked up his toolbox. "Listen, I want to ask you something." He walked slowly across the barnyard toward the path, and Griff kept pace with him. "Isabel Fennel came by this morning and offered to sell me her pa's ranch. She even offered to swap houses with me."

"Wow. Good opportunity for you."

"Yeah." Hiram shook his head in doubt. "I told her I don't have the money, and then. . .well, she asked if I'd think about living out at the ranch and acting as foreman. She'd pay me. Trudy says I should do it, but I don't know. . . ."

"Well, I'll help you move if you do it. And I'll help Miss Isabel move her things, too."

"Chances are she'll go live in one of Cy's empty houses here in town, or at the boardinghouse. I got the impression she doesn't like living out at the ranch, at least not now that she's alone."

They'd reached the boardwalk on the street, and Griff stopped. Hiram paused, too.

"She asked me to keep the stage line running. Offered to let me take over her pa's contract with Wells Fargo."

Hiram whistled softly. "You going to do it?"

"Don't know yet. I kind of feel sorry for her."

"Yeah. She seems a lot more mellow since her father died." Hiram smiled up at his friend. "Maybe you ought to think about calling on her."

"Oh no. Not a chance." Griff held up both hands and backed off a step. "You're not going to marry me off, so quit thinking that way. I like my life just fine the way it is."

Hi chuckled. "Aw, Griff, she's a nice young woman. And Trudy says she's coming right along with her shooting lessons. She may not be the prettiest gal in town, but she's not so bad."

Griffin laughed and shook his shaggy head. "Not me, mister. I'll start courting a lady the day you do."

Hiram eyed him soberly. Griffin stopped laughing and peered at him suspiciously. Hiram felt a blush washing up from his neck to his hairline.

Griffin's eyes popped wide. "You wouldn't."

"Yes, I would. As a matter of fact, I'm going calling tonight."

"No."

"Yes."

Griffin stared at him. "Might I ask who?"

Hiram couldn't help it. He must look like a fox that just raided the henhouse, but he couldn't stop grinning. "The prettiest woman in town. She's a good shot, too." He swung his toolbox by the handle and headed up the sidewalk whistling.

From behind him came the stunned words, "I don't believe it. I just don't believe it."

Bitsy came out the front door of the Spur & Saddle and walked over to admire Hiram's work. He had repainted the sign and was adding a gold stripe around the edge of the board.

"Oh, that's fine." Bitsy grinned at him. "Can you hang it back up tonight?"

"The paint's not dry, and one of the screws is stripped. I don't have quite the hardware I need."

"Hmm. The emporium's still open."

Hiram glanced up at the westering sun. "Not much longer, and if I ask Mrs. Adams to stay open to sell me hardware, she and I will both be late to dinner tonight. I'm bringing her here."

Bitsy stared at him for a moment then playfully shoved his shoulder. "Go on."

"It's true."

"Well, I never." She eyed the sign critically. Beneath the shaded Gothic lettering of "SPUR & SADDLE" and Hiram's rendition of a roweled spur, smaller block letters spelled "FINE MEALS SERVED" and "MR. & MRS. A. MOORE, PROPS."

"I like it," Bitsy said. "Looks dignified."

Hiram nodded slowly. "Refined."

"The picture really looks like a spur, and the gold stripe gives it an aristocratic touch." She chuckled. "Who'd have thought it?"

"Bitsy, your place is as proper as a church now."

"Well, thank you. I don't need folks to feel all inhibited, but I want them to know we're decent now."

"How's business?"

Bitsy scrunched up her face. "I'm not sure yet. We don't make nearly so much as we did when we sold liquor. I probably shouldn't have bought so many new dishes. Might have to cut the girls' pay, but I hate to do that."

Charles and Orissa Walker strolled over from their house across the street.

"New sign?" Charles asked as they mounted the steps.

"New paint on the old one," Bitsy said.

Orissa eyed it closely. "Looks fine."

"What's the special tonight?" Charles asked.

"We've got chicken and dumplings or roast beef." Bitsy watched the Walkers enter the building. She looked anxiously at Hiram. "Do you think we ought to put, 'No LIQUOR' on there, too?"

Hiram twitched his lips back and forth, thinking about it. "No, I think it's good."

"Magnolious. I'm going to go get Augie so he can see your handiwork. Of course, he'll say he's too busy and want to wait until the dinner rush is past."

"Say, I'd better get moving." Hiram gathered his tools.

Bitsy headed for the door grinning. "I'll be looking for you a little later."

★ CHAPTER 42 ★

Ethan ambled down the sidewalk toward the Dooleys' house. The sun had sunk behind the mountains, leaving the valley in soft twilight. Across the street, Libby shut the door to the emporium and turned the placard in the window. Ethan strolled around to the kitchen door and mounted the steps. When he knocked, Trudy let him in.

"Am I late?" he asked.

"No. At least no later than anyone else."

To his surprise, the table was set for only three. A vase of fresh wildflowers stood on a doily in the middle.

"Isn't Rose joining us tonight?" He hung his dusty hat on the peg rack.

"Yes—at least I think she is. She went down to the store beside the telegraph office."

"What store?"

Trudy scowled. "The empty one between the telegraph and Bitsy's."

"Why'd she go there?"

"That's the one she wants to lease from Isabel for her millinery shop. Isabel told her she could go in and measure the windows for curtains."

"Rose is really planning to do it?"

"I guess." Trudy set a plate of sliced, cold ham on the table. "I didn't want to heat up the oven today."

"Can't say as I blame you." He eyed the place settings. "Er. . .if Rose is going to be here, am I one too many?"

"What? Oh no." Trudy pushed her hair back. "Hiram's going out."

"Out?" Something wasn't right. Ethan frowned, certain he had missed something.

Trudy smiled and peeked around the parlor doorjamb. She turned back and whispered, "With Libby. He finally asked her. I think he's going to court her."

Ethan's jaw dropped.

She laughed and went to the stove. "Don't look so shocked."

"Sorry. I just didn't. . ."

"Didn't think he'd have the nerve?"

"Something like that."

"Well, he found it someplace. Maybe you inspired him when you asked me to marry you."

Now, that was something worth discussing. Ethan stepped closer and wrapped his arms around her from behind. For a moment, she leaned back against his chest. He bent and kissed her cheek.

"Hey, now." She gently disentangled herself from his embrace. "I do think Rose will be home any minute, and Hi might finish with his preparations and come out here, too."

"What's he doing?"

"Having a bath. Though he came home later than I expected. He'll have to make it a quick one. I had the water ready for half an hour before he showed up. Didn't want to keep the stove going, so it was only lukewarm when he got to it."

Ethan laughed.

"Why is that funny?" Trudy placed her hands on her hips. "Don't you dare make fun of him. You've been known to bathe once in a blue moon yourself."

"I know it." He grinned. "I think it's great."

"Good. He can't pick Libby up until a half hour after she closes the store."

"She getting a bath, too?"

Trudy slugged his shoulder and picked up the bread plate. "Maybe you could run out to the street and see if you can tell whether she's closed shop yet."

"Don't need to. I saw her closing up right before I got here."

"Good. I can tell Hiram when he's dressed."

Ethan followed her to the table. "Hey, listen, I've got some news for you. They caught Wilfred Sterling."

She whirled to face him. "*Who* caught him?"

"The marshal in Boise. They're holding him in a bank robbery. And he did have a wound that hadn't healed. Guess Arthur Tinen was right when he said he thought he'd hit him."

"Well, what do you know?" Trudy said.

Ethan nodded in satisfaction. "I might ride up to Boise when Sterling goes to trial. I wired the marshal some details about Isabel's kidnapping. And I told him to ask Sterling why he was so interested in Milzie Peart's land."

"Did they get anything out of him?"

"Sterling said Kenton put him up to it, thinking he could get Frank's mine and make some featherhead think it was worth something and sell it to him. But when I started all the inquiries, it wasn't worth the trouble, so they gave up on that."

"Hmm. If he's telling the truth."

"Right."

"I suppose it fits with what Isabel told you she heard them talking about."

"Trudy, can you—" Hiram appeared in the parlor doorway, his hair damp and his face pink and clean shaven. "Oh hello, Eth. Trudy, I can't make this tie sit right." He fumbled at the black ribbon below his collar.

"Here, let me." She untied the ribbon and gritted her teeth as she set about tying it correctly. "There. But you can't go yet. You're too early."

"You sure?" Hiram glanced anxiously toward the window. "I don't want to be too early. But I don't want to be late either."

Ethan chuckled. "Maybe you need a watch."

"Can't afford one."

"Well, maybe for Christmas." Ethan closed his mouth, but he couldn't help where his thoughts led. If Hiram succeeded in wooing Libby, he'd probably have a very nice pocket watch by yuletide.

"Ethan says Libby closed up about ten minutes ago," Trudy said. "Relax and give her time to prissy up."

Hiram glared at her and went to the stove. He hefted the coffeepot and reached for a mug.

"So. . ." Ethan watched him. "I thought maybe we could ride out to the Fennel ranch this evening and dig up that tin for Isabel. I asked her if she wanted me to check the place where her pa had buried something, and she said she'd be grateful if she didn't have to do it herself. But I don't suppose you'd want to go now. I mean, you'll probably be tied up till all hours, and—"

"Yes, he'll be busy," Trudy said. "You and I could go, though."

"Yeah, I like that idea." Ethan smiled at her. Trudy and moonlight, always a good combination.

"What are you going to do with the paper that's in there?" Hiram asked.

"Get rid of it," Ethan said.

Hiram nodded. "Probably best."

"And I'll take Isabel the money. I was thinking I could tell her that when I dug up the hole, I found that pouch in the tin. She doesn't need to know it wasn't the only thing in there."

"That's a good idea." Trudy beamed at him. "That way she'll stop fretting. Let's do it tonight."

Hiram sipped his coffee and looked at them over the rim of his cup. "You kids have fun. But just remember, Ethan—you might be getting married in a couple of weeks, but I still expect Trudy home at a decent hour."

Ethan saluted. "Yes sir. We'll be in by curfew."

Hiram grunted and set his mug down. "Guess I'll get going."

"Wait!" Trudy lifted the flowers from the vase and wiped the dripping stems on a linen towel. "Hold on. Let me wrap a handkerchief around these." From her apron pocket, she produced a white square of cotton edged in blue tatting. "There, now." She held the bouquet out to Hiram.

He swallowed hard and stared at them.

"Take it. And don't ask me what you're supposed to do with them." Trudy scowled at him.

At last he raised his hand and took the posy. "Thank you. Shoulda thought of it myself."

"Yes, you should, but I wouldn't say so." She nodded firmly.

Ethan hid a smile by turning to open the back door for him.

"Have a pleasant evening, my friend."

"No doubt." Hiram walked down the steps and around the house.

"I was afraid he wouldn't go through with it," Trudy whispered.

From outside, Rose's high-pitched tones reached them. "Why, Hiram, where *are* you going? And just look as those delectable blossoms!"

Hiram muttered a reply.

Before Rose came into their line of sight, Ethan leaned down and kissed Trudy. "You're a good sister."

She smiled and nodded. "He makes it easy, but yes, I am."

★ CHAPTER 43 ★

Libby turned before the beveled mirror, anxiously regarding as much as she could see of the back of her dress.

"Are you sure I'm all buttoned correctly?"

Isabel smiled at her in the mirror. "You look marvelous."

"Thank you." Libby put a hand to the smooth wing of hair at her temple. "I'm nervous, I guess."

"I could tell."

"Yes, well it's been a long time since I've had a gentleman caller."

Isabel sat down on the cherry-framed settee and picked up the skirt she was sewing. "I hope you and Mr. Dooley have a very pleasant time."

"I hope so, too." Libby glanced in the mirror again then made herself move away from it. "You know, I think it's a good idea for you to rent Rose that little shop near the telegraph office. It will be income for you, and she'll be out of Hiram and Trudy's hair."

"I'm glad you think so." Isabel frowned as she pushed her needle through the fabric. "I don't like to admit it, but sometimes I find it difficult to think charitable thoughts toward Mrs. Caplinger. But she is a sister in Christ, and I'm sure her business will be an asset to the town. I told her she could fix the rooms above the shop and move in if she wants and live there."

Libby tried not to let her face show the full extent of her delight. Seeing Rose move out from under Hiram's roof would be pure pleasure. "That sounds good. She has such a flair for decorating, I'm sure she'll improve the building's value for you."

"Yes, if she doesn't pester me about repairs and such." Isabel waved a hand in dismissal. "What am I saying? I shall have to educate myself on what it means to be a landlady. I have several tenants, after all."

"I'm sure you can hire someone to make repairs to the buildings your father left you."

"True. And I'm thinking of reserving one of the houses on Gold Lane for myself."

"Oh! You'd be right near the Bentons. How delightful."

"Yes. I don't want to live at the ranch anymore. I've made that decision, at least. And I'm trying to negotiate with a gentleman I'm sure would like to have the ranch."

"That's good." A quiet rap sounded on the kitchen door, and Libby caught her breath.

"That must be your gentleman caller." Isabel laid her sewing aside and rose. "Shall I let him in?"

"Oh! Yes, I guess so." Libby tried to breathe evenly as Isabel walked briskly into the next room. She glanced again at the mirror then resolutely turned her back. Too late to change anything now. As Isabel's greeting rang throughout the apartment, she clenched handfuls of her embroidered pink muslin skirt. She'd loved the fabric when it first came in and had hired Annie to stitch her a gown. Then she'd wondered if she'd have a place to wear it. The dress was too fine for workdays in the store. She'd decided to wear it to church on Sunday—and then Hiram had invited her to dinner.

He stood in the doorway, beaming at her and holding the dearest nosegay of bouncing bet and fleabane she'd ever seen. His freshly shaven face fairly glowed, and his hair was neatly parted and combed. Libby's stomach fluttered. She would be proud to be seen on his arm tonight.

"Evening," he said.

She let go of her skirt and crossed the room to meet him, trying to rein in her smile so she wouldn't look foolish. "Good evening."

"You look fine, Elizabeth. Mighty fine."

"Oh thank you." She felt the blood rush to her cheeks. He'd given her Christian name a lyrical lilt, and suddenly she was glad to be wearing pink again and to hear a man say *Elizabeth* in that deep, profound voice.

He thrust out the flowers and opened his mouth then closed it.

"For me? How lovely!" Libby took the bouquet, noting that the stems were folded in one of Trudy's handkerchiefs. The blossoms in varied pinks and mauves complemented her gown. "Thank you so much. I shall wear a sprig if you don't mind." Isabel hovered in the doorway behind him, grinning at her over his shoulder. "Perhaps dear Isabel would put the rest in water."

Libby pulled one of the fuller stems free and took it to the table beneath the mirror, where she found a pin. After fastening it to her bodice, she turned.

Hiram gazed at her, unblinking. His usually mournful eyes seemed younger. Libby even thought she glimpsed a bit of a twinkle there. His mouth curved in a fetching smile that demanded an answer. How long they stood like that, she couldn't tell, but Isabel entered the room with the posies in a small, milk-glass vase.

"These are delightful. I'll set them here on the side table."

"Thank you, Isabel." Libby sucked in a breath and reached for her gloves and handbag. "I'm ready if you are."

In reply, Hiram offered the crook of his arm.

"Good night," Isabel called as they went through the kitchen.

"Good night, dear," Libby said. Somehow they went through two doorways and started down her rear stairway, and she was still holding on to Hiram's arm. She shot a glance at his face. He was only three inches or so taller than she was, but she felt he was just the right size. They stepped across the back porch and down to the ground, then rounded the corner and entered the alley between the emporium and the stagecoach office.

"Griffin seems to be doing a good job keeping the stages running on schedule," she said.

"Yes."

She smiled. One word from Hiram was as good as ten from any other man.

★

After supper Rose retired to work on her plans for the millinery shop, and Trudy quickly did the dishes with Ethan's help. The two of them sauntered out to the barn, and Trudy hummed as she saddled Crinkles. Ethan untied Scout's reins and led his mount away from the fence.

"You all set?"

"Sure am." Trudy swung into the saddle and stroked Crinkles's neck as she looked up at the almost-full moon. "Going to be a pretty ride tonight."

The horses trotted side by side, snorting now and then. When they reached the Fennels' barnyard, a man came from the bunkhouse.

"Evening, Brady," Ethan called.

"Sheriff. Can I help you?"

"Miss Dooley and I have a bit of business for Miss Fennel."

"Anything I can help you with?"

"You could bring me a shovel."

Brady's eyes widened, but he nodded and turned toward the barn.

"They'll want to know what's going on," Trudy said.

"I'll just tell them Isabel knew her daddy had a stash behind the barn, and I'm digging it up to see if he left any cash there for her."

Trudy nodded and smiled as Brady came from the barn hefting the spade.

Fifteen minutes later, they left the ranch and rode back toward town. Ethan carried the tin box in his saddlebag.

"Thought we wouldn't get away without opening it in front of Brady," Trudy said.

"Me, too. He sure was curious."

"Good thinking to tell him he could ask Isabel all about it when he sees her."

Ethan grinned over at her. "She'll tell him she found a pouch of hard money, and that was all."

"Right."

As they passed his own ranch, Ethan said, "I don't s'pose you want to stop in and take a look at your new kitchen?"

"Well. . .it's tempting." *Too tempting,* Trudy thought. If anyone else in town heard she'd gone into Ethan's house alone with him before they were married, the gossip would fly. "We'd probably best go home. Rose will be there even if Hiram's not back yet."

"All right." They rode along in companionable silence to the Dooleys' house. A light shone in the front bedroom window.

"Rose must be upstairs," Trudy said as they rode behind the house to the barnyard. The oppressive heat was gone, but the breeze that flowed down from the mountains was almost too cool.

Ethan halted Scout near the corral fence. "I'll take care of Crinkles. You take the box inside and stoke the fire." He dismounted and opened the saddlebag.

Trudy lit beside him on the ground and exchanged Crinkles's reins for the tin they'd unearthed. He came in five minutes after she did. By then she'd lit the lamp and had the kindling snapping. She added a couple of good-sized sticks to the firebox and smiled at him.

Shadows lay dark under Ethan's eyes. He looked tired, and she knew the outcome of the shootout still bothered him.

"It wasn't your fault," she said.

He didn't ask what she meant. He only set his lips together and shrugged. "Shoulda been some way to get Isabel out without killing anyone."

Trudy put the lid on the stove. "You can't let that nag at you. It's over."

"I know." He exhaled in a puff and shook his head. "And I know that God is in control. He could have stopped it." He still stood by the table, staring off at nothing.

"You sure you're ready to get married? Next Saturday, I mean. It's not too soon?" Trudy's own question appalled her. Why was she giving him the chance to back out?

He focused on her, his dark eyes glittering in the lamplight. "Trudy, it's not too soon. I don't want you thinking that way."

"What way?"

"That I don't want to tie the knot."

"I'm not thinking that."

"Good. Because the closer it gets, the happier I am that we're going through with it. A week from Saturday is *not* too soon."

She shivered as his voice cracked with emotion.

"I love you, Ethan."

He stepped closer and pulled her to him. She wrapped her arms around him and met his kiss eagerly, hoping her lips would transmit her own anticipation and joy.

After a long moment, he pulled away. "Guess we'd better get down to business."

She ducked her head and ran a hand over her hair. Her face must be five shades of red. Why hadn't anyone ever told her how wonderful it was to kiss the man you loved?

Ethan picked up the tin and worked the lid off. The pouch of coins clinked as he set it on the table. Carefully, he took the rolled-up paper out.

Trudy opened the stove lid. "Let's not even look at it again. Those pictures are burned into my brain, and I need to forget about them."

"All right." He brought it over and paused a moment, holding the paper above the open firebox.

"This is the right thing to do," she whispered.

He tossed it into the stove, and the blaze flared up. She closed the lid.

"Trudy, is that you?" Rose came into the parlor doorway. She saw Ethan and pulled her wrapper closer around her. "Oh, excuse me. I didn't know Mr. Chapman was here."

"I'm just leaving, ma'am." Ethan tucked the tin under his arm.

Trudy saw him to the door. "Good night, Ethan."

He winked at her as he clapped his hat on. "I'll see you tomorrow." He nodded vaguely at Rose over Trudy's head and went out.

With the door shut behind him, Trudy turned to face her sister-in-law. "What is it, Rose?"

"I've decided to rent the shop from Miss Fennel, and I wondered. . ." She looked down at the floor for a moment. "It's just filthy. All dust and cobwebs. And. . .well, I wondered if. . .do you know someone I could hire to help me clean it?"

Trudy smiled. That certainly wasn't what Rose had intended to ask, but for whatever reason, she had changed her mind and her approach.

She walked across the room and squeezed Rose's arm gently. "I'd be happy to help you without pay, and I know a few other gals who might pitch in, too."

Rose's eyes flared. "Really? I hated to ask you with the wedding coming up and all. I know you're busy."

"Yes, I am, but I can give you a day's work. Rose, there's something else. Would you consider making me a new bonnet for the day of the wedding?"

"Why. . .I'd love to."

"Nothing too fancy, now."

"Of course not. You're not a modish person. Yet I think we can come up with some fetching design befitting a new bride that will bring out the blue in your eyes."

Trudy nodded. "That'd be nice. Thank you."

They stood for a moment watching each other.

"I don't believe I've thanked you for your hospitality in putting me up this summer."

"You're welcome." Trudy smiled and walked toward the stairs.

★ CHAPTER 44 ★

At the Spur & Saddle, quiet music floated from the piano in the corner. Hiram sat across from Libby at a small table, carefully eating his soup. It wouldn't do to be sloppy this evening or to accidentally make slurping noises.

Sitting opposite Libby was distracting enough, but he knew all the other patrons—not to mention Bitsy, Augie, and the two girls waiting on tables—kept an eye on them. The Walkers lingered over their cake, and Dr. Kincaid ate alone at a small table near the piano. Someone probably watched them every second. It wasn't exactly the quiet, romantic dinner Hiram had imagined.

Vashti set their plates of roast beef, mashed potatoes, gravy, and fresh peas on the linen tablecloth. Oscar and Bertha Runnels came in, greeted the Walkers loudly, and pulled chairs over so they could share their table. Hiram could tell the precise instant Bertha spotted him and Libby. She turned and leaned close to Orissa Walker's ear and whispered something. Orissa cast one of her pinched glances in their direction. Hiram looked away.

They ate in silence for a few minutes.

"This is delicious," Libby said.

"Mm. Do you need anything?" He probably should have thought to ask sooner. He was too used to his sister waiting on him all the time.

"No, I'm fine." A moment later, Libby said, "Trudy stopped at the store today, after she'd been to see Annie Harper about her wedding dress."

"Oh?"

"Yes. I've never seen her so happy. These days she might as well be walking on air. If her feet touch the ground, she's insensible of it."

Hiram smiled and wiped his lips on his napkin. The china and linens looked new and very elegant. Bitsy and Augie must have laid out a lot of cash to refit the restaurant. "I'm glad she and Ethan are getting married."

"So am I, but I'll miss having her right across the street. You'll miss her, too."

"I expect so." Hiram laid his napkin in his lap and leaned forward a little. "Elizabeth?"

Her shapely eyebrows flew up. "Yes?"

"There's something I'd like to discuss with you. Maybe this isn't the time. . . ." He glanced around. Everyone seemed to be eating and enjoying themselves, but even so, two or three people caught his gaze.

"Is it a private matter?"

"Yes."

"Hmm." She looked around. "I would be surprised if folks could hear you over the music."

He gulped in a big breath. "Isabel invited me to be foreman at her daddy's ranch. That is, she suggested swapping houses first, but when I said that wouldn't be fair, she came up with this other plan."

Libby cocked her head toward her right shoulder and studied him. "She's told me she wants to move into town, but I didn't know about this. Is it something you'd like to do?"

He shrugged. "I haven't worked for someone else for a long time. I did want to ranch when I came here, but. . ." So many things to consider. Did he know enough about it to do a good job? Could he boss the men and not look like an idiot? Could he live contentedly on his wages? And could he stand being farther from Libby now that they'd stepped into a different relationship? "There's a lot to think about."

"Indeed." Libby took a bite of roast beef.

Hiram just watched her and waited. Libby did everything delicately, even chewing. He wished he could look at her all the time. Her golden hair shimmered in the lamplight.

After a minute, she took a sip from her water glass. "You'd be closer to Trudy and Ethan out there."

"And farther from Rose." He could feel his ears going red. "I'm sorry. I shouldn't have said that."

"If it's important to you. . ."

"I don't mind her, I guess, but I'd rather not be under the same roof with her."

Libby nodded thoughtfully. "You'd be good at ranching."

"Would I? I don't know. If I'd worked with cattle the last ten years or so, maybe. But I don't want to do it and lose a lot of money for Isabel. And I might go crazy out there by myself."

She didn't answer for a long time. Instead, she cut off another piece of beef and slowly put it into her mouth and chewed it. Hiram took a bite, too, but his appetite had dulled. *I'd be farther from you,* he wanted to say. The bite of potato didn't want to go down, and he reached for his glass.

"If you were lonely, you could do things with the ranch hands," Libby said. "Invite them into the house for coffee and checkers, maybe."

Hiram thought about that. "I don't know."

"You could ask Isabel for some time to think about it."

"Maybe I should."

"Good evening, folks." Dr. Kincaid stood by their table with his hat in his hands.

"Well, hello, Doc." Hiram stood.

Libby favored the doctor with one of her glowing smiles.

"Sorry to interrupt, but I thought I'd inquire about Miss Fennel. Is she still staying with you, ma'am?"

"Yes, she is. She's making plans for a place to live here in town, but I've told her she's welcome to stay with me as long as it's convenient and agreeable to her."

"That's kind of you. Is she feeling well?"

Libby's whole face softened. "She's grieving, of course, but physically, I'd say she's doing well. And her father's estate is a good distraction for her."

Kincaid nodded. "She's an interesting woman. Very well read for a woman in this territory."

"Indeed," Libby said.

Hiram felt a sudden pang of guilt. "I reckon we should have invited her to come and eat with us tonight."

"I'm sure she wasn't offended," Libby said. "However. . ." She looked expectantly from him to the doctor and back. "I do wonder if she'd enjoy having a piece of Augie's chocolate cake with us."

Dr. Kincaid smiled. "Now, that sounds like a good idea. I'd decided to skip dessert tonight, but if Miss Fennel could be persuaded to join us, I might change my mind."

Hiram had been puzzling in his mind ever since he'd noticed Doc eating at the restaurant, and his curiosity got the better of him. "Say, why are you eating here, anyway? I heard Mrs. Thistle is a good cook."

"Oh, she is. But I, uh. . ." Kincaid glanced around and leaned closer. "I did a little professional consultation here yesterday, and Mrs. Moore asked if they could pay me in meals. I didn't want to embarrass her, so I said yes."

Hiram nodded. Doc wouldn't be one to point out that he already paid for three meals a day at the boardinghouse. But if Bitsy and Augie were short on cash, that might mean they were hurting even more than Bitsy had let on this afternoon.

"Well, say," Libby said with a broad smile, "I think it would be delightful to ask Isabel to come and join us. What do you gentlemen think?"

Hiram nodded and looked toward Doc.

"If you agree, I could step over to your lodgings and invite her," Kincaid said.

"Sounds good." Hiram resumed his seat as Doc headed for the door. He looked across at Libby and chuckled. "Well, what do you know about that?"

"It was unexpected," Libby said. "At least on my part."

"Mine, too."

Vashti approached, her satin skirt swishing. "Can I give you folks some coffee?"

"Yes, thank you," Libby said. "And we expect two more people to join us momentarily for dessert."

"Why, ma'am, that's lovely. I'll bring over a couple more chairs." The girl brushed her dark hair back and poured both their cups full.

"The place is busy tonight," Libby said.

"Yes ma'am. This is the way we like it."

Vashti went off with the coffeepot.

"You don't mind that I suggested we invite Isabel and Jim Kincaid, do you?" Libby asked.

"Not a bit."

"I hope Isabel isn't too overcome when he shows up at the door. I don't know if she's ever had a gentleman caller before." Libby's face went pink. "Oh dear. I just thought—what if she decided to retire early? And she might be frightened if someone knocks on the kitchen door."

Hiram tried to imagine the schoolteacher's reaction to the unexpected arrival of a man on the doorstep. "If you think we ought to, we could step over there and..." He let it trail off. Libby was already shaking her head.

"No, Isabel is not overly timid. I know she's been through a lot recently, but I think Dr. Kincaid is intelligent and polite enough to overcome any awkwardness."

Hiram let out a sigh. "That's fine, then. Because if we're going to have company soon, there's something else I'd like to say."

"Oh?" She fixed her vivid blue eyes on him with an air of expectancy.

"Yes. That is...Elizabeth..."

Her lips curved in a gentle smile. "Yes Hiram?"

His heart pounded like the hooves of a running pony. "I wondered if you ever thought about...about a different life."

"What sort of life?"

"Away from the Paragon."

She was silent for a long moment. Goldie ended her song at that instant, and the entire room seemed breathless.

"Yes," Libby said. "I often think of it."

Hiram felt a warm wave of satisfaction wash through him. The music began again, a slower tune. A rogue thought crossed his mind of dancing with Libby to that music. Of course, they didn't have dancing in here, and he wasn't sure his strict New England upbringing would allow him to come here if they did.

She still watched him. "As a matter of fact," she said, "the last time I was in Boise, I received an inquiry about my business."

He had to breathe carefully to keep his chest from hurting. "I've been thinking of life at the ranch," he said, barely above the music.

She nodded.

"But not alone. Isabel's right about that. It's not a life for the solitary."

Her lips parted, and his pulse soared.

At that moment, the door to the Spur & Saddle opened, and Isabel walked in wearing her gray schoolroom dress, her spine as stiff as a ramrod, followed by dapper Dr. Kincaid. She darted nervous glances about the room while he closed the door. When she located Hiram and Libby, her back seemed to unkink and let her stand like a normal woman.

"I believe our guests are here." Hiram stood beside the table and gave Isabel a slight nod.

Isabel noticed and nodded back. She looked behind her for Dr. Kincaid. He caught up to her and touched her elbow lightly, looking toward Hiram.

Just before they reached the table, Libby said softly, "Indeed, that is a topic we should discuss further."

Hiram glanced at her, not wanting to plunge into conversation with Doc and Isabel. But there would be another time. Libby's approving eyes told him that.

"Yes," he said, "and soon."

He found it easy to work up a smile for the new arrivals.

On a fine day at the end of August, Hiram stood outside the haberdashery building with Trudy and Libby. Too bad the new church wasn't ready for the occasion, but his crew had only begun to hoist the rafters for the building on Gold Lane.

From inside the makeshift sanctuary came the strains of the hymn "Savior, Like a Shepherd Lead Us." Goldie had a way with the piano. Oscar Runnels and a crew of volunteers had hauled the instrument over from the Spur & Saddle for the wedding. The effort expended probably wasn't worth it, especially considering the men would just have to move it back again after the celebration. But Bitsy's gesture in lending the piano and pianist showed her love for Trudy, and that's what this day was all about.

Libby, too, hovered over the bride, brushing a bit of dust off Trudy's powder blue dress. "All set?" she asked.

"Yes." Trudy's smile was more eager than anxious, and Hiram's own butterflies settled down a little.

Libby held on to her own bonnet and ducked under the edge of Trudy's astonishingly wide-brimmed hat to kiss her cheek. Wearing the same pretty pink gown she'd worn to her first dinner with Hiram, Libby made a perfect companion for Trudy. The two of them ought to sit for portraits.

"I'll see you inside," Libby said softly.

Trudy squeezed her hand and nodded.

Hiram realized the music had changed to a slow, solemn tune he didn't recognize. Libby smiled at him and headed for the door. It closed behind her, and he exhaled. Wait thirty seconds—those were their orders.

Trudy adjusted her bouquet of wildflowers.

"Trudy?"

"Hmm?"

He sucked in a deep breath. What would Pa say now if he were here, not back in Maine at the boatyard? "I. . .love you."

Her blue gray eyes glittered, mostly blue from the reflection of the dress's fabric, but a watery blue. "Don't make me all weepy now. I love you, too."

He nodded and crooked his arm. She grasped it firmly, and he patted her hand. "Guess it's time."

They walked down the aisle slowly. Goldie laid on the trills and arpeggios. Ethan stood at the front of the room waiting for them with Pastor Benton. On both sides of the aisle, the people of Fergus stood and stared at them, grinning. Some of the ladies already had their handkerchiefs out. Libby had reached her position opposite Ethan and watched them with her chin high and her cheeks flushed. The thought that she was the most beautiful woman in the room caused Hiram a pang of guilt—but Trudy wasn't far behind. His little sister had never looked better.

They stopped before the pulpit. Hiram stood between Ethan and Trudy as Pastor Benton puffed out his chest and began the "Dearly Beloveds." Not looking over at Libby took all Hiram's concentration.

When it came to the question, "Who giveth this woman in matrimony?" Hiram caught his breath. That was his cue. He gazed down at his little sister. Her eyes gleamed. He nodded and spoke up.

"Her parents and I do."

Over Trudy's head, Libby smiled at him. Hiram stepped back, placing Trudy's hand in Ethan's, and stood on the other side of his friend to act as Ethan's best man.

As the pastor recited the vows, Trudy and Ethan responded as they should. Hiram couldn't help imagining another wedding—one that would take place in the new church. And after that, a new life with Libby at the ranch. . .

Suddenly Ethan was kissing Trudy, and everyone clapped.

"Ladies and gentlemen," the pastor intoned, "I now present to you Mr. and Mrs. Ethan Chapman."

Hiram grinned as the couple walked down the aisle. Time for the reception over at Bitsy and Augie's, with the Ladies' Shooting Club serving cake and punch. He moved over and crooked his elbow for Libby. She smiled up at him as she took his arm.

"Well Mr. Dooley," she murmured.

Hiram winked at her with his right eye—the one no one but the pastor could see, if he were looking—and straightened his shoulders. He and Libby strode smartly down the aisle and out the door together. Ethan was kissing Trudy again, right there in the street.

Hiram looked down at Libby. Well, why not, he thought. He bent toward her and kissed her, and a jolt of fire shot through him. But by the time the haberdashery door opened, they stood discreetly next to the bride and groom, ready to accept good wishes with them.

Discussion Questions

1. Given the constraints of their culture, were the women of Fergus right to insist on shooting against the men at the box social? In what other ways do the women show their independence in this story?

2. Was it unwise to allow the single young women to put their lunches in an auction attended by all sorts of men, some of whom were known ruffians? Should the organizers have taken steps to make the picnic safer and more pleasant for the women? Would the women have let them?

3. Hiram Dooley is a quiet man who believes it's better to be silent than to put your foot in your mouth. Are there times when Hiram should have spoken up, but didn't?

4. Gossip plays an important and harmful role in this story. How are Trudy and Isabel hurt by gossip? How can the Ladies' Shooting Club enjoy their fellowship without letting their tongues harm others?

5. Ethan bides his time in courting Trudy—to the point of exasperating Hiram, who is also a slow mover. How does his delay hurt Trudy? Is there a right time to act? What can you do if you feel you've missed the ideal moment to strike in a sensitive situation?

6. Rose feels that Hiram and Trudy have grieved too long. They are uncomfortable when she decides to appropriate Violet's clothing. How have you handled disposing of a dead loved one's belongings? Would you keep quiet, as the Dooleys did, and let Violet's sister have her things?

7. How does Libby's secret grief over her childlessness color her memories of Mary Fennel? Should she have told Isabel what her mother said to her in the past?

8. The five friends, Hiram, Libby, Trudy, Ethan, and Griffin, agree never to reveal Isabel's past to her. Are they right in doing this? If not, at what point should they tell her?

9. Though Hiram and Libby have been acquainted about twelve years, there is much they still don't know about each other. What issues should they discuss before they enter marriage?

10. Ethan berates himself for handling the siege at the Martin Ranch badly. What could he have done differently? If you were sheriff, how would you have approached the situation?

✪ THE BLACKSMITH'S BRAVERY ✪

Dedication

For all the women who dream big—
and for those who wish they dared.

⭐ CHAPTER 1 ⭐

Fergus, Idaho
October 1887

Griffin Bane picked up the big bay's foot. He stretched the gelding's hind leg back and rested the hoof on his leather-aproned knee. Reaching with his long arm, he pulled a rasp from his toolbox. The horse had chipped its hoof so badly that the nails had come loose. As he filed away at the remaining clinches on the nails, a shadow blocked his light.

"Morning, Griff."

"Ethan." Griffin didn't have to look up to recognize the sheriff's voice.

"Scout lost a shoe. I wondered if you could tend to him."

"Did you find the shoe?"

"Yeah, got it right here."

Griffin glanced up at the worn shoe Ethan held. Bent nails dangled from the half-dozen holes on each side.

"Front foot," Griffin noted.

"Yep. There's some bad footing out Silver City way. I rode up there yesterday."

Griffin grunted, placed the rasp in his toolbox, and pulled out the shoe pullers. "Reckon I can do it after this one." As he fitted the pincher ends under the edge of the horseshoe he was removing, he added, "Got to do the coach horses first."

"That's all right. I plan to stay in town this morning."

"Is his foot all right?"

"I think so. He's not limping."

643

Hurried footsteps echoed on the boardwalk that ran up the street from the feed store. They pattered softly on the ground after they reached the spot where the walkway ended. Griffin looked up. The dark-haired girl from the Spur & Saddle—Vashti—scurried toward them.

"Morning, Mr. Bane. Morning, Sheriff." She stopped a couple of yards away.

"Miss Edwards," said Ethan, tipping his hat.

Griffin grunted. Odd green eyes she had, almost like aspen leaves.

"Miss Bitsy wanted me to buy her a ticket to Boise. She's got business there and wants to take the afternoon stage, but you weren't at the office."

Griffin clenched his teeth and twisted the pullers, prying the remaining nails out of the bay's hoof. The shoe came off, and he tossed it on the ground near Vashti's feet. He reached for the hoof nippers and began clipping off the ragged horn around the edge of the hoof. "Tell her I'll be up to the office in a couple of hours. I've got two horses to shoe, but I'll be there in plenty of time before the stage leaves."

"All right." Vashti didn't move.

Griffin clipped all the way around the hoof and exchanged the nippers for a rasp so he could smooth the surface of the hoof wall before he put a new shoe on. "You want something else?" he growled.

"No, sir. I'll tell her." Vashti turned away and hurried back up the street.

"Pretty thing," Ethan said.

"I'm surprised at you, Sheriff, you being married and all."

Ethan grinned. "I said that on your behalf."

"Ha." Griffin finished smoothing the horse's hoof and set it down. He straightened and tossed the rasp into the toolbox, then pressed both hands to the small of his back.

"You getting the rheumatiz, Griff? A young fella like you?"

Griffin grunted. At thirty-five, he didn't think he ought to be having old folks' ailments. "Reckon it's all the hours I spend bent over."

Around the corner of the smithy from the livery stable came

Marty Hoffstead, who had lately been working for Griffin, though he never had much to show for the hours he claimed he put in.

"Kin you come look at the brown wheel horse? I think he's favoring his off forefoot."

Griffin sighed. "I hope you're wrong, because I don't have a replacement for him today for the stagecoach team. I'll come look when I finish this job, but then I've got to reset the shoes on the sheriff's paint."

Marty nodded. "Oh, and Ned came over from the boardinghouse. Says Bill's got the heaves and he's shaking all over. Doesn't know if he can make the run to Boise this afternoon."

"Wonderful." Griffin lifted his eyes skyward and shook his head. "I'll probably end up driving myself. Again." He frowned at Marty. "You tell Bill if he's not dead, he'd better be on the box of that coach at two o'clock."

"I'll tell him, but I wouldn't count on it." Marty walked away.

"Looks like you could use more help around here," Ethan noted.

"You're telling me. Ever since I took over the stage line, I've been running nonstop. Can't get anyone to work the forge, and I can't get enough help running the livery. And keeping good drivers? Let's not even get started on that."

"Maybe you should advertise for help."

"Maybe so." Griffin scooped up the horseshoe he'd just removed from the coach horse and stalked into the smithy.

At half past eleven, Vashti scurried about the dining room of the Spur & Saddle with a wet dishrag, making sure all the tables were clean. Already a few folks had come in for lunch and seated themselves. Bitsy Moore, who owned the establishment with her husband, sauntered over to the table where Mayor Peter Nash and his wife, Ellie, sat.

"Good morning, folks. What'll it be?"

Bitsy could charm anyone with her sunny smile. Though Vashti reckoned Bitsy was twice her own age—approaching fifty—she still showed signs of the pretty woman she'd been. Her reddish hair had faded, but she no longer dyed it. She wore one of the satin gowns she'd purchased back when the Spur & Saddle was a saloon, but she'd recently added a creamy lace insert across the top of the bodice. Bitsy had gone more modest since she got religion, and she insisted the hired help adjust their fashions, too. She kept her bright lip color and rouge and her flamboyant jewelry. Bitsy did enjoy decking herself out.

"What's Augie cooking today?" Ellie asked.

"Thought I smelled fried chicken." Peter smiled hopefully at Bitsy.

"Oh yeah, he's got fried chicken. Venison stew, too. Biscuits and sourdough bread. And we've got us some carrots and Hubbard squash."

"I fancy the squash, myself." Ellie smiled across at her husband. "Of course, Peter never cared for winter squash."

"Bring me the fried chicken. You got potatoes with that?"

"Yes, sir, Mr. Mayor."

"Good. And the carrots."

Vashti scurried behind the serving counter that had been made out of the old bar. She poured two glasses of water. Bitsy paused beside her on her way into the kitchen to give Augie the Nashes' order.

"Before it gets busy, could you run across and see if Griffin's got the ticket office open yet? I don't want to get there at the last minute and not have my ticket."

"Yes'm." Vashti delivered the water glasses with a smile to the Nashes and ducked out the door and across the street.

She hiked up her skirt and ran past the emporium and across the alley to the stagecoach office. The big blacksmith had shed his apron and was tacking a notice to the wall beside the door.

"Mr. Bane, Miss Bitsy sent me for her ticket to Boise." Vashti halted beside him, panting.

He looked up. "Oh sure. Just a second." He hammered a final tack into the poster and went inside. "You got the money?"

"Yes." Vashti stared at the notice he'd posted:

HELP WANTED
STAGECOACH DRIVERS
BLACKSMITH
LIVERY STABLE HANDS
INQUIRE WITHIN

She pulled in a deep breath, squared her shoulders, and stepped inside. Griffin sat at the desk, fumbling at the ticket book with his big hands.

"You said she's going through to Boise?"

"That's right. On business. Taking the two o'clock."

Griffin wrote in the book and tore out the ticket. "Three dollars and six bits."

Vashti handed over the money Bitsy had given her that morning. "I noticed that poster you put up."

"Uh-huh." Griffin gave her the ticket. He put the ticket book in a drawer and, in the process, knocked his pen off the desk. He bent to retrieve it.

"It says you're hiring."

He sat up and squinted at her. "That's right. I need some more manpower."

She ignored the *man* part and plunged on. "Mr. Bane, I'd love the chance to drive. I learned how when I was a kid, and I've always been good with horses. I know I could do the job."

His jaw dropped.

"If you'll give me a chance, I can take the stage through. I know I can, easy as pie."

Griffin stood and stared down at her with such a thunderous expression that Vashti faltered to a stop and waited.

"You want to *drive?*"

"Yes, sir."

"Stagecoaches?"

"Yes, sir."

He threw back his head and laughed.

★ CHAPTER 2 ★

Something must be funny."

Griffin Bane looked past the saloon girl. Ned Harmon, one of his shotgun messengers for the stage line, stood in the doorway to his office.

His office. Griffin still found it hard to believe he had one. But since the former division manager of the Wells Fargo branch line had died, he'd taken over running the coaches, office and all.

"It's downright balderdash, Ned. This here gal thinks she can drive a stage."

Ned's eyes narrowed, and he looked Vashti up and down. The girl had enough decency to blush.

"Mr. Bane, I really can drive." She turned to him, clutching the pasteboard ticket. "I used to drive my daddy's team when I was eight or ten years old. Sometimes I even drove a four-in-hand. I haven't had much chance to work with horses these last ten years or so, but—"

Griffin held up one hand in protest. "Gal, you can't be more than—what?—seventeen? Eighteen?"

Vashti stopped short and eyed him cautiously. A gentleman never asked a woman her age, but Griff had never counted himself a gentleman, and he didn't reckon Ned was one, either.

She clenched her teeth. "I'm twenty-four, and if you two spread that around town, you'll live to regret it, but not much longer."

Ned howled with laughter. "Maybe you'd best hire her, Griff."

The blacksmith shook his head. No way was he going to hire a girl, even if she was older than she looked. He'd be the laughingstock of the Idaho Territory if people saw her driving one of his stagecoaches. Passengers would refuse to ride with her, and the shotgun riders would want to start a flirtation. She was pretty enough, after all. And if they knew she used to work in a saloon...

Nope, he wasn't going to think about that. He put on a firm face and said, "No."

He strode past her and Ned, ducked his head, and escaped out into the sunlight. Behind him, Ned was still laughing. He was halfway to Walker's Feed when he realized light footsteps pattered after him down the boardwalk. He swung around, and the girl almost plowed into him. She stopped so short, her earrings swayed.

"You followin' me?"

"Yes, sir."

Well, she had spunk. "I thought you were still working for Bitsy and Augie."

"I am."

"Then you don't need a job."

"Well, sir, it's like this." She glanced over her shoulder.

Ned had come out of the Wells Fargo office and ambled off across the street toward the boardinghouse. Griffin wondered vaguely what he'd wanted. He'd better not have come to tell him Bill couldn't drive today.

"Bitsy and Augie aren't doing so good," Vashti said. "This is just between you and me. Bitsy would have a conniption if she knew I'd told anyone. But they're not making nearly the profit they were when they sold liquor. Goldie's started clerking at the emporium, and I figured to look around for another job myself. Miss Bitsy says we're welcome to board with them as long as we want to, but it wouldn't hurt to look for another position. She figures she and Augie can support themselves but not much more than that unless we get more people in this town to patronize the restaurant."

Griffin frowned. He didn't like to hear his friends were having trouble. "That right? Augie came by the smithy day before yesterday, and he didn't say anything."

"He wouldn't. They're proud, both of 'em."

"Reckon that's so. But I can't let a girl drive a stagecoach. It wouldn't be fittin'."

She sighed. "Please, Mr. Bane. I really do know how to drive."

"Maybe so, but driving six is a whole lot different from driving two. Or even four. It takes drivers years to master it."

"Then let me start."

He shook his head. "I can't. I might find something else for you, though."

"Well, I can't shoe horses."

"Could you work at the livery?"

She wrinkled her nose. "I suppose I *could*, but. . ."

"What? You're too dainty to shovel manure?"

"I wasn't going to say that. I don't know as I'd want to work with Marty Hoffstead. I heard he goes over to the Nugget every night and puts back a few, and when he's got a brick in his hat, he treats those girls over there shamefully."

"That right?"

"Yes, sir, and I wouldn't make up stuff like that."

"I don't imagine you would." Griffin had heard Marty tell some coarse stories, and he'd seen him stagger out of the Nugget on a few occasions, but lately he couldn't be fussy about whom he hired. He scratched his chin through his beard. It was getting long—he ought to trim it, or soon it would be catching sparks from the forge. As if he had time. He didn't even get a minute to work with the colt he'd hoped to start training this fall. "Well, it'd help me some if you could sit in the office for a couple of hours every morning, say ten to noon, when folks want to buy tickets. I'd give you two bits for every ticket you sold."

"Well. . .I usually help Bitsy set up for lunch, but if she can spare me—how many tickets do you think I'd sell?"

"Maybe none. Maybe two or three."

"Hmm."

He could see she didn't think much of the idea. "You think about it. I've got to make sure the team's ready for the afternoon stage. If you want to try it, come see me later."

Without waiting for a response, he turned and walked swiftly toward the livery. All he needed was a pretty girl flitting about, getting in the way. The thought of that little bit of a thing handling a stagecoach made him laugh again. As if she could hold down six horses.

Of course, she was part of that shooting club Trudy Dooley—that is, Trudy Chapman now, since she married the sheriff—had started for the ladies. Unless he misremembered, Vashti had placed pretty well in the shooting match at the last town picnic. If someone could take Ned Harmon's place riding shotgun, then Ned could drive—he wasn't half bad in a pinch, though he needed more finesse to become a really good driver. Why, then Griffin might get by with the drivers he had. Provided Bill recovered from whatever ailed him.

He shook his head. What was he thinking? A girl for a shotgun messenger. He must be mad-brained. He stomped into the stable. Marty was just bringing in the two wheelers. They'd never have the team ready in time. Griffin dashed out back to get the swing horses from the corral.

Loco. That's what he was to even think of hiring a woman for this business. Crackbrained.

The next day, Vashti served lunch to three patrons. Bitsy wouldn't be back until the following afternoon, but there was barely enough work to keep Vashti busy, even though Augie had cooked a scrumptious roast beef dinner. The restaurant business was mighty slow now that the days were getting shorter. People were trying to get things ready for the coming winter and not thinking about eating in town.

When Oscar Runnels, Doc Kincaid, and Parnell Oxley had finished their meals and sauntered out of the Spur & Saddle, Vashti whisked their dishes into the kitchen and had them washed, dried, and put away before Augie had covered the stew pot and put the leftover lemon meringue in the pie safe. Augie walked over to the corner shelf where he and Bitsy kept the cash box. He opened the cover and stared down into it.

"Things are getting tight, aren't they?" Vashti asked.

"A mite." Augie slapped the lid shut. "We've been through hard times before."

"Still, you have to buy enough food for twenty, in case they come, and if nobody shows up, it goes to waste."

"Mrs. Thistle wants four pies for the boardinghouse." Augie pulled his sifter out of the flour barrel. "Guess I'll get started."

The boardinghouse down the street, owned by schoolmarm Isabel Fennel, was feeding more people than the Spur & Saddle. Terrence and Rilla Thistle, who ran the place, could count on their boarders. The stagecoach drivers and messengers usually slept and ate at the Fennel House, and sometimes passengers from the stagecoaches did, too. A few would wander out in the evening for dinner at the Spur & Saddle, but most of the Moores' customers were townsfolk who wanted a change of pace. Some of them probably came to help Augie and Bitsy. The Sunday chicken dinner was still the big event of the week at the Spur & Saddle, but that didn't generate enough to support the Moores and their two hired girls.

"I'm going out for a minute." Vashti took off her apron and hung it up. "Do you need anything?"

"No, I don't think so."

Augie sounded so glum that Vashti reached the decision she'd been chewing on for twenty-four hours. She'd take Griff Bane up on his offer and sit in his office two hours a day. If she sold eight tickets a week, she could give Bitsy two dollars for her board. And she could still help out at the supper hour, when the Spur & Saddle generally got more traffic than at noon. That would square what she should be paying for her room. Right now, she was living for free with the Moores, but her friend Goldie had started paying them every week for room and board when she began working at the Paragon Emporium. Vashti hoped in time she could do the same.

She went up to her room and put on a hat and shawl. She didn't want Griffin to think she wasn't proper enough to deal with his customers. Since she'd trusted in Christ, she'd stopped serving drinks to cowboys and poker players. Bitsy's decision last summer to turn her saloon into a family restaurant had made that part easy. Vashti felt cleaner now—almost decent again. But she knew some folks still pegged her as a barmaid. As a last thought, she wiped off most of the lip rouge she'd put on that morning.

She hurried down the stairs and across the empty dining room. Outside, the sun felt good on her shoulders, and the shawl was almost too much. She slowed down and took ladylike steps as she crossed the street and headed for the Wells Fargo. Reaching the office, she stopped and pulled in a deep breath. The door was closed. She knocked and then tried the latch. Locked. That figured. Griffin was probably down at the livery stable or the smithy. She'd go find him.

She held the ends of her shawl close as she turned. The poster on the wall caught her eye again, and she gasped. That man. That exasperating lunk of a man!

After HELP WANTED, Griffin had scrawled, MEN ONLY NEED APPLY.

She turned on her heel and marched up the street toward the smithy. No smoke came from the chimney, and she didn't hear the clang of Bane's hammer. He mustn't be working at the forge. A quick glance inside confirmed her conclusion. She strode around the corner toward the livery stable.

Marty Hoffstead was bringing in two big geldings from the back paddock. He walked between them, holding one halter with each hand.

"Whoa now." He stopped them in the middle of the barn floor. He let go of one, and the horse immediately put its head down, snuffling the floor. It walked along, picking up stray wisps of hay with its lips.

"Whoa, you!" Marty spotted Vashti standing in the door and waved his arm. "Can you get that nag and hook him up? There's a rope tied to the ring over there." He nodded toward the side wall.

Vashti stepped smoothly into the dim barn, without any sudden moves, and stooped to catch a leather strap that ran along the horse's cheek. "Come on, big fella." The gelding raised his head. She pushed gently on his nose. He backed up, and she was able to lean over and snatch the end of the dangling rope. How Marty had expected to get it and hitch the two big horses without help, she didn't know.

"Thanks," he said. "This is a two-person job, for sure." He hooked the other horse to a rope on the other side of the barn floor.

"Where's Mr. Bane?" Vashti asked.

"Gone to Silver City on the morning stage."

She arched her eyebrows. "Oh?"

"Yup. Ned Harmon caught whatever Bill Stout had yesterday and was too sick to go, so Griff had to ride shotgun for Bill this morning."

"Why didn't he send you?"

"Me? I'm not a good enough shot to hold off road agents. But I don't know as I can hitch up the six for the Boise coach alone." Marty eyed her speculatively. "Guess you're too scrawny. Would you step across to the Nugget and see if anyone over there can help me?"

Vashti scowled. She didn't especially want to get her good clothes smelling like a stable. On the other hand, she resented the implication that she couldn't hitch a horse or two. And while she disliked Marty and didn't trust him farther than she could throw an anvil, a little voice inside her egged her to show him just what *he* knew.

"I can do it. You want me to harness these two, or to bring in the next two?"

Marty's eyes narrowed. "Well, missy, the harness for the two wheelers is hanging yonder." He nodded toward the barn wall. "Iffen you want to try to sort that out, I'll go bring in the swing team."

By the time he'd brought in the next pair, Vashti had the first harness over the near wheeler's back and was buckling the belly band. Marty somehow managed to get the two new horses into place and came to survey her work. He grunted and went out the back again.

She had two horses done before he had the team all lined up. Marty grabbed the next harness off the wall and went to work. They labored without speaking. Occasionally Marty said, "Get over, you," to a horse or swore quietly. Vashti scratched each horse's forelock as she slipped on their bridles. They were good horses. Cyrus Fennel had always bought good stock for the line, and Griffin seemed to be keeping up the standard. Vashti loved to watch the coaches come thundering into town. The drivers always had them run up the main street while they cracked their whips, just for looks.

The lead horses didn't have breech straps, and the harnesses went on quickly. Marty was still messing with a buckle on his side. Vashti took an extra moment to caress the two leaders' silky noses.

"Guess you're all set," she said.

Marty came around and cast a critical eye over the work she had done. "It appears I am." He nodded at her grudgingly. "Thank you, missy."

"You're welcome. Do you expect Mr. Bane back today?"

"Nope. Not until the stage comes in tomorrow. I've got to get up to the office and see if anyone wants tickets for the two o'clock. When the next coach comes in, someone has to be there to meet the passengers. Then the driver will bring the coach around here to switch the teams, so I'll have to run back over here. . . ." He pushed his hat back and sighed. "Best get going."

"I can tend the office," Vashti said.

Marty's brow furrowed.

"I can," she said. "Mr. Bane offered me a position to sell tickets for him. That's why I came here this afternoon. Wanted to tell him I'd do it. So if you want, I can start now. Give me the key, and I'll open the office and meet the incoming coach."

"You know how to make out the tickets?"

"Well. . ." She gritted her teeth. "Not especially, but it can't be too hard."

Marty shook his head. "Griff's got a table telling the prices for all the stops. It changes every now and again, and Wells Fargo sends him a new one. You have to look up the destination and put the price on the ticket."

"I can do that."

"You sure?"

"Sure as sunup."

Still he hesitated. "I'd best go over there with you. Griff didn't say nothing to me about a gal getting to have the key to the office. I'll unlock for you. Most likely there won't be any tickets sold, anyhow. We hardly get any passengers going out on Thursday."

At a quarter past ten the next morning, the stagecoach rattled up Fergus's main street. Driver Bill Stout flourished his cowhide whip, and the horses obliged by stepping along smartly. On the box next to Bill, Griffin dug in his pocket for the watch that had once been Cyrus Fennel's.

Griff squinted down at the hands. It always took him a minute to work it out. He'd learned to tell time as a kid but hadn't practiced in more than twenty years. After Cyrus died, his daughter gave Griff the watch when he took over her father's Wells Fargo contract.

The coach was late. He'd known that since before they pulled out of the stop at Dewey. Bill was a good driver, but last night's rain had left the roads a little sloppy, so the delay had increased.

If he was figuring the time right, they were twenty minutes late. Griff sighed and closed the watchcase. Could be worse. Of course, if Cy Fennel were alive, he'd threaten to fire Bill for being late.

They pulled up hard in front of the office. Griff climbed down carefully to open the door for the three passengers—a rancher's wife returning home and two miners coming into town to dispose of their meager findings. Ned Harmon would have jumped down from the box like a monkey, but Griff was too big and too old—yes, he was feeling his age after hours of jolting along on the hard box—to do that.

When he reached the ground and turned around, a vision in blue satin skirts stood on the boardwalk. Vashti Edwards again, complete with a ridiculous feathered bonnet that must have come from that Caplinger woman's millinery shop. She may have quit wearing knee-high skirts and plunging bodices, but she hadn't parked her vanity at the church door when she found her faith, had she?

"Morning, Mr. Bane," she said. "I hope you had a nice trip down from Silver City."

He grunted and turned to open the door. Mrs. Tinen grabbed his hand, gingerly climbed down, and stepped toward the rear of the coach to claim her bags. That was the messenger's job, too. Griff waited while the two miners eased down to earth; then he shut the door and shuffled around to the back. Bill had climbed over the top of the coach and opened the boot. He didn't have to, but maybe he did it because the boss had been riding with him.

Griffin went over and caught the bags as Bill tossed them down. He set them on the edge of the boardwalk. "There you go, ma'am.

Thanks for riding with us." As if she had another choice in these mountains.

Bill scrambled back across the roof to the driver's box.

"Tell Marty I'll be over in a few minutes," Griffin called.

Bill raised his whip in salute and flicked the reins. The horses started off at a jog, knowing they were nearly home. The two miners hoofed it for the Nugget. Arthur Tinen Sr. had driven his wagon into town to meet his wife. Griffin waved to him and lifted one weary leg, setting his right boot squarely on the boardwalk.

"Bye, Mrs. Tinen." Vashti still stood on the boardwalk, waving at Jessie and Arthur and looking as pretty as a circus horse in her fancy trappings. Griffin looked her up and down.

"You want another ticket today?"

"No, sir. I came to tell you we sold two tickets while you were gone. One on yesterday's Boise coach, and the other to go to Lamar today. The money's in the tobacco tin in your desk drawer."

Griff closed one eye and considered her again. "We?"

"We, the Wells Fargo line, Fergus branch."

"Ah." He looked past her and noted for the first time that the office door was open. "Where's Marty?"

Her smile slipped for the first time. "Over to the livery, waiting to help Bill swap out the horses. I opened the office yesterday morning, like you said I might, and again today. Well, Marty unlocked for me, but I wrote the tickets and greeted the one passenger who came in yesterday afternoon and directed him to the boardinghouse. I think it's important that passengers see a friendly face when they disembark in a strange town, don't you?"

Griffin grunted.

Orissa Walker and her married daughter came out of the emporium and walked toward them. Orissa always reminded Griff of a fussy crow. The skinny, white-haired woman moved down the walk in a pause-jerk rhythm. Her arthritis must be getting worse.

"Hello, Vashti. Morning, Mr. Bane."

"Miz Walker. Ma'am." Griff touched his hat brim, groping in his mind for the daughter's married name and coming up short.

"Good day," said the daughter. Her brown dress was brightened by red trim, unlike her mother's totally drab gray fashion. "I'd like to purchase my return ticket to Portland."

"Oh, you're leaving us," Vashti said with a regretful smile. "I hope you've enjoyed your stay with your folks, Miz Hodges."

Hodges. That was it.

"Yes, thank you," the woman said with a smile. "I've had a delightful stay, but my husband wrote and told me he's lonesome, so I guess I'd better head on home tomorrow."

Orissa cackled. "I guess it didn't hurt Clay any to cook for himself this month."

"Well, step right into our office." Vashti smiled broadly and shot Griff a quick glance. "I can write up your ticket now, and you'll be all set to board the coach tomorrow."

"Why, thank you." Mrs. Hodges and her mother followed Vashti to the door.

Griffin opened his mouth and closed it again. Orissa was saying, "Vashti, I'd no idea you'd begun working on this side of the street."

Vashti's musical chuckle floated out from his office. "Yes, ma'am, Mr. Bane offered me the position a couple of days ago to free him up so's he can tend to his smithing and livery duties better. Now, let me see, you're traveling all the way through to Portland. . . ."

Griff worked his jaw back and forth a few times. He was bone tired. Seemed like he ought to tell Vashti she presumed a hair too much. On the other hand, she appeared to be handling the job well. And dealing with ladies wasn't his strong suit. He stepped a little closer to the doorway and leaned against the wall. Vashti named the price of the ticket, and he thought it sounded right. She acted as though she'd been doing this job for years. He didn't like to remember how befuddled he'd felt the first few times he'd tried to figure out the rate table. Maybe he should leave well enough alone and let her carry on. At a quarter per ticket sold, it would be a cheap way to cut down on his headaches.

"Griffin!"

He whirled around.

Maitland Dostie waved a piece of paper as he hurried across the street. "Telegram just came in for you."

Griffin stepped uncertainly to the edge of the boardwalk. He wasn't the type of person to get telegrams. That was for the sheriff or maybe the preacher or Doc Kincaid. Who would spend fifty cents a word to send a telegram to a blacksmith?

"You sure?"

"Of course I'm sure." Maitland stopped and held out the paper. "Sorry to be bringing you bad news."

"Bad news?" Griffin searched the telegrapher's face. "How bad?"

"Well, you know I have to read these things when I take them down. That is, I can't take them down without seeing what they say. And I'm sorry, Griffin."

"Wha—" Griffin quit staring and opened the folded sheet of paper. The top was a mess of letters and numbers and his name, followed by FERGUS, IDAHO, and the word CINCINNATI. Below that, set off in stark importance, were the words JACOB DIED. He stared at it for a long moment.

"Some of your kin?" Maitland frowned as if trying to look suitably sad.

Griff nodded. The only Jacob he knew in Cincinnati was his sister's husband, Jacob Frye. "My brother-in-law."

"Oh. I'm sorry." Maitland looked down at his dusty shoes. "Would you. . .er. . .like to send a reply?"

"Yeah." Griffin cleared his throat, thinking what to say to Evelyn. "You need me to come over to your office?"

"If you want to write it out, I'll take it from you here."

Orissa and her daughter and Vashti came out of the Wells Fargo office, still chattering about Mrs. Hodges's forthcoming journey.

"I'll step over with you," Griff said. He followed Maitland across the street, mulling how to word his message frugally and still offer a brother's proper support and sympathy. Evelyn was five years his elder. She'd married Jacob Frye nearly twenty years ago, and they had five children. Jacob had never earned much as a schoolmaster. How would Evelyn support those kids now? He seemed to recall that the eldest girl, Rachel, was pledged to be married soon.

He stood holding the pencil for a long time and staring down at the blank telegram form. At last he scrawled, "Very sorry. Anyway

I can help?" He hoped Maitland would let him get away with making *any* and *way* one word, though he supposed it wasn't correct usage. He scowled down at it. The deceased was a teacher, after all. His sister would likely tell her friends she'd gotten a telegram from her brother out West, and he'd used poor grammar. He erased the second sentence and replaced it with "Need anything?" There. He'd saved two words. And Evelyn couldn't complain if he only spent two dollars—she'd cut her message to the bare minimum for a dollar.

He shoved the form across the counter. "Guess that'll do. I'll write her a letter this evening."

"That'll be two dollars. I'll send this right out." Maitland set the message beside the telegraph key and reached out to take the money.

When Griffin stepped outside again, the stage was coming down the street from the livery. Apparently Marty had managed without him. The drivers and messengers weren't supposed to have to change the teams, but sometimes they had to do it, or it wouldn't get done. Griff glanced up at the sun. He was glad they hadn't waited for him, as his sister's telegram had driven all thoughts of the stage from his mind.

Across the street, Vashti stood on the boardwalk near a drummer who'd come into town yesterday. Griff decided to let her see the passenger off and go get something to eat. He'd give Augie and Bitsy a little business. And he'd worry about what to do with his new employee later.

★ CHAPTER 3 ★

A week later, Vashti met the stage from Silver City. No one got out, as Johnny Conway had made the run with an empty coach. He pulled up in front of the Wells Fargo office and touched his whip to his hat brim. He was a young man, a cowpoke turned stage driver, who thought he knew more about driving and horses than any man on earth, and more about women, too.

"No pigeons today, Miss Vashti. We'll get the box inside."

The shotgun messenger, Cecil Watson, bent to slide the treasure box out from under the seat.

"You'd best wait until Mr. Bane can come open the safe," Vashti said.

"Naw, he gets mad if we take the strongbox over to the livery. Cecil will have to stay here and guard it until Griff comes."

Vashti blew out a breath. "All right." She hurried inside and took her handbag from the hook behind the door. From its depths, she produced the pearl-handled pistol she'd bought the year before when she'd joined the Ladies' Shooting Club of Fergus.

"What's that peashooter for?" Cecil gasped out the words between breaths as he lugged the heavy wooden box to the desk.

"Thought I could help protect the box."

Cecil laughed. "Aw, go on, missy. Nothing so funny as a woman all dolled up and flashing a gun around."

Vashti scowled at him. "Oh yeah. Very funny." She turned on her high heels and strode out onto the boardwalk. Johnny was about to drive off to the livery. "Hey, Conway! Wait a second."

He froze with his whip poised. "What d'ya want?"

"I want to drive." She shoved the pistol back into her bag and grabbed the handhold on the side of the coach.

"You crazy?" Johnny asked.

"No. It's only up the street to the livery."

"No."

"Pretty please?" She hoisted herself up and plopped into the seat beside him.

Johnny's eyes narrowed. "I ain't never let no one else take the reins when I was on duty. Griff Bane would fire me."

"I'll give you two bits."

He hesitated, and she was pretty sure she had him.

"Two bits and a kiss." His blue eyes glittered.

"Four bits and you keep your lips to home."

He laughed and handed over the reins. As Vashti took them, her blood rushed eagerly through her veins. At last! She tucked one rein under each pinkie and held the other two on each side together.

"No, no. You've got to thread them through your fingers right." Johnny reached over and pried open her left hand.

"Sorry. I used to drive four."

"Six is different. A lot different. You've got to keep some tension on all of them all the time. Be ready to climb those ribbons if you have to." He fussed at the leathers until she could feel they were in place.

"Am I ready? It feels like I am."

"Hold on—"

She was afraid he would change his mind and take the reins back, but he only leaned over and took the brake off. She moved her hands forward a little to put the tiniest slack in the lines and chirruped to the horses. They took off at a trot, and Johnny grabbed the edge of the seat.

"Hey! I said wait."

"Well, we're moving now."

"Yeah. Don't let 'em put on too much speed or they'll try to take you right into the barn, coach and all. Unless you want to lose your head, that's a bad idea."

They clipped along so fast they were already passing the feed store. The leaders bent around the corner by the smithy and pounded toward home.

"Slow 'em down," Johnny yelled.

Vashti pulled back on the lines, but it seemed to have no effect.

"Lay right down on 'em!"

She put all her weight into her pull, rising up on her heels.

"Tighten the near leader's rein."

There wasn't time for her to figure out which ribbon led to the near lead horse's mouth as and they came abreast of the livery. Johnny reached over and added the strength of his muscular forearm to her tugging and gave a loud, firm "Whoa!"

The six horses stopped so fast the wheelers nearly piled up on the swing horses' tails.

"Quick," Johnny said. "Gimme the lines. Bane's coming."

As she untangled the reins from her hands, Vashti saw two men coming from the interior of the big barn.

"I'll come by for the four bits later," Johnny hissed. "Don't talk about it."

"What's going on here?" Griffin's bushy dark eyebrows met in a frown over the bridge of his nose.

Vashti felt her face flush. "Hello, Mr. Bane."

"I said, what's going on?" Griffin glared at Johnny, who refused to meet his gaze. "Conway, did you let this woman drive my stagecoach?"

Johnny's Adam's apple bobbed up and down. "Well, uh. . ."

"I've got a mind to fire you, except we're so shorthanded I can't. Get down off the box, and get out of my sight."

Johnny dropped down over the side of the coach, thrust the lines into Griffin's hands, and disappeared. Vashti craned her neck to see where he went. It appeared he was headed over to the Fennel House for some lunch—that is, if he didn't detour into the Nugget first.

"Miss Edwards."

She turned back and found Griffin had climbed up on the step and was eye-to-eye with her.

"Yes, sir?"

"What do you think you're up to?"

"Please, Mr. Bane, I told you I can drive. Let me learn to handle the six. I know I'd be the best driver you ever had." She stared into his smoldering dark eyes. For a long moment, neither of them said a word.

At last, Griffin's beard twitched, and he opened his mouth. "No." He stepped down and backed up two steps, then turned around. "Come on, Marty. Let's get the teams switched. Move!"

Vashti sighed. For a moment, she'd thought he was wavering. She gathered her skirts and climbed down on the side away from the barn door. No sense trying to get him to change his mind today. She'd walked a few yards before she remembered the treasure box. Reluctantly she turned back.

"Oh, Mr. Bane?"

He paused in unhitching the off wheeler from the whiffletree. Though he said nothing, his dark eyebrows rose in question.

"Mr. Watson's up to the office guarding the treasure box because the safe wasn't open."

Griffin frowned.

"If you don't want to give me the combination, you could go over there, and I'll help Marty switch the teams."

Griffin laughed. "First you think you can drive, and then you think you can wrangle these critters."

"Don't laugh, Griff," Marty said from the other side of the hitch. "She helped me while you were gone. She knows how to harness a team better'n Ned or Bill does."

"I doubt that." Griffin pulled out his pocket watch and scowled at it. "Time I get up there and back, we could have these horses changed." He looked at Vashti. "Just tell Cecil to stay there until I come."

"Yes, sir."

Vashti walked swiftly back to the office. When she walked in, Cecil jumped up off the edge of the desk with his shotgun in his hands. "Where's Griff? I'm hungry, and the next stage will be ready before I get anything to eat."

"He's working with Marty. Shorthanded, as usual." Vashti looked around. "Any customers wanting tickets?"

"Nope."

"All right. You stay here, and I'll run over to the Spur & Saddle and get you something."

"Mrs. Thistle feeds us."

"All right, I'll go to the boardinghouse. Maybe she'll let me bring you a plate."

Cecil nodded. "That'd be good. I don't want to head out on the next leg with an empty belly."

Vashti hung her handbag behind the door and plodded over to the Fennel House. She was no closer to becoming a driver—in fact, she may have lost ground where Griffin was concerned. Johnny would regret putting the reins in her hands, and while Marty had unexpectedly come to her defense, Griffin hadn't listened to a word he'd said. It was just as well. She didn't really want to get her dress all dirty.

By the time she got back to the Wells Fargo stop with Cecil's plate, the coach was coming around the corner by the smithy. Cecil gulped a few bites and left his dinner half eaten on Griffin's desk without so much as a thank-you. Johnny came back from his own dinner and wouldn't let Vashti catch his eye. It made her boil, but she knew he was trying to get out from under Griffin's ire. He and Cecil loaded the strongbox and climbed into their seats on the front. As the coach rumbled away, she let her shoulders droop. No tickets sold today. She'd put in more than two hours for nothing. Nothing but the feel of the lines in her hands for less than two minutes.

A heavy step made the boardwalk vibrate. She turned. Griffin stood two paces away.

"Don't you be thinking you can drive the stage again."

She gulped and looked away. "No, sir."

"Good. Because if you try, I'll fire the driver who lets you. And it'll be your fault."

Griffin dashed about his one-room home, the other half of the smithy building. He always intended to get to church in plenty of time, but sometimes he lost track. Even though he had a watch, he couldn't get used to being at the new sanctuary on the hour. For that matter, he still had trouble making sure the stagecoaches left at precisely the right time.

He wet his comb and slicked down his unruly hair. He'd have to cut it again soon. Someone had mentioned that Augie Moore would cut hair for a dime. Maybe he should get the brawny restaurateur to do it. Augie was a good friend, and he was having a hard time financially, so it would be a good arrangement all around.

By the time he got his hair to lie flat, it was soaked, with drips drenching the collar of his one good shirt. Griffin sighed and tried to pull the comb through his beard. The tangles put the brakes on that plan. He threw the comb down. No time to put on a tie. He grabbed his hat and ran out the door. Why had they built the church two blocks over, anyhow? When the congregation met in the old haberdashery on Main Street, he usually made it on time.

The bell rang out over the town as he hit the boardwalk beside the Fennel House, and he lengthened his steps. Nice thing, that bell. The ladies had campaigned for it and raised money all last winter with bake sales and a quilt raffle. The preacher took three special offerings, and the bell had arrived on one of Oscar Runnels's freight wagons a month ago. The sound of it made him feel as though he lived in a civilized town.

A few stragglers climbed the church steps as he approached. That made him feel a little better. Of course, he'd never make it to Sunday school, though the preacher encouraged everyone to come out for that an hour earlier than the worship service. Griffin puffed up the steps behind the Nash family. Peter saw him coming and held the door open.

"Thanks," Griff said.

"Morning, Griff. There's a letter for you over to the post office. Stop by my house tomorrow, why don't you?"

Griffin reared back and stared at him. "All right." Probably from his sister. It had been two or three weeks since he'd received the disturbing telegram. That must be it. She'd most likely written him the details of Jacob's demise.

He looked over the nearly filled sanctuary before sliding toward his usual pew—second from the back, on the left. In the row ahead of him, the sheriff sat on the aisle, beside his wife. Those two made quite a pair, Griff had to admit. He'd never expected Ethan to get married, but it seemed fitting that the best shot in town had won his heart. Trudy Chapman's brother, Hiram, the gunsmith, sat in the middle of the row, beside Libby Adams, the emporium's owner. No doubt they'd tie the knot soon. Romance seemed to have discovered Fergus. Griff shook his head. More and more so-called confirmed bachelors fell to the call of Cupid.

The two girls who worked at the Nugget Saloon slipped in and found seats in the back row. They wore their low-cut satins to church but covered up with their shawls. Seemed nearly everyone in town came to church these days. Griffin supposed that was a good thing.

The folks from the Spur & Saddle had claimed a pew just ahead of the sheriff and his party. That was a case where the last folks you ever expected to see in church had turned to Christ and flipped their lives head over heels. Vashti Edwards and Goldie Keller sat with Bitsy and Augie, and you'd have never thought to look at them that they'd ever been anything but respectable. Bitsy and the girls still had a heavy hand with the rouge and lip color, and they were too frugal to throw out their fancy dresses, but they'd altered them a bit. No one would think they'd been saloon girls for years.

That set Griffin's mind off on a rabbit trail. A passenger who occasionally rode the line on business had come in from Boise Friday. He'd complimented Griffin on the polite and beautiful young woman who now ran his ticket office. Griffin hadn't let on about Vashti's past. If anyone didn't know, they'd assume she'd always been decent. She didn't have a hoity-toity Eastern accent like Rose Caplinger, the milliner, but neither did she speak coarsely like the guttersnipes at the Nugget. And Goldie—why, that blond girl at the Spur & Saddle could play the piano like a professional. Last Christmas, she'd played a concert of carols at the church, and the whole town had lauded her. The reverend's wife was getting up a new collection to buy a piano for the church so they could have Goldie play the hymns every Sunday.

The Reverend Phineas Benton rose to open the service, and Griffin focused his attention on the front of the large room. The first hymn, "Amazing Grace," helped. Griffin tended to let his mind wander when he was sitting still, listing all the things he needed to do when church was over.

Of course, he never worked at the forge on Sundays. Not since the preacher came. People would hear his hammer and know he worked on the Sabbath. But if he didn't putter around the livery on Sunday afternoon, some things would never get done. The horses needed to be fed, watered, and groomed. And Wells Fargo and Company had never heard of the no-Sunday-labor rule. The stagecoach schedules must be kept no matter what day of the week.

Everyone around him sat down, and he realized the singing was over. He sat down on his pew.

Preacher Benton gazed out over the congregation. "My fellow believers, this morning we'll look at Paul's second letter to the Corinthians and contemplate the virtue of benevolence. Gracious giving where it is perhaps not merited. Of course, if someone we love is in need, we do all we can to help them out. But what of the stranger or, even more, the person we know slightly and do not like? Can you be gracious when you don't feel like it? My friends, if you see someone unsavory in need, can you meet that need without resentment and bitterness? Ask yourself what Christ would do in this situation. Unto the least of these. . ."

Griffin tipped back his head and gazed up into the rafters. He dealt with unsavory men all the time. And the good Lord knew he'd been gracious to one of his drivers. He ought to have fired Jules Harding the first time he showed up for work drunk. But Griffin had tossed him in the watering tank behind the livery to sober him up and put him on the box of the stage dripping wet. The second time, he'd turned him away and driven the run to Dewey himself—big mistake. As experienced as he was with horses, Griffin wasn't much of a hand with a six-horse hitch. But they'd made it through. It wasn't until time number three that he'd given Jules the boot. That was benevolence, wasn't it? Giving a man three chances when old Cy Fennel would have cut him loose the first time.

"I submit to you, dear people," the reverend said, "that sometimes God would have us give our fellow man another chance. Remember the question about forgiveness?"

For some reason, Griffin's mind drifted to Vashti Edwards. Should he give her a chance at driving coaches? She was no more a stagecoach driver than he was. Less of one, if the truth be told. He'd be foolish to allow a girl who used to drive her daddy's farm wagon to climb up on the box. The passengers' lives would be at stake. No, he'd done the right thing to turn her down. And hadn't he shown grace by letting her work at the office? Of course, he paid her a pittance—and only when she sold tickets. A dim spark of guilt flickered deep in his heart.

Phineas Benton wasn't through yet. "We've all had times when we were down—when another person reached out and gave us a hand. When someone gave us a boost we needed but didn't deserve."

That was true enough. Griffin liked to think he'd built his own career. He'd been apprenticed to a blacksmith back in Pennsylvania when he was an awkward kid. His master had been tough on him, but he'd shaped Griffin into a competent farrier and ironworker. When his apprenticeship was over, Griffin had stayed on long enough to earn the money to buy his own tools. Then he'd come west. Opportunity lay in the West, he'd heard. The little town of Fergus, Idaho, had given him the chance to build his smithy and run his own business. Five years later when the livery stable owner moved on, Griffin had saved enough to buy him out, so he became one of the town's most prominent business owners.

But how much of that was due to his own hard work? To hear the preacher tell it, none. It was all God's doing, and in a way, Griff could see that viewpoint. God could have kept him from succeeding. But the Almighty had blessed him and first made it possible for him to get started and later made him able to buy the livery.

Then there was Isabel Fennel. Her father was once the richest man in town. When Cyrus died, she could have hired anyone she wanted to fulfill the Wells Fargo contract, or she could have simply told Wells Fargo they needed to find a new man to oversee the Fergus branch line. But no. She'd turned to Griffin and offered it to him. He had a lot to be thankful for. But did that mean he should turn around and put a green-as-grass girl who wasn't strong enough to control a newborn filly on the box to drive six coach horses? Griffin shuddered.

"All rise, please, for the benediction."

As they filed toward the church door, Vashti craned her neck. Griffin wasn't hard to keep track of—he stood several inches taller than anyone else in the line ahead of her.

Her friend Goldie nudged her. "Who you staring at?"

"Mr. Bane."

"You're mooning over your new boss?"

Vashti frowned at her. "No, I most certainly am not."

"What are you doing, then?"

"Trying to figure out how to make him let me drive the stage."

"You might as well forget about that. He's told you more than once he won't let you."

A lanky young man stepped into the aisle beside them. "Morning, Miss Vashti. Or should I say, 'afternoon'?" Johnny Conway cracked a broad smile at her.

"I expect it is past noon," Vashti said absently.

"You're one of the stagecoach drivers, aren't you?" Goldie asked, gazing up at Johnny with her overlarge blue eyes.

"Yes, ma'am. Have we met before?"

"Maybe." Goldie fluttered her lashes. Vashti had scolded her for continuing to flirt with men since they gave up being saloon girls, but the habit seemed ingrained in Goldie. "Ever been to the Spur & Saddle?"

"Well, sure. You're the gal who plays the pianner." Johnny's smile slipped. "I ain't been there since they changed over—well, you know."

"That's all right," Goldie said.

"You still work there?" Johnny asked.

"No, I work in the Paragon Emporium now, but I still board at the Spur & Saddle, same as Vashti."

"Oh." Johnny looked from her to Vashti and arched his eyebrows as though he expected something.

"Her name is Goldie Keller." Men were always fascinated by Goldie's china-doll looks. Vashti didn't mind, so long as they didn't get fresh with her friend. But Goldie had been around saloons long enough that she knew how to keep most fellows in line.

"I haven't seen you in church before," Goldie said, smiling up at him.

"Well, I don't usually stay over Sunday in Fergus. Most weeks I'm over to Murphy."

They had reached the door. Vashti turned her back on Johnny and Goldie and shook the pastor's hand.

"Good day, Miss Edwards." Pastor Benton always greeted the girls cheerfully, but it was his wife who soothed Vashti's heart. Though Vashti smiled at the preacher, she turned eagerly to Apphia.

"Hello, Mrs. Benton."

"Vashti, so good to see you again. You must come visit me this week, if you have a chance."

"I'd like that, thank you."

"Why don't you come Tuesday afternoon, if that won't interfere with your work? I understand you have two jobs now."

"I'm putting in a few hours at the Wells Fargo. But I could come over around two thirty."

"Wonderful. I'll have the teakettle on."

Vashti stepped out into the sunlight, feeling warm to her toes. Mrs. Benton genuinely cared about the ladies in this town, whether they were rich or poor, refined or crude. Vashti had seen her reach out to women many would consider among the least desirable residents of Fergus. She'd befriended the girls from both saloons back when there were two in town. At the time, Vashti had been jealous of the attention Apphia paid the girls from the Nugget. But now she understood. That was Apphia's nature: to love them all impartially. Even so, whenever she spent time with the pastor's wife, Vashti felt almost as if she were Apphia's only friend and certainly the one she loved best.

She went down the front steps. Griffin Bane had disappeared, probably going back to the livery or the smithy. She waited while Goldie greeted the Bentons. Johnny Conway didn't leave her friend's side. He shook the pastor's hand, too, and spoke to Apphia. He came down the steps with Goldie.

"Say, Miss Vashti, why are you so keen on learning to drive?"

Vashti bristled. "I already know how to drive."

He laughed, and it stung a little. "All right, then. Why do you want so badly to drive a stagecoach? Griff told me you've been hounding him to hire you to drive."

"So?"

"So, you're not ready."

Vashti held back her retort and gazed up at him. She liked Johnny in a way. He was boyishly handsome and had a fun-loving streak, but he'd be trouble for the woman who lost her heart to him.

"So how did *you* get ready?" What she really wanted to know was how he'd convinced Griffin Bane to hire him. Maybe it amounted to the same thing.

"When I was a kid, my pa put up a rig for me in the barn, so's I could practice handling the reins without anyone—or any horses—getting hurt."

"What kind of a rig?"

"It's just a frame with six reins attached like they are on a real hitch. You can pretend to drive for hours at a time, working those lines with your fingers until you can tighten or ease up on any one of the six without affecting the others. That's what you need to do if you're going to control all six horses 't once. You can't drive them all like you would one horse. They'd learn to take advantage of you worse than a tinhorn gambler."

Vashti scowled at him, but what he said made sense. Already her mind was groping for a place where she could have someone make a rig for her. It couldn't be at the livery—Griff would see it. Besides, she wouldn't want to be over there for hours on end, practicing.

Trudy Dooley would let her have it in her barn if she still lived with her brother. But she'd married the sheriff last summer, so she was Mrs. Chapman now and lived out on the sheriff's ranch. It wasn't far out of town, but it was too far for Vashti to trot out there every day.

Augie and Bitsy didn't have a barn. They had a woodshed, though. She wondered if there'd be room out there. They'd burned all of last winter's wood, so the shed was pretty nearly empty. But Augie would be filling it soon and ordering a ton of coal, too.

The pastor and his wife stepped outside. All of the church folks must be finished shaking their hands. The reverend closed the church door, and they turned to walk down the steps together.

Vashti smiled as another option came to mind. She hurried toward the couple.

"Mrs. Benton, Reverend—I've got a favor to ask."

Apphia paused and waited for her to reach them, a smile hovering on her lips. "What is it, Vashti? You know we'll do anything feasible for you."

Vashti wasn't quite sure what *feasible* meant, but she knew the Bentons were bighearted when it came to folks in need.

"You folks have a stable you're not using."

The minister's eyes widened. "Are you getting a horse, Miss Edwards?"

Vashti shook her head. "No, sir, that would be nice but too expensive. This is cheaper and easier to clean up after."

Mr. Benton laughed.

Apphia squeezed her hand. "Well, my dear, you have us on pins and needles. What is it you want to use the stable for?"

"For a place where I can learn to drive my imaginary stagecoach."

★ CHAPTER 4 ★

The next day as the coach came in from Reynolds, Vashti stood in front of the Wells Fargo office, ready to make sure the disembarking passengers had their needs met. Sure enough, a couple got out and turned expectantly toward her.

Too bad—it was nearly time for her to set out for the shooting club's regular practice. But Mr. Bane had made it clear that directing the passengers to food and lodging and hearing any complaints they might make was part of her job, for which he now grudgingly paid her a dime a day, plus the commission on tickets she sold.

"May I help you folks?" she asked, remembering belatedly that Griffin had also specified she smile when addressing customers. She tacked on a perfunctory curve of her lips.

"I think you might be able to." The man doffed his bowler hat, revealing his balding head. After a quick glance at his companion, Vashti catalogued them as man and wife, in their sixties, probably come to visit grandchildren.

"Do you need a place to eat lunch? Because the Spur & Saddle, over yonder, has the best food in Fergus."

"Thank you, that was to be my first question," the man said. "The second was where we might find Mrs. Elizabeth Adams."

Vashti grinned. "Well, that sure is easy. Turn around."

A couple of doors down, Libby was just coming out of the Paragon Emporium with Florence Nash, who clerked for her in the store.

"Miz Adams," Vashti called.

As usual, Libby wore a fashionable but modest dress made of good material. The powder blue gown brought out the vivid blue of her eyes, and her golden curls were topped by a matching bonnet. Florence, who was quite pretty, looked almost ordinary next to the lovely lady.

Libby advanced toward them with a smile. "Yes, Miss Edwards? May I help you?"

Her well-modulated tones inspired Vashti to speak as smoothly as the emporium's owner. "Yes, ma'am. These folks would like to see you."

Libby looked at the couple, favoring them with a hesitant smile. "Hello. Have you just arrived in Fergus?"

"Yes, ma'am." The man gestured toward his wife. "We're the Hamiltons. We've corresponded with you."

"Why, yes, of course." Libby's reserve melted, and she extended her hand, first to the lady and then to the gentleman. "Forgive me. I wasn't expecting you so soon." She turned to include Florence and Vashti in her explanation. "Ladies, this couple is interested in viewing the emporium with the prospect of buying it."

Vashti caught herself so she didn't let out an unladylike whoop. It was no secret that Libby Adams planned to marry the shy gunsmith, Hiram Dooley, but she couldn't until she sold her business. No one in Fergus could afford to buy it—with the possible exception of the schoolmarm, Isabel Fennel, who had inherited a large estate from her father. But Isabel enjoyed teaching and had no desire to run a store, thank you, so Mrs. Adams had advertised the emporium in several Eastern newspapers. Goldie had told Vashti all the details she'd learned while stocking shelves in the store.

"You must be tired." Libby addressed the lady. "Did you folks come all the way from Boise today?"

"Yes, we did," Mrs. Hamilton said. "We were anxious to get here and meet you and see the emporium."

"Of course. But you must be hungry." Libby looked to Mr. Hamilton.

"Well. . ."

"Of course you are. Please allow me to entertain you at our finest restaurant." Libby looked apologetically at Florence. "My dear, I fear I must let you go to the club without me today. Please make my excuses to Trudy. She will understand."

"Yes'm," said Florence.

"Let me give you folks a quick look at the emporium before we eat." Libby turned her head and raised her eyebrows in Vashti's direction. "Miss Edwards, could you possibly run ahead and see if the Moores can accommodate three late diners? We shall be over in ten minutes."

"I surely can." Vashti gathered her satin skirt and leaped off the boardwalk. She ran across the street.

When she charged into the dining room, Bitsy was just picking up her husband's shotgun. Dressed in her red bloomer costume, she looked the part of a sharpshooter.

"What's happened?" she asked, eyeing Vashti with trepidation.

"Nothing bad. There's a couple off the stagecoach, and they want to buy Miz Adams's store. She wants to bring them here to eat. Do you have anything left?"

"Praise the Lord," Bitsy shouted. "Augie! You hear that?"

Augie poked his shiny bald head out from the kitchen. "Hear what?"

"We've got customers coming. Is the stew still hot?"

"Yes, I've got it on the back of the stove."

"Well, heat up those leftover biscuits, too, and put the chicken pie in the warming oven." Bitsy stuck the shotgun under the serving counter. "I'll have to stay here to serve them. Tell Trudy."

"Do you want me to stay?" Vashti asked.

"No, child, you go on. But I need to get out all the luncheon things we put away. We didn't have a single customer to lunch. I thought today was the first day of our decline and bankruptcy."

"That day happened last year, when we got married and closed the bar," Augie muttered as he shuffled for the kitchen.

"Don't pay him any mind." Bitsy pulled three of the best china plates off a shelf. "Go on now, Vashti. Tell Trudy I'll be there Thursday, for sure. And you see if you can't win the prize today."

Griffin tore open the envelope as he left the post office on Mayor Peter Nash's closed-in porch. He felt bad for his sister, Evelyn. Five kids, and no grandparents nearby to help her out. He'd written to her, offering to help in a small way—he could probably send her a few dollars a month if she needed it.

He pulled the closely written sheet of paper from the envelope and stopped walking to steady it. Squinting down at her spidery writing, he immediately felt a glow of satisfaction. Offering his brotherly generosity had been just the right thing to do. It would help Evelyn and make him feel good.

My dear brother,
> *I cannot thank you enough for your sympathy and your offer to help us. You cannot know how your letter affected me. I confess, I burst into tears as I read it.*

Griffin felt the sting of tears in his own eyes, just knowing the good he'd done.

> *Dearest Griffin, I think you are aware that Jacob's father passed on two years ago and left my late husband his property. Since that time, we have lived a little better than before, and I am happy to say that I do not need financial assistance at this time.*

Griffin frowned over that sentence. If she didn't need money, what did she need? Just his kind thoughts from three thousand miles away?

> *There is a way you can help me immeasurably, however, and that is with my eldest boy, Justin. It grieves me to tell you this, but he has given me great pain this past year. He's become friends with an undesirable group of youths, and since his father's passing I've not been able to control his behavior at all. He comes and goes as he pleases. I don't like to mention it, but*

I fear he stole some money from my reticule last week. Not only that, but he's taken up smoking. He thinks I don't know, but the odor clings to him. Dear brother, I fear the worst for my boy, and thus your letter offered a ray of hope to my grieving heart.

Griffin's chest tightened and he feared to turn the page.

I've purchased a train ticket for Justin to depart on Wednesday next. He will ride to Salt Lake City, from where he can get the stagecoach up to your territory. I expect he will arrive in Mountain Home, Idaho, about the fifth of October.

Griffin looked up in a panic. People walked along the main street as though everything was normal. A wagonload of women approached from the north. Shooting practice must be finished. Libby Adams and a middle-aged couple came out of the Spur & Saddle, chatting amicably as they headed across to the Paragon Emporium.

Sucking in a deep breath, Griffin turned and hurried back to the post office.

"Peter!" He threw the door open, but the postmaster-mayor was no longer behind the counter. He stepped to the inner door and pounded on it.

Ellie Nash, Peter's wife, opened it. "Hello, Mr. Bane. I thought you came for your mail earlier."

"I did."

"Well, Peter's out back tending the—"

"What day is it?"

"It's Monday."

"No, no, what day of the month?"

"Oh. Let's see, I believe it's the fourth."

"October fourth."

"Yes, that's right." Ellie eyed him curiously.

Griffin ran his hand through his thick beard. He still hadn't trimmed it. Why on earth hadn't Evelyn telegraphed him with this news, not to say asked permission to send the boy? He had to get to Mountain Home by tomorrow to meet his nephew, and Mountain Home wasn't even part of his branch line. He'd have to ride up to Boise and change to the main line there. That or ride a horse across country. But then what would his nephew ride back on?

"Mr. Bane? Are you all right?"

"What? Oh. Yes, thank you." He turned and staggered out the post office door and down the steps. Where would he keep the boy—Justin? He checked the letter to be sure he had the name right. His bed wouldn't hold both of them. He could give it up for Justin, he supposed. But why should he? Yet there wasn't room in his small lodging for another bed.

Could he let the boy sleep in the loft over the livery? The stage drivers slept there before the boardinghouse opened. But he'd be so far away, Griffin wouldn't hear him if he cried out in the night. How old was the lad, anyway? Evelyn hadn't said. She'd mentioned smoking. . . . He must be at least fifteen.

Griffin scrunched up his face, recalling the first and last time he'd tried smoking. His father had caught him out behind the barn and tanned his backside but good. He'd been twelve.

What was his sister doing to him?

His breath came in quick gasps, and his boots thunked loudly on the boardwalk. When he came even with the Wells Fargo office, Annie Harper had pulled her wagon over and was letting the shooting club ladies climb down. He ducked quickly inside the office and shut the door.

How could he go to Mountain Home tomorrow? He was still shorthanded. He needed to round up a shotgun messenger for tomorrow's run to Silver City, and if the man who came in on the Boise stage wouldn't do it, Griffin would have to do it himself. And what if he did go to Mountain Home? What if he got all the way over there, and Justin didn't show up? He sat down heavily. There must be a good way to handle this. It occurred to him that he didn't pray much, but now might be a good time.

Uh, heavenly Father. . .uh. . .I know I don't talk to You as much as I should. But I'm thankful for. . .for everything You do for me. And I was wondering. . .well, could You help me figure out what to do with Evelyn's boy? It's too late to tell her not to send him. Uh. . .thanks.

A soft knocking sounded on his door, and he jerked his head. "It's open."

The door creaked on its hinges. Vashti Edwards stood there in her usual crinkly finery. He guessed that was all she had to wear—satins and taffetas left over from her saloon days, but no soft cotton housedresses like the ranchers' wives wore. She was probably being frugal, wearing her old dresses until they wore out, but it was distracting.

"What do you want?" He pushed himself to his feet, not caring whether he sounded rude. He had a family crisis to deal with.

"Mr. Bane, I wondered if you'd reconsidered letting me learn to drive the coaches. I'm willing to—"

"No."

"Please, Mr. Bane? I've done a good job for you here in the office, haven't I?"

He looked her over grudgingly. "Yes, you have, but that doesn't mean you could handle a team. Besides, at the moment it's not a driver I need."

"What do you need, sir? Maybe I can help."

"I need a place for a boy to stay. And a shotgun rider for to-morrow's run to Silver City."

"A boy?"

"That's right. My nephew is coming to stay here for a while."

"That's wonderful."

"It is?"

Vashti smiled. "Of course. You have family. That's a mighty precious gift, Mr. Bane."

"Well, I suppose so." It was a long time since he'd thought deeply about family. "My sister's husband kicked off, and she doesn't know what to do with all the kids, so she's sending me her big boy."

"Does she want you to apprentice him?"

Griffin snapped his gaze to meet hers. "I didn't think of that. She wants me to keep him in line, I guess. Keep him out of trouble. She didn't say anything about teaching him a trade."

"Seems to me that would be the best thing for him."

"Well. . .it would take a lot of time."

She stepped farther into the office and stood before the desk. "Yes, it would, but you know you need someone to help with the forge work. Once you've taught him, he could maybe take that over one day. Or if he wants to move along, he'd have a skill so's he could support himself when he's grown. How big is this boy?"

"I don't know." Griffin eyed her uneasily, fearing she would berate him for neglecting his kinfolk, but she seemed deep in thought. "I don't even know for sure he's on the stage," Griffin added, "but he's supposed to come in to Mountain Home tomorrow. Guess I'll have to ride over there and fetch him."

"Where's he coming from?"

"Salt Lake. Took the train that far."

Vashti smiled. "Why don't you telegraph the Wells Fargo division manager in Salt Lake and see if he boarded the stagecoach there as scheduled? It would be worth the money the inquiry would cost you. If he's on the stage, you go get him, or else tell them to send him on to Boise. It would be easier to get him there. And if he's not on board, you won't waste the trip."

He gave that a full five seconds of consideration. "Not a bad idea. Thank you."

"You're welcome."

He rose and stepped toward the doorway, but Vashti moved into it and stood her ground. She tipped her head back so she could look up into his face. "If you write out the telegram, I could run it over to Mr. Dostie for you, and I'm sure Mrs. Thistle would have a vacant room a young man could stay in, if that suits your situation."

Griffin frowned down at her. Why was she being so helpful?

She smiled. "As to the shotgun messenger, I'd be happy to fill in for your man tomorrow. I'm a pretty good shot, if I do say so. I won the ribbon for personal best at today's shooting club meeting."

He stared down into her new-leaf-green eyes. After a long moment, he said, "I can take care of the telegram myself. And I suppose I could put him up at the boardinghouse for a few days till I figure out something better."

Susan Page Davis

Vashti didn't move out of the way. "What about the Silver City run? I'd love to do it."

He huffed out a breath and shook his head. "You don't understand, do you? I cannot—I *will* not hire a woman on my stage line. I'd be laughed out of Idaho Territory. Besides, I have a responsibility to the U.S. Mail."

"But you're in a bind. You said so yourself. It's only for one day. One run. And I can do it. Just ask Trudy Chapman or Bitsy. They'll tell you I'm a good shot."

"I don't doubt that. It's just—"

"I know. It's because I'm a girl."

"Well, yes. I don't know any other way to put it. Do you think a gang of outlaws would hang back and say, 'Oh my, look at that! They've got a lady on the box today. I guess we'd better not rob that stagecoach'? Of course not! They'd be nudging each other and saying, 'Look, Billy. Easy pickings today, and a pretty little skirt, too.'"

Vashti's face paled, and he immediately regretted the words. "I'm sorry. Shouldn't have said that." His own face began to feel warm. "I'm just trying to make you understand why I can't let you do it."

She squared her shoulders and hiked up her chin. "And I'm telling you they would never get near that coach with me on the box."

"Sure. With your fiery hair and shiny satin gown calling out to them."

Vashti stamped her foot. "I'll put my hair up under a hat. I'll even wear *your* hat if you want. They wouldn't think a lady would be wearing *that*."

"What's wrong with my hat?"

"Just everything."

"Ha!"

"And I'd borrow a drab-colored dress from Isabel Fennel or Apphia Benton. They've got enough of them."

Griffin chuckled. Feisty little thing, she was. "Tell you what, Miss Pushy, I'm going to go send my telegram. You mosey on over to the Fennel House and see if Mrs. Thistle could put my nephew up for a few nights. If she says yes and if I get a telegram back saying Justin's on his way, I'll take what you said under consideration."

Her eyes glowed. "Really?"

"Said so, didn't I?"

"Oh! Thank you!" She squeezed his wrist and tore off across the street.

"Wait!"

She stopped and turned in a swirl of skirts. "Yes, sir?"

"*If* this happens, and I'm not saying that it will, you'll have to fill out some paperwork required by the Wells Fargo company for all employees."

She grinned. "I'll come back after I speak to Mrs. Thistle." She tore for the Fennel House.

Griffin stared after her. Was he nuts? Well, at least he hadn't promised her. Maybe he could back down later. Or maybe Justin was delayed, and he wouldn't have to go to Mountain Home, or even Boise. But if he did. . .

He shook his shaggy head. He had to be crazy to consider this. He'd actually listened to her and halfway said she could ride the stage tomorrow with Bill Stout. How could he have done that?

Must be the green eyes.

★ CHAPTER 5 ★

That evening after the supper rush of six diners, Vashti pondered long over the paper Griffin had given her. Goldie came in about six thirty, after her stint at the emporium, and found the plate Bitsy had put by for her in the kitchen. She carried it over to the rough table where Vashti was seated and plopped down across from her.

"Whatcha doing?"

Vashti sighed. "Mr. Bane has practically agreed to let me ride shotgun on the Silver City stage tomorrow, but I have to write down all kinds of information first."

Goldie frowned. "What sort of information?"

"Well, name, age, address—I can do that. But the last question is 'Next of kin.' What do I put down?"

"Don't you have any kin?"

"I'm thinking on it."

Goldie bowed her head for a moment, asking the blessing on her food. As she raised her head, Bitsy breezed in from the dining room. "Mr. Dooley and Mrs. Adams just came in wanting pie and coffee. This is turning into a good night for us."

Vashti pushed her chair back. "Want me to help?"

Bitsy waved her offer aside. "I can serve two pieces of pie and two cups of coffee with one hand tied to a bucking horse. Relax and eat."

"Did you know Vashti's riding shotgun tomorrow?" Goldie asked.

"She told me."

"What do you think?"

Bitsy took half an apple pie from the pie safe. "Not my cup of tea, but if that's what she wants to do. . ."

"I think she's very brave." Goldie dove into her roast chicken and baked potato.

Bitsy put two plates on a tray and reached into the crock of forks. "I said to her, 'That could be a step toward the job you really want.' I think it's progress."

Vashti smiled her thanks across the room. "Now, if I can just figure out who to put down as next of kin."

"What's that for?" Bitsy frowned with her knife hovering above the pie.

"In case I get killed on the job, I reckon."

"Humph."

Goldie nodded. "That's what I think, too."

Vashti looked down at the paper again. At the top, she'd written as neatly as she could, *Georgia Edwards, age 24, Fergus, Idaho.* But for "next of kin," she had few options. The one relative she could think of was the last person she'd want notified on her behalf.

Bitsy poured the customers' coffee and set the pot back on the stove. "You've lived with me for more than four years, and you're like kin to me and Augie. Why can't you just put me down on that paper?"

Vashti looked over at her. For a moment, she couldn't speak. Her breath was knocked out of her, and tears filled her eyes. The weathered old Spur & Saddle building had indeed become her home, and Bitsy was closer to her than any legal family had been since she was a small child. "I like that."

Bitsy smiled at her. "Go ahead. If Griffin makes a fuss, send him to me. I'll take care of him."

"Thanks!" Vashti quickly wrote, *Mrs. Augustus Moore, Fergus, Idaho,* and folded up the paper.

The next morning, Vashti ran along the dirt street, holding her skirt above her ankles. She turned in at the path to the pastor's house, ran up the steps, and knocked, panting for breath.

Apphia Benton opened the door. "Well, good morning, Vashti.

I didn't expect you until later."

"I can't come this afternoon. I just wanted to let you know—I'll be away."

Apphia stepped back and gestured for her to step inside. "Away? Where are you going?"

"Sorry, but I can't stop long. Mr. Bane's nephew is coming, and he has to go and get him. He's taking the Boise stage today. But he'd been planning to ride shotgun to Silver City, in the other direction, so I'm taking his place."

"What? My dear, do come sit down and explain this to me. Surely you're not—"

"Yes, ma'am. The shotgun messenger who usually has that run quit and headed for the Yukon."

"Oh, I heard they'd found gold up there."

"That's right, so Mr. Bane is short a messenger, and he can't send the coach without one today, on account of something I'm not supposed to tell you."

Apphia arched her eyebrows but said nothing. Vashti gulped. She'd almost blabbed about the treasure box coming down from one of the mines tomorrow. One of the first and most important rules Griffin had taught her when he let her tend the Wells Fargo office was to never reveal to anyone when money and other valuables would be on a stagecoach. Not that the minister's wife would tell anyone, but it was the principle. That, and if Griffin found out, he'd fire Vashti immediately.

"Anyway, he says I can do it this once, and I'm hoping that if everything goes well, he'll let me try driving."

Apphia nodded slowly. "You told me you hoped for a chance to be a driver. I still think it's a rather rough way for a young lady to earn her living, but—"

"But I love driving," Vashti said. "I've prayed it over, like you told me I should, and I still want to do it. I don't think God would put this in my heart if He didn't want me to try it, do you?"

"Well. . .sometimes the Lord lets us do things that aren't especially good for us. We need to be careful not to think our wants are the same as God's will."

"But I've always loved horses." Vashti eyed her friend uncertainly. "All the time I worked in saloons, I thought that if I could just be out working with horses—animals are so much kinder than people, don't you think?"

Apphia touched her shoulder gently. "Sometimes that's true, I admit. But stagecoach driving—that's a rough-and-tumble world."

"Not so bad as selling whiskey and putting up with the men drinking it."

Apphia did not answer, but her eyes held a troubled cast.

Vashti smiled at her. "If I could drive, I'd be perfectly happy. And if I show Mr. Bane I can do a good job as a messenger, that's one step closer to driving."

"Ah, Vashti. I'll continue to pray for you. For your safety, and also that God will show you clearly if He wants you to pursue this. I know you haven't always had it easy. Just please, come see me tomorrow after you come home, to let me know you're all right."

"I will." Vashti gathered her skirts. "Now I must run. Mr. Bane says I have to sign another paper at the Wells Fargo office before I leave."

"Say, did you find someone to build that driving rig you were talking about?"

"Not yet, but I will. You don't mind, do you?"

Apphia cocked her head to one side. "I'm not sure it's the best thing, but we'll let you use the barn. I'll trust to God to stop this adventure if He doesn't want you to do it."

"Hey, Griff, I see you're busy." Hiram Dooley stepped into the dim livery barn and walked over to stand beside his friend.

"I'm always busy these days." Once again Griffin had to help Marty hitch up the stagecoach team. "Got to get these horses ready, then get over to the office and sign some paperwork with Vashti Edwards, and I'm heading to Boise later today."

"What for?"

"My sister's boy's arriving. He's going to stay with me for a while."

Hiram whistled softly. "Big change for you. What's the business you're doing with Miss Edwards? Not that it's my never-mind."

"She thinks she can ride shotgun on the Silver City stage. I'm making her sign a paper that says I'm not responsible if she breaks her neck or gets shot by road agents."

"You're really letting her do it? I knew she'd been pestering you to let her drive."

"I'm not letting her do that. But I'm in a bind, and it's common knowledge she's a good shot." Griffin finished buckling a strap and snapped his fingers. "I meant to ask Libby Adams if she had some pants that would fit Vashti. I don't want her riding in one of those flashy dresses of hers, advertising to the criminal world that my shotgun messenger is a female."

"I can go over and ask Libby if you'd like."

"That'd be a big help, since time's getting short." Griffin grinned at him. "Not like you'd mind a reason to pop in and see Libby, eh?"

Hiram smiled and stuck his thumbs under his suspenders. "Don't mind a bit. Actually, she's the reason I'm here. Wondered if you'd keep an eye out for a nice, calm saddle horse for Libby."

"Your wedding present to her?"

"Something like that."

Griffin headed toward the barn wall for the next set of harnesses. "Sure, I'll look for something. You set a date yet?"

"Nope, but she's got a likely prospect to buy the store."

"That couple that's staying at the boardinghouse?"

"They're the ones. Mr. and Mrs. Hamilton." Hiram stepped back. "So what else do you need for Vashti? A pair of pants and. . . ?"

"Anything that will make her look like a man."

"You want me to *what*?" Vashti glared at Griffin, but he refused to back down and glared back.

She put her hands on her hips. "I figured out who to name as my next of kin, and I agreed to sign that ridiculous paper swearing you wouldn't get in trouble if I get killed. Bitsy loaned me this old, drab brown dress—don't ask me where she got it from. I even told you I'd wear this bowler hat of Augie's. But apparently that's not enough."

"It's just a pair of trousers," Griffin said.

She clenched her fists and mimicked his tone saucily, "Just a pair of trousers."

Griffin scowled down at her from his height. His conscience reproached him slightly, but he ignored it. So he was demanding something of her that she didn't want to do. He did that to the drivers all the time. They lived by the stage line's rules—or else. Could he help it if Vashti saw him as a shaggy Goliath who held her future in his hands? He rather liked the idea that he was the only man in town who could boss her around.

"Look, it's very simple. If you don't want to do it, all I've got to do is tell Hi Dooley I'll pay him twice the normal rate, and he'll take this run for me. The stagecoach leaves in fifteen minutes, with or without you. What do you say?" He glared steadily back into those icy green eyes. Of course, he hadn't asked Hiram if he'd do the run, but he probably would, now that he thought of it. In fact, Griff wished he *had* asked his friend this morning. It would have been worth paying a double wage to avoid this conflict, and Hi could probably use some pocket change. He'd have to remember that for next time. There was always a next time.

He kept up the stony glare, and Vashti's face squirmed into a mask of distaste.

"I ought to refuse, but that's what you want, isn't it?" She snatched the neatly folded pants and flannel shirt off Griffin's desk. "Where do I change?"

"Mrs. Adams says you can go over there and use her back room."

Vashti turned on her high-heeled shoes and strode out the door.

Griffin didn't know whether to smile or swear.

Five minutes later, Vashti opened the door of Libby's back room and cautiously peered out into the emporium. Libby waited behind the counter.

"All ready? Let's take a look."

Only when she'd flung the door wide and taken two steps did Vashti realize Mr. Dooley was leaning on the far side of the counter.

She felt a flush speed up from the collar of the huge buffalo plaid shirt.

Hiram let out a sort of gasp and turned around.

Vashti's chest hurt. She looked anxiously to Libby. "What? Is it that bad?"

"He's just surprised. Hmm." The elegant lady looked her up and down. "You need men's boots, that's for sure. Maybe a boys' size. And how about a leather vest over that shirt? It will disguise your. . .er. . . gender better." Libby swung around and hurried between the racks of merchandise toward the far corner where boots lined one set of shelves.

Hiram glanced at Vashti then away. "I, uh, need some twelve-penny nails." He all but ran toward the hardware section.

Vashti steamed as she pulled her shoes off. Did she look so shocking in trousers? Libby had found a pair in a smaller size than the voluminous ones she'd tried first, and a belt to bring in the waist. The big shirt hung down over it. Maybe she ought to tuck that in if she was going to wear a vest, too.

Libby dashed back, holding out a pair of stiff leather boots. "Try these. I'll find a vest."

As she turned away, Griffin Bane strode in. "Hey, gal, the stage is here, and we need to load the box. We're waiting on you to stand guard while we do it."

"Uh. . ." Vashti darted a glance toward Libby.

"She's ready, Griffin," Libby called. "I'm just getting her a vest to complete her ensemble."

Quickly Vashti pulled on the boots. Libby hurried over, holding a black leather vest made for a middle-sized boy. Vashti slipped her arms into it.

"There," Libby said. "Put your hat on."

Vashti grabbed the hat off the counter. Libby had replaced Augie's overlarge bowler with a smaller cowboy hat in creamy felt with a braided leather band. Vashti loved it at first sight but wondered if her first wages as a messenger would pay for all these clothes. Boots now, too, and the soft leather vest.

Griffin stood motionless, staring at her. He opened his mouth, but no words came out.

Libby chuckled. "Makes a fine-looking boy, doesn't she, Mr. Bane?"

Griff cleared his throat. "I reckon from a couple hundred yards away she'd pass. And remember, you're not letting any outlaws get that close."

"No, sir, I'm not. Thanks, Libby. I'll settle up with you when I get home tomorrow." Vashti put on a little swagger as she left the store. Griffin came along behind her—she could feel the boardwalk shake under his heavy tread.

Two passengers were already in the coach when she reached it. Bill Stout, the white-haired veteran driver, sat on the box with his whip in its stand and the lines of the team of six horses in his hands. To Vashti's surprise, the sheriff leaned against the side of the stage line office.

Ethan Chapman straightened and stepped away from the wall. "Morning."

"Hello, Sheriff."

Vashti felt a firm hand on her shoulder. She stopped and turned to look up at Griffin.

"I told Bill to call you Sam, so people wouldn't know you're a girl," he said in as soft a voice as she imagined that barrel chest could emit.

"Sam?" she hissed. She looked around quickly. The passengers and Bill didn't seem to have heard.

"What, you don't like that name?"

She considered for a moment. "I have another name, you know, if Vashti's too feminine for this outfit."

"You mean Edwards?"

"No. I mean. . ." She leaned closer and stood on tiptoe so she could get within a foot of his ear. "My Christian name was Georgia. So whyn't you all just call me George?"

His dark, bushy eyebrows rose. He blinked. "George?"

"Is that any worse than Sam?"

"No, I s'pose not."

"Good. Didn't you read that paper I signed all legal-like for you?

If you look close, you'll see that's what I put. Georgia Edwards. Only I smeared the I-A a tad, so's anyone might think it said George."

He nodded slowly. "All right then. Let Bill in on it once you get going."

She nodded and winked. He jerked his head back.

"Come on inside. I've got your shotgun in there. I'll carry the strongbox out, and you look sharp, up and down the street, while I load it."

They stepped into the office, and Griffin took a gleaming shotgun with a cherry stock from a rack on the wall and placed it in her hands. Vashti held it to the light streaming in the doorway and admired the fine tracery on the lock. Any man or woman in Fergus would be proud to own this gun. She nodded and hefted it. Not too heavy.

"Thank you."

"That's on loan while you're working for me." Griffin crossed the room and stooped to open the safe. He brought out a sturdy wooden box, painted green and bound with bands of steel.

"You go out first and make sure it's clear."

Vashti stepped out onto the boardwalk. As if anyone in Fergus would hold up the stagecoach right in town. Especially with the sheriff loafing around.

She glanced at Chapman. He stood with his hands on his belt, his right hand close to his six-shooter, looking up the street toward the Nugget Saloon. Vashti looked the other way, southward along the boardwalk and the dusty street. Beyond the emporium, Oscar Runnels, the freighter, was climbing the steps to the post office.

Griffin came out and went straight to the coach. He heaved the treasure box up and settled it on the boards where the driver and messenger rested their feet. Bill helped him slide the heavy box under the seat. They fussed for a moment, making sure it was secure; then Griffin stepped back and turned to her.

"All right, George. Time for you to go."

Vashti walked over to the step at the front of the coach and climbed up. Settling onto the seat beside Bill, she smiled at him. "Morning, Mr. Stout."

"How do, Sam."

"It's George, but that's all right." She looked down at Griffin, whose head came up as high as where her feet were braced. A strange look crossed his face. Was he thinking he ought to tell Bill to take care of her, instead of the other way around? For a moment, Vashti was afraid he'd make her get down again and tell her she couldn't go.

"We'll be just fine, Mr. Bane," she said. "I hope you and your nephew have a nice trip."

"Godspeed." Griffin stepped back.

Bill lifted the reins and let the horses have an inch or two of slack. "Get up!"

They rolled out of Fergus with the wind whistling in Vashti's ears below the hat's brim. As they passed the Spur & Saddle, she glimpsed Augie and Bitsy standing at the front door. She raised the shotgun in triumph and waved.

★ CHAPTER 6 ★

Griffin paced the porch in front of the Wells Fargo office in Boise. He had another half hour before the stage was due. He could step down the street for refreshment, but he wanted to make sure he was here when Justin arrived.

After a few minutes, he went inside. The ticket agent looked up and smiled. "Cup of coffee, Mr. Bane?"

"Thanks."

The man nodded toward the potbellied stove in the corner. "I make a fresh pot before the Mountain Home stage comes in. The cups on the shelf are clean."

Griffin poured himself a serving of the boiling, dark brew. The stove's heat made the room too warm, and he stepped away from it, toward the counter. He set the hot cup down for a minute to let the grounds settle.

"How's business up to Fergus?" the agent asked.

"Tolerable. I'm having a little trouble keeping enough drivers and messengers lined up."

"We've had a big turnover here, too," the man admitted.

"Thought I might talk to your division manager to see if he had any suggestions."

The agent shook his head. "Mr. Nelson's gone to Glenn's Ferry. I don't expect he'll be back for two or three hours at least."

Griffin picked up his tin cup. The small, curved handle was hot, but not so bad he couldn't hold it. The worst part was that the curve

694

was so tight he couldn't get his large finger through it. He managed to raise the cup to his lips and took a cautious sip. He'd had worse coffee. Once. He grimaced and set the cup down.

"Did you get the new rate table?" the agent asked.

"Yup."

The door opened. Two men came in.

"Afternoon," one of them called. "We need tickets to Mountain Home."

Griffin stepped outside, leaving his cup of brew on the counter. He paced back and forth, ignoring the passing wagons and foot traffic. If he were home, he could be shoeing Oscar Runnels's mules, or working with the bay colt, or mending harness.

And what about the Silver City run? He'd put Vashti with his steadiest driver, but maybe he'd lowered Bill's chances of a safe run by giving him a green shotgun rider. What if road agents tried to stop them and she panicked? Griffin turned and walked the length of the porch again. Best not to think about the Silver City stage when it was too late to change things.

Ten minutes later, the ticket agent came out and piled luggage and mail sacks near where the stagecoach would halt. The two men who'd come for tickets and a few other prospective passengers milled about, making small talk.

Right on time, a bugle blew. Griffin heard the pounding hooves and rattling wheels before he caught sight of the stage. His chest swelled a little, and his throat tightened as the red and gold coach flew down the street. People scattered and stood admiring the sight or cursing the driver, who popped his whip more for show than practicality. The six bay horses—nearly matched—slowed to a trot then drew up right where the pile of luggage waited.

Griffin laughed. Those horses' flanks were dark with sweat, but their breathing wasn't labored, and no foam had formed along the harness straps. The good drivers knew how to pace the team and still put on a performance when they neared each stop.

The messenger hopped down and flung the door open.

"Welcome to Boise, folks." The ticket agent offered a hand to a middle-aged woman who climbed stiffly down from the coach. She was followed by a string bean of a boy. Griffin looked no further. The gawky lad had the Bane chin and his sister, Evelyn's, dark doe eyes, with which he warily scanned the people on the boardwalk.

"Justin." Griffin stepped forward and held out his hand.

The boy snapped his head around and caught a quick breath. "Uncle Griff?"

"That's right." His hand closed over the boy's. "Glad you got here safe. Do you have a trunk?"

"No, sir. Just a satchel."

Griffin turned to the back of the coach, and they waited for the messenger to toss down the luggage.

"We'll stay in a hotel here tonight," he told Justin. "Then we'll take the stage back to Fergus in the morning."

A battered leather bag landed with a thud beside them, and the boy stooped to grab the handle. As he straightened, he flipped his overlong hair back from his forehead.

"Just so's you know, I don't want to do no smithing."

Vashti clung to the curved metal on the side of her seat. The coach swayed on its leather straps as they barreled around a corner. She was grateful that the sheer drop-off was on Bill's side, not hers, but she realized two things: If she was going to become a top-notch driver, she'd have to get used to flying along these precarious roads. And coming back downhill tomorrow, she'd be on the side edging what amounted to a cliff.

The horses slowed to a walk as the grade increased. Bill let them lumber along up the incline. He reached into the pocket of his jacket, brought out a small hunk of tobacco, and bit off a piece. Stuffing the wad back into his pocket, he glanced over at Vashti.

"I like a chaw while I'm driving."

She nodded.

"Griff says you want to learn to drive."

"I know how to drive."

"That so?"

"I can drive two and four."

"So you could drive a stage on the flat, with four horses?"

"I could."

"Huh." They rode on in silence until the horses gained more level ground. Bill snapped the reins. "Up now." The team picked up a steady jog. "We'll trade for mules at the next stop. It's a little over halfway to Silver. The last half's the worst."

Vashti clenched her teeth and nodded. She'd never been up to the mining town before, and the road was a bit rougher than she'd imagined. The hairpin turns and sheer drops gave her pause. And Bill said the worst terrain lay ahead of them.

She watched his hands as he worked the lines gently, making fine adjustments with subtle movements she could barely see. Not one horse broke stride as they clopped through a wooded area and splashed across a shallow creek.

"Pull now," he called, and the six leaned into the harness to carry the coach up the next grade without losing speed.

"How'd you learn to drive so well?" she asked.

"Oh, I been driving since I was one-sixteenth your size."

She smiled.

"Hold on."

She grabbed the metal bar again and tried not to look toward the far edge of the road as the coach careened down a dip and up the other side. The wind tugged at her sleeves and whistled past her ears.

"That gully took my hat off the first time I ran it," Bill said with a laugh.

The horses slowed to their businesslike jog for another half mile. Bill bent down and took a bugle from beneath the seat.

"Are we nearly to the swing station?" Vashti looked ahead but saw no signs of civilization.

"Around the next curve." He put the horn to his lips and blew a long blast. Lowering the shiny instrument, he smiled at Vashti. "Now Jules Harding, he could play a right smart tattoo on the horn. I just give it a lungful."

They swept into the yard of the stage stop, and Bill pulled the team up.

Two men came running from the cabin to help unharness the blowing horses. Vashti jumped down and winced as her feet hit the ground. She hadn't realized how long she'd braced her legs on the footboard. She took a few steps to get her blood flowing and opened the coach door. "Do you gentlemen want to stretch your legs? We'll leave in about ten minutes."

The two passengers climbed down. One of them eyed her keenly as he made his exit. Vashti looked away, hoping she wouldn't blush. That would surely give away her secret. As the two men ambled toward the house, the one who'd stared at her said something to the other. The second man turned around and looked at her. Vashti turned her back to them and shut the door of the coach. Bill came around from behind the coach.

"The necessary's out back. I suggest you wait until the passengers come back."

She nodded, staring at the ground. Her face was scarlet for sure.

"You want some coffee?" Bill asked.

She shook her head.

The hostler led a team of mules out of a corral, where he'd had them hitched up and waiting in their harness. In no time flat, the bay horses had been turned out and the six mules put in their place before the stagecoach. Bill came around the corner of the cabin and nodded to her. Vashti ran around the other side of the little building. Within two minutes she was back, panting as she climbed up. The passengers had boarded, and the station agent and his helper stood leaning against the corral fence.

Vashti felt their eyes on her as she climbed aboard. The rough boots made her feet feel clumsy, but she sprang as quickly as she could up to the seat beside Bill. "What are they staring at?"

"You, of course. They think you're awfully young to be riding shotgun. I told them you're a top marksman." He spit tobacco juice over the side. "Melvin said, 'Oh, that's what you call it in Fergus.'" He laughed.

"So he knows I'm a woman?"

"I'd say so. He guessed."

"I think the passengers are suspicious, too."

"Makes no difference, so long as the lawless part of the population doesn't know."

"Word will get around."

"Mebbe so." Bill gathered the reins. "Up now, you lazy mules!"

The team began the merciless uphill pull. Another eight miles of hard going.

"You ever been held up?" Vashti asked.

"Sure."

She eyed him in surprise. "Really?"

"Every driver who's been around awhile has been."

"Here? I mean, on the Fergus line?"

"Once. Before that I was down on the Wyoming run. Wild, oh, that route was wild, especially during the war."

"You mean the War Between the States?"

"That's right. It was like the Injuns knew most of the soldiers were busy elsewhere, and they attacked all up and down the line. Stole horses and food—burned everything else. Hay, grain, stations. Everything. Times were hard then, and it cost a pretty penny to keep the line running."

"Mr. Bane told me it cost a lot more then to ride the line."

"Sure it did. But most people were afraid to ride anyway, at least on certain parts. If it hadn't been for the mail contracts, the stagecoach companies would have folded."

Vashti clung tightly to her shotgun and the edge of the seat as they took a curve.

"So what was the worst scrape you were in?"

Bill spat over the side. "About twenty Injuns come after me. Old Ben Liddel was sittin' where you are. He pumped the lead, I'm telling you."

"How'd you get away? Outrun 'em?"

"Nope. A team of horses hitched to a coach can't outrun their horses. Mules even less likely. No, we drove into a piece of road between some rocks and stood 'em off for three hours. We weren't far out from Julesburg. Finally, half a dozen men came riding out to see what had happened to us. They ran the Injuns off. Good thing, because Ben and me were about out of lead."

Vashti eyed him for a long moment. "You telling it straight?"

"I sure am."

"Did you have any passengers?"

"Not that day. Had five sacks of mail, though. And we got it through, yes sirree. 'Course, I took a bullet in my hand."

Vashti stared down at his tanned, leathery hands. "Which one?"

"That one. The right."

"Did it heal up good as new?"

"Pretty good. Still bothers me some, especially in cold weather or when it's going to rain. But I was mighty glad they didn't hit me in a worse place."

The wheels hit a rut, and Vashti lurched forward, nearly flying over the footboard.

"Hold on, there, Georgie!" Bill grabbed the back of her vest and yanked her back up onto the seat.

Vashti gasped and looked up into his placid blue eyes. "Thank you, sir."

"Don't need no 'sir.' I'm just Bill."

"Thank you kindly, Bill."

He nodded. "So, you want to drive."

"I do. I surely do." For a split second, she thought he might offer to let her take the reins.

Bill spit a stream of tobacco juice off into the brush. "What'd you ever drive before?"

"My daddy's horses."

"How long ago?"

She couldn't hold his gaze. "Awhile."

"Like ten years or more?"

"Something like that."

"Hmm." They were approaching a steep incline. Bill let out a little rein and called to the mules, "Hup now. Step along, boys."

Vashti held on and kept quiet. When they got to the top of the rise, the road leveled out for a short stretch.

"Driving a farm wagon h'ain't like driving a stage," Bill said.

"No, sir, I expect you're right. My daddy had a carriage and four."

Bill's eyes narrowed, and he shot her a sidelong glance. "That true?"

"Well. . .the team of four is."

"Ha."

"Johnny Conway said when he was a nipper, somebody made him a rig to practice driving on."

"That's a passable way to learn. At first. If you can't learn on real horses."

"Well, I don't see how I can learn on real horses when I don't have any of my own and Mr. Bane won't let me drive his."

"Hmm."

Vashti watched him cautiously for a bit then cleared her throat. "Would you make me a rig, Bill? I've got a place to put it."

"Do you?"

"Yes, sir. I mean Bill."

He pursed his lips and, after a moment, shot more tobacco juice over the side. "I'll think on it."

They rode along for another hour without much talk. Vashti stared out over the valley below them and across at the distant peaks and rock formations. Some of the stone columns had fanciful shapes. She imagined one group as a quartet of trolls, watching them strain up the ribbon of road.

"Look ahead now," Bill said.

She turned forward. They approached a place where a huge boulder crowded to the edge of the road.

"Anyplace there's cover, you need to be watching."

"You think there might be outlaws hiding behind that rock?"

"You just never know. They say that back in the old days when the most ore was coming down, this was a favorite spot."

Vashti's neck prickled. The road was so steep, the mules walked slowly, leaning into their collars. She sat straighter and flicked glances at every conceivable hiding place along both sides of the road, always coming back to the base of the boulder. The only sounds were creaking leather, the mules' labored breathing and snorting, and the crunch of the wheels on the sandy ground.

When they'd passed the spot, she sighed and relaxed a little.

Bill nudged her with his elbow. "It also makes a good courting spot, on top of that boulder."

She laughed. "Did Mr. Bane tell you his nephew's coming?"

"I heard."

"He's boarding him at the Fennel House."

Bill grunted. They reached a somewhat flat spot in the road, with no trees or large rocks about, and he halted the team. "I like to let them take a breather here. More uphill ahead."

Vashti nodded. "What would you have done if bandits jumped out from behind that rock back there?"

He frowned and spit again. "It's a bad place. Can't run away from 'em, 'cause the road's so steep. Can't turn around. Reckon I'd have to stop and give 'em what they wanted—unless you shot 'em first."

She gulped. "You think I should shoot if that happens?"

"If someone jumps out, aiming a gun at us, I'd just as soon you let off a round and didn't wait to parley. If they's only one or two of 'em, that might be enough. If they's a whole gang. . .well, that's different. At a tight spot like that, it's better to give in than get killed." He shrugged. "Just be glad we don't have to worry about Injuns anymore in these parts."

By the time they reached Silver City, every muscle in Vashti's body ached. The passengers grinned at her as they left the coach.

"Thanks, young fella," one of them said.

"You're welcome." She kept her hat on as Bill drove the coach around to where the liveryman would unharness the team.

As she climbed down again, she heard the man say to Bill, "You've got a new messenger."

"That's right." Bill came around to her side of the coach. "All right, George, let's get over to the hotel."

Vashti quietly walked alongside Bill, carrying the small canvas bag she'd brought.

"I generally share a room with the shotgun rider," Bill said as they reached the steps of the Idaho Hotel.

She paused with one foot on the bottom step. "Mr. Bane said to get a separate room."

"He paying for it?"

"I reckon."

Bill shook his head. "He won't want to keep doing that."

"Well, he was in a bind today."

"So this is a onetime thing for you?"

She raised her chin and met his gaze just below her hat brim. "No, sir. I want to learn to drive and do this regular, like I told you."

"Then you need to think about your bunking arrangements. Folks will think it's odd if you have a separate room. And that Griff pays for it, or pays you enough for you to do it. People will think about that."

"What do you think I should do?"

Bill lifted his hat and scratched his head. "Don't know. There's a widow woman over on Placer Street. Maybe if you told her who you are, she'd let you board with her whenever you come up here."

"Then wouldn't folks wonder why the widow took in a boy as her boarder?"

"Maybe so." Bill spit off to the side of the steps. "You got any ideas?"

"Well, I'm not sleeping in the same room with you."

He pulled back, frowning. "Didn't mean to suggest you should."

"Then let's get in there and ask for two rooms."

He threw his hands in the air, managing to keep hold of his whip as he did so. "Fine with me, Georgie. Come on."

★ CHAPTER 7 ★

Griffin kept in his anger all the way to the hotel. What right did this upstart boy have to tell him what he was and wasn't going to do? Evelyn had sent him here to get straightened out. Well, Griffin didn't know much about parenting, and he'd be the first to admit it. But he knew about hard work. Hard labor had made a man of him, and he figured it could do the same for Justin. But what if the boy wouldn't work? He couldn't force him to do it.

He had a mind to wire Evelyn and tell her he was sending the boy back. But that wouldn't solve any of the problems that had traveled across the country with his nephew. He'd have to give it some thought. Calm down, that was it. Keep from getting mad and saying things he'd regret later.

"When did you eat last?" he asked as he pushed open the door to the Pacifica Hotel.

"I had breakfast."

"Breakfast? What about dinner?"

Justin shrugged. "Some folks bought dinner where we stopped last."

"What? You didn't have any money?" Griffin eyed him closely.

The boy shrugged and squinted his eyes.

"Well, we're going to have us a whopping big supper, I'll tell you that." Griffin tromped to the desk. "We'd like a room, my nephew and me."

"Yes, sir." The clerk turned the guest registry toward him. "Sign here, please. That'll be a dollar."

"Thank you. And we'd like supper as soon as possible."

"Our dining room opens at four thirty for early diners."

"Can't get nothing now?"

"No, sir. Unless you go into the bar, but your nephew looks a bit young for that. If the marshal came along while you were in there, I couldn't guarantee you wouldn't face charges."

Griffin looked over at Justin. "How old are you?"

Justin hesitated. "Seventeen?"

"I doubt it."

The boy hung his head and muttered, "Fifteen and a half."

"Right. We'll go down the street and find a place where we can get something to tide us over till supper. Let's go put our kit in the room first."

They found a boardinghouse down the street, and the proprietor was willing to heat up some leftovers for them. A bowl of beef stew and a brace of biscuits went down quickly. Griffin considered ordering a refill, but decided it would benefit the boy more to have a small meal now and another later, rather than to stuff himself.

"How about apple pandowdy?" the woman who had served them asked.

"Surely." Griffin looked over at Justin. "You could do with a dish of that, couldn't you?"

"I guess."

Griffin scowled. "That's no way to answer. You say, 'Yes, sir.'"

"All right, yes, sir. I'd like coffee with it, if it's all the same to you."

Shouldn't boys drink milk? Griff tried to remember back when he was fifteen on the farm. He'd drunk a lot of milk. But somewhere in there, he'd started drinking coffee with his father, too. "All right." He looked up at the woman. "Another cup of coffee, please."

When she'd gone, Justin said, "How far is it to Fergus?"

"About forty miles. We'll get there tomorrow afternoon."

"Ma said you've got a smithy and a livery stable."

"Yes, and this past year I've been running the branch line for the stagecoach company. Guess I didn't tell your mother about that." He ought to write to Evelyn more often, but he seldom had time to sit down and craft a letter.

Justin's chin came up a notch. "Are you rich?"

Griffin laughed heartily. "That's a good one, son."

The boy's face clouded. "You're not my pa. In case you didn't hear, my pa's dead."

"Yes, I heard. I'm sorry about that."

"Well, just so's you know, I don't plan to be your boy."

Griffin studied him for a long moment. About the time he'd decided silence was the prudent thing, the woman came back with their dessert and coffee.

Maybe he was doing his nephew a disservice by feeding him. Maybe he'd ought to invoke that Scripture verse Pastor Benton mentioned a few weeks back—the one about people who didn't work not eating. He'd give that some thought.

"I've got a few errands to do before supper." He lifted his thick china mug and sipped the coffee. It was much better than what he'd gotten at the depot. And better than what he made in the old tin pot he kept on the shelf near the forge. His always tasted a little burnt.

"I can amuse myself while you're at it," Justin said.

That didn't seem right in Griff's mind. He recalled Evelyn's words about the boy getting in with the wrong friends. *"He comes and goes as he pleases. I don't like to mention it, but I fear he stole some money from my reticule last week. Not only that, but he's taken up smoking."*

Just recalling those lines made Griff's nose wrinkle. He hadn't smelled any tobacco on the boy, but then, Justin wouldn't likely smoke on the stagecoach with other passengers present. And he appeared to have arrived broke. But if he wasn't above stealing, he might get himself into trouble if Griff turned him loose in Boise. Yep, a young fellow like Justin could find a heap of trouble in this half-grown, half-tamed town.

"You stay with me." He took a gulp of coffee.

"What?" The boy obviously took the command as an insult.

"I said, you come around with me. See what I do. I'm going to do a little livestock shopping. We could use an extra team of six, and I need another riding horse or two for the livery trade. After that, I'll go around to the Wells Fargo office again and see if the division agent is back. I need to talk to him about some stagecoach business."

"I don't want to stand around while you do all that."

"What would you do?"

The line of Justin's mouth hardened. "Explore."

"Oh yes, I can just envision that. You stay with me." Griff took another sip.

Justin cautiously slurped his coffee. He didn't make a face or ask for sugar. Maybe he'd been drinking coffee for a while, though Griff couldn't imagine Evelyn allowing it. Of course, he had no idea how Jacob Frye had raised his children; didn't know Jacob at all, for that matter. Griff tackled his apple pandowdy.

"Your pa let you drink coffee all the time?" he asked when he'd scraped out the last bite.

"Nope."

Griff drained his cup and pushed his chair back. "Come on. Let's get over to the stockyard."

The ride down from Silver City went twice as fast as the long pull uphill had gone. Vashti clung to the edge of the seat at least two-thirds of the way. Sometimes Bill drove faster than she'd have thought prudent, but on some of the slopes, it would be impossible to make the mules walk. By the time the road flattened out some, her hands ached from gripping the seat and the shotgun. Despite the warm sunshine, she could feel the tang of winter in the mountain breeze.

"Hey, young George, you done all right this trip," Bill said with a lopsided grin.

"How long till we get home?"

"Another hour."

Vashti nodded. They had no passengers on the return trip, but the heavy treasure box was always on her mind. That cargo had to make it safely to Fergus, and someone else would take it on to Boise.

"Think Mr. Bane will let me do it again?"

"No idea. But if he asks me, I'll tell him you did good."

"Thanks." She lifted her hat and let the sun shine on her head for a moment. It was warmer down here than it had been up at Silver.

She shot a glance at Bill. "What are you laughing about?"

"Don't ever do that when there's men about. No way they'd think you was a boy when they saw that pile of red hair."

"My hair is not red," she said with precision and dignity.

"That right?"

"It's auburn."

"Ha." Bill drove on for a bit, still smiling. "How'd you come to be with Bitsy, anyhow?"

Vashti hesitated. No one in Fergus knew her story. Not even Bitsy and Goldie, her two closest friends.

After about half a minute, Bill looked over at her. "You don't need to tell me. I just thought. . .well, you know. You could have gotten some other job besides working in saloons."

"You don't know anything about it."

"That's right, I don't."

Her joy in the sunlight, the breeze, the trotting mules, and the creaking coach crumbled. Her stomach began to ache. They came to another steep hill, and Bill let the mules extend their trot but kept the reins taut so they wouldn't break into a run and go out of control. Vashti clapped her hat on. They flew down the grade, with her clenching the edge of the seat once more and bracing with her feet.

When they slowed to a businesslike trot, she said, "My folks died when I was eleven."

"Didn't know that."

She nodded.

"Didn't you have no kin?"

"I did." She didn't like thinking about those times. For a good many years, she'd tried to forget.

"Guess they didn't treat you right."

"Something like that."

They rode in silence for another mile.

"We're almost to town." Bill leaned down and reached under the seat for his horn.

"Is this where I plug my ears?"

"You'd better not. If you do, it'll mean you're not holding on to that shotgun."

Up ahead, she glimpsed the roofline of the Spur & Saddle. Beyond it, the steeple of the new church pierced the achingly blue sky.

Bill put the horn to his lips.

She'd have to go back to see Libby at the emporium. Next time, she'd have some cotton wool in her pocket to stuff in her ears when they approached a stop.

The mules broke into a canter as the blast of the horn rang out. They charged into town in a flurry of dust. Vashti wished Griffin could see them, but he wasn't due back for another four hours at least.

"How we going to open the safe?" She turned to Bill, but he didn't seem flustered.

"Miz Adams says we can put it in hers until Griff gets back."

"Oh." Vashti looked ahead to where they would stop and unload the strongbox. There on the boardwalk in front of the Wells Fargo office and stretching up the street before the emporium almost as far as the post office, waving and calling congratulations, stood the members of the Ladies' Shooting Club of Fergus.

"I thought we were going to take the stage to Fergus." Justin scowled as he eyed the mule his uncle expected him to mount.

Just like a kid. They wanted change and excitement, but when it came along as someone else's idea, they balked. Speaking of mules...

"We were. But I need this string, so I bought it, and I don't know another way to get 'em home. So get in the saddle and let's move."

The boy had no idea that he had it easy. Griffin rode the one horse he'd purchased—he'd considered letting Justin take it, but if anything went wrong, he had to be able to get around quickly. Besides, this was the horse he'd chosen for Hiram to give his bride as a wedding present. The ten-year-old palomino gelding looked flashy, but he was settled and well behaved. Libby could handle him with no problems.

Griffin would ride the palomino and lead along the string of three more mules he'd bought. Six new mules would have been better, but he'd settle for four. These looked healthy and strong, and the seller had guaranteed they'd pull a coach. Griffin had already strapped Justin's satchel to one of them and his own small pack to another. The sun was up, and the day was a-wasting.

"Come on," Griffin said. "Mount up."

Justin held the mule's reins and turned to face the saddle. He wiggled this way and that and finally raised his left foot to the stirrup. Griffin almost called out to him but held back. Was the boy really as green as he seemed? He'd lived in the city. Maybe he hadn't ridden much.

When he landed in the saddle with a thud, the mule stood still and blew out a breath as though resigned to a tedious day. Justin stared down at the reins in his hand as if he knew something wasn't quite right, but he couldn't pinpoint the problem. He separated the reins and put one in his right hand.

Griffin adjusted his hat and said as calmly as he could, "You need to get the off rein on the off side. Lean forward and run it under his neck. Grab it with your other hand."

Justin sat still for a moment, like an equestrian statue, but Griffin had never seen a general cast in bronze on a mule before.

After a good half minute, Justin leaned forward along the mule's neck and fumbled with the lines under the animal's throat latch. It was all Griffin could do not to ride over, grab one rein, and pass it to the correct side. Instead he looked toward the distant hills. He counted silently to ten and then looked back. Justin had dropped the off rein and now leaned over the mule's withers to the right, groping for it. But in doing that, he pulled the mule's head around to the left without meaning to.

"Let up on the near rein," Griffin said.

Justin looked over at him.

"I said, let him have some slack."

Justin dropped the other rein.

Griffin sighed. "Good thing that's not a fresh horse, or he'd be halfway to Nampa, and you'd be eating dust." He walked his new horse over, and the other three mules went with him. He angled the horse so that he could get close to Justin's mule without jostling it. With a swoop of his long arm, he caught the near rein and held it up for the boy. "Hold on to that loosely, and bend over the other side and get the off rein."

Finally Justin had both reins again, one on each side of the mule's neck.

"All right, let's move." Griffin headed his horse toward the road. He looked over his shoulder to make certain Justin followed.

Although the boy continued to hold the reins so slack they looped down below the mule's neck, the mule seemed content to fall in with the others and keep pace. It was going to be a lengthy process to teach his nephew to ride well—but the owner of a livery stable couldn't allow his kin to be so ignorant about animals. Of course, if Justin couldn't stay in the saddle without a struggle, he'd be unlikely to ride off and get himself into trouble. Perhaps there were advantages to not teaching him to ride.

The boy's sour expression stayed in place for the first mile or two. Griff ignored it and set a steady pace, jogging along. It was as good as he could expect when leading three mules. Justin kept his seat, though he jarred up and down in the saddle. That boy was going to be sore come tomorrow.

Finally Griffin called out, "The trail gets narrow up ahead. You go ahead of me."

Justin looked ahead and then back to him. "What if there's outlaws in those rocks?"

Griffin patted his sidearm. Since he'd ridden to Boise on the stage, he hadn't packed a long gun, but he had worn his pistol. He'd had the same thought as Justin, but he wasn't about to tell the boy that.

"Reckon there won't be. If there are, I've got my Colt, and it won't be much longer until the stage comes along behind us."

Justin hesitated, his eyes squinted into slits. After a moment, he gritted his teeth and turned forward. "Come on, mule. Get up!"

Griffin smiled. That was progress.

Vashti entered the emporium, carefully holding her basket level. In it, she carried four of Augie Moore's famous cinnamon buns wrapped in clean napkins—two for Griffin and two for his nephew. They'd be hungry when they got off the stagecoach from Boise. She intended to wait at the office and greet them when the stage came in, but first she had business to tend to with Libby Adams.

"Good afternoon, Vashti," Libby called from the hardware section of the store. "Don't you look pretty!"

"Thank you, ma'am." Vashti had taken special care in her grooming after she and Bill brought the stage in from Silver City late that morning. She'd bathed and arranged her hair in feminine waves about her face. Then she'd put on her most conservative dress. Even so, when she'd mentally compared her image in the gilt-framed mirror to the way Libby and some of her other friends looked, she knew she'd still missed the bull's-eye when it came to dressing like a lady. The hem of her dress was too short, the fabric too gaudy, and the neck too low—though she'd basted a row of lace along the edge.

"I wondered if I could have a moment of your time." Vashti looked about the dim interior of the store. A couple of women shopped among the groceries; Mrs. Walker was engrossed in yard goods, assisted by Florence Nash; and it appeared that Goldie and Libby were sorting out nails and bolts.

"Of course." Libby touched Goldie's shoulder. "Just keep counting each size, dear, and write the totals down as we've been doing." She smiled and walked toward Vashti. Even her workaday outfit was a soft blue dress with black braid and buttons—a gown any lady could wear proudly to church or on a stroll about town. "How may I help you?"

"I didn't mean to interrupt your work."

"Think nothing of it. Goldie and I are taking inventory. I'm selling the emporium to the Hamiltons—that couple who came in on the stage the other day. We're counting all the merchandise so we can give them a list of what they're buying." Libby pushed back a strand of her golden hair.

"That's a big job."

"Yes, but not too bad. I've kept good records. It shouldn't take us more than a couple of days. They can't move here immediately, but we've signed the paperwork. They'll come back in the spring and take over the store." She smiled, and her teeth showed pearly white against her pink lips. Vashti was sure Libby wore discreet cosmetics—never enough to overpower her lovely features. Libby was the most beautiful woman she knew, and she hardly needed enhancements.

Vashti gulped. "Well, ma'am, I wanted to settle up with you on the bill for the clothes you provided for me yesterday, and"—she looked down the aisle toward the yard goods—"well, I wondered if you could help me pick out a pattern for a regular dress."

"A regular. . . Oh, I see." Libby smiled. "The one you have on is very becoming."

"Thank you, but I know it's too short, and the fabric isn't at all suitable for. . .well, for most occasions." Vashti pulled her shoulders back and looked Libby in the eye. "I don't serve drinks anymore, Miz Adams. I want to look like a lady. I want to *be* a lady. Just because I want to drive a stagecoach and Mr. Bane is making me wear pants to do it doesn't mean I shouldn't look nice the rest of the time."

There. She'd said it. She didn't want to look like a boy when she worked and a floozy when she didn't.

Libby stepped toward the counter. "Why don't you set your basket here? I have several patterns that would suit you, but we also have some very nice ready-made dresses. The winter fashions just came in. There's a green woolen dress with a smart overskirt that I considered keeping myself, but it was a bit too short for me. On you, however. . ." She leaned back and considered Vashti's attributes. "Yes, I think it would just skim your ankles. Very practical, if it's not too plain for your taste."

"I'd like to see it."

They walked the length of the store together. The other women looked up. Emmaline Landry, a regular member of the shooting club, called, "Afternoon, Vashti."

"Hello, Miz Landry." What a difference from the way the townspeople used to treat her. Not so long ago, Vashti and the other saloon women used to come to the emporium after hours when none of the regular customers would see them. Now Goldie worked here, and Bitsy and Vashti came to shop whenever it struck their fancy.

Florence left her customer's side and came to join them. "Vashti! You looked so cute in that vest and hat this morning. If I hadn't known you were a girl—"

"Now, Florence," Libby said gently, "Miss Edwards wants to look at some more feminine apparel this afternoon."

"Oh, have you seen the silk and wool shawls that came in? I told Mother she and I both have to have one."

"Yes, one of those might go well with the green woolen dress." Libby paused before a rack of dresses, skirts, and coats. She pulled out the dress in question and held it up for Vashti to see.

"That's. . .that's beautiful, ma'am. How. . .how much?"

Libby flipped the little pasteboard tag that dangled from the cuff of the gathered sleeve. "Three dollars and fifteen cents."

"Try it on, Vashti," Florence said. "I'll bet it will fit you perfectly."

"Is there time before the Silver City stage comes in?" Vashti glanced anxiously toward the front window. "I want to be out front when Mr. Bane gets here with his nephew."

"Perhaps not," Libby said. "You can come back later and try it."

Vashti nodded, disappointed. She wanted to make the best possible impression on Griffin. To her way of thinking, the buns would help, and she would tell him how smoothly everything went on the Silver City run. Bill would confirm what she told him, but she wanted to be the one to tell him first. "I was hoping. . ."

"What were you hoping, my dear?" Libby's smile left no doubt of her affection and empathy for Vashti.

"The last time he saw me, I was decked out like a boy. I wanted him to see me as a woman—a neat, professional woman. But my clothes. . ."

"What about your clothes?" Florence asked.

"They're not like yours and Mrs. Adams's. Not suitable for business. Like when I sell stage tickets." She glanced across the store toward where her friend was still diligently counting screws and nails. "Even Goldie. Since she started working here, she's bought regular clothes, and she looks fine. We were always trying to catch attention in the old days, but now I just want to look *nice*."

Libby smiled and squeezed her arm. "You come back after the stagecoach comes in, and we'll talk."

"Thanks." Vashti started to leave but turned back. "Oh, and I almost forgot. I owe you for the boy clothes. I want to settle up with you for those."

Libby spread her delicate fingers. "Mr. Bane told me to put them on his account."

Vashti opened her mouth. For years she'd turned down men's offers to buy her fancy things—laces and ribbons and silk petticoats—knowing they'd want more than a pretty thank-you in return. Now a man was buying her clothes, but they were thick work boots and a leather vest.

"It's part of his business expense," Libby said quickly.

Vashti gulped and nodded. "All right. I'll come back later."

"Don't forget your basket."

"Thank you!" She grabbed the gathering basket with the buns in it and hurried outside and down the boardwalk to stand before the office door. A man walked across the street from the Fennel House.

"Ticket to Dewey."

Vashti went inside and made out his ticket. She took his money and put it in the cash box Griffin kept in his desk drawer. The man watched her, unblinking, the whole time, and she cringed as she handed him the ticket. If only she were wearing that green dress. She rose and stepped toward the door, wondering what she'd do if he didn't move.

"You're all set for your ride to Dewey, sir. Excuse me."

He stepped back, and she exhaled. She went out again to wait for the stagecoach. Peter Nash came out of the post office. He usually met the Boise coach to claim the town's sack of mail. His presence put Vashti more at ease.

"Hello, Mayor," she called. The traveling man took a few steps down the boardwalk and leaned against the office wall.

"Good afternoon, Miss Edwards. How did your run to Silver City go?"

"Just fine."

Mr. Nash smiled and chatted pleasantly with her. Soon she heard the stage coming. Johnny Conway, the regular driver on the Boise run, didn't blow a horn when he came into town. He just ran the horses like a pack of demented wolves were after them. Griffin didn't like that. Come to think of it, why was Johnny racing the team like that with the boss inside the coach? Vashti peered down the street, trying to see through the cloud of dust that approached with the stage.

Johnny pulled up with his usual showmanship—yelling to the team to whoa and stopping them on a dime—if there'd been a dime lying in the street, that is. Vashti shook her head and scowled at him. He looked down and grinned at her, touching his whip to his hat brim.

"Afternoon, Miss Edwards. Don't you look fine?"

"Where's the boss?" Vashti had already noticed that Lenny Tucker, one of the regular messengers, rode the box with Johnny, and none of the faces she could see through the coach window had her boss's exuberant beard and shaggy head of hair.

"He didn't take the stage back."

"What?" Vashti stepped closer to the coach. Lenny jumped down on the other side and hustled around to open the door. "Where is he?"

"He told the station agent in Boise he was buying some stock for the line and driving it home."

"Oh." Vashti sagged and let out a big sigh. So much for the buns and careful toilette.

"We passed him an hour out of town," Johnny said.

She straightened. "So he'll be here soon?"

"Soon enough."

"Is his nephew with him?"

"Yup."

"What's he like?"

Johnny shrugged. "He's a kid."

Lenny set a sack of mail on the walk. "There you go, Mayor."

"Thanks, Lenny." Mr. Nash hefted the sack and swung it over his shoulder. "I guess a few folks in Fergus will be getting mail today." He ambled off up the street.

Two passengers got out and headed for the Nugget.

"We've got three more sacks of mail to go on to the mining towns," Lenny said.

Vashti looked into the coach and counted the sacks. "All right, go switch out the team."

"All set, Johnny," Lenny said moments later as he climbed back up on the box.

Johnny touched his whip to his hat again and lifted the reins.

Vashti realized she might have time to try on the green dress. She started to the emporium, then remembered the cash box and the ticket money she'd put in it. She couldn't leave any money in the Wells Fargo office unattended. Griffin would skin her alive. She ran inside and took the small amount she had collected and shoved it into her pocket. Then she dashed to the emporium.

Mrs. Adams was talking to the couple who planned to buy the store, but Goldie saw her and strode over to meet her.

"Hey! Florence told me you were coming back to try on that green dress. That would look wonderful on you."

"Thanks. I'm not sure I can afford it. I mean. . .Mr. Bane hasn't paid me yet, and I feel as though I should be the one paying for the boy's clothes, not him."

"Miz Adams thinks it's all right," Goldie said.

"Well, I want to talk to her about that. Because I don't want anyone in town getting the wrong idea."

"I s'pose." Goldie smiled. "Well, I've got hinges to count. I'm trying to be extra careful so's the Hamiltons will want me to keep working for them when they're the owners."

Vashti eyed her friend closely. "I'm sorry, Goldie. I hadn't even thought about how it will affect you if Miz Adams sells the emporium. Do you think you might not have a job anymore?"

"I don't know. Miz Adams said she'll ask them to keep Florence and me on, but it's up to them."

"We can pray about it," Vashti said.

Goldie smiled. "We surely can." She tossed her head. "Isn't it funny? A year or so ago if you'd have said that, I'd have thought you were loco. But I believe that if I lose this job, God will help me find another one."

"Well, you know you won't go hungry. Bitsy and Augie will see to that." Vashti looked down the length of the store. "Think Florence can wait on me?"

"Surely. Just tell her you want to try the dress. And I want to see you in it."

Five minutes later, Vashti stepped timidly from Libby's back room, wearing the green woolen dress. Mr. Hamilton had disappeared, but Libby and Mrs. Hamilton stood near the counter, still talking.

"There you are." Libby stepped toward Vashti. "Come on out here, dear. That looks lovely on you."

"Oh my, yes." Mrs. Hamilton smiled at her as though Vashti were a special customer.

Florence and Goldie left their tasks and came near. A couple of customers browsing the shelves glanced their way, and Vashti began to feel like a sideshow exhibit.

"It is supposed to be this long?"

Libby held up a fold of the skirt. "You could stand to have two or three inches off the hem, but for the most part, that's a good fit."

Vashti liked the way the bodice buttoned up, snug but not too tight, to her throat.

"Come look in the mirror," Florence said.

The customers made no pretense of not gawking at her.

"That's a pretty dress," said a rancher's wife.

"Thank you," Vashti whispered.

Florence led her to the long mirror mounted on the wall between the yard goods and the tinware. When she saw her reflection in the glass, Vashti caught her breath.

"Oh."

"Yes." Florence beamed at her.

I look like one of the regular women. No one would think I'd worked in saloons. Tears burned her eyelids. She'd kept wearing the old dresses because she had nothing else, and she didn't like to ask Bitsy for money when she knew cash was tight at the Spur & Saddle.

"I'll have to see if Mr. Bane pays me today. If he does, I'll come back. If not, I'll just have to see if it's still here when I get some more money."

"I'll see that Mrs. Adams doesn't sell it to anyone else," Florence whispered.

"Oh, I couldn't let you do that."

"Why not? Mrs. Runnels and Mrs. Walker ask her to hold things all the time. And Mrs. Adams says big stores back East do it regularly."

Vashti gulped. She still wasn't certain about the boots, hat, and other clothes she'd received for her role as stagecoach guard.

"I'd better take it off before I muss it." She hurried to the back room, and within five minutes she was back out on the boardwalk in her old satin. She tugged at the skirt, hoping the hemline wasn't too garishly short for daytime in a decent town. The alluring fashions she'd been expected to wear in her former life had never bothered her as much as they did now.

The door to the Wells Fargo office was still closed, but far down the street at the corner by the smithy, she could see a large man riding a horse into town. As he turned the corner toward the livery, she saw plodding behind him a string of three mules, and at the tail end of the procession came another mule with a slight figure on its back.

Griffin was home. She squared her shoulders. Time to face the giant.

★ CHAPTER 8 ★

Mr. Bane?"

Griffin finished fastening the gate to the corral before turning around. He knew who called his name, and he was in no hurry to face Vashti "George" Edwards.

He swung around. "Yeah?"

"Welcome home," she said.

She stood in the back door of the livery, wearing one of those short, shiny dresses that made him feel as though he should look elsewhere. He shot a glance toward the haystack where his nephew had sprawled the moment he climbed stiffly from his saddle. Justin sat up, eyeing Vashti like a cougar watching a plump little prairie dog. Marty leaned on his shovel just inside the dim stable, ogling her, too. Griffin scowled at him, and Marty turned and ambled farther into the barn.

"Can I help you?" Griff yanked his hat off and shot another glance at Justin, who by this time had scrambled to his feet and brushed compulsively at the straw on his clothes.

"I thought you and your nephew would be hungry after your trip, so I brought you a couple of Augie's sweet buns."

Griffin wanted to chase her off, but his belly had been growling for the last two hours, and he'd tasted Augie's sticky, cinnamon-shot buns before. They were not to be turned away lightly.

"That's nice of you."

Justin edged closer.

Griffin cleared his throat. He hadn't considered the way a fifteen-year-old boy would look at Vashti and some of the other girls in town. How in the world was he supposed to steer the boy right when the kid didn't want to be steered?

"Uh. . .this is Justin Frye, my nephew. Justin, that's Miss Edwards, one of my employees."

Justin snatched his hat off and held it over his heart. "It's a pleasure to meet you, miss."

There, now. He could be polite if he took a notion to. But if he'd quit staring at her ankles, Griffin would be happier.

Vashti folded back the napkin that covered the basket. "Would you like these now, or should I leave them inside?"

"Uh. . .reckon we ought to wash first." Griffin thrust his hand out and collared Justin, who already had reached toward the basket. "There's a basin and a bucket of water around the corner. Come on."

He marched Justin around the side of the livery, where a battered tin basin sat on an upended barrel. A bucket of water stood on the ground beside it, and he tipped it up, pouring the basin half full.

"Be my guest."

Justin eyed him with one cocked eyebrow, then plunged his hands into the water. He took them out and accepted the grayish towel Griffin held out to him.

Griffin sloshed his hands through the water and dried them. Maybe Vashti had left the basket and disappeared while they were gone.

"Come on."

"Does she really work for you?" The boy grinned at him.

Griffin felt a knot in his stomach just behind his belt buckle. What was Justin thinking? Nothing good, from the look on his face.

"She sells tickets at the stage office." Griffin marched past him and around the corner. Vashti still stood there with the basket. Marty was forking straw around inside the barn, pretending to be busy but waiting and watching.

"It was mighty nice of you to bring that," Griff said.

"No trouble." She handed him the basket. "I didn't think to put in extra for Mr. Hoffstead."

"Who, Marty?" Griffin peeked into the basket and saw four plump, odiferous buns oozing cinnamon and sugar icing. Men like Marty would kill for something less tempting. "Guess he can have one."

"Miss Edwards, you ought to join us," Justin said with a charming smile Griffin had never seen before on his face.

"Thank you, but those are for you fellows." Vashti smiled back at the boy and cast a tentative glance Griffin's way. "I. . .uh. . .had a couple of things I hoped I could talk over with you, Mr. Bane."

He tried not to scowl when she'd just done something nice, but it seemed Vashti always had a reason beneath the obvious for doing what she did. "I need to get Justin settled at the Fennel House. Maybe you can meet me at my office later?"

"Of course. In an hour?"

"That's fine." Griffin lifted out one of the sugary buns and offered the basket to Justin. Marty stood in the barn doorway, practically drooling. "Come on, Marty. Can't have you starving while we're eating high on the hog."

Vashti laughed as Marty came out of the shadows. "I'll see you later, then."

Justin's gaze followed her every step until she'd walked through the stable and out the front door.

When Griffin entered the office, Vashti leaped up from the chair behind the desk. She moved away from it to the corner nearest the safe, suddenly aware that the boss was in the room and she'd been sitting in his place.

He stopped inside the door and looked her over. Perhaps he was waiting for his eyes to adjust to the dimmer light, but it seemed to her that they narrowed in a rather critical expression.

"All right, what do you want to talk about?"

Not ready for such an abrupt conversation, she said, "Your nephew seems like a nice young man."

"Huh." Griffin walked around the desk and sat down. "He's all right, I guess."

"Did you leave him at the boardinghouse?"

"Yes, the kid was tuckered out after riding all day. Probably sore, too. I don't think he did a lot of riding back in Pennsylvania. He'll probably sleep until suppertime."

Vashti wondered how to ease around to the topic she wanted to discuss. "I believe his father died recently."

"Yes."

"My father's dead, too. You know, taking care of a half-grown kid has its challenges."

"What am I here for?"

She winced at his gruff tone and folded her hands before her. "I wished to speak to you about the Silver City run."

"Oh. How was it?"

"Fine. Everything went fine."

He grunted.

"Bill Stout and I got along fine."

"So everything was fine."

"Yes. Absolutely. And I. . .well, I wanted to ask you about the clothing that Mrs. Adams gave me for the ride."

"What about it? It fit you."

She felt a flush climb up her neck. Why should it bother her that he'd noticed the fit of those boys' trousers, when she'd dressed for years to draw men's eyes to her figure? "Yes, but. . .am I to keep those things?"

He shrugged. "I don't care. I'll pay for them, if that's what you're getting at."

"It's not. What I mean is"—she stepped over in front of the desk—"will I be making another run?"

"Oh." His gaze slid away from her toward the door, the window, the lantern on the shelf—anything but her face. "Well, I don't know. I wasn't planning on it. On the other hand, sometimes it's hard to come up with an extra messenger."

"Or driver?"

He brought his fist down on the desktop with a *whap* that made her jump. "I told you—you can't drive a stagecoach. You're not good enough."

She frowned but managed to keep down the anger building

inside her. "I realize I have a lot to learn. An old hand like Bill could teach me a lot."

"That so?"

"Yes, it's so. And...well, to be honest, after making that ride up to Silver City, I know I couldn't drive that route myself. Not yet. You're right about that."

"I am?" He scowled. "I mean, I know I am, but I'm surprised you'll admit it."

Vashti picked up the ticket book she'd left on the desk that afternoon. "As I said, I know I have a lot to learn." She laid the book down and met his gaze head-on. "All I'm asking is the chance to get that knowledge."

He watched her in silence. At last, he shifted in the chair and crossed his legs at the ankles. "I'm not going to let you practice on the stage teams."

"Didn't ask you to."

"Humph."

They stared at each other for half a minute. Vashti decided it might be a good idea to let him win, and she looked away.

"I also wished to know..." She gulped, suddenly losing confidence. Griffin was a very large man, and sometimes men like him had hair-trigger tempers. She didn't want to vex him. Neither did she want to go back to the Spur & Saddle without her pay. "I wished to know when you would pay me for making the run."

"I pay on Fridays."

"Oh. All right. That's it, then."

"Fine."

"Yes. Fine."

"Bane, you in there?"

Vashti whirled toward the doorway. Ted Hire, the owner of the Nugget Saloon, stood there, sweat beading on his forehead.

Griffin stood. "What do you want, Ted?"

"There's a boy over to my place—says he belongs to you."

Griffin stalked into the Nugget with smoldering fire in his chest.

Justin leaned on the bar, blinking dewy-eyed at Hannah Sue, the blonde Ted had hired a few months back. She wasn't as young or as pretty as some of the saloon girls who had come through Fergus, but she wasn't homely, either, and Griffin knew from experience that she listened well.

Probably Justin was filling her full of tales of how mean his uncle had treated him, while Hannah Sue poured him a drink of—what?— out of a clear bottle.

In three steps, he stood beside Justin and clamped his huge hand over Hannah Sue's on the bottle. "What have we got here?"

Hannah Sue's eyes widened, and she jerked her chin up. Her startled expression slid into a smile. "Well, hi, Griff. I was just making the acquaintance of your nephew. Justin here tells me he arrived in town this afternoon with you. Come all the way from Pennsylvanie, he says."

As she talked, Griffin yanked the bottle away from her so he could read the label.

Sarsaparilla.

He set it down on the bar with a sigh and turned to Justin.

"This ain't no place for a kid."

Justin straightened and thrust his shoulders back. "I ain't no kid. I'm a man now. My ma said so."

"Yeah?"

"Yeah. She wouldn't have sent me all this way by myself if I was a kid."

"That right?" Griffin glared down at him. Justin was nearly a foot shorter than him and weighed about a third as much—hardly more than a sack of feed. "Tell you what, boy: If you were a real man, you'd have stayed home and taken care of your mama and the other kids, instead of worrying her sick."

Justin's jaw clenched. "Miss Hannah Sue knows I'm ready to take a man's place in the world, don't you, ma'am?" He looked at the bar girl, innocent appeal spilling out of his big brown eyes.

"Well now, Justin, I think you could do that, I surely do." Hannah Sue's honeyed drawl soothed the boy a little, and his face relaxed. "But you've got to understand that no matter how mature you are, you have to be a certain age to come into the Nugget. Mr. Hire knows that, and he also knows that if we served you liquor, the sheriff could lock him up and close down his business."

"Even in the West? I thought it was different here."

"Not so different as you might think," Ted said from behind Griffin. "Especially when we've got a sheriff who takes the law seriously."

"That's right," Hannah Sue said. "So he went to get your uncle. Now, he could have gone for the sheriff and got you tossed out and your uncle charged with child neglect or some such tomfoolery, but he's a nice man. So instead of getting you and Mr. Bane in trouble, he just fetched your uncle, and it's up to you to play the man's part. Go on home, and don't come back here until you're older."

Justin's frown had returned. He looked down at the glass on the bar. "But you poured me a drink."

"Honey, that ain't whiskey. Go ahead and drink it if you want. On the house. Then you go on home with Uncle Griff and behave yourself. In a couple of years, I'll see you back in here." She winked at Justin, a little more provocatively than Griff thought seemly, but then, nothing about the Nugget was seemly. "Go on, now."

Justin picked up the glass and sniffed it. He set it down with a thud that slopped sarsaparilla over the edge. His shoulders slumped, and he turned toward the door without another word, shrinking back as he passed Griffin.

"Thanks, Hannah Sue," Griffin said. He knew she and Ted had both stretched it a little about the law. Most folks wouldn't have cared whether or not a fifteen-year-old boy was served liquor in a frontier town. But in Fergus, people had ideas about decency and helping friends, and he figured they'd done it for him as much as for Justin.

"No trouble," Hannah Sue said.

Griffin fished in his pocket and found a lone dime. He handed it to her and nodded at Ted. "Thank you, too. If he comes here again. . ."

"He won't."

Griff allowed that was probably true. He followed Justin out into the thin autumn sunshine. The chill of winter danced in the breeze, and a drink wouldn't have been unwelcome. But with the boy around. . .

Yes, with the boy around, Griffin was going to have to consider his habits carefully.

Justin waited at the bottom of the steps with his hands shoved into his pants pockets.

"Where's your coat?"

"Over to the boardinghouse." Justin's eyes still had the sullen cast.

"Come on. Let's go get it."

"Where are we going after that?"

"You're coming with me to the smithy."

Justin's eyes were slits of brown. "Can't I just stay in my room?"

"Like you did last time I put you there? Come on, I've got four mules to shoe."

★ CHAPTER 9 ★

Dusk hovered over Fergus, reaching long, cold fingers of shadows between the buildings, as Vashti hurried down the street toward the smithy. After the feed store, where the boardwalk ended, she lifted her skirts and quickened her pace. Winter surely was on its way.

The sound of Griffin's hammer told her that he was still at work. It wasn't the loud, musical ring of his rounding hammer on the anvil, but the *tap-tap-tap* of the smaller nailing hammer he used to fasten horses' shoes onto their hooves. As she rounded the corner, he turned the hammer's head toward him and with its claws grabbed the end of a nail protruding from the side of a mule's hoof. He twisted the pointy end off and went around the hoof, repeating the motion five times, then tossed the hammer into the toolbox. Out came another tool, with which he clinched the jagged ends of the nails he'd broken off. Then came the rasp.

Vashti wasn't sure how many more tools he needed to use in the process. Shoeing a horse—or a mule—was a lot lengthier and more complicated than she'd realized. She stepped forward and cleared her throat, but the rhythmic humming of the rasp over the clinches drowned out the noise.

"He don't hear you."

Vashti whirled toward the open smithy. Inside, Justin sat on a barrel close to the forge, no doubt soaking up its warmth.

She nodded to him, and Justin spoke again.

"You got to yell when he's working."

Griffin looked up then, taking in her presence and shooting a glance toward his nephew. He lowered the mule's foot and stood slowly. "Miss Edwards."

"Good evening. Bitsy sent me to invite you and Justin to take dinner at the Spur & Saddle tonight. It's on her and Augie."

"Well, that's right nice of her." Griffin slid the rasp into a special slot on the side of the toolbox. He pulled a bandanna from his pocket and mopped his forehead. Even in this cold air, he was sweating.

"Shall I tell her you'll come?"

Griffin looked toward Justin. "What do you say?"

"Is the food any good?"

Griffin scowled at him. "That's no way to talk!"

The boy shrugged. "Sorry. I just thought the smells at the boardinghouse were pretty good."

Griffin nodded at Vashti. "Tell Bitsy we'll be there after I clean up. And you, boy." He sent Justin another glare. "Can I trust you to go and tell Mrs. Thistle you're eating with me tonight?"

Justin's mouth went pouty. "Yes, sir."

"All right, you go, then. If you're not back by full dark, I'll come after you, and this time I'll bring the sheriff."

His harsh tone took Vashti aback. Then she recalled Ted Hire coming over to fetch Griffin earlier. The episode at the Nugget must not have gone well. She managed to smile at them. "All right. We'll look for you soon at the Spur & Saddle."

Griffin carried his toolbox inside the smithy and set it down near the door, where he always left it. A glance at the forge told him the fire had burned down enough so he could safely leave it. He opened the door to his living quarters to let some of the heat in there.

Walking back through the smithy, he shut the outside door and unhitched the mule he'd shod. The mules he'd purchased looked good, if a little thin. And the palomino—he'd show the horse to Hiram next time he came around. If his friend didn't want it, Griffin could let it out as a livery horse, but he thought Hiram and Libby would both be pleased.

He led the mule around to the corral behind the livery and headed into the barn for a couple of lead ropes. To his surprise, when he came out again Justin was waiting for him.

"Did you get washed?" Griffin growled.

"No, sir."

"Wash your hands and comb your hair." He turned toward the smaller enclosure, beyond the corral where he kept the stage teams. He'd put the palomino out there, along with a colt he'd taken in trade last summer.

"I could lead that spotted horse in for you."

He looked askance at Justin, hardly knowing how to respond to an offer of help. "Whyn't you take Mrs. Adams's palomino? I'll get the colt."

"I thought that was the horse you just bought."

"It is." Griffin opened the gate to the small corral. The palomino walked placidly toward him, and the colt trotted over, swinging his head and snorting. "I bought it for a friend of mine, Hiram Dooley. He's getting married soon, and he asked me to find a nice horse for his fiancée."

"So. . .does the spotted one belong to you?"

"Yup." Griffin clipped a lead rope to the palomino's halter and placed the end in Justin's hands. "Careful, now. Don't let him step on you. Put him in the first stall on the right."

The colt tried to duck past Griffin.

"Hold it, buster." Griffin snagged his halter and pulled his head down. "There we go." He hooked the snap on the end of the rope to a ring in the halter. "All right, mind your manners." He walked on the colt's left, holding back and downward on the rope, forcing the colt to walk beside him. This one had fire.

As he stepped inside the barn, Justin called, "Now what?"

"Hook the chain that's hitched to the wall to his halter and unhook the rope." Griffin took the colt into the stall next to the palomino's. "I'll get them some feed and roll the doors shut."

Justin came out of the stall. "Want me to close the front door?"

"Thanks. That would be good."

By the time he'd fed the two horses, Justin had both big doors closed.

"All right. Now we need to clean up."

"That paint horse sure is pretty," Justin said.

Griffin grunted and eyed the boy in the dim light. "He's too young to ride yet."

"Really? He's big."

"He'll be two in the spring. I'll start training him then. And until I do, I don't want anyone messing with him, you understand?"

"Yes, sir."

Griffin relaxed a little. "Come on." He opened the rear door just far enough to squeeze through, and he and Justin went out. Darkness had fallen, and he shivered in the chilly breeze. "I thought you didn't like horses."

Justin shrugged. "I never been around them much."

"Guess you saw more of that mule than you wanted to today."

Justin let out a short laugh.

"You sore?" Griffin asked.

"Some."

"It'll be worse in the morning." They walked over to the smithy. Griffin jerked his head toward the open door. He hated to let the boy see his disorderly living quarters, but he didn't see a way around it. "Come on, we're heating the outdoors."

Griffin and the boy appeared in the dining room half an hour after Vashti had left them. Both had damp comb marks through their hair, and Griffin had changed his shirt. The hot smell of the forge lingered on him, but Vashti didn't mind it. She smiled broadly as she led them to a table in the corner near the fireplace. In chilly weather, Augie kept the heater stove ticking, but Bitsy still liked to have a fire on the grate for atmosphere. "People feel warmer when they see the logs burning," she said.

Justin stumbled a bit as he pulled out his chair. Vashti figured he wouldn't be so clumsy if he'd quit staring at her. She couldn't wear her shawl while waiting on tables.

"I'll bring you water," she said. "Would you like coffee, Mr. Bane?"

"Lots of it, and strong."

"Yes, sir." She smiled at Justin. "And you, Mr. Frye?"

Justin glanced at his uncle, then back at her. "The same."

"Very good. Our dinner special tonight is roast chicken, but we also have a venison stew simmering."

"Bring me some of both," Griffin said. "And plenty of biscuits."

Vashti tucked in her smile and turned her attention to the boy. "And you, sir?"

"I'll have the chicken, please. And some of those biscuits."

"I'll bring a basketful."

She walked briskly to the kitchen. Bitsy was picking up two full chicken plates for Oscar and Bertha Runnels.

"Mr. Bane and his nephew are here," Vashti said.

"Oh good. I can't wait to see the boy." Bitsy lifted her tray and brushed past her with her taffeta skirts swishing.

"I'll need a basketful of biscuits for those two," Vashti said to Augie. "Hope you and Bitsy don't go broke from your charitable efforts."

"Giving away samples is good for business. If the boy likes my cookin', Griff will have him over here at least once a week. Bachelors don't want to have to cook for kids."

Vashti chuckled. "That's true. But he is putting Justin up at the Fennel House."

"Oh." Augie's bald head glistened in the lamplight as he reached to stir the big iron kettle on the stove. "Well, maybe they'll still come around now and again."

"Let's hope so. Two chicken dinners and one stew."

"Who's the third person?"

"Griffin."

Augie laughed. "He always did like my venison stew."

A few more customers drifted in, and Vashti stayed busy for several minutes. When she got back to Griffin and Justin, both had cleaned their plates.

"That was good food," Griffin said.

"Yes'm." Justin looked up at her with a shy smile. "Did you cook it?"

Vashti laughed. "No, not me. That would be Mr. Moore. He's the finest cook in Fergus."

"A man?" The boy's face stretched to new lengths.

Griffin let out a bellow of laughter. "You've never seen Augie, kid, or you wouldn't say that. He could make hash out of you with one hand."

"Would you like dessert?" Vashti asked Justin. "Mr. Moore makes delicious cakes and pies, too. You had one of his cinnamon buns earlier today."

"Two," Griffin said.

She flashed him a smile. So the boss had given one to Marty and eaten one himself and let the boy have the other two. Somehow, that warmed her feelings toward Griffin.

"What have you got for pies?" Justin asked.

She pointed to the bar that Hiram Dooley had remodeled into an efficient serving counter. "Why don't you step over and see for yourself? There're several varieties." She raised her eyebrows at Griffin.

"Just bring me apple pie with a hunk of cheese," he said. "And more coffee."

Justin pushed back his chair. "Uh, will you please excuse me, Uncle Griff?"

"To pick out your pie? Why, surely."

The boy walked away, and Vashti said softly, "Well now, he's got manners."

"Yes, when he chooses to dust them off."

She hesitated a moment then said, "You know, leaving home at that age isn't easy. Chances are, he feels as though his mother didn't want him around anymore."

Griffin's bushy eyebrows drew together. "I can understand why. I had him here ten minutes and had to go pull him out of a saloon."

"I can see he was a handful for her."

"That's putting it mildly." Griffin watched Justin as he walked slowly along the counter, eyeing each confection. "Truth is, my sister was a little scared of him and of his friends, I think. The trouble they might bring on her and the other young'uns."

Vashti nodded. "You can be a good influence in his life, Griffin Bane."

Griff sighed. "I'm beginning to think he'll be a bad one on me."

She chuckled. "I'll get that pie and coffee for you."

"Wait a sec."

"Yes?"

He shot another glance at Justin. "You've mentioned before that you had a tough time of it as a youngster. Someday, maybe you'll tell me about that."

Vashti looked at him for a long moment. "You'd really want to hear?"

"I'm starting to think I should listen to people who know about kids. What it's like to be a kid." He shrugged in apology. "Seems like a long time ago, and. . .well, he's not like I was."

She nodded, though she thought, *Maybe more like you than you realize.* Justin headed back their way, carrying a plate with two pieces of pie on it. "We'll sit down sometime. But not tonight. You look exhausted, and I think you need to make sure Justin's safe for the night."

Griffin shook his head. "I can't watch him every minute."

"No, but you've gotten him banned from the worst place in town, and there's no stagecoach out until tomorrow. Unless he steals a horse, he's stuck here."

"I've thought of that, and I wouldn't put it past him."

She hurried away to get Griffin's dessert and coffee. Doc Kincaid and the Hamiltons had come in while she talked, and Bitsy threw her a glance begging for help. Vashti took Griffin a generous slice of pie with cheese on the side and refilled his coffee, and then she turned to the Hamiltons' table.

"Sorry to keep you waiting, folks. We have a delicious roast chicken dinner tonight and a savory venison stew."

"Oh, the stew sounds good," said Mr. Hamilton. "What'll you have, dear?"

Vashti glanced back at Griffin's table. His eyelids drooped as he reached for his coffee mug, but he seemed to be listening as Justin talked with more animation than she'd seen so far on the boy's face.

Mrs. Hamilton said, "I believe I'll try that stew as well."

Vashti smiled at them. "Very good. Would you like coffee?"

"Could you bring us a pot of tea?" Mrs. Hamilton asked, cringing almost as though she were asking for something very rare and difficult to produce.

"Of course. I'll be just a moment." As she turned away, Vashti looked once more at Griffin. He was still listening to his nephew, but a tolerant smile lit his face.

That's the way you ought to look all the time, she thought. *Griffin Bane, you could be a very handsome man.*

★ CHAPTER 10 ★

Vashti stayed on her feet, serving the customers long after Griffin and Justin left the Spur & Saddle. About seven thirty, Goldie came in from the kitchen. Though she'd spent the entire day working at the emporium, she smiled at the diners and sat down before the piano. Soon lilting music filled the restaurant. Mr. Hamilton gave her fifty cents to play "Jeanie with the Light Brown Hair." Next, Dr. Kincaid requested "Silver Threads among the Gold." After several more numbers, Goldie covered the keyboard and accepted the people's applause with a becoming blush.

Vashti had taken away all the dirty dishes but the coffee cups by then, and the diners soon ambled home. As she cleared off the last table, Goldie came to help her.

"You go on up to bed," Vashti said. "I know you're tired."

"The people are so nice now." Goldie's eyes reflected the light of the lamps and the candle chandelier. "In the old days, the cowboys wanted me to play my fingers to the bone, but they never applauded like that—like they respected me, I mean."

Vashti gave her a hug. "You deserve that respect. And a good night's sleep. Go on—Bitsy and I will get these done in no time."

As Goldie drifted up the staircase, Vashti looked up in surprise to see Griffin again coming through the doorway.

"Mr. Bane!"

"I guess you're closing."

"Well. . .the coffeepot's still on the stove."

"Would you join me for a cup?"

Vashti hesitated, her pulse tripping. "Let me just take these to the kitchen. I'll be right back."

Bitsy had already washed most of the dishes, and Augie was drying them and stacking them on the shelves.

"This is the last of them." Vashti held out a pile of cups and saucers.

Bitsy took them and plunged them into her pan of sudsy water.

"Uh. . .Mr. Bane came back."

"Oh?" Bitsy frowned. "What does he want?"

"Coffee. And conversation, I guess. He asked me to sit with him. Earlier he said he'd like to talk to me about Justin."

"Can't see any harm in that." Bitsy looked over at Augie. "What do you think?"

"Well, I dunno. Has Griff got designs on our adopted daughter?"

Bitsy flicked some soapsuds at him. "The day Griffin Bane falls in love is the day somebody finds the Blue Bucket Mine."

Augie laughed at her reference to the legend of a "lost" gold mine. "Stranger things have happened."

"That's right. You finally convinced me to marry you, didn't you?"

"Yup. Mighty strange, but I'm tickled pink." Augie squeezed her.

Vashti laughed. "I'm pretty sure it's not romance Mr. Bane has in mind. The boy's giving him headaches, and he's only been here half a day."

"Go on, girl," Bitsy said. "Just don't let him stay too late."

Vashti ran a hand over her hair, wondering if it looked all stringy and scraggly. She hadn't noticed her reflection in the big mirror for hours. What if Griffin really was interested in her? Would that be so bad? More likely, he'd tell her again why she couldn't hold a man's job and ask for more advice on dealing with Justin. Her past had taught her not to count on good things happening out of the blue. She took off her apron and went back to the dining room, a bit wary.

Griffin stood by the woodstove, pouring himself a big mug full of coffee.

"Hope you don't mind."

"No, that's fine." Vashti walked over and sat down at the table nearest the stove, where Griffin and Justin had sat earlier. "We put the pies away, but I could get you a piece."

"That's all right. I ate plenty."

"Where's Justin?"

"In bed at the Fennel House. I made sure he was sleeping this time."

"First night in a strange bed. You sure?"

"Oh yeah. I tickled his foot to see if he was faking it. What you said earlier about him stealing a horse made me think. He might do that—just take one from the livery—if he doesn't like it here."

"Do you want him to like it here?"

Griffin winced. "Not sure." He sipped his coffee and set the mug down. "I guess what I really want is for him to apologize to his mama and go home and take care of her like a man should."

"What are the chances?"

"Slim to none."

Vashti nodded. "That's about the way I saw it. That boy's got a lot of growing up to do."

"Well, I'm not sure I know how to help him do it."

"Put him to work, but not too hard. Let him see that he can do things—make things. Like you do."

"I don't know as I can get him to work around the smithy."

"Did when you were his age?"

"Yes, but I was interested in it. I'd go by the smithy in our town after school and watch old Jack Hogan shoeing horses. And when he'd put a piece of metal in the fire and bring it out all yellow-hot and glowing and hammer it into a hinge or a spoon or something else useful, well, that seemed like magic to me." He picked up his mug. "But Justin's got no such inclination."

"Does he like horses?"

"I would have said not overly—he acted a little scared of riding at first. But he did perk up when he saw that yearling colt I've got in my barn."

"Hmm."

"He rides like a sack of flour in the saddle."

"Ouch. And he rode all the way from Boise?"

"Yeah. Maybe that was a poor decision on my part. We could have stayed over at Nampa or Reynolds, or I could have sent him on in the coach. But think how much mischief he could have gotten into until I got here."

"True. He'll get over the sore muscles in a few days." She thought about Griffin's situation. "There ought to be lots of things a boy could do around your place. Lots more than a girl can. And if he likes horses. . ."

"Yeah. If I give him a few pointers and give him decent mounts, he might get to be a good rider. The thing is, he's here, and I'm responsible for him. I couldn't just turn him loose, even if I felt like it. He's too young to take care of himself."

"Didn't you take care of yourself at his age?"

"Yes, but Justin—he doesn't seem to have any common sense, and he wants to butt heads with life, not learn how to make things work for him."

Vashti smiled ruefully. "Sounds like me in some ways."

Griffin focused on her with a pensive frown. "I've been wondering about you. How you got to be on your own so young. Didn't you have anyone to take care of you?"

She shook her head. "I was eleven when my folks died."

"What'd you do then?"

"Went to live with some kinfolk—my mother's cousin. I called her Aunt Mary. But I—I couldn't stay there."

"Why not?"

She hesitated, wondering how much to spill. "Mostly because of Uncle Joshua."

Griffin was quiet for a moment, then took a sip of his coffee. He set the mug down and met her gaze. "I see."

"Do you? I told Aunt Mary when he bothered me, but she didn't believe me. Said I was a bad girl for making up such tales. I ran away after less than a year. Headed west." She gave a little chuckle. "I thought maybe I could find a place where I'd fit in and could get a job of some sort. I found out quick enough there aren't any jobs for twelve-year-old girls."

"That's awful young to be on your own, boy or girl." Griffin's voice had taken on a gentle tone, and his eyes were velvety like an elk's.

"Yes. Far too young." Vashti stood, suddenly unable to sit under his scrutiny. "I believe I'll have some coffee, too." She went to the stove and took her time pouring a cupful. When she sat down again, she took a sip. Too hot and too strong. She blew on the surface of the dark liquid.

"You want to tell me the rest? How you got here?"

She considered whether she wanted to or not. "It was a long journey. But looking back, I believe the Lord brought me here."

He nodded slowly. "I can understand that. I reckon He wanted me here, too, at a time when I didn't know I needed Him. And now the boy..."

"Yes." Vashti thought about the path they had all followed to Fergus. "I know Justin wasn't in the same situation I was, but I believe you can help him avoid going down a dark road."

"How? What can I do to keep him out of trouble?"

"Take care of him. Teach him to do honest work. And maybe, sooner or later, you'll learn to love him. Because he is your kin."

Griffin lowered his head. "I would have kept him with me at my place, but it's a wreck. I figured he'd be better off at the Fennel House. I mean, I've got that one little room behind the smithy, and it's hardly as big as a tobacco tin. Can't turn around without bumping something. And...well, it's not the cleanest, either. I admit I've never been much at housework."

"You could stay with him at the boardinghouse."

He pressed his lips together for a moment. "That'd cost a lot. Winter's coming—my slack time."

"Well, maybe you'll think of some other arrangements. But you need to show the boy that you care about him."

"So far, that's been kind of hard." Griffin squinted at her and squirmed a little in the chair.

"Hard to like a boy who's not likable?"

"I guess I thought he'd be glad to see me. That he'd want to live out here and learn what I do and...well, that he'd take to the West. And to me."

"He still might."

Griffin cleared his throat. "Look, it won't be long before we get snow in the mountains. The road to Silver City will close. They used to keep it broken all winter, but since the bigger mines shut down. . ."

She nodded.

"The road to Boise might stay open another month, if we're lucky. But I still can't let you drive."

"I understand, Mr. Bane. It's still a dream of mine, but I know I'm not ready."

"Look, I. . .maybe I can let you do the Boise run—as far as Nampa, that is—as a shotgun messenger for the next couple of weeks. You'd ride with Johnny Conway. I could put Ned Harmon on with Bill until the Silver City road closes."

She nodded, trying not to show her excitement. She'd rather ride with steady old Bill Stout than with Johnny Conway, but at this point, she'd take whatever run Griffin would give her.

"Thank you. I promise you I'll defend the stage as well as any man."

"All right. It's a twice-a-week run this time of year, and I can only promise you two weeks. After that, it depends on the weather, because Ned's one of my regular men, and if he can't do the run to Silver, I'll give him whatever's open to keep him working as long as I can. He's been faithful to me. But you can be ready Monday, and if nothing drastic happens, you can ride with Johnny."

Vashti scarcely heard anything after he said, "All right." The joy that welled up in her threatened to burst out in a wild laugh. She wanted to hug him and kiss him and shout to Bitsy and Augie that he'd hired her. Instead, she clamped her teeth together and smiled serenely. "Thank you."

★ CHAPTER 11 ★

Johnny Conway looked Vashti up and down as she climbed up to the box to sit beside him. When she sat down, he spat tobacco juice off the side of the stagecoach and said, "You look better in your fancy dresses, darlin'."

"Don't call me that, and don't talk about me bein' a girl."

"Oh, pardon me." Johnny looked ahead to where Griff and Marty were holding the leaders' bridles and nodded. "Get up now!"

The holders released the team, and they sprang forward, breaking into their road trot. Vashti was a little surprised that Johnny didn't make the horses canter to show off in front of the people watching from the sidewalk.

They rolled up Main Street and out of town, and she settled back, watching the road ahead and cradling the shotgun in her arms. "Mr. Bane said you might give me some driving tips."

"Ha! Why should I teach you to drive? Next you'll be wantin' my job."

"Mr. Bane says he has trouble keeping steady drivers."

"I'm steady," Johnny said.

"Didn't say you wasn't."

"Humph."

They rode in silence for a good hour. The coach swayed along. The horses' hooves clopped on the packed road. They passed the ranches to the north of Fergus and came down out of the mountains to rolling hills. Gradually the air warmed a bit, and Vashti peeled her gloves off. They passed a horseman headed toward Fergus—one of the cowboys from the Landry ranch. Vashti and Johnny waved. The cowpoke waved back then turned his head to follow Vashti with a perplexed stare.

Johnny laughed. "He's wondering who my new guard is."

"Well, you'd best keep it quiet. Don't go telling people when you unwind tonight with a whiskey or two."

"Me? I ain't no blabbermouth."

"Humph," said Vashti, and he scowled at her.

"You sure look better in a dress."

"You said that. And I said—" She broke off, catching the glint of sun on metal ahead, among the rocks to the left of the road. "What's that?"

"What?"

"In those rocks."

Johnny peered ahead. "I don't see anything."

Ten seconds later, they'd come within a hundred feet of the rocks. A man jumped from behind the biggest boulder and stood in the middle of the road, aiming a rifle at them.

"Hang on!" Johnny laid the whip on. "Yee-haw!"

The horses leaped forward, tearing toward the gunman. Vashti had to cling to the edge of the seat to keep her perch.

"How'm I supposed to aim?" she screamed against the wind of their speed.

"Just sit tight."

At the last possible moment, the man let off a round and leaped aside. Vashti's heart pounded so hard she thought it would burst. When she looked back, she couldn't see the man. Johnny drove on for another half mile at full speed, then began to talk the horses down until they fell once more into their road trot, snorting and shaking their heads.

Vashti pulled in a deep breath and eyed him askance. "You seen that fella before?"

"Uh-huh. He tried it three or four times last summer. He's so stupid, he tries to get you coming downhill. Anyone with half a brain would know to stop the coach when the horses are going uphill so they're already going slow and can't get into a run."

"Is he dim-witted?"

"Don't know. We never stuck around long enough to find out. The first time, Bill was driving. Got his hat shot off. But Bill was carrying treasure to Boise, and he told me he just made up his mind he wouldn't stop for one outlaw, not no-how. Ever since then, if we see him, we just try to run him down."

"What if he hits one of you?"

"Hasn't yet."

Vashti huffed out a breath and stared at him. "If you hadn't lashed up the horses like that, I could've got a shot off. Put an end to his nonsense."

Johnny shrugged. "Remind me next time."

"Oh sure."

He laughed. "One of these days, he won't move fast enough, and I'll roll the coach right over his weaselly little carcass."

"Who is he, anyway? Does he live around here?"

"I dunno. He just showed up one day last June, and ever since, we watch for him."

"And he always jumps you going downhill?"

"Naw, he tried it once the other way, but Ned emptied his shotgun at him and grabbed his revolver. Thought he might have got him with a couple of pellets. The robber ran into the rocks. That was the last time I've seen him until now. But it's the same fella."

Vashti puzzled over that. "Why doesn't the sheriff come out here and scour those rocks and arrest him?"

"He tried, but the popinjay wasn't there. He's showed up on a couple different stretches of road, too."

"Well, he must live somewhere."

Johnny shook his head. "We've asked the tenders at every station, and nobody around here knows who he is. Probably just some drifter who's hiding out. Once it gets real cold, he'll probably clear out."

Vashti thought about that for the next mile, while she searched the roadside for movement that didn't belong. At last she said, "One of us could have been killed."

"Yup." Johnny grinned at her. "If'n you get shot, you want to be laid out in them clothes, or in your swishy dress?"

Griffin and Justin rode side by side toward the Chapman ranch on Wednesday morning. Justin still looked ill at ease in the saddle, but he didn't complain the way he did when he'd had to ride a mule all the way from Nampa. Griff had picked a gentle little chestnut gelding for him out of his string. "Red" was a horse he could rent out to a tinhorn and not worry about the rider breaking his neck.

Of course, Justin bounced all over the saddle.

"Sit yourself down, boy," Griffin called.

"I'm trying."

Griff shook his head. "Whoa. Here, pull up for a minute. Whoa, Red."

Justin hauled back on the reins, and they stopped. Griff's horse, Pepper, stopped next to Red.

Griffin adjusted his hat and studied the boy's posture. "Look, when you trot, you've got to set yourself in that saddle like you weigh a thousand pounds."

Justin grimaced. "How do I do that?"

"Think about how heavy you are. You weigh a ton."

"I thought you said a thousand pounds. That's half a ton."

"All right, then, half a ton. You weigh a lot. And while you set there, every ounce of you is pressing down on your feet."

"My feet?" Justin frowned at him.

"That's right. Don't keep all the weight on the horse's back. Put it down on your feet. Five hundred pounds on each foot. Heavy as lead. Heavier."

Justin's brow furrowed as he scowled toward Red's ears. He rocked forward a little so that he was almost standing in the stirrups.

"That's it," Griff said. "When Red picks up his trot, you think about that. Weight pushing down into your boots. You're so heavy you'll probably break the stirrup leathers before we get to the sheriff's house."

"How come we got to help the sheriff, anyway?" Justin's petulant words made Griff want to slap him, box him up, and ship him back to Pennsylvania.

"Because he's a friend. Ethan's as good a friend as you can get, and don't you forget it."

"Never had no use for lawmen," Justin said.

"Well, that's a mistake on your part. There'll come a day when you need a lawman on your side, and when that day comes, you'll be mighty glad Ethan Chapman's your friend."

Justin muttered something.

"What'd you say?" Griffin snapped.

"Nothing."

Griff leaned toward him. "Look here, boy, I don't know what your folks tolerated, but I don't take to letting a kid sass me."

Justin's face went stony.

Griff clenched his jaw. Light into him or let it go? He inhaled slowly then shrugged, trying to relax his tight muscles. "Hey, you and me, we can get along, or we can go our separate ways. If you're going to stay here, you'd best learn to get along."

Justin watched him from slits of eyes. "So. . .what if I don't want to get along? Are you saying I can leave?"

"Well now, that depends." Griff pushed his hat up in the back and scratched his head. "You got enough money to take the stage home?"

"No, sir."

"You got other transportation, then? I don't cotton to horse thievery."

Justin's face grew longer and darker.

Griffin straightened and clucked to Pepper so that he began to walk again. Red kept pace, though Justin hadn't cued him to move.

"On the other hand," Griff said, "I've been known to let a fella work off the cost of a horse before. You think you'd like to own a nice little horse like Red?"

Justin eyed him suspiciously. "What'd I have to do? Shovel manure for three years?"

"Nope. Maybe a year, for one hour in the morning. Or half a year for two hours. Plus bookkeeping."

"Bookkeeping? What's that? You got so many books you can't keep track of them?"

Griffin smiled. "No, sir. That's keeping records of money and such. You should know that."

"Oh, that kind of bookkeeping." Justin yawned. They rode on for a minute before he asked, "What sort of work would I do for that?"

"Well, you seem to be a hand with numbers. Maybe you could help me keep track of who owes me for smithing work and keeping their horse at the livery. And maybe even for the stagecoach business if you show yourself apt and trustworthy."

"Huh." Justin frowned and flicked a piece of straw off Red's withers.

"Come on," Griffin said. "Let's practice that trot again. Remember, five hundred pounds on each foot." He waited while Justin shifted in the saddle and took on an air of concentration and then clucked to Pepper and eased up on the reins.

They clipped along for the last half mile with Justin trying to weigh more and keep his weight low. When they reached the lane leading to the ranch, Griff called, "You're doing fine."

Justin gave him a fractured smile. "It's hard."

"Sure is." Griffin grinned as they trotted up to the ranch house.

While they tied their horses to Ethan's hitching rail, Trudy and Ethan came out of the house. Trudy had on a warm coat and hood and her split riding skirt, and she had a bundle of fabric under her arm.

"You going somewheres this morning, Mrs. Chapman?" Griffin asked.

Trudy smiled at him. "Good morning, Griff. Yes, I've got business with the shooting club." She turned her gaze on Justin. "Hello, Justin. How do you like it here so far?"

Justin wrapped Red's reins around the hitching rail. "It's cold."

Trudy chuckled. "It's a little chilly. Winter's coming."

Griff scowled at his nephew. "Here, now, don't tie him up by the reins."

Justin threw him a dark look. "Why not?"

"Because if he gets scared, he'll pull back and hurt his mouth and maybe break the leather."

"What do I tie him with?"

Griff didn't like to admit he'd brought his own lead rope, as always, in his saddlebag, but hadn't thought to add an extra for Justin.

"Here." Ethan walked down the steps and lifted the end of a rope dangling from the far end of the rail. "Use this one. I leave it tied here all the time for folks who don't bring one."

Justin hesitated, then led Red over a few steps to get it. "Thank you, sir."

Griffin beamed. Maybe there was some hope for the boy yet.

"All right, ladies, we have to hurry," Bitsy called to the other six women who'd gathered in front of the smithy. "Remember, what looks like trash to us might be a treasure this man has saved for twenty years. We don't throw anything away unless it's got mold all over it."

"Are you sure it's legal for us to do this?" Annie Harper asked, swinging her broom down off her shoulder.

Bitsy looked at Trudy. "Your husband's the sheriff. What did he say about this?"

Trudy laughed. "Ethan said he'll keep Griff and Justin busy all morning, bringing the herd down from the high pasture for the winter—but I'd better be there to dish up dinner at noontime, so let's get at it. We've only got a couple of hours."

"Yes, I have to be to work at the emporium then," Goldie said. She and Vashti had come with Bitsy. Along with Annie and her daughter Myra, and the mayor's wife, Ellie Nash, they made up the cleaning brigade.

Trudy looked toward the livery stable. "We'd best get inside, or Marty will see us."

"Yeah, we don't want him to come around asking what we're up to," Vashti said.

Bitsy picked up her scrub bucket and opened the door of the smithy. The women followed her across the dim workshop, past the anvil and the forge. Vashti looked up at the big bellows overhead. She'd always been fascinated by the forge and all the tools Griffin had in this workshop and the things he made out of plain metal bars. She'd never had a chance to watch him work, though. It would be unseemly for ladies to stand around and watch a man working.

Bitsy opened the door to the room behind the smithy. She stood still on the threshold.

"Well?" Annie said. "Are we going in, or aren't we?"

Bitsy turned with a pained expression. "The question is, *can* we?"

Vashti eased between them and looked into Griffin's home. The tiny room was jammed with junk. A rumpled bunk was nailed to one wall. Wadded blankets and clothes covered the straw tick. All around the room were stacks of boxes, kegs, and cartons. A bucket half full of water stood beside a small box stove. Hanging from the rafters were bunches of corn drying on the cob with the husks peeled back and braided together, clusters of onions, a few strings of dried apples, and squash.

"Griff got a garden somewhere?" she asked.

"I think folks pay him in foodstuffs sometimes," Annie ventured, "same as they do Doc."

Trudy nodded. "Well, it's none too fresh in here. Can we open that window, Bitsy?"

"I don't know. Maybe if we wash it, I can see where the latch is."

Vashti unrolled her apron. Inside it were a bar of soap and several rags.

"All right, ladies," Bitsy said. "We all know how to work hard. Let's get started."

For the first few minutes, they straightened things enough to make a path to the window and the bunk.

Ellie pulled the covers off the bed. "I declare, there is a sheet in there, all wound about in knots. Needs a good washing, though. I'll take all this bedding over to my place and scrub it."

"It won't be dry by noon," Trudy said.

"No, I don't expect it will."

"Well, I brought a quilt." Annie went back to the doorway, where she'd left her bundle, and brought it over. "It's a shame to put it on a dirty bed, though."

Vashti pondered the problem while Annie brought out the colorful log cabin quilt.

"That's a nice one for a man." Bitsy reached out and touched the brown and green squares.

"Thank you," Annie said. "I was going to put it on my boy Tollie's bed, but I can make him another one this winter."

"Mighty generous of you," Ellie said.

Annie shrugged. "Griffin does a lot for folks in this town. Time he was blessed."

Goldie laughed. "That's what we're doing. Blessing him. I wish we could see his face when he comes home."

"Well, we'd best get to work." Bitsy gave the quilt one last pat. "I never did any quilting."

"It's easy," Annie said. "Do you want me to tell you next time I'm working on a quilt and show you how?"

Bitsy blinked rapidly. "Why, thank you. I'd like that excessively."

Vashti hauled in a breath and took courage. If Mrs. Harper could be that nice, she could do her part. "Ma'am, I could dump the old straw out of that tick and air it out, and then I could get some fresh from the livery."

"What about Marty Hoffstead?" Annie asked.

"I'll tell him I need straw for a tick, but I won't tell him whose."

Trudy held out two nickels. "This is all I've got on me, but I reckon Marty will make you pay for the straw."

"Say, maybe I should go with you," Myra said. "Can I, Ma?"

Annie frowned. "Well. . ."

"It'd be better if both of them went," Bitsy said. "Marty ain't the kind of man a gal wants to be alone with."

Annie's frown lines deepened. "That's exactly why I don't think Myra should. . ." She pressed her lips together and shrugged. "If you stick together. Vashti, you'll look after each other, won't you?"

"Of course." Vashti and Myra seized the dank straw tick and dragged it outside. "Let's dump the old straw out back of the livery on the manure pile," Vashti said.

"How we going to rip the seam?" Myra asked when they'd reached their destination.

Vashti reached into her pocket for the small, mother-of-pearl-sided pocketknife she carried.

"Ooh, that's purty," Myra said.

"Thanks." Vashti quickly slit open one end of the tick where it had been rudely stitched together. They tipped it up and shook it. The clumped, smelly straw fell out onto the manure pile.

"What are you gals doing?" Marty stood in the back door of the livery, watching them.

"We're cleaning. Thought we'd get some fresh straw from you for this mattress," Vashti said.

He studied them for a moment, and a smile slid across his face. "Surely. Help yourselves. It's yonder." He pointed over his shoulder into the livery.

Myra looked at Vashti and swallowed hard.

"Don't worry," Vashti whispered. "If he tries anything, I'll clobber him but good." She shook the tick out again.

"We ought to let it air for a while," Myra said. "Ma always washes them before she puts new straw in."

"No time," Vashti said.

She gathered the fabric and headed for the barn, trying not to show her apprehension. There were two of them, after all.

Marty watched as Vashti led Myra across the barn floor to the enclosed area where Griffin kept bedding straw. They knelt and began to stuff armfuls into the tick.

"You ladies need any help?"

Vashti spun around. Marty was two feet from her. "We're fine."

"I could—"

"Marty! Marty, you in here?" The man's voice calling from the front of the livery was unmistakably Oscar Runnels's.

Marty grimaced. "Sounds like I have a customer. If you need anything, let me know." He turned and walked toward the front of the barn.

Myra let out a long breath. "That man makes my skin crawl."

"I know," Vashti said. "For once, Oscar Runnels played the delivering angel."

"Mr. Runnels isn't bad." Myra peered around the board partition at Marty and the stocky freighter talking in the barn's doorway.

"And his son's not bad, either, eh?"

Myra's cheeks flushed, but she smiled. The ongoing flirtation between her and Oscar's son Josiah was no secret.

"Here, we just need a little more." Vashti stood and shook the straw down into the tick. "Shove more in."

"Are you going to drive the stagecoach again soon?" Myra scooped up a huge armful of straw.

"Not driving, but I'm going along as messenger tomorrow. It's my job twice a week until the snow closes the roads."

"Really? That's so exciting! And you look cute in those boy clothes."

Vashti shook her head. "I don't like pretending to be a boy, but it's easier to do the job in that outfit. I wouldn't want to climb up onto the box many times in a skirt."

"Wish I could wear pants." Myra looked at her with a little gasp and wide eyes. "Don't tell Ma I said that, will you?"

"I won't."

They shoved in a few more handfuls of straw.

"If we put in any more, we won't be able to stitch it shut," Vashti said.

"Oh dear. How are we going to get it back to Griffin's?" Myra surveyed the bulging mattress. "We can't ask Marty to help us, or he'll know what we're doing."

"We can do it," Vashti said. "Come on, while the men are still talking." They wrestled the unwieldy tick out onto the barn floor. Each picked up one end and carried the awkward burden out the back door and around to the smithy. Both were puffing and red-faced when they reached the back.

"Hey, they've got the window open," Myra said.

Vashti set down her end of the tick and strode to the window. "Goldie, come help us!"

Her friend looked out the open window. "Well, look at that. Old Marty let you have the straw."

Vashti grinned. "Yep, and he didn't charge us a penny."

★ CHAPTER 12 ★

Even though he was bone tired, Griffin brushed Pepper and made sure Justin did a good job of grooming Red. The boy didn't have to be shown twice—he seemed to take to it. In fact, he rubbed the chestnut's flanks carefully and smoothed his mane and tail. Griff watched him over Pepper's back and saw Justin actually pet Red's neck.

"Red's a good horse." Griffin put his brush back on the shelf between the studs in the barn wall.

"Yeah. He's not bad." Justin brought his brush over and stuck it on the shelf beside Griffin's. "Now what?"

"They've about finished their oats, so we'll put them out in the corral for the night."

"Don't they get hay?"

"There's a rack full in the corral, and a water trough. Marty should have filled it, but I'll check to make sure. Unhitch Red and lead him out." Griffin unhooked Pepper's lead rope and didn't look back to see how Justin did, though it was tempting. It was dark already, and colder than it had been all day. Griffin led Pepper to the corral gate, opened it, and released the gelding. Half a dozen other horses whickered a greeting.

Justin came cautiously out of the barn, holding Red's halter with one hand. Griff waited until he got right up to the gate and swung it open.

"Walk him in and turn him around. Then you get yourself out

here with me and let him go so I can shut the gate."

The boy managed to follow instructions and didn't let go of the halter until he had Red completely inside the corral and turned toward the gate.

Griff shut the swinging gate and latched it. "Feels like snow."

"Sure does." Justin shivered and shook himself.

"I'll get the colt. Can you take the palomino again?"

"Sure. But why do you keep those two inside at night?"

"They're special. Until I deliver that palomino to Mr. Dooley, I need to make sure nothing happens to it. And the colt. . .well, he's special. I don't want to take a chance of him getting loose or somebody stealing him."

"When will he be old enough for you to ride him?"

"Well, someone who doesn't weigh too much will likely be able to ride him next summer—after his training. But me?" Griffin laughed. "I wouldn't want to put my weight on a two-year-old. Another year, and his back will be strong enough, but not yet."

"So how will you train him if you can't get on his back?" Justin asked.

"You'll see." Griffin hitched the colt in his stall and left him with his feed to munch. His plans for training would fall into place when the time came. He didn't want to get too optimistic—things could change in a hurry—but he thought he might have an eager helper close by. "You ready? I need to stop at my place before we go to the Fennel House."

"You eating over there with me tonight?" Justin asked.

"Reckon so." Griffin didn't like spending as much on meals as he had been lately, but he'd been gone all day, helping Ethan, and his fire would be out. He didn't think he had much to eat in the place except a few dried apples and such. He'd never cooked much, anyway. "Come on." He grabbed the lantern he'd left hanging inside the back of the livery and shut the rolling door.

They went in through the smithy. When he got to the door to his room, he paused.

"Uh, wait here. I'll just be a second."

"All right." Justin looked doubtful, but he stood there between the anvil and the forge, shivering.

So far, Griff had managed to avoid taking the boy into his private quarters. Sometime he'd get around to redding up the place, and then Justin could see it. Not until.

Shoving the door open, he held the lantern high. And stopped in his tracks.

"What—" His heart lurched. Had he been robbed? The place looked almost bare. The floor between where he stood and his bunk was clear. And his bunk! The covers were smooth and. . .not his covers. A quilt he'd never seen before lay over the mattress, and his pillow actually had a linen cover on it. That was odd. When did thieves leave things behind?

Justin touched his arm. "Uncle Griff? Something wrong?"

"I'm not sure." Griffin stepped into the room and swung the lantern around slowly. The room felt fairly warm, like someone had kept a fire in the stove today. His extra wool pants and dungarees, along with his two other shirts, hung from nails on the wall. All his boxes and kegs were neatly stacked, and the shelves, while crowded, had an orderly look. He could actually see the surface of the small plank table he'd lost sight of months ago, and sitting in the middle of that table were a covered basket and a green bottle holding a cluster of dried weeds and red berries. It was kind of pretty.

"This place isn't so bad," Justin said. "I thought you said it wasn't fit to live in."

"Well, I. . ." Griffin swallowed hard. He didn't know who'd done this, but his initial shock had faded. Now anger vied with gratitude in his heart. Insight flashed in his brain, like the sparks that flew from his hammer when he struck white-hot iron. He could get mad at the scrubbing bandit, or he could accept an anonymous friend's act with humility. The first course would be easiest. But someone had cared about him enough to spend a lot of effort making his place nicer. And he had a feeling it wasn't done for Griffin Bane alone.

He whipped around and eyed Justin suspiciously. Had the boy complained to someone that his uncle had farmed him out to the boardinghouse? Had he told other people the room behind the smithy was too filthy to take a boy into?

"You, uh, didn't say anything to anyone about not liking the Fennel House, did you?"

Justin shrugged. "Don't think so. Why would I? It's not half bad."

Griff nodded and looked around again. He strode to the table and lifted the napkin that covered the basket. Biscuits. And a jar of jam.

"Hmm."

"Hmm, what?" Justin came over and looked down at the basket. "Say, those look mighty good. Did you make 'em?"

"Nope." Griff laid the napkin back over the tempting biscuits. "I'd say we had company while we were out to the Chapmans' ranch."

"You mean someone brought you those biscuits while you were away?"

"No, someone brought *us* those biscuits." Griffin thought he might have an idea of whom. Vashti had known they'd be gone today. But how could she have done all this by herself and still made the stagecoach after lunch? He looked cautiously at Justin. "Do you think this place is too small for the both of us?"

Justin looked around. "Well. . .there's only one bunk."

"True. But I *could* build another one over the top."

"You mean. . ." Justin cleared his throat. "You mean you'd want me to stay with you, after all?"

"If you'd like that. But if you wouldn't, you can stay over to the boarding—"

"I would!"

"Oh." Griffin nodded slowly. "All right then. Let's go over and have supper, and I'll tell Mrs. Thistle that tonight's your last night with them. And tomorrow we'll scare up some lumber and build another bunk. How does that sound?"

"Sounds good, Uncle Griff."

Griffin smiled. "Great. And for breakfast we'll have biscuits and jam."

Griffin tried to think where he could get some lumber. He didn't want to go clear out to the sawmill, but maybe he'd have to. On Thursday morning, he rose with the sun and stoked his woodstove.

He'd promised Justin he'd get him from the boardinghouse and they'd build a new bunk. The basket of biscuits all but called his name as he pulled on his trousers, suspenders, and boots. But if he ate some before Justin came, the boy would know. Best wait.

A knock came at the door.

"Hey, Griff, you up?"

He clomped over to the door as he slid on his heavy wool overshirt. "Hiram Dooley, you're out early." Griffin opened the door wide and let his friend enter.

"Oh? I need to make a firing pin for Emmaline Landry's gun." Hiram looked around the small room and nodded. "Mighty spruce, Griff."

"That's what I think, too." Maybe getting a visit from a scrubbing genie wasn't so bad. Griffin chuckled. "Used to be you were always fixing the men's guns. Now the ladies are keeping you in business."

"There's truth to that," Hiram said.

"Well, I haven't fired up the forge for two days, but help yourself."

Hiram held up a burlap sack and shook it. It clinked.

Griffin shook his head. "You didn't have to bring your own coal."

Hiram shrugged. "Might need a piece of steel if you've got one that's right."

"Sure. Let me just grab my gloves and hat. I've got to go over and get my nephew."

"I heard the boy was here. How's that working?"

"All right. I'm going to bring him over here to stay with me today, but I need to make him a bunk." Griff stopped and whirled around. Hiram was the perfect person to ask. "Say, you don't have any leftover boards and such from building the church or something like that?"

Hiram nodded. "Over to my old place there's lots of lumber in the barn. Look it over and take what you want. I'll swap you for the steel."

"All right. And I've got a palomino gelding in the livery that I think you'll like the looks of. I bought it in Boise, with Mrs. Adams in mind. Rode him all the way up here. He's steady and well mannered, and he doesn't look half bad, either."

"Terrific. Do you have time to show me now?"

"All right, let's go."

They walked to the back door of the livery, and Griffin rolled the door open. He went into the palomino's stall and unhooked him. When he led the horse out onto the barn floor, Hiram's eyes lit up.

"He looks fine, Griff."

"You want to try him out?"

"I'll take your word. How much do I owe you?"

Griffin named the price he'd paid in Boise.

"I'll get it to you later today," Hiram said.

"You want to keep him here or take him out to your place?"

"I might as well take him to the ranch. All right if I take him later when I'm heading home?"

"Sure." Griffin put the horse away and came out of the stall. "Say, I've got a riddle for you."

Hiram silently raised his eyebrows and waited.

Griffin pulled in a deep breath. Did he really want to spill it? Hiram was the quietest man in town. He wouldn't tell anyone.

"Come on back to my place." They walked over to the smithy and into Griffin's living quarters. He turned to face Hiram. "Yesterday a funny thing happened. Justin and I rode out to Ethan's ranch to help him all day. When we came back at suppertime, my place was. . .well, it was the way you see it now. Except the bed was made up fresh."

Hiram glanced at the rumpled bunk and nodded.

"Don't you think that's odd?" Griffin asked.

"That your bed was made? Mighty odd."

"Yes, well, somebody came in here while I was gone and cleaned the place up." Griffin looked around again at the neat supplies and the clean window and lamp chimney. "You know what else?"

Hiram shook his head.

"My blankets were gone, and my bed was all made up with linen sheets and a new quilt. That one there."

"It's not your quilt?"

"Nope. I think they even put fresh straw in my mattress."

Hiram's eyes widened, and he looked around again. "Know who did it?"

"I've got my suspicions." Griffin picked up the basket of biscuits.

"They left this. And that there posy of weeds."

Hiram peeked under the napkin and grunted.

"Biscuits," Griff said, as if he couldn't see them.

"They any good?"

"Don't know. Justin and I ate at the Fennel House last night, and I saved these for breakfast."

"Well, it's not Trudy's basket," Hiram said.

"Hmm. But she left the ranch as soon as Justin and I got there yesterday."

"I could probably tell you who made the biscuits if I tasted one," Hiram said.

"Now, that's a thought." The two single men had eaten biscuits made by nearly every woman in town at church functions and such. Griffin laid back the napkin. "Try one."

"Thank you." Hiram took one out.

Griffin reached for one and pulled his hand back. "I'd better not. Don't want the boy to think I ate a bunch without waiting for him."

Hiram took a bite and closed his eyes, chewing slowly. Then he took another bite.

"Well?" Griff asked.

"Flaky. I'd say Augie Moore's, but there's a heavy touch with the lard. He wouldn't do that." Augie was the undisputed best cook in Fergus. Hiram broke off a piece and handed it to Griffin. "Try it. I'm guessing Ellie Nash."

"Ellie?" Griffin frowned as he took the quarter biscuit. "Why would she—" He stared at Hiram. "No. Oh no."

Hiram grinned. "I think you're right."

"Not the whole shooting club."

"Why not? They helped redd up Doc Kincaid's new house and gave him a pound party. Why not you, too?"

"I don't want all the women in town talking about—" Griffin looked wildly around. How many of them had been in here and seen his. . .habits? He moaned.

"Eat the biscuit," Hiram said. "It's good."

"Be better with some of that strawberry jam."

"Jam? You should have said so. That clinches it. Ellie made a bumper batch of strawberry this year. Remember she brought some to the harvest dinner? And Annie Harper makes quilts quicker'n you can shoe a mule."

Griff looked toward the bed again. "You must be right."

Hiram laughed. "That's gotta be it. Trudy mentioned last time I saw her that you were boarding your nephew out and how it was too bad you couldn't keep him to home." He slapped Griffin on the back. "Say, I've got an idea."

"What?"

"This place is awfully small for two men."

"I'll say. It's awfully small for me by myself."

Hiram nodded. "How much are you paying to board him?"

Griff winced. "Twelve dollars a week. Way too much, but Rilla says boys eat a lot."

"Right. My old house is sitting empty since I moved out to the Fennel ranch this fall. Libby and I—well, we intend to live at the ranch." His face flushed a little as he mentioned his upcoming nuptials. "When you go to get the lumber, take a look around my house. The back door's unlocked. You and Justin could stay there, and if you think it's worth twenty dollars a month. . ."

"You mean it?"

Again Hiram nodded.

"Say, that's a good idea. And close to the boardinghouse if we want a hot meal. Close to the jail, too." At Hiram's puzzled look, Griffin added, "I think Justin took a shine to Ethan yesterday. I want to encourage him to look on Ethan as a friend."

"Sounds reasonable. Let me know what you think."

Griffin put the basket on the table. They walked out into the smithy. Hiram moseyed over to the corner where Griffin kept steel stock. "How's your new shotgun rider doing?"

"Oh, you know about that?" Griffin asked.

"Whole town knows you hired her."

"Ah. So far, so good."

Hiram selected a small scrap of bar stock and carried it and his sack to the forge. Griffin left him as he dumped his ration of coal into the firepot.

On the road to Nampa that afternoon, Vashti wore a warm jacket Libby had provided. It was made of green wool and lined with fleece, and it buttoned up snug under her chin. Vashti had insisted on paying for it herself—she didn't want to be beholden to a man again, even if Griffin had said he would pay for it. It kept her warm, though light snow fell all around them, deadening the sound of the wheels on the road.

She reminded herself many times not to watch Johnny drive. Her job was to watch the road ahead and the rocks and trees along the sides. It was tempting to sneak glances at his hands, though, especially when they came to a curve or had to cross a stream. She would drive as well as Johnny someday—better!

"What you looking at?" Johnny asked with a sly grin.

"Nothing." She turned away from him and studied the gulley beside the road.

"Yes, you was. You like looking at me?"

"Not hardly."

"Huh."

Vashti felt her face flush. If Johnny noticed, he'd think she liked him.

"The passengers know you're a girl," he said a mile later. "I heard 'em talking back at the Democrat station."

Her heart thudded. "What'd they say?"

"One of 'em asked the tender about you, if you was really a girl."

"Which tender?"

"Jake."

She scowled and turned her face away again. The swing station was owned by a man everyone said was the only Democrat in the valley. When they'd stopped to change the team, she'd noticed a man called Jake watching her and stayed away from him.

"He told the passenger you used to be a saloon girl," Johnny said.

"Oh, wonderful." She exhaled and focused on the road, but tears stung her eyes.

"I reckon you'll know how to handle him if he tries to get fresh."

She glared at him. "Be quiet, Johnny."

He laughed. "What, you think you can get away from the past that easy? Everybody in these parts knows who you are. What you are."

"And just what do you mean by that?" She felt like smacking him.

"You know." He shrugged. The horses took the slight flapping of the reins as permission to break into a canter. Johnny jerked to attention. "Here, now! Whoa, boys. Slow down."

They careened toward a downhill curve. Vashti caught her breath and jammed the butt of the shotgun against her thigh, holding it tight with one hand and grabbing the edge of the seat with the other. She knew better than to say anything at that moment, though she wanted to scream at Johnny.

As they reached the curve, the leaders began to slow, but the swing team hadn't caught on yet, and they tried to keep running, nudging the leaders' tails. Johnny tried to hold them steady and work the brake lever, too. Even so, they hit the turn way too fast. As the leaders turned, the coach wheels slid and the whole framework swung wildly to one side.

Vashti gasped as she slid over and slammed against Johnny's hip.

"Whoa now! Whoa, Rolly! Sam!" He sawed at the reins.

Vashti wanted to tell him to keep his voice even, but she couldn't breathe.

"Hey!" The muffled cry came from one of the passengers inside the coach.

Before Vashti could grab another breath, the seat fell out from under her and she was falling.

★ CHAPTER 13 ★

Vashti and Johnny hit the ground in a heap.

With no time to think about injuries or indignities, Vashti sat up. The coach had tipped over on its side. The terrorized horses dragged it, with the upper wheels spinning wildly, across the snow.

"Whoa, you lummoxes!" She clawed her way to her feet and found the shotgun lying in the snow. She'd lost her hat. "Johnny! You alive?"

Johnny sat up and shook his head. "Oh man!" He was on his feet in a flash and tore off after the horses.

Vashti gulped. There wasn't a thing she could do—she'd never catch up to him, let alone the horses. She looked around and found her hat a few yards back. After brushing the snow off it, she clamped it on her head and set off. Her hip and elbow smarted where she'd landed on them. A couple of hundred yards away, the horses had come to a halt and stood steaming and shivering. By the time she'd limped to where they'd stopped, Johnny was talking to them and running his hands over their sleek sides and down their legs.

"There, boys. Calm down now. It's all right."

She walked over to the scarlet coach. "Ahoy there, passengers. You in there, gentlemen?"

The door on the top side of the coach cracked open, then swung upward, and a man's head appeared, minus his hat, with his disheveled hair hanging down about his ears.

"Yes, ma'am. Sir. Uh—" He blinked at her. "Sorry. We're shook up, but we're all right."

Vashti nodded. "Let's get you out of there, and we'll see if we can right the coach. I'm sorry you got tossed around like that."

Johnny unhitched the team and secured them to the only tree within sight. He continued to talk to them and pet them.

When the two passengers stood on firm ground, one of them asked, "What do we do?"

Vashti eyed the overturned coach. Griff wasn't going to like this. "I'll have to see what Johnny says. He has more experience than I do."

"Oh, is that right?"

Something about the amusement in the man's gaze made Vashti flush and her blood boil. She turned on her heel and walked over to Johnny. "Whatcha reckon we should do?"

"After the horses are calm, we can hitch them to the coach broadside and let them pull it up onto the wheels again."

"Sounds like you've done this before."

"What driver hasn't?"

She let that pass. "What about damage?"

"What about it?" He glared at her. "This ain't my fault."

"Oh yeah? Whose fault is it?"

"Ice. There was ice on the road, underneath the snow."

"Whatever you say, Johnny."

A few minutes later, they led the horses over to the coach, and Johnny took a coil of rope from the boot. He hitched it to the luggage rack on the top and tied the other end to the evener. Vashti held the leaders' heads while he worked, speaking softly to the horses.

"So that gal's got a nighttime job in a saloon, I hear," one of the passengers said to Johnny, but Vashti had no trouble hearing him.

Her chest tightened, and she clamped her fingers around the bridle straps.

Johnny shook his head. "I don't know what you've been hearing, but Georgie's all right."

"She's a woman, isn't she?" asked the other passenger. "Hard to tell with that coat she's wearing."

Vashti kept her face turned away from them.

"I saw her red hair after you two fell off the coach," said the first man. "She didn't get it all up under her hat."

"Bet she's a stunner in silk stockings," said his companion.

"Look, gents," Johnny said firmly, "Georgie's a girl, it's true. But she ain't that kind of girl. So just leave her alone, you hear?"

Vashti leaned her forehead against Sam's bony muzzle. "Thank You for Johnny, Lord." Her tears fell on the horse's nose, and he snorted. She wiped her face with her sleeve before the next few tears could freeze on her cheek.

Griffin walked around the stage three times, searching out every scratch and scrape. His eyes narrowed when he looked at the cracked door panel and the broken spoke on the off front wheel. They were lucky the coach hadn't been ruined. Vashti stood perfectly still, waiting for him to explode. Johnny began to fidget. Justin stood in the shadow of the livery doorway, watching in silence.

The third time around, Griff stopped in front of Johnny. He stood six inches taller than the driver and outweighed him by at least fifty pounds, most of which was muscle made by hefting iron. He gazed down at Johnny through slits of eyes.

"Want to tell me again what happened?"

Johnny cleared his throat and looked away. "It's like I told you, boss. We came up on that corner two miles out from Democrat's, and it was slippery, and the horses got het up."

"Uh-huh." Griffin nodded. "You think that road's too treacherous for us to run any more this season?"

Johnny swallowed. "No, sir, I don't."

"Then how are you going to keep this from happening next time, Conway? Answer me that."

"I...uh..."

"You recall when Cyrus Fennel was your boss."

It wasn't a question, but Johnny said, "Yes, sir."

"What do you suppose he'd do if he were here now?"

Johnny's face lost its color. He opened his mouth and closed it again.

Griff nodded again. He took two steps and squinted down into

Vashti's face. "You get hurt?"

She gulped. "No, sir."

"Good." His momentary softening was gone. "All right, Georgie-boy, let's hear your version."

Vashti's pulse raced. Surely Griffin wouldn't punish her. Or would he? She'd never seen him so dangerously quiet.

"We, uh, we left Democrat's, and everything was fine, but the horses were frisky. The snow and all, you know."

He nodded.

"We, uh. . ."

"You *what?*"

She jumped. "On that downhill, the team started running. Johnny tried to pull them in, but then the wheels slipped, and the stage overset."

Griff held her gaze for a long moment, his dark eyes simmering. He paced back to Johnny. Each word distinct, he said, "You two will sand down the side of that coach this evening and repaint it. I will do the other repairs. The cost of the materials and my time will be deducted from your wages, Conway."

Johnny winced. "Yes, boss."

"And if this happens again while you're driving, I'll suspend you for a month of Sundays." Griffin turned away.

Vashti sneaked a glance at Johnny. His mouth drooped, and he wouldn't meet her gaze.

An hour later, Vashti knelt in the straw on the barn floor, gently scrubbing at the door panel with a piece of fine sandpaper. Griffin had removed the damaged wheel and taken it over to the smithy. The axle was propped up on a chopping block.

Johnny worked on the body panel below the window. He swore softly.

Vashti cleared her throat and threw him a pointed glance.

"Sorry," he said.

"Swearing doesn't help."

Johnny made a face at her. "If you was a boy, it wouldn't matter.

I'm as bad as that passenger—can't remember when you're a girl and when you're a boy."

She clenched her fist. "Quit it, Johnny. You're a good driver. Most of the time, anyway."

"Yeah?"

"Yeah. But you got sloppy today. We both know it. The whole world knows it."

"One second. That's all it took. One second."

"Yeah, that's about right. It takes one second for a team of horses to get out of control."

"Oh, so now you know more about driving than I do."

She straightened and faced him. "I'm not saying that."

"Sure sounds like it." He stood and towered over her, scowling.

Vashti let out a deep breath. "At least the horses didn't get hurt. Come on. Let's get this done."

"You really think I'm a good driver?"

"When you're not being reckless. And it *was* slippery on that hill."

"So it wasn't entirely my fault."

She pressed her lips together and went back to rubbing the scrape on the door.

"Thanks for not telling Griff it was my fault," Johnny said. "He'd have taken your word if you had."

"I'm not out to get you in trouble."

"You're not?"

She shook her head. "You can do that easy enough yourself."

"Ha!" He smiled ruefully. "Thought you wanted my job."

"I wouldn't mind it, but I wouldn't want to do you out of your livelihood."

He began rubbing the wood again. "Thanks."

"Well, thank you for setting that passenger in his place."

"You heard what he said?"

"Every word." She rubbed harder. She had no reason to feel guilty. God had forgiven all her past transgressions. He'd sanded away every scratch and repainted her soul a pure, sparkling white.

"You still want a driving rig to practice on?" Johnny asked.

"Bill's going to make me one."

Johnny blinked at her. "He is?"

"Yes. He thinks I'm tenacious enough to master the art."

"I reckon maybe you are."

Vashti and Apphia Benton watched as Bill Stout threaded the six long reins through the wooden rack he'd constructed in the Bentons' stable. He gathered the ends and backed up, letting the leathers slide through his hands until he'd reached a wagon seat he'd mounted on two big rounds of a log.

"All right, missy, you come over here and sit on this wagon seat."

Vashti shot Apphia a smile and walked over to the seat. She eased down and smoothed her full skirt.

"Here you go." Bill handed her the lines.

She laced them between her fingers and took up the slack.

"It's got a weight hanging from each line, to keep some tension. If you let off, it will fall down a few inches." Bill stood back and cocked his head to one side.

Vashti tried to feel each weight through the lines.

"The off leader's too tight," Bill said. "Let it out just a hair." Vashti painstakingly pushed the rein for the imaginary front right horse forward with her thumb.

"Oops," Bill said. "Now the swing is too loose."

She frowned in concentration, trying to catch the rein to the middle horse on the right side of her "coach" with her third finger and inch it up.

"Better." Bill nodded. "You look fine. I should have put the seat up higher, though."

"Vashti, how did you learn to hold the reins?" Apphia asked. "I'd get confused first thing. And you only have one line for each horse. I don't see how you can keep them under control."

Vashti glanced over at her and smiled. "When my daddy was still alive, he used to let me drive his team."

"Uh-uh." Bill shook his head. "You relaxed your hands when you spoke to Miz Benton, and you let the reins go slack. Your team just ran away with you and tipped the stage over on its side."

Vashti frowned and looked down at her hands. Bill was right. She firmed up her wrists and put a light tension on each of the six lines. The one for the near wheeler had slipped, and she worked it up until the rein ran straight from her hand to the rack again, but not too tight.

"That's better," Bill said.

"How do you use your whip, if you need both hands to drive?" Apphia asked.

Vashti determined not to look at her again so Bill wouldn't scold her. "You answer that, Bill."

He chuckled. "Good stage drivers don't use the whip much. It's more for show when you're setting out or for times when the horses need to be reminded to keep the pace up. If you're driving through mud, for instance, or if you see outlaws coming up on you. Then you take the reins in one hand, loose enough so the horses can get their heads down and run, and you crack the whip with the other."

"Oh my."

Vashti figured she'd get a talking-to about outlaws later from Apphia.

Bill watched Vashti in silence for several seconds as she moved her hands and let the weights in and out slowly. "You practice for two hours every day, and by snow melt, mebbe you'll be ready to drive one of Griff's sixes."

"Two hours a day?" Apphia stared at him. "She'd get charley horses in her hands."

"When I'm driving, I'll hold the lines longer than that at a stretch," Vashti said.

Bill nodded. "Yes, ma'am. She needs strong fingers and springy wrists. Can't have those without working 'em."

Vashti smiled up at her mentor. "Thank you so much, Bill. I'll practice every day, and I promise that next spring I won't embarrass you and overset my coach."

His eyes twinkled. "I expect you'll make me proud. You've got a sight of determination, young lady."

"She can come over and practice anytime she wants," Apphia

said, "but I'm afraid she'll get cold."

"I'll be fine." In her mind, Vashti was dashing along the Nampa road behind a team of six matched bays. She moved her hands slightly as they galloped, and tucked up the near leader's rein a bit.

"I heard the boss is moving," Bill said.

"What?" She lowered her hands and swung around to stare at him.

"Your team's running away."

"Very funny. What's that you said about Mr. Bane?"

"He's going to rent the old Dooley place, next to the jailhouse."

"Really?" Vashti looked over at Apphia.

Bill gathered up his tools. "Reckon I'd better get over to the boardinghouse. If you're late for supper there, you're apt to miss out on the pudding."

When he'd left the stable, Vashti carefully wound the lines around a stick Bill had attached to her wagon seat for a brake handle. She gathered her skirts and climbed down. "Miz Benton, do you know anything about why Mr. Bane is moving?"

"I expect it's for the boy."

"Then all the work the ladies did at his little house was wasted."

"Why do you say that?" Apphia put her arm around Vashti. "My dear, what you and the other women did was a nice gesture. I understand why you didn't tell me until it was over."

Vashti hung her head. "We figured you'd say we oughtn't to do it without his permission."

"I probably would have. Griffin is a very private man, and if his room was as filthy as you say it was, then I suspect he was embarrassed to know a group of ladies had been in there."

"He never said anything to me about it afterward."

"No, but the whole plan could have gone awry. It might have made him angry."

Vashti nodded slowly.

Apphia smiled. "You should rejoice and thank the Lord that Griffin accepted your gesture for what it was—an honest effort by a group of friends to help him. And it accomplished just what you hoped—he's got the boy living with him now."

"Yes." Vashti frowned. "I suppose moving over to Mr. Dooley's would be good for them. They'd have more space."

"That's right. Justin can have his own chamber."

"And that little room behind the smithy was drafty and cold the day we were there. The nearest water is over beyond the livery, at the well where they draw it for the horses—"

Apphia pulled her toward the door. "Come, dear. I'm cold. Let's have a cup of tea together. I think what you did was admirable, and it made Griffin consider how he could better take care of Justin. That's what you hoped, isn't it?"

"Yes. I suppose they'll be much more comfortable at the Dooleys' old place." Vashti looked back at her new rack. "God is good, isn't He, Miz Benton?"

"Yes, dear. He's very good."

★ CHAPTER 14 ★

With the first heavy snow in December, Griffin quit sending the stagecoach to Silver City. Enough mines were operating that their outfits kept the road from Fergus to Nampa rolled and packed down, which made for good sleighing, and the stages kept running through to Boise. Vashti, however, was out of a job until spring.

It was just as well. Griffin spent entirely too much time fretting when she took to the road with Johnny. He told himself it was the responsibility weighing on him, not her determination or her sparkling eyes.

On Christmas Eve, he and Justin fed the horses and buttoned down the livery for the night. In the morning, they could feed the stock and ride on out to Ethan's without having to worry about keeping a stage schedule or shoeing mules.

They'd developed an evening routine where Justin measured out the oats and Griffin threw the hay down from the loft. When the snow was deep, most of the horses stayed in the barn, though Griffin had taken four stagecoach teams to Nampa and left them there with Jeremiah Gayle for the winter. Come spring, he'd bring them back up to Fergus. He'd given Marty a month off, but even so, his workload seemed a lot easier. Part of that was due to Justin's help. The boy had lost some of his sullenness, especially while working around the horses.

Ethan's invitation to the ranch for the holiday had surprised Griffin, considering Ethan and Trudy had family close by. Hiram and Libby would join them for dinner as well. In response to the gesture, he'd stopped at the emporium the day before and picked up a box of ribbon candy to take to Trudy.

"Are we picking up Mrs. Adams in the morning?" Justin asked as he shut the grain bin.

"Yes. I'll harness two of the horses to the sled."

"Can I ride Red?"

Griffin eyed him in surprise. "I guess so." He walked over to the wall where he kept brushes and hoof picks. "How'd you like to brush the colt tonight?"

"You mean it?" Justin's eyes fairly glowed in the lantern light.

"Sure. Just speak to him soft-like, and don't do anything sudden."

Justin took the brush from him and went to the colt's stall. "Hey, fella. I'm coming in." He touched the colt's flank while standing to the side, as Griffin had taught him to.

Griffin smiled to himself. That boy could make a good hand with horses by next summer. He strolled over and leaned on the divider between the colt and Red. "That's right. Everything nice and easy. And remember, I still don't want you going in the stall with him when I'm not around."

"I won't. I promise."

"You brush him all over every night, and next week I'll have you picking up his feet."

"What for?"

Griffin chuckled. "So he'll let you."

Justin looked quizzically over his shoulder.

"You have to get a colt used to everything," Griffin said. "If you rub him all over, he gets used to being touched. Then he won't jump when a rein or a piece of rope touches him. You want him to be calm. And you practice picking up his feet and putting them down easy, so he won't mind you doing it when you need to."

"Think he'll ever be calm?" Justin asked, stroking the colt's spotted withers with the soft brush. "He's always jumping around and kicking and bucking in the corral."

"That's because he's young. He needs to learn that it's all right to play around when he's out to pasture, but when it's time for work, we get down to business."

Justin paused his strokes. "I never thought about horses needing to learn to work."

"They do, just like people. They learn that when the bridle goes on, that means you don't run and jump however you feel like it. You stay quiet and do what your master tells you. And you have fun together."

Justin began brushing the colt's mane. "You think they like it when people ride them?"

"Some of them do. When I get on Pepper, I can feel him pulling, ready to go."

Justin nodded. "I think Champ will make a good saddle horse."

"Champ?" Griffin asked.

The boy swung around and faced him. "That's what I call him in my head. Does he have another name?"

"No. No, Champ's a good name."

Justin smiled.

Justin rode ahead on Red while Griffin drove the sleigh placidly down the road. Libby sat beside him, mostly covered by a woolen quilt, cradling a large basket on her lap.

"Your nephew was very polite this morning," she said.

"He's progressing," Griffin replied.

"Have you heard anything from his mother?"

"I telegraphed her when Justin arrived, to tell her he'd gotten here safe, and we had one letter after that. To be frank, she seemed relieved to have Justin off her hands."

"That's too bad." Libby threw Griffin a smile. "It might be the best thing for you, though, and I think Justin will benefit from being with you."

"I hope you're right, ma'am."

Libby had long been known as the most beautiful woman in town, and Griffin had always felt intimidated in her presence, especially since her husband died. All the single men in Fergus had watched her, but none he knew of had dared to approach her in the first two years of her widowhood. Then, all of a sudden, Hiram Dooley was courting her. How that had come about, Griffin couldn't quite fathom. Hiram spoke so little, he couldn't imagine how the two of them passed the time when they were alone. In fact, Hiram would have been the last man in Fergus he'd have put money on to win Libby's hand. Maybe Hiram knew something he didn't.

"Will you send him to school during the winter term?" Libby asked.

Griffin jerked his head up, startled. "I hadn't thought about it. He reads and ciphers better than I do."

"He might do well with more education."

"What do you mean?"

She shrugged. "Doctors and lawyers start somewhere, Mr. Bane. Many have humble beginnings. Do you know what interests your nephew?"

"Can't say as I do."

"Maybe you should ask him."

Griffin felt he'd been mildly rebuked—but she was right. Justin had been with him more than a month, and he didn't know how the boy had spent his free time back in Pennsylvania or what he aspired to do when he was grown. Griffin had worried about keeping him away from a life of crime but hadn't considered how to keep him occupied.

By the time he turned in at the lane to the Chapman ranch, Justin had far outdistanced them, and he was unsaddling Red in Ethan's barn when Griffin drew the sled up in front of the ranch house.

"Welcome," Trudy called from the porch. Ethan and Hiram stood with her.

Hiram came down the steps and offered Libby his hand. She took it and climbed out of the sled, smiling all over.

"Drive right to the barn, Griff," said Ethan. "I'll come help you unhitch."

The McDade boys were helping Justin hang up his tack and stable Red.

"Thought those boys only worked for you in summer," Griffin said to Ethan.

"I kept them on this fall. I've been running a lot more cattle since

Trudy and I got married. They're doing my chores today and going home tomorrow to have a late Christmas with their folks. I'm giving them a couple of weeks off."

"Hey, boss," Johnny McDade called, "is it all right if Justin comes over to the bunkhouse until dinnertime?"

Ethan looked at Griffin and arched his eyebrows.

"I guess so," Griffin said.

"Sure," Ethan told Johnny. "Just come when Mrs. Chapman rings the dinner bell." They put Griffin's team away and hung up the harness. As they walked back toward the house, Ethan said, "They're high-spirited boys, but they're good workers."

Griffin sat down with his hosts in the big sitting room for a few minutes. Trudy wanted all the town gossip.

"You'll have to get the news from Libby," Griffin told her. "I don't exactly hear all the rumors."

Libby and Hiram sat off to one side, talking in low tones, holding hands, and smiling a lot. Ethan and Griffin discussed Ethan's ranching and sheriffing, and Griffin's smithing and stage coaching.

After about twenty minutes, Trudy jumped up. "I'd better go see if that goose is done."

Libby rose, too, still smiling at Hiram. "Let me help you, Trudy."

The two women disappeared through an archway. The savory smells increased, and Griffin's stomach rumbled.

"You got yourself a good one there, Hi," Ethan said.

"I know it." Hiram came over and sat down where Trudy had been. "So how are you and Justin doing at the old house?"

Griffin ran a hand across his beard. "Not too bad. It's a sight better than my little place."

Hiram nodded. "Glad it's working out for you."

Griffin still couldn't believe the change that had come over Hiram these past few months. "When are you and Libby going to tie the knot?"

"As soon as Mr. and Mrs. Hamilton come back and pay her for the store."

They talked for a while longer, until Libby came and told them dinner was ready.

"Is Trudy going to ring the bell for the boys?" Ethan asked.

"I can mosey out there and tell them," Griffin offered. He was curious as to how Justin was getting along with the McDades. He'd only met the boys once or twice at church. Both were older than Justin and seemed much more mature.

"Hold on. I'll go with you." Ethan handed Griffin his coat and hat and grabbed his own from pegs near the front door.

They ambled across the barnyard, talking about the chance of more snow. Ethan opened the bunkhouse door and stepped inside.

"Well, boys, dinner's about ready."

Griffin followed him. Justin had been seated with his back to the door, but he jumped up and whirled around with as guilty a face as Griffin had ever seen.

"All right, boss," Spin McDade said, shoving his chair back and throwing down a hand of cards.

"You boys playing poker?" Ethan sounded slightly scandalized.

"Just having fun," Johnny said with a shrug. "We don't usually get someone else to take a hand with."

Griffin frowned but decided to say nothing. He didn't want to embarrass Ethan by making a fuss, and anyway, he'd played his share of poker games. Evelyn probably wouldn't approve, but she'd given Justin's care entirely over to him.

"You're not taking Justin for every penny he's got, are you?" Ethan threw Griff an apologetic glance.

"I don't have any money, sir," Justin said. "We're playing for matchsticks." His face flushed, and he had trouble meeting Ethan's gaze.

"Aha. Well, come on and get washed up."

The boys ran ahead of them to the house.

"Sorry about that," Ethan said as he and Griffin followed.

Griffin shrugged. "His mother probably wouldn't like it, but they were just passing time. How old are those boys?"

"Spin's almost twenty. Johnny's seventeen. I never thought—"

Griffin held one hand up. "If they'd been in the Nugget playing, that'd be one thing."

"I always tell them to watch themselves in town. They know I won't put up with any nonsense. I can't. I mean, I'm the sheriff."

"I know," Griffin said. "Don't worry about it."

Ethan stamped his feet to get rid of the snow before climbing the steps. "Did you get Justin a present?"

"Yup. I'm giving him a bridle for the spotted colt he's going to help me train. And a pocketknife."

"Nice gifts for a boy that age."

"What'd you get Trudy?"

"A dress from New York. I had Libby pick it out and order it. Trudy will probably say it's too fine for her to wear."

"What'll you do if she won't wear it?"

"Oh, I think she will, though she might hang it up and look at it for a while first." Ethan chuckled. "And I got her something else she'll like real well."

"What's that?"

"A sweet, tooled leather scabbard to go on her saddle."

"Oh yeah, she'll like that. I guess Hiram's giving Libby the palomino today."

"That's the plan."

Griffin half wished for a moment that he had a special lady to give things to. It would be kind of fun to order something fancy from back East for someone pretty. He had a fleeting vision of putting a sparkly chain around the neck of an auburn-haired girl with green eyes. He shook his head as they entered the house. That would only mean spending more money, and he'd had enough trouble getting Christmas gifts for Justin. Besides, he had no intention of getting tangled up with a woman anytime soon—even one as pretty and spunky as Vashti Edwards.

At the Spur & Saddle, Christmas Day overflowed with visitors. Terrence Thistle had declared it a holiday for his wife, Rilla, at the Fennel House. Consequently, all the boarders walked down the street for dinner. Dr. Kincaid and Isabel Fennel also came to enjoy Augie's lavish ham dinner, as did Charles and Orissa Walker. Vashti and Goldie helped the Moores serve ten for dinner and then sat down together at three in the afternoon to celebrate with their own small "family."

Augie came from the kitchen carrying a covered dish. "I held back a sweet potato apiece."

"Oh good!" Goldie jumped up and planted a kiss on his cheek. "I thought sure the guests had gotten them all, and I wanted one something fierce."

After the blessing, they tucked into the ham, gravy, biscuits, cranberry sauce, squash, and carrots, along with the sweet potatoes.

"I believe I'm too full to eat any pie." Vashti leaned back and patted her stomach with regret.

Augie looked over at Bitsy and winked. "Maybe we should hold the sweets until after we see what Santy Claus brought."

Goldie chuckled. "Augie, you haven't let the fire go out long enough for Santa to come down the chimney."

" 'S'all you know. Santy's magic. Isn't that so, darlin'?" Augie appealed to Bitsy with such a hopeful face that she laughed and reached over to pat his cheek.

"You're just a kid in big boots. We can have the gifts now, if you want."

They took their dishes to the kitchen then slipped into the Moores' sitting room. Bitsy guarded their private quarters closer than she did her purse. Company was generally entertained in the public dining room. The sitting room remained a place where they could retreat from the turmoil of the business.

Augie had brought in a scraggly little fir tree early in December. Though Bitsy had scoffed at it, by nightfall, she'd clothed it with strings of popcorn and a few bits and baubles. Goldie had come home from work the next day with a dozen shimmery gold glass balls the size of plums, and Vashti had strung a garland of dried cranberries. The little tree stood in splendor now, with several small packages resting at its base. Each of the residents had stolen in sometime during the morning to add their gifts to the pile.

They took their time opening them, lingering to look and exclaim over each item as it was unwrapped. Vashti felt the presents she'd chosen went over well. Goldie put on her silver cross pendant at once, thanking Vashti prettily. Bitsy and Augie declared it was a right pretty necklace and suited her well. Bitsy's face flushed with pleasure when she opened a package of cosmetics that Vashti had asked Goldie to help her select at the emporium—hand cream, face cream, and two shades of rouge.

"There, now, you knew I was getting low, didn't you?" Bitsy opened the little pot of scarlet rouge. "What a pretty color."

Buying cosmetics had long been an expenditure for business in Bitsy's life, but her lower income for the past six months had made them a splurge. Vashti was satisfied that she'd chosen something Bitsy would appreciate.

"Miz Adams has ordered in some pretty new colors of lip rouge," Goldie said. "That 'poppy petals' is my favorite."

In the past, Vashti had given Augie a bag of penny candy for Christmas, but this year was different. He and Bitsy were married now, and they'd unofficially claimed Vashti as part of their family. She'd felt something more consequential was indicated, and after a great deal of thought and observation in the kitchen, she'd made her selection.

Augie's big hands fumbled with the ribbon and brown paper on her package. She almost warned him to be careful but held her tongue. She'd wrapped it carefully to prevent an accident.

"Well, there." Augie's smile spread across his face as he gazed down at the new butcher knife. "I can't wait to cut up a few chickens. This looks like a mighty fine blade. Thank you, missy."

Vashti hugged herself, pleased with the pleasure she'd brought those she loved.

"Here's what we got you. It ain't much, but I hope you like it." Bitsy placed a package in her hands.

Vashti opened it and stared down at a pair of silk stockings folded on top of a book.

"My own Bible." She fingered the black leather cover and smiled at them. "Thank you both."

"That was Augie's idea," Bitsy said. "I got the stockings."

"I needed a new pair desperately."

Goldie, who had the comfort of regular wages, pushed another parcel into her hands. "Open mine."

Vashti tore the paper off the squishy package and laughed. Inside was a boy's woolen cap with earflaps.

"That's in case you get to ride the stagecoach this winter. I didn't want you to freeze your ears. But look inside."

Vashti turned the cap over and tugged at the wad inside it. Out came a pair of kitten-soft leather gloves. "Oh! Thank you!"

She and the Moores settled back to watch Goldie open her gift from them. Vashti thought she'd never had such a cozy, contented Christmas. Not since her parents had died, anyhow.

Her thoughts drifted to Griffin and Justin. Were they having a good time today? Trudy had told her after the last shooting club meeting that she and Ethan had invited them to the ranch for the day. Would they have asked Griffin if his nephew wasn't living with him, or if Griffin wasn't renting the Dooleys' old house? How had Griffin spent his past Christmases, anyway? It made her sad to think he'd been alone in that grubby little room behind the smithy.

Things had changed for the better this year—for both of them. She sent up a silent prayer of thanks.

"Who's ready for dried apple pie?" Augie asked.

Vashti realized she'd hardly heard a word as Goldie opened her gift of a Bible and stockings like hers. She jumped up. "I'll help you, Augie."

Only one thing could make this day more perfect. That would be Griffin forgiving her part in the stagecoach upset and looking on her as a capable driver. More than ever, she determined to keep up her practice and be ready to step into a driving job in the spring. If he would only look at her with a smile in those big brown eyes.

"What are you sighing over?" Augie asked as he opened the pie safe.

"Nothing. Just Christmas. You and Bitsy are awfully good to me and Goldie."

"You've done as much for us as we have for you. We won't ever have any kids, so you girls kind of fill a gap there. For Bitsy especially." He shrugged. "She'd be terrible sad if you was to leave. That's not to say she wouldn't want you to find matrimonial happiness of your own, you understand. She'd love some grandchildren one day."

Vashti smiled and reached for her apron. "If that happens, I won't go far. I promise." *Maybe no farther than two blocks up the street.* She shoved that thought aside. Griffin was still mad at her. He'd never look at her as marriageable. With a shock, she realized she almost wished he would. But would she rather he saw her as a sweetheart or as a potential driver? That would be a difficult choice.

★ CHAPTER 15 ★

On the last Sunday in February, Griffin and Justin had an invitation to dine with the Reverend and Mrs. Phineas Benton after services. Griffin trimmed his beard and sponged the worst spots off his good shirt that morning. He eyed Justin critically as the boy combed his hair back with water.

They'd lived in Hiram's old house for two months. Griffin liked having a solid roof over their heads and space to put their stuff—though he didn't like having to heat such a big house. It took far too much coal, in his opinion. They hardly used the parlor, but they did use the kitchen, and they both had bedrooms. He'd let Justin take the downstairs chamber, which was closer to the stove. Griff slept upstairs by himself, where there were two good-sized rooms and a large landing.

He didn't suppose he would ever have enough furniture to fill the place. Trudy Chapman had given them a table for the kitchen, and Isabel Fennel, whose father used to own the stage line, boardinghouse, and various other concerns, had told him to take a bedstead and two chairs from the Fennel House. Terrence and Rilla Thistle, who ran the boardinghouse for Isabel, weren't too happy. They'd not only lost a steady-paying customer during the slack wintertime, but now they were losing furniture, too. Still, Isabel owned the stuff, so Griffin guessed she had the say-so.

Isabel wasn't so bad. The skinny schoolmarm had scared him to death last year when she'd visited him at the smithy and babbled on about marriage and such. But nothing had come of it, and now she seemed to fancy Doc Kincaid, so that was all right. Personally, Griffin preferred females a little less bookish. And ones with a little roundness to them.

A certain female with auburn hair came to mind, but he banished the notion. He'd tried not to think any more appreciative thoughts about Vashti. After all, she and Johnny Conway were the two responsible for staving up his Concord coach back before Christmas. When he reminded himself of that, it was easy to stay slightly perturbed with Vashti.

"You ready, Justin? We'd best get over to the church. Don't want to miss Sunday school."

"Aw, do we have to?"

"Yes, you have to."

"Mayor Nash is teaching my class about the forty years in the wilderness. It's more boring than dry corn bread."

"Well, just you wait until you get into Judges. Then things will perk up." Griff grabbed Justin's hat off a hook near the back door. "Put those earflaps down. It's cold this morning."

Justin had been pretty good about going to church ever since Griffin had moved him out of the boardinghouse. He didn't complain much, and he seemed to like Pastor Benton. Too bad Peter Nash's lessons fell on the dry side. The truth was, Griffin had only started attending Sunday school himself since Justin came. Prior to having a youngster in the house, he'd gone to morning worship only. But he couldn't send the boy off alone when the pastor taught a perfectly good class for grown-ups. So they went each week, and Griff had picked up quite a few tidbits from the study of Proverbs that he hadn't known before. Like the verse that said getting into someone else's fight when you shouldn't was like grabbing a dog by the ears. He liked that one. He'd picked a few fights in his day.

Someone had shoveled the sidewalk all the way from the Spur & Saddle at the south end of town to the Nugget on the north end. Snow was heaped between the walk and the street. The wind whistled cold and sharp up from the prairie, and Griffin leaned into it until they got around the corner, where several houses shielded them.

"Do you think it was wrong to put all the Indians on the reservations?" Justin asked as they trudged along.

"What put that notion into your head?"

Justin shrugged. "Pastor Benton said last week that we're supposed to be kind to folks, no matter what color they are."

All sorts of thoughts zipped through Griffin's mind—how his father had fought in the War Between the States; what the outcome of that meant to all the slaves; and the more recent Indian conflicts. Ethan Chapman had served in the Bannock War, and Griffin had gone with a group of men to help when Silver City was attacked. How could he tell Justin it was wrong to fight the Indians? Was it?

"I don't know," he said. He didn't suppose that answer would satisfy a fifteen-year-old boy.

But Justin only nodded, frowning. A few steps later, he said, "I don't know, either. Ma used to be kind to the black washerwoman that came to do laundry for us, and she let her bring her little girl with her. But them Injuns. . ."

"You didn't see any Indians on your way here, did you?" Griffin asked.

"A few at Fort Laramie. And we passed some on the road."

"Well, some folks say we ought to get rid of them all, but I can't agree with that."

"You can't?" Justin asked.

"No. They're people, same as us. Some of 'em steal. But then, some white men do, too." He really should have sent Justin to school this winter. Then Isabel could answer these prickly questions.

"You know any Injuns?" Justin asked.

Griffin nodded. "A few. And they're Indians, not Injuns. Blackfeet, Snake. . .I know several, as a matter of fact."

"Any of them good?"

"Yes. One of them used to scout for the army. Probably some other Indians think he's bad because he helped us. But I've talked to him several times, and he seems like a decent person. Doesn't believe like we do, but he actually bought a horse off me once—didn't try to steal it."

"So he was an exception."

"I didn't say that. But some folks think all Indians are thieves."

They'd reached the church, and Griffin was glad. He hoped Justin would forget the issue and not bring it up later. Did all parents go through this?

During the worship service, Justin fidgeted a lot. The boy hadn't said much about Sunday school, but he kept swiveling his head to look at other people. Across the aisle, the Nash boys sat with Tollie Harper. Ben and Silas Nash were close to Justin's age, and Tollie was a few years younger. Justin had asked once if he could sit with the boys. Griff had almost let him go, but then he envisioned the mischief he'd have gotten into at that age—and remembered why Evelyn had sent Justin out here in the first place—and he'd told him, "You stick with me."

Griffin tried to set a good example for the boy by paying close attention to the sermon. That was kind of hard, since Vashti and Goldie sat right in front of them, along with Augie and Bitsy Moore. Vashti wore a very modest green dress that came right up to her neck. He thought it must be new this winter—he wasn't sure. But she looked nice from his vantage point, with her auburn hair wound up on the back of her head, above the high collar. He could just glimpse a little white strip of skin at the nape of her neck. A tiny brown mole contrasted with the whiteness of her flesh. Did she even know it was there?

Justin stared at him, and Griffin jerked his eyes straight ahead and squared his shoulders. The pastor was talking about why Jesus had to die on the cross. Griffin determined to pay close attention in case Justin asked any questions later. Pastor Benton had a way of explaining things. Within fifteen seconds, he'd forgotten all about the little mole on the back of Vashti's neck. Almost.

That afternoon, after a delicious dinner of ham, cornpone, and carrots, Pastor Benton invited Griffin into the parlor with him. Somehow or other, Mrs. Benton had cajoled Justin into helping her wash the dishes—something he griped about at home. Griffin was glad to have a few minutes of respite from the boy's constant surveillance. Besides, as long as Apphia kept him in the kitchen, Justin couldn't bring up controversial topics.

"What did you think of the message this morning?" the pastor asked.

"Oh, you did fine, Preacher." Griffin sipped his coffee.

"No, I don't mean my delivery. I mean, what did you think of the sermon itself?"

Griffin swallowed and set his cup down on a bitty little table that sat between their chairs. "Well, I. . ."

"Yes?" The minister leaned forward eagerly.

"It's a subject I've wondered about before."

"How so?"

"Well, you said nothing we do can get us to heaven—that it was all Christ's doing."

"That's right."

Griffin shook his head. "My ma used to tell me to be good. You know, don't lie, don't steal, do my chores well. If I didn't, she said I wouldn't go to heaven."

The pastor smiled regretfully. "I'm afraid a lot of people have that misconception."

"But isn't that what real religion is? Obeying God?"

"Yes, in one sense. But you can't truly obey God if you don't believe in Him first."

Griffin squeezed up his eyes and looked that one over. "Yup. Reckon that's right."

"And you do believe in God, don't you?"

"Of course." It was almost insulting that the preacher would ask. "How could anyone not believe in God?" Even the miners who used to come to town Saturday night and shoot up the saloons believed there was a God. They just weren't acquainted with Him.

"And do you believe in Jesus Christ as your Savior? That He died for your sins?"

"Well. . .sure."

Pastor Benton looked as happy as a pup with a hock bone. "What about Justin? I'm delighted that you've been bringing your nephew to church and Sunday school. Do you think he knows the Lord?"

Griffin puzzled over that one. "Well. . ." He had no answer.

"Griffin, since you're responsible for Justin now, it's your duty to consider his spiritual education."

"Ah. . ." Griffin wasn't quite sure what that meant. "We pray before we eat."

"That's good. Have you talked to him about God and sin and right and wrong?"

"Maybe some. Right and wrong, I mean." Griffin winced and glanced toward the kitchen. "Justin was in some trouble back in Pennsylvania."

"I see. And his mother hopes he'll behave better out here?"

Griffin scratched his chin through his beard. "I'm not really sure what she hopes. Sometimes I think she just doesn't want to hear if he gets into any more scrapes."

"So she's transferred her obligations as a parent to you."

That didn't sound very complimentary of his sister. "Evelyn was having a hard time after her husband died, and she's got other young'uns to consider."

The pastor nodded gravely. "I want you to know that I'm praying for you, and I'll be here to help you in any way that I can."

"Well, Justin likes you. That's good. Oh, and if he asks you about the Indians. . ."

Phineas Benton's eyebrows rose. "Indians?"

"Yeah. Whether reservations are right or wrong and such."

"Ah. I see the boy is a thinker."

"You might say that."

"Well, as I said, I'm here to assist you anytime you need it."

"Good. I appreciate that. And if you hear about Justin sneaking into the Nugget or smoking behind the schoolhouse, or anything like that, you tell me, all right?"

"I surely will, but it's my hope that you won't have to deal with such things."

"Oh, I've already dealt with one of them."

The pastor's eyes flared, but Mrs. Benton and Justin came in from the kitchen just then.

"There, the dishes are all clean until the next meal," Apphia said with a bright smile. "Justin was a big help."

"That's wonderful," said the pastor.

The boy plopped down on a chair. "Reverend, I heard that they don't let Mormons vote in Idaho Territory. What do you think of that?"

The glance Benton threw at Griffin was near panicky. Griffin almost laughed.

On Monday morning, Vashti bundled up and walked over to the Bentons' house. She didn't go to the door but walked around back in the crunchy snow, to the stable behind the house. She came every morning that Bitsy didn't need her help. Augie had rigged up a little box stove so she could have some heat while she practiced her driving. She didn't like to burn much fuel, as firewood and coal were expensive. But Bitsy said it was an investment in her future and a better job, so she kept coming.

She rolled the door open and jumped back. Three figures huddled together on the board floor near the stove. Cautiously, she poked her head back inside and eyed the young men critically.

"What are you boys doing here?"

"Uh. . ." Ben Nash stared at her, clearly groping for a believable explanation.

Justin, on the other hand, just looked at her with his jaw set in a determined frown.

Will Ingram spoke up. "We're meeting here for a clubhouse, ma'am."

"A clubhouse?" Vashti focused on Will. "Shouldn't you be in school?"

"I ain't going anymore. Justin doesn't go to school, and he's my age, so I told my pa I'd had enough learning."

"Oh really." She turned her gaze on Justin. No sense blaming him. It wasn't his fault that Griffin hadn't enrolled him in school.

"How about you, Ben? Has your father let you quit school, too?"

"Uh. . .no, ma'am. I just ran over here on recess, and. . ." He trailed off, his face flushing.

"Mighty long recess." Vashti stepped forward and closed the rolling door, then held her hands to the stove. "Thanks for making my fire up for me. What are you doing?"

"Uh. . ." Ben seemed to be stuck on that syllable. It didn't matter. She'd seen them shove cards and coins into their pockets when she'd arrived.

"Well, let me tell you something," she said, looking around sternly at the three. "Mr. and Mrs. Benton are friends of mine. They let me use this stable to practice my driving." She nodded toward the rig hanging from the rafters and the reins threaded from it to her wagon seat. "I'm pretty sure they wouldn't like it if someone else came in here without their permission. Especially not if those people were doing something they would consider immoral."

"Like what?" Will asked with a smirk.

"Oh, like drinking, or smoking, or. . .gambling."

"Huh. You should talk."

Vashti glared at him. "I beg your pardon."

Justin whirled on Will. "Hey, quit that. She's a nice lady. And she works for my uncle."

Will scowled at Vashti. "Well, I've had enough for today, anyhow. You kids need to grow up." He walked to the door and let himself out.

Ben gulped and edged toward the gap. "I'd best get back to the schoolhouse."

"Yes, I'm sure Miss Fennel wonders what's keeping you," Vashti said.

Ben scooted out. She turned to face Justin.

"Well now, it's just you and me. How'd you come to be trespassing with them?"

Justin gulped. "Are you going to tell Uncle Griff?"

"Should I?"

"No, ma'am. Because it will never happen again."

"Here? Or anyplace?"

Justin was silent for a long moment, holding her gaze.

"You know your uncle cares about you, Justin. He wants to see you grow into a responsible man."

Justin's chin sank, and he lowered his gaze. "I don't want to make him mad."

Vashti considered that. Was he afraid Griffin would punish him harshly? At last she said, "Griffin treats you all right, doesn't he?"

"Yes, ma'am. And I don't want to make him sorry that he took me in."

"Then you shouldn't sneak around places you shouldn't be, doing things you know you shouldn't do."

Slowly Justin nodded. "I know that's right. And I'm sorry I did it. I'm sorry Ben got involved, too. He's a good kid, and his dad would be really upset if he found out Ben skipped school."

Vashti walked over to the wagon seat and climbed onto it. She found it very important that Griffin should succeed as a father and that Justin shouldn't go astray. But would he listen to her?

"This is a very small town, Justin. Ben's father sees most of the residents several times a week. If you don't think that one of them— or Ben's younger brother or the teacher—will tell him Ben wasn't in school this morning, then you underestimate the power of the wagging tongues in a small town."

He stood still, staring at the floor for a minute.

"Where's your uncle this morning?" Vashti asked.

"He had to drive down to the swing station to pick up a wagonload of oats. I wanted to go, but. . ."

"But what?"

He flicked a glance at her. "He told me to stay and clean up the barn."

"Did you do it?"

"Partly."

"Hmm. Do you wish you were in school with Ben and his brother?"

Justin shrugged. "I don't mind being done with it. I like helping at the livery. Didn't think I would, but I sort of do, now that I'm not afraid of the horses anymore."

She untied the reins and laced them through her fingers. "Let me ask you something. How do think Griffin will feel if he comes home this afternoon and you haven't done the work he set you?"

"Disappointed, I guess."

"Now imagine him coming home and finding the livery all

cleaned up, even neater than he asked you to make it. How would he feel then?"

Justin pressed his lips together. "Good, I guess."

"Mmm. And you'd feel good, too. Griffin's not a hard man, Justin. I thought he was at first, but I was wrong. He's got a big heart, and he's got a soft spot for you."

He took two steps toward her and looked her in the eye. "I didn't mean to do anything bad today."

"Maybe you should tell Mr. and Mrs. Benton that."

He sucked in a breath. "Do they have to know?"

"The way I see it, if you don't tell them and I don't tell them, and then their stable burns down or they find something broken or missing from here, that wouldn't be good, would it?"

"I won't come back. Honest."

"No, but Will might. If not here, then somebody else's barn where they don't go very often. Will's a kid who has a nose for trouble. You don't want to be like him, Justin." She looked him up and down. "I think you want to be a man, not a brat of a kid that folks hate to see coming."

"Is that what people think of Will?"

"I didn't say that."

Justin stood frowning for a moment, then went over near the stove and picked up his hat. "I guess that was your wood we burned."

"I'll make good use of what heat's left."

He nodded and went to the door. "If you're going to tell Uncle Griff. . ."

Vashti smiled. "Why don't you just make things so that it won't matter whether I tell him or not?"

He eyed her suspiciously, then gave a nod and went out. He rolled the door shut behind him.

Vashti laid down the reins and hurried to the entrance. She pushed the door over an inch and squinted through the crack. Justin walked to the back door of the pastor's house and knocked. Mrs. Benton opened the door and greeted him with a wide smile. Vashti pushed the door shut and went back to her imaginary stagecoach, sending up a prayer for Griffin and Justin. Even if Griffin didn't like her, she wanted to see that family turn out all right.

★ CHAPTER 16 ★

Spring came slowly to Fergus, a gradual shrinking of the snow and a hint of red on the ends of branches as buds swelled. Mud the length of Main Street heralded the thaw, and suddenly ranchers were putting their wagon boxes back on the axles and leaving the sleigh runners in the barn.

As the bare earth appeared, ground squirrels came out, and large flocks of birds winged overhead. Vashti spent more time in the Wells Fargo office, selling tickets for the stagecoaches to the flat regions and telling folks who wanted a ride up to Silver City or Delamar that they'd have to wait a little longer.

Bill Stout came in one morning, his eyes twinkling. "Well now, Miss Edwards, you been practicing your driving skills?"

"I surely have. Missed a few days during the coldest of the cold spells, but I've been out there every day this past month and more."

"Want to try driving real horseflesh?"

She caught her breath. "You mean it?"

Bill nodded. "Hiram Dooley's got a team of four we can borrow this afternoon with his wagon. Thought we'd take them out the Mountain Road, just to let you get the feel of them."

"I'd love to!" She'd rather drive a six-horse hitch and a fine Concord coach, but this would be experience driving genuine, living horses.

She and Bill bundled up in their overcoats, woolen hats, and mufflers, and she pulled on her trousers beneath her skirt. Bill borrowed two saddle horses from the livery, and they rode out to the ranch Hiram Dooley managed. The rancher met them in the dooryard to help hitch up the horses. Vashti doffed her gloves when she took the reins. Bill joined her on the wagon seat, and they set off. The exhilaration of really driving kept her warm for the first half hour on the road, but then her hands began to chill.

"How do you keep your hands warm on a cold day?" she asked.

"Sometimes you've got to wear gloves, but unless it's a flat, smooth road and a steady team, I wouldn't recommend it. What I have in my gear is a blanket with slits in it for the reins. It's not ideal, but it lets me thread the reins through and keep my hands under the blanket. It's awkward, but it's a sight better than frostbite. Short of that, in a pinch you can take all the reins in one hand for a short time and put the other hand in your pocket, but you're not really in control if you do that."

Vashti nodded. Maybe sitting out the winter driving season hadn't been such a hardship, after all.

The horses shied as a small herd of pronghorns appeared in the road ahead.

"Easy now." She kept firm pressure on the lines and talked calmly to the team. The pronghorns skipped off across the hillside, and the horses gradually fell back into their road gait.

Bill nodded. "Spring's coming, for sure."

"Seems like it took its time."

When they returned from their drive, Bill nodded toward the hitching post before the ranch house, where a buckskin mare was tied. "Looks like Miz Chapman's here to see her brother." He helped Vashti down from the wagon. "Go on into the house and visit with her. I'll put the horses away."

"Oh no," Vashti said. "You're not doing all the work."

He frowned at her flowing skirt. "But you're not wearing your boy togs."

"Well, it won't be the first time I've unhitched a team while wearing a dress."

While they worked, Hiram came into the barn. "How'd your driving go?"

"Wonderful," Vashti said. "Thank you so much for letting me use your team."

Hiram nodded and looked to Bill.

"She did fine," Bill said. "I reckon she can handle six if she gets a chance."

Vashti glowed inside. "That's nice of you."

Bill shrugged.

"Trudy's here," Hiram said. "She's putting the kettle on."

"Go on." Bill reached to unbuckle the last harness. "We'll take care of this. Scoot."

"All right, since you gentlemen insist." Vashti hurried to the back door of the house. The ranch had belonged to Cyrus Fennel, the schoolteacher's father. Mr. Fennel had owned half the town in the old days, and now Isabel did. But after her father's death, Isabel had reached some sort of arrangement with Hiram to run the ranch for her so she could live in town. Vashti wasn't sure what Hiram's duties entailed, but she knew his job made it possible for him and Libby Adams to get married soon. At one of the shooting club meetings, Libby had told the ladies of her engagement amid blushes and prompts from Trudy.

Vashti had never been to the ranch before. She couldn't tell much so far. The barn was huge, and several outbuildings circled the barnyard. A bunkhouse, she supposed, and maybe a smokehouse and a woodshed. And the house was fine. Nicer than any in town, with the possible exception of Charles and Orissa Walker's yellow frame house.

She knocked timidly on the kitchen door. Trudy opened it, grinning. A large, flower-print apron covered most of her blue wool dress, and her hair was done up in braids, wrapped on top of her head.

"Hello! Come right in. How was your drive?"

"Magnolious," Vashti said. "Not like sitting on the box of a stage, but closer than I've been all winter."

Trudy chuckled and led her to the table. A plain brown teapot sat steaming in the middle, and two ironstone mugs and a jug of cream waited for them.

"Isn't this the grandest kitchen you ever saw?" Trudy asked.

Vashti looked around. "It's almost as big as the one at the Spur & Saddle."

"Yes, and that nickel-trimmed stove cost old Cy Fennel a pretty penny, I'll wager."

"Must have taken a lot of effort for Oscar Runnels to haul it up here with a mule team," Vashti said.

Trudy sat down and poured the tea. "Isabel took the fine china with her to her new place in town, but she left a lot of dishes and things here for Hiram. Of course, Libby has her own dishes, too, and furniture and linens. I'm not sure where they'll put everything when they get married."

"I've been in Mrs. Adams's rooms," Vashti said. "She's got beautiful things."

"Yes. Hiram's going to move it all out here before the wedding. The whole shooting club can help them move."

"That will be exciting. When's the day?"

Trudy shrugged. "The Hamiltons said they'd come back in the spring and bring her the rest of the money for the emporium. When they take over, she'll be ready to marry my brother. And the Hamiltons want to buy her whole building and live in the apartment upstairs, so it's perfect."

"Say, maybe you could give some of the extra things to Griffin and Justin."

"That's a good idea."

The men came in and joined them for hot tea, but as soon as he'd downed his cupful, Bill said, "We'd best push off, Georgie. It'll be getting dark soon."

"Georgie?" Trudy eyed him askance.

"It's actually my real name," Vashti said. "Georgia. When I'm riding the stage, the fellows call me George so the passengers won't know I'm—" She broke off and felt her face warm. "I guess it's no secret. Folks hereabouts know, anyway."

"Might protect you some," Hiram said.

Vashti looked over at him. It was the first thing Hiram had said since he came in from the barn. She'd rarely heard him speak, but she guessed he'd found enough words to convince Libby Adams to accept his suit.

When she and Bill got back to the livery stable, Griffin had one of the stagecoaches on the main barn floor and was greasing the axles. Its red paint and gold trim glinted in the afternoon light. He glanced up as they led their mounts in.

"Road to Silver's open."

Bill smiled. "Well now."

"You up to taking the run tomorrow?"

"Sure."

Griffin straightened and picked up the grease bucket. "If it doesn't rain, you should be able to go all the way through. There's a couple of real soft spots, though. If we do get some weather, you might have to lay over at Sinker Creek."

"I can handle it, boss."

Griffin nodded and fixed his gaze on Vashti. "What about you? You ready to shake out your pants and boots?"

She caught her breath. "You want me to ride shotgun for Bill tomorrow?"

"No, I've got another job in mind for you." He came over and stood facing her soberly. "I'm taking over the mail run as far as Catherine. Johnny's going to drive that route for the time being. Thought I'd put you on the Reynolds-Nampa run."

Vashti almost said, "Who's driving?" but Griffin said, almost as an afterthought, "With Ned Harmon."

Her heart raced. "You mean—"

"That's right, missy. You'll drive and Ned will watch your back."

She could hardly breathe. "Oh! Oh! Thank you!" She flung herself at him and reached up to embrace him. His bushy beard tickled her cheek.

"Hey! Watch it!"

She backed away, mortified.

Griffin laughed. "I'm holding a bucket of axle grease, gal. Don't think you want that all over your pretty dress, do you?"

"No, sir." Vashti laced her fingers together and squeezed her hands tight. She was going to drive the stage. And she'd hugged Griffin. But maybe it didn't matter. He thought her dress was pretty. Did that mean anything?

She gulped and looked over at Bill.

His eyes twinkled. "Well, there. I guess your hard work paid off."

The next morning, Vashti came down the stairs at the Spur & Saddle in her masculine attire. Augie and Bitsy were laying out clean dishes for the noon traffic, which had been dismally slow, and Augie was polishing the big mirror behind the serving counter that used to be the bar.

"Look at that, dearest," Augie said to Bitsy. "It's our little boy going out to play."

Bitsy laughed. "Don't mind him, honey." She came over to stand before Vashti and placed both hands on her shoulders. "You take care."

"I will. And they treat me nice at the home station in Nampa."

"Good."

"Who's riding shotgun for you?" Augie asked.

"Ned Harmon."

"Well, he's not so bad. Just don't let him go carousing tonight. Remind him he's got to bring you home safe tomorrow."

"She can't stop Ned if he wants to drink." Bitsy frowned. "I expect knowing Griffin will be watching him when you get back here will keep him from doing too much damage."

"I hope so." Though Vashti had never ridden with Ned before, she remembered nights when he'd come into the saloon and drunk himself under the table. But those weren't times when he had to go on duty the next morning. Cyrus Fennel ran the line then, and he wouldn't have stood it. "I'm just glad I'll finally be sitting in the driver's seat."

"Well, don't you get too cocky," Bitsy said. "There's more to life than driving stage and showing up men who don't drive as well as you."

Vashti laughed. "I'm as green as they grow, Bitsy. I know I've got a lot to learn before I'm as good as Bill, or even Johnny."

"Well, at least you've got an old hand riding shotgun. Ned's all right, and he's been riding these roads for twenty years." Bitsy pulled her close and kissed her. "We'll see you tomorrow."

Vashti arrived at the livery an hour before the stage was scheduled to leave. She inspected the coach. It had sat idle all winter, but Griffin had gone over it and touched up the paint. The glass in the side lantern gleamed, and every piece of hardware shone.

Griffin grinned at her as he came in the back door with two large mules. "You want to brush these fellows down?"

"I'd love to." Vashti stowed the bag with the few things she'd need for her overnight stay in Nampa and went into the first stall.

Griffin brought in two more mules then stopped at the opening to the stall. "That's Blackie. He'll be your off wheeler. I'm giving you mules because there's still some heavy going in places."

"I don't mind." She didn't really, though she'd always imagined driving horses. But mules were surefooted, and they ate less than horses. They pulled better in mud or sand. "What's the other wheeler's name?"

"Elijah."

She smiled and ducked under Blackie's neck to brush his other side. When she'd finished with him, she went to Elijah's stall to groom him and check his feet. By the time she'd done with him, Marty Hoffstead was grooming the swing mules, so she headed across the barn floor to where the leaders were hitched.

Bill Stout came in, looking about in the dim, warm barn. "There you are." He walked over to Vashti. "Came to wish you luck."

"Thanks, Bill. That means a lot."

He brought his left hand from behind his back and held out a coiled driver's whip.

"Brought you this."

Vashti looked down at it, her eyes filling with tears. "Aw, Bill! That's the nicest thing you could have done." She sniffed.

He held the whip away from her and cocked his head to one side. "You ain't gonna cry now, are you?"

"No, sir." She straightened her shoulders and smiled. "I'm going to drive like a man."

Bill chuckled. "Don't know as you need to go so far as that, but the passengers might lose confidence in you if you're bawling all the way to Nampa."

"I won't be. I'll be singing inside."

Griffin, who had brought Blackie out to hitch to the coach, called, "Don't sing out loud. They'd really get nervous if they knew they had a soprano driving them."

If she heard one more word of caution or advice, Vashti might just pop her cork. With effort, she kept smiling and holding in her eagerness to be on the road.

When the mules were harnessed, Griffin walked over to her. "I reckon you want to drive the rig up to the office."

"I sure do, if you don't mind."

"Not a bit. I'll ride along with you. Marty will come over to the office, too, to hold the team while the passengers load."

Bill touched her shoulder lightly. "Godspeed, Georgie. I'm heading up to Silver in a couple hours, but I'll be thinking of you."

"Thanks, Bill." She lifted the whip in salute and hurried out to mount the box.

Marty held the leaders' bridles, and Griffin stood beside the coach.

"Ordinarily I'd help you up, but. . ."

She grinned. "It'd look pretty odd if you did." With a bound she was in her seat and gathering the reins.

Griffin climbed up beside her.

"Where's Ned?"

"He'll join us at the stop."

She adjusted the leathers along her fingers and looked ahead between the leaders' twitching ears, then nodded to Marty. He let go of their heads, and she clucked and slackened the reins.

"Let's go, boys!"

The mules set off at a laconic walk. Vashti felt her cheeks warm. This was no way to start her first official drive. Stubborn mules. She passed the near reins into her right hand and grabbed the whip Bill had brought her. She shook out the coiled lash and snapped her wrist, making the lash pop. At once, Blackie and Elijah picked up a trot, and the other four mules followed their lead.

She tucked the whip behind her boots and sorted out the lines again. When she had the six reins in position and felt the slightest tension on every one, she dared to look up again. The mules were still trotting as they passed Walker's Feed Store, almost to the Wells Fargo.

"Not bad," Griffin said.

She laughed. "Thank you."

"You'll have one sack of mail going out."

"Oh." She gulped. Carrying the mail was a heavy responsibility.

"There'll be more when you come back tomorrow."

She nodded. "All right. Ned and I can handle it."

"Nothing stops the U.S. Mail. Nothing."

"Yes, sir."

"You mind that place where the rocks are on both sides of the road?"

"Yeah. Where the outlaw hides."

"That's the spot. If he's there, you're not giving up the mail."

"I'm not giving up anything, Mr. Bane."

His eyes narrowed. "That's the spirit. But you know, if it comes down to it, the mail. . .well, it is the U.S. Mail, but it's not worth your life or Ned's."

"I'll keep it in mind."

"You got a weapon?"

"Got my pistol in my bag."

"I'd feel better if you and Ned both had long guns. I'll let you take that rifle I keep at the office."

"If you want."

"I do."

She guided the mules ever so slightly, and they eased on over to the boardwalk in front of the stage line office nice as you please. Several people had gathered to wait for them.

"Whoa now!" They stopped in formation and stood swishing their tails. Vashti exhaled. So far so good. She wouldn't be so nervous with Ned beside her instead of the boss. She glanced up at Griffin.

His brown eyes glittered. "Nice job, George. I think you'll do."

He hopped down and she stared after him, feeling hot all over. Who'd have thought a good word from the boss would mean so much to her?

Ned was waiting near the office door, his shotgun over his shoulder, but he straightened as Griffin stepped up on the walk. He gave Vashti a nod, and she returned it. Marty came trotting up the sidewalk, went to the front of the team, and held Blackie's cheek strap as a precaution. Ned followed Griffin into the office. The mail sack went into the coach first. The mail always took priority over passengers. If there was a lot of mail, sometimes passengers had to sit on the roof. But since this batch originated in Fergus, there wasn't much. The hundred residents hadn't written more than a couple of dozen letters.

Griffin plopped the sack into the coach while Ned stood by, watching the people milling about. The boss stood back and smiled at those who waited.

"Passengers can board now."

Ralph and Laura Storey climbed into the stage, along with two miners who'd walked down from Booneville. When all were in, Griffin shut the door and went back into the office. Ned came over to the front of the coach and mounted the box beside her, holding his shotgun.

He eyed Vashti critically. "They tell me I'm s'posed to call you George."

"Right. That's my name. George Edwards."

He laughed. "Can't fool me. Take it away, George."

At that moment, Griffin emerged from the doorway carrying a Spencer rifle. He handed it up to Ned.

"Pass that to the driver."

Vashti took it and slid it into the space behind her feet, where her small bag lay.

"It's all loaded," Griffin said quietly, "and here's a box of extra cartridges."

Ned stowed the ammunition under their seat. Griffin stood back and nodded soberly.

Vashti took up her whip, gave Marty a nod, and cracked the lash in the air. "Up now!" The mules broke in a smooth trot. She shot one glance over to the boardwalk. Griffin smiled, and she smiled back before facing the road.

★ CHAPTER 17 ★

Aside from oozy mud in the low spots and a washed-out roadbed near a creek, the drive wasn't too bad. Every stream filled its banks nearly level as snowmelt thundered down from the mountains. Even as they bowled along past the rock formations with Ned keeping a sharp eye out for the bandit, Vashti's heart sang, and she noted patches of brown grass as they came down to the flat land, with hints of green beginning to show.

The river crossing on the ferry threw her heart into her throat. She'd never ventured on the water when it flowed this high and fast. Though the mules were firmly hitched, she and Ned stood at their heads and stroked them as they were pulled across the roaring, swirling flood.

They made it through to Nampa without mishap. When they pulled up at the home station and the tender came to open the door for passengers, Vashti let out a deep sigh and coiled her whip.

"Not half bad," Ned said. He climbed over the top of the coach to get the luggage out of the boot.

Vashti scrambled down. The stationmaster was handing over the mail sack to the postmaster.

Mr. and Mrs. Storey were staying with the coach all the way to Boise. Laura leaned out the window and called, "Nice driving, George."

Vashti turned and grinned at her, and Laura winked.

"Thank you kindly. I hope you folks have a pleasant journey," Vashti said.

The home station in Nampa was run by a married man, and his wife and three children helped with the animals and the meals. A hearty dinner and a bunk in the ten-year-old daughter's room awaited Vashti. Ned went off to bunk in a room they kept for the usual stage drivers and messengers. The whole Gayle family knew she was a woman, but even the youngsters were careful to keep quiet about the open secret. When Vashti retired, young Becky was already asleep in the top bunk. Vashti put on her flannel night-gown, snuffed the candle, and slid in under a pile of quilts on the lower bed.

"Thank You, Lord." She yawned, letting the warmth and her full belly and the comfort of a safe home lull her into sleep without being more specific about her gratitude.

The next morning when they set out for Fergus, four horses pulled the stage. They would change to a team of six mules again at the Democrat Station.

Vashti was confident they'd have a good trip. True, they had to cross the swollen river again, but the ferrymen knew what they were doing. They took on two bulging sacks of mail and five passengers. One of the riders was Emmaline Landry, a member of the shooting club. She rode in the coach with three miners going to Silver City and a cowboy hoping to get a job in the hill country. When Vashti climbed to the driver's seat, Emmaline was already quizzing the cowhand about where he'd previously worked.

Early in the afternoon, they approached the rock formations again. The breeze off the mountains chilled Vashti. She buttoned her fleece-lined jacket around her neck and wrapped her black knit muffler snugly beneath her chin, wishing she'd worn a knit cap instead of her cowboy hat.

They changed the team for four different horses at a swing station and headed steadily uphill toward Fergus. They breezed along on the flatter stretches. The Democrat Station was next, where they'd get a late dinner while the tenders swapped out the team. Then the road would be mostly uphill.

Ned slumped down in the seat, but his eyes continually roved the landscape. His leathery skin made him look old, but his hair still held its medium brown color. Vashti figured he had to be past forty, but nowhere near as old as Bill.

"How long you been doing this job?" she asked.

"Too long. I'm thinking of quitting after this summer."

Vashti looked over at him in surprise. "What would you do?"

"Maybe take a swing station. Griffin has trouble keeping good tenders in some spots. I think I could make a go of it and have a garden and maybe some beef."

They approached the uphill grade, heading toward where the rocks were, and Vashti urged the horses not to slacken their pace.

"Think that outlaw's out here?" she asked.

"Too early. Another month or so, when it's warm enough to sleep out and be comfortable. The ground's not even dry yet."

That was some solace. The leaders tried to slow down. One of them broke stride. She grabbed her whip and cracked it. They surged forward. She eased up on the reins, keeping the lightest touch possible, and called out to them.

"Move, you! Get along."

Ned jerked his shotgun to his shoulder.

Vashti caught some movement in her peripheral vision and shot a glance off to the left side of the road ahead, where Ned was aiming.

"It's that outlaw." She reached for the whip again.

"If it's him, he's got friends."

Vashti's chest ached. She snapped the whip, popping the lash between the lead team's heads. "Hee-yah! Up now!"

She didn't look to the side again but watched the road ahead. In the distance, a report sounded above the creaking of harness and the pounding of hooves.

"What was that?" yelled one of the passengers.

"Land sakes, are we being held up?" Emmaline called.

"Easy, folks," Ned replied. His shotgun went off and Vashti jumped. The horses sprang into a canter, outrunning the acrid smoke. Vashti's heart hammered and her hat flew off.

Above the noise, Emmaline screeched. Vashti gritted her teeth.

Emmaline belonged to the Ladies' Shooting Club. Now would be a good time for her to stay calm and produce a weapon. She wished she could use Griffin's rifle, but she'd best concentrate on keeping this stagecoach rolling. The road passed closest to the rocks about three hundred yards ahead. If they could get past that, the road was clear to the Democrat Station.

She raised her whip, tempted to let the horses feel the lash. But that wasn't the way of a stagecoach driver. She cracked it again, first on the off side, then the near side. The team tore along the road with the coach swaying behind them on its leather thoroughbraces. Several shots powed behind her, loud and close. The passengers must be firing out the windows.

"How many?" she yelled at Ned.

"Three that I can see. One was on foot, but one's riding up behind." He braced himself and rose so he could fire over the top of the coach. The blast deafened Vashti for several seconds.

As they neared the boulder closest to her route, a mounted man emerged from behind it. He planted his dark horse facing her, directly in their path.

Vashti gasped. She shot up a prayer and determined to use Johnny's strategy. *I'll run right over him!*

"Hee-yah! Hee-yah!" She half stood and cracked her whip repeatedly. What she wouldn't give for the team of six matched bays Bill was likely driving today. They held the speed record for this stretch of road. She could feel the leaders' hesitation through the reins. They were almost on top of the rider. Could she hold them steady and pull out Griffin's rifle at the same time?

The outlaw turned his horse slightly sideways and trained his rifle on them.

"Ned?" Vashti called.

Ned's shotgun went off again with a crash. Emmaline screamed.

A horseman charged up beside them and edged past the front of the coach, up next to the wheelers. The rider had a cloth tied over his mouth and a hat pulled low over his eyes. As he gained on the stagecoach team, Vashti stared at the gunman in her path straight ahead.

Another shot cracked, and Ned dropped his gun. It slid down the box and lodged next to her feet.

"Ned!" She looked over at him as he crumpled on the seat, hugging his arm to his side.

★ CHAPTER 18 ★

The horses gave up suddenly, with the leaders stopping in their tracks before the steely-eyed gunman in their path. The wheelers ran into them and stopped, too, with loud oofs and squeals. The second outlaw rode up to the leaders and grabbed the near horse's bridle. The gunman who'd sat his horse square in the path rode forward.

"Throw down your weapons." He held his rifle aimed at Vashti.

She gulped, measuring their chances.

"Do it now, Driver."

"I need to help my messenger. You've shot him." She glared at the outlaw.

"Land, Benny, she's a girl." The man holding her team laughed.

"Shut up. I got eyes in my head."

Vashti hadn't realized until that moment that after her hat flew off, her hair had tumbled down. Strands of it flew loose about her face in the breeze.

"Hand the gun down," the one called Benny ordered.

A third outlaw had walked up to the side of the coach and stood just below her. He must be the one with no horse. Even in the chilly wind, beads of sweat stood on his brow. Vashti reached down and took Ned's shotgun. She was tempted to blast one of them.

The man on the ground must have sensed her thoughts. He pointed his gun at her and snarled, "Don't even think it, darlin'."

She held the shotgun out barrel first, and the man took it. Would they find Griffin's rifle and her pistol? She tried not to give away any more by staring coldly into his eyes, but it was hard not to think of the guns behind her feet.

"Now get down," the one called Benny said.

Besides Benny, the man holding the team, and the man on foot, a fourth outlaw had dismounted and stalked over to the door of the coach. "Time to get out, folks."

Vashti half hoped one of the passengers would let loose a barrage of gunfire so she could dive for Griff's rifle. The man covering her with his weapon glared at her.

"Move."

She looped the reins around the brake handle and turned to Ned. He huddled on the box, squeezing his arm. Blood soaked the sleeve of his wool jacket.

"Ned, are you hurt bad?"

"Hurts like blazes but could be worse." His teeth never opened as he ground out the words.

"I said get down, and I meant it. Both of you."

"Best do as they say." Ned winced.

"I'll help you." Vashti went over the side backward and groped for the step, keeping her eyes on Ned. "Can you come over this way?"

He groaned and slid into her seat.

Vashti hopped down and stood, anxiously staring upward and trying to ignore the gunman at her back. She held up her hands in a futile gesture of aid. Ned's boot found the step, and he oozed over the side of the box, sliding down in a rush. As she tried to catch him, she got knocked to the ground for her trouble.

"Take it easy, folks. Just get out nice and slow," the fourth robber said.

Vashti picked herself up and crouched beside Ned. "You okay?"

He moaned and blinked up at her.

One of the horses whinnied, and she glanced over to see one of the outlaws cutting through the leaders' harness. She opened her mouth to protest, but a stern voice behind her said, "I wouldn't try anything if I were you."

A quick assessment told her that one of the outlaws guarded her and Ned while another cut the horses free of their harness and a third one terrorized the passengers on the other side of the coach. Their outraged spluttering was all she needed to hear. The outlaws were robbing them blind.

Vashti focused on Benny, the leader. She tried to memorize as much about him as she could, but he'd masked his features well.

The one who'd cut the lead team free called, "All right, Benny. These two look good. Did you check for a money box?"

"Not yet." He dismounted and came over to the coach.

On the ground beside Ned, Vashti could see his feet as he went to where the passengers stood. "We don't have a treasure box. No money today."

"Shut up," said the one standing over her.

Vashti watched him. When he shifted so he could see Benny checking the inside of the coach, she leaned close to Ned. "Can you help if I make a move?"

His eyes widened. "Don't. They'll shoot you."

"Well, this ain't worth much." Benny threw the two mail sacks out of the stage and hopped to the ground. He and one of the other outlaws cut open the sacks and turned them upside down, dumping the mail on the ground. Letters and advertisements fluttered in the breeze and skimmed over the damp earth.

Another outlaw crowed. The one who'd cut the harnesses had mounted the coach and found Griffin's rifle.

A bitter taste filled Vashti's mouth. "I should have dropped the reins and gone for the gun first thing."

"We didn't know there were four of them." Ned grimaced and closed his eyes. "Don't do anything stupid."

She gritted her teeth and watched, but the man jumped down from the box with Griffin's rifle and extra ammunition.

"Got me a nice Spencer."

The robbers gathered, showing each other their plunder. The one who'd robbed the passengers had taken two pistols, some money, and a pocket watch. The others had collected Ned's shotgun, Griffin's rifle, and the two lead horses.

"All right, let's get out of here," Benny said.

The man who had guarded Vashti and Ned backed away from

them. From behind his neckerchief mask, he said, "You know, if we leave those other two horses, they'll be at the next station in ten minutes."

"We don't need four horses," said Benny. "Two is enough."

"We could shoot the extras," another man offered.

Heat surged through Vashti. She leaped up and faced them with clenched fists. "How could you be such monsters? I understand you wanting money, and even shooting Ned, because he'd have shot you if you didn't. But to kill innocent animals?"

Benny laughed. "Little spitfire. Maybe we should take her along with us."

"She's got grit," one of his friends admitted.

"Hey, can you cook?" Benny called.

"Let's go," the fourth man said, looking up the road toward the Democrat Station. "Someone else could come along any minute."

"Come on. Bring the other nags." Benny took the rope his cohort had tied to one of the lead team and rode off with the two horses in tow.

The man with no mount ran to the tongue of the coach and unhitched the wheelers from the whiffletrees. He stood on the tongue and swung onto the near horse's back, coiling up the long rein, and rode off after his comrades with the off wheeler still hitched to his mount and keeping stride.

Vashti stood staring after them. Tears streamed down her cheeks.

"My dear, are you all right?"

She turned. Emmaline and the other passengers had come around the coach.

"I'm fine, but I'm mad. They shot Ned and stole all our horses."

Emmaline pulled her into her embrace. "We're all alive. That's what counts."

"They took my gun and my watch," one of the men said.

Another of the passengers knelt beside Ned. "Are you all right, sir?" Ned groaned.

"Do any of you have medical experience?" Vashti asked.

None of the men spoke, but Emmaline came forward. "I've tended the sick and wounded. I can take a look."

Vashti sobbed. "I have to collect the mail."

One of the miners shook his head. "What next? Girls driving stagecoaches!"

"We'll help you, ma'am," said the cowboy. He stooped and grabbed an empty mail sack. "Come on, boys, let's get as much as we can. This little dab of a gal will probably be in trouble if we don't save the mail."

Vashti wiped the tears from her cheeks and walked over to where Emmaline was prodding Ned's arm.

"I think we should take his coat off and try to stop the bleeding."

Vashti knelt beside her. "How bad is it?"

"I'm not sure, but it's possible he could bleed out while we wait for help." Emmaline touched Ned's cheek. "Ned, can you hear me?"

He let out a groan, and his eyelids fluttered.

"Help me," Emmaline said to Vashti. The two of them struggled with Ned's coat but at last got him out of it. He began to shiver.

"It looks real bad." Vashti swallowed down her revulsion at the bloody mess.

"It must've hit the bone," Emmaline said. "We'd best wrap it tight and run to the station."

"Yes. And get his coat back on if we can. I'll see if there's a rug or a blanket in the boot of the stage."

She hurried to the back of the coach but found nothing useful. The cowboy came over with a full mail sack.

"Here's what we've got so far, ma'am. Picked up the easy piles first. The other fellows are chasing letters that blew away."

"Thank you. That's extremely good of you. I wonder if any of you have anything in your bags that we can use to keep Mr. Harmon warm?"

He tipped his hat back and looked into her eyes. "I could build a fire."

"That would be wonderful. Thank you." She hurried back to Emmaline. "The cowboy is going to try to find enough combustibles to light a fire. I think I'd better leave for the Democrat Station."

"Ned needs the doctor." Emmaline frowned down at the patient. "If he loses too much blood. . ."

Vashti nodded. "All right. I'll check to see if those outlaws found my pistol. I think it's still in my bag."

"I sure wish I'd had my gun with me. I was going to take my rifle, but Micah said we'd be fine with the stagecoach guard to protect us. Only two of the other passengers had weapons, and as far as I could see, they couldn't shoot worth beans. Of course, the stage was lurching and bumping."

Vashti went to the front of the coach. Most of the harness had gone off with the horses, but the coach itself seemed unscathed except for some splintered wood on the front corner. She hugged herself and shivered. That must have been a bullet meant for her.

"Thank You, Lord."

She climbed onto the box and rummaged under the seat. Her small canvas bag was intact. Nestled between her spare socks and pantalets and her hairbrush was the revolver she'd bought from Libby Adams last year. She tucked it in her belt and climbed down.

She walked back to Emmaline and Ned. "Guess I'd better hoof it for the next station. It'll probably take me a half hour, so don't expect anyone to come too soon."

Emmaline stood. "I'll try to keep Ned comfortable. I was thinking we should get him off the ground, but if that fella's going to light a fire. . ."

Vashti squinted up the road. "Someone will come along before dark, I'm sure, but we can't count on it. If I get to the Democrat Station, we can bring the relief team of mules to come and haul the coach in."

Emmaline nodded. "Makes sense to me. They don't have a telegraph, do they?"

"No. But they might send a rider for Sheriff Chapman—or back to Nampa for the lawman there."

"And the doctor. Don't forget to tell Ethan to bring Doc along."

"Right."

Vashti could see the cowboy on the hillside, breaking low branches off a small pine tree. The miners had scattered, chasing the mail. She was thankful for that, but Ned's condition worried her. She waved at Emmaline and set out.

When she was out of sight of the stagecoach, the vastness of the land swept over her. She quickened her steps. These hills could swallow up a woman—or a stagecoach full of people or a band of outlaws.

Years ago, she'd felt alone like this—when she'd left home. She'd set out alone then, too, but not in a desolate place like this. Her only thought then had been to escape Uncle Joshua. Aunt Mary didn't believe her when she'd told her that her uncle had grabbed her in the barn and kissed her. Vashti was Georgia then, and eleven years old. The kiss had repulsed and confused her.

Aunt Mary confronted her husband when he came in later. "What did you do to this child?"

"Nothing. Just teased her a little. What did she say?"

"Said you kissed her."

He laughed. "She doesn't like me. She'll say anything."

She'd avoided him for weeks but saw him watching her. Aunt Mary sent her out to gather eggs before school one morning. He caught her as she came from the chicken yard.

"No, no!" she screamed. As she writhed in his grip and tried to pull away, the seam of her dress tore at the waist. At last she got away and ran for the house. She burst through the back door, crying.

"Why are you running, Georgia? And where is your egg basket?"

She halted before Aunt Mary's disapproving glare.

"I. . .I dropped it."

"Oh, look, you've torn your dress."

Uncle Joshua came through the back door. "Is the little girl all right?"

"She ripped her dress." Aunt Mary looked at him questioningly.

"I told her not to climb over the fence like that." He shook his head.

Georgia stared at him.

"Go on," Aunt Mary said with a sigh. "You'll have to wear your Sunday dress today. And if you come home with a tear in it, young lady, you'll be in trouble."

"Yes, ma'am." Georgia scurried to her attic room and changed. She hoped Uncle Joshua would be gone when she went down the ladder and took the torn dress to Aunt Mary, but he was sitting by the cookstove, drinking coffee and talking about planting corn. Vashti snatched her lunch pail off the windowsill and ran out the door. But she didn't go to school that day. Instead, she took the road for Cincinnati.

Now she wasn't terrified the way she had been then, but she'd be lying if she said she wasn't afraid. Ned could die before she got back. The outlaws' brazen thievery and disregard for life angered her, but it might have been worse. They could have killed her and the passengers as easily as not.

"Thank You, Lord, for preserving us. Please keep Ned alive until we get him some help." She began to jog, but the cool wind tore her breath away. She'd heard it was harder to breathe, the higher you got in the mountains. Wolves might lurk out here, and there were outlaws, though they'd probably ridden off a good ways to divide their plunder. Was one of the four in the gang the same man who had tried unsuccessfully to rob the stagecoaches last year? Maybe Ned was right and he'd rounded up some friends to come and help him.

She reckoned she was halfway to the station when she heard footsteps behind her.

★ CHAPTER 19 ★

Griffin paced the boardwalk in front of the Wells Fargo office. He shoved his hand in his pants pocket and pulled out Cy Fennel's old watch. No getting around it. The stage was an hour late.

Micah Landry came out of the Nugget and strode across the street toward him. "No sign of them?"

Griffin shook his head and came to a decision. "I'm going for the sheriff."

Micah tailed him over to the jailhouse, next to where Griffin and Justin now lived. Ethan's paint horse was tied out front. Griffin hurried up the walk and threw the door open. Justin was seated across Ethan's desk from him, playing a game of checkers with the sheriff. The small potbellied stove kept the office toasty, and a pot of coffee steamed on top.

"Howdy, Griff." Ethan straightened and smiled at him.

"The stage is late."

"Oh?" Ethan frowned. "How late?"

"A whole hour."

Micah came in behind Ethan and shut the door. "That's right, Sheriff, and my wife is supposed to be on it."

"Let's telegraph Nampa and see if they left on time."

"Good thinking."

Ethan slapped his hat on and reached for his jacket. Justin tagged along as they left the jail. They reached the boardwalk, and Bitsy Moore met them in front of the old haberdashery. Beneath her wool coat she had on her red bloomer costume, and a jaunty red hat with a dyed pheasant feather graced her head.

"Griffin Bane! Where's Vashti?" She hurried toward them, her high-buttoned boots clomping on the walkway.

"Don't know," Griffin said.

"So I was right and the stage is late?"

"Looks that way."

Bitsy seized Ethan's wrist. "What are you going to do, Sheriff?"

"Send a telegram to Nampa. If they left on time, we'll ride out and see if we can get word of them."

Maitland Dostie's cramped office barely held them all. They waited in silence after Maitland sent Ethan's message off.

After ten minutes, Micah Landry swore. "I could have been halfway to the first stage stop by now."

"Take it easy," Ethan said.

Griffin started to speak but thought better of it. The river was high this time of year. Maybe they shouldn't have started running the stages yet. But it hadn't rained for several days, and the ferrymen didn't take foolish chances.

The telegraph clicked. "Here comes something." Maitland picked up his pencil and began to write. After a moment, he sighed and shook his head. "Not for you."

They all let out a pent-up breath.

"I've got to take this message to Ted Hire at the Nugget," Maitland said.

Griffin grabbed his arm. "You can't leave now. This is an emergency."

"I could deliver the telegram," Justin said.

Griffin had almost forgotten he was there. "To the Nugget? I don't think so."

"I'll run it down there," Micah said. "But if you hear anything while I'm gone, make sure you let me know."

Maitland held out the sheet of paper, and Micah ran out the door.

Griffin resumed pacing. Bitsy leaned against the counter and drummed her fingers, while Ethan leaned against the wall with his arms folded. Justin stood in the corner, quiet for once.

Micah came back five minutes later, and as he opened the door, Maitland's telegraph key began to click again.

"That's your message," he said after a moment. The others crowded up to the counter and watched him. After a minute, the clicking stopped, and he looked up and read: " 'To Sheriff Chapman, Fergus, from Wells Fargo agent Gayle, Nampa. Confirmed stage left 9:00 a.m., crossed river safely.' "

Griffin exhaled again. "They got across the river."

Ethan nodded. "That's good news. I guess we'd better ride out and see where they are."

"I'm coming with you," Bitsy said.

Ethan frowned. "Best not, Miz Moore."

"My girl is on that stage. If something's happened, you may need a woman along."

"My Emmaline's on it, too," Micah said. He and Bitsy eyed each other.

Bitsy nodded. "I hope they're a comfort to each other. Sheriff, we're going with you."

Ethan threw his hands in the air. "All right, but hurry."

"Will you lend me a horse, Griffin?" Bitsy asked.

He nodded. "Let's not waste any more time."

"Me, too?" Justin jogged along beside him, down the street toward the livery.

Griffin shot him a glance. "You'd best stay home."

"He's nearly a man grown," Ethan said quietly.

Griffin frowned. "All right. But if there's trouble, you do what I say, you hear?"

"Yes, sir." Justin sped ahead of them to the stable.

Vashti whipped around, holding her pistol in front of her. Fifty feet behind her was the cowboy who'd gathered the fuel for a fire. He held his hands up and stopped walking, but he smiled.

"Hey, there! Didn't mean to scare you. I thought, in light of what happened, it might be good for you to have some company."

Vashti let out her breath and stuck the holster back in her belt. "Come on, then. It's not much farther."

"A gal like you shouldn't be out here alone."

"It's broad daylight," she said.

"Yes, and we was robbed in broad daylight."

She walked along, kicking at a stone now and then. When it came down to it, she was glad it wasn't dark, but she didn't say so. "Think those outlaws went far?"

The cowboy shoved his hat back a little. "I dunno. They could have a hideout somewhere close."

"There's a lot of stage lines around here," Vashti said. "Could be they'll strike again."

"They didn't get much today."

"Huh. They got four good horses. I don't know what my boss will say."

"He won't fire you or anything, will he?"

She shrugged. Her innards dragged, and she'd have turned back if Ned weren't hurt so badly. Griffin had gone white-hot angry when Johnny had tipped the coach over last fall. She could picture his face when she told him what had happened this time.

"My name's Clell," the cowboy said.

"Oh." She looked full at him for the first time. He was about thirty, medium height, and spare. "I'm George."

He laughed. "Right."

Vashti shrugged. She didn't care what he thought.

"What do you do when you're not driving the mail coach?" Clell asked.

Was he trying to flirt with her? What was he thinking, when Ned lay bleeding to death?

"Come on if you're coming." She hurried her steps as they rounded a corner. Up the slope, she saw the northernmost fence line of the Democrat's pasture.

Griffin and the others saddled their mounts quickly and added Marty to the group. Three miles out of town, they met a lone rider.

He cantered toward them and pulled up when he got close. "Hey, Sheriff!"

"What is it?" Ethan called.

Griffin recognized one of the tenders from the Democrat Station. "Where's the Nampa stage?"

"Robbed. My boss took two men and a fresh team out. It's not supposed to be far from the station, but we didn't hear any gunfire, so it must be a piece."

Griffin swallowed hard. "Where's the driver?"

The man grinned. "The boss made her stay at the station with his wife. She didn't want to, but she was wore out and cold. Boss said they'd bring in the coach and passengers and then she could drive on to Fergus. But she says they need a doctor bad."

Griffin urged Pepper into a gallop. As he rode away he heard Ethan telling Justin to ride back to town as fast as he could and find Doc Kincaid and his deputies.

At the stage stop, Griffin jumped to the ground and ran inside.

Mrs. Jordan turned from where she was tending the stove. "Mr. Bane, you scared me."

"Where's my driver? Georgie Edwards."

"She's yonder." Mrs. Jordan nodded toward a doorway. "Poor thing was plum tuckered out." She stepped to the closed door and tapped on it. "Miss Edwards? You awake, honey? Mr. Bane's here."

A moment later the door swung open. Vashti stood blinking at him, wearing her green woolen trousers and tan shirt, with the vest hanging open and her auburn hair spilling all rumpled about her shoulders. Her green eyes looked suspiciously red-rimmed.

"I'm sorry."

"For what? Getting held up?"

"Everything." Tears coursed down her cheeks. "They wouldn't let me ride back to the stage with them. I wanted to."

"Of course you did."

"She walked up here to tell us what happened," Mrs. Jordan said.

Ethan knocked at the front door and stuck his head in. "Should we go on, Griff?"

"Yeah. I'm coming. Just wanted to hear from Vashti what happened."

"Four men, in the rocks. Three of them had horses, and the other one was on foot. They shot Ned and stole all four of our horses." She raised one hand to her mouth. "He needs a doctor, Griff."

"We sent for Dr. Kincaid," Ethan said.

Griffin reached out and ran his hand over her tangled hair. "Are you all right, Georgie?"

She nodded. "And the miners that rode with me tried to save the mail. I think they got most of it."

"All right. You rest, and we'll head out there."

"Please let me come." Her eyes brimmed with tears. "I hated to leave Ned like that."

"Anyone else hurt?"

She gulped and shook her head. "They shot him in the arm, but it's an awful mess. He's bled a lot. Emmaline was tending him when I left. Please let me come with you."

Griffin looked at Ethan, and Ethan shrugged.

"The men took all the horses we had here," Mrs. Jordan said. "That fella that walked in with Georgie took one, and my husband and Buddy. We sent Hank to find you, Sheriff. That and the team of mules was all the critters we had."

"You can ride with me." Griffin wasn't sure where the words came from, but they popped out of his mouth. Vashti dashed back into the bedroom and came out hauling on her coat.

He made sure she had a hat, her muffler, and gloves before he let her swing up behind him on Pepper's back. She reached around him and hugged his middle as Pepper began to trot.

"You going to be okay?" he yelled over his shoulder.

"Yes. But loping would be better."

He loosened Pepper's reins, and Vashti clung to him like a little burr. She was warm against his back, and when the road got steep and Pepper slowed down, she leaned her head against him. Griffin wished they could keep on riding like that a ways, but the coach wasn't far. Ethan, Bitsy, Micah, and Marty reached it before he did.

From a distance, he could see Emmaline run into her husband's arms. Those two might bicker, but when it counted, their marriage was solid.

The passengers surrounded Ethan. All of them talked at once, but he held up his hands.

"Easy, folks. I want to hear from all of you, one at a time. First I want to take a look at Mr. Harmon and assess the damage. As soon as the rest of my deputies get here, I'll be going after those outlaws. Anything you can tell me about them will help."

Griffin pulled up near where Ned lay on the ground, turned, and grasped Vashti's hand. She held on to him and slid to the ground.

"How's Ned?" she asked Emmaline.

"Not very good, but the men from the station said they'd sent for a doctor."

"That's right, and a couple of my deputies, too."

Emmaline nodded. "Well, I hope Ned makes it. Mr. Jordan brought two blankets when he came with the mule team, and we've got Ned lying on one, with the other bundled around him."

Vashti knelt beside Ned, and Griffin crouched on his other side.

"Ned, can you hear me?" Vashti's tone was a wheedling plea, but Ned didn't open his eyes.

Griffin clenched his teeth. He didn't want to lose Ned, especially not this way. Vashti would never stop blaming herself, though it wasn't her fault.

"Harmon!"

Ned twitched.

"Harmon, open your eyes," Griffin barked. "I want to know what happened here."

Slowly Ned's eyelids lifted. "Sorry, boss. We tried."

"I know you did." Griffin reached out a hand to clap him on the shoulder, but stopped. It would probably hurt Ned. "I'm not blaming you or Vashti. Listen, we've got Doc Kincaid coming, and some men are hitching up a new team. Will you let me lift you into the stage?"

"Whatever you say, boss."

Griffin slid an arm under the wool cocoon, judging where Ned's knees were. His other arm he carefully snaked under Ned's back. Ned moaned, and Vashti reached from the other side to help lift him enough for Griffin to get his arms in place.

"Make sure the coach door's open," Griff said. He stood with the limp burden in his arms and walked toward the stagecoach.

★ CHAPTER 20 ★

Vashti's stomach fluttered as Griffin counted out her pay. As each bill hit her palm, the tickle rose until she felt she'd burst. She'd be able to pay Bitsy and Augie for a month's board and room and also pay what remained on her bill at the emporium.

"Twenty-eight, twenty-nine, thirty."

"Thanks, Mr. Bane."

"Griffin. And you earned it."

She ducked her head. "I still feel like I ought to help pay to replace the horses and harness."

"Unfortunately, that's part of my business expense." Griffin's eyes narrowed. "Are you sure you want to do the mail run again next week?"

"Yes, sir. I'll be ready."

"Because I could maybe find someone—"

"I want to do it."

He looked down into her eyes for a long moment. Vashti felt the tickle move toward her heart. He looked handsome today, less shaggy. Must have trimmed his beard.

"Vashti, I don't want anything to happen to you."

She nodded. "Thanks. But don't you think they'll go more for the stages carrying treasure? Some of the mines will be shipping out gold again, and payrolls will be coming through regular."

"Yes. And you'll be carrying some of them."

She gulped. "Think the outlaws know when we're carrying something valuable?"

"It'll be pretty much even odds this summer. If they hit often enough, they'll get something eventually." Griffin scrunched up his mouth. "I guess I'd better line up some more guards. If we've got to deal with an outlaw gang this year, it's going to be rough going, no matter what run you're driving."

"Sheriff Chapman didn't find any trace of them, did he?"

"No. He was able to track them until they got into the rocks."

"I'm really sorry they got your rifle and Ned's shotgun."

Griffin sat down on the edge of his desk. "Well, don't fret over it. I'll put in my claim to the government for the guns and horses, since it was a mail coach. And I'll make sure you've got a good messenger next time."

She looked up at him. "Who will ride with me now that Ned's laid up?"

"We'll see." He looked worried, and she didn't press him.

"I'm really sorry we lost the horses, but I especially regret that Ned got hurt."

"Have you seen him since we brought him in?" Griffin asked.

"Yeah, I went over to Doc's yesterday. Ned was in a lot of pain."

"I saw him this morning." Griffin's brown eyes darkened. "The doc says his arm may never be right again. And he'll need several weeks to recuperate."

"He lost a lot of blood," Vashti said softly. "I should have stayed and helped Emmaline."

"You couldn't do that and go for help, too. Besides, she had the other passengers. Doc said there wasn't much else they could have done besides what she did—making a bandage and trying to stop the bleeding."

Vashti looked down at the money in her hand. Maybe she'd spend a dollar or so on a new petticoat for Emmaline, to replace the one she used to cover Ned's wound.

On Monday morning, Vashti mounted the stage box outside the livery and prepared to drive around to the Wells Fargo office. She had a team of four sorrel horses for a mostly downhill run. Warm sunshine beat down on her. She couldn't see any snow left in town, though the mountains still wore their snowy cloaks, and the north slopes probably still held pockets of it. The horses stamped and nickered, ready to go. If not for the fresh memory of the robbery, she'd have sung a tune under her breath.

To her surprise, when the mail and nine passengers were loaded and a green wooden treasure box was lodged in the front boot, behind her feet, Griffin himself mounted the box and sat down beside her, holding two guns. He slid a Sharps rifle under their seat and held the shotgun up against his shoulder.

"Ready, Georgie?"

She swallowed hard. "*You're* riding with me?"

"Yes, I am."

Her pulse rate doubled. Could she ride twenty-five miles with Griffin Bane sitting next to her? How would she ever concentrate on the horses? It was bad enough sitting next to her boss, but lately her heart had done strange things when he was close by. She'd pondered far too much on the brief ride she'd taken on his horse with him the day of the robbery.

"What about Justin?" she asked. "What'll he do tonight?"

"Mrs. Thistle is happy to have him as a guest once more."

Vashti gathered the reins. If she put it off any longer, they'd start late, and keeping the conversation going wouldn't put a different shotgun rider at her side. She signaled Marty, and he let go of the leaders' heads. They broke into a smooth trot. This was her dream— good horses, a fine coach, and an open road. She wouldn't think about the stretch that ran through the rocks.

The first few miles flew by, and she felt Griffin's gaze on her often while they were still near town. Of course he was watching her, evaluating her performance. She tried not to let it bother her, but she couldn't help being conscious of him every moment.

After their brief stop at the Democrat Station, where Mrs. Jordan ran out to say hello to "Georgie," Griffin sat tall, constantly scanning the broken landscape. Neither of them mentioned the rocks, but as they approached the site of the robbery, Vashti felt his tension. He sat alert and tight as a bowstring, holding the shotgun at the ready.

She kept the horses moving at a swift trot. Her heart raced as they came to the spot where she'd first seen the lone outlaw six months ago.

"I think the robber who didn't have a horse last week was the one who was out here last summer," she said suddenly.

"Ned told me as much."

She looked over at him in surprise. "He did? I thought of it that day, but I paid more attention to their leader. Benny." She shivered.

The horses kept on, never once breaking stride. She wondered where the others were now—the ones that were stolen. Would their own faithful coach horses be used to attack them?

Ahead was the narrow place where rocks loomed on both sides of the road. Vashti's lungs ached, and she held her breath.

Griffin never took his eyes off the rocks as they rolled smoothly toward the danger point. Of course, if that gang were to stop them again, the outriders would likely have shown themselves by now. You just never knew. And the coach traveled downhill. Far more likely they'd be attacked going the other way, as Vashti and Ned had been. A team plodding uphill was much easier to stop than one barreling down an incline. Still, he remained vigilant, aware of the nine passengers, the mail, and the treasure box. The weight of his responsibility pressed on his broad shoulders.

All of that and Vashti.

If his small part of the Wells Fargo line suffered another holdup, who knew what would happen? He might lose the mail contract. That could ruin him financially. Already he was hard pressed, and if he wasn't reimbursed for last week's losses, he'd have a difficult time of it. But worse—people's lives were at stake. Was he foolish to run a stage here when danger lurked?

The coach rumbled through the narrow place, and he exhaled heavily. Ahead lay more rocks—the ones most of the outlaws had hidden behind. But the best place to waylay them was now behind.

He glanced over at Vashti. A drop of sweat trickled down her temple, though it wasn't overly warm.

He wanted to assure her that they were safe, but he couldn't say that for sure. Not yet. So they rode on in silence, down out of the hills and toward the river.

As the rocks fell farther behind, Vashti uncoiled. Her jaw relaxed and her shoulders fell a little. She resumed talking to the horses now and then, as she had during the first part of the ride. He admired the way she kept all the reins almost taut—but without pressure on the horses' mouths. Gentle contact, that was all. She may not have driven long, but she had a feel for the horses.

He relaxed just a hair and scanned the terrain on both sides of the road. After looking ahead for a long minute, he allowed himself another glance at her. Watching Vashti drive was like listening to rippling music with auburn hair and green eyes.

She shot a reproachful glance at him, and he looked quickly away. When had he started caring for her? He'd known her for years in a general way—had let her bring him drinks when he visited the Spur & Saddle in the old days, before Bitsy got religion. She was a bar girl, that was all. Then she became a churchgoing member of the community. A sister in Christ, according to Pastor Benton, and Griffin supposed that was right. It had taken everyone awhile to get used to thinking of Bitsy and "the girls" that way.

Now she was much more. His employee. A member of the Ladies' Shooting Club. A holdup survivor. And one tough stage driver.

His gaze strayed to her face again, and she glanced over. She bit her bottom lip as she adjusted the reins. Was she nervous because he was here? He smiled.

Her green eyes widened for an instant, and she looked forward again, frowning slightly. The ferry lay a half mile ahead. Across the river, and they'd be nearly there. Griffin almost regretted that the end of their ride together approached. But there was the return trip tomorrow. And tonight in Nampa.

Normally if he rode one of the stages, he had a couple of drinks after dinner and hit the hay early. He didn't have enough spare cash to get into a poker game. He'd always figured he shouldn't gamble unless he wouldn't miss the money if he lost. Now and then, he found a saloon where they had a singer or dancers. One time in Boise, he'd been to the theater. That was something he still thought about two years later. Colorful costumes, music, pretty ladies, and a magician who wasn't half bad.

But tonight...he made himself not look at Vashti, but he knew he wouldn't stray far from the home station if she stayed there tonight.

They rolled up to the ferry, and Vashti called, "Whoa now." The team halted smoothly. The ferryman and his two helpers came out of their shack.

"How many passengers?" the ferryman called.

"Nine," said Vashti.

The man looked sharply at her.

"Good afternoon," Griffin said, louder than he'd intended. At least he distracted the ferryman.

"Oh, Mr. Bane. How are you, sir?"

"Fair to middlin'." It pleased Griffin to see the man straighten his shoulders and snap orders to his men. The ferryman knew who would pay him at the end of the month for the Wells Fargo coaches, employees, and passengers he carried.

Griffin climbed down and watched Vashti scramble to earth. If one didn't know, he supposed one might think she was a young man. But how many people between Fergus and Boise didn't know? The ferryman's helpers sneaked glances her way as they prepared to load the stage onto the ferry. After the horses and coach were aboard, the passengers and a few locals who'd been waiting to cross the river got on.

"Sir," said one of the men who'd ridden the stage.

Griffin paused beside him. Vashti went forward to make sure the horses were calm.

"Can I help you?"

"Yes, sir. I want to get to Mountain Home as quickly as possible, and I wondered if I should have bought a ticket all the way through."

"When you get to Boise you can get it, but I think you'd do better to take a train from there." He looked toward Vashti.

One of the ferryman's helpers leaned on his pole, smiling at her. The ferry was pulled across the river with ropes and a team of mules on the other side, so the men didn't have to work too hard during the crossing. This one seemed to think that gave him license to bother the passengers.

"So, you got plans for tonight, honey?" The man leaned toward Vashti and arched his eyebrows coyly.

Vashti appeared to notice him for the first time and moved around to the other side of the lead horses. The man followed her.

Griffin nodded to the man who was still talking to him. "Excuse me." He cut behind the horses and came up behind Vashti. Over the swirling river, the ferry worker's sugary tones were clear.

"You shy, darlin'? 'Cause I know some fun places we could go."

Vashti, with her back to Griffin, stood boulder still. "Leave me alone."

"It'd be more fun if we was alone *together*. I heard you know how to be a fun kind of girl."

Strange, Griffin had always thought his bulk was too great to ignore, but this fellow had zeroed in on Vashti and didn't appear to see anything else.

Griffin reached out, grabbed the back of Vashti's vest, and yanked her back a step, putting her behind him. He stood in silence, glowering down at the man.

The ferryman's helper looked up at him with his mouth hanging open. "H–h—"

"You plaguing my driver?" Griffin roared.

"N–n–n—"

"Good. Because I could hurl you into the Snake with one pop."

The man gulped and edged away between the horses. Griffin watched him, not moving a muscle until the man had disappeared behind Prince's head.

He turned around. The ferryman clung to the rudder at the other end of the boat, staring at him. Every passenger stared. Vashti stood two feet from him, her lips clamped together.

"You okay?" he asked.

"I could have handled it," she said between clenched teeth.

Griffin blinked. Her face was red, and her eyes were slits of green fire.

"Uh. . ." He glanced up and saw the others still watching. He leaned toward Vashti and said quietly, "Did I do something wrong?"

"You might say that."

"I was just protecting you. You're my employee."

"I told you, I could have handled it."

"He knew—"

"That's right. He knew. And now *everybody* knows." She shook as she spat the words out in ragged whispers. "I could have put him in his place without making a three-ring circus out of it."

He glared down at her. "Fine. Next time I'll just let the womanizers and the drunks hang all over you."

The lines of her face congealed. "He didn't touch me."

"No, but he would have."

"Oh, now you're a prophet."

A man couldn't win. Nothing he could say right now would pacify her. Griffin stomped past her toward the far end of the ferry. The passengers ducked out of his way and grabbed the railing. His shifting weight actually made the ferry rock. He slowed his steps and stayed to the middle of the craft, until he was face-to-face with the ferry's owner.

"Your man was bothering my driver."

The ferryman seemed to concentrate on steering the boat, though it was guided mostly by the pulley system.

"I'll speak to him, but I expect he was just trying to see if the rumors were true."

"What rumors?"

"That you had a loose woman driving stage for you."

Griffin clenched his fists. "I could kill you for saying that."

"That's the word I heard. I saw her last week when she came through with Ned Harmon on the box. The boys didn't catch on till afterward, when I told 'em."

Griffin squinted down at the much smaller man, trying to make sense of that. "Why'd you tell 'em?"

The ferryman laughed. "It's a nine-days' wonder, Mr. Bane. Something curious."

"Yeah. Curious."

One of the stagecoach passengers edged in beside Griffin.

"Curious, all right. I had no idea a woman was driving us. She did a good job."

"She's a good driver," Griffin said. "And she's *not* a—" He glanced over his shoulder. Vashti had kept to the other end of the boat. "She's not what you said. I'd appreciate it if you didn't spread rumors to that effect."

"I beg your pardon. I'd heard tell her last job was in a saloon."

Griffin hesitated. "Well, that's not a lie. But there's respectable saloons, you know."

The male passengers standing nearby broke out in laughter.

Griffin gritted his teeth and decided he'd said enough. He kept his distance from Vashti as the ferryman and his helpers brought the boat to shore. Once they'd unloaded and the passengers were back in the coach, he climbed up to the box. Vashti waited until he was settled and lifted the reins. She didn't look at him or speak as she drove toward Nampa. Griffin held his shotgun and watched the edges of the road.

Finally he couldn't stand it any longer.

"Vashti, listen to me. I didn't mean to embarrass you or make things worse for you. I honestly thought you could use some help." He sighed. "You're such a little bit of a thing, and that fellow had the wrong idea about you. I just figured I'd set him to rights."

She looked over at him. "What do you think would have happened if you hadn't been there? You think I'd have gotten mauled?"

He didn't know what to say.

"I'll tell you. I told him to leave me alone. If he hadn't respected that, I'd have gone back to where there were other people, so's he couldn't keep bothering me. If that wasn't enough, I'd have appealed to his boss."

Griffin nodded slowly. "Sounds like it might have been enough."

"Well, if it wasn't, I pack a decent punch."

He chuckled. "I'll bet you do. I'm sorry. I should have let you tend to your own business."

They rode on in silence. When they were a mile out from the home station in Nampa, she looked over at him, her green eyes anxious. "Are you going to stop me from driving?"

"Why would I do that?"

She didn't answer.

His mind whirled. There would be no hiding the fact now that one of his drivers was a female. Would that make his stages more vulnerable? Would robbers throng to the Owyhee Valley to take a crack at the girl driver? He mulled that over as Vashti drove up to the stop. He supposed outlaws might think it would be easier to rob a woman than a man. Or would they find it humiliating and tease each other about how they had to pick on a girl because the men who drove were too tough for them?

He climbed down from the box wearily. He'd had some vague notion this morning of asking Vashti to see the town with him tonight. He almost laughed aloud at the thought now.

Businesslike, Vashti gathered her personal possessions and clambered down. The station agent had opened the door for the passengers, and they piled out, exclaiming about the smooth ride the "girl driver" had given them. Each of the nine men made a point of thanking Vashti before they scattered. She stood there and took it well, smiling and returning their comments.

When the last one walked away with his luggage, she sighed and turned back toward the coach. One tender was leading the team away, and another led out the new four-in-hand.

"How many of the passengers thanked you when they thought you were a man?" Griffin asked.

Vashti's lips twitched. "Nary a one. But then, they'd been terrorized and robbed, so you can't really blame them."

Was this really only her second run? Griffin stared after her as she headed for the house.

Vashti walked slowly and deliberately. She knew Griffin was watching her. She'd hardly had a moment all day when she wasn't conscious of his gaze. Well, she intended to ignore him until time to mount the stage again in the morning.

The next driver, who wasn't under Griffin's supervision, ambled out onto the porch. He nodded at Vashti.

"You George?"

"That's right." Vashti stuck out her hand. "George Edwards, of Fergus."

The other driver, a man of about forty, gripped her hand. "Buck Eastman. I heard you had a holdup last week."

"Yes."

"An' I heard Ned Harmon got shot."

"He did. Our doctor thinks he'll recover all right, but his arm's pretty stove up."

"Too bad."

"Yes, we miss him."

"Who's riding with you?" He looked toward the stage.

"Griffin Bane."

Eastman turned wide eyes on her. "Your boss?"

"That's right."

He shrugged. "I heard he's fair. Maybe doesn't run as tight a ship as old Fennel did."

"Mr. Bane's all right," Vashti said.

Buck nodded. She expected him to move on, but he just stood there.

"Well, I'm hungry, Mr. Eastman, so if you'll excuse me—"

"I heard other things, too, and I guess I heard right."

She pulled back and eyed him suspiciously. "What sort of things?"

"Heard Bane had a woman on his Fergus-to-Nampa run."

"Well?"

He looked her up and down. "I reckon you're the one."

She set down her bag and put her hands on her hips. "Mr. Eastman, I'm a driver. The rest doesn't matter. If you want to make something of it, you go right ahead. But I'd hate to see one driver make trouble for another, even if they work on different branch lines, and even if one dislikes the other."

"I didn't say I disliked you."

"Maybe I wasn't talking about you."

His eyes narrowed, and he held her gaze for a moment. Vashti wondered if she'd made a mistake. He no doubt had a friend nearby—he must have a shotgun messenger going with him. And she'd told

Griffin not to mix into her business.

About the time she'd begun to wonder if she ought to apologize, Buck threw back his head and laughed. "Ain'tchou somethin'? Wait'll I tell Jack."

"Tell anyone you want," Vashti said. "It's no secret anymore."

Buck pulled his hat off and slapped it against his thigh. "Good luck to you, missy. I reckon you're a good driver. I heard it took a whole gang of outlaws to stop you. You take care, now, y'hear?"

"I will. Thanks."

She watched him swagger down to the coach. Griffin stood next to the wheelers, watching as usual. When Eastman stopped to speak to him, Vashti turned away and went inside. Supper and a bunk sounded mighty good. For a brief moment, she wondered what Griffin would do for the evening. The sun was just going down behind the distant mountains. Would he make the rounds of the saloons in Nampa?

She walked to the dining table. "Not even going to think about it."

★ CHAPTER 21 ★

Vashti went downstairs for breakfast early the next morning, wearing her driving clothes. The station agent's wife handed her a plate full of eggs, fried potatoes, and sausage.

"You've got a full stage this morning, Georgie."

"Oh?"

"Five fellows going up to Silver City stayed at the hotel last night. They're going to look at the Poorman mines."

Vashti arched her eyebrows. "That outfit's been shut down for years."

"I know. Wouldn't it be something if they got things running again?"

"Isn't the gold all gone?"

"Oh no. Most of the mines that closed did it because of the bank trouble in California. The owners mostly moved on. Oh, they say the easy pickings are done, but if these fellows have investors, they could get the machinery going again. The money's in ore you have to crush."

Vashti nodded. She didn't know much about stamp mills and all of that, but any investment in the Owyhee Valley would be good news. It would mean more travel on the branch line and more business at places like the Spur & Saddle.

After eating quickly, she went out to the stable. She didn't like to eat when the passengers did. She couldn't politely wear her hat in the house, and if she sat at the table without it, they'd all stare. Of course, she hadn't much hope of keeping her secret any longer.

Her favorite way to spend the last half hour before they left was getting to know the horses. The tenders were harnessing the team. Vashti took a brush and a hoof pick and checked over the leaders. With a pang of regret, she thought of the horses she'd lost last week.

When the stage from Boise rolled in, she was ready. She climbed the box and waited while the tenders hitched up the team—six horses this time—and loaded the mail and the luggage. Eight passengers climbed into the coach, and two men climbed up to sit in the seat on the roof, behind her and the shotgun messenger—Griffin. He was the last to board, looking chipper this morning. He'd greeted the mining men enthusiastically. Vashti eyed him sideways and decided he hadn't been out drinking last night, or not much, anyway. That was good. He'd be alert this afternoon when they hit the stretch leading up to Democrat's. Perhaps she'd misjudged him. Come to think of it, she couldn't remember him ever drinking more than a glass or two. Why had she assumed he'd cut loose last night? Didn't she know him better than that by now?

"Ready, Georgie?"

"Yes, sir." She uncoiled her whip and cracked it. The horses sprang forward. Vashti settled into the rhythm of the stage. Good horses, plenty of paying passengers, and splendid weather. If not for the large man sitting next to her, she might have felt lighthearted. The hulk of a blacksmith had somehow become the man who occupied her thoughts and called to her heart.

Late that afternoon when the team was put away and Marty had reported on business at the livery, Griffin plodded across the street to the Fennel House. His hips and legs felt stiff from sitting so long on the box of the stage.

"Howdy, Mr. Bane," Terrence Thistle called from the front porch. "The boy's over to the jailhouse with the sheriff."

"Thank you kindly. I expect we'll eat supper here." Griffin changed course and headed for Ethan's office.

Sure enough, Justin sat across the desk from Ethan, pushing checkers. Hiram sat on a stool in the corner, whittling and watching the game.

"Well, look at the no-accounts we got here," Griffin boomed.

Justin leaped from his chair. "Uncle Griff! I didn't know you were back, or I'd have come and helped with the team."

"That right?" His statement pleased Griffin, and he smiled at the boy. "You hungry?"

"Gettin' there."

"He's whomping me at checkers," Ethan said.

Griffin touched the top of the stove. It was cold, so he sat on the edge. "Go ahead and finish the game."

Justin eyed him for a second then resumed his seat.

"Your turn," Ethan said.

"Hey, we brought a whole flock of mining men up from Nampa," Griffin said.

Ethan and Hiram looked interested.

"Five fellows from back East. They're looking into reopening the Poorman mines."

"Well, that's news." Ethan nodded, still watching the checker-board. "I'll keep my ears open when I make my round of the saloons tonight."

Griffin pushed his hat back. "They told me they represent a syndicate in London and they've been negotiating with the owners. They'd like to start taking ore out again."

"That'd be a boon to the valley." Ethan frowned as Justin moved a checker.

"Yup, we need more paying jobs," Griffin said. "They'd put the roads back in shape, too." Of course, some of the mines were still operating, but the population of the Owyhee Valley was far below what it had been two decades earlier, and only a trickle of silver and gold found its way out these days.

Ethan picked up one of his pieces and jumped over two of Justin's checkers. "There! I guess you won't get me this time."

"Did you find out any more about those outlaws?" Griffin asked.

Ethan shook his head. "I took Hi and my two ranch hands and

spent all day yesterday looking for a place they could have holed up, but we didn't find anything. Could be they swooped in here for one job and then cleared out."

"Doubt it," Griffin said. "They'll probably show up on another one of my lines—or wait until they know we've got a payroll in the box."

"Well, if the mines open up again, we'll get some soldiers in here to escort the shipments."

"True."

Justin made his move and hopped all the way across the board. "King me, Sheriff."

Ethan moaned. "How'd I not see that coming?" He slapped a checker on top of Justin's piece.

"I talked to the deputy marshal in Nampa," Griffin said. "He says a gang that used to operate in Cheyenne may have moved up here."

"You think those are the ones who held up Vashti and Ned?" Ethan asked.

"Could be. But one of them was that fella who camped out there in the rocks last summer. Somehow, either he got some men with horses and guns to join him, or they moved in on him and took over his territory."

"Maybe they recruited him into their gang and helped him get a horse."

"Yeah, one of my stage horses."

Ethan ran a hand through his hair and studied the checkerboard. "What I'm trying to figure out is how to prevent it from happening again."

"You and me both," Griffin said.

Hiram folded his knife and tucked it in his pocket. "You two eating at the boardinghouse?"

"Thought we would," Griffin said. "But we'll cook at home tomorrow." He looked at Justin as he said it.

"Mrs. Chapman sent us a pie." Justin smiled, and Griffin thought for the first time that he looked a little like Evelyn—that is, like the Banes.

Hiram fetched the broom from the corner and swept up his

shavings. "Reckon I'll head on home. Come and visit anytime."

Justin finished the game in a matter of minutes, leaving Ethan complaining good-naturedly about getting beat again.

"It's a sort of mathematical game, Sheriff," Justin said solemnly. "You can only move so many ways, and if you think them all through, you can see what will happen."

Ethan stared at him. "You see the whole game in your mind?"

"Not the whole game, but a ways down the road."

Griffin laughed at Ethan's baffled expression. "That's why I've got this boy setting up a ledger for me. I want him to see down the road until I'm making money again." He slapped Justin on the shoulder. "Come on, champ."

They walked out into the street.

"Uncle Griff?"

"Hmm?"

"Marty showed me how to clean the horses' feet. Well, he showed me on a mule, but I learned how."

Griffin eyed him cautiously. "So, you think you like working with horses now?"

"Yes, sir. I'm getting used to them. If I do well with the bookkeeping, would you give me some more riding lessons?"

Griffin rested a hand on Justin's shoulder. "I surely will."

Vashti sat in the Wells Fargo office the next morning, selling tickets. Seemed everyone wanted to go somewhere now that spring had arrived. She'd have a day off before her next run to Nampa, and she'd enjoy the luxury of sleeping in. Having a bath last night and putting on a dress this morning had brought back all her feminine instincts.

Griffin had finally given her the combination to the safe, and when she closed the office at noon, she locked away the morning's proceeds. She stopped in at the emporium before heading home.

"Vashti! How are you doing?" Libby came from behind the counter to take her hands. "I haven't seen you since your last run. How did it go?"

"Fine. No problems."

"That's a relief. I hope that incident last week won't be repeated." Libby smiled. "Say, you should have some special passengers next time you come from Nampa."

"Oh?"

"Yes. I had a letter from Mr. and Mrs. Hamilton in the mail you brought yesterday. They expect to arrive in Boise tomorrow, and they'll ride up here with you the next day."

Vashti tingled with excitement just from watching Libby's shining face. "Oh, Miz Adams, I'm so happy for you. This means you'll be getting married soon."

Libby's cheeks went a delicate pink. "Yes, it does. I don't mind admitting that I'm delighted."

"You and Mr. Dooley have been waiting a long time."

"Not so long as some, but long enough."

"Have you set a date?" Vashti asked.

"Not for certain, but I shouldn't think we'd wait more than a few weeks, if all goes as planned."

Vashti picked up a sack of sugar for Augie and carried it, along with Libby's news, toward the Spur & Saddle. As she reached the sidewalk on the west side of Main Street, Maitland Dostie hurried out of the telegraph office. When he saw her, he pulled up short. "Is Mr. Bane at the Wells Fargo? I have a telegram for him."

"No, sir. I believe he's working at the smithy today."

Dostie frowned. "I don't suppose you'd have time to take it to him? I don't like to leave the office that long."

"Surely. Just let me give this to Augie, and I'll be right back."

Vashti hurried into the restaurant. Bitsy scurried about, serving several traveling men and a few local residents.

"Oh dear," Vashti said as she plopped the sugar sack down on the serving counter. "Today you need me, and Mr. Dostie asked me to take a telegram over to Griffin."

"Best run and do it," Bitsy said. "Goldie's in the kitchen filling glasses of cider for me. We'll be all right."

Vashti dashed back to the telegraph office.

"Here you go." Dostie handed her an envelope. "He may want to send a reply."

Vashti's curiosity prickled, but she didn't ask questions. She hurried down the street. Griffin was shoeing one of the coach horses when she rounded the corner. Justin hovered nearby, watching everything he did. She waited until Griffin stopped nailing and reached for a rasp.

"Mr. Dostie asked me to bring you a telegram."

Griffin lowered the horse's hoof to the ground and straightened. "Me? A telegram?"

"Yes, sir." She held it out, watching his wary face. Telegrams were almost never good. She recalled his last one had announced Justin's imminent arrival.

Griffin looked down at his filthy hands. "Can you open it, please?"

"Surely." She ripped open the envelope and fished out the yellow paper.

"What's it say?"

She looked down at it and froze. "Oh no."

"What?" Griffin's features went hard. "Read it."

" 'Passengers, driver, and messenger fought off outlaws in ambush Catherine Road. One passenger killed. Advise.' "

Griffin let out a deep sigh and bowed his head. Vashti waited, her heart aching. Nick Telford, an experienced driver, had that run now, on the same branch line with Johnny Conway. She sent up a prayer for him and the passengers, and for the safety of all the drivers and messengers on the road today. Though she wouldn't like to admit it, an icy stab of fear struck her.

Griffin jerked his chin up and glared at her.

"You're not driving tomorrow."

★ CHAPTER 22 ★

Griffin moved his toolbox farther from the horse and looked at Justin. "Stay here. I've got to send a telegram. If Marty comes over, tell him I'll be right back and I'll have the team ready in time." He strode toward the street.

Vashti tagged after him in a swirl of green skirts. "What do you mean, I'm not driving?"

"Just what I said." Griffin didn't look at her. If he did, those eyes would make him think twice.

"But if they're over on the Catherine Road now—"

"They could be back here tomorrow."

"Oh, come on." Vashti grabbed his arm, but he kept walking. "You don't think they'd pull another job tomorrow, do you?"

He paused and glared down at her. "I don't know what they'd do. If I did, my men wouldn't have been attacked today, would they? And a man wouldn't have been killed."

That shut her up, at least temporarily. He marched on to Dostie's office, not wanting to think about the ambush or what could have happened if it had been on Vashti's route. He'd have to scare up another driver for her run tomorrow. He couldn't go off himself again—not so soon. Justin needed him. He guessed he'd better advertise in the *Avalanche* and the Boise paper for more drivers, though he hated to. But if a lot of businessmen and geologists were going to be coming through to get to the old mines, he'd better make the stages keep their timetable. If traffic increased, they might

844

even need a three-times-a-week schedule from Boise to Silver City and De Lamar.

He pushed into the telegraph office. Dostie sat behind his desk at the telegraph key.

"I'm sorry, Griffin. Tough luck."

"No luck about it," Griffin said. "Send back to the station agent. 'Hire extra guard and send stage on time.' Oh, and you'd best tell him I'll ride over tomorrow and catch my men at Sinker. I need to talk to them personally." He brought his fist down on the counter. Tomorrow was the day he'd hoped to take Justin for a leisurely ride to Reynolds Creek and check in with the station agent there, who stored extra feed for Griffin. That would have to wait.

A sound behind him alerted him that Vashti had followed him in. She cleared her throat delicately, but in a manner not to be ignored.

"Yes, ma'am?" Dostie asked, peering at her.

"Has the sheriff been informed?"

"I expect it's a bit out of his territory," Dostie said.

"Yes, but he'll want to know."

Griffin nodded. "You're right. He might even take some men over to help look for those scoundrels."

"I could tell him," Vashti said.

"All right. I'd go myself, but I've got two more horses to shoe." She started for the door.

Griffin called, "Oh, wait a sec."

Vashti turned toward him.

"Would you tell Ethan we'll need extra guards tomorrow? Maybe he can help me round up a few extra men to make the run with you."

She smiled then. "Yes, sir."

As she closed the door, Griffin kicked himself mentally. Why had he said that? He'd had no intention of letting her drive to Nampa tomorrow.

"That all you want to say in the telegram?" Dostie asked.

"Reckon so."

"Eight dollars and fifty cents."

Griffin winced. "Let me see that." He studied the spare message but couldn't see how to eliminate more than one word. "All right," he said at last. "I'll have to come around later and pay you. Don't have that much on me."

Vashti put on her trousers and boy's shirt the next morning. She frowned at herself in the mirror as she braided her hair and pinned it up. What if she got to the livery and Griffin had found another driver? She clenched her teeth. After he'd had her tell Ethan he needed more guards to go with her, she'd avoided seeing Griffin for the rest of the day. That way, he hadn't had a chance to tell her that he didn't mean it.

She eyed her reflection critically. The shirt had shrunk a little in the wash. She pulled the vest on and surveyed her figure from the front and the side. Maybe she had time to run into the emporium and buy a baggier shirt. Even if everyone local knew she wasn't a man, she couldn't drive in a dress, and she didn't want to give the tenders or the passengers reason to think she was immodest. It was too warm to wear her coat.

She pulled on her boots, grabbed her hat, whip, and overnight bag, and dashed down the stairs. In the kitchen, Bitsy and Augie were peeling vegetables for the day's guests.

"I'm heading out," Vashti called. "Need me to bring you anything?"

"Just bring yourself back, honey." Bitsy smiled at her.

"You want to take my shotgun?" Augie asked.

"No, thanks. I'll be fine." She patted her canvas bag, where her pistol lay. The last thing she needed was to lose Augie's shotgun the way she'd lost Griffin's rifle.

"Take your coat," Bitsy said. "It's fixing to rain."

Vashti smiled at her. "It's nice to have someone who cares whether or not I get wet." She walked over to the dry sink and kissed Bitsy's powdered cheek. Bitsy squeezed her.

Vashti waved at Augie and hurried over to the store. Goldie was helping Libby this morning, while several customers stocked up on groceries. Vashti went to the ready-mades section and pulled a men's shirt off the rack. She sidled up to Libby, who was pouring out a quart of milk for Mrs. Walker.

"Would it be all right if I tried this on in the storeroom?"

Libby looked at her and the shirt and nodded. "Help yourself."

The new shirt hung loosely on her, but Vashti figured that was good. She tucked it in and put the vest on over it. If this one shrank, it would still fit. She stuffed the old one into her bag and went out into the store.

Goldie was totting up a large order for Terrence Thistle. She shot a sidelong glance toward Vashti. "Whatcha got today?"

"The shirt on my back."

Mr. Thistle laughed. "You should hear the men when they come in off the stagecoach, arguing over whether you're a girl or not."

"Really?"

"My, yes. Last week I was afraid they'd come to fisticuffs over it. And then Griff Bane come in with his boy, so I says, 'Fellas, here's the division agent for the stage line. Whyn't you ask him?'"

Vashti gulped. "Did they?"

"Oh yes. And Griffin says, real somber-like, 'What's that? A woman driving one of *my* coaches?' He shook his head and said, 'What next?'"

Goldie laughed. "What did the men say?"

"Not much after that. Griff's so big, I think they was afraid to say any more."

Vashti smiled, but she wondered how much ragging Griffin would take on her account. If he was stacking up reasons to fire her, he probably had quite a stockpile by now.

"All right, Mr. Thistle, you're all set." Goldie gave him a piece of paper with his total on it.

He picked up a small crate of groceries. "I'll come back for the rest."

Vashti watched him go out the door, struggling to shut it behind him. "Too bad he lost his arm in the war."

"Yeah, but he does all right. Now, let's see, one man's cotton shirt." Goldie named the price, and Vashti laid the money on the counter.

"Think this one will shrink much?"

"Oh, I wondered why you needed a new one." She eyed the cuffs that fell down over Vashti's wrists. "That one's plenty big."

"Good. Got to run." Vashti whisked out the door and down the sidewalk. To her surprise, the door to the Wells Fargo office was open, and three people were lined up outside. She slowed her steps. As she came even with the office, she stepped down off the boardwalk to avoid the customers, but she could still hear Griffin's loud voice from within the building.

"I'm telling you, Manny, it'll be safe. I'm sending two outriders with the stage, and I'm putting an extra guard on the roof."

So that was it. People had heard about the holdups and were afraid to ride the stage. She picked up speed and ran past the feed store and down the street, cutting behind the smithy to the livery. Marty was hitching up the last of the six-mule team. Vashti wished she hadn't dawdled so long at the emporium. It must be nearly time for her to drive up to the office.

"Morning, Marty." She stopped and stared at the two riders sitting astride their horses and the young woman standing near the coach. "Hello, Trudy. Mr. Dooley. Mr. Tinen."

"Howdy," Trudy said. "My brother and I and Arthur Jr. are riding along with you today. Hope you don't mind."

"I heard Mr. Bane say he was sending extra guards with me. Didn't expect you folks."

"Well, Ned's still laid up," Trudy said. "Griff asked for my husband this morning, but he's over on Catherine Creek, helping the marshal's deputies look for the outlaws. So I said I'd go."

"I'm surprised Mr. Bane agreed."

Trudy shrugged. "He said I couldn't ride point, but I could ride on the stage with you. I suggested he stop at Hiram's place and see if he felt like an adventure."

Hiram smiled and nodded, but said nothing. He and Arthur Tinen Jr. had rifles in scabbards on their saddles, and Art also wore a sidearm.

Art said, "That's about the way of it. I was over to Hiram's to see if he could fix my leather punch for me when Griff came by, and we both thought it sounded like a noble thing to do."

"Noble," Trudy scoffed. "You only came because Griffin offered you five dollars for the trip, and even then you're lucky Starr let you go."

Arthur grinned and shrugged one shoulder. "We'd best get moving. Griffin said we had to be on time."

"Right. Climb up, Trudy." Vashti mounted the box. She stowed her canvas bag under the seat and readied her whip.

Trudy climbed up cautiously and took the seat Ned usually had. She held her rifle on her knees. "So far, this is fun. Wish I had trousers, though." She smoothed down her brown divided skirt.

"All ready, Georgie," Marty called from his place at the lead mules' heads.

Vashti gathered the reins and gave him a nod. Hiram and Arthur rode out just ahead of them, and she put the mules into a trot. As they rounded the corner by the smithy, she looked over at Trudy.

"I have to admit it feels good to have two outriders. . .and to have the best shot in Fergus sitting beside me on the box."

Trudy smiled. "I can see why you like this job."

"Think Ethan will mind you doing it?"

"By the time he hears, I'll be home. Besides, Griffin says we've likely got the safest route in Idaho today. Those outlaws are off east of here, hiding from the law."

"I hope he's right." Vashti felt a flicker of fear but shook it off. "Will you stay at the stage stop with me tonight?"

"Yes, Griffin gave us money for our room and board."

Vashti thought about that as she guided the mules to a stop before the Wells Fargo office. The holdup had cost Griffin a lot—more than just the horses and his rifle.

He stood, grim and foreboding, on the boardwalk. "Four of your six passengers decided not to go."

Vashti gritted her teeth. "I'm sorry. I suppose you had to refund their ticket money."

He nodded. "You okay with your new messenger?"

"Oh, sure. Trudy's great."

Griffin stepped closer and looked up at them earnestly. "You know I wouldn't let the two of you go if I didn't think the road would be safe today."

Vashti nodded. "Thanks for giving us an escort."

Griffin eyed Hiram and Arthur, who sat their horses ahead of the coach, waiting for the passengers to board. "Well, I don't like putting my friends at risk, but I didn't have anyone else on hand. I can't go off and leave Justin again so soon. Guess I could have sent Marty, but. . .well, you know Marty."

"Yeah, and he can't shoot straight, either."

Griffin cracked a smile. "All right then, Georgie. I'll load the mail sacks and tuck the passengers in. Be safe."

Vashti raised her coiled whip to her hat brim.

He turned away, and Trudy said, "That man cares about you."

Vashti chuckled. "He cares about all his employees."

"That's not what I meant. He's worried about you personally."

Vashti tucked that comment away to examine later. The mail sacks thudded on the coach floor, making the stage sway; then the two hardy men who hadn't demanded refunds climbed in. Griffin waved, and Vashti turned forward. "Up now!"

Ethan rode in tired, sweaty, and chilled. He'd been in the saddle all day, in the rain. He only wanted one thing: home. Home meant a hot meal to fill his belly, hot water to wash in, a cozy, comfortable bed to sleep in—and Trudy. He smiled as Scout plodded down the lane toward the ranch house. No smoke came from the chimney. That was odd on a chilly evening like this. The sun was bedding down for the night behind the mountains, but no lights shone from the kitchen window—or any other window.

Scout would have gone on toward the barn, which meant a meal and a dry bed for him, too, but Ethan pulled back on the reins.

"Whoa!" He stared at the silent house.

Across the sodden barnyard, a lantern glowed in the window of the little bunkhouse where the McDade brothers slept. He turned Scout toward it. Dismounting, he dropped the reins. After a brief knock, he opened the door a few inches and stuck his head into the gap.

"Spin?"

"Yeah, boss." Spin jumped up from his chair near the stove and hurried toward him. "Didn't expect you tonight."

"Where's Trudy?"

"Uh. . ."

Ethan scowled at him. "What's the matter with you?"

Johnny set his tin plate down and came to stand beside Spin. "Miz Chapman's gone."

Ethan scowled even harder at Johnny, so hard it hurt. "What do you mean, gone? Did she go over to Hiram's this evening?"

"Nope. She went to Nampa."

Ethan cocked his head to one side and considered whether the young man was teasing him or not.

"That ain't funny."

"It's true," Spin said. "She went on the stagecoach. Mr. Dooley and Arthur Tinen Jr. went along on their horses."

Ethan swiveled his gaze to Spin. "Whatever for? Did somebody die in Nampa?"

"Nope, but Griff Bane needed extra guards for the stagecoach," Johnny said.

Ethan let that sink in. Very slowly, deliberately, as if the boys were still cutting their teeth and wearing short pants, he said, "Are you telling me that my wife is riding shotgun on a stagecoach?"

Spin nodded, a gleam in his eyes. "She said you wouldn't know till after she came home tomorrow, but if you did get home first, to tell you not to worry."

"That's right," Johnny added. "Griff said you was keeping them outlaws so busy they wouldn't come anywhere near the stage today, so they'd be safe."

Ethan narrowed his eyes. "Well, if it's so all-fired safe, why did he send Hiram and Art and *my wife* along to protect it?"

Johnny looked away.

Spin shrugged. "Word is, folks don't want to ride the stage unless they have extra guards."

Johnny perked up again. "Yeah. I wanted to go. Griff was paying five bucks a man."

"Or woman," Spin put in.

"Yeah. Only he said I was too young."

"That right?" Ethan was feeling a mite testy by this time. He glared at Spin. "Why didn't you go?"

"Well, boss, I didn't think you'd want me to. Not with the missus gone. I mean, would you want me to leave the ranch in the hands of a seventeen-year-old rapscallion?"

Ethan looked from him to his younger brother. "Guess not." He let out a long, slow breath. "You boys got any grub?"

Vashti and Trudy chattered as they neared Nampa. The rain had slacked off, but the breeze was still chilly. Trudy rubbed at her gun barrel with a handkerchief.

"I hope this rifle doesn't rust from getting wet today."

Vashti looked over at her. "Too bad we had to drive most of the way in the rain. Are you all right?"

"I'm fine. I dressed for it. What do you do when you stay over in Nampa?"

"I usually have the rest of the day free. Once I walked up the street a little and looked in the shops, but mostly I stay at the station. I get my supper and go to bed early. I'll ask if you can be in the same room with me tonight."

"That would be fun."

Vashti called out to the riders, "Mr. Dooley! Mr. Tinen!"

They turned in their saddles.

"Station's just over that rise." She uncoiled her whip and cracked it. Had to make a good showing when you came into the station. Hiram and Art pulled off to the sides and let her pass them, then fell in behind the coach. The road was a bit muddy, but the mules managed to jog into the yard at a respectable pace.

"Whoa, boys," Vashti called and laid on the reins a little. These mules needed a firmer touch than most horses.

The station agent came out. "Well, George, I see you made it."

"Yes, sir."

"Well, well, well." He looked Trudy over. "I see Mr. Bane's hired a new messenger of the distaff side."

Trudy laughed. "Ned Harmon was injured last week. My brother and I and Mr. Tinen, back there, rode along to give Mr. Bane peace of mind."

"And you had no trouble on the road?"

"Just rain and mud," Vashti said, bending down to retrieve her bag from beneath the seat.

"Good. Got a meal ready for you, but don't get too comfortable."

Vashti paused. "What do you mean?"

"Buck Eastman busted his leg."

Vashti caught her breath.

"Who's Buck Eastman?" Trudy asked.

"He's the driver on the run from here to Boise," Vashti said.

"That's right." The station agent made a sympathetic face. "Sorry, but you'll have to drive on to Boise. You've got twenty minutes to eat while we change the teams."

★ CHAPTER 23 ★

You don't have a choice?" Art Tinen asked.

"I'm afraid not. The contract I signed says if the next driver up the line can't make his run and they don't have a replacement ready, I have to make it." Vashti shoveled mashed potatoes into her mouth.

Trudy frowned at her across the table. "But what if you get to Boise and the next driver's sick?"

"They can't make me do more than two runs in a row."

Trudy, Hiram, and Art watched her eat for a minute. They'd get fed, too, but they'd have plenty of time. Vashti had to be on the box and ready to roll in ten more minutes.

Hiram rested his arm on the back of his sister's chair. His eyes matched Trudy's perfectly—stormy gray blue. "Do they have an escort for you?"

Vashti gulped down a swallow of milk. "Yes, the fellow who usually rides with Buck Eastman is here. And it's fairly civilized along the road from here to Boise. I don't think we'll see any road agents."

"So. . .what should we do?" Art asked.

"Vashti, if you want us to go with you, we can," Trudy said quietly.

"Don't be silly. You don't need to do that. I'll be fine. Stay here and rest. Besides, Ethan and Starr will worry their heads off if you don't come home tomorrow afternoon."

"But won't you drive back here tomorrow and take your regular run back to Fergus?" Hiram asked.

She hadn't thought of that. Did they expect her to drive four legs

854

in two days? Of course, the run to Boise was only twenty miles, and the road was pretty good. "I'd better speak to the station agent."

She shoved her stool back and rose. Though she was tired, she knew she could drive as far as Boise with a fresh team. A couple of more hours wouldn't kill her. She'd spend the night in the territorial capital and head back in the morning. "It's really not that far."

Outside, the tenders had the fresh team in place—four matched bays. Vashti found herself eager to drive them. She walked to where Jeremiah Gayle, the station agent, stood talking to another man.

"Here's your driver," he said as Vashti approached. "George Edwards, meet Harold Day. He's your messenger as far as Boise, and he'll go on with the next driver from there."

Vashti shook the shotgun rider's hand. "Nice to meet you, Harold. So they have someone ready to take over in Boise?"

Harold just stood looking at her with a half smile pasted on his face.

Mr. Gayle said, "Yes, they telegraphed. Sid Carver's there, rarin' to go. He's young, but he hopes to get a permanent driving job. This will be a little test for him. You'll just go as far as Boise and stay at the hotel there."

"A hotel."

"Yup. They put drivers up at a fancy place there, right, Harold?"

Harold spat on the ground. "Wouldn't call it fancy."

Vashti gulped. She wanted to ask if it was safe for women. "And will I drive back here in the morning?"

"That's right. You'll have a different messenger with you. Likely Tom McPherson. You'll come back here and take your regular drive back to Fergus. You good with that? It means double pay."

She hadn't thought of that. "Sure. And if my friends who came along from Fergus want to go, is that all right?"

"Well, we've got a full coach for you. And we wouldn't pay for the extra riders, though I understand you needed 'em to get here safely."

"I'll be right back." She turned toward the house.

"Be quick," Gayle called. "You're scheduled to leave in three minutes."

She hurried inside and explained the situation. Passengers

bustled about, gathering their belongings.

Art looked at Hiram. "What do you think? We could just stay here and join Vashti again when she leaves here for Fergus tomorrow. Our room and food are all paid for here."

Hiram nodded. "To be honest, I didn't come prepared to pay for a hotel and meals in Boise."

Trudy's mouth drooped.

"How long since you've been to Boise City, Trudy?" Vashti asked.

Her friend looked at her and shrugged. "Quite a while."

"You could probably share my room with me, if you wanted to ride along. Mr. Gayle says the coach is full, but there's always room outside." She glanced toward the window. "Of course, the rain could start up again."

Trudy's eyes glittered. "Hiram, can I borrow your hat? It'll keep the rain off better than mine."

He sighed mournfully, but his lips quirked into a little smile as he handed her the old felt hat. "If you're going, maybe there's something you can check on for me. Can I talk to you for a second?"

Trudy followed him a few steps away from the others. Vashti tapped her foot. Mr. Gayle was probably looking at his watch and steaming. Hiram put something in Trudy's hand, and she shoved it quickly into her purse. She came back to Vashti smiling.

"I'm ready."

"Mind you don't let her get into trouble," Hiram said.

"I assure you, we'll be proper ladies. Well, as proper as I can be in these clothes." For the first time, Vashti regretted not bringing a dress along on her stagecoach runs.

"Come on, then." Trudy clapped the hat on. "Hiram, you boys be good."

Hiram and Arthur laughed.

When they got outside, the coach was loaded and two men were sitting on the roof.

Vashti threw Trudy an apologetic glance. "Sorry—I didn't know we had *that* many passengers."

"Don't fret." Trudy was always game to lead the shooting club into adventure, and the prospect of an uncomfortable ride among strange men didn't seem to daunt her. She climbed up to the box and smiled at the passengers. "Excuse me, gentlemen. I'll be joining you."

Harold Day already sat on the box. He caught Vashti's eye. "Your friend can sit here with us, if you don't think it'll interfere with your driving."

At once Vashti said, "Hey, Trudy, sit with me and Harold."

"Oh. All right."

Vashti climbed up and considered whether she ought to sit on the outside or in the middle for the best control of the horses. At last she settled between Harold and Trudy and took up the reins.

"You're two minutes late leaving," Mr. Gayle said from the ground.

"I'm sorry." Vashti looked ahead to the tenders and nodded. As they released the horses' heads, she flicked her whip, careful not to jab Trudy with her elbow as she did. "Up, you." The four bays broke immediately into their road trot, and the coach rolled forward.

Though the quarters were a little close, she found the ride to Boise almost as pleasant as her earlier drive with Trudy. They soon had Harold laughing with their tales of life in Fergus. Trudy drew out the messenger, looking past Vashti to question him. They learned he was a family man living in Nampa, and the father of three children. By the time they reached the swing station where the horses were changed, Trudy and Vashti had learned all the children's names and ages, and the fact that one of them had celebrated his fourth birthday the day before.

"That reminds me," Trudy said. "Libby's birthday is next week. I'd like to get her something. Nothing big. Just something she doesn't have in the emporium, you know?"

"She and Hiram will have a cause for wedding gifts soon, too." Vashti picked up her whip, ready to set out again with the new team. "The folks who are buying her business are supposed to return with us to Fergus tomorrow."

Trudy gave her a mysterious smile and bounced a little on the seat. "Remember when Hiram asked to talk to me at the last minute?"

"Yes."

Trudy leaned closer and whispered in Vashti's ear, "He asked me to look for a wedding ring for Libby, so's he wouldn't have to buy it at her store."

"That sounds like a fun errand."

"Do you suppose the stores will still be open when we get to Boise?" Trudy looked up, but gray clouds blocked the sun.

"Should be," Harold said. "The schedule puts us there at four."

"Then let's be on time," Vashti said. The new team was swiftly put in place, and she figured they might have made up their lost two minutes. One more passenger had climbed to the roof behind them. "Next stop Boise City," she called and nodded to the tenders. The horses tried to jump into a canter, but she steadied them. No need to rush.

A raindrop plinked on her nose.

As soon as Vashti was free to leave the stagecoach stop, she and Trudy headed for the nearest cluster of shops. With the promise of double pay when she got home, Vashti splurged on a large umbrella.

"We can both fit under it," she said.

They asked the clerk at the haberdashery what stores would be open latest and planned their itinerary accordingly. Carrying their meager luggage, they visited those between the stage stop and the hotel. Vashti found a serviceable black bombazine skirt, which she wore out of the store, carrying her trousers stuffed into her canvas bag.

"All the wedding rings they have look the same," Trudy said when Vashti came out of the fitting booth at the back.

"Well, of course. They're supposed to, aren't they?"

"I guess. Hiram didn't give me much money, but I can get one."

"I've got a little extra, if you need it."

"No. . .but they have different sizes. What size do you suppose Libby wears?"

"Hmm. Her fingers are slender."

"That's what I'm thinking." Trudy perked up suddenly. "Let's try them on."

Trying to hide their laughter, they slipped ring after ring onto their fingers as the clerk watched.

"This one, I think," Trudy said at last. She held it out to the clerk and slipped her own wedding ring on again.

Vashti turned away from the counter with a sigh. That was probably as close as she'd ever get to wearing a wedding ring.

By six o'clock, they were ready to sign in at the hotel and have dinner.

The desk clerk made no comment about the extra guest Vashti was taking to the room with her, but he did eye their headgear—men's hats on both ladies' heads—with an air of disapproval. They found they could lock their possessions in their room, so they freshened up and descended to the dining room.

"I can pay for your supper," Vashti offered as they sat down at a table near the front windows.

"I have enough," Trudy said. "I wasn't sure until I got Libby's birthday gift, but it wasn't too expensive, so I have plenty left for supper and breakfast. Do you think she'll like it?"

"I certainly do. I've heard she loves to read, and you got the very latest book from New York. She can't possibly have read it yet."

"I do hope she likes poetry."

"She'll love it," Vashti said.

A woman in a dark brown dress and ecru apron came to their table. "Good evening, ladies. What may I bring you?"

They ordered two servings of chicken pie and a pot of tea.

"I wish I could have found a good wedding present for them," Vashti said.

"There's still that store down beyond the bank," Trudy said. "We could walk down there."

When the waitress came back with their plates, Vashti asked, "Would we have time to go shopping at that big store down the street?"

"Hubbard's generally stays open until nine," the woman said.

"Would it be safe for us to walk down there?" Trudy asked.

"I'd think so, if you stay together and don't loiter."

Vashti wished the men had come with them. "What do you think?"

Susan Page Davis

Trudy shrugged. "I'm willing if you are."

The waitress poured tea for them. "There is one saloon on the other side of the street, shortly before you get to Hubbard's. Just be aware and keep moving."

When they'd finished the meal, they got their wraps. Trudy put her pistol in her purse. Vashti hadn't brought a handbag, but she tucked her gun into her waistband, beneath her vest and coat. She took the umbrella, but the rain had let up.

"I don't suppose we dare leave this here."

Trudy shook her head. "If we do, it will pour just when we're ready to come back."

They walked quickly down the street. Few pedestrians were out. A wagon occasionally rattled past them. As they approached the store, it was easy to pick out the saloon. On the far side of the street, a dozen or more horses were tied to a hitching rail before a low log building. Laughter and tinny music reached them. Vashti swallowed hard at the vivid reminder of her past life.

"Come on." Trudy hung on to her sleeve and steered her quickly onward, to the quiet store. "I'm glad we didn't have to walk on the same side of the street as that place."

Inside, ready-made clothing for the entire family was displayed. Vashti hadn't been in a store bigger than Libby's Paragon Emporium since she'd come to Fergus five years ago, and she suspected that for Trudy it had been longer. They walked slowly around the perimeter, stopping to look at whatever caught their fancy—a silk shawl draped over an open chest, a pair of children's overalls on a large doll, or row after row of shoes.

"This place could outfit everyone in Fergus," Trudy said.

Vashti nodded, eyeing the headless display form that vaguely resembled a woman's body. The shimmering gown it wore caught her eye, but the decapitated figure made her shiver. "They say there wasn't even a town here thirty years ago."

"It wasn't nearly so big when I last came here," Trudy said. She fingered a challis blouse in a muted pink and white print. "Sort of wish I'd brought more money. But that's silly. I have all the clothes I need."

860

"It's fun to get something new now and then." Vashti turned to her with a smile. "Help me pick out a nice gift for the bride and groom."

Trudy joined her quest, and fifteen minutes later they left the store with an imported china platter, hand-painted with flowers and nesting birds, wrapped with several layers of newspaper and tied up in brown paper. Vashti had spent a little more than she'd planned, but the birds were so dear she couldn't resist it.

"When Libby and Hiram have you and Ethan over at Thanksgiving, she can serve her turkey on it," she said to Trudy.

Her friend laughed and pulled on her gloves as they left the store. They walked toward the hotel.

"Know what I'm going to do with the ring tomorrow?" Trudy asked.

"What?"

"Now, mind you, I don't think we'll get held up. But just in case we do. . ." She leaned closer and whispered, "I'm tying it into my corset."

Vashti laughed.

"You think it's funny," Trudy said, "but I heard about a robbery down in California where a lady put nine hundred dollars in her bosom. All the men got robbed. She gave the outlaws her reticule with a couple of dollars in it, and they never suspected she had more."

"Right." They were even with the saloon, and Vashti flicked a glance toward it. A man came out the door. He appeared to be sober, and he headed diagonally across the street toward Hubbard's. She would have kept going without another thought, but he turned his face into the light flowing out the store's front window, and she caught her breath. Her step faltered, and she nearly dropped the platter.

★ CHAPTER 24 ★

"Are you all right?" Trudy asked, putting out a hand to steady her friend.

Vashti whipped her head around, her heart racing. "Quick," she whispered and dashed along the sidewalk, hugging her awkward burden.

Trudy raced along beside her, craning her neck to look back and then turning forward again. "What is it? That man? He went into the store."

"Good." Vashti slowed to a brisk walk, panting. "I'm sorry."

"It's all right. Do you know him?"

Vashti felt a sick knot in her stomach. "I'm not sure. He looked like someone I used to know. But not here."

"Let's get back to the hotel, and then you can tell me about it."

They hurried along, slightly uphill. The platter grew heavier, and Vashti's feet began to drag.

"Here, let me take that." Trudy reached for the package.

Vashti didn't protest. She climbed the hotel steps wearily and went to the front desk to retrieve their room key. One more flight of stairs, and she could relax. Trudy held the package and the umbrella while Vashti unlocked the door.

Their room would be their fortress. With the door closed and locked, Vashti sank down on the edge of the bed.

"I'm sorry. I shouldn't have let him scare me like that. It startled me, though."

"Are you sure it was the man you knew?"

"No. I hope it wasn't." Vashti gulped and pulled off her gloves. "The man he looks like is one I never want to see again."

Trudy laid the platter carefully on the dresser and came around to sit beside her on the quilt. She put her arm around Vashti. "I'm sorry. We were having such a good time." Her eyes filled with sympathetic tears, and Vashti felt a pang of guilt.

"I didn't mean to get you upset, either."

"I'm all right. Do you want to tell me about this fellow, so that I'll know how to act if we meet him again?"

Vashti pulled in a long, slow breath. "I thought he was Luke Hatley."

Trudy frowned. "Don't know that name."

"He was a gambler. I met him back in Independence."

"Was he good at it?"

"At gambling? Very. But not so good at winning."

Trudy snorted a laugh. "So what happened?"

"I first met him when I was thirteen, outside a bakery. I was sniffing the bread baking and wondering if I could steal some." She tugged off her coat and laid it, with her hat and gloves, on the bed. "Anyway, I was young, and I was desperate. I figured being with him was better than being with half the men in town, so to speak. He liked me, and he seemed decent. I guess that must sound funny to you—a fellow who would do to a thirteen-year-old what he did to me. But he seemed like a way out for me. A way to survive without. . ."

Trudy stroked her back gently. "And then what? Did he leave you?"

"Sort of." Vashti jumped up and turned to face her. "Look, I didn't mean to tell you all this. Haven't told anyone but Bitsy. Well, I told Griffin some, but not this part." Trudy seemed surprised, and Vashti felt she needed to explain. "He came to talk to me shortly after Justin came. I wanted him to understand how it is if you're young and alone. If you don't have a good, honest person like Griff to take care of you."

Trudy nodded. "Justin could have gotten into all sorts of trouble, I suppose."

"He'd already started to back where he came from. It wouldn't take much for him to run away from Griffin and try to make it on his own. And then what? He'd end up with some toughs like those road agents or take to gambling and drinking. But one person—one good person—can turn a kid's life around."

"I think you're right."

"I thought Luke might be that for me, but I was wrong. He took me deeper into. . .what the reverend would call lasciviousness. And then crime."

"So you left him?"

Vashti walked over to the dresser and opened her canvas bag. "No. He left me. When it was convenient, he dumped me and rode out of town, never looking back. See, he'd gotten into debt to a fellow who owned a place."

"What kind of place?"

"A saloon."

"Oh."

Vashti turned to look at her face. Would Trudy still want to be her friend if she knew everything?

"I shouldn't have told you."

"No, I want to know. It helps me to understand some things."

Vashti pulled out her bandanna and dabbed at her cheeks. "Well, Luke gave me to this fellow Ike to cancel his debt. Ike said I had to work for him. I tried to get away, but he kept a strict eye on me and the other girls he had working there."

"You mean—"

Vashti turned away, unable to meet her gaze.

Trudy cleared her throat. "Well, obviously you got away after a while."

"Yes. Thanks to Bitsy. I ran away, and she helped me. But just seeing Luke tonight—or someone who looked a lot like him—gave me a turn. I. . .Trudy, I don't want to see him again. Ever."

"That was—what? Five years ago?"

"More like eight."

"So you worked for that Ike person for three years."

The tears flowed steadily, and Vashti nodded. She mopped her face again with the bandanna, conscious that Trudy was studying her profile.

"I'm so sorry," Trudy said.

Vashti tried to shrug it off, but she couldn't stop the tears. The intensity of her dread when she thought she'd seen Luke surprised her. Still, he hadn't been mean to her during their time together. But at the end, he proved that he didn't really care for her as much as he cared about money and winning and a good hand at the poker table. "It could have been worse, I guess. At least Luke, taking me with him like he did, put off the inevitable for almost three years." She sat down again with a sob. "I thought he'd marry me someday. Was I ever wrong."

"You said Bitsy helped you."

Vashti sniffed. "Yes. My life is good now. I have a family. I have a good place to live and a real job and friends."

Trudy smiled and stood. "Let's not think about that man we saw. It probably wasn't him, anyway. A lot of men drift around the West, especially since the gold craziness."

"True."

Trudy eyed her anxiously. "Are you sleepy? You've got a long drive again tomorrow."

"Not really."

"Tell you what: I'll go downstairs and see if we can get a pot of tea and maybe some cookies."

Vashti smiled. "That sounds good." She fished in her pocket and brought out two dimes. "Take this and use it if they won't add it to my bill."

"All right. Lock the door while I'm gone. I'll be back in two shakes of a lamb's tail."

She whisked out the door. Vashti walked over and locked it. She hung up her coat and put her hat and Trudy's on hooks beside it.

The window fronted the street. She walked over and moved the curtain aside with one finger. Lamplight lit the hotel's dooryard and several other buildings down the street. At least they were a good distance from the saloon. But that man could have a room right here in this hotel. She shuddered and let the curtain fall into place.

"Dear God, I guess this is one of those times when I should call on You. Please don't let me see that fella again. Help me not to even think of him. And if he is Luke. . ." She stopped, not knowing what to say next.

Griffin dashed for the smithy, holding a mule's bridle in his hand. How on earth did Marty do it? He was always busting something. Griffin grabbed his leather punch off the wall of tools and rummaged in a crate of leather straps for one the right width. At least the mule's mouth wasn't torn up. A shadow fell across his work as he lined up the new strap with the one on the bridle.

"Anything I can do to help, Uncle Griff?"

The blacksmith paused and looked at the boy. "That's nice of you to ask, Justin. You can run up to the office and tell Josiah Runnels we've got a small delay, but the team should be ready when the stage comes in. Ten minutes. And ask him how many passengers today. We've got two sacks of mail going out."

Justin sped off without another word. Griffin punched a couple of holes in the straps and turned to his workbench for rivets. His quick fix might chafe the mule's cheek, but what else could he do? He didn't have another harness bridle on hand to fit the mule. That robbery had really cut into his assets.

At last the bridle was patched together. He'd have to stitch it tomorrow, when this harness came home to him with the stagecoach. He dashed out the door and headed for the back of the livery. Ethan was dismounting near the corral gate.

"Hey, Griff! Thought I'd turn Scout out while I wait for the stage."

"Sure, go ahead." He hoped Ethan wasn't upset with him for letting Trudy act as a shotgun messenger. "They'll be here any minute. I've got to have this team ready, or I'd stop to chew the fat."

Ethan waved. "No problem. I'll mosey on up there."

Griffin bridled the near swing mule. Done. He turned and looked for Marty. Found him sitting on a barrel of oats, chewing a straw. Griff felt like tearing into him. The man moved slower than a snake in winter.

"Uncle Griff?"

Justin stood in the open front door of the barn.

"Yeah?"

"Josiah says seven passengers to Silver City."

"Good." There'd be room for all seven inside the coach, along with the mail sacks.

At last the team was ready. Griffin pulled out his watch. The stage should arrive any minute.

"Marty, you step lively when they bring the stage in."

"Sure, boss."

Griffin tried not to let that rankle him. Pastor Benton's last sermon had included some warnings about anger. As he strode up the sidewalk to the Wells Fargo office, he tried to think about better things. Technically, Isabel still owned the building, but if his application for the mail contract came through for another year, he could buy it from her. That and a pile of new harnesses and maybe even another coach. He could hire more drivers and messengers. . . .

Ethan lolled against the wall of the office, and a few people who planned to meet passengers milled about on the walkway. Griffin went to the door. Peter Nash stood inside talking to Josiah Runnels. Two sacks of mail sat on the desk.

"Hey, Griffin," Peter said. "I'd better get back to the post office."

Griffin nodded. "We'll take care of the mail, Mayor."

"Do you need me to help with the team?" Josiah asked.

"Wouldn't hurt. Marty moves slower every day."

"I'll get over to the livery, then." Josiah put on his hat and went out.

Griffin took out his watch again. The stage was five minutes late. His stomach started doing odd things. Those outlaws—he couldn't stand another robbery. Especially not with Vashti driving. Trudy was on the stage, too, and her husband waited outside, looking relaxed but probably tied up inside. At least it wasn't raining today.

As if Griffin's thoughts had drawn him, Ethan appeared in the doorway, squinting into the dimly lit room.

"Are they late, Griff?"

Griffin snapped the watchcase shut. "Not much."

Ethan came in and leaned on the edge of the desk. "Can't help fretting. Guess that doesn't do any good, though."

"I know what you mean."

Ethan bit his lip and nodded. "Maybe I should ride out and meet them."

"They'll be fine." Griffin wished he believed it. He kept seeing that narrow place in the rocks.

"Trudy's pretty headstrong, but I didn't expect her to go off overnight like this."

"I guess that's my fault. Hiram and Arthur were going, and she was keen to go, too. I figured it wouldn't hurt to have another crack shot along. Besides, I didn't expect anything to happen. I'm sure they're all right." Griffin walked around the desk and sat down. "You like being married?"

Ethan smiled. "Shoulda done it a long time ago."

Griffin took his hat off and laid it on the desk. He ran a hand through his bushy hair. "Sometimes I think about it."

"You surprise me."

"Have to admit there's a gal I'm a little sweet on." Griffin shot a glance at his friend. "Haven't said anything to her. Yet."

"Might that be a certain person on the stagecoach?" Ethan asked.

Griffin couldn't help smiling as he thought of Vashti in her boy clothes, cracking her whip like the best of the old-time drivers. "She's got pluck. I thought she was crazy when she first asked me for a job. But she really can drive. Bill Stout came around when he knew I was hard pressed to find drivers this spring and told me I should look twice at her. She'd been practicing." He shook his head. "Didn't expect her to mean anything to me, other than a driver."

"Well, take your time, Griff. Make sure it's not just an infatuation. She's pretty, and she's independent, given her past."

"What about her past?" Griff scowled at him. How dare Ethan bring that up?

"Easy, now. I'm just saying. . .a gal who's been forced to take care of herself most of her life can find it hard to let other folks do things for her. She might have some ideas that aren't quite like yours." Ethan strolled to the doorway. "Your nephew's running up the street."

"Justin?" Griffin jumped up. He'd forgotten all about the boy and left him at the livery.

Justin hit the sidewalk as he reached the door and Ethan stepped aside.

"Uncle Griff! The stage is coming!"

Griffin walked past him, out onto the boardwalk. Sure enough, he could hear the team's thudding hoofbeats and the sound of the wheels skimming over the road. He looked at his watch again. Nearly fifteen minutes late. But here, just the same. Passengers who planned to ride on up to Silver City, along with those there to meet folks getting off the stage, looked eagerly toward the sound. Libby Adams stood outside the emporium's door watching.

Hiram Dooley and Arthur Tinen Jr. rode around the corner by the smithy on their horses. They looked none the worse for wear. As the coach came into view, Griffin half expected to see arrows sticking out of the sides, but that was silly. Hadn't been Indian trouble in ten years. He blew out a deep breath. Ethan came and stood beside him, bouncing on his toes.

Trudy sat on the box beside Vashti. Trudy's dark blond hair hung in a braid over her shoulder, but Vashti had her hair hidden beneath her felt hat, as he'd demanded she do. Too bad. She looked much better when she let her womanly charms show.

Griffin frowned at his thoughts. He wasn't about to let her start driving in a dress, with her hair all shiny and soft around her face, like it was that night he ate at the Spur & Saddle. She would make far too tempting a picture that way, and she traveled miles and miles of isolated roads. No, she'd best keep dressing like a boy, even if everyone in the territory knew she was anything but a man.

Trudy started waving and grinning, and Griffin looked over at Ethan. His face looked about to crack, the sheriff was smiling so big.

The coach eased to a stop, and Griffin opened the door. He took out the bag of mail for Fergus and entrusted it to Josiah to take over to Peter at the post office, then let the passengers out. The couple who'd come last fall to see Libby about buying her store got out first. Libby hurried down the boardwalk to greet them.

"The stage will leave for Silver City in twenty minutes, folks," Griffin said. "If you're traveling on, coffee and a quick meal can be had at the Fennel House or the Spur & Saddle. If you're late getting back, the stage won't wait for you."

Four men tumbled out, and those who planned to ride on after the stop looked around and headed quickly across the street. Last out was a salesman with a large sample case.

"I'd like to stop here overnight," he said. "Is there a clean, reasonable place to stay?"

"Fennel House." Griff pointed across the street. He turned to those planning to board the coach. "Folks, we need to swap the team out. I know we're a few minutes late, and I'm sorry about that. Let the driver take the stage around to the livery. They should be back so you can climb aboard in ten minutes." He glanced up at Vashti, and she nodded at him. Trudy still sat on the box with her. Arthur and Hiram waited a few paces away on their horses. "Did you have any trouble?" Griffin asked in a low voice.

Vashti shook her head and smiled. "It was muddy in the creeks because of the rain, but not too bad. The ferry held us up. Had to wait nigh half an hour for it."

"All right. Good job, and I'll see you after the stage leaves again." He waved to Hiram and Arthur. "Come see me at the livery, boys. I'll be down there soon." Getting Vashti back in one piece—not to mention the livestock and equipment—was well worth their wages. He wished he had enough money to pay extra guards every day. If only the postmaster general would come through with that new contract. . .

He went into his office and opened the safe. He'd be very low on cash once he paid off this week's crew. Had Wells Fargo sent him money to buy new equipment? He hadn't given up hope yet that the government would reimburse him for what he'd lost on the mail run, either, but it was probably too soon to look for a bank draft in the mail.

Someone came in and stood behind him. Griffin was suddenly conscious of how vulnerable he was, bending over his open safe like that. He looked over his shoulder. Justin stood blocking the light from the doorway.

"Anything I can do, Uncle Griff?" He sounded lonesome.

Griffin took most of the cash that was in the Uneeda Biscuit box and closed the safe. "Sure. As soon as we see off the Silver City coach, you can go back to the livery with me. Vashti and the messengers will tell us about their run. I always have the drivers give me the details, so I know how the roads are and hear any news they picked up. Then we'll go over the team that just came in, check their feet, and brush 'em down real good." Tight times or not, he determined he'd find a way to pay the boy something, now that he'd started showing a will to work.

"One of the farmers brought in a great big chestnut horse after you left. Said it needs shoeing. Mr. Robinson."

"Rancher," Griffin said. "Not a farmer, a rancher."

"Yes, sir."

Griff smiled and shoved the cash into his pocket. "Come on. Let's go outside. The stage should be back soon, ready to leave for Silver."

"Uncle Griff?"

"Hmm?" He hoped this wouldn't be another philosophical question.

"Do you s'pose I could learn to drive a four-in-hand?"

"Maybe. It takes a lot of practice. A six takes even more."

"Well, then, can I learn to drive one horse at a time?"

Griffin laughed. "I'm sure you can. And when you're comfortable with that, we'll go to two. I don't s'pose you'd care to learn to make horseshoes?"

Justin winced. "If I have to."

"You don't have to."

They walked out onto the sidewalk as the coach came up the street with Bill Stout on the box.

Trudy and Vashti waited in the barn at the livery after the coach headed out with its new team and crew. Hiram and Arthur leaned on stall dividers and told Ethan about their journey. After a while, Griffin and his nephew came into the barn. Marty, who'd been sitting on a stack of hay bales listening to Arthur's tale, jumped up, grabbed a dung fork, and disappeared into the nearest stall.

Susan Page Davis

"Folks, I sure do appreciate your help." Griffin pulled his wad of bills out of his pocket. He looked at Vashti first. "I'll settle with you on Friday. You need any cash right now?"

"Nope, I'm fine until my usual payday. Thanks."

He counted out five dollars and handed it to Trudy. "Thanks a lot."

"It was fun. First time I've been out and about for a long time, and I enjoyed having some time with another woman."

He turned and gave five dollars each to Hiram and Arthur.

"Much obliged," Arthur said.

"Did they take care of you at the home station?" Griffin asked as he handed over Hiram's pay.

"Very well. Of course, Trudy went to Boise with Vashti."

"Boise?" He swung around and stared at Vashti. "You drove to Boise?"

She nodded. "Buck Eastman broke his leg. Mr. Gayle told me I had to keep going, but I didn't mind. It didn't put me off schedule. And he said I'd get double pay." She looked at him hopefully.

"Yes, all right, but why didn't you wire me?"

Vashti shrugged, wondering if she'd done wrong. "I thought Mr. Gayle had. And I didn't think you'd want me to spend money like that, anyway."

Griffin sighed. "Guess I'd better ride to Nampa tomorrow. I'll need to hire more drivers and guards for sure now." He looked over at Hiram and Arthur. "You boys want extra work?"

Arthur said, "I'll have to talk to Starr. Things are getting pretty busy on the ranch, but we are a little short on cash."

"I didn't mind doing it," Hiram said, "but Art's right. We've got spring roundup and fences to fix and all kinds of chores to see to. But if you're in a bind. . ."

"I'll find somebody."

Trudy stepped toward him. "Griffin, I think I know a way you could have plenty of guards without spending too much money."

"How's that?"

"Let the members of the Ladies' Shooting Club ride free on the stagecoaches. Some of the ladies would love a chance for a free trip

872

to Nampa or Boise to shop, and they'd surely be willing to take their weapons along and watch out for trouble."

"I don't know. Putting ladies at risk like that."

Art laughed. "If ever there were women who could take care of themselves, it's our shooting club ladies."

"That's right," Trudy said. "Give them a free seat, and I'll bet they'd be happy to buy their own meals and lodging. Some of these women haven't been out of Fergus for upwards of five years."

Griffin scratched his chin through his beard. "I'll take that under consideration."

"Good. Now, I'm heading home with my husband."

"Finally." Ethan straightened and walked over to her. "Where's Crinkles?"

"I left him out in the corral yesterday."

Ethan walked to the back door. "I'll go get him and Scout."

Justin dashed after him. "I'll help you, Sheriff."

Trudy turned to Vashti and hugged her. "Again, thank you for showing me a good time in the city."

Vashti laughed. "Maybe we'll get to do it again."

Griffin scratched his head. "Do you think that if two or three ladies rode along, they'd pay attention to the road, or would they just. . ."

"Just what?" Trudy glared at him.

"Yeah," Vashti said. "Are you insinuating that our women would get caught up in conversation instead of keeping watch?"

"No. I, uh. . ."

Trudy fairly bristled. "Griffin Bane, our women are not only the best shots in town; they also take their duty seriously."

Ethan stepped into the doorway at the rear of the barn, frowning. "Trudy? I can't find Crinkles out there."

"What?" Trudy ran past him toward the corral. A moment later she came back. "Griffin, my horse is gone."

✦ CHAPTER 25 ✦

Griffin frowned and pushed his hat back. "I saw that palomino gelding out there an hour ago." His mouth twitched. "Marty! Oh, Marty!"

"Yeah, boss?" Marty leaned around the stall divider and peered at him.

"Where is Mrs. Chapman's horse?"

"Uh. . ."

Griffin stomped over and stood before him, glaring down from his superior height. "Where is the palomino?"

"A miner came in from the Nugget, wanting a horse to take him up to De Lamar. I told him to pick one out of the corral."

Griffin stared down at him for a long, smoldering moment. "Who saddled the horse?"

"I. . .uh. . .I guess he did."

"Did he pay for it?"

"Uh—yeah." Marty shoved his hand in his pants pocket and pulled out two bits.

"That's not the overnight rate."

Marty gulped and went prospecting for another quarter. When he finally plopped it in Griffin's hand with a grimace, Griffin said in a tight, quiet tone, "Thank you. Come by my office tomorrow and get your wages. You're done here."

Marty's head jerked up. "What? Come on, Griff, you can't fire me."

"Who says I can't? You rented out a horse that wasn't ours, and you would have kept the money if I hadn't found out. Get your stuff out of the loft and hit the road."

"Griff, you can't—"

Griffin turned his back and walked out the front door of the barn.

Vashti tugged at Trudy's sleeve. "Maybe now is a good time for us to leave."

"Come on, darlin'," Ethan said. "You can ride double with me to the ranch."

Justin came in the back door. "Mrs. Chapman, the sheriff's right. Your horse is gone."

Trudy smiled at him. "I know, Justin. We just found out Marty rented him out."

Hiram said, "I reckon I can ride up to De Lamar and get your horse, Trudy."

"You're tired," she said. "Just go catch the stagecoach and ask Bill to tell that man to bring Crinkles back tomorrow."

"I'll go with you, Mr. Dooley," Justin said. He shot a glance at Griffin. "If my uncle says I can."

Marty moved out of the shadows and slunk toward the door.

"Hey, Marty," Arthur called. "Whyn't you get on Hiram's horse and I'll get on mine, and we'll go catch the stagecoach? You can ride the stage to De Lamar and bring Trudy's horse back, and I'll lead Hiram's paint back after you're on the stage."

"Oh, I don't think. . ."

Arthur, Hiram, and Ethan silently moved into position around him.

"I think that's a fine idea," Ethan said. "Because if you don't go, I might have to arrest you for horse thieving."

"What? No!"

Ethan nodded at Arthur. "Get going, boys. And that palomino better be back in my pasture by noon tomorrow, Marty."

Arthur shoved Marty toward the front of the barn, where his pinto and Hiram's horse were tied. Justin kicked at a hay bale.

"What's the matter, Justin?" Vashti asked.

"I wanted to go."

Ethan laid a hand on his shoulder. "I've got a feeling your uncle's going to need you. He just fired his only full-time employee here at the livery. It's a big job. Now, if you were to show that you could handle it—and I don't doubt you could, maybe better than Marty—why, there's no telling what kind of arrangement you could come to."

"You mean, he'd hire me regular?"

"He might. I can't speak for Griffin, but he's a fair man. You've got to start thinking like a businessman, though."

Justin's eyes gleamed. "Well, I think a good businessman would want to make his customer happy." He walked over to Trudy. "Mrs. Chapman, there's an old mare yonder that my uncle lets me ride whenever I want. Would you like to borrow her at no charge to get you home, and return her to us when it suits you?"

Trudy smiled. "That's a very nice offer, Justin. Thank you. I'll do that."

Ethan sighed. "Finally. Let's go home."

Vashti opened the door to her bedroom and leaned against the jamb. The big tin tub sat in the middle of the floor, full of steaming water. Bitsy must have had the water heating and watched for the stage to pull in.

She placed her package containing the wedding platter on her bed, then walked over and stuck her hand in the water. Not too cool, though she'd lingered at the livery. She closed the door and scrambled out of her masculine clothing. On the chair near the tub was a clean towel, a dish holding a bar of soap, and a small bottle. She picked up the bottle. Bath salts. Bitsy's way of reminding her she could feel feminine, even though she'd played the role of a man for two days. She shook a little into the bath and stirred it with her hand.

As she sank down into the warm, fragrant water, she closed her eyes. Rich women probably bathed every day, but this was a luxury in Fergus, where every drop of water had to be hauled from a well or the river.

Thank You, Lord, for blessing me with friends like Bitsy and Trudy.

She smiled as she remembered Trudy's delight at seeing a town bigger than Fergus for the first time in years. Their unintended time together in Boise had strengthened their friendship. Vashti was certain now that Trudy accepted her as an equal. The trip would have been completely uplifting if not for the man from the saloon.

She slid a little lower in the tub, until the water came up to her chin. He'd looked like Luke, but older. That was what really scared her. If he'd looked the same age as the man who'd sold her years ago, she would have known at once that it couldn't really be him.

Tears coursed down her face, and she splashed them away. Why did she have to get so mixed up when she thought about Luke? She'd loved him, hadn't she? Or was that really love? She'd trusted him, certainly, and depended on him, to her regret. The man who'd seemed her angel turned out to be the one who sold her into vile slavery. Yet during their time together, he'd treated her well. Mostly. And he'd said many times that he loved her. Was it a lie?

She took the washcloth and scrubbed her face and arms, determined not to let Luke into her mind again. She would think about the soggy ride to Nampa and Boise and Trudy's invitation to visit her at the ranch this weekend. The way Trudy and her brother and Art Tinen had stepped up to help yesterday amazed Vashti. Of course, they were being paid. But they had done it for Griffin as friends, too, not just for the pay. And Trudy had gone on to Boise with her for adventure, yes, but also to keep her company and ease her mind.

She hoped Griffin would seriously consider Trudy's suggestion of filling his coaches with ladies from the shooting club. Those outlaws who'd stopped her and Ned wouldn't have had a chance if Trudy, Libby, and Bitsy had been inside the stage. Those three women could have picked them all off. Ned, on the other hand, had let off several rounds and hit nothing.

Luke's face flashed across her mind again, unbidden. Would she see him again? Why would he come to Idaho? She knew he didn't need a reason. While she was with him, they'd drifted around from town to town, wherever he saw a chance to get some money. Luke wasn't above stealing, but he preferred gambling. So long as she stayed away from Boise and kept close to her lodgings when she was on the road, she ought to be fine. Provided Luke didn't decide to hop a stagecoach to Silver City. That was entirely possible if more of the mines opened up again. Where there was gold dust, the saloons multiplied, and that brought more gamblers.

She certainly didn't want to see Luke again. She'd look twice at only one man if he came around to call, and he wasn't Luke Hatley.

What was she thinking? She stood in the tub of water and reached for her towel, telling herself sternly, "It wasn't even him."

When Vashti went downstairs, refreshed and dressed in her old red taffeta gown, several guests were already eating in the dining room. Vashti scooted to the kitchen and donned an overall apron that hid the neckline she now found embarrassing.

"Sorry I'm so late coming down. That warm water was just too heavenly. I wanted to stay there all night."

Bitsy laughed as she picked up two platefuls of the evening special—meat loaf with mashed potatoes and gravy. "You'd have frozen if you stayed there much longer."

"Yes, it was quite cool when I finally got out." Vashti smiled. "What shall I do first?"

"Put on another pot of coffee, and then I'll let you help me serve." As she headed out the door, Bitsy called, "Augie, we might need more biscuits. Two more people just came in."

When Vashti entered the dining room a few minutes later, Hiram Dooley was holding the door for Libby Adams. She smiled at them and looked around for an empty table that would be out of the traffic, so they could talk quietly. The dining room was half full of patrons, a good turnout for Thursday supper.

Bitsy hastened to the couple and led them over to a secluded corner. Perfect. Vashti poured two glasses of water. She recalled that Libby liked a glass of water with her meal.

"Good evening, Mrs. Adams. Mr. Dooley." Vashti set the water glasses before them.

"Hello, Vashti." Libby smiled up at her. "Hiram was just telling me about your uneventful trip to Nampa."

"Blessedly boring." Vashti nodded toward the chalkboard that Augie had recently hung as a way to list the daily specials. "We've got meat loaf tonight or baked chicken. Oh, and fresh dandelion greens. Augie just told me Ruth Robinson picked a mess and brought them into town this morning. He bought all she had."

"By all means, I'll have those," Libby said. "I've been hankering for fresh greens."

"How about you, Mr. Dooley?"

He gave her his shy smile. "You can call me Hiram. I'll try some, with the meat loaf."

"Yes, meat loaf sounds good," Libby said.

"I brought your party in this afternoon." Vashti watched Libby's face.

"Yes, and I appreciate it. They said that a cute boy drove them and they didn't think he could be over sixteen." Libby laughed. "We're going ahead with the sale. The Hamiltons will take over the emporium a week from Monday. They'll stay at the boardinghouse until I've moved out of my apartment."

Libby's face was the picture of joy. Vashti felt a stab of envy. It must be wonderful to have the love of a good man. She might never find that. Even though she knew some decent men, they all knew her past—or thought they knew.

She went to the kitchen, where Augie was putting a pan into the oven.

"Big crowd tonight, my darlin' tells me."

"She's right," Vashti said. "I've got two meat loaves for Mr. Dooley and Miz Adams. And they both want the dandelion greens."

"They make a right sweet couple." Augie took a china plate from the stack and ladled a mound of mashed potatoes onto it. "Good thing I made plenty of gravy."

When she took their plates out on a tray, Hiram was holding Libby's hand on the tablecloth. As Vashti approached, he let go and picked up his water glass. So cute. Vashti could see why Libby had fallen for the quiet man. He had a romantic spirit, that one.

"Here you go, folks. I hope you enjoy your meal."

Libby glanced at Hiram then smiled up at her. "Vashti, I'm bursting to tell someone my news. Mr. Dooley and I just set the date for our wedding."

"Well now." Vashti stood there holding the tray and grinning. "I'm very happy for you. When is it?"

"Two weeks. From Saturday, that is." Libby laughed and reached out to Hiram. He grabbed her hand again, beaming but saying nothing.

"Oh my," Vashti said. "That sounds like an excuse for a new hat to me."

Libby's laugh burbled out, and other diners turned to look. She covered her mouth with one hand and continued to chuckle.

"May I tell Bitsy and Augie?"

"You certainly may. Goldie, too, if you like. It's no secret."

"Or anyway, it won't be for long," Hiram said with a wink.

When Vashti reported to the livery on Monday morning, Griffin greeted her with an anxious nod.

"You've got a shotgun messenger I pulled from the Mountain Home line, but I'm also letting Zach and Annie Harper and Opal Knoff go along, provided there are enough seats, as guests of the line. All heavily armed, and they've signed a paper saying they won't sue us if they're injured."

"Terrific. I'm a little surprised Annie's going."

Griffin shrugged. "She wanted to real bad, but Zach said he wouldn't let her go without him. Zach's a fair shot, and he's packing a hundred rounds for that shotgun of his."

"And Opal?"

"Ted says if she's not back serving drinks at the Nugget by sundown tomorrow, she's fired."

"Oh, that's accommodating of him." Vashti made a face as if she'd bitten into a crabapple. "At least he gives her a day off now and then. I'll make sure she's back on time."

Griffin slapped her shoulder lightly. "That's what I told Ted. And that he can't stop his employees from doing what they want on their own time. Of course, Art Tinen's different. Starr wanted to go, and he put his foot down. He said she's not going out and mixing it up with outlaws when they've got a baby in the house."

"Can't blame him there." Vashti imagined that when it came down to it, Starr couldn't leave the nursing infant overnight, anyway. "She's probably just jealous that Art went last time and feeling a little deprived."

"Cabin fever." Griffin nodded. "Well, you stay on guard, especially near those rocks and when you're coming to bridges. They hit the stage on the Catherine road by the bridge. I've had the station agent over there hire an extra man for Johnny Conway's run tomorrow."

"I'll keep it in mind. What are we carrying today?"

Griffin looked around and leaned toward her. "Got some ore samples and a bit of gold dust coming down from Silver, and a bank deposit for Walker's Feed. Libby Adams might want to send in the check those Hamiltons are giving her, too. I told her to bring it to the office, so I can stash it in the box when I load the mail."

Vashti gritted her teeth. Her first time carrying a significant amount of valuables. "We can handle it."

"Sure you can." Griffin held her gaze for a moment then sighed. "If I could, I'd go myself. But I've got too much to do here."

She almost wished he was going. But that was crazy. "Don't worry. We'll get through just fine."

"There's something new you'll notice when you climb up to the driver's box."

"What's that?"

"I bolted the treasure box to the floor of the driver's boot. That way, if you do get stopped and they tell you to throw down the box, you tell 'em you can't. They're doing this on other lines, and sometimes it's enough to stop the outlaws, or at least slow 'em down. And with the armed passengers and your messenger, that might be enough to tip the scales your way."

Vashti gulped. What if that only angered the robbers? "My plan is to not let them stop us in the first place."

"That's the best way, all right. You want to grease your axles while Justin and I get the team hitched up?" he asked.

"Yes, sir." Bill had taught her how to do this, assuring her that any driver worth his pay would grease his own wheel fittings and do it liberally, thus ensuring that he wouldn't have a "hot box" from the friction of the axle. Vashti didn't especially like that part of the job, but she accepted it as one aspect of caring for the equipment. When she'd finished all four wheels, she handed the dope pot to Justin and wiped her hands on a rag.

"Uncle Griffin's going to hire some more men if we get the mail contract," Justin said.

"More drivers and messengers?"

"Yes'm, and more help here at the livery, too. But he says I can keep on working for him. He's paying me now."

Vashti raised her eyebrows. "That's a fine thing. Is this your first paying job?"

"Except for stacking wood for some neighbors back home."

She nodded. "Your uncle's a fair-minded man, and I'm proof of that. Work hard, do a good job, and he'll treat you right. He appreciates people who do their job well and do it on time."

"Not like Marty."

"Well, no. Marty wasn't the best at either diligence or punctuality."

Justin frowned. "I guess. Anyhow, we heard he's gone to California."

Twenty minutes later, Vashti drove the coach to the office. Griffin loaded the mail and put a small sack and an envelope in the green treasure box and locked it. Vashti shivered. If she lost the Walkers' money, would the aging couple have enough to make do? And what would they do to her? She could envision Orissa Walker screeching at her and demanding that Griffin fire her, or even have her locked up.

"That envelope has to go directly to the bank," Griffin said. "Instructions are written on it. Make sure the driver who takes over at Nampa understands."

"Yes, sir."

Griffin drew a deep breath and held her gaze. His eyebrows pulled together the way they did when he wasn't pleased. "It doesn't seem right, sending a woman off like this. Georgie, if you want to change your mind..."

She scowled at him. "Change my mind? What would you do if Johnny or Bill came to you and said, 'Mr. Bane, I don't want to drive today.' Hmm?"

He gave her a tight smile and looked away. "I wouldn't blame them right now, I guess. Not with this gang plaguing our lines."

"Well, I'm in this for the long haul. And we'll get through just fine." She nodded. "I'll see you tomorrow."

She looked forward. Justin was holding the leaders' heads. They were well-behaved mules, and he hardly needed to do it, but it made the boy feel important. She smiled and nodded firmly, and he let go of their bridles and jumped up on the boardwalk.

Vashti cracked her whip three times before the mules settled into a road trot. Behind her, Opal, Annie, and Zach called good-bye to their friends who'd come to see them off. It seemed like a frolic as they breezed up the street. But once they'd passed the smithy and the Nugget, Vashti hunkered down and concentrated on driving and watching. Now and then, she shot a glance at the messenger, Cecil Watson. She half wished Griffin was beside her. Cecil had to be at least forty, but she didn't hold that against him. Bill Stout was older than that, and he was still one of the best drivers in Idaho. She just hoped Watson had good eyesight—and an even better aim.

★ CHAPTER 26 ★

Three hours after leaving Fergus, Vashti stood on the steps at the home station in Nampa, waving to the folks traveling on to Boise.

"Have a good time, and be sure you get into Hubbard's if there's time this evening."

"No fear," Opal called, waving her handkerchief. "Miz Harper and I both have shopping lists to fill."

Annie waved. "I've got a lot of things to buy for the wedding party dresses, not to mention gifts for the happy couple."

Vashti ran closer to the coach and spoke to her through the window. "I got them a china platter, so don't get that, will you?"

Annie smiled. "How lovely. We'll remember, won't we, Opal?"

"Couldn't forget."

The driver cracked his whip, and Vashti leaped back as the stage jerked forward. She would never start without warning like that, and she wouldn't jump the horses into a canter, either. At least the coach was full of passengers. Several of the men on board were packing pistols. They ought to be all right. She'd heard the Boise run had been a favorite route for holdups back in the heyday of the mines. Was it coming to that again?

Lord, keep them safe. She wished for a moment that she'd traveled on with them, but she knew she needed to rest. And she didn't really want to jounce along another two hours and sleep at the hotel. The station here in Nampa was more comfortable, to her way of thinking.

Mrs. Gayle kept a small loft chamber for her and other ladies who traveled through. The male drivers and messengers slept out in the bunkhouse with the hostlers.

She climbed the steep stairs to her room. A framed mirror hung on one wall and a crewelwork sampler on another. The bottom bunk was made up with linen sheets and a woolen quilt, with an extra blanket folded at the foot of the bed. Vashti set her canvas bag on the wooden crate below the mirror.

"Home away from home." She gazed into the mirror at her dusty face. A sixteen-year-old boy? She smiled at the thought and tried to picture herself next to Justin. How could anyone mistake her for a boy, even in this getup? She frowned and turned her head at different angles, trying to see herself the way the passengers saw her. Her appearance might fool the unsuspecting and nearsighted.

A layer of dust dulled her complexion. Her eyebrows were caked with it. No leisurely scented baths here. But it was a homelike, snug place, and she felt safe. She took off her hat and pushed the pins out of her hair, letting it cascade onto her shoulders. Mrs. Gayle had left her a white china pitcher of water and a chipped washbowl with green flowers traced on it. Vashti poured the bowl half full and found a washcloth on the rough shelf in the crate. She brushed her face with the dry cloth first, to get the worst of the dust off, then wet the fabric and carefully washed her cheeks, forehead, and chin. It took several rinsings of the cloth before the image in the mirror satisfied her. She took her hairbrush from her bag. The light from the small window at the end of the room wasn't enough to show up the auburn glints in her hair, but she kept brushing vigorously for several minutes. Finally she went down to supper.

She turned in early and slept deeply for several hours. The sun was peeking between the mountains when she jerked awake, gasping. For a moment, she wondered where she was, missing her familiar room at the Spur & Saddle. As she oriented herself, she sat up slowly and swung her feet over the edge of the bunk. Her dream had already faded, but one thing she remembered vividly—Luke's face, sneering as he shoved her toward Ike Bell to settle his gambling debt.

"No trouble?" Griffin asked anxiously as he carried the mail from the stage up the boardwalk toward the post office.

Zach Harper walked beside him, puffing at a cigar. "Not a bit. That little Georgie girl is quite a Jehu."

"Oh yeah?" Griffin didn't remember Vashti pushing the horses too hard when he was along.

"We had to wait at the ferry landing, and once we were over, she made up some time, I'll tell you. And not a sign of those bandits." Zach laughed. "I think Annie was almost disappointed. But didn't she and Opal have a time in Boise."

"Big doings?" Griffin asked as he mounted the Nashes' steps.

"Big spending is more like it." Zach opened the door for him.

Griffin entered the post office and plopped the sack on the counter. "Here you go, Mayor."

"Thank you very much, sir. Sorry I didn't get down to the stage stop to get it myself."

"No trouble."

Peter nodded. "I take it the stagecoach didn't have any trouble this time?"

"Not a lick."

"Good. Maybe that gang has moved on."

"I hope so." Griffin settled his hat by way of a farewell.

For two weeks the ladies of the shooting club and a few of their husbands rode the Nampa stage for free. Once it was known they could ride that far in comfort and pay only for the short leg from Nampa to Boise, it became a favorite outing for the club members. They always took their role seriously and avoided idle chatter during the ride through the desolate territory between towns, but once they got to the city, they kicked up their heels. Micah Landry and Zach Harper laid down the law after their wives had done two runs each. They needed their women to home, in the kitchen.

Even Bitsy went once, and after Libby had given over ownership of the Paragon Emporium to the Hamiltons, she rode to the city to shop for a trousseau and stayed over an extra day. Starr Tinen gave her husband no end of grief because he wouldn't let her go, though her mother-in-law, Jessie, went along one sunny May day with Florence Nash and Apphia Benton. Not to be outdone, a few men had come in and offered their services.

With no new robberies causing him headaches, Griffin began to wonder if he was a fool to let folks ride along for nothing and pay for their room and board in Nampa. Some of them just went for the novelty, he was sure, like Ollie Pooler. He wasn't known to be a good shot, so why should he think Griffin would allow him to go along as an extra guard? Things were getting out of hand. Everyone in town seemed to think that if they carried a gun, they could get free passage.

"Uncle Griff?"

"Yeah?"

"What's the matter?" Justin asked.

"Nothing. Why do you ask?"

"You're holding your face all pinched up while you do that."

Griffin had been hammering away for an hour, making a stack of horseshoes. He hadn't realized he'd been holding his mouth in an odd position, but now that he thought about it, his cheeks were sore.

He relaxed for a moment, letting his pritchel and rounding hammer hang loosely in his hands. "Truth is, I'm wondering if I'm going to go broke running this stage line."

"You should hear about the mail contract soon, right?" Justin brushed his hair back from his forehead.

The boy needed a haircut. Griffin wondered if he could do it himself. Annie Harper would do it if he asked, but then he'd feel as though he should pay her. That was why he usually hacked away at his own when it got so long it bothered him.

"Yes, we should. And you've been a big help. So have the Nash boys. But unless we get that contract, pretty soon I won't have any money left to pay you boys for keeping the livery clean and feeding the horses and all the other chores you've been doing."

Justin eyed him solemnly. "If you go broke, I'll still help you for nothing."

Griffin smiled. "Thanks. That means a lot. And I guess if we *don't* get the contract, I won't need so much help around here, right?"

Justin nodded slowly.

"Well, I'll still need you to help me train Champ."

That brought a smile from his nephew. "Have you thought about selling the smithy?"

"Some." Griffin put down his pritchel and used his tongs to pluck a hot bar of steel from the forge. As he began shaping it with his hammer, wrapping it around the horn of the anvil, Justin watched closely.

When the metal cooled so that it was no longer malleable, Griffin stuck it back in the coals. Justin hadn't moved a muscle.

"The outlaws haven't shown themselves since the holdup on the Catherine road."

"Maybe they got enough, and they've gone away," Justin said.

"Maybe." Griffin pumped the bellows.

"Uncle Griff?"

"Yeah?"

"I'm glad I'm working in the livery, not out there with the robbers."

Griffin inhaled deeply. "Me, too."

The Dooley-Adams wedding was the talk of the town. Every woman in town with money to spend ordered a hat from Rose Caplinger. Annie Harper skipped shooting club practice because she had so much sewing to do. Apphia Benton organized a bevy of women to clean the church thoroughly the week before the ceremony, and Isabel Fennel promised to take her schoolchildren out to gather armfuls of flowers the morning of the wedding.

On Monday and Tuesday, most of the women of the Ladies' Shooting Club met upstairs over the Paragon Emporium to help Libby pack up everything she was taking to the ranch. Griffin, Ethan, and Oscar and Josiah Runnels helped Hiram carry it all down to their waiting wagons and take it to the old Fennel ranch.

"I expect it will take us awhile to unpack and settle in," Libby murmured to Vashti and Goldie as they watched a procession of wagons drive off.

"I hope that ranch house is big," Goldie said.

"It's much bigger than my apartment." Libby frowned. "Of course, Isabel left most of the Fennels' furniture there when she moved to town. Hiram said he hardly had to take anything at all from his old house."

Vashti laughed. "The way folks in this town are playing musical houses, I wouldn't be surprised to see your furniture show up at the Chapmans', or Mrs. Benton's Scripture sampler hanging in Isabel's parlor."

Goldie elbowed her sharply, and Vashti clapped a hand over her mouth. She'd forgotten Apphia Benton was stitching a sampler for Libby and Hiram as a wedding gift. She'd shown it to some of the ladies at shooting practice the week before, after Libby had left.

Goldie had walked about with a dreamy expression ever since Libby had asked her and Florence, her other clerk, to be her brides-maids. Libby was even paying for fancy gowns for them and Trudy Chapman, who was to serve as her matron of honor. Goldie had sworn Vashti to secrecy and told her that the gowns were rose-colored silk, finer than anything Goldie had ever seen. Finer even than Bitsy's purple silk that came from Paris.

Rumor had it that Libby's wedding gown would dazzle the entire population of Fergus, but she and Annie were close-lipped about it. During the last few days before the wedding, Libby scurried about town—from the Chapmans' ranch, where she was staying her last few days as a single woman, to Annie's for dress fittings, to the Spur & Saddle to discuss the wedding cake with Augie, to the Bentons' to speak to the pastor about the vows. Hiram went about his odd jobs—building a chicken coop for the Bentons and fixing a rifle for Oscar—with a smile on his lips.

"What are you wearing to the wedding?" Goldie asked Vashti on Tuesday afternoon.

"I haven't had time to think about it." She'd just returned from the Nampa run and was preparing to bathe and help Bitsy serve the supper crowd.

"Well, come on! It's only four days away."

"Do you think my green wool would work?"

"No! That would be too hot. It's June, Vashti! You need something lighter." Goldie shook her head. "This is what comes of you wearing boys' clothes half the time. You've lost your sense of fashion."

Vashti shrugged. "I don't care so much about fashion. But you don't have to worry—I won't wear trousers to the wedding. I guess I can wear the same dress I wore to Bitsy and Augie's wedding last year."

"Don't do that. Everyone will remember that you were a bridesmaid. And you're not a bridesmaid for Miz Adams."

"So?"

"So you want to look nice, but not as nice as the bridesmaids."

Vashti laughed. "All right, so I have to look nice but not nicer than you."

"I didn't mean it that way."

"I know you didn't. Right now I'm more worried about whether Griffin's going to get the mail contract or not. He should have heard a couple of weeks ago."

"Well, you've got plenty of pay now. Why don't you come over to the Paragon tomorrow morning and look at the ready-mades? One of the last things Miz Adams did was order in some new summer dresses, and they're very attractive."

Vashti decided not to tell her that she'd told Griffin not to pay her last Friday. She did have quite a stash from her previous paydays, even though she'd paid Bitsy board every week and bought a few things. Griffin was finding it hard to meet his payrolls.

He'd put on an extra run each week to Silver City. Since the mining men had come through and dropped hints that a couple of the big mines up there might be reopened, traffic between Boise and Silver City had tripled. It was the one stage run that more than paid for itself with passenger fares these days.

Vashti looked on it with mixed feelings. If the mines got up to full production again, her job as a driver would be secure. But the output of the gold mines would also draw more bandits.

They wouldn't go after the wagons hauling ore down to the railroad head. It was too bulky and too hard to process. But bullion or gold dust from the stamp mills, now that was a different story.

The stagecoaches usually had passengers carrying pouches of gold dust and sometimes payrolls for the mines and other businesses. Robberies were so common that the territorial government wouldn't reimburse lost equipment unless someone was killed. Vashti wasn't sure she wanted to drive in those circumstances.

She set off on her Nampa trip Wednesday, still uncertain of her attire for the wedding. Rose Caplinger rode the stage as a passenger, going to Boise to purchase supplies for her millinery business, and Myra Harper and Ellie Nash were scheduled to go as extra messengers if seats were available.

As it turned out, Rose was the only paying customer that day. They reached Nampa in safety, and Rose got out to eat a hasty dinner before boarding again for the leg to Boise.

"Do you have a hat for the wedding?" she asked Vashti as they ate the stew and cornpone Mrs. Gayle provided.

"Oh no, I—"

"I can make you a fetching chapeau for three dollars and a half." Rose squinted at her then nodded. "That blue dress you wear to church sometimes—it's too short, but you could add some tatted lace edging, and I can dye feathers to match the fabric."

Vashti felt her face warm. A man sitting down the table on the other side stared at her, neglecting his bowl of stew. She realized he was listening to their conversation and trying to reconcile it with her appearance. Her cheeks burned hotter, and she lowered her voice.

"Rose, people aren't supposed to know I'm not a man. Could we talk about this when we're back in Fergus, please?"

"Oh. Of course. But you won't have time to get up a new outfit." Rose eyed her clothing and curled her lip. "How do you stand it?"

Vashti didn't deign to answer. "Have a pleasant ride to Boise, Mrs. Caplinger. I'll see you tomorrow on your return trip." She took her empty tin plate to the side table where Mrs. Gayle liked diners to leave their dirty dishes and went to her small room at the back of the house. Mrs. Gayle had made up a pallet on the floor so that Myra and Ellie could spend the night in her room. Myra had insisted that she be the one to sleep on the floor, and Vashti had given the bottom bunk over to Ellie. Both women came in a few minutes later.

"The stage just left, and Rose with it," Myra reported.

Vashti had taken down her hair and was brushing the dust out of it. "I hope she has a good time in Boise."

"Yes, and finds all sorts of notions to make hats from," Ellie said with a smile.

"Wish I could have gone to visit the capital." Myra sat down on her makeshift bed.

Vashti didn't ask why she hadn't gone on. She knew the nineteen-year-old had come along for the adventure and to earn a little pocket money. If she went on to Boise, she'd spend more than she earned for her ticket, lodging, and meals in town.

"Maybe someday, Myra." Ellie sat on her bunk and opened her small traveling bag. "We're trying to economize. Peter didn't want me to come at all. He thinks it's too dangerous. But his salary as postmaster isn't covering all the expenses we've had lately, what with the two boys growing like weeds and prices going up."

"We'll have fun here." Vashti nodded firmly. "There's a grocery store up the road and a new hotel."

Ellie raised her eyebrows. "Nampa's getting to be quite a town."

"Yes. They're thinking of digging a canal to irrigate the farmland here, and there's a doctor who's opened up a drugstore."

"That's something," Myra said. "The Paragon always carries basic health needs, but a drugstore! Wouldn't Doc Kincaid love to have one in Fergus?"

"I'll bet he would," Vashti said. "Several houses are being built, too. If we get overly bored, we can walk around and see how the construction is coming."

Myra crinkled up her face. "No, thanks. But I wouldn't mind seeing the drugstore."

Vashti almost mentioned that the drugstore sold ice cream and phosphates, but recalling the ladies' pinched budgets, she kept quiet. If they got to the store before it closed and the right moment presented itself, she'd offer to buy them both a dish of ice cream. She smiled at the thought. Having enough honestly earned money in her pocket to consider treating her friends gave her a new sense of what she could be. She could support herself without serving drinks or worse. In Fergus, she was accepted as respectable. She'd never be as refined as Libby or as wealthy as Isabel Fennel, but she called nearly every woman in town her friend and could sit anywhere she liked in church without getting snubbed.

"I could use a walk, too," Ellie said. "Is it far?"

"Not at all. Just let me change into my skirt." For the past two weeks, Vashti had carried the black skirt and a plain blouse with her when she drove. This was the third time since Trudy's trip that other ladies had ridden with her, but usually they wanted to go on to Boise. Vashti was glad for the chance to get to know Myra and Mrs. Nash better.

The only troubling aspect was that she found the more time she spent with wives and mothers—and young women from proper homes like Myra's—the more she longed for a home of her own. As grateful as she felt for what Bitsy and Augie had given her, she yearned for a true family. But that would mean a husband, and she wasn't sure she could ever trust a man enough to commit to him for the rest of her life.

She ran through a cold mist, uphill toward Fergus, but the lights of the Spur & Saddle kept sliding farther away. Behind her, footsteps pounded, and a man's labored breathing came closer and closer. She snatched a glance over her shoulder. Luke chased her through the chilly, wet darkness, carrying an impossibly huge umbrella. "Georgia! I love you, Georgia!"

"You're lying!" she screamed back. She slammed into someone. Ike Bell. He laughed and grabbed her by her arms. "Let me go," she cried, twisting and pulling against his grip. "If you lose another harness, you're fired," he said. She jerked her head back and stared up at him. Ike had turned into Griffin. Raindrops dripped off his beard and splashed on her face. "I love you, Georgie."

"Honey? Wake up. You're dreaming."

Someone shook her, and Vashti climbed slowly through the mist and confusion toward candlelight and Ellie's soft voice.

She hauled in a deep breath.

Susan Page Davis

"Are you all right?" Myra asked, climbing up with her feet on the bottom bunk so she could get closer to Vashti. "You groaned."

"I was trying to scream, I think."

"Oh, honey, I'm so sorry. It's only a dream." Ellie patted her hand.

"Yes. A nightmare." Vashti tried to calm her heart's hammering. "I'm sorry I woke you both up."

"It's all right," Ellie said. "I'm glad we were here."

Myra got down and blew out the candle. Vashti rolled over.

She lay staring into the darkness. How long until sunup? She didn't want to sink back into slumber. Luke might not be in her life anymore, but he'd ruined her haven of sleep. And what was that craziness with Griffin at the end? Insanity, that's what it was. She pulled the quilt up to her chin and prayed for peace.

★ CHAPTER 27 ★

The new church was jammed with the citizens of Fergus. Folks drove into town from outlying ranches. Hardened cowpokes and old sourdoughs rode down out of the hills to see the beautiful Mrs. Adams married. Most of them wondered how Hiram Dooley had snagged her.

As he waited for the hour to strike and the parson to start the doings, Griffin monitored his pocket watch. The stage was due in from Silver City at two. After the one o'clock ceremony, the nuptial celebration would move over to the Spur & Saddle. In case they weren't done at the church by then—though Griffin couldn't in his wildest imaginings see how a wedding could last more than an hour—he'd bribed Josiah Runnels to meet the stage for him.

He wouldn't have been in this situation, but it seemed Libby had to have three bridesmaids. That in itself wasn't a problem—Trudy Chapman, Florence Nash, and Goldie Keller were tickled to serve. But someone somewhere had made a harebrained rule that said there had to be a groomsman for every bridesmaid. And Hiram had called on him.

Sheriff Chapman was his number one choice, of course. Hiram and Ethan were best friends. Ethan looked fine, wearing the suit he'd bought for his own wedding last year. Now, that wedding had been simple. One bridesmaid—Libby—and one best man—Hiram. No fuss. Where was this "got to have three bridesmaids and three groomsmen" coming from? Libby must have seen it in *Godey's Lady's*

Book or some such Eastern convention.

Anyway, here he was. He didn't have a true suit, but Libby had allowed he could wear the black jacket he wore for funerals and a pair of black pants. He'd bought a new white shirt, and Hiram had brought him a tie just like his own and Ethan's and Augie's. Augie was the other groomsman. Griffin looked over at him and almost laughed aloud. Augie was completely bald. He stood about five feet, nine inches, and he had more muscle than anyone Griffin knew— with the possible exception of himself. But that was understandable. He pounded iron. Augie, on the other hand, pounded biscuit dough. How did he keep those muscles?

Griffin scanned the crowd, looking for Justin. Finally he spotted him near the back, squished in on a bench with the Nash boys. That might spell trouble. Peter and Ellie sat farther toward the front, so they could get a good look at Florence when she came down the aisle. Griffin guessed he'd be the one to walk out of the church with Florence. That didn't bother him any. He just hoped those boys would sit still during the wedding and not cause a disturbance. A memory of his cousin Amelia's wedding twenty years ago made him squirm. Was there any way Justin could have gotten his hands on fireworks?

Music started, and Goldie came up the aisle. She was a pretty little thing, all pink and gold in her fancy dress. Her blond hair cascaded down in back, below her white straw hat. She carried pink and white flowers and smiled all the way down the aisle. Behind her came Florence Nash. With her orange-red hair up on her head underneath her hat, she didn't clash too badly with her pink dress. It was just like Goldie's, but Florence looked ganglier and less graceful than Goldie.

Trudy Chapman had come a long way from the homely tomboy who test-fired guns for her brother. She looked good in the pink dress, too. Ethan stood watching her and grinning from ear to ear. You'd have thought he was at a horse auction and they'd led in a leggy, thoroughbred filly.

But none of the bridesmaids looked as nice as Vashti, sitting in the second row on the groom's side with Bitsy. She wore a shimmery blue dress Griffin thought he might have seen before. Maybe at church—or not. But it was far too proper to be one of her made-over barmaid dresses. She looked fine, and it was a chore to take his eyes off her.

The music changed, and all of a sudden the congregation stood, startling Griffin back to the moment. In the church doorway, Libby stood, resplendent in ivory silk, clinging to Charles Walker's arm. That was fitting. Charles had been a close friend of Libby's departed first husband.

Griffin had to admit Libby eclipsed all her bridesmaids. Not many women in Idaho would get married in a dress she could never wear anyplace else. The pale silk glimmered with tiny little beads and embroidery. Way too fancy for any other kind of outing. But he guessed Libby could afford it.

As Charles walked her down the aisle, trying hard to conceal his limp, Libby smiled at the folks on both sides, then focused on the front. Griffin turned his head and saw Hiram's face. Now there was a man in love. Griffin almost wished he knew what it felt like to be that happy.

Vashti couldn't help it. Tears gushed from her eyes as the parson pronounced Libby and Hiram man and wife. Hiram stooped to kiss his magnificent bride, and Libby raised her hands to his shoulders and kissed him back. It was the most romantic thing Vashti had ever seen. The gold band glinted on Libby's finger. Did she know Trudy had transported it from Boise tied to her corset lacings?

And Griffin! Who would have thought he could look so handsome? Augie had trimmed both his and Justin's hair in the kitchen last night. Griffin had trimmed his beard, too. He looked almost like a gentleman in his church clothes. Even Augie looked solemn and presentable.

She leaned over and poked Bitsy. "Your man looks mighty fine."

"Yes, and isn't Goldie gorgeous?"

Bitsy's eyes were full of tears, too. Vashti dabbed at her face with a new lawn handkerchief.

Pastor Benton beamed at them all. "I now present to you Mr. and Mrs. Hiram Dooley."

Everyone clapped and cheered as Hiram and Libby swooped down the aisle and out the door. Trudy took Ethan's arm and walked more sedately. Behind them came Griffin with Florence. Vashti felt the tiniest twinge of envy for the girl on Griffin's arm, but Griffin didn't seem to care much which lady he escorted. Last came Goldie, in step with Augie, grinning and swishing her rose satin skirts.

"Well, I guess we'd better scoot, or the guests will all be over to the Spur before we get there." Bitsy stood and picked up her mesh reticule. "Nice wedding."

"Yes. Very nice." Vashti followed her into the aisle.

"Hey, there."

She looked up into Johnny Conway's face. "What are you doing here?"

"No stage on my run today," Johnny said. "Griff asked me to come take over from Bill when the Silver City stage comes in. I'll take it on all the way to Boise."

"They should be coming in soon."

"I figure I've got just time for a piece of wedding cake. Say, Georgie. . ."

She frowned up at him. "What?"

"You look real good today."

"Thank you."

He nodded and pressed on through the crowd.

At the Spur & Saddle, Augie had already unlocked the door, and folks crowded into the dining room. The gifts were piled on a table to one side, where the town councilors used to have their weekly poker game. Libby had requested wedding cake, lemonade, coffee, and tea, which Bitsy had set up on the bar, with baskets of candy and dainty cookies on the tables. Since folks had eaten dinner an hour before the wedding, it was plenty.

Vashti ducked into the kitchen and found an apron. She took charge of the lemonade bowl, ladling cup after cup of the stuff. Libby and Hiram sat at the central table, receiving congratulations, and the bridesmaids and groomsmen sat with them. Myra Harper and her younger sister, Phyllis, had agreed to help serve, since Augie and Goldie were occupied. Bitsy gave them instructions and circled the room with a coffeepot in her hand.

After ten minutes or so, Augie got up and made the rounds of the tables, talking to the men. Vashti had figured he wouldn't sit still long. Griffin was the next to defect. He came over and held out his empty cup.

"More lemonade, Mr. Bane?" she asked.

"Don't mind if I do, thanks."

She could feel him watching her as she poured.

"You look fine in that dress."

She felt her cheeks heat up. "Thank you." She held out the cup but couldn't quite meet his gaze. He took the lemonade but didn't walk away. Finally she glanced up at him. "Can I get you something else?"

"I was wondering. . ."

His voice sounded odd, not at all like his usual confident self. She raised her chin and looked up into his eyes. Big, chocolate brown eyes. The haircut and clothes certainly suited him. And the expression deep in those eyes. . . Not the shameful one men used to rake her with in saloons. A wistful, yearning look. It touched her heart, and her knees shook. Griffin was one of the decent men in this town. Could he ever think of her as a decent woman?

"Yes?" It came out a whisper.

The door flew open. The wedding guests stopped in mid-chatter. Josiah Runnels looked wildly around the room and homed in on the big blacksmith.

"Griff! The stage just pulled in, and Bill's been shot."

★ CHAPTER 28 ★

The Spur & Saddle had never emptied so fast. Doc Kincaid and Augie were the first two out the door, but the whole town poured onto Main Street in fifteen seconds flat.

Vashti ran, trying to stick to Griffin's coattails, but his long legs carried him much faster than she could go. When she got to the coach, Doc was already inside. Griffin, Johnny, Augie, and Ethan stood in a tight group before the door, keeping folks back. Pete Gilbert, who'd been Bill's messenger, still sat on the box, the reins slack in his hands and his head bowed.

Vashti scooted around Ethan and climbed up beside Pete. She put her hand on his slumped shoulder. "What happened?"

"Road agents. Bill whipped up the mules and tried to run through them, but they shot him first thing. The mules were tearing by then, and I had to drop my gun and try to slow them down, or at least keep them from flinging the coach off one of those hairpin turns."

Vashti shuddered, recalling the steep drop-offs along the road to Silver City. "Where was it?"

"This side of Sinker Creek, maybe a mile out. Uphill. They always try to get you when you're going uphill."

She nodded. Some of those grades were worse than a pitched roof.

Ethan's head and shoulders appeared on the other side of the stage. "Pete. Want to tell me about it?"

Vashti grabbed a handful of skirts and prepared to climb down.

900

"I'll leave, Sheriff, and you can sit up here with him."

She dropped to the street. Doc Kincaid was backing out of the stagecoach. He turned and faced Griffin.

"I'm sorry, Bane. Does he have family to notify?"

Vashti caught her breath. Her stomach wrenched. She turned away and took a few steps to the off wheeler's head.

Bill couldn't be dead. Sweet old Bill who'd built her driving rig for her and taken her out to Hiram's ranch to practice. The white-haired driver who'd treated her like a daughter. Her first run, she'd ridden with him, and he'd helped keep the secret of her disguise at least for that first trip. She clung to the sweaty mule's harness and sobbed.

How long she stood there, she didn't know. She found her handkerchief, tucked in her sleeve—the same one she'd used an hour ago at the wedding. The voices around her faded as people moved away from the coach. Unable to stop crying, she clenched her hands around the tug strap and gritted her teeth. Dear old Bill.

A large hand rested on her shoulder.

"Come on, Georgie. Let go, so's Johnny can take the team around to the livery."

Griffin. She'd never heard his voice so gentle. Her throat was hot and achy. She stared at her hands, curled around the strap so tightly that her knuckles were white. She sobbed again.

"There now." His hand stroked her hair lightly and came down on her shoulder again. "Come on." His large, warm hands closed over her stiff fingers. He gently pried her hand from the harness. "Let Pete and Johnny take the team."

Her fingers came loose, and she backed away from the mule into Griffin's solid form. She turned and looked at the front of his shirt, clean white for the wedding. Her gaze traveled slowly up to the necktie that looked so foreign around Griffin's neck, to his neatly trimmed beard, his grim mouth, and at last his compassionate eyes.

She dove toward him, a new sob racking her body. He folded her in his arms and pulled her close against his wedding shirt.

"There now."

He eased her away from the mules and the stage. A whip cracked,

901

and Johnny Conway clucked to the mules. The wheels rolled as the mules started forward.

Griffin held her for a minute, stroking her back softly. Finally she pulled back and took a deep breath.

"Where did they take Bill?"

"Over to the boardinghouse. Mr. Thistle said they can lay him out in the parlor."

Vashti sniffed. "Not the livery?" Somehow it seemed odd that, with all the bodies they'd laid out at the livery, a stagecoach driver should be taken somewhere else.

"The sheriff's getting up a posse. The livery's going to be busy."

She pulled away from him and turned to survey the crowd. Now that Bill's body had been removed and the coach was gone, the people focused on Ethan Chapman. The sheriff stood on the boardwalk in front of the Wells Fargo office.

"If you need to change your clothes, be quick about it," he called. "I'll leave from the livery in about ten minutes. I'll take any man who's ready to ride up to Sinker Creek with me, but you have to supply your own weapons and horses."

A dozen men broke from the crowd and ran toward the livery or their homes. Vashti hauled in a deep breath and turned toward the Spur & Saddle. Before she took one step, Griffin's hand clamped on her shoulder.

"Where you going, Vashti?"

"To get changed. I'm going with Ethan."

"That's not a good idea."

"I think it's an excellent idea." She wrenched away from him and ran.

The Boise stage pulled out ten minutes late, with Johnny Conway and Pete Gilbert on the box. Pete still looked shaken, and Griffin almost replaced him. But whom could he ask? Not any of the women after this catastrophe, and not Hiram Dooley on his wedding day.

Griffin dashed about the stable, saddling every spare horse. Even though Ethan had specified that the posse supply its own horsepower, some men like Dr. Kincaid depended on him for transportation. Justin ran back and forth from the corral to the barn, fetching tack and bringing in the few available mounts.

"Uncle Griff?"

Griffin tossed his own saddle over the back of his gray gelding. "What?"

"Can I go this time?"

Griffin eyed him over Pepper's withers. Instead of showing boyish eagerness, Justin's face was troubled.

"I don't think so, son."

"I liked Bill."

"We all did. But I need you to stay here. Folks will come around wanting news, and the stock will need to be fed at sundown. You can get Ben and Silas Nash to help you. Oh, and Justin. . ."

"Yeah?" The boy—no, the young man—didn't argue, but his mouth drooped in disappointment.

"If I'm not back by eight o'clock, you go over to the Fennel House and ask Mrs. Thistle to put you up."

"I can stay by myself. I'm old enough."

Augie ran in through the front door of the livery, with his wife on his heels in her bloomer costume and Vashti wearing her dungarees and boy's shirt, vest, and hat.

"Griff, you got any extra mounts? I know folks are supposed to have—"

"Sure, Augie, but no women." Griffin looked sternly at Bitsy and Vashti.

"Please, Griff," Bitsy said. "We're good shots. We won't slow you down."

"Trudy's outside. She's riding with her husband," Vashti said.

Griffin snatched his hat off and slapped it against his thigh. "Next I'll have the bride and groom coming around, wanting to ride out on their wedding day."

"Nope." Augie shook his bald head. "The sheriff told Hiram absolutely no way would he let him go along."

Ethan's voice sounded at that moment, out front. "All right, men, let's move!"

Griffin shot a glance at Justin. "Give Augie the chestnut and Mrs. Moore the paint mare. There's two spare mules out back. You and Vashti can take them. Don't know if they'll keep up, but it's all I've got left. The team that just came in from Silver needs to rest."

He walked Pepper out of the barn and swung into the saddle. Ethan and a band of twenty or so men already cantered toward the Mountain Road. He urged Pepper to follow, half hoping Justin and Vashti wouldn't catch up. Justin wasn't even armed. Griffin had had a couple of shooting sessions with him, but his nephew was nowhere near being a marksman, even if he had a weapon.

He clamped his teeth together. What would Evelyn say if she knew he was teaching her boy to use a gun? Out here, it was a necessary skill for a man.

Hoofbeats drummed behind him on the packed road. He looked over his shoulder. Augie and Bitsy were coming already. No. A second glance made him say something he tried not to say when Justin was around. The second rider wasn't wearing the bright red suit. It was Vashti, riding the horse he'd said Bitsy could take, and she was pulling ahead of Augie's chestnut.

"Too bad we couldn't pick up their trail." Bitsy held her hands out to the campfire that evening.

"Bill deserves better than this," Vashti said.

"It could have been you."

Vashti didn't respond. She preferred not to discuss that angle.

Ethan came to the fire, carrying his tin cup.

"More coffee, Sheriff?" Bitsy asked.

"Much obliged." She rose and poured it for him.

"I still don't know how you folks managed to grab so much stuff so fast," Ethan said.

"That's why we were late. While Augie and I were getting out of our glad rags, Goldie was down in the kitchen packing supplies for us."

Ethan smiled. "Sounds like Trudy. I wasn't of a mind to let her

904

come, but she'd ridden in for the wedding and stashed her riding skirt at the Bentons'."

Parnell Oxley and Micah Landry sauntered over.

"What's the plan for morning, Sheriff?" Parnell asked.

"We'll look around a little more after daybreak, but most of these men have families and businesses they should be tending to."

Vashti's spirits plummeted even lower at Ethan's words. This was for Bill! They ought to be able to do better for him.

The other men drifted over, some still chewing their meager meal of jerky and a biscuit apiece.

"We found that mask," Josiah said.

"Yes. But that was before we got into the rocks. Awfully hard trying to track anything in these mountains." Ethan sipped his coffee.

The rough cloth mask was a gray hood with eyeholes cut into it. Josiah had found it among the brush near the creek bank. It matched what Pete Gilbert had said the robbers wore.

"Think they'll hit another stage while we're up here?" Micah asked.

Ethan shook his head. "So far they've gone two or three weeks between holdups. And they got quite a bit of money off the passengers today, as well as two thousand dollars from the treasure box. That'll keep them going for a while, I expect."

Justin and Griffin stood next to each other. Their dark eyes reflected the firelight—the giant of a man next to the slender boy. Justin had grown since he'd come last fall. In six months, he'd shot up several inches. Vashti had noticed how short his trousers were and mentioned to Griffin that the boy needed new clothes.

"Hate to head back with nothing to show for it," Griffin said.

Parnell nodded. "That's right. I say we keep after 'em."

Ethan shook his head. "I know how you feel. We all want to bring these men in. But they could be halfway to Salt Lake by now. We can't stay out here for days on end looking for them."

"Then what *can* we do?" Micah asked.

Ethan turned to Griffin. "Can't you ask for military escorts for the mail coaches?"

"I put in a request a few weeks ago, but I haven't heard anything yet. Maybe if we send a telegram and put your name on it, and Peter Nash's."

"Yeah," said Augie. "The sheriff and the postmaster ought to carry some influence."

"We can try it." Ethan dumped the dregs from his cup and set it on the rocks by the fire. "I could stay out here another day or two, but we don't have supplies, and most of you men need to get back to your regular work."

"I hate to give up," Griffin said. "After what they did to Bill. But you're right. I need to be where I can contact other people along the stage line and make sure all the routes are covered for Monday."

"We should go home and open up tomorrow," Augie said, looking at Bitsy.

Vashti reached for Bitsy's hand and clasped it. The Moores would lose money for every meal they didn't serve at the Spur & Saddle. She ought to go back with them first thing in the morning and help prepare the usual Sunday chicken dinner. Would Goldie get things ready tonight?

As much as she hated to give up the chase, she knew Ethan was right.

"You all right?" Bitsy asked her. "I know Bill was special to you."

"I'll be fine." She gritted her teeth thinking of how the brave white-haired man had died. "But I'll honor Bill's memory the best way I know how—and that's to never let my stage be held up again."

Bitsy eyed her thoughtfully. "You think you can make sure of that?"

She shrugged. "I'll do whatever I can."

"Bill probably did whatever he could, too."

Vashti didn't want to think about that. If an experienced driver like Bill was vulnerable, even with a good shotgun messenger, she would be even more so.

"It's a risky business," Trudy said.

Vashti looked over at her. She hadn't realized Trudy had come near enough to hear their conversation.

"I know, but we're sworn to protect the mail. And the passengers, of course. But the federal government gets involved when you're carrying mail."

"So why isn't the federal government out here combing these hills for that gang of road agents?" Bitsy asked.

"I don't know."

Vashti shivered and leaned closer to the fire. None of them had brought bedrolls or enough food for breakfast. Bitsy and Trudy had their husbands along to nestle up to until morning. Vashti would have to make do with her horse blanket, and nights got freezing cold this high in the mountains, even in early June.

"You've got to trust in God," Trudy said firmly. "Only He can keep you and the passengers safe. Oh, and let's not forget the U.S. Mail, too."

That hurt a little bit. Vashti was used to insults, but not from Trudy.

"I didn't mean that the mail is more important than the passengers. I just meant. . ." Tears filled Vashti's eyes, and she shook her head.

Trudy sat down beside her. "I'm sorry. I know you care about the passengers, too."

"I do." Vashti put her hands to her head. "It's just that Bill— why did it have to be him? Why does it have to be anyone? First Ned, now Bill. Those robbers are killers. We need to bring them to justice."

"Only if God wants us to," Trudy said. "But I'll tell you one thing: Until you get a military escort, the Ladies' Shooting Club will be riding your coaches, whether Griffin can afford to pay us or not. If he says no, we'll buy tickets and ride anyway. And if the stages are full, we'll ride on top, or go alongside on our own horses. We're not going to lose you, Vashti."

"Your husband—"

"Ethan knows I'm right. We have to do this. You'd do it if I were the one driving."

"Yes, I would. But I don't expect other women to risk their lives for me."

Trudy nodded, her face sober in the firelight.

Griffin and Justin walked around the fire ring and stopped near where they sat.

"Are you all right, Vashti?" Griffin asked.

"I'm fine."

He nodded. "I've been talking some more to Ethan. We'll head back in the morning. You ride with me and Justin."

Trudy stood and faced him. "Griffin, I'm going to call a meeting of the Ladies' Shooting Club about this. After shooting practice on Monday, in my kitchen at the ranch. If you're able to come address us, we'd appreciate it. And we'll set up a roster of members to ride with Vashti on every single one of her runs—like we've been doing, only more shooters. We've got to put a stop to this."

"We'll be there," Bitsy said.

"Not me. I'll be in Nampa." Vashti looked up at Griffin's glowering face.

"No, you won't. I don't want you to drive anymore."

Bitsy caught her breath.

Vashti jumped to her feet. "Why are you doing this?"

"Isn't it obvious?"

"Not to me."

Griffin glared down at her. "It's too dangerous. I'll put a man in your place, and if I can't find one at short notice, I'll drive your route myself."

"You can't."

"Can't I? Let's see, last time I looked, I was the division agent for this line. But I won't be known as the one who let women get killed driving his stages."

"I've earned the right to keep my route."

"Oh, you have? Been driving six weeks, and you're a veteran?"

They stood smoldering at each other for a long moment.

Bitsy laughed. "Come on, you two. Do I have to get my husband to bust your heads together? Settle down. You can talk about this in the morning."

"That's right," Trudy said, a little shakily. "Things will look better by daylight. Vashti, come sleep over here beside me. Ethan's going to sit up awhile with the men."

Vashti wasn't ready to give up the fight, but Griffin had already turned away and was walking off with his hand on Justin's shoulder.

Slowly she unclenched her fists and let out a long breath.

"Come on," Trudy said again.

"He can't do this."

"Well, yes, he can," Bitsy said. "I'm not so sure it's a bad thing, either. Honey, lots of people care about you. And unless I'm greatly mistaken, that man is one of them."

Impossible. If he cared, he'd know how he'd hurt her. If he cared, he'd show everyone he believed in her and let her keep driving.

★ **CHAPTER 29** ★

On Sunday morning after a long, difficult ride in the dawn, the posse trotted grimly into Fergus. Griffin and Justin led the procession, and the Chapmans brought up the rear.

Vashti and the Moores left their borrowed mounts at the livery and walked down the street to the Spur & Saddle. They'd have time to get cleaned up for church and, with Goldie's help, prepare the chickens for the dozens of patrons they expected for dinner. A lot of people who hadn't ridden with the posse would come, hoping for news.

Vashti hadn't slept well on the cold mountainside, and she was sure Augie and Bitsy hadn't either, but they all arrived at church on time. As Vashti followed Goldie into the pew, Hiram and Libby came in the door.

"What are you doing here this morning?" Oscar Runnels's loud voice carried throughout the sanctuary, and the newlyweds blushed scarlet.

"Good morning to you, too, Oscar." Hiram shook his hand and guided Libby into the nearest vacant pew.

Justin came in with the other boys from his Sunday school class. Griffin may not be the ideal parent, but he was doing something right with that boy.

Vashti swung around to face forward, but she heard his voice when he entered the church. Someone greeted him near the door, and Griffin's hearty "Good morning" rang off the rafters. She didn't turn around, but she could tell by the bustle and cheerful comments that accompanied him up the aisle that he was close by.

His large form moved between her and the window across the aisle. His dark shadow lingered on her, and all grew still around them. She looked up.

Griffin stood with his hat in his hands and his Bible tucked under his arm.

"Mr. Bane," she said.

"Morning. I'd like to speak to you after church."

"I'll be helping with the chicken dinner."

"Then I'll come eat some. Can I talk to you after that?"

She hesitated. He'd only hammer home his declaration that she was done driving. She wouldn't make that easy for him. "I'll likely be washing dishes until three o'clock."

"Then I'll help you."

That surprised her. She'd expected him to say he'd wait, or he'd come around later. She squinted up at him. The sunlight from the window made his hair glow around his head. He was clean shaven— the first time she'd ever seen him without a beard. She wished he wasn't standing with his back to the light that way, so she could see his face better.

Everyone in the neighboring pews waited to hear what she would say, making no pretense of disinterest.

"Fine," she said. "Augie might have an apron that will fit you."

Several people chuckled, and Griffin cracked a smile.

"All right. We'll talk then."

Griffin paid for his dinner and Justin's and turned to his nephew. "You go on home and change now. Go over and check the livery— make sure everything's quiet there. I'll be along after I wash a few dishes and settle Miss Vashti's hash."

"Can't I do dishes, too?"

Justin's brown eyes were only a couple of inches lower than his own now, Griffin realized with a start. The boy was filling out and would likely end up as big as Griffin. He grinned. "I doubt they've got two aprons in the jumbo size."

"Can I work with Champ?"

"Sure, but don't get on him until I'm there." They'd begun saddle training a couple of weeks ago, and both colt and boy seemed to enjoy it.

"All right," Justin said. "See you later."

Anyone who saw him from the back would think he was a grown man. Griffin shook his head and turned toward the kitchen door.

Bitsy came out carrying two slices of pie on small plates. Her bright red lips curved in a grin. "I hear you're helping out with the dishes today."

"That's the plan."

"Your boss is yonder." She jerked her head toward the kitchen and passed him.

"Very funny," Griffin muttered. He reached the doorway in three steps and stood there looking in. Augie bustled about between the stove and a worktable with platters and dishes spread over it. In one corner, Vashti scraped used plates, putting the leavings in a bucket. She wore her blue satin under a big white apron, and her hair was up in a bun. When it wasn't covered by her cowboy hat, her hair looked shimmery and feminine.

"Howdy, Griff." Augie lifted a chicken leg out of a big frying pan and laid it on a platter with other crisp pieces of meat.

Griffin nodded to him and strode over to Vashti.

"Well, hello. Where's Justin?"

"I sent him home. Where's my apron?"

She smiled then, just a little smile. "You don't have to do dishes."

"I don't mind."

"All right then." She took a couple of steps and opened a drawer full of folded linens. "Let's see. . ." She pulled one out and shook it to unfold it. "This one's pretty big."

It was the kind of apron that hung around the neck with a bib to cover the wearer's shirt.

"Maybe you should take your jacket off first. Hang it over there." She indicated a row of hooks near the back door.

Griffin sauntered over and shed his coat, then went back to her and reached for the apron. She held it up, holding the neck strap away from the apron. He hesitated a second then stooped a little. She popped it over his head and smoothed the strap behind his collar.

"Turn around."

He felt silly with her tying the apron strings behind his back. Silly and a little on edge. Her light touch against the back of his shirt made his skin tingle. He pulled in a quick breath.

"There you go. What did you want to talk about?"

She seemed softer than she had this morning, more ready to listen. He turned around. She had already lifted a stack of plates and plunged them into a pan of soapy water.

"About your work for the stage line."

"What about it?"

A clean towel lay on the counter beside the dry sink, and he picked it up.

"Rinse first," she said. "You have to get the soap off. There's a kettle of hot water over there."

He went to the stove and lifted the steaming teakettle.

"She putting you right to work?" Augie asked with a wink.

"Regular slave driver," Griffin said.

Vashti put the clean dishes into another pan, and he poured the boiling water over them. She was watching out of the corner of her eye, but she didn't say anything, so he guessed he'd done it right. He grabbed the towel and began drying the first plate.

He cleared his throat. "Listen, you've been doing a good job driving."

She was quiet for a moment, then squeaked out, "Thank you," as she placed another plate in his rinsing pan.

"I mean that. You're good with the horses, and you're getting better all the time with the reins. And the passengers love you. More than one has told me you gave them a mighty smooth ride."

Her hands stilled, and she sniffed. "Do you recall what Pastor Benton spoke on this morning?"

Griffin had to think for a minute. "You mean about how we shouldn't do rash things?"

"Rash—oh yes, he did mention that." She chuckled. "Paul had a

913

whole list of things we aren't supposed to do over in Timothy, didn't he? Funny how we each picked out different ones."

"Well, yeah, I suppose so. I'd been feeling kind of guilty—like I'd acted hastily and got mad over things I shouldn't be mad about." He eyed her cautiously. "So what one did you mean? Not loving money too much?"

"No, not that, either. It was 'boastful and proud' that hit me. Right smack in the face."

He frowned. "That doesn't sound like you."

"Doesn't it, though?" She put the last plate in his pan and reached for a pile of dirty forks. "I've been strutting around like I was the finest stagecoach driver who ever cracked a whip, when we both know I'm not." She looked up at him with earnest green eyes. "Griffin, if I were to drive every day for the rest of my life, I'd never be as good a driver as Bill Stout. Never."

"Bill was born to it." Her words made him uneasy. "That doesn't mean you can't be a fine driver one day."

"That's right. One day. Not now. I'm as green as the grass along the riverbank. I'd like to think I'm an old hand at driving, but I'm not."

"You learned a lot from Bill in a short time."

"Yes, I expect I did. But I still have a long way to go. And so. . ." She pressed her lips together for a moment, then looked up at him again. "So I'm telling you I'm sorry. I don't have a right to drive for you, like I was making out I had last night. It's a privilege, and you have the final say because you're in charge. That's fittin'."

Griffin turned around and leaned against the counter and studied the planks of the floor while he considered that. She had actually come to the place where she could stand back and let him decide what was best for the stage line. And for his drivers.

Bitsy strode in from the dining room with a tray of dirty dishes and set them down beside him.

"How's the dish crew doing?"

"Fine, ma'am."

She went over to the stove to speak to Augie.

Griffin looked over at Vashti. "I came to apologize for acting rashly and telling you that you couldn't drive anymore."

She washed another fork and plinked it into his pan. "You mean you would let me?"

"Do you still want to?"

"Yes. Very much."

He nodded, noting how pretty she looked with the steam feathering the little wisps of hair that had come loose from her bun. He could see that tiny brown mole on the back of her neck, too. He inhaled sharply and picked up the teakettle. "Let me make a suggestion. The robbers have never hit the run between here and Reynolds Creek. What if you drive that far and back every day?"

"And not go on to Nampa? What's the sense in that? You'll need another driver if I just do a short run."

He poured hot water over the soapy forks and put the kettle down. "I don't want to lose you, Vashti. I don't want to lose Georgie the driver, either, but it's not just because you're a driver. Mostly. . ." He cleared his throat. "I don't think I could live with myself if you got hit like Bill did."

She was staring at him, her pink lips parted. "Thank you. But I don't think giving me a shorter route will solve your problems."

"It won't. But it might keep me from adding to the list of ones that need solving. I could switch you with Johnny—"

"Johnny's run was hit once last month."

Griffin nodded reluctantly. "But there's not so much treasure on that route as there is over here. And with all the traffic up to Silver and the Poorman opening up again—"

"It's definite, then? They're reopening the mine?"

"That's what they tell me. And if it happens, there'll be more money going back and forth."

Vashti turned back to her dishpan and washed a few more forks. "If you put me on another route, I won't be at home between my runs, and the shooting club members won't be able to give us extra protection."

"I've been thinking about that, and I wonder if it's wise to let those women—"

"Now don't start that. You know they want to help, and they're better shots than any men you could hire. The price is right, too."

Griffin dried a fistful of forks while he thought about it. "Part of me doesn't want you driving at all, though I don't know who else I'd get to do it. And part of me wants you to go on doing it because I know it means so much to you. You're a good driver. It's true you don't have a lot of experience, but you've got a good touch."

He didn't feel he'd done the best job of explaining his reasons, but she seemed satisfied. If he told the complete truth, he'd be saying wild things about the way her eyes shone when she took the reins, and how warm it made him feel inside just knowing he'd made her happy.

"I want to keep driving," she said at last.

He nodded. "All right. We'll work something out."

"What about tomorrow?"

He sighed. "You drive to Nampa. I'll put Cecil Watson on with you until Ned's healed up. Cecil's got sharp eyes, though I'm not sure he's as good a shot as you or some of the other ladies."

"I'll put the word out that we'll take extra riders, if it's all the same to you."

"So long as there are empty seats. I won't turn away any paying customers to make room for shooters."

"Done." She wiped her hands on a towel. "I think we're caught up on dishes for the moment. Thank you for helping. Oh, and I like the new look." She nodded toward his whiskerless chin and smiled.

"Vashti. . ."

She arched her eyebrows and gazed up at him, but he couldn't think of anything else he wanted to say out loud.

★ CHAPTER 30 ★

A week later, Vashti arrived at the livery early as usual, to grease her axles and check over the harness and the horses' hooves.

"You've done a great job of grooming the team," she told Justin and the Nash boys.

"Thank you," Justin said, and the Nash brothers smiled at her. Ben was about Justin's age, and Silas was thirteen. They both seemed eager to please Griffin and earn a little pocket money. Since school was out for the summer, Griffin had decided to let Ben and Silas keep working for him at the livery with Justin until the fall term began. In the meantime, he'd scout around for a man to take over then. Vashti had never told him about the gambling incident, and so far as she knew, Justin and Ben had stayed out of trouble.

Griffin came out of one of the stalls and glanced her way. "Vashti, how's it going with Cecil?" He came over to stand directly behind her.

"Not bad." This would be her third run with Watson. Their first time out, he'd made one remark that was a bit on the crude side, and Vashti had let him know at once that she wouldn't tolerate it. It hadn't hurt that four women of the Ladies' Shooting Club were riding the stage that day. Since then, he hadn't gotten out of line, but she had the impression he resented being paired with her. On nights they were in Nampa, he disappeared shortly after supper. He always showed up on time in the morning, so she didn't ask questions.

"You've got a water run today."

She nodded. A stagecoach run with no treasure in the Wells

Fargo box suited her just fine. Of course, the passengers usually had valuables on them, and the coach would carry mail, which might also contain some money or bank drafts. But she always felt easier when they weren't carrying a payroll or precious metals.

"You didn't see anyone in those rocks last week," Griffin said.

"Nary a soul." Griffin had continued to shave, and she found it hard not to stare at him. He'd turned out rather handsomer than she'd imagined, and she was still getting used to the change.

She fixed her gaze on the front of his shirt. It struck her that she'd never seen him wear that one before—a black and white plaid that looked crisp and maybe even new. Why had Griffin taken up shaving and buying new clothes? Was it because of the mine executives who'd been coming through his office lately? Or maybe he expected an inspector for the postal service. He was now one of the handsomest men in Fergus, no doubt about it.

"I heard from the territorial governor."

That startled her into meeting his gaze. "Really?"

He nodded. "Telegram. He says we'll have a military escort in two weeks. They're giving me eight troopers."

"Eight? Fantastic."

Griffin shrugged. "That's for all my line."

"Oh."

"I figure the runs to Silver City and Boise are the most vulnerable, but I want to put two men on your run and two on the Catherine run." He frowned, and his eyebrows pushed together. That made Vashti smile. He may be well groomed, but his bushy brows still formed a hedge over his dark eyes. "I wish they'd give me more."

"It may be enough to keep the robbers away."

When she drove up to the Wells Fargo office, four women decked out for travel waited eagerly on the boardwalk. Cecil stood guard while Griffin loaded the mail. He admitted three paying passengers to the stage, then allowed the four ladies to fill the coach. Vashti hummed as he gave his signal to start. Probably Ellie and Florence Nash, Jessie Tinen, and Isabel Fennel would all go on to Boise for the night, but that was all right. Just knowing they'd be on her coach today and again tomorrow gladdened Vashti's heart.

When they approached the rocky section of the road she thought of as "the gauntlet," Cecil sat tall and watched both sides of the road like an owl, swiveling his head and staring—always staring at the boulders. Vashti kept the horses moving down the slope at a quick, controlled trot.

When they were safely through it, Cecil sat back and relaxed. "They never stop you going downhill, but it doesn't hurt to be aware."

"The last holdup happened at a bridge," Vashti said.

He nodded. "Anywhere you have to slow down and there's no houses in sight."

"Well, we should be all right at least as far as the ferry now."

They rode in silence for a ways.

"Any of those women staying over with you at Nampa?" he asked.

Vashti eyed him askance. Cecil hadn't engaged in much conversation with her since she'd put him in his place that one time.

"I don't think so. Why?"

He shrugged. "They've got a minstrel show at the school building. Thought you might want to go over and see it."

"Maybe. If any of them stay in Nampa." It might be fun, especially if Florence and her mother opted to stay.

"I meant with me."

She locked her neck muscles to keep from turning and gawking at him. The man was older than Griffin—way older. And he certainly wasn't the type she'd want to step out with.

"Oh. You mean—you and me?"

"Is that so far-fetched?"

She stared at the leaders' twitching ears, trying to form a reply that would be clear but not rude. "Thank you, but I don't think so."

"You could wear them clothes, and no one would know you was my lady friend."

The idea of being Cecil Watson's lady friend made her head swim.

"We could get a drink after," he said.

"No, thank you." She should have known there was to be an "after" to this proposed outing.

"I heard your old employer stopped serving. Too bad. The Spur & Saddle was a top-notch watering hole."

"Well, now it's a top-notch restaurant. And I don't drink, no matter where it's served."

"You're joshing me."

"Do I look like I'm teasing?" She gave him her best glare.

"Huh."

It rankled her that he assumed because she used to work in a saloon that she would go out drinking with a man she barely knew—namely himself.

"Don't you like to have a little fun now and then?" he asked, scanning the countryside.

"I'm not sure what you consider fun."

"You know. Just—" He whipped his shotgun to his shoulder.

Vashti's heart raced and she stared in the direction he was aiming, but the ground sloped down on Cecil's side of the road.

"What is it?"

He relaxed and lowered the gun. "A couple of pronghorns grazing on the hillside yonder. When I first saw movement, I wasn't sure what it was. Reflex."

"It's a good one to have in this job."

The horses had slowed to a jog. She unfurled her whip and cracked it in the air. "Move along, you." She looked over at Cecil as she stowed the whip again. "I get all the excitement I can use driving this route."

"So that's a no?"

"That's a no."

The four female passengers went on to Boise, as Vashti had anticipated. She ate her supper early, with Cecil sitting across the table from her. He wolfed down his pork roast, potatoes, and gravy, ignoring the mess of fresh greens Mrs. Gayle served with them. After that, he put back two pieces of pie and half a pot of coffee.

When he was done, he shoved his chair back. "You sure you don't want to see the show with me, George?"

"I'm sure. You go ahead, Cecil."

He slapped his hat on and shuffled out the door.

Vashti finished her pie and carried her dirty dishes and Cecil's to the kitchen.

"Bless you, child," said Mrs. Gayle. "I'll have seven sitting down in a few minutes."

"So many?"

"Three men who came this afternoon and are staying over to take your stage in the morning, along with Mr. Gayle and the tenders. And myself, of course."

"Allow me to set the table for you," Vashti said.

"I won't refuse." As Mrs. Gayle counted out the forks for her, she kept talking. "I wrote my sister's girl and asked her to come help me out here, but she said she expects she'll get married before fall. I really do need some help."

"If I hear of any likely ladies needing work, I'll tell them."

"Thank you. Decent girls only." Mrs. Gayle put the silverware in her hand, and Vashti went to the dining room and laid places for seven. Was Mrs. Gayle saying that a woman with Vashti's background wouldn't be suitable for the job? She doubted that. The hostess was kindhearted and always treated her with respect. More likely she was only saying she didn't want to take on an employee who would cause problems with the men about the place.

When she'd finished, Vashti went to her little chamber with the bunk beds. She wished one of the women had stayed. She wouldn't have thought it, but she longed for female companionship. Back in Fergus, she had Bitsy and Goldie to talk to, and sometimes Mrs. Benton. She wondered what the minstrel show was like. It might be fun to see it. If she went by herself, no one would bother her—they'd think she was a young man.

At once she knew that was a bad idea. Cecil might spot her. Besides, enough people in Nampa knew her secret by now that she couldn't count on going out alone in the evening without fear of being bothered. When the dining room quieted below and she knew the crew and guests had been fed, she went down and helped Mrs. Gayle wash the supper dishes.

"You're such a lovely young lady," the hostess said. "Why haven't you married, child?"

Vashti hesitated. Surely this woman knew her background. "I don't expect the Lord has that in mind for me," she said at last.

"No reason why not."

Vashti turned the topic, and when they finished, she borrowed an old magazine from Mrs. Gayle and retired to her room. Why hadn't she married? The question came back to her as she sat staring at an advertisement for shoes. If only that option was open to her. If she had the chance, there was only one man she'd consider now—one she had come to trust—and she doubted he'd ever look at her with marriage in mind. Though he had looked at her a few times with a sober, wistful air.

She turned the page of the magazine and began to read an article on cooking, something she loathed. Anything to keep from thinking of Griffin.

The next morning, she rose and dressed, knowing she had a couple of hours until the Boise stage arrived for her to take over. She went to the kitchen and found Mrs. Gayle brewing the morning coffee.

"That shotgun rider of yours never came in last night," Mrs. Gayle said.

Vashti stopped in her tracks. "Are you sure?"

"Yes. My husband's gone out to look for him."

Vashti's throat went dry. "What'll happen if he doesn't find him?"

"He'll telegraph Mr. Bane. I suppose he could send one of our tenders along as a guard."

Vashti took an apron from a peg near the back door. "My friends who went to Boise yesterday should be back this morning. They can serve as my shotgun messengers."

"Those women?"

"Yes. They all belong to the Ladies' Shooting Club of Fergus."

"I heard about that club." Mrs. Gayle shook her head. "Well, chances are my husband will find Watson, but whether he'll be sober or nay, who can tell?"

When the stage rounded the corner and rolled down the street toward him, Griffin let out a great sigh. Vashti was on time, coming in from Nampa. On the box beside her sat Florence Nash, her red hair flying. Vashti kept the mules at a spanking trot to the very last second. They pulled in and stopped on a dime, with the door of the coach directly in front of him. Ben Nash ran to take the near leader's bridle.

"You help with the bags," Griffin said to his nephew. He opened the door and mustered a smile he didn't feel.

"Welcome to Fergus, folks."

Jessie Tinen, Ellie Nash, and Isabel Fennel exited first.

"Ladies, thank you so much. If you can stick around for a few minutes, I'd love to have a word with you all."

They nodded and smiled and allowed they could do that. Griffin turned to the other passengers.

"Thank you for riding with us, gentlemen. I trust you had a good trip up from Nampa."

"Couldn't have asked for a smoother ride or more congenial company," said the first man out. A dapper man with graying hair peeking from beneath his derby, he walked over to Isabel. "Miss Fennel, may I offer you lunch? I'd love to talk with you further about your fine town and the real estate you're considering selling." He carried a black case, and Griffin pegged him for a drummer.

Isabel's face went pink, and she fluttered the fan she held. "Why thank you, Mr. Madden. My boardinghouse, just across the way, offers a fine luncheon."

"Excellent. Let me fetch my suitcase."

By this time, three other men had climbed out of the coach. Justin had scrambled to the roof and was tossing luggage down to Silas. The boys were doing a first-class job, Griffin noted.

When the passengers had cleared, he took out the mail sacks. Peter had arrived by then and hugged his returning wife and daughter.

"Did you have a good time?" he asked.

"Yes, we did." Ellie's eyes glowed with satisfaction. "We got in a little shopping, and we ate in a restaurant fancier than the Spur & Saddle, if you can believe that."

"Wait until you see what I brought you, Papa." Florence bounced on her toes.

"I shall have to," Peter said. "I need to take care of the mail first, but I'll do it with great anticipation."

"Your boys can help you take the sacks to your house," Griffin said. He looked up at Vashti. "Anything in the box?"

"Just Mrs. Tinen's handbag."

"Oh dear, I nearly forgot. I asked Vashti to put it in there so I wouldn't have to keep track of it." Jessie stepped over and accepted her leather purse from Vashti's outstretched hand.

"Well, ladies, we're very grateful that you were along on this run. As I'm sure Miss Edwards told you, our shotgun messenger disappeared on us in Nampa."

"Shocking," said Isabel. The drummer waited near her, listening avidly.

"Yes. Well, I'm happy to say that in a couple more weeks we should have a military escort for the mail coaches. Meanwhile, we appreciate your services more than I can tell you. And as a token of my gratitude, even though I said I couldn't pay you, I'd like to give you each a silver dollar, which I'm docking from Cecil Watson's wages—if he ever shows up to collect them."

"You don't need to do that, Mr. Bane," Florence said. "We had a grand time."

"Yes, we did," Jessie said.

"I'm glad that you enjoyed yourselves. Because we had no regular messenger aboard, and because you were willing to step in and fill the role of protectors for our passengers if needed, I want to do this." Griffin reached into his pocket and distributed the four silver dollars he'd put there for the purpose.

The ladies accepted gracefully and said good-bye. The Nash family headed up the street toward their house, carrying the mail sacks and the ladies' luggage. Isabel walked across to the Fennel House with the drummer, and Jessie waved to her husband, Arthur Tinen Sr., who was just rumbling into town in his buckboard.

Griffin walked around the coach and climbed up beside Vashti. Justin had taken over the tender's place from Ben.

"Hold them long enough for Justin to jump in," Griffin said.

"Yes, sir." Vashti nodded to the young man, and he released the mule's bridle.

"Climb aboard and ride over to the livery with us," Griffin yelled.

The mules fidgeted while Justin ran to the side of the coach, scrambled in, and closed the door. Vashti eased up on the reins and clucked to the team.

When she stopped the coach a minute later in front of the livery, Griffin said, "Let the boys unhitch the team. I need to talk to you."

"All right." She eyed him uneasily.

"I just want to know what happened with Cecil."

"I don't know."

"Uncle Griff?" Justin was out of the coach and looking up at him. "You want me to take the team in?"

Griffin had forgotten the Nash boys went home with their parents. "Start unhitching. I'll be right there." He looked back into Vashti's green eyes. "Everything go all right on the way to Nampa?"

"Yes, sir. And Cecil and I ate our supper first thing when we got there."

"Then what?"

"I'm not sure. Cecil went out." She frowned. "He did say something earlier about going to see a minstrel show in town."

"Did you tell Mr. Gayle that?"

"Yes, sir. When he came back this morning and said he hadn't found Cecil at any of the saloons or. . .well, other places he'd checked, that's when I remembered. I told him, and Mr. Gayle went to see the people in charge of the show."

"But he didn't pick up Cecil's trail."

"No, sir." She gritted her teeth.

"What aren't you telling me, Vashti?" He tried to keep his voice gentle, so he wouldn't spook her, and quiet enough that Justin wouldn't hear.

"Nothing, really. Just. . .he wanted me to go to the show with him. He asked me on the way if the ladies were staying in Nampa with me. Said we might want to see the show. I thought he meant all of us at first, but it turned out he meant just me and him. He wanted to make sure the others wouldn't be there, I guess."

"That snake."

"Why do you say that? He wasn't too obnoxious about it."

"But I told him to leave you alone." How much should he tell her? He'd given Cecil the same ultimatum he'd given Marty last fall: Keep away from Vashti or be fired. Had he walked off the job to avoid being fired?

She scrunched her lips together—shapely lips no boy would ever own up to—and looked down at the whip in her hands. "I can—"

"I know. You can take care of yourself."

She glanced up. "Actually, I was going to say, I can appreciate your doing that. As an employee."

He nodded slowly. "Let me know if you think of anything else, all right?"

"Yes, sir."

"Good. Let's get these nags unhitched."

He clambered down, and Vashti unwound the reins from the brake handle.

When Vashti walked to the livery in her driving outfit on Thursday, she looked about the shadowy barn. Justin and Griffin were bringing in the coach horses. Dr. Kincaid was saddling a dun gelding in one of the stalls, and the Nash boys were filling a wheelbarrow with manure.

Vashti walked over to meet Griffin. "Who's my messenger today?"

He hitched the near leader's halter to a tie rope. "You're looking at him."

"You?"

"Me."

"Bitsy plans to ride inside," she said.

"Good. The Dooleys are riding along, too."

"Hiram and Libby are coming?"

"That's right," he said. "They're taking a little trip."

Vashti bit her lip.

"What?" Griffin asked. "You don't like it?"

"It's so soon after their wedding."

"That's the idea. It's called a honeymoon."

She glared at him.

"Well, we're not getting stopped," he said. "Right?"

"Right."

"And the lovebirds will be well armed; you can count on that."

"No doubt. So...no word on Cecil?"

"Nope. Maybe Jeremiah Gayle will have some news when we get to Nampa."

Vashti went to get the pot of axle grease. When the team was harnessed and she'd inspected the fittings on the coach and horses, she climbed to the box.

Griffin sprang up beside her. "The boys can ride up the street inside."

"All right." Vashti waited until Justin, Ben, and Silas were inside the stage, then set out for the Wells Fargo office. "Where will Justin stay tonight?" she asked. "At the Fennel House?"

"No, the Nashes invited him to spend the night. Ellie sent a note over with Ben saying it was all right."

"It's nice that Justin's made some good friends."

"Yes. I've had a few talks with Peter and Ellie about raising boys. They know heaps more about it than I do."

"I'm proud of you. You've made great progress with Justin." She smiled at him. "Are you starting to feel like a father?"

Griffin's lips twitched. "Maybe more like an uncle should. I admit I wasn't keen on the setup when he first arrived."

"It's obvious things are going better. You've both come a long way."

He nodded soberly. "I think we turned a corner back around Christmastime."

"I'm glad."

She pulled up at the office, and he said offhandedly, "I'll load the treasure box."

"We're carrying money today?"

"A deposit for Ted Hire and another for the Paragon."

He climbed down, and Vashti noted that the sheriff stood near the office door. Griffin must have told him they'd be carrying treasure. The Dooleys and Bitsy waited to one side with a couple of other passengers. Justin hopped out of the stage and ran to the horses' heads. Ben and Silas approached the passengers.

"Load your luggage, ma'am?" Ben asked Bitsy.

"Thank you, but I just have this little bag, and I thought I'd keep it with me."

"You may load ours, Ben," Libby said, and he took a tapestry satchel Hiram held out to him.

Vashti wrapped the ends of the reins around the brake handle and climbed down. She walked over to her friends. "I'm glad you folks are coming along."

"Thank you, Vashti," Libby said, all smiles.

Bitsy elbowed Libby. "That's Georgie," she whispered, a bit too loudly for a secret.

Libby covered her mouth with one dainty, gloved hand, and Hiram's lips twitched.

One of the male passengers, a cowboy from the Tinens' ranch, peered at her through half-closed eyes. Vashti looked away, but he took a step closer and stared at her openly.

"You can't be that gal from the Spur & Saddle."

His comment flustered Vashti. "You're probably right," she managed.

He pulled his head back and frowned. "You ain't the one that plays the pianner."

"Right again."

Hiram and Libby laughed.

"That there is George," Bitsy said sternly. "He's one of Mr. Bane's best drivers."

"Are you folks traveling on to Boise?" Vashti asked Libby.

"Yes, we decided to spend a few days in town."

Griffin came out of the office carrying a sack, and Ethan straightened and scanned the waiting passengers and the street beyond. Peter walked toward them carrying a mail bag.

"Excuse me, folks." Griffin nudged the cowboy aside and climbed partway up to the box.

"Maybe we'd ought to pray together." Bitsy looked around at them timidly, as though expecting her suggestion to be rejected.

"Good idea." Vashti looked toward Libby and Hiram.

"I could lead us if you wish," Libby said. "My husband can join the sheriff in keeping watch."

"Thank you," Vashti said.

Hiram nodded and took a step away, cradling his Sharps rifle in his arms and gazing out over the quiet town.

Vashti bowed her head, determined not to think about the other waiting passengers and their opinions.

"Our heavenly Father," Libby said softly, "we thank Thee for this opportunity to help our friends and to travel. We ask Thy protection as we go. Bring us safely here again. In the name of Jesus we pray. Amen."

"Amen," said Vashti and Bitsy.

Vashti opened her eyes and turned around. Griffin was locking the treasure box in the driver's boot. Since he had bolted the chests to his coaches, he couldn't lift them down to load and unload them. It made the transfer of treasure a little awkward, but that was a minor inconvenience.

When he'd finished, Griffin stepped down to the boardwalk and glanced at the boys. All the luggage was loaded. He took the mail sack from Peter and placed it in the coach, then walked over to Vashti and the volunteers.

"Folks, we thank you for offering your services. Just remember, lives are the most precious thing we're carrying, then the U.S. Mail. The front box is important, but it's nothing to die for."

They nodded.

"I suggest you keep your weapons loaded and close at hand, but ride with them pointing in a safe direction. I'll be on the box, watching the road all the time, but it wouldn't hurt to have you folks paying attention, too."

"You want me to ride on the roof?" Hiram asked.

Griffin smiled. "I think you should stick with your bride. I don't anticipate trouble today, but lately things haven't been exactly predictable."

They all nodded soberly. Griffin turned and walked to the coach and opened the door. "All aboard." The men stood back to allow the ladies to enter first.

Susan Page Davis

Vashti hurried to the front of the coach and climbed up. A moment later, Griffin loomed beside her and settled into his seat, holding a new shotgun. The driving box seemed much smaller with him sitting there.

Though his presence set her on edge, the feeling was not entirely unpleasant. The more she saw of him, the more she liked him. Lately, she had begun to think that she might be persuaded to love him.

The very thought sent a flood of heat to her face.

"Anytime, Georgie," he said softly.

She gathered the reins and picked up her whip.

★ CHAPTER 31 ★

A mile out of Fergus, the stagecoach passed the Dooleys' ranch, then the Chapmans'. Griffin wished Hiram sat on the box with him to talk cattle and horses. On the other hand, he didn't mind being near Vashti. She concentrated on her driving and stayed aware of what each horse did. He watched the road ahead, but there wasn't much chance of a holdup on this stretch.

They wound down out of the hills, with the horses trotting steadily.

"How's Justin doing with the bookkeeping?" Vashti asked.

"Good. He made out my monthly report for Wells Fargo at the end of May. Did a fine job."

"I'm glad to hear it. His attitude has changed since he came."

"I think the colt helps."

"You told me Justin seemed interested in him last fall." She flicked the reins to keep the horses from lagging on a slight upgrade.

"Yes, he up and named it first thing. Champ." Griffin smiled. "He took to that colt right away. I let him take care of it, and he does a fine job. Of course, I told him that if he got into trouble or tried to jump ahead of the training program, I'd take the colt away."

"And how's Champ doing?"

Griffin smiled. "He's terrific. We've started saddle training, and Justin loves it. He's still green, but he's learning as fast as the colt is."

She grinned at him. "I'd like to see Justin work with him sometime."

"All right. I'll tell him."

When they stopped at the Democrat Station, the passengers got out to use the necessary while the tenders switched teams. Griffin stayed out near the coach while the tenders unhitched the team and brought out the new horses—four well-muscled bays that matched except for their leg markings. In just twenty minutes the coach was ready, with one new passenger added.

"Hello, Rice," Griffin greeted the man as he boarded the stage. "Going to town?"

"Yeah, just a quick jaunt in and back."

Griffin shut the people in. There were six inside now, not crowded, though they did have the mail sack to contend with. He mounted the box, and Vashti took them out with a stylish flurry of whip cracking.

After they'd gone a short ways and settled into the rhythm of the road, Griffin eyed her frankly. "You're doing well, Georgie."

"Thank you."

When she smiled, her face took on decidedly feminine lines. He realized no one who looked closely would believe she was a man. Maybe she could wear a false mustache. The thought made him smile. No, a beard would be needed to disguise her dainty chin and the smooth curve of her neck.

"What?" she asked.

He snapped his gaze forward, realizing they would soon be at the rocky stretch of road where the outlaws sometimes lurked. "Nothing. Just admiring your skill." He could feel her sneaking glances at him as he scanned the terrain ahead and to the sides.

The next time he looked at the driver, her mouth was set in a determined scowl. She was watching, too. Watching and probably remembering the other holdup.

"They don't stop you going downhill," he said.

"That fellow tried once when I was with Johnny. And if he's got friends now. . ."

She said no more, but Griffin renewed his vigilance. No chatter could be heard from within the coach. The others must also know this was one of the most dangerous spots on the road.

When they emerged on the downhill side of the tumbled boulders, Vashti sighed. Her shoulders fell slightly, and she cast Griffin a glance.

"I appreciate the good stock you keep for the teams."

"It pays in the long run."

"Well, I'll always be sorry for the horses Ned and I lost you."

"Can't be helped." He took a broad view, swinging his head all around to inspect the vista spread below them. The desolate country lay empty for the most part. A few ranches lay farther on, but the rocky foothills remained largely unsettled. He turned the other way, and Vashti's gaze met his. Her leaf-green eyes smiled at him. He couldn't think of any other way to describe it, and his heart jolted.

She looked forward again. "This stretch of road will be pretty when the flowers come out."

Griffin inhaled deeply. Was he out of his mind, putting a beautiful woman like her in danger day after day? His hands tightened on the stock of his gun. Was this danger any worse than what she'd lived through to get this far?

"You started telling me a bit about your past once." He looked over at her, trying to judge her reaction. "I don't want to pry, but I admit I'm curious, and I'd like to know more about you. How you came here, and why. If you don't mind telling it."

Her smile was not a happy one, and he regretted broaching the topic.

"Why did you come here?" she countered without looking at him.

"Work. A chance to be my own boss."

She nodded. "Well, I've never had that. I tried being on my own when I ran away from Aunt Mary and Uncle Joshua, but I wasn't ready to take care of myself. I tried asking for work, and a man in St. Joe actually let me sweep the front stoop of his store for him and gave me some food. But his wife found out and wouldn't let me stay on. I kicked around town, first asking for work, then begging... then stealing."

Griffin eyed her narrowly, thinking of the desperate twelve-year-old girl, but said nothing.

"Then I stole from the wrong person."

"You got caught?"

She nodded. "I'd been swiping food, but it was getting on for fall and the cold was setting in. I needed money, so I practiced lifting things out of sacks and pockets. I did all right the first couple of times. I got a coin purse out of a lady's handbag, and I picked up the change off a store counter. But when I tried to lift a man's wallet, he grabbed my wrist and wouldn't let go. I'd surely picked the wrong mark."

"A lawman?"

"Nope. He owned a saloon."

"Oh." Griffin frowned and looked away. He'd known it had to be in there somewhere, that plunge from petty crime into hopeless, inky darkness.

"I was there near two years," she said. "He had me sweep and scrub and wash glasses. I wasn't allowed to go out in the barroom when there were men out there drinking."

"So he had some sense of morality."

Vashti shrugged. "Not much." The pace had lagged a little, and she clucked to the horses. They quickened their trot. "After a while I caught on to what the bar girls were up to when they took a fellow upstairs. I heard one of them arguing with the owner about me one day. She kept saying I was too young. I wasn't fourteen yet. He said youth was worth big money. Well, I didn't need to hear more. I lit out first chance I had. And this time I didn't take his wallet. I knew where to get some cash from a box he kept in the kitchen." She raised her chin and looked Griffin in the eye. "I could have taken fifty dollars, but I didn't. I took three dollars and fifty cents—enough to get me out of St. Joe."

"You should have taken more."

"Yeah. That's what I figured when I got to Independence. I'd been really stupid, and now I was in worse straits than I was before. Because now men were looking at me like I was more than just an orphaned little kid."

She faced forward. The breeze past his ears, the creak of leather, and the rattle of the wheels on the hard-packed road were the only sounds he heard. Griffin's heart had gone all mushy and mournful.

He shifted on the seat and watched her as she adjusted the reins. "I'm sorry."

She shrugged it off. "I didn't pay much account to God back then, but in a way, I guess He looked after me. At least, He sent along a fella who kept me with him for a long time. He took pretty good care of me. Mostly." She flicked a glance at Griffin.

He didn't buy it. A man who took advantage of a girl that young was *not* taking care of her.

"Well, he asked for favors in return," she admitted, though he hadn't asked. "But that was better than working for somebody like my next employer." She made a face, as though she'd tasted foul medicine.

Griffin drew in a deep, painful breath. "You didn't stay with him—the fellow you said took care of you."

She shook her head. "He owed someone money, and he. . .he gave me to the man he was in debt to. The wrong kind of man." She blinked rapidly and turned her face a little to the side, but he saw a tear escape and trickle down her cheek. Did she regret revealing how far she'd sunk before she came to Fergus? Surely she wasn't actually missing the fellow who'd debauched her and sold her into slavery.

"Look, I don't want to talk about this anymore, all right?"

"Sorry. I respect that. But a man who'll give over the woman he's been protecting to settle a debt—that ain't right."

"Yeah." The horses started down a gradual slope toward a creek bottom, where they would cross a wooden bridge. Vashti took in a little rein and focused on the leaders. He was surprised when she spoke again.

"I'll just say that Bitsy Shepard was my angel. I met up with her at the dry goods store in Cheyenne, and she asked me what I was doing there. I told her I was working at the Pony, and she got this look on her face. Asked me how old I was. I told her twenty, because I was, by then. I told her I'd been with Ike—he's the one who owned the Pony—for nigh on three years. Felt like a century. You know what she did?"

Griffin shook his head. Vashti lifted a shoulder and scrubbed away the errant tear with the shoulder of her vest.

"She got me out of there. She gave me five dollars and said, 'I've got a place in Idaho Territory. I'm headed back there tomorrow. If you can get out of that filthy place in the morning without anyone seeing you, come to the depot, and I'll take you with me.' I told her I thought I could, but I might not be able to get out with my things, or Ike would catch me. Or one of the other girls would see me, and they'd tell him. She said not to worry about my clothes. She'd outfit me—and I wouldn't have to. . .to. . .to entertain men." She flushed scarlet. "Anyway, that's all I needed to hear."

"Good old Bitsy." Griffin smiled, pleased that the brusque saloon keeper had come through for the desperate girl.

"She's the best. I've been here with her four years now, and she's kept her word. Augie, too. They've protected me and let me earn an honest living."

"The Spur & Saddle has always been a high-class place, even when it was a saloon."

Vashti nodded. "It's home now. And Bitsy and me, we both found God here. I'll always believe He put me in her path that day at the dry goods. Ever since I learned to pray, I've been thanking Him." She smiled at him, though tears still glittered in her eyes.

Griffin returned her smile. Somehow they'd crossed a line—dismantled a barrier between them. He glanced ahead, down the slope to the bridge. Trees overhung the road before the short span, and he looked into the shadow beneath the branches of the pines. They were nearly halfway from Democrat's to Nampa. Laughter issued from the coach behind them—Bitsy's loud guffaw. He glanced at Vashti, and she grinned with him.

Beyond Vashti's hat brim, Griffin caught a glimpse of movement in the trees. Automatically he swung his gun barrel toward it. Vashti's eyes flared and she turned, snapping the reins and clucking to the team.

The leaders were only five yards from the bridge when two men jumped from beneath the pines, one on either side of the road.

"Ye-ha!" Vashti slapped the reins on the wheelers' sides as the outlaws took aim. The horses lurched forward then stalled for a second as the leaders saw the men and the bridge.

"Up!" Vashti yelled, and the lead team plunged toward the span. If they would just charge onward, maybe they could cross the bridge and leave the outlaws behind.

Griffin fired toward the robber on his side of the road, and she knew it might be the only shot he got off. Another gun went off somewhere behind her. Wood splintered between her and Griffin. A horse screamed. On the far side of the bridge, another man stood squarely in their path.

One of the two men she'd seen first ran toward her side of the coach. Vashti unfurled her whip, jerking the tip off to the side. Beside her, Griffin half stood, bracing his feet, as she cracked her whip at the outlaw on the ground. The masked man leaped back from the stinging lash. His gun fired, but the bullet went wide.

The horses thundered toward the bridge. The outlaw on the far side of the span drew a bead and fired. The off lead horse veered left and crashed into his harness mate, throwing the near leader off balance only a few feet short of the bridge. The two horses went down in a tangle, pawing and whinnying shrilly, while the two wheelers plowed into them. The stage swayed. Griffin and Vashti flew forward.

Vashti grabbed wildly as she landed on the off wheeler's rump. Somehow she managed to keep hold of the reins and clutch the backstrap of the harness. A moment later she felt Griffin's huge hand as he clenched a fistful of her vest and yanked her up beside him. She sprawled between the seat and the footrest.

"You hurt?" he asked.

She stared up at him, gasping. "I don't think so." She still held the reins in her hands.

"Stay down." He shoved her head lower.

"They shot one of the horses."

"I know."

The horses plunged and clattered, trying to get their footing—all but the wounded one, who neighed piteously and thrashed about on the ground. Two more men had appeared out of the brush and leveled pistols at Griffin. Someone was keeping up fire from within the coach.

"Throw down your weapons," the man at the far end of the bridge yelled over the noise.

"Griffin!"

He looked down at her, and she reached a hand toward him.

"Don't give them the mail."

"We've got no choice, Georgie. There's five of them at least."

Griffin laid his gun down in the driver's boot. They'd take it, just like they had his other gun. Scowling ahead at the outlaw across the bridge, Griffin slowly raised his hands.

"Put 'em up!"

Vashti realized he meant her, and she straightened enough so that she could obey. Raising her hands over her head was the hardest thing she'd ever done. A lull in the shooting brought a stillness broken only by the horses' breathing and struggling.

"All right, you two. Throw down the box."

Vashti caught her breath and stared toward the man on the bridge. He seemed to be the leader. She rose on her knees and wrapped the reins around the brake handle, staring all the while toward the outlaw. She squinted, eyeing his tall, lanky form closely. It couldn't be—

"Hurry up!" His boots thudded on the bridge as he walked toward them. "Get that box down here." He stepped carefully around the fallen horse and off the bridge.

When she heard his voice, Vashti was sure. After eight years, she was looking into the eyes of Luke Hatley, the man she'd at one time hoped to marry. The man who'd sold her to settle his two-hundred-dollar poker debt.

★ CHAPTER 32 ★

Pain stabbed through Griffin's knee as he tried to straighten it. When he'd catapulted forward, he'd slammed into the metal rail on the footrest. Good thing, or he'd have sprawled on top of the wheel team, the way Vashti had, but he'd smashed his knee in the process.

A quick glance around told him that two outlaws stood on the near side of the stage—his side—and one on Vashti's side. One of their men must have gone down, but whether it was the one he'd shot at first, he had no idea. Maybe one of the passengers had hit a robber.

He focused on the leader, who walked deliberately toward them with his gun pointed squarely at Griffin's chest.

"We can't throw the box down," he called.

The leader stopped and stared at him through the eyeholes in his rude sack of a mask. "Why not?"

"The box is bolted to the frame of the stagecoach." Griffin waited, his hands still at shoulder level, half expecting the man to shoot him point-blank. He glanced uneasily at Vashti. She still crouched between the driver's seat and the footrest, staring at the man. "You all right?" he asked, low enough that he hoped no one else heard.

Her lips twitched, but she didn't answer.

"All right, get down," the outlaw said, gesturing with his rifle. "Nice and easy. Get over the side and stand a couple yards away from the coach. And don't try anything."

"Come on, Georgie." Griffin lowered his hands slowly and gripped her shoulder. "With one horse down, we're not going anywhere, so we

939

may as well do this peacefully."

"But we can't let them take the mail!"

"Yes, we can," he said between clenched teeth. "Come on. I'm not letting you get shot because of your stubbornness." Her eyes snapped. That was good. She was mad at him now, and that anger would get her moving. "Climb down on my side. I don't want the coach between us so I can't see you."

He turned to get his footing. One of the outlaws, wearing a mask, stood just below him. He jerked his rifle, indicating that Griffin must get down. He looked back at Vashti. "Come this way. Stay close to me."

She nodded but kept her gaze fastened on the leader, who now stood near the wheelers.

Griffin hopped down. Another outlaw had opened the coach door and was herding the passengers out.

"Leave all weapons and belongings in the coach, folks," he said, as if this were a sightseeing trip.

Griffin looked up. Vashti was at the edge of the messenger's seat, about to lower one foot over the side.

"Get over there," the outlaw near Griffin said, nodding toward where Hiram, Libby, Bitsy, and the other three passengers huddled.

Griffin ignored him and stayed close until Vashti hopped down from the steps to the ground. "Come on, Georgie." He placed himself between her and the outlaw and walked beside her toward the others.

"That one's Benny," she hissed.

"The one behind us?"

She nodded. So she recognized one of the robbers from the earlier holdup, even though they wore masks this time. If they ever got the chance, she might be able to identify him in court.

"I'm sorry, Griff," Bitsy said when they reached the knot of passengers.

"Nothing to be sorry for," he said.

"Hiram got one of them, but—"

"Shut up!" The man guarding them lunged toward Bitsy, pointing his gun at her midsection.

Bitsy clamped her lips together and glared at him. The red feather on her hat quivered.

Griffin noted the checkering on the stock of the gun the outlaw held. That was his shotgun—the one the robbers had stolen weeks ago. He looked away.

"Keep your hands up," growled Benny.

Griffin turned slowly, his hands in the air. Vashti stood between him and Bitsy, her mouth set in a hard line. He looked down the line at the others. They stood still in the sun with the breeze fluttering the spruce boughs. Leo Rice, whom they'd picked up at the Democrat Station, had blood on his cheek. Not shot, Griffin decided. A splinter must have caught him when the outlaws peppered the coach.

The leader and the fourth outlaw climbed up to the driver's box and rummaged around. One of them lifted Griffin's shotgun and examined it. The other held up the little canvas bag Vashti carried on her trips. He pulled out a skirt and a pair of pantalets and held them up, laughing. "Well, boss, I guess you was right."

Griffin scowled. He expected them to pull out Vashti's pistol next, but he didn't see them do that. Instead, the leader used his own handgun to shoot the lock off the treasure box. Griffin winced. More repairs to the coach. The two outlaws whooped.

"Well, boys," the leader called, "we hit pay dirt this time."

"All right," said the one who'd threatened Bitsy. "If you folks have anything of interest in your pockets, now's the time to hand it over."

Griffin sighed and reached into his pocket for Cy Fennel's watch. He handed it to Benny, with a few coins and his case knife. "That's it."

"And you, young fella?" The outlaw shifted his attention to Vashti.

"I've got nothing of value," Vashti said, stony faced.

"That right?"

"Yeah, that's right."

While Benny relieved the cowboy, Hiram, and the third male passenger of their cash, his companion looked Vashti up and down. "I heard they was a girl driving stage out here, but I didn't believe it."

Vashti said nothing, but her cheeks colored.

"Leave the driver alone," Griffin said.

"I just want to know what he's got in his pockets." The outlaw reached toward Vashti's vest.

"Here! You want this? You can have it." She swiftly unbuttoned the front and wriggled out of the vest.

The shocked outlaw stared at it and then at her cream-colored shirt. "Well now."

Griffin caught his breath and made himself look away. When she'd peeled off the vest, Vashti had turned her back slightly toward him. Stuck in the back of her trousers' waistband was her Colt revolver. The outlaw crumpled the vest in his hands and then explored its pockets, pulling out a snowy cotton handkerchief. While the robber was occupied, Griffin snaked his hand out and slipped the pistol from Vashti's waistband. She never twitched, but he knew she felt him take it. Her body shielded his action as he tucked it behind him, in his own belt. He wished he had Libby's voluminous skirts to hide it in. If the robbers decided to search him, he'd had it.

The leader and his companion climbed down from the stage laden with treasure and Griffin's new shotgun.

"You got everything?" the leader called.

"There's two sacks of mail in the coach, boss," Benny replied.

"Could be some money in it," said the man holding Vashti's vest.

"Leave it," said the leader. "We've got plenty. But bring the driver."

They all stared at him.

Vashti's stomach lurched. He knew. That was why he'd attacked this stage. But she wouldn't go with Luke, not if it meant losing her life.

Libby spoke first. "You can't take Georgie."

"Can't I?" Luke strode forward, holding his rifle trained on Griffin. "Step back, mister."

Griffin hesitated.

"I'd as soon shoot you as not," Luke snarled.

Griffin took one step back. Vashti wondered if she could distract Luke and give Griffin time to bring out her pistol. But it would be one gun against four.

"Cover the others, Benny." Luke seized Vashti's wrist and yanked her toward him. "Come on, Georgia, you're coming with me."

"No. You left me in Cheyenne, Luke Hatley. I'm not going anywhere with you." She twisted her arm, but his grip clamped her wrist like a vise.

He twisted her arm and pulled her closer. "Oh yes, you are, sweetheart. You can come along peaceful, or you can watch these good people die one by one. Which is it?"

Sick dread shot through her. The Luke Hatley she'd known wasn't a violent man, but that was eight years ago. She'd changed immeasurably. Perhaps he had, too.

He pulled her arm back farther, and she gritted her teeth.

"All right."

Luke loosened his grip but kept hold of her wrist. "That's better. Come on. I've got a horse for you across the bridge." He looked at Griffin and the passengers. "Don't try to follow us, folks, or your darling little driver will wind up dead."

He pulled her toward the bridge. The other three outlaws followed, walking backward and still brandishing their guns. Vashti stared at Griffin. He stood stock still, watching, a look of pain and disbelief on his face. Would she ever see him again, or would Luke take her far away? And if he did, would Griffin even try to find her? No man she'd trusted had ever come through for her before.

"Come on now." Luke jerked her around and dragged her past the horses.

Griffin watched in shock as the outlaw leader pulled Vashti with him. Luke Hatley must be the man who had given her to a brothel owner. He wanted to kill the man, but with three others holding him at gunpoint, he was helpless. The only thing he would accomplish by drawing the pistol would be to get himself and his unarmed friends killed. Then who would help Vashti?

When Luke got to where the team still stood, with one lead horse down and moaning, he hauled Vashti around the horses, onto the span of the bridge. The other three outlaws turned and ran after them.

Griffin whipped the pistol from behind his back.

"Hiram!" Bitsy called. She bent and pulled the right leg of her bloomers up to her knee.

"Griff, wait," Hiram said.

Griffin looked over at him. Bitsy thrust her tiny, genuine Deringer pistol—made by the master gunsmith Henry Deringer himself—into Hiram's hand.

"All right, now!" Hiram ran a few steps forward.

The outlaws were still on the bridge. Hiram took cover behind the horses and aimed. The Deringer popped, and one of the outlaws fell.

The leader had reached the far end of the bridge. He looked back and saw one of his men had fallen. He raised his rifle. Vashti wrenched away from him and leaped over the side of the bridge.

Griffin fired once and ducked behind the team, near Hiram.

"They'll likely drop the rest of the horses," Hiram said.

"You got another shot left?" Griffin asked.

"Nope. Single shot."

"Then take Vashti's sixer." Griffin handed him the revolver. Hiram was a better shot than he would ever dream of being. "There should be five shots left. I'll distract them."

"How?"

"Don't know."

Griffin glanced over his shoulder. Libby, Bitsy, and the other passengers had retreated into the trees, out of sight. He peeked around the lead horse's muzzle, preparing if necessary to run into the open and draw Luke's fire.

Luke stood on the bridge, looking down over the side. The other two outlaws were scrambling for the far side.

"He's going to get Vashti." Griffin leaped into the open. "Hatley!"

As Luke swung toward him, Hiram stepped out from the shadow of the near wheeler's side and took aim, holding Vashti's Colt with both hands, and squeezed the trigger.

✭ CHAPTER 33 ✭

Vashti lay in the icy water, stunned. The fall was farther than she'd bargained for, and the bottom rockier. She'd had the breath knocked out of her. Both ankles and one wrist throbbed, but she didn't move. She lay with her head to one side, hauling in gulps of air and concentrating on keeping her face out of the six-inch-deep water.

Above and behind her, several shots rang out. She didn't care. She only wanted to breathe.

A closer explosion jerked her into reality. She craned her neck and looked up at the bridge. Luke was up there, still wearing the ridiculous mask. He'd spotted her in the creek. He raised his rifle to his shoulder and pointed the barrel at her.

"What's the matter, Georgia? You used to like me."

She turned her face away. Let him shoot her if he wanted. That would be better than going with him again. *Lord, if You want to take me home, I'm ready,* she thought. Then she remembered Griffin and the others. She looked around at Luke again. He was still aiming at her.

"Come on. I haven't got all day. Get up."

She closed her eyes.

Two more shots rang out. Something splashed in the water beside her. She opened one eye. A rifle was caught in the current but snagged on the rocks. It lay there in the burbling water. Had Luke dropped his gun?

A bigger splash threw gallons of freezing water over her. She raised her head. Luke lay facedown in the creek, on top of his rifle.

945

Vashti huddled, shivering in the stagecoach. Libby and Bitsy rubbed her hands and feet. Both had donated their shawls to keep her warm, and they'd recovered her leather vest.

"You're going to be all right," Bitsy said, wrapping Vashti in her arms. "Griff and the other men will get the team straightened out, and we'll take this coach back home."

"No," Vashti said. "We've got to get the mail through to Nampa."

"We'll go back to the Democrat Station, and they'll get a new team," Libby said. "Then we'll take you home. Someone else can drive to Nampa."

They wouldn't have an extra driver on hand, but Vashti knew it was useless to explain the quirks of the stage line.

A gunshot sounded, very close and loud. She jumped and grabbed Bitsy's hand.

"There now, honey. Griff said they'd have to put the one horse down. I'm sorry."

Vashti squeezed her eyes tightly shut. A tear escaped and ran down her cheek.

Hiram came to the door of the coach. "How are you doing, ladies?"

"We're all right." Libby's usually cheerful voice was subdued as she looked to her husband for news.

"Griff's unhitching the lead horse that wasn't hurt. He's going to send the cowboy to get the men from the Democrat Station."

"What about the outlaws?" Bitsy asked.

"Mr. Rice and the other passenger are guarding the two that Griffin captured."

Bitsy frowned. "So. . .two dead?"

"Three. That one we got first thing—" Hiram stopped and swallowed hard.

"The one you shot out the window? What about him?" Bitsy asked.

"We took all their masks off. It's Cecil Watson."

Vashti stared at him for a moment, then collapsed against the back of the seat. The man who'd run out on her in Nampa had joined the outlaws. She felt as if every ounce of energy had been drained from her.

Outside, receding hoofbeats told her the cowboy was leaving for the swing station. A moment later, Hiram stepped aside and Griffin appeared in the doorway.

"We've decided to wait until they bring another team out. One of the wheel horses has a flesh wound. He'll heal up, but I don't want to ask him to pull right now."

Vashti sat up, finding new strength. If Griffin could keep going with his knee all smashed up, she could, too. "What about the leader? The one blocking the bridge?"

Griffin winced. "We'll have to move him. I figure when Mr. Jordan and his boys get here, we'll hitch the new team to the horse and drag him off the road. Maybe we can get a crew out here this afternoon to dig a hole. Don't want to leave something dead that big so close to the road."

She nodded, thankful for that. She wouldn't have to pass the horse's carcass every time she drove this road.

Griffin leaned his big body inside so that he was half in the coach and blinked in the dimness. His gaze focused on Vashti. "How you doing?"

She nodded, frowning. "I'll be all right. I'm a little sore in places."

He reached out and touched her cheek gently. "You sure?"

"Yes."

"We'll have Doc check you over."

She nodded and on impulse grabbed his hand. "How about you? Hiram said one of the outlaws was Cecil Watson."

"That's right. He's dead. Him and Hatley and the one they called Benny. So now we know: They had an insider who knew when there would be treasure in the box."

She sucked in a breath. "Thank you, Griff. You and Hiram." Her tears let loose, and she turned her face away.

Two hours later, Griffin and Vashti rode together in the stagecoach. Mr. Jordan had insisted he could drive a team of mules back to his station. It wasn't that far, and the injured parties needed to sit inside, in relative comfort.

Libby, Bitsy, and Hiram opted to ride on the roof with Jordan, and the other passengers rode the two healthy horses from their original team. Griffin thought they'd all gone to great lengths to put him and Vashti alone in the stage together, but he didn't mind. If his knee didn't hurt so much, he'd have been tickled.

"You'd better have Doc check out that knee," Vashti said. She hadn't protested when he sat beside her on the cushioned seat at the back of the coach, instead of one of the other seats. He took that as a good sign.

"My knee will be fine. It's you I'm worried about."

"I'm just bruised up. Nothing's broken." Her clothes were still damp, but she'd dried out considerably. She probably would heal up within a couple of weeks, but it wasn't her bumps and bruises that worried him.

"What about Luke?" he asked.

"What about him?"

Griffin drew in a deep breath. "Did you know he was in these parts?"

She was quiet for a moment; then she looked at him. "I thought I saw him in Boise, that one time I drove through. Trudy was with me. I saw a man come out of a saloon, and I thought it was Luke. Scared me something awful."

"Did you tell Trudy?"

Vashti nodded. "I decided it wasn't really him—just my imagination."

"Do you think he came here looking for you?"

"No. He probably came looking for a chance to make some easy money. When he heard about me, he probably thought it was a streak of luck."

"Folks have been talking about the female driver," Griffin said.

"Yes. And if he heard my name was George Edwards. . ."

"He knew you as Georgia?"

"Yes. I changed my name after I left Ike's." She sighed and shrank away from him, into the corner of the seat.

Griffin reached over and found her icy cold hand. He cradled it in his and stroked it with his thumb. "That's all in the past."

"I know." Her voice had gone tiny, but she didn't pull her hand away.

He inhaled deeply and let the breath out in a puff. "So why did you pick the name Vashti?"

She blinked at him. "You sure you want to chitchat now?"

"Might as well."

She looked out the coach window. They were going uphill, only half a mile or so from Democrat. She sat back with a sigh, still letting him hold her hand. "When I came here to Idaho, I wanted a new name. Somebody told me once that Vashti was the name of a queen in the Bible."

"I reckon that's right."

"Yeah. But see, after we got the parson and I started going to church, I found out the king got mad at Vashti and kicked her out. He got himself a new queen."

Griffin nodded. "Esther."

"That's the one. And Esther was the really pretty one, and she ended up being the honorable queen. Vashti was thrown out of the palace in disgrace. Esther saved her people."

"That's true, but I wouldn't be so hard on Vashti if I were you."

"You wouldn't?"

"Nope. From what Reverend Benton says, I'd say Queen Vashti was quite a lady."

"You think so?"

"Yes. Her husband wanted her to act in an unseemly manner, and she refused."

Vashti pondered that. "I thought she was bad because she wouldn't do what the king said."

"Maybe. But I think she had a reason for that. Maybe if you ask Miz Benton, she can tell you more about Queen Vashti."

"I might do that."

"Good. Because I happen to think the name suits you more than you know."

"Really?"

"Yup. You don't stand by convention, and. . .well, if anyone was to ask me, I'd say you had a regal way of moving, and you're pretty enough to show off, too."

She eyed him critically, as if she thought he was making fun of her.

"I mean it," he said softly. "I think a heap of you, Vashti Edwards."

She sucked in a breath. "Honest?"

He squeezed her hand. "Honest."

Halfway back to Fergus they met the welcoming party. Jordan had taken the stage and its paying passengers on to Nampa himself, driving the mule team and taking one of his hostlers along as shotgun messenger. He'd loaned Griffin his farm wagon. With Hiram driving, they'd headed out with the two sound horses from the stage team in harness. Libby and Bitsy sat on the seat with Hiram, and Griffin and Vashti sat in the back on a quilt.

From the road ahead, a whooping broke out with the sound of pounding hoofbeats. Vashti held on to the side of the wagon and raised herself until she could see three horses approaching at breakneck speed.

Ethan and Trudy Chapman galloped toward them, and out in front came Justin on Griffin's gelding, Pepper.

"Uncle Griff!" When Justin saw his uncle in the wagon, he halted Pepper and slid to the ground. Hiram stopped the team, and Justin climbed over the wheel into the wagon bed. He flung himself into Griffin's arms. "What happened? Mrs. Chapman and I were worried, so the sheriff telegraphed Nampa. They said you were late."

"We got waylaid." Griffin slapped the boy on the back. "We're all right, so quit fretting."

Justin looked at Vashti. "You, too, Miss Edwards?"

"I'm going to be fine, Justin," she said.

Ethan and Trudy rode up to the wagon and greeted them all. Bitsy launched into a colorful account of the day's events.

"So where are all these road agents you whipped?" Ethan asked.

"Down to Democrat's," Bitsy said. "Two living and three killed."

Ethan looked them over solemnly. "You folks all right?"

"We're fine," Hiram said. "One of the passengers was grazed, but he wanted to go on to Nampa."

"Griffin and Vashti both need to see Doc when we get home," Libby said.

Trudy rode Crinkles around the wagon. When she came close, Vashti reached out and petted the mare's nose, glad to see Trudy's mount had been returned to her.

"You sure you're all right?" Trudy asked.

"Scrapes and bruises," Vashti said. "Griffin hurt his knee, but we'll make it."

"I guess I'd better go on to Democrat's," Ethan said.

"They've got the prisoners locked in the corn crib," Hiram said. "Maybe you'd better get a few men to help you take them to Boise."

"I'll loan you a wagon, if you want to come to the livery," Griffin said.

"You're not going alone to take two prisoners in." Trudy eyed her husband sternly.

"I'll get a couple of my deputies." Ethan returned her stubborn look. "My male deputies. This isn't a job for ladies."

"For once, I'm going to agree with you," Bitsy said. "Can we go home now?"

Two nights later, Griffin walked slowly down the street to the Spur & Saddle. He still limped, but his knee didn't hurt so bad anymore. He went slowly up the steps and into the building. Bitsy was wiping off a table. Doc Kincaid and Isabel Fennel sat in one corner, chatting softly. Rose Caplinger lingered at a table across the room, sipping coffee with Maitland Dostie. Griffin looked, then looked again. He supposed it made sense—Rose had opened her millinery shop last year in the vacant storefront next to the telegraph office. The two must see each other every day.

Bitsy looked up and smiled. "Hello, Griff. Where's your shadow?"

"I left Justin over to the Nashes' playing Chinese checkers with Ben and Silas."

Bitsy nodded. "Have you eaten?"

"Yes, ma'am."

"Piece of pie, then? Coffee? Or did you just come for the company?"

Griffin smiled and glanced toward the kitchen. "I came to see one of my drivers."

"She's in the dishpan, as usual."

"Is my apron hanging by the door?" Griffin asked.

She laughed and shooed him toward the kitchen. Griffin found Vashti scrubbing Augie's saucepans.

"Evening, Griff," Augie called. He picked up a bucket of slops and went out the back door.

Vashti smiled at him but kept on scrubbing the pan. "What brings you out?"

Griffin grabbed an apron off a hook and walked toward her. "I came to see how you were doing and if you'll be ready to drive again Monday."

"You mean you'd let me?"

He smiled. "I don't think we'll see any outlaws on the Nampa run for a while." He held out the apron.

She took it and pulled up the neckband. Griffin stooped toward her. She slid it over his head, then leaned close and kissed his cheek.

He straightened, eyeing her closely. "What's that for?"

"You saved my life. I've already been to see Hiram and thanked him personally."

"Did you kiss him?"

Her face went scarlet. "No, I. . ."

Griffin laughed.

She eyed him askance and began to laugh, too. "That was just for you." She turned back to her dishwater.

"Aren't you going to tie my apron strings?"

"If you want."

"Vashti. . ."

"Yes?"

He could look into those leaf-green eyes forever. He reached for her, and she came into his arms before he even knew what he was going to do. Her kiss was sweeter than Augie's cinnamon rolls.

He held her close against his apron front and sighed. "You can drive anytime you want, sweetheart."

She reached all the way around him and squeezed him tight. Griffin held her, wanting never to let go. After a while, he dared to reach up and stroke her hair. "You know I only opposed your driving because I wanted to take care of you."

"Is that so?" Her tone held amusement.

He pulled back a little and looked down at her. "Maybe not at first. But. . .well, you're a strong woman. I didn't know how strong. But I'd still like to take care of you. For the rest of my life, if you'll have me."

Her lips curved into a smile. "What kind of talk is that? *If* I'll have you."

"I mean it."

She shook her head. "I'm the one who's got a load of baggage. Are you sure you can overlook everything?"

"It's in the past. I'll make sure it stays in the past."

She looked away, frowning, then turned back to face him. "I never. . ." Tears glistened in her eyes. She cleared her throat. "I never got close to a man except those that had bad intentions."

"Well, my intentions are honorable."

She nodded slowly. "And you won't make me quit driving?"

"No." A sudden thought came to him. "Well, not unless. . .well, you know." Blood rushed to his cheeks, and he wished he still had his beard to hide it. "If you were in a delicate way. . ."

She reached up and stroked his stubbly cheek. "I love you, Griffin Bane."

It was the one thing he'd meant to say, but hadn't been sure how—and now she'd said it first. "I love you, too. Can we go see the parson after services tomorrow?"

"That would be lovely."

He kissed her again, and the dishes would have sat unwashed for hours if Augie hadn't come in with his empty slop bucket and slammed the back door.

"Well now! Wait till Bitsy hears about this! She'll be some tickled."

Vashti stood beside her bridegroom in the dining room of the Spur & Saddle, ready to cut the wedding cake. Augie had outdone himself.

With help from Rose Caplinger, he'd fashioned a garden of sugar roses and topped the four-tiered masterpiece with two feathery white doves.

Ethan Chapman came over near the table and raised his hands. "Folks, if I could interrupt for just a minute, I have an announcement to make."

The murmuring quieted as everyone focused on the sheriff. Ethan looked over at Griffin, and he shrugged. Vashti took that to mean he had no idea what was going on, but he was in a mellow mood and didn't care how many announcements people made today. The vows were said, and nothing could change that. She reached for his big hand, and he squeezed hers, smiling.

"Some of you know I got back from Boise yesterday. I delivered some prisoners to the U.S. Marshal there a few days ago. Those outlaws are two of the gang we believe held up the stagecoach twice on the Nampa run and once each on the Catherine and Silver City runs. The postal service had sent notice of a reward to the marshal before Griff Bane and Hiram Dooley caught the outlaws."

"We had some help," Griffin muttered.

Ethan swung around and grinned at him. "Yes, you did. In fact, I have orders to give a share of the reward to the following people: Griffin Bane, Hiram Dooley, Leo Rice, Buck Ashley—"

Arthur Tinen Jr. let out a whoop at the mention of the name of one of his cowhands. Ethan smiled and nodded at him.

"Yes, Buck was on the stage that day, and other witnesses say he acquitted himself well. The same with the drummer who was a passenger, Mr. John Sedge. The marshal will send his part to him. Also receiving a share of the reward will be Miss Georgia Edwards, Mrs. Hiram Dooley, and Mrs. Augustus Moore."

Libby, Bitsy, and Vashti exchanged looks across the room. Hiram beamed, and Augie said, "That's my darlin' girl." He gave Bitsy a loud smack on the cheek.

Griffin let go of Vashti's hand and slid his arm around her waist. "You deserve it, Queen Vashti."

Ethan grinned. "If each of you will please see me when it's

convenient, I'll give you a bank draft for your share in the ten-thousand dollar reward."

"Ten thousand!" Bitsy's jaw dropped.

"What's that make your share?" Augie asked.

"That's $1,250," yelled Justin, who had been sipping lemonade in a corner with his friends.

Ethan smiled at the boy. "That's exactly right, and spoken by Mr. Bane's accountant."

Everyone laughed.

Goldie called out, "And the newlyweds get a double share."

"That's fittin'," said Bitsy.

Vashti looked up into Griffin's brown eyes. With that and the money Wells Fargo had sent for new equipment, they wouldn't wonder where the money to keep the stage line running would come from. Griffin nodded, contentment oozing from him. She snuggled close and hugged him around the waist.

Johnny Conway stepped up beside Ethan with his driving whip in his hand. "Folks, I have an announcement, too."

The crowd quieted.

"I know it's not far to the happy couple's new home," Johnny said, "but when they've finished their cake and are inclined to leave this jolly gathering, Ned and I have a carriage waiting outside to carry them home."

Griffin's bushy eyebrows shot up. "What?"

"Take a look out the window, boss," Ned Harmon called.

Griffin seized Vashti's hand and strode to the front window. They both looked out at their transportation for the two-block ride home: the red and gold Concord coach, with roses twined all along the top luggage rack and tucked into the horses' harness.

"Anytime you're ready, just say the word, and we'll drive you home," Johnny said.

Vashti tugged the whip out of his hand. "Oh no, you won't. You can ride along as far as the house if you want, but *I'm* driving."

Discussion Questions

1. Griffin is overworked and understaffed. In short, he's frazzled. What do you do when you feel this way?

2. Vashti has a dream of driving a stagecoach. She thinks she'll be perfectly content if she gets to do this. What aspects of her life will the driving job help her to overcome? What ones can she not escape?

3. Griffin gives a couple of reasons for not hiring Vashti. Is it common sense or pride that makes him reject her pleas?

4. Are there some jobs women should not do? Explain your reasons, pro or con, for thinking that way.

5. Vashti at first resists dressing like a boy when riding the stagecoach. Her former positions required her to look ultra feminine. Is Griffin wrong to require this of her? She felt she would lose the job if she refused. Did she make the right choice?

6. Were the women right to clean Griffin's house without his permission? If you were Trudy, how would you have handled the situation?

7. Vashti's friends want to help her after the first holdup. The club members offer to ride unpaid as extra guards. Are they realistic in their expectations of what they can do to help and what the consequences might be? What things should you consider before offering your help to someone in need?

8. Bitsy and Augie suffer some difficult times after closing the bar at the Spur & Saddle. Honoring the Lord in practical ways isn't always easy. Have you made hard decisions that hurt you financially? Was it worth it?

9. How does Griffin measure up as a single parent? What advice would you give him if you were a member of the Ladies' Shooting Club of Fergus?

10. Bill's death is a turning point in Griffin and Vashti's relationship. How does each one grow emotionally and spiritually?

11. Vashti chose her name because she heard that Vashti was a beautiful queen in the Bible. How are her assumptions dashed? Should she choose another name? What did you think of Griffin's response?

About the Author

SUSAN PAGE DAVIS is the author of more than thirty published novels. She's a Carol Award Winner and a two-time winner of the Inspirational Readers' Choice Award. In 2011, Susan was named Favorite Author of the Year in the 18th Annual Heartsong Awards. A native of Maine, she and her husband, Jim, now live in western Kentucky. Visit her website at: www.susanpagedavis.com.